A Rebecca Harding Davis Reader

D0278989

Lt

"Life in the Iron-Mills,"

Selected Fiction, & Essays

Edited, with a Critical Introduction

by Jean Pfaelzer

University of Pittsburgh Press

Pittsburgh & London

A
Rebecca
Harding
Davis
Reader

Published by the

University of Pittsburgh Press

Pittsburgh, Pa., 15260

Copyright © 1995

University of Pittsburgh Press

All rights reserved

Manufactured in the

United States of America

Printed on acid-free paper

Library of Congress Cataloging-in-Publication Data

Davis, Rebecca Harding, 1831–1910.

A Rebecca Harding Davis reader : "Life in the
iron-mills," selected fiction, and essays / edited, with a
critical introduction by Jean Pfaelzer.

p.   cm.

ISBN 0-8229-3887-1 (cl)

1. United States — Social life and customs — 19th
century — Fiction.   2. Women iron and steel workers —
United States — Fiction.   3. United States — Social
conditions — 19th century.   4. Working class women
— United States — Fiction.   5. Domestic fiction,
American.

I. Pfaelzer, Jean.   II. Title.

PS1517.A6   1995

813'.4 — dc20   95-3296

CIP

A CIP catalogue record for this book is available from the
British Library.

Eurospan, London

To my daughters

JOHANNA JUSTINE PFAELZER

and

SOPHIA MEIRA PANUTHOS

 Contents

Acknowledgments

In this process of recovery, rediscovery, and interpretation, many have hunted and gathered, photocopied, cut and pasted, listened and read. I am particularly grateful to Sandy Hawke, Jen Johnson, Sue Serra, and Johanna Pfaelzer for their wit, perseverance, attention to detail, and enthusiasm for the anthology. The pioneering work on Rebecca Harding Davis of Sharon Harris and Jean Fagan Yellin continues to shape my thinking. I appreciate the inspiration and observations of Violet Lippett, my mother and—as always—my first reader. Jane Flanders of the University of Pittsburgh Press has monitored this book with knowledge of the era as well as tolerance for the messy uncertainties of archival materials. Peter Panuthos continues to light my work with enduring care and warmth.

My writing on Rebecca Harding Davis is made possible by the provision of a research office at the Library of Congress and by financial support from the National Endowment for the Humanities, the American Philosophical Society, and the University of Delaware. I am very grateful indeed.

The Common Stories
of Rebecca Harding Davis

AN INTRODUCTION

On April 12, 1861, the Civil War began. With the smell of jasmine in the air, families with laden picnic baskets watched from their carriages as secessionist Edmund Ruffin fired the first shot at Fort Sumter in a war in which six hundred thousand people would die and four hundred thousand would be maimed. As Harriet Tubman recalled the war, "And then we saw the lightning and that was the guns; and then we heard the thunder and that was the big guns; and then we heard the rain falling and that was the drops of blood falling, and when we came to get in the crops, it was dead men that we reaped."

In 1861 the debate over slavery, national identity, and the nature of American labor—whether chattel or industrial—was yet to be resolved. Nonetheless, in April 1861, the *Atlantic Monthly* published "Life in the Iron-Mills," an unsigned story that foretold the brutal victory of industrial labor and industrial consciousness over a craft-based, farm-based, and slave-based economy. In her first published story, Rebecca Harding Davis, its anonymous author, would, like Harriet Tubman, describe the degradation, invisible pain, and inevitability of another system proffered as benevolent. Later that year in *Margret Howth*, her first novel, Davis explained, "You want something, in fact, to lift you out of this crowded, tobacco-stained commonplace, to kindle and chafe and glow in you. I want you to dig into this commonplace, this vulgar American life, and see what is in it. Sometimes I think it has a new and awful significance that we do not see." [1]

With the war and with the publication of the early writings of Rebecca Harding Davis that would dig into the commonplace, one could say that April 1861 marked the end of American romanticism. It also marked the end of a set of repressive cultural expectations for women. Late in the night shift in "Life in the Iron-Mills," the mill overseer leads a journalist, a doctor, and a wealthy friend on a tour of the works. Through the startled gaze of these middle-class visitors, readers of the *Atlantic Monthly* suddenly encountered "the white figure of a woman . . . of giant proportions, crouching on the ground, her arms flung out in some wild gesture of warning" (14). This ominous and prognostic female is a statue which a desperate Welsh mill hand carved from "korl"—like himself, the pink refuse of the mill. "There was not one line of beauty or grace in it; a nude woman's form, muscular, grown coarse with labor, the powerful limbs instinct—with some poignant longing. One idea there was in it: the tense, rigid muscles, the clutching hands, the wild eager face, like that of a starving wolf's" (15).

This story of the psychological effects of American industrial labor is narrated by an unnamed middle-class spinster who identifies the emotional and creative suffocation of urban poverty in a raw factory town with her own arid intellectual and sexual life. Early in the development of American realism, an aesthetic that attempts to represent common social practices and languages, Davis would borrow a variety of literary tropes from the popular domestic novel—plots of orphans, broken families, class barriers, physical disfigurement, and unjust imprisonment, and infuse them with intense feelings of sentimentalism—abandonment, isolation, and inadequacy—in order to stimulate our sympathy for industrial workers. Crossing class and gender lines, she adopted sentimental images of intense loss, hunger, silence, and confinement to build a unifying motif of industrial "soul starvation." But in place of the sentimental telos of romantic closure—contented wife—Davis portrayed a defiant hunchback "mill girl" who, after a backbreaking shift at a factory loom, treks from her hovel to the iron mill in the dirty rain to carry her own meager dinner to her beloved cousin who is working the night shift, giving lie to the rationalization that home is woman's refuge.[2] Further, in this first of many stories that question the romantic significance of the self, Davis used the sentimental invocation of feminine sympathy to condemn a culture of individualism. She thus exposed the tension between sentimentalism, a genre predicated on the repression of the self, and realism, a genre predicated on the search for individual identity.

James Fields, the new editor of the *Atlantic Monthly* and Davis's first literary mentor, attempted to contain the implications of "Life in the Iron-Mills." In a role he played throughout his tenure at the journal, he refused to let Davis entitle her story "Beyond," a name that invited political interpretation, or "The Korl Woman," a name that focused on gendered interpretation.[3] Indeed, in May 1861, one month after the successful publication of "Life in the Iron-Mills," he rejected Davis's next piece, her first version of *Margret Howth*,[4] as too gloomy. Davis replied, "I am sorry. I thank you for the kindness with which you veil the disappointment. Whatever holier meaning life or music has for me, has reached me through the 'pathetic minor.' I fear that I only have the power to echo the pathos without the meaning. When I began the story, I meant to make it end in full sunshine—to show how even 'Lois' was not dumb, how even the meanest things in life, were 'voices in the world, and none of them *without* its signification.' [Lois's] life and death were to be the only dark thread. But . . . in my eagerness . . . I "assembled the gloom" you complain of. . . . [Do] you think I could . . . make it acceptable by returning to my original idea. Let her character and death (I cannot give up all, you see) remain, and the rest of the picture be steeped in warm healthy light. A 'perfect day in June.' " [5]

This tension between realism and repression, authenticity and sentimentality, history and literary tradition, would shape the long career of Rebecca Harding Davis, who wrote from 1861 until her death in 1910. Critics such as Jean Fagan Yellin find in her career a pattern of "feminization" whereby she accommodated her views and style to the demands of Brahmin male publishers.[6] Judith Fetterley goes further, suggesting that Davis "chose a form of suicide; artistic compromise turned her pen against herself."[7] In my view, despite economic pressures to support her husband (an impoverished young lawyer) and despite editorial pressures to erase uncomfortable and "unfeminine" social realities from her work, Davis refused to be silent about, as she put it, the "signification [of the] voices of the world." She survived as a compelling author by weaving aesthetic traditions of realism and sentimentalism to create powerful tales of frustrated "hack" women writers, child prostitutes, isolated fishermen, slaves who fear rape by their masters, sexually frustrated women in celibate utopian communities, lonely female doctors, women circus performers, and victims of enforced institutionalization in mental hospitals. The stories and essays of Rebecca Harding Davis included in this anthology support Jane Tompkins's view that domestic fiction of the nineteenth century is "remarkable for its intellectual complexity, ambition and resourcefulness, and . . . offers a critique of American society far more devastating than any delivered by better-known critics such as Hawthorne and Melville."[8] Textures of sentiment and realism in Davis's stories are resourceful strategies through which she both encoded and struggled to change the attitudes of her time.

In one way or another, almost all of Davis's stories are about the lack of power. Social and political suffering, the "echo [of] pathos," stimulates a sympathetic reaction in her characters that in turn stimulates their desire and capacity to change consciousness and, occasionally, to change the world. By turning to the vocabulary of feelings, a permitted female discourse, she managed to evade the advice of James Fields, who continued to be an ambivalent midwife at the birth of realism, encouraging its aspirations but toning down its incipient tendencies toward social criticism. But Davis persisted in explaining intense feelings as appropriate reactions to social causes—rooting the political in the emotional. Her conceptualization of power provides the link between sentiment and realism in her fiction. She did not, in my view, undermine the serious with the banal, but rather, rooted the objective in the subjective, appealing to emotions as well as data, to criticize social systems that authorized, for example, the persistence of racism in the North, the desperate plight of slaves, the harsh division of sexual spheres, men's abandonment of wives as they fled their homes and rural communities in search of work and adventure, the isolation of housework and child rearing, the futility of wifely resistance, the loneliness of single women, and the muteness of poverty. For Davis, home was neither utopia, nor even, in women's eyes, a retreat from worldly consciousness. Instead, home was a realm of somewhat limited female power that could, through sympathy, stimulate affection and responsibility. In sympathy Davis sought to model the appropriate social reaction. Thus the narrator in "Life in the Iron-Mills" chides the reader, "You laugh at [Deb's pain]? . . . Are pain and jealousy less savage realities down here in this place I am taking you to than in your own house or your own heart,—your heart, which they clutch at sometimes?" (10). Our task, as modern readers, is to understand how Davis's gendered conventions represent social history, how the traumas in her stories are symbolic of other traumas, and how they would have been understood in the second half of the nineteenth century.

Whether a study of an industrial town, a fictional exposé of mental institutions, a novel about the Tweed Ring, or a story about the painful divisions among southern families during the Civil War, nearly all of Davis's tales are primarily about women, all are shaped by a strong sense of place, and many are about the historical determinants of ethnicity and race. To the degree she left a record of her feelings, we sense that Davis saw life through its restrictions. Because her letters are generally reticent and her journal resides in an envelope of hundreds of snippets, because no letters exist between her and her husband, and few remain between her and figures with whom we know she was in touch—Lucretia Mott, Harriet Beecher Stowe, Louisa May Alcott, for example—the facts of her biography are, to my mind, frustrating to analyze.[9] Nonetheless, letters do remain between Rebecca and Annie Fields (first known to Davis as the wife of her publisher) and between Rebecca and her son, popular author

Richard Harding Davis. We also have correspondence with her publishers, her many essays, and her reminiscences published at the end of her life, under the belittling title *Bits of Gossip*. Taken together, they reveal Davis's concern that in the second half of the nineteenth century, with the close of the Civil War and the opportunities of industrialization, women were still illiterate, uneducated, unemployed, lonely, impoverished, and dependent on ineffectual, if kind, men. Race, which Davis often constructed in terms of gender, still begot abuse, rage, and the repression of creativity. Finally for Davis, geography—defined through botany, weather, local history, landscape, and the economics of place—continued to shape character and consciousness.

Rebecca Harding Davis wrote from 1861 to 1910. During this long career, she produced over 275 stories, 12 novels (most published serially), 125 juvenile stories, over 200 identifiable essays, and perhaps an equal number of unsigned essays.[10] Her work was published in journals such as the *Atlantic Monthly*, *Harper's New Monthly*, *Scribner's Monthly*, the *Independent*, the *Saturday Evening Post*, as well as in more widely circulated magazines such as *Lippincott's* and *Peterson's*.

Born in 1830, Rebecca Blaine Harding lived first in the cotton plantation country of Big Spring (now Huntsville) Alabama, whence her father, Richard Harding, a quixotic, displaced, and unsuccessful British businessman, had taken his young bride, Rachel Leet Wilson.[11] Her father was stern and distant, a man, in her view, with "no energy or business ability whatever."[12] Still, she acknowledged that she acquired his social conscience, his hatred for "vulgar American life," and his love of telling stories. A rather unsettled but whimsical man, Richard Harding would take his children on fanciful flights into the Middle Ages with Monsieur Jean Crapeaud, a twelve-inch knight who lived in a locked closet cut into the dining room chimney. Released only by her father, M. Crapeaud would carry a drawn sword and a banner, blazoned with the lilies of France, into dungeons, high towers, and gilded salons.

By contrast, Davis recalled her mother as "the most accurate historian and grammarian I have ever known [who] had enough knowledge to fit out half a dozen modern college bred women."[13] It was Rachel Harding who bestowed on Rebecca a sense of history and a love of literary style and precision. Unlike Richard, Rachel rooted her tales in regionalism and realism, early correctives to the myths of pastoralism, southern romanticism, and the prevailing fascination with transcendentalism. Rebecca would recall, for example, "I . . . often heard my mother describe the mixed magnificence and squalor of the life on the plantations among which we lived;

the great one-storied wooden houses built on piles; the pits of mud below them in which the pigs wallowed; the masses of crimson roses heaped high on the roofs; . . . the bare floors, not too often scrubbed; the massive buffets covered with magnificent plate, much of it cups and salvers won on the turf." Southern women, as described by Rachel, were not the belles of romanticism: "The women of these plantation families did not lead the picturesque idle life which their Northern sisters imagined and envied. Much of the day was spent in weighing provisions or cutting out clothes for field hands. They had few books—an odd volume of poems and their Bibles, which they read devoutly—and no amusements but an occasional hot supper to which they went in faded gowns of ancient cut." [14]

When Rebecca was five, the family moved to Wheeling (then in Virginia) where she would live until she married at age thirty-one. Like Big Springs, Wheeling was a village: "The world that we lived in when I was a child would seem silent and empty to this generation. There were no railways in it, no automobiles or trolleys, no telegraphs, no sky-scraping houses. . . . There was not, from sea to sea, a trust or a labor union. Even the names of those things had not yet been invented." [15] The town of Wheeling and the surrounding mountains of the Alleghenies would become compelling influences on Davis's writing. During Rebecca's childhood Wheeling would grow before her eyes into a booming industrial town. Yet in many senses it would always remain a border town. Built at the crossroads of the Ohio River and the National Road, Wheeling stood at a line between west and east, Confederacy and Union, industrial and rural—tense contrasts that would impel Davis's best fiction. As a young girl she would gaze down at steamships bound for St. Louis or New Orleans, and watch as huge vans, laden with bales of cotton, trundled from the slave plantations of the South toward the northern mill towns. As she saw the white-topped Conestoga wagons carrying emigrants from Norway, Poland, and Germany to "the Ohio" (which, as she observed, the whole West was then vaguely called), real history became more exciting than her father's fables: "These wagons were full of romance to us children. They came up with these strange people out of far-off lands of mystery, and took them into the wilderness, full of raging bears and panthers and painted warriors, all to be fought in turn. We used to look after the children peeping out at us with bitter envy for . . . we never left home." [16] As an adult, however, she would find this border conflicted and emotionally dangerous, its complexities misunderstood by New England intellectuals.

At her mother's insistence, Rebecca received considerably more education than most girls of her time. Rachel Harding was also her daughter's first and perhaps most influential teacher. She urged Rebecca to read Shakespeare's *Julius Caesar* and *The Tempest* when she was eight years old. Early on, Rebecca also read "Bunyan and Miss Edgeworth and Sir Walter."[17] One day she found a cheap collection of tales that included two or three stories pirated from Nathaniel Hawthorne's *Twice Told Tales*: here she first discovered that the "commonplace" had a place in literature. As Rebecca grew older, the Hardings hired tutors for Rebecca and her eldest brother, Wilse. Finally, for three years, from 1845 to 1848, she attended the Female Seminary Society in her mother's hometown of Washington, Pennsylvania. Although Rebecca was valedictorian and graduated at the head of her class, this marked the end of her formal education, which thereafter depended on that of Wilse, who enrolled in Washington College in Pennsylvania. In his summer breaks he would pass along to Rebecca his recent knowledge of the German language and his growing fascination with German romanticism, in particular the works of Johann von Goethe and Johann Gottlieb Fichte. Rebecca would soon reject the German romantics as obsessive and egoistical, but Rachel Harding's and Nathaniel Hawthorne's interest in "commonplace folk" would most profoundly influence the course of her writings.

Davis's literary apprenticeship began sometime in the late 1850s, when she met Archibald W. Campbell, editor of the local Wheeling *Intelligencer*,[18] a daily paper with the largest circulation in western Virginia. During these years, the *Intelligencer* reprinted national news, reported secessionist proceedings, covered local events and trade reports, reprinted best-selling fiction, and twice a week published poetry.[19] During the late 1850s Rebecca apparently sent the *Intelligencer* reviews, poems, and of greatest pleasure to herself, editorials, because, as she wrote to Campbell, "I have the most insane ambition that way."[20] As biographer Sharon Harris observes, this was truly an "insane" idea because, at the time no woman held editorial power in a periodical unless it was specifically intended for children or "ladies."[21] In any case, since none of these early pieces have been identified there is nothing really to prepare us for "Life in the Iron-Mills."

Written when sentimental fiction still reigned over the literary marketplace, "Life in the Iron-Mills" was, and remains, innovative and compelling both in its subject matter and in its experiments with literary form. Within the frame tale, Davis tells analogous stories of emotional and artistic confinement and repression. Sympathy shapes both the structure and desired reaction. As Glen Hendler astutely observes, sentimental narratives do not just describe sympathetic identification, they "perform" it.[22] But unlike the tall tale, often seen as a formative genre in American realism, in which a gentleman narrator distances himself from the local characters he describes in order to enhance their humor and contain their plebeian energy, Davis's narrator identifies with the emotional suffocation and the creative rebellion of the industrial poor. What is also unique in "Life in the Iron-Mills" is that the narrator is not a man and the "folk" are not comic rural yokels. Thus the tension Davis creates between realism and sentimentalism forces the reader to question the social assumptions behind both genres.

This is a story about analogous forms of deprivation in the family and at work. The narrator, "stifled" by the foul air of the factory town, is confined in her room throughout the story. Like the women in the illustrated magazines of the time, she stands alone, "idle," removed from the action, watching the world of work and activity through a window and sympathetically repeating, "I know." Nevertheless, while she identifies with the impoverished life outside, she also invites her readers to "come down and judge." "Life in the Iron-Mills" works through a series of narrative paradoxes; it encourages identification across class lines, invoking sympathy to undermine the sanctity of the home and then it distances the reader from the working-class characters through dialects, foreign phrases, elevated vocabularies, and a series of spectators who guide us "downward" and interpret for us. The "frame" mediates conflicting class values and conflicting literary styles. This putative synthesis of class and gender, and the putative sympathy across class lines, undermines the sanctity of a separate sphere for middle-class women.

As Elizabeth Langland has observed of sentimental fiction, "the very signifiers of powerlessness in the gendered frame of reference become eloquent signifiers of power in a class frame."[23] Throughout her writings Davis would question the tenets of sentimentalism—the joy of selfless love, motherhood, and the society of the family, the redemptive power of love, the home as refuge from the tensions of the workplace, and capitalism's protective covenant for women. Recurrent images of domestic hunger deconstruct sentimentalism's telos of nurture and build toward unifying images of "soul starvation." In the figure of a "mill girl" who works a twelve-hour shift and tries to feed a family and stay responsible for the emotional connections within it, "Life in the Iron-Mills" also introduced into American fiction the double oppression of working-class women.

Deborah's nighttime visit to the iron works is also one of the first detailed pictures of a factory in American fiction. In this early study of industrial labor, Davis introduced a presumedly uninformed reader to the night shift—the disruptive result of the new Bessemer process for making steel, in which it became too expensive to let the huge vats of molten pig iron cool down each night. In my view, Davis's images of industrial activity and heat take us well beyond Herman Melville's symbolic portrait of work in "The Paradise of Bachelors and the Tartarus of Maids," published six years earlier, in which an extended sexual metaphor of the machinery in a paper mill subsumes his descriptions of female labor.[24] Davis's local narrator will serve as interpreter for readers of the *Atlantic* because "Not many even of the inhabitants of a manufacturing town know the vast machinery of a system by which the bodies of workmen are governed, that goes on unceasingly" (7).

Davis also embedded her portrait of industrialism in the literary conventions of sentimentalism. Sentimental fiction and the domestic novel anticipated the depiction of daily life and domestic power struggles often credited to realism. In many of her stories, Davis included signs of what Elaine Showalter terms female "covert rebellion," already popularized in the highly sentimentalized domestic novel. For example, to undercut images of stoic womanly suffering and to record acts of female resistance, she portrayed images of sexual solidarity among women, the plight of unmarried women, feminized male heroes, and the attractiveness of a rebellious woman.[25] At the same time, pollution and poverty render the town "pregnant with death," a metaphor that fuses the gendered and economic readings. Located at the center of "Life in the Iron-Mills," the korl statue represents the era's most forceful attack on the Cult of the True Woman, as well as on factory life: "There was not one line of beauty or grace in it: a nude woman's form, muscular, grown coarse with labor the powerful limbs instinct—with some poignant longing. One idea there was in it: the tense, rigid muscles, the clutching hands, the wild eager face, like that of a starving wolf's" (15). This statue is the first of many of Davis's female characters whose body is not confined by bustle and bodice, whose existence is not defined by her maternal role, whose morality is not derived through avoidance of the outside world. Hers is a working woman's body. Created by the mills, it is strong, tired, and dissatisfied. And none of the male characters, including her male sculptor, can say for sure what she wants. They can only interpret the statue by her absences: she wants "summat [something] to make her live" (16). It makes one wonder why James Fields refused to let Davis entitle this story "The Korl Woman."

Critics have suggested that "Life in the Iron-Mills" hovers on the edge of naturalism. Published six years before Émile Zola's early and influential experiment in naturalism, *Thérèse Raquin* (1867), it began Davis's lifelong exploration of the effects of heredity, race, economics, gender and environment on character.[26] Unlike her realist contemporaries, Davis's characters must frequently navigate these inexorable pressures in a web of malignant purpose—economic, sexual, or geographic. Yet unlike Stephen Crane's or Frank Norris's characters, Davis's characters enact her commitment to free will and the existence of rational choice; their actions have meaning and shape the plots. Despite their ignorance, deformities, and even animalistic attributes, they are never in danger of slipping into the grotesque.[27] If in Davis we find impotent characters we also find characters who can conceptualize their situation and who survive. The frequent presence of an ironic narrator also implies that Davis does not intend to evoke amoral reactions in her readers.

In Davis's eyes, the blame for the personal and environmental plight of the emerging industrial society also resides in romanticism. "Life in the Iron-Mills" anticipates her later stories by firmly resolving the question that haunted Emerson and Thoreau, the romantic conflict between duties to the self and duties to the world, between solipsism and commitment. If indeed "there is no hope that it will ever end" (11), the fault lies in the self-absorption of the reader, who, like the midnight visitors to the mill, has gone out slumming in her story: "You, Egoist, or Pantheist, or Arminian, busy in making straight paths for your feet on the hills . . . do not see it clearly" (4). Two endings mark the romantic choice between solipsism and commitment—one promises social rebirth through Quakerism, a community identified with Abolition and reform, the second offers the persistent image of the unsatisfied statue which refuses to remain hidden, parodying the sentimental figure of the repressed narrator and decrying the frustrations of Davis's own life.

The politicization of sympathy and the feminization of public life would be the subject of narrative explorations for the rest of Davis's long career. In her first novel, *Margret Howth*, Davis would again investigate the relationship between female identity and historical change. By 1862, with the issues of Abolition and the Civil War storming through Wheeling, Davis became one of the few authors of American fiction to write about slavery and the war and to consider the impact of slavery on white identity. As William Dean Howells observed, the Civil War "laid upon our literature a charge under which it has . . . staggered very lamely."[28] Yet Davis's experiments in realism in "Life in the Iron-Mills" and *Margret Howth* gave her tools for writing about slavery in ways most others, with the exception of Lydia Maria Child or Harriet Beecher Stowe, could not. Furthermore, living in Wheeling gave Davis a closer knowledge of slavery and the Civil War than most northern writers had. Wheeling flanked the North and South; it had an active slave trade, yet, located across the river from the free state of Ohio, it also had become a station on the underground railroad and was picked by John Brown as a site for his insurrection. In 1861, after a painful debate over the issues of slavery and union, Wheeling also became the political center of the split from Virginia. Just a few blocks from Rebecca's house a citizen's convention voted to nullify Virginia's Ordinance of Secession and pass a new constitution granting gradual emancipation of slaves. By 1862, General Rosecrans had headquartered the Mountain Garrison across the street from the Harding house, and Davis spent the early war years under martial law, living on the edge of a battleground.

Daniel Aaron suggests that the literature of the American Renaissance begot a generation of authors who found it difficult to write about the Civil War because American literature could not shape "soldierly" activities, which require discourses of action rather than speech and avoid ambiguity and ambivalence.[29] But this recipe of certitude, violence, and closure was particularly unsuitable to the creation of fiction about the Civil War, which appeared to lack the noble purpose that give holy wars an "epic character."[30] The noble purpose of the Civil War, the abolition of slavery, was concealed in the rhetoric of union. The slave, and hence the war itself, figures only peripherally in most fiction written during the early 1860s, even in the North.[31] Northern authors also repressed the black character as "an uncomfortable reminder of abandoned obligations, a shadow of guilt and retribution."[32] Slavery, wrote Nathaniel Hawthorne, was "one of those evils which divine Providence does not leave to be remedied by human contrivances" but which will one day, "by some means impossible to be anticipated . . . vanish like a dream."[33]

Rebecca Harding Davis, however, wrote a series of stories during the war and the early years of Reconstruction that portrayed the oppression of slavery, the role of Abolition, the brutalities of the war itself, and its divisive impact on border communities. Although she was limited by the cultural distortions of slavery within romanticism and sentimentalism, in 1862 she would write three stories, "John Lamar," "Blind Tom," and "David Gaunt," which uniquely challenge Jane Tompkins's assessment that women confronted slavery only in the " 'closet' of the heart."[34] Struggling to create a realist discourse, Davis attempted to go beyond contemporary stereotypes that pictured black people as contented slaves, comic minstrels, and wretched freedmen. Despite the informative material of slave narratives and abolition literature, such popular images of blacks were tainted by contempt, dread, guilt, and sympathy. All stereotypes, Werner Sollors reminds us, reflect a form of universalist or essentialist thinking which is always a "thin camouflage" for power relations.[35] Raised in slaveholding Virginia, Davis's portraits of blacks are tinged with ambivalence, while her portraits of the institution of slavery clearly expose its brutality. In her Civil War stories, two discursive traditions collide: rhetorics from Abolition, Quakerism, transcendentalism, and the social gospel conflict with rhetorics of early eugenics, southern romanticism, and the proslavery movement. The representation of black characters becomes the site of her contested understanding and loyalties. Images of blacks as lazy, subservient, at times bestial confront portraits of blacks that reveal Davis's belief in human rationality, conscience, and growth.

Like many abolitionists, Davis also believed that women's moral superiority, which she identified with domestic work, gave them an understanding of the best needs of a community. Along these lines she believed that female suffering promoted an understanding of other sorts of oppression; domesticity positioned women to understand slavery as repression and exile. In her stories of slavery and the Civil War she developed the view that the line between the home and the work place is thin; in "John Lamar," "Blind Tom," and in her novel about reconstruction, *Waiting for the Verdict* (1867), she showed how slavery erased the border between private life and economic life. For the slave, neither the home nor the plantation offers refuge. In Davis's Civil War fiction she would challenge the notion that women and slaves thrive in confinement. However, while Davis would repudiate sentimental gestures of survival, in her studies of white women, that is, lying, manipulation, madness, and creativity, she would invoke these same gestures as understandable forms of slave resistance—dissembling, running away, fantasizing about freedom, enlisting in the Union Army, and committing acts of violence against slaveholders.

Written during and soon after the Civil War, these tales explore analogies between race and gender. In rejecting sentimental images of slavery as a form of holy martyrdom[36] she challenged the mutually enforcing romanticization of domesticity and slavery. As historian William Chafe observes, the parallel between race and sex functions "not in the *substance* of material existence which women and blacks have experienced but in the *forms* by which others have kept them in 'their place.' "[37] In Davis's narratives these parallel forms of control of women and blacks include physical abuse, psychological intimidation, economic deprivation, unrealizable goals, and painful limits on aspirations.

"John Lamar" is the story of a Confederate officer and his slave, Ben, who have been captured by the Union army. Ben must decide whether or not to help Lamar, his owner, escape, ensuring his master's freedom at the expense of his own. Throughout the story Davis uses the conventions of domestic fiction—child abandonment and abuse, powerlessness, homelessness, resistance and flight—to build sympathy between Ben and the Union soldiers, and between Ben and the reader. Unlike Lamar, Ben recalls the plantation as a place of abandoned children, brutality, intellectual loss, and sexual exploitation. Undermining Lamar's memory of the plantation as a protective home is Ben's rage at his orphan status and the vulnerability of his family. Through Ben's story Davis deconstructs the sentimental power of the home. Slavery shapes Ben's profoundly American longing for an absent father. His anger derives from a child's longing for his lost father, a runaway slave, rather than from an inherent feature of his race:

> He was this uncouth wretch's father.—do you understand? The flabby-faced boy, flogged in the cotton field for whining after his dad, or hiding away part of his flitch and molasses for months in hopes the old man would come back, was rather a comical object, you would have thought. Very different his, from the feeling with which you left your mother's grave,—though as yet we have not invented names for the emotions of those people. We'll grant that it hurt Ben a little, however. (42)

Thus descriptions of the cruelty of Ben's childhood compete with later references to him as a "brute negro."

Images of repression and self-concealment, conventionally assigned to women, also mark Ben's experience. With his "dull eluding word of something you could not tell what in the points of eyes" (35), Davis suggests that the meaning of slavery is hidden and unutterable. Yet Ben understands that to survive a slave, like a white woman, must understand power and learn how to lie and mask reactions. Davis thus portrays the internalization of servitude. As Ben contemplates revenge, he daintily (like a woman?) bends down to polish Lamar's boots and sees himself in the shoe—a slave narcissus whose image is shaped by dependency. The domestic codes of caretaking—protection, sympathy, and selfless identification—here suggest that sympathy endangers one's sense of self. Of greatest significance, however, is that while Ben's eyes render him a difficult text, his body, scarred "where the lash buried itself" (49) plainly exposes his brutal history. Slavery to Davis is neither paternalistic nor compatible with domesticity.

The most complicated image of the story surrounds the figure of Lamar's young orphaned sister, Floy, who has been left on the plantation in charge of 300 slaves. Both Lamar's and Ben's visions of freedom will take the shape of sexual fantasies about this child. In this Davis evokes domestic codes in order to point to female vulnerability and expose the false promise of the protective code. Both Lamar's incestuous fantasy, posed as chivalric romanticism, and Ben's eroticized dream of violence reverse the real sexual danger of slavery—white men's freedom to rape their slaves. For Davis, the ideology of sexuality—of virginity, chastity, and infantilized women—represents an interesting (and enduring) confusion of the erotic and the ethnic. In the mid-nineteenth century, civil marriage and the family were supposed to regulate men's sexual passion. As many abolitionists pointed out, however, a master's legal sexual accessibility to his female slaves undermined the family's ability to control his "licentiousness." Further, as Davis would observe in *Waiting for the Verdict*, during an era that allegedly revered chastity, the facts of rape, concubinage, and the presence of mulatto children testified to the false pretenses of domesticity and plantation chivalry as protective codes. Slaves, lacking relationships sanctioned by law, were accused of lacking the restraints of moral and religious culture.[38]

Interracial sexuality has long functioned in the white cultural imagination as a site for ethnic ambivalence.[39] E. Franklin Frazier once commented that "the closer a Negro got to the ballot box, the more he looked like a rapist."[40] A reference to black sexuality was a sanctioned reference to sexuality per se; it provided a window into the erotic. Although there is no documentation to prove that slaves or ex-slaves frequently raped white women, the stereotype of "Buck," the oversexualized male slave, was common. Elizabeth Fox-Genovese observes that this image both caricatures the economic value of a strong male slave and reflects an attribute that white men sought for themselves. The convention of "Buck" also severed black sexuality from social responsibility and atrophied black men in the white cultural tradition as perpetual adolescents.[41]

The final bond in "John Lamar" thus appears between woman author and female child, not between woman author and slave. Throughout the story we are meant to identify with Ben as a man who suffers the loss of his own mother, wife, daughter, and sister. The absence of such women in his life deprive Ben of the reforming power of love. Davis's messy synthesis of domesticity and slavery exposes the limited capacity of the private sphere to influence the public sphere; domesticity offers no sanctuary from masculine mastery. Although the sexual does not directly displace the racial in Davis's work, in 1862, the right to control one's own body would suggest the abolition of slavery. Her fusion of gender and race externalizes the possibility of black violence in order to give moral purpose to a reluctant war.

Marianna Torgovnick suggests that race and ethnicity are pliable cultural constructions; contemporary needs continually redefine the value and the nature of the ethnic or nonwhite person. Race does what the dominant culture asks it to do: "Voiceless, it lets us speak for it. It is our ventriloquist's dummy—or so we like to think. . . . It asks us what we want it to tell us."[42] Davis, however, writing as a white woman, has not simply appropriated slavery; in posing the identification of the woman and the slave, she has posited a reciprocal discourse of repression and liberation.

In "Blind Tom," a character sketch, the slaveowner attempts to make a slave his ventriloquist's dummy, channeling the culture of white society through the slave's musical talent. In this study Davis also makes the slave her own dummy, channeling a story of her own artistic repression, deformity, and loss of control through a study of a slave's repressed genius. "Blind Tom" is a portrait of Thomas Greene Bethune, a slave who was born blind, deformed, and suffering from *savant syndrome*, a form of autism. One night, when Tom was seven, he awakened the plantation family by ecstatically playing complicated music on the piano. His owner soon discovered that this child could instantly mimic, memorize, and play any music he heard. He also could compose his own music, which filled audiences with a sense of discordant beauty and pathos. As soon as Tom's master realized that his slave's talent was clearly more profitable than tobacco, he exhibited him in concert halls throughout the South, although never in a free state or Europe.[43] Within a year he took Tom on his first tour, which apparently earned Colonel Bethune $100,000.

After seeing one of Tom's performances, Davis began her own investigations into his biography. While her depiction is essentially accurate, she shapes Tom's life as a study of white projection, a portrait of repressed creativity, thereby undercutting the stereotype of the black performer as a comic fool. Tom also engages Davis's ongoing analysis of the sentimental figure of the body. Tom's body signifies love and protection as terms of ownership, exposes the ways in which the body can simultaneously be a source of creative freedom and an object in an involuntary transaction. It too suggests the physical hunger for artistic expression. Defined through his body, nature and nurture compete in Tom, but his representation is ultimately distorted by Davis's racist assumptions about black nature.

Like many of Davis's female characters, Tom suffers both physical subjugation and exclusion from intellectual stimulation. He, too, defies his designated identity and creates a form of his own freedom that, in the end, guarantees his enslavement; his creativity becomes the means of his appropriation and display. Yet, paradoxically, the absence of culture and training is what keeps Tom's music pure. The image of Tom's repression thus illustrates what Jean Fagan Yellin has observed as the paradoxical way slavery gave white women access to speech.[44] In the nineteenth century, the figure of a bound and silent slave allowed a female abolitionist political discourse that was denied the slave; her representation of the slave also suggested her own repression.

Tom is the first of a series of Davis's characters whose body both is and is not a useful sign of his identity. The description of Tom's deformities confirm the sentimental notion that the body offers a stable grammar of social and psychological signs. However, in terms that anticipate the vocabulary of Social Darwinism, Davis shapes the concept of natural selection to include the physical abuses of slavery.[45] At the same time, Davis, who sees herself as unattractive, identifies with a series of homely but artistic characters whose creative and sexual passions are stymied by their bodies—female, plain, deformed or black. In "Blind Tom," images of silence and repression project Tom's isolation across lines of gender and class. What distinguishes this figure from many of Davis's other pitiable enslaved or female characters is the fact that Tom is not ultimately silenced.

In this regard, "Blind Tom" confirms what Philip Fisher has termed the "sentimental procedure," the conflation of the categories of class and gender into figures of abused prisoners, children, animals, and slaves.[46] By means of this analogy, he suggests, the weak will gain representation through the moral category of compassion. Davis would use the textured figure of the prisoner, like the slave, in tales such as "The Story of Christine" (1866), which tells of a young Dutch woman abducted by a ship captain and sold in America as an indentured servant, and *Put Out of the Way* (1870), a gripping novella about the involuntary institutionalization of mental patients.

Fisher aptly warns us, however, to distinguish the successful politics of sentimental representation from the representation itself. Sentimentality, he suggests, extends "normal states of primary feeling to people from whom they have been previously withheld . . . [who] earn the right to human regard by means of the reality of their suffering."[47] Through sympathy, the conventions of sentimentality modify the representation of slavery as difference. But Tom's suffering also deconstructs our projection: his performances have a titillation, a fascination with bondage that he, at times, attempts to resist.

Realism further complicates the sentimental procedure by frustrating its promise that virtue will earn material reward. In realist fiction, powerlessness does not necessarily guarantee justice; indeed, powerlessness often requires public rather than private responses. Unlike the martyrdom of Harriet Beecher Stowe's Uncle Tom, Davis's Blind Tom does not suffer a spiritual predicament. His pain, like the suffering of Ben in "John Lamar," requires a secular solution. Through realism Davis also avoids what Wernor Sollars terms sentiment's "typology of ethnicity," the assumption of reciprocal events that transform and elevate history into a shared biblical drama.[48] In addition, through realism Davis can confront the sentimental motif that pictures confinement as safety and suffering as heavenly wrath. Her representation of slavery externalizes suffering; the pain of slavery is historical, political, institutional, and public. Thus she compelled her readers to conceive of the elimination of slavery as the true role of the Civil War. She examined the tenuous future of Abolition and Reconstruction in her finest novel, *Waiting for the Verdict*, the story of a mulatto surgeon who practices in Philadelphia.

In addition, Davis rejected facile or romanticized images of the Civil War itself. She was haunted by the suffering she saw on both sides:

The histories which we have of the great tragedy give no idea of the general wretchedness, the squalid misery, which entered into every individual life in the region given up to the war. Where the armies camped the destruction was absolute. Even on the border, your farm was a waste, all your horses or cows were seized by one army or the other, or your shop or manufactory was closed, your trade ruined. You had no money; you drank coffee made of roasted parsnips for breakfast, and ate only potatoes for dinner. Your nearest kinsfolk and friends passed you on the street silent and scowling; if you said what you thought you were liable to be dragged to the county jail and left there for months. The subject of the war was never broached in your home where opinions differed; but, one morning, the boys were missing. No one said a word, but one grey head was bent, and the happy light died out of the old eyes and never came to them again.[49]

With the publication of "David Gaunt" in the *Atlantic* in 1862, early in the war Davis sent north a portrait of a West Virginia village painfully divided in its loyalties over union, religion, and the role of women. A pioneering tale in American antiwar fiction, "David Gaunt" tells the story of the relationship between a lonely mountain woman and three men—a Union officer, an itinerant preacher, and her grieving father, whose Confederate son has just been killed in battle. The tragic ironies of the war force all the characters to become open to new ways of thinking—that is, to openness itself, which, in the end, allows them all to recognize the larger implications of religious and political freedom. Peripheral to the narrative of war, religion, and romance, but central to the meaning of the story, is Bone, a slave, who also moves from an unquestioning acceptance of his assigned role to a new sense of his right to freedom. Davis, pained by her Virginia roots and her growing abolitionist sensibilities, well understood that the Civil War signified national fratricide. As such, it cast political actions in personal terms and personal actions in political terms. With its inherently insurrectionist and, at the same time, interfamilial overtones, the Civil War served Davis as an appropriate metaphor for resistance to social proscriptions, including evangelical religion and sex roles, which she continued to define through the constructs of sentimentalism.

In "David Gaunt" Davis invokes sentimental conventions of romance, reunion, and reform to question the meaning of sacrifice: should an amorous, political, or religious goal justify the death of father, brother, or friend? Initially, male certitude about these compelling issues seems more reasonable than female ambivalence; however, Davis sets this tale of men fighting for their cause against the story of a woman who refuses to be the prize for their political rectitude. Despite the men's political disagreements, they agree that Dode, the heroine, represents home, a utopian repository for their justifications for war—dissimilar though their rationales may be. Increasingly, the men's political convictions appear to be instances of masculine individualism, which are challenged by female images of tolerance and true community—home and hospital. Soon the men's debate about secession (not, in this story, a debate about slavery) devolves into senseless killing. While the men are represented through their actions—fighting battles, delivering patriotic sermons—the female characters are represented through images of pregnant silence, palpable but in wait. If the man's war is about conviction and honor, the woman's war is about isolation, ignorance, and repression. Women, Davis observed, absorbed the war "as women greedily do anything that promises to be an outlet for what power of brain, heart, or animal fervor they may have. . . . [They] had no poetic enthusiasm about it. . . . Their sleazy lives had wanted color and substance and they found it in a cant of patriotism, in illuminating their windows after slaughter, in dressing their tables with helmets of sugar."[50] It is through the figures of the village women that Davis speaks to the brutalities of war—of women and children, naked and homeless, fleeing in the snow, or a mother who finds her boy's half-charred body left tied to a tree by rebel scouts. Moreover, the men's war seems meaningless; immediately after a bloody Union victory, the federal army evacuates the village, leaving it in the hands of the Confederates.

"David Gaunt" is also the story of a father who repeatedly misunderstands his daughter's intelligence and independence and who is "savagely" jealous of her lover. It may have been an emblem for Rebecca, who was finally leaving home at thirty-one to marry a young attorney, L. Clarke Davis, who had written her a fan letter after he read "Life in the Iron-Mills." With her career taking shape during a moment of great political upheaval, painfully felt at the most local level, and with her marriage to Clarke a few months away, in "David Gaunt" Davis wrote a story of the discovery of female courage, independence, intellectual tolerance, and political romance.

On January 10, 1863, Rebecca wrote to Annie Fields that soon she was to be married and would move to Philadelphia: "It isn't easy for me to tell you this. I don't know why. I would rather tell other women's stories than my own."[51] But to some degree, these stories would become one and the same. Finally anticipating career and children, it never occurred to Davis that marriage would mark the end of her writing. Late in January she again wrote to Annie, "I must have leave to say my word in the Atlantic as before, when the spirit moves me. It is necessary for me to write—well or ill— you know every animal has speech and that is mine."[52] Within six months of the wedding, despite her contentment with Clarke and her pleasure at her research desk at the Philadelphia Free Library, Rebecca suffered an acute attack of nervous exhaustion which stemmed, it seems, from a difficult pregnancy, from sharing a small house with Clarke's family, and from tending to Clarke and his sister, who were both ill. During this breakdown, Rebecca was treated by Dr. S. Weir Mitchell, who prescribed for her the rest cure that Charlotte Perkins Gilman so formidably evokes in "The Yellow Wallpaper" (1891).

With "The Wife's Story" (1864), her first major work after her recovery, Davis launched a series of short stories that focus on women's isolated and frustrated lives; others included in this anthology are "The Harmonists" (1866), "The Story of Christine" (1866), "Earthen Pitchers" (1873-1874), "Dolly" (1874), "Marcia" (1876), "A Day with Dr. Sarah" (1878), and "Anne" (1889). These stories engage the most subversive elements of sentimentalism, exposing the painful consequences of an ethos that represses women's independence and individuality.[53] In describing several women's attraction to lives of creativity and self-definition, Davis rescripts the sentimental heroine's "progress" from autonomy to subservience, from independence to abjection, from initiative to stasis. She undercuts the paradigm of obligatory self-abnegation, and uses her characters' power and pain to undercut her own plots, giving lie, along the way, to her stories' endings of masculine superiority and social control. Thus does Davis follow a trend of earlier sentimental tales, in which critic Joanne Dobson finds "a strong emotional undertow that pulls the reader in the opposite direction."[54] Davis's stories expose her profound ambivalence about the domestic contract in which women gain authority by redeeming men rather than by pursuing their own lives and power. Her ironic voice lets us know that women's pursuit of autonomy results in unearned punishment and unmerited self-doubt.

In these stories Davis also attacked the notion that a "separate female sphere" offers women a zone of refuge, community, culture, and, in a restricted sense, freedom. Ultimately, Davis's stories of mill girls, child prostitutes, female journalists, utopianists, opera singers, and circus performers call into question the very existence of a world untouched by the marketplace. The distinction between public and private breaks down. Not only do many of her working women inhabit both worlds: her wives and mothers also understand that romance and the protective covenant of marriage are threatened by a disorderly public world in which businesses collapse, husbands are fired, and mortgages foreclosed. Davis refused to remove subjective experience from its place in economic history. The family—the sentimental metaphor for desire and the image of material respite—emerges as an analogue of economic and gender tensions, rather than as an alternative social geography. Femaleness is rarely a straightforward sign of domestic authority.

While Davis locates domestic plots in authentic historical contexts, the narrative activities themselves transform political situations into psychological dilemmas. Davis's plots work themselves out on the psychological plane, and hence they reinforce the notion that resolution lies in the subjective realm. Because she ultimately represents social conflict as personal history, we must decide whether Davis returns us to the social plane in the end, or whether in such stories as "The Wife's Story," "Anne," and "Earthen Pitchers" she continues to conceal power in the domestic plots, subversive though they may be.

Davis's first critique of marriage as an elusive promise appeared in "The Wife's Story" (1864). Here the image of the family as sanctuary confronts the image of marriage as intellectual suicide. Hester Manning, a middle-aged New England woman, has recently married a widower who has five children. Soon after the birth of her daughter and the discovery that her husband's business has failed, she is offered the chance to launch her musical career as a composer and to have a singing part in the premiere of her first opera. Raised in New England on Margaret Fuller's doctrine of a woman's right to growth, Hester chooses career over family, delivers her colicky baby to a nurse, and moves to New York. But her brief night at the opera turns into a terrifying dream sequence of shame, abandonment, and death.

There are strong autobiographical elements in the "The Wife's Story," written during Davis's difficult first pregnancy—her despondency at middle-class poverty, her concern that her talent was unauthentic, and her guilt-laden fear that her new career would be thwarted by the pressing needs of her husband and forthcoming child. In her earliest use of a first-person narrator she announces, "I will tell you the story of my life" (112), although there seems to be no evidence that Clarke Davis tried to impede Rebecca's career. "The Wife's Story" also develops Davis's critique of romanticism. She frames the tension between Hester's creative needs, motherly duties, and sexual attraction to her husband as the tension between Christian sympathy and transcendental egotism. While true femininity represents social commitment, martyrdom, and life in the commonplace, the creative life is self-indulgent and solipsistic. It becomes impossible, it seems, to reconcile sentimental femininity with liberal individualism. By equating a woman's artistic autonomy with transcendentalism, Davis has extended the contradictions within sentimentalism into a more complicated ideological debate. Through sexuality and motherhood, marriage, which is initially seen as the death of the unique self, offers community and intimacy.

Like Nathaniel Hawthorne's Hester Prynne, Davis's Hester must also choose between idealism and materialism, artifice and nature, the self and others. Davis, however, compounds these romantic tensions with references to the influences of gender and class. Hester recalls from her childhood in her New England, where there was more "mental power" than necessary for the work that needed to be done, intellectualism constantly fed upon itself. By contrast, her Western husband and his son seem "but clogs of flesh, the mere hands by which the manual work of the world's progress was to be accomplished" (115). When she finally allies herself with her adult family, she accepts them as the industrial and masculine present. She comes to understand that her husband's lack of apparent introspection does not imply a lack of feeling. In the end, she finds resolution by redefining gender differences as differences of class and region.

"The Harmonists," published two years after "The Wife's Story," extends Davis's attack on romanticism as solipsistic, individualistic, and hostile to women's real needs. An early critique of utopianism, "The Harmonists" shows how Economy, a celibate experimental community in rural Pennsylvania, perpetuated industrial alienation, and along the way repressed female subjectivity. Here Davis suggests that the community of Economy (based on the theories of George Rapp) represented a sexual exchange that promised women economic security through the benevolent patronage of male authority. While utopia protected women from public and political decisions, it also deprived them of authority over domestic life, pictured as the loss of reproductive and sexual control of their bodies.[55] The celibate Rappite women, marked by their shriveled breasts, are assigned to impersonal "families" of seven where they mourn the children they never bore.[56] Although George Rapp argued that celibacy represented the subjugation of personal desire in preparation for the Messiah, in "The Harmonists" Davis suggested that his male followers used chastity to create a barrier between themselves and women. In contrast, she found that sexual desire to the Rappite women signified intimacy and maternal longing. In the village of Economy, the separation of personal and public life becomes a utopian paradigm for male dominance. By perpetuating separate spheres for men and women and calling it utopia, Economy also perpetuated the romantic notion that the self, even the utopian self, is separate from the society. Throughout her career, Davis would remain suspicious of any formula whereby the dreams of a single man would shape the community as a whole.[57] Ultimately, Davis would seek philosophies forged through dependence, conflicted though it may be.

During the time when Davis was intensely involved in raising her active and winsome two-year-old son, parenting becomes the central metaphor for the debate over social organization. Dr. Knowles, a single father, is a parody of the romantic motif of a man on the run from civilization, still marked as women's space.[58] He is seeking "the old patriarchal form for its mode of government, establishing under that, however, a complete community of interest" (170). But Davis questions the possibility of a community of interests for men and women in a society that is hierarchical, celibate, and hostile to children. Dr. Knowles vows that he knows no child, no wife, nor any brother except his brother man and gives his son to the community. He is seeking a place "a sphere of infinite freedom . . . a home where a man can stand alone" (171–72)—not a sphere, as Davis was well aware, that included a young child. Women in the nineteenth century did not conceive of the home, practically or ideologically, as a sphere of one's own.

"The Harmonists" explores how Dr. Knowles, a highly feminized man, came to understand the meaning of dependence. To undo the alienation, isolation, and economic obsession of industrial consciousness, he must return to the family rather than join utopia. Through this androgynous mother-father figure, Davis rescripts the oedipal plot; in Knowles she recovers both the mother, whom the son must reject in order to realize his sexual identity, and the unavailable industrial father. In restoring the intimacy of father and son through their visit to Economy, Davis calls into question the idea of identity based on a denial of domestic connection rather than identity forged within relationships.[59] Theorist Jessica Benjamin suggests that such a denial often leads to domination because the absolute assertion of independence requires regressively possessing and controlling the needed objects—traditionally the repudiated parent.[60] In "The Harmonists" Davis anticipated modern feminist psychoanalysts who observe that because girls do not have to relinquish maternal dependency, they are free to presume that intimacy is healthy. In his visit to the lonely communards, Davis's androgynous traveler Dr. Knowles comes to understand the paradox of identity which, as Jessica Benjamin puts it, is "that in being with the other, I may experience the most profound sense of self."[61]

The image of the maternal figure is unusual in Davis's opus. Like many female authors of her time, Davis usually repressed the figure of the mother, who is often absent, silenced, or dead.[62] While Sandra Gilbert and Susan Gubar argue that fictive motherlessness is often a textual emblem for female disinheritance and powerlessness,[63] and while Adrienne Rich argues that motherlessness *frees* the Victorian heroine from a model of subservience,[64] I find that the nonmothers in "The Harmonists" represent women's political oppression and sexual repression. As Knowles, his son, and the narrator come upon the community for the first time, the narrator predicts, "Nature was about to take me to her great mother's bosom"

(172). The breast, the visitor's projection of female desire as social tele-ology, is in fact empty; utopia is a sterile and unloving mother. Davis refused to portray women's desire through their ability to attract or repel; unless the utopian women, with their shriveled breasts, are political and sexual *subjects* rather than political and sexual *objects*, we have dystopia. In this, Davis anticipated the later nineteenth-century matriarchal utopias of Mary E. Lane's *Mizora* (1890) and Charlotte Perkins Gilman's early twentieth-century feminist utopia, *Herland* (1915).

Utopia disappoints Knowles because it has reified gender roles at the expense of the natural self. Redeemed by "mother love," he reclaims his son, "growling caresses like a lioness who has recovered her whelp" (172); maternal behavior takes precedence over male theory in determining social relationships. The traveler rejects autonomy, the telos of the patriarchal utopia, in favor of family. The sexual contract, the gendered split between the public and private worlds, universalized as utopian telos, has disguised the competitive and incompatible natures of men's and women's interests. In "The Harmonists" Davis exposes autonomy, reveals the true nature of women's work, and encourages the expression of female desire. "The Harmonists" also deconstructs the utopian space between independence and community, self and society, reality and possibility, to transform a political state into a psychological condition and to recast political distinctions as gender differences. In contrast to the fears of the Rappites, for Davis the mother figure is neither menacing nor engulfing. Utopia need not involve her repudiation.

"Marcia," written in 1876, tells the story of a young woman writer who desperately tries to challenge the powerful literary province of sentimentality. Marcia has come to Philadelphia from her impoverished farm in Mississippi, "vowing herself to literature," a play on the marriage metaphor by a woman who has chosen the "business" of authorship over the "business" of marriage. She attempts to rebel against the sentimental prototype of a "literary domestic,"[65] but publishers reject her regional stories in which she portrays her dreary home on the Yazoo River, the unbearable heat, the poverty, the reptiles in the swamps and stagnant ponds, the dirt and monotony of the big house and the quarters. Nevertheless, the narrator, a publisher, finds that her stories remain in his mind with the vivid strength of Thomas Hardy's moors—unlike other stories he receives that linger only as a blurred memory of sunsets, duchesses, violets, bad French, and worse English. Although he acknowledges that those other stories are unreal, impossible, and show not a hint of common sense, he believes that the literary industry is unprepared for Marcia's realism.

Davis, enacting the publisher's goals for American literature, grounds her study of Marcia in the material realities of a woman writer. Marcia has refused to write tales of countesses and romance, matters of which she knows nothing. That is to say, she has refused to join Hawthorne's "damned mob of scribbling women." Nonetheless, she must figure out how to survive in Philadelphia as a writer, a crisis of style that Davis struggled with when she decided to write for women's magazines such as *Petersen's*, which appealed to mass audiences. Ann Wood argues that women writers succumbed to pressures to produce children's literature, books on child care, household management, and "works of sensibility steeped in depoliticized and lofty patriotism and misty, death-oriented and nonsectarian religious fervor." Unlike Marcia, the "feminine writers responded gallantly to the call, and turned out such works in staggering numbers to the polite applause of their reviewers, who complacently praised their piety, lack of energy and resolute disregard of conflict." [66] But rather than betray her craft, Marcia takes a job stitching socks and accepts a meager writing assignment collecting jokes for the humor columns. Thus, while many sentimental authors announced that their tales issued from an unconscious and irresistible flow of creativity (Harriet Beecher Stowe reported that God wrote *Uncle Tom's Cabin*),[67] Davis insists that writing is a skilled, competitive, and deliberate job.

In this story of a destitute woman who fails at this job, Davis conflates the choices for Marcia with the situation of American literature. Sentimentalism, observes Ann Douglas (Wood), "asserts that the values a society's activity denies are precisely the ones it cherishes." [68] Or claims to cherish. Davis's portrait of Marcia's public and professional vulnerability contrasts with her portrait of Marcia's mother, a bright but uneducated rural woman who learned from her husband that wives are "like mares— only useful to bring forth children" (311). Living on a poor plantation, she sees from her window a view of the graves of her dead babies, a haunting landscape of her capitulation to female activity. With her acute but untutored mind and her unfulfilled instinct for beauty, Marcia's mother has nothing to think about and takes opium to "quiet" herself; again Davis uses the metaphor of silence as the repository of women's material discontent.

True to the paradigm of sentimentality, in the end Marcia, like Anne in the story of the same name, or Jenny in "Earthen Pitchers," denies her literary ambitions and accepts the proposal of Mr. Biron, the abrasive overseer of her family's decaying plantation who has come north to rescue her. But the character of Mr. Biron exposes Davis's ambivalence about this resolution. As Marcia lies comatose with hunger and fatigue, he undresses her, his big hairy hand shaking as he opens her tattered dress in a suggestive violation. Images of ownership surround their marriage, a business transaction arranged by her father. Allusions to Biron's role as a slave overseer and hunter of slave fugitives further complicate his rescue of Marcia.

Marcia's final punishment is to suffer literary silence. Like the korl woman, Marcia is also starving, a condition that represents her unfulfilled artistic and intellectual quest. Clearly culpable is the cowardly publisher-narrator who acknowledges the creative power of Marcia's story even as he refuses to publish it. The fact that Marcia and her mother cannot survive in either the world of writing or the world of marriage suggests Davis's conflict about the prevailing literary tradition and the ideology that constitutes it. "Marcia" is a self-reflexive story about writing that profoundly questions the tradition to which it succumbs.

As early as the 1860s, however, Davis began to explore an alternative vision to the culture of northern industrialism. In "Life in the Iron-Mills" the narrator remarked that the "dream of green fields and sunshine is a very old dream—almost worn out, I think" (3). But it was not worn out for Davis. Rooted in her childhood in the mountains of West Virginia and in her frequent trips to a farm in Manasquan on the barren New Jersey coast are a series of stories of rural life. Here, in polarized images, Davis would consider the city and the country, civilization and wilderness, mind and body, yet she always remained well aware that literary tradition shapes our perception of nature. In these stories she explores the tensions between the pastoral motif and the realities of rural life, and exposes the cultural conventions that suggest that rural life is simple, static and continuous. Davis saw that assumptions about nature are inescapably bound to commerce, slavery, post–Civil War nationalism, and patriarchy.

Throughout her stories of rural life, Davis identifies society with masculinity.[69] In "Out of the Sea" (1865), "Earthen Pitchers" (1873-1874), "The Yares of Black Mountain" (1875), and "The House on the Beach" (1876), and in the novel *Dallas Galbraith* (1868), she explores how political, economic, and cultural relationships between city and country signify relationships between men and women. Based on years of visits to Point Pleasant on the New Jersey coast, to Lewes on the Delaware coast, and frequent travels through the rural South, Davis introduces and then resists the view that nature and woman are available and vulnerable to human intervention, control, or even definition.

I hope that the reissue of Davis's rural stories will help to undermine the idea that women's regional writings in the late nineteenth century were emasculated tales produced by " 'New England spinsters . . . driven to extremes of nostalgic fantasy' about 'imaginary pasts.' "[70] As early as 1919 the *Nation* charged that women's local color stories showed a "triviality of observation . . . connected with [a] strongly, often stiflingly domestic atmosphere,"[71] immured, George Santayana would add, from the "rough passions of life."[72] Robert Spiller, in his influential *Literary History of the United States* (1974 edition) similarly observed, "It is fair to say that as a group [female local colorists] avoided the commonplace, concerned themselves chiefly with the unusual, were incurably romantic, obsessed with the picturesque, and accurate only to the superficial aspects of their chosen materials."[73] Ann Douglas would likewise find in them "paranoid and claustrophobic" tendencies.[74]

For Davis, however, rural life is not local color, but is constructed, culturally and economically, in its relationship to urban life. Nature is a site of work and politics. Nature is also an imagined territory, a fantasized landscape of gendered values. Annette Kolodny suggests that if a woman writer who lived on or visited the frontier saw it as the metaphorical landscape of someone else's imagination, she could not locate herself in nature.[75] To feminize the frontier, she would confine herself to an "innocent amusement of a garden's narrow space" and, with equanimity, welcome the disappearance of primal wild spaces.[76] When Davis wrote of nature, she seems to have avoided not only these female tropes, but also several recurrent male constructions of nature—as the place of a brutal exodus to an unpromising land, as the eroticized site of violent conquest, and as the source of guilt for its destruction. In "Earthen Pitchers" Davis sees the wildness in nature as a dangerous and layered symbol of a woman's unconscious that she must conquer and domesticate, and in "The Yares of Black Mountain" she views the wilderness as a complex metaphor for female community, maternal power, and political resistance.

As L. J. Jordonova reminds us, distinctions that pose woman as natural and man as cultural inevitably appeal to ideas about the biological foundation of woman.[77] Davis's stories of rural life challenge the essentialist analogy between woman and nature in which both are seen as mutually backward, ignorant, innocent, and fertile. Neither woman nor nature is the repository of an uncorrupted morality. Not even her female rural characters can completely transcend the artificiality of society and culture. Yet Davis seems to maintain the gendered tradition in her representations of urban life; civilization itself is rational, exploitative, dominating, and competitive, and in itself is often a metaphor for masculinity. The struggle between the sexes in her stories thereby takes on a historical dimension, as human history—the rise of civilizations through domination over nature—represents the realization of masculine ways of being.[78]

Davis inherited the sentimental critique of America's passage from a decentralized agrarian life to industrial capitalistism. Yet she never resorts to a generalized and nostalgic view of the preindustrial or nonindustrial world. Nor does she turn toward a romantic discourse that severs rural life from urban life through fantasies of a natural home in an earlier moment of economic development. Hence, she rejects the evocation of nature as home, a space where women can find meaning and where men can avoid the world of trade. It is not a safe spot where Eve might cultivate her New England garden, as in the fictions of Alice Cary, for example. Rather, Davis recorded the dangers to rural life that she saw in southern nostalgia, in the growth of industries in mountain towns in West Virginia, in hardships in fishing villages on the Jersey coast, and in the brutal mountain battles of the Civil War.

In stories of Union mountain women and men living in the southern Cumberlands, of isolated Delaware fishermen, of "wrakers" who scrounge for the salvage from wrecked sailing ships, of impoverished women in coastal villages compelled to take rude tourists into their homes as boarders, life close to nature provides neither nurture, abundance, nor unalienated labor. At times, her characters succumb to fantasies of a space of harmony with nature where they might find a maternal and feminine presence, an enclosing receptive environment that offers gratification and painless satisfaction.[79] But Davis quickly goes on to deconstruct visions of nature as a regressive site away from adult (read *masculine*) responsibilities, a return to the primal warmth of womb or breast in a feminine landscape, an abundant, tempting if vulnerable image of filial homage and erotic desire.[80] Hence, because nature is not home, neither are her rural women, in Kolodny's phrase, unauthorized presences in landscapes to which they do not belong, as in the fictions of E.D.E.N. Southworth or Maria Cummins.[81]

Between 1857 and 1898, a series of editors of the *Atlantic*, from James Russell Lowell, James Fields, and William Dean Howells through Thomas Bailey Aldrich and Horace Scudder, promoted a realist aesthetic that could depict authentic regional details. Influenced by T. W. Higginson, they sought an American literature that would debunk the overgeneralized descriptions, the essentialist characterizations and the pastoral nostalgia of sentiment.[82] Among these authors, Davis has most in common with the grim antipatriarchal indictments of Rose Terry Cooke, the ironic ambivalence about matriarchal pastoralism of Mary E. Wilkins Freeman, the early class consciousness of Elizabeth Stuart Phelps, and the close observation of southern botany, geology, and language of such later regional writers as Mary Noailles Murfree and Constance Fenimore Woolson.

As a realist, Davis altered the pastoral landscape (which is not to say, as critic Roger Stein wryly reminds us, that nature doesn't still "mean").[83] Davis repopulated arcadia with intelligent and competent female figures who survive through their knowledge of tides, herbs, clouds, rock formations, and the dangers of storms, quicksand, and rural marriage. Her heroines can track a horse, build a log cabin in a blizzard, rescue a wounded lover in a blinding snowstorm, and row out to sea in a gale to save a shipwrecked son. Abandoning the "heroine's text" of seduction, betrayal, and marriage, Davis describes the realities of rural relationships—at times comfortable, caring, and mutually involved in the projects of agrarian work and rural survival, and at other times lonely, repressive, and intellectually barren. But nature alone does not determine the course of romance.

Refusing to divorce nature from society, Davis explored the economic and technological links between the country and the city and grounded her rural tales in local history. In "The House on the Beach" (1876) she traces the financial and ethical pressures to build lighthouses and lifesaving stations along the Jersey shore and describes how new inventions for predicting weather have united rural communities across the country; in "David Gaunt" she pictures the ravishment of the land during the Civil War; in "Out of the Sea" (1865) she refers to the role of insurance companies in shaping the moral meaning of shipwrecks; in "Earthen Pitchers" she talks of female inheritance and property rights; and in "The Grey Cabins of New England" (1895) she describes how men have abandoned the barren land, leaving the women similarly forsaken. At the same time, Davis's descriptions of nature itself are realistic and authentic. Her descriptions of botany, climate, geology, and color appropriately picture coastal and mountainous regions, altitudes, and seasons. Similarly accurate is her use of local dialect, customs, and dress.

In these stories, Davis recasts the rhetorics of romanticism in order to portray rural life and nature as a female community. Nature emerges as an image of dependence rather than autonomy, intimacy rather than isolation, speech rather than silent awe. The female traveler cannot remain a voyeur or outsider and will find, through whatever natural epiphany the plot provides, an organicism in nature. To the degree Davis pictures nature as maternal, it motivates the heroine not through quest to conquest but through quest to transcendent recognition of her own identity. As Simone de Beauvoir observes,

> Nature is one of the realms [women writers] have most lovingly explored . . . for the woman who has not fully abdicated, nature represents what woman herself represents for man: herself and her negation, a kingdom and a place of exile: the whole in the guise of the other. It is when she speaks of moors and gardens that the woman novelist will reveal her experience and her dream to us most intimately.[84]

It is in this feminist sense of transcendence that Davis builds on the narcissism of romanticism. By submission to nature and acknowledgment of friendship with a rural woman, her characters receive an image of unity and suffer the dissolution of ego.

"Earthen Pitchers" (1873–1874) is Davis's most sustained exploration of the assumptions about the masculinization of culture and the feminization of nature. This is the story of two young women who struggle with the meaning of "earthen pitchers," the teleological image of women as nature's vessels. Jenny, a Philadelphia journalist, lives by writing book notices, women's columns, portraits of country life, and reports of expeditions to Indian country; hence she suffers the poverty and isolation of a single career woman. Audrey (her name evokes a pastoral shepherdess), who lives in a fishing village and has a deep knowledge of the sea and the legends of the Barnegat pirates, wants to pursue a career as a singer. But for both the urban and the rural woman, life as an artist is not only masculine but masculinizing. Barely able to get by, Jenny tries to ingratiate herself into the Bohemian society of Philadelphia, only to be seen as a sharp woman pushing into a man's place. But in this man's place, nature has become a fashionable artistic trend—a pretty effect. Yosemite, the Rocky Mountains, the Maryland countryside, and Indian country are merely attractive new settings to replace Europe, the Nile, and Australia— by this time exhausted by Dickens, Kingsley, and their followers as interesting literary "backgrounds." Thus, pressures of literary convention and economic necessity have given Jenny a utilitarian view of rural life; she confesses that she has concealed her true literary style in order to write "shop work." Jenny cannot afford to write her poetry, even though "it tells," and she spends her time scouring the countryside for "ideas and facts as capital" (226).

In "Earthen Pitchers" Davis explores the confused relationship between nature and gender. Both Jenny and Audrey are initially perceived as masculine and feel a pressure to become more feminine. The story is colored with images of dressing, cross-dressing, mistaken gender identities, and hints at homoeroticism. In contrast to Audrey, whom Jenny first mistakes as a free-spirited boy, is Neil Goddard, an effete landscape artist whom Jenny longs to marry and protect. Clever, incompetent, and parasitic, Neil represents the urban misunderstanding of nature and the masculine misunderstanding of woman as nature. He invokes the vocabulary of sentimentalism to define his misinterpretations: "To be with [Audrey] is to breathe a new and alien air" (234). To Neil, Audrey is nature: "How can I tell what she is to me? Say that you go out and see the sea and the mountains for the first time, can you map and paint and label them out for your parlor at home? I cannot map out Audrey Swenson for you" (234). Because Audrey is identified with nature, she is available to anyone's definition. To the visitors from the city she represents the pastoral promise of woman as primal, maternal, living in indolent harmony with nature, the return of a vanished Eve. But Audrey well understands that none of these images will give her a career. Through the figure of Audrey, Davis also invites us to explore the confusion a woman suffers as the object of projection. Like Sara Orne Jewett, Davis examines how women yearn for a full identity that is at once bound and free. The ending of the story, however, marks both Jenny's and Audrey's acceptance of loss; farms, marriage, and children become middle borders between isolation and identity, nature, and civilization.

"Earthen Pitchers" is among the most formless, modernist, and—to my mind—difficult of Davis's stories. The landscape of Lewes, Delaware, like the landscape of Jewett's "Dunnet's Landing" or Constance Fenimore Woolson's "St. Clair Flats," is a watery indeterminate place where an outsider can lose her bearings in the shifting dunes, the quicksand, and the rural characters who merge indistinguishably into the landscape. In a romantic dissolution of the self, Jenny relinquishes her masculine and urban need to control. Unlike the detached narrator in "Life in the Iron-Mills," Jenny immerses herself in the world of Lewes, forced by nature to melt, if only for a time, the barriers between subject and object. Ultimately, however, Jenny's romantic diffusion of self emerges as sentiment's traditional female deference for others; although the ironic narrator clearly sees marriage as betrayal and loss, Jenny trades art for a husband, and creative autonomy for the illusion of domestic authority. Thus has she exchanged the individualistic and competitive values of the town for the coastal legend that promises that the "sea stretches out its hands to punish selfishness. Sand or wave creeps over every man's life who lives for himself alone" (247). But in fact the waves threaten only every *woman's* life; although Jenny and Audrey will live for others, the sentimental moral is at odds with the ironic voice, the imagery of nature, and the representation of men who continue to abuse and betray their wives.

In "The Yares of Black Mountain" Davis continued to explore romantic assumptions about nature in a story of a young Civil War widow who travels into the mountains of North Carolina. Hoping to heal her sickly infant in the high balsam forests, she overcomes her isolation as she discovers the political history of the impoverished family that shelters her. Through three female characters—the widow, a political journalist who has come to find material for her book on "Causes of Decadence of the South," and the powerful matriarch of the Yare family—Davis juxtaposes romantic preconceptions about nature and rural life with the history of a family of resistance fighters in the southern Appalachian mountains during the Civil War. Through the widow's quest for healing and integration, Davis portrays nature in a poignant and dramatic exploration of the complex relationship between nature and society and nature and history.

The story begins with a group of summer tourists who find themselves at the end of the railroad line, thirty miles from Asheville, North Carolina. "Civilization stops here, it appears" observes an industrialist (292). But this is a false appearance, as the travelers are welcomed into a generous rural community. Nonetheless, most of the travelers are disappointed with what they see. The mountains, they find, offer neither inspiration nor industry—the cloud effects are less dramatic than those of the White Mountains, the scenery "lacks the element of grandeur," and a speculator from Detroit finds the balsam lumber so spongy that "a snake couldn't get his living out of ten acres of it" (292). Even the travelers' fantasy of venison cooked over an open campfire is frustrated by the "civilized beastliness" of fried meals in a local barroom (293).

After just one morning in the mountains, the female journalist, Miss Cook, who has briefly visited the village jail and purchased a bundle of photographic postcards, decides that she has "done the mountains and mountaineers" and announces that she has enough Carolina material for her book and is moving on to Georgia. Unlike Davis, who closely observed and carefully researched details of geological, botanical, and social life in the mountains, Miss Cook claims, "I can evolve the whole state of society from a half a dozen items. I have the faculty of generalizing" (299). She confesses, however, that she has quite forgotten to ask people about the Civil War, a portentous omission.

Davis juxtaposes Miss Cook's superficial and preconceived impressions of the rural South with those of the widow, Jenny Denby. Unlike the lone male traveler of literary convention who leaves civilization (read *women*) behind in his quest for adventure in an eroticized wilderness, Jenny discovers that she has come "unbidden into Nature's household." As she travels higher into the mountains, she moves between sublime and overwhelming visions of the wilderness and allegorical images of nature as female sanctuary. When Jenny first leaves the village, she sees the mountain as a beckoning virgin: "The very earth seemed to blush . . . the tupelo thrust its white fingers out of the shadow like a maiden's hand." But as she "penetrates" the high summits of the Appalachian range, her sense of nature as seductress merges into an image of nature as a mother figure: the enticing heights become the "the nursery or breeding-place" of all the mountains that wall the eastern coast (301–02). Paralleling the shift in Jenny's perception from nature as sexual to nature as maternal is the deconstructive shift from nature as luminous and sublime to companionable and familiar:

> She could not help observing how unusually clear the light about her was from the thinness of the air, although the sun was out of sight in a covered, foreboding sky, and black ragged fragments of cloud from some approaching thunderstorm were driven now and then across the horizon; . . . the baby's mother suddenly became conscious that the river was a companion to whom she had been talking and listening for an hour or two. (301)

Like Mary Wilkins Freeman, Sara Orne Jewett, and Willa Cather who would follow her, Davis pictures Jenny's voyage into the mountains as a female quest for wholeness and community in a rural world.

The companionable and loquacious river, traditionally a feminized symbol in any case, reappears in the figure of Mistress Yare, who welcomes the widow to her rugged mountain hut and who takes over the narration to tell Jenny the "terrible history" of the Yares. Initially she tells of her sons who refused to serve in the Army of the Confederacy and instead spent the war years as mountain guides, leading southern deserters and Union soldiers who had escaped from the brutal prisons at Andersonville and Salisbury across the mountains to the federal lines in Tennessee. Mistress Yare is even more proud of the courageous wartime deeds of her daughter Nancy, who rescued hundreds of federal refugees and Confederate deserters trekking through icy mountain gorges. When one of the Yare brothers lay wounded in the woods, Nancy evaded the Confederate soldiers, and, on her own, built a log cabin to shelter him in the icy woods. Eventually Nancy was captured and held in Andersonville prison, where the rebels threatened to hang her because she refused to disclose her brother's whereabouts. In the end, when Jenny urges the Yares to move to the North where they will be rewarded for their service, the mother replies, "It must be powerful lonesome in them flat countries, with nothing but people about you. The mountings [sic] is company always, you see" (309).

Through the voice of Mistress Yare, Davis shifts the story from an emblematic to a dramatic social narrative, undercutting her own discourse that has equated women with nature. Whereas in the narrator's text, Jenny Denby regressively identifies with nature as female, immanent, communal, and available, in Mistress Yare's text Nancy emerges as an autonomous rural subject who lives within and works on nature to shape her rebellious deeds. In the mother's story, nature refuses to be used for tourism, moral instruction, isolation, or even inspiration. Nature is populated. The "Yares of Black Mountain" begins with the portraits of travelers who debate how to experience and interpret nature—for amusement, instruction, inspiration, or healing. First parodying the picturesque conventions through her portrait of Miss Cook, and then deconstructing the magnificent subjectivity of the sublime in Jenny's cart ride up the mountain, Davis suggests that the real meaning of nature lies in its connection with history and its role in forming true communities. Teased and frightened at first by the untold tale of the "terrible history of the Yares," Jenny finally hears a story of complex actions of rural people who are defined in and through the land as political territory. Dislocated from her worldly affiliation by her sense of the sublime, she is able to be receptive to the symbiosis of land and politics. Rather than find romance with one of the rugged mountain sons, she is rewarded with the female grail, an intimate relationship with a mother figure. Her quest into the Cumberland mountains from her lonely apartment in New York has led her to engagement with a woman who teaches her the priority of history over allegory. In a story about the disjunction between the perceived images and the historical meanings of the wilderness and rural community, Davis erodes the patriarchal assumption that nature is primitive, knowable, and separate from culture.

The 1870s marked a major transition in Davis's work. As her fiction became increasingly political, she began to write numerous articles, essays, and editorials that established her as a serious commentator and social historian. She would serve in this role for four productive decades. Between 1870 and 1910, her concerns about such topics as alcohol addiction, political corruption, the condition of mental institutions, the premature demise of Reconstruction, the treatment of Native Americans, restricted opportunities for women's work, and the role of women in utopian communities appear in her essays as well as in the plots and characters of her serialized novels and short stories. Throughout her literary career, Davis would continue to focus on the lives and psychological realities of women who were denied the chance for career, marriage, creativity, and adventure. For the next three decades she would also publish travel narratives based on well-researched discussions of rural life and local history. These focus on cultural differences between North and South, England and the United States, and among African Americans, Native Americans, and whites. Of particular interest is her long study of the people of the mountain wilderness of Virginia, West Virginia, and Maryland in "By-Paths in the Mountains" (1880), which mingles narrative, adventure, character sketches, botany, and social analysis.

Davis's fiction was also consistently topical. She was intensely interested in the impact of demands for social change on personality, perhaps because she was able to examine and manipulate the psychological and personal effects of social theories through characterization and plot. Among her novels, four that deserve new readings and critical attention are *Margret Howth* (1862), a pioneering novel in the development of American realism that speaks to the poverty, drudgery, and emotional suffocation of women in a small mill town in Indiana; *Waiting for the Verdict* (1867), which describes racism within personal relationships during the Civil War and Reconstruction; *Dallas Galbraith* (1868), a regional novel set on the Manasquan coast that challenges many of the era's gendered male stereotypes, and *John Andross* (1874), a fictional expose of the Tweed Ring. During the seventies, partly for financial reasons, Davis also began to publish regularly in such children's periodicals as *Youth's Companion* and *St. Nicholas*, where she incorporated many of these same social and antiracist concerns in rather didactic tales.

It was also during the seventies that Davis began her long affiliation with the *New York Daily Tribune* and the *Independent*. Because it is nearly impossible to assign authorship to most editorials in the *Tribune*, we cannot yet republish any of those pieces. The essays in this anthology, drawn mainly from the *Atlantic Monthly* and the *Independent*, have been selected both to contextualize her fiction and to draw attention to her contribution in areas other than abolition, suffrage, reproductive rights, prostitution, temperance and child welfare—topics in which women's contributions have been acknowledged. Taken together, the stories and essays included here should redefine Davis's place in the canon of American literature and mark her as a significant political journalist, social novelist, feminist, anti-imperialist, and reformer.

A major concern of her essays that also runs through her fiction was the intellectual and artistic suffocation of the uneducated and disenfranchised, whom she saw as creative but mute. Perhaps anticipating Freud, in "Men's Rights," in the persona of a man, she asks of women: "What is it they want? What is it they do *not* want? . . . Suffrage, they cry; emancipation from a bondage as old as the world; equal wages and property-rights; work to save them from prostitution; and—God help us!—food for them and their children" (344). Her response throughout was that women suffered a "savage reality," a kind of "mental hunger or unused power. Unused, and therefore unwholesome power" (346).

While Davis would continue to support suffrage, in "Men's Rights" she justifies her emphasis on economic changes as the way to remedy women's financial plight and afford opportunities to satisfy their creative hunger. Financial independence would give women enough confidence either to choose good husbands or remain single. She saw a large surplus of women who have no man on whom to lean for support, and who believed that traditional women's employments such as sewing and teaching would not provide many of them with food. Women's "urgent and immediate necessity" was simple: "more work, and more wages." Suffrage and reform of the property laws were of secondary importance (354). It is through this pragmatic view that Davis understands the behavior of women, both the coquettes and the "silly Madonnas" who live solely for a man because they believe that only in the home can a woman live and move and find "her being" (352). Nearly thirty years in advance of Charlotte Perkins Gilman's *Women and Economics*, she described the financial pressures that determine what Gilman would later see as women's oversexualization. Davis's portrait of women who, in their effort to please men, degrade themselves by wearing revealing clothing or permitting unwanted sexual contact is an astute view of the relations linking economics, woman's objectification, and the painful loss of self-esteem. She suggests that a "pink-and-white doll" stands in the way of the woman who is "clear-eyed, large-brained, large-hearted, fitted by nature and training to be either seeress, orator, sea-captain, or clerk in a cooperative grocery" (352). Nonetheless, although Davis's studies develop the social causes of women's troubled lives, her solutions, unlike Gilman's, are individual. She argues that while women wait for the arrival of suffrage and women's colleges, they should begin humbly, find a trade, and quietly learn printing, stenography, beekeeping, and paper hanging. In "Men's Rights," as elsewhere, Davis seems to avoid the political implications of the portraits she has drawn, shifting topics when she moves from problem to solution, and insisting, through her sardonic title, that the solution lies not in the responsibility of men but in the efforts of each woman taking care of her own life, a view that jars with her fictional images of female community.

Davis's focus on economic individualism emerges in her other essays on the woman question. "In the Gray Cabins of New England" (1895) she describes single women and widows who have remained behind in abandoned New England villages, stifled and repressed, compulsively cleaning or taking opium, and she argues that these women need training, industries, or emigration to the West. Yet despite her commitment to women's equality, education, and finances, often posed through the metaphor of the recovery of women's artistic voice, in her essays we find ambivalence and tension about political women who could lead the way in improving women's lot. "The Newly Discovered Woman" (1893) suggests that Davis was intimidated by what she saw as the "shrill feminine hurly-burly" (405). She decries the new "sex-consciousness" of the modern woman exultant in her congresses, guilds, Chatauquan circles, colleges, and charities, and like Virginia Woolf she wants this woman to be aware of the contribution of women who lived before the industrial revolution. She hopes the new woman will also study the power of such early "warlike queens" as Margaret of Anjou or Joan of Brittany and the influence of earlier female writers such as Madame de Maintenon or Madame de Stael. Yet in her own essays and stories, she writes often of the middle-aged woman, with "crows' feet at either temple and yellowish blotches on the flesh below the soggy under-jaw," who creatively survives "the prison house of nature." As a realist writer, she saw the "genius of the commonplace" in the mountain woman feeding a family on corn-cakes, fried opossum, and rye coffee. The female journalist who sits all day in a little closet of an office of a publishing house, still managing to run a home for a large and demanding family, embodies "the history and social condition of the country" ("The Middle-Aged Woman," 374–79).

Davis was particularly concerned with the situation of impoverished and dislocated blacks. In her many essays about racial inequality, remedies emerge that mirror her solutions for women. From "Blind Tom," written early in the Civil War, through a series of essays on the economic failure of Reconstruction written around the turn of the century, Davis analyzes how racism shapes economic inequality for blacks and concludes that political rights without financial security are irrelevant. Anticipating the views of Booker T. Washington, she argues in "Some Testimony in the Case" (1885) that the freedman needs training in mechanics and carpentry rather than in Latin and metaphysics, and she questions the utility of higher education for African Americans. Davis's later articles on race, such as "Two Points of View" (1897) and "Two Methods With the Negro" (1898), are explicitly shaped by the debate between Booker T. Washington, who founded schools for trade and technical training for blacks, and W.E.B. Du Bois, who argued for rights and the merits of higher education for blacks. In a view quite consistent with her position on women, she repeatedly argued, as in "The Black North" (1902) that "the negro to live must find work" (441). Thus, siding with Washington, Davis considers various job possibilities in the industrial age, discusses the comparative opportunities for blacks who migrate north or remain in the South, analyzes the failure of Reconstruction in terms of the black middle class, and decries the economic damage of demeaning racial stereotypes. While understanding the justice of Du Bois's rage over the social and economic failure of Reconstruction, she argues that blacks must put away anger and cease striving for white recognition. Then, following Washington, Davis urges blacks to found and attend black industrial schools, train for available jobs in industry and service, and buy land. The Hampton Industrial School, which trained carpenters, joiners, plumbers, and mill hands for the new industries in the South, is a model for Davis. At the same time, as in "Some Testimony in the Case," she speaks forcibly against the "puerile prejudice" of southern apologists for convict labor, which she calls just another species of slavery, and against northern trade unions who refuse to admit blacks. Taken as a whole, in these essays Davis concludes that because African Americans have freedom, suffrage, and education, it falls to the individual to find work. Nevertheless, throughout her articles, penned for a northern audience, she insists that there is a diversity of analyses, voices, and histories that undercut cultural stereotypes, on the one hand, and monolithic solutions on the other. Most particularly, Davis decries those attitudes, north and south, that look at black people as a "unit . . . prophesying defeat or victory of it as a whole people" ("The Black North," 339). Throughout, as in "Two Points of View," she urges blacks to build cohesion within their own community.

In three essays written at the turn of the century, Davis returns to the theme of the dangers of imposing one culture's values upon another and reconsiders an issue with which she launched her literary career—the romanticization of war. In "The Work Before Us" (1899) she describes how, following the massacre at Khartoum, the British plan to Anglicize tribal Africans by founding a university where they might teach them to speak English, wear Western clothes, copy British manners and, in general, "force [their lives] into our mold of life" (427). Davis observes that Lord Kitchener, backed by the enthusiastic applause of Queen Victoria and the English people, "thinks that the Sudanese can be as easily turned into an Englishman as into a corpse" (427). She compares this British spurt of cultural imperialism to our own treatment of Native Americans. In a gendered metaphor Davis refers to those Americans who would put a football sweater on a Sioux or Cheyenne boy, change his Indian name to "Sam Jones," and erase his memories of nature and of his tribal traditions and concludes, "If that does not make a man of him—what will?" (427)

In "The Mean Face of War" (1899), Davis returns to the theme of the dangers of a military mentality as she watches the American people eagerly support the invasion of Cuba and "policing" actions in the Philippines. She predicts that politicians, held captive to monopolies and trusts during the ongoing depression of the 1880s and 1890s, would make war our "regular business." To unemployed young men, they are offering the flag in lieu of jobs. Davis describes the jingoist rhetorics by which the government and industry sought to persuade Americans that this country ought to join the imperialist family of nations, and reminds her readers of how the eroticism of violence and heroism tempted immature boys during the Civil War. Davis would return to the issue of pacifism in "Lord Kitchener's Methods" (1901), where she decries the hypocrisies of the British people who loudly protest fishermen's slaughter of albatrosses but, as they did during the massacres in Ireland and India, remain silent when British soldiers are ordered to starve the Boer people into surrender by burning their homes and crops and driving families into the barren veldt. Recalling Sherman's march through Georgia, she warns that Americans, too, should be aware of the long hatred that follows brutal suppression—in Ireland, India, or the American South.

Davis's essays are also studies in literary culture and reveal her acute sense of her place within American literature. "Boston in the Sixties" is a chapter from her reminiscences, *Bits of Gossip*, published toward the end of her career in 1904. It recounts her first foray, in 1862, into the literary milieu of Boston at the invitation of James and Annie Fields, following the publication of "Life in the Iron-Mills." In this essay Davis describes her early repudiation of romanticism and her search for a rhetoric of the commonplace. She recalls her childhood reading of Hawthorne's *Twice-Told Tales*: "There was no talk of enchantment in them. But in these papers the commonplace folk and things which I saw every day took on a sudden mystery and charm, and, for the first time, I found that they, too, belonged to the magic world of knights and pilgrims and fiends" (444). By contrast, she describes her first meetings with Emerson, Lowell, Holmes, and Bronson Alcott as encounters with "memorable ghosts" who "while they thought they were guiding the real world, they stood quite outside of it, and never would see it as it was" (445). Bemoaning the visionaries who talked in "strained high notes of exaltation" of a Civil War they had never seen (445) and who analyzed the spiritual influence of fruit, she traces the distortions and political inertia within romanticism to the narcissism of its philosophers. Transcendentalism, she held, was a philosophy that lacked the backbone of fact; its theories were like bubbles blown from a child's pipe, "queer reflections of sky and earth and human beings . . . all a little distorted" (446). In particular, Davis criticizes Bronson Alcott, who had covered miles with paper while his home was bleak and his children hungry, and—along similar lines—Emerson, who studied souls as "a philologist does words or an entomologist beetles," only to forget that "the negro or I were in the world—having taken from each what he wanted" (448-49). Such personal insensitivity make Davis question the transcendentalists' faith in their discovery of the "new god" within themselves (450). For Davis, the disengaged and mythologizing literary practices of romanticism are inseparable from the male egotism of its authors.

By contrast, in "Undistinguished Americans" (1906) a review of an anthology of short autobiographies by working-class men and women, Davis draws a manifesto for realism as the representation of the commonplace in literature. She values those writers from across the spectrum of races and classes who see their ordinary lives not as a moment in a drama or as an emblem of history but as "simply what they purport to be" (459). This summarizes Davis's philosophy of the ordinary—represented, for example, in "A Faded Leaf of History" (1873) in which Davis tells the story of colonial life in the "commonplace" and describes details of household duties, spiritual ambivalence, financial greed, and troubling contact with Native Americans by early settlers in Philadelphia.

Rebecca Harding Davis believed in the power of the word, for both writer and reader. In 1891 she wrote, "I have a hope that this body of women who have the habit of broad and accurate thought will not always be content to expend their force in society, or even in charitable work. They will be stirred by the ambition to leave something more permanent behind them than Reports of Sanitary or Archeological clubs, and will paint as they only can do, for the next generation, the inner life and history of their time with a power which shall make that time alive for future ages" ("Women in Literature," 404).

Taken as a whole, Davis's stories and essays involve an ongoing critique of the literary and philosophical systems of romanticism and transcendentalism, which, in their formal structures and social textures remove us from life in the commonplace, both its inner life and history of the time. Romanticism, as Nina Baym reminds us, promises an *idea* of America where we can achieve complete self-definition because we can exist in some meaningful sense prior to and apart from history; society is artificial, secondary to human nature and destructive of individuality.[85] This romantic idealization of autonomy, Davis would find, particularly threatened women's self-definition and identity as social subjects.

The narrator of *Margret Howth* observes, "Once or twice I have rashly tried my hand at dark conspiracies, and women rare and radiant in Italian bowers; but I have a friend who is sure to say, 'Try and tell us about the butcher next door, my dear'" (104). Davis developed the rhetorics of realism as a way to talk about the butcher next door. She sought, thereby, to challenge the restrictive tenets of sentimentalism—its illusion that domestic culture can transcend political culture, that the self can be divorced from social circumstances, and that domestic life guarantees women status, power, or moral redemption. But in fastening the emerging strategies of literary realism onto felt experience, Davis reclaimed from sentimentalism its subjectivity and intensity of feeling; she thereby successfully linked a new literary genre to the traditions of social practice. In her fiction, the defining experiences of gender, race, and region authorize emotional appeals as they shape her character's identity and our experience of history. Throughout her stories, images of difference—working-class women, freed slaves, destitute fishermen who scavenge along the barren Jersey coast—build on the traditions of vernacular fiction and, in my view, launch American realism as an indigenous political narrative. By bringing into the fictive world the issues of class and gender, race and power, and the colonization of rural life, Davis showed how emotions and sensibilities involve the imperatives of economics and place. History legitimates the feelings of characters who, like Rebecca Harding Davis herself, were unfinished, hungry, and eager to know.

Fiction

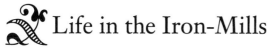
Life in the Iron-Mills

Atlantic Monthly, April 1861

"*Is this the end?*
O Life, as futile, then, as frail!
What hope of answer or redress?"[1]

A cloudy day: do you know what that is in a town of iron-works? The sky sank down before dawn, muddy, flat, immovable. The air is thick, clammy with the breath of crowded human beings. It stifles me. I open the window, and, looking out, can scarcely see through the rain the grocer's shop opposite, where a crowd of drunken Irishmen are puffing Lynchburg tobacco in their pipes. I can detect the scent through all the foul smells ranging loose in the air.

The idiosyncrasy of this town is smoke. It rolls sullenly in slow folds from the great chimneys of the iron-foundries, and settles down in black, slimy pools on the muddy streets. Smoke on the wharves, smoke on the dingy boats, on the yellow river, — clinging in a coating of greasy soot to the house-front, the two faded poplars, the faces of the passers-by. The long train of mules, dragging masses of pig-iron[2] through the narrow street, have a foul vapor hanging to their reeking sides. Here, inside, is a little broken figure of an angel pointing upward from the mantel-shelf; but even its wings are covered with smoke, clotted and black. Smoke everywhere! A dirty canary chirps desolately in a cage beside me. Its dream of green fields and sunshine is a very old dream, — almost worn out, I think.

From the back-window I can see a narrow brick-yard sloping down to the river-side, strewed with rain-butts[3] and tubs. The river, dull and tawny-colored, (*la belle rivière!*) drags itself sluggishly along, tired of the heavy weight of boats and coal-barges. What wonder? When I was a child, I used to fancy a look of weary, dumb appeal upon the face of the negro-like river slavishly bearing its burden day after day. Something of the same idle notion comes to me to-day, when from the street-window I look on the slow stream of human life creeping past, night and morning, to the great mills. Masses of men, with dull, besotted faces bent to the ground, sharpened here and there by pain or cunning; skin and muscle and flesh begrimed with smoke and ashes; stooping all night over boiling caldrons of metal, laired by day in dens of drunkenness and infamy; breathing from infancy to death an air saturated with fog and grease and soot, vileness for soul and body. What do you make of a case like that, amateur psychologist? You call it an altogether serious thing to be alive: to these men it is a drunken jest, a joke,—horrible to angels perhaps, to them commonplace enough. My fancy about the river was an idle one: it is no type of such a life. What if it be stagnant and slimy here? It knows that beyond there waits for it odorous sunlight,—quaint old gardens, dusky with soft, green foliage of apple-trees, and flushing crimson with roses,—air, and fields, and mountains. The future of the Welsh puddler[4] passing just now is not so pleasant. To be stowed away, after his grimy work is done, in a hole in the muddy graveyard, and after that,—*not* air, nor green fields, nor curious roses.

Can you see how foggy the day is? As I stand here, idly tapping the window-pane, and looking out through the rain at the dirty back-yard and the coal-boats below, fragments of an old story float up before me,—a story of this old house into which I happened to come to-day. You may think it a tiresome story enough, as foggy as the day, sharpened by no sudden flashes of pain or pleasure.—I know: only the outline of a dull life, that long since, with thousands of dull lives like its own, was vainly lived and lost: thousands of them,—massed, vile, slimy lives, like those of the torpid lizards in yonder stagnant water-butt.—Lost? There is a curious point for you to settle, my friend, who study psychology in a lazy, *dilettante* way. Stop a moment. I am going to be honest. This is what I want you to do. I want you to hide your disgust, take no heed to your clean clothes, and come right down with me,—here, into the thickest of the fog and mud and foul effluvia. I want you to hear this story. There is a secret down here, in this nightmare fog, that has lain dumb for centuries: I want to make it a real thing to you. You, Egoist, or Pantheist, or Arminian,[5] busy in making straight paths for your feet on the hills, do not see it clearly,—this terrible question which men here have gone mad and died trying to answer. I dare not put this secret into words. I told you it was dumb. These men, going by with drunken faces and brains full of unawakened power, do not ask it of Society or of God. Their lives ask it; their deaths ask it. There is no reply. I will tell you plainly that I have a great hope; and I bring it to you to be tested. It is this: that this terrible dumb question is its own reply; that it is not the sentence of death we think it, but, from the very extremity of its darkness, the most solemn prophecy which the world has known of the Hope to come. I dare make my meaning no clearer, but will only tell my story. It will, perhaps, seem to you as foul and dark as this thick vapor about us, and as pregnant with death; but if your eyes are free as mine are to look deeper, no perfume-tinted dawn will be so fair with promise of the day that shall surely come.

My story is very simple,—only what I remember of the life of one of these men,—a furnace-tender in one of Kirby & John's rolling-mills,[6]—Hugh Wolfe. You know the mills? They took the great order for the Lower Virginia railroads there last winter; run usually with about a thousand men. I cannot tell why I choose the half-forgotten story of this Wolfe more than that of myriads of these furnace-hands. Perhaps because there is a secret underlying sympathy between that story and this day with its impure fog and thwarted sunshine,—or perhaps simply for the reason that this house is the one where the Wolfes lived. There were the father and son,—both hands, as I said, in one of Kirby & John's mills for making railroad-iron,—and Deborah, their cousin, a picker[7] in some of the cotton-mills. The house was rented then to half a dozen families. The Wolfes had two of the cellar-rooms. The old man, like many of the puddlers and feeders of the mills, was Welsh,—had spent half of his life in the Cornish tin-mines. You may pick the Welsh emigrants, Cornish miners, out of the throng passing the windows, any day. They are a trifle more filthy; their muscles are not so brawny; they stoop more. When they are drunk, they neither yell, nor shout, nor stagger, but skulk along like beaten hounds. A pure, unmixed blood, I fancy: shows itself in the slight angular bodies and sharply-cut facial lines. It is nearly thirty years since the Wolfes lived here. Their lives were like those of their class: incessant labor, sleeping in kennel-like rooms, eating rank pork and molasses, drinking—God and the distillers only know what; with an occasional night in jail, to atone for some drunken excess. Is that all of their lives?—of the portion given to them and these their duplicates swarming the streets to-day?—nothing beneath?—all? So many a political reformer will tell you,—and many a private reformer, too, who has gone among them with a heart tender with Christ's charity, and come out outraged, hardened.

One rainy night, about eleven o'clock, a crowd of half-clothed women stopped outside of the cellar-door. They were going home from the cotton-mill.

"Good-night, Deb," said one, a mulatto, steadying herself against the gas-post. She needed the post to steady her. So did more than one of them.

"Dah 's a ball to Miss Potts' to-night. Ye 'd best come."

"Inteet, Deb, if hur 'll come, hur 'll hef fun," said a shrill Welsh voice in the crowd.

Two or three dirty hands were thrust out to catch the gown of the woman, who was groping for the latch of the door.

"No."

"No? Where 's Kit Small, then?"

"Begorra![8] on the spools. Alleys behint, though we helped her, we dud. An wid ye! Let Deb alone! It 's ondacent frettin' a quite body. Be the powers, an' we 'll have a night of it! there 'll be lashin's[9] o' drink,—the Vargent be blessed and praised for 't!"

They went on, the mulatto inclining for a moment to show fight, and drag the woman Wolfe off with them; but, being pacified, she staggered away.

Deborah groped her way into the cellar, and, after considerable stumbling, kindled a match, and lighted a tallow dip, that sent a yellow glimmer over the room. It was low, damp,—the earthen floor covered with a green, slimy moss,—a fetid air smothering the breath. Old Wolfe lay asleep on a heap of straw, wrapped in a torn horse-blanket. He was a pale, meek little man, with a white face and red rabbit-eyes. The woman Deborah was like him; only her face was even more ghastly, her lips bluer, her eyes more watery. She wore a faded cotton gown and a slouching bonnet. When she walked, one could see that she was deformed, almost a hunchback. She trod softly, so as not to waken him, and went through into the room beyond. There she found by the half-extinguished fire an iron saucepan filled with cold boiled potatoes, which she put upon a broken chair with a pint-cup of ale. Placing the old candlestick beside this dainty repast, she untied her bonnet, which hung limp and wet over her face, and prepared to eat her supper. It was the first food that had touched her lips since morning. There was enough of it, however: there is not always. She was hungry,—one could see that easily enough,—and not drunk, as most of her companions would have been found at this hour. She did not drink, this woman,—her face told that, too,—nothing stronger than ale. Perhaps the weak, flaccid wretch had some stimulant in her pale life to keep her up,—some love or hope, it might be, or urgent need. When that stimulant was gone, she would take to whiskey. Man cannot live by work alone. While she was skinning the potatoes, and munching them, a noise behind her made her stop.

"Janey!" she called, lifting the candle and peering into the darkness. "Janey, are you there?"

A heap of ragged coats was heaved up, and the face of a young girl emerged, staring sleepily at the woman.

"Deborah," she said, at last, "I'm here the night."

"Yes, child. Hur 's welcome," she said, quietly eating on.

The girl's face was haggard and sickly; her eyes were heavy with sleep and hunger: real Milesian [10] eyes they were, dark, delicate blue, glooming out from black shadows with a pitiful fright.

"I was alone," she said, timidly.

"Where 's the father?" asked Deborah, holding out a potato, which the girl greedily seized.

"He 's beyant,—wid Haley,—in the stone house." (Did you ever hear the word *jail* from an Irish mouth?) "I came here. Hugh told me never to stay me-lone."

"Hugh?"

"Yes."

A vexed frown crossed her face. The girl saw it, and added quickly,—

"I have not seen Hugh the day, Deb. The old man says his watch lasts till the mornin'."

The woman sprang up, and hastily began to arrange some bread and flitch [11] in a tin pail, and to pour her own measure of ale into a bottle. Tying on her bonnet, she blew out the candle.

"Lay ye down, Janey dear," she said, gently, covering her with the old rags. "Hur can eat the potatoes, if hur 's hungry."

"Where are ye goin', Deb? The rain 's sharp."

"To the mill, with Hugh's supper."

"Let him bide till th' morn. Sit ye down."

"No, no,"—sharply pushing her off. "The boy 'll starve."

She hurried from the cellar, while the child wearily coiled herself up for sleep. The rain was falling heavily, as the woman, pail in hand, emerged from the mouth of the alley, and turned down the narrow street, that stretched out, long and black, miles before her. Here and there a flicker of gas lighted an uncertain space of muddy footwalk and gutter; the long rows of houses, except an occasional lager-bier shop, were closed; now and then she met a band of mill-hands skulking to or from their work.

Not many even of the inhabitants of a manufacturing town know the vast machinery of system by which the bodies of workmen are governed, that goes on unceasingly from year to year. The hands of each mill are divided into watches that relieve each other as regularly as the sentinels of an army. By night and day the work goes on, the unsleeping engines groan and shriek, the fiery pools of metal boil and surge. Only for a day in the week, in half-courtesy to public censure, the fires are partially veiled; but as soon as the clock strikes midnight, the great furnaces break forth with renewed fury, the clamor begins with fresh, breathless vigor, the engines sob and shriek like "gods in pain."

As Deborah hurried down through the heavy rain, the noise of these thousand engines sounded through the sleep and shadow of the city like far-off thunder. The mill to which she was going lay on the river, a mile below the city-limits. It was far, and she was weak, aching from standing twelve hours at the spools. Yet it was her almost nightly walk to take this man his supper, though at every square she sat down to rest, and she knew she should receive small word of thanks.

Perhaps, if she had possessed an artist's eye, the picturesque oddity of the scene might have made her step stagger less, and the path seem shorter; but to her the mills were only "summat deilish to look at by night."

The road leading to the mills had been quarried from the solid rock, which rose abrupt and bare on one side of the cinder-covered road, while the river, sluggish and black, crept past on the other. The mills for rolling iron are simply immense tent-like roofs, covering acres of ground, open on every side. Beneath these roofs Deborah looked in on a city of fires, that burned hot and fiercely in the night. Fire in every horrible form: pits of flame waving in the wind; liquid metal-flames writhing in tortuous streams through the sand; wide caldrons filled with boiling fire, over which bent ghastly wretches stirring the strange brewing; and through all, crowds of half-clad men, looking like revengeful ghosts in the red light, hurried, throwing masses of glittering fire. It was like a street in Hell. Even Deborah muttered, as she crept through, " 'T looks like t' Devil's place!" It did,—in more ways than one.

She found the man she was looking for, at last, heaping coal on a furnace. He had not time to eat his supper; so she went behind the furnace, and waited. Only a few men were with him, and they noticed her only by a "Hyur comes t' hunchback, Wolfe."

Deborah was stupid with sleep; her back pained her sharply; and her teeth chattered with cold, with the rain that soaked her clothes and dripped from her at every step. She stood, however, patiently holding the pail, and waiting.

"Hout, woman! ye look like a drowned cat. Come near to the fire,"—said one of the men, approaching to scrape away the ashes.

She shook her head. Wolfe had forgotten her. He turned, hearing the man, and came closer.

"I did no' think; gi' me my supper, woman."

She watched him eat with a painful eagerness. With a woman's quick instinct, she saw that he was not hungry,—was eating to please her. Her pale, watery eyes began to gather a strange light.

"Is 't good, Hugh? T' ale was a bit sour, I feared."

"No, good enough." He hesitated a moment. "Ye 're tired, poor lass! Bide here till I go. Lay down there on that heap of ash, and go to sleep."

He threw her an old coat for a pillow, and turned to his work. The heap was the refuse of the burnt iron, and was not a hard bed; the half-smothered warmth, too, penetrated her limbs, dulling their pain and cold shiver.

Miserable enough she looked, lying there on the ashes like a limp, dirty rag,—yet not an unfitting figure to crown the scene of hopeless discomfort and veiled crime: more fitting, if one looked deeper into the heart of things,—at her thwarted woman's form, her colorless life, her waking stupor that smothered pain and hunger,—even more fit to be a type of her class. Deeper yet if one could look, was there nothing worth reading in this wet, faded thing, half-covered with ashes? no story of a soul filled with groping passionate love, heroic unselfishness, fierce jealousy? of years of weary trying to please the one human being whom she loved, to gain one look of real heart-kindness from him? If anything like this were hidden beneath the pale, bleared eyes, and dull, washed-out-looking face, no one had ever taken the trouble to read its faint signs: not the half-clothed furnace-tender, Wolfe, certainly. Yet he was kind to her: it was his nature to be kind, even to the very rats that swarmed in the cellar: kind to her in just the same way. She knew that. And it might be that very knowledge had given to her face its apathy and vacancy more than her low, torpid life. One sees that dead, vacant look steal sometimes over the rarest, finest of women's faces,—in the very midst, it may be, of their warmest summer's day; and then one can guess at the secret of intolerable solitude that lies hid beneath the delicate laces and brilliant smile. There was no warmth, no brilliancy, no summer for this woman; so the stupor and vacancy had time to gnaw into her face perpetually. She was young, too, though no one guessed it; so the gnawing was the fiercer.

She lay quiet in the dark corner, listening, through the monotonous din and uncertain glare of the works, to the dull plash of the rain in the far distance,—shrinking back whenever the man Wolfe happened to look towards her. She knew, in spite of all his kindness, that there was that in her face and form which made him loathe the sight of her. She felt by instinct, although she could not comprehend it, the finer nature of the man, which made him among his fellow-workmen something unique, set apart. She knew, that, down under all the vileness and coarseness of his life, there was a groping passion for whatever was beautiful and pure,—that his soul sickened with disgust at her deformity, even when his words were kindest. Through this dull consciousness, which never left her, came, like a sting, the recollection of the dark blue eyes and lithe figure of the little Irish girl she had left in the cellar. The recollection struck through even her stupid intellect with a vivid glow of beauty and of grace. Little Janey, timid, helpless, clinging to Hugh as her only friend: that was the sharp thought, the bitter thought, that drove into the glazed eyes a fierce light of pain. You laugh at it? Are pain and jealousy less savage realities down here in this place I am taking you to than in your own house or your own heart,—your heart, which they clutch at sometimes? The note is the same, I fancy, be the octave high or low.

If you could go into this mill where Deborah lay, and drag out from the hearts of these men the terrible tragedy of their lives, taking it as a symptom of the disease of their class, no ghost Horror would terrify you more. A reality of soul-starvation, of living death, that meets you every day under the besotted faces on the street,—I can paint nothing of this, only give you the outside outlines of a night, a crisis in the life of one man: whatever muddy depth of soul-history lies beneath you can read according to the eyes God has given you.

Wolfe, while Deborah watched him as a spaniel its master, bent over the furnace with his iron pole, unconscious of her scrutiny, only stopping to receive orders. Physically, Nature had promised the man but little. He had already lost the strength and instinct vigor of a man, his muscles were thin, his nerves weak, his face (a meek, woman's face) haggard, yellow with consumption. In the mill he was known as one of the girl-men: "Molly Wolfe" was his *sobriquet*. He was never seen in the cockpit, did not own a terrier, drank but seldom; when he did, desperately. He fought sometimes, but was always thrashed, pommelled to a jelly. The man was game enough, when his blood was up: but he was no favorite in the mill; he had the taint of school-learning on him,—not to a dangerous extent, only a quarter or so in the free-school in fact, but enough to ruin him as a good hand in a fight.

For other reasons, too, he was not popular. Not one of themselves, they felt that, though outwardly as filthy and ash-covered; silent, with foreign thoughts and longings breaking out through his quietness in innumerable curious ways: this one, for instance. In the neighboring furnace-buildings lay great heaps of the refuse from the ore after the pig-metal is run. *Korl* we call it here: a light, porous substance, of a delicate, waxen, flesh-colored tinge. Out of the blocks of this korl, Wolfe, in his off-hours from the furnace, had a habit of chipping and moulding figures,—hideous, fantastic enough, but sometimes strangely beautiful: even the mill-men saw that, while they jeered at him. It was a curious fancy in the man, almost a passion. The few hours for rest he spent hewing and hacking with his blunt knife, never speaking, until his watch came again,—working at one figure for months, and, when it was finished, breaking it to pieces perhaps, in a fit of disappointment. A morbid, gloomy man, untaught, unled, left to feed his soul in grossness and crime, and hard, grinding labor.

I want you to come down and look at this Wolfe, standing there among the lowest of his kind, and see him just as he is, that you may judge him justly when you hear the story of this night. I want you to look back, as he does every day, at his birth in vice, his starved infancy; to remember the heavy years he has groped through as boy and man,—the slow, heavy years of constant, hot work. So long ago he began, that he thinks sometimes he has worked there for ages. There is no hope that it will ever end. Think that God put into this man's soul a fierce thirst for beauty,—to know it, to create it; to be—something, he knows not what,—other than he is. There are moments when a passing cloud, the sun glinting on the purple thistles, a kindly smile, a child's face, will rouse him to a passion of pain,—when his nature starts up with a mad cry of rage against God, man, whoever it is that has forced this vile, slimy life upon him. With all this groping, this mad desire, a great blind intellect stumbling through wrong, a loving poet's heart, the man was by habit only a coarse, vulgar laborer, familiar with sights and words you would blush to name. Be just: when I tell you about this night, see him as he is. Be just,—not like man's law, which seizes on one isolated fact, but like God's judging angel, whose clear, sad eye saw all the countless cankering days of this man's life, all the countless nights, when, sick with starving, his soul fainted in him, before it judged him for this night, the saddest of all.

I called this night the crisis of his life. If it was, it stole on him unawares. These great turning-days of life cast no shadow before, slip by unconsciously. Only a trifle, a little turn of the rudder, and the ship goes to heaven or hell.

Wolfe, while Deborah watched him, dug into the furnace of melting iron with his pole, dully thinking only how many rails the lump would yield. It was late,—nearly Sunday morning; another hour, and the heavy work would be done,—only the furnaces to replenish and cover for the next day. The workmen were growing more noisy, shouting, as they had to do, to be heard over the deep clamor of the mills. Suddenly they grew less boisterous,—at the far end, entirely silent. Something unusual had happened. After a moment, the silence came nearer; the men stopped their jeers and drunken choruses. Deborah, stupidly lifting up her head, saw the cause of the quiet. A group of five or six men were slowly approaching, stopping to examine each furnace as they came. Visitors often came to see the mills after night: except by growing less noisy, the men took no notice of them. The furnace where Wolfe worked was near the bounds of the works; they halted there hot and tired: a walk over one of these great foundries is no trifling task. The woman, drawing out of sight, turned over to sleep. Wolfe, seeing them stop, suddenly roused from his indifferent stupor, and watched them keenly. He knew some of them: the overseer, Clarke,—a son of Kirby, one of the mill-owners,—and a Doctor May, one of the town-physicians. The other two were strangers. Wolfe came closer. He seized eagerly every chance that brought him into contact with this mysterious class that shone down on him perpetually with the glamour of another order of being. What made the difference between them? That was the mystery of his life. He had a vague notion that perhaps to-night he could find it out. One of the strangers sat down on a pile of bricks, and beckoned young Kirby to his side.

"This *is* hot, with a vengeance. A match, please?"—lighting his cigar. "But the walk is worth the trouble. If it were not that you must have heard it so often, Kirby, I would tell you that your works look like Dante's Inferno."

Kirby laughed.

"Yes. Yonder is Farinata [12] himself in the burning tomb,"—pointing to some figure in the shimmering shadows.

"Judging from some of the faces of your men," said the other, "they bid fair to try the reality of Dante's vision, some day."

Young Kirby looked curiously around, as if seeing the faces of his hands for the first time.

"They're bad enough, that's true. A desperate set, I fancy. Eh, Clarke?"

The overseer did not hear him. He was talking of net profits just then,—giving, in fact, a schedule of the annual business of the firm to a sharp peering little Yankee, who jotted down notes on a paper laid on the crown of his hat: a reporter for one of the city-papers, getting up a series of reviews of the leading manufactories. The other gentlemen had accompanied them merely for amusement. They were silent until the notes were finished, drying their feet at the furnaces, and sheltering their faces from the intolerable heat. At last the overseer concluded with—

"I believe that is a pretty fair estimate, Captain."

"Here, some of you men!" said Kirby, "bring up those boards. We may as well sit down, gentlemen, until the rain is over. It cannot last much longer at this rate."

"Pig-metal,"—mumbled the reporter,—"um!—coal facilities,—um!—hands employed, twelve hundred,—bitumen,[13]—um!—all right, I believe, Mr. Clarke;—sinking-fund,—what did you say was your sinking-fund?"[14]

"Twelve hundred hands?" said the stranger, the young man who had first spoken. "Do you control their votes, Kirby?"

"Control? No." The young man smiled complacently. "But my father brought seven hundred votes to the polls for his candidate last November. No force-work, you understand,—only a speech or two, a hint to form themselves into a society, and a bit of red and blue bunting to make them a flag. The Invincible Roughs,—I believe that is their name. I forget the motto: 'Our country's hope,' I think."

There was a laugh. The young man talking to Kirby sat with an amused light in his cool gray eye, surveying critically the half-clothed figures of the puddlers, and the slow swing of their brawny muscles. He was a stranger in the city,—spending a couple of months in the borders of a Slave State, to study the institutions of the South,—a brother-in-law of Kirby's,—Mitchell. He was an amateur gymnast,—hence his anatomical eye; a patron, in a *blasé* way, of the prize-ring; a man who sucked the essence out of a science or philosophy in an indifferent, gentlemanly way; who took Kant,[15] Novalis,[16] Humboldt,[17] for what they were worth in his own scales; accepting all, despising nothing, in heaven, earth, or hell, but one-idead men; with a temper yielding and brilliant as summer water, until his Self was touched, when it was ice, though brilliant still. Such men are not rare in the States.

As he knocked the ashes from his cigar, Wolfe caught with a quick pleasure the contour of the white hand, the blood-glow of a red ring he wore. His voice, too, and that of Kirby's, touched him like music,—low, even, with chording cadences. About this man Mitchell hung the impalpable atmosphere belonging to the thorough-bred gentleman. Wolfe, scraping away the ashes beside him, was conscious of it, did obeisance to it with his artist sense, unconscious that he did so.

The rain did not cease. Clarke and the reporter left the mills; the others, comfortably seated near the furnace, lingered, smoking and talking in a desultory way. Greek would not have been more unintelligible to the furnace-tenders, whose presence they soon forgot entirely. Kirby drew out a newspaper from his pocket and read aloud some article, which they discussed eagerly. At every sentence, Wolfe listened more and more like a dumb, hopeless animal, with a duller, more stolid look creeping over his face, glancing now and then at Mitchell, marking acutely every small-est sign of refinement, then back to himself, seeing as in a mirror his filthy body, his more stained soul.

Never! He had no words for such a thought, but he knew now, in all the sharpness of the bitter certainty, that between them there was a great gulf never to be passed. Never!

The bell of the mills rang for midnight. Sunday morning had dawned. Whatever hidden message lay in the tolling bells floated past these men unknown. Yet it was there. Veiled in the solemn music ushering the risen Saviour was a key-note to solve the darkest secrets of a world gone wrong,—even this social riddle which the brain of the grimy puddler grappled with madly to-night.

The men began to withdraw the metal from the caldrons. The mills were deserted on Sundays, except by the hands who fed the fires, and those who had no lodgings and slept usually on the ash-heaps. The three strangers sat still during the next hour, watching the men cover the fur-naces, laughing now and then at some jest of Kirby's.

"Do you know," said Mitchell, "I like this view of the works better than when the glare was fiercest? These heavy shadows and the amphitheatre of smothered fires are ghostly, unreal. One could fancy these red smoulder-ing lights to be the half-shut eyes of wild beasts, and the spectral figures their victims in the den."

Kirby laughed. "You are fanciful. Come, let us get out of the den. The spectral figures, as you call them, are a little too real for me to fancy a close proximity in the darkness,—unarmed, too."

The others rose, buttoning their overcoats, and lighting cigars.

"Raining, still," said Doctor May, "and hard. Where did we leave the coach, Mitchell?"

"At the other side of the works.—Kirby, what 's that?"

Mitchell started back, half-frightened, as, suddenly turning a corner, the white figure of a woman faced him in the darkness,—a woman, white, of giant proportions, crouching on the ground, her arms flung out in some wild gesture of warning.

"Stop! Make that fire burn there!" cried Kirby, stopping short.

The flame burst out, flashing the gaunt figure into bold relief.

Mitchell drew a long breath.

"I thought it was alive," he said, going up curiously.

The others followed.

"Not marble, eh?" asked Kirby, touching it.

One of the lower overseers stopped.

"Korl, Sir."

"Who did it?"

"Can't say. Some of the hands; chipped it out in off-hours."

"Chipped to some purpose, I should say. What a flesh-tint the stuff has! Do you see, Mitchell?"

"I see."

He had stepped aside where the light fell boldest on the figure, looking at it in silence. There was not one line of beauty or grace in it: a nude woman's form, muscular, grown coarse with labor, the powerful limbs instinct with some one poignant longing. One idea: there it was in the tense, rigid muscles, the clutching hands, the wild, eager face, like that of a starving wolf's. Kirby and Doctor May walked around it, critical, curious. Mitchell stood aloof, silent. The figure touched him strangely.

"Not badly done," said Doctor May. "Where did the fellow learn that sweep of the muscles in the arm and hand? Look at them! They are groping,—do you see?—clutching: the peculiar action of a man dying of thirst."

"They have ample facilities for studying anatomy," sneered Kirby, glancing at the half-naked figures.

"Look," continued the Doctor, "at this bony wrist, and the strained sinews of the instep! A working-woman,—the very type of her class."

"God forbid!" muttered Mitchell.

"Why?" demanded May. "What does the fellow intend by the figure? I cannot catch the meaning."

"Ask him," said the other, dryly. "There he stands,"—pointing to Wolfe, who stood with a group of men, leaning on his ash-rake.

The Doctor beckoned him with the affable smile which kind-hearted men put on, when talking to these people.

"Mr. Mitchell has picked you out as the man who did this,—I'm sure I don't know why. But what did you mean by it?"

"She be hungry."

Wolfe's eyes answered Mitchell, not the Doctor.

"Oh-h! But what a mistake you have made, my fine fellow! You have given no sign of starvation to the body. It is strong,—terribly strong. It has the mad, half-despairing gesture of drowning."

Wolfe stammered, glanced appealingly at Mitchell, who saw the soul of the thing, he knew. But the cool, probing eyes were turned on himself now,—mocking, cruel, relentless.

"Not hungry for meat," the furnace-tender said at last.

"What then? Whiskey?" jeered Kirby, with a coarse laugh.

Wolfe was silent a moment, thinking.

"I dunno," he said, with a bewildered look. "It mebbe. Summat to make her live, I think,—like you. Whiskey ull do it, in a way."

The young man laughed again. Mitchell flashed a look of disgust somewhere,—not at Wolfe.

"May," he broke out impatiently, "are you blind? Look at that woman's face! It asks questions of God, and says, 'I have a right to know.' Good God, how hungry it is!"

They looked a moment; then May turned to the mill-owner:—

"Have you many such hands as this? What are you going to do with them? Keep them at puddling iron?"

Kirby shrugged his shoulders. Mitchell's look had irritated him.

"*Ce n'est pas mon affaire.* I have no fancy for nursing infant geniuses. I suppose there are some stray gleams of mind and soul among these wretches. The Lord will take care of his own; or else they can work out their own salvation. I have heard you call our American system a ladder which any man can scale. Do you doubt it? Or perhaps you want to banish all social ladders, and put us all on a flat table-land,—eh, May?"

The Doctor looked vexed, puzzled. Some terrible problem lay hid in this woman's face, and troubled these men. Kirby waited for an answer, and, receiving none, went on, warming with his subject.

"I tell you, there 's something wrong that no talk of '*Liberté*' or '*Égalité*' will do away. If I had the making of men, these men who do the lowest part of the world's work should be machines,—nothing more,—hands. It would be kindness. God help them! What are taste, reason, to creatures who must live such lives as that?" He pointed to Deborah, sleeping on the ash-heap. "So many nerves to sting them to pain. What if God had put your brain, with all its agony of touch, into your fingers, and bid you work and strike with that?"

"You think you could govern the world better?" laughed the Doctor.

"I do not think at all."

"That is true philosophy. Drift with the stream, because you cannot dive deep enough to find bottom, eh?"

"Exactly," rejoined Kirby. "I do not think. I wash my hands of all social problems,—slavery, caste, white or black. My duty to my operatives has a narrow limit,—the pay-hour on Saturday night. Outside of that, if they cut korl, or cut each other's throats, (the more popular amusement of the two,) I am not responsible."

The Doctor sighed,—a good honest sigh, from the depths of his stomach.

"God help us! Who is responsible?"

"Not I, I tell you," said Kirby, testily. "What has the man who pays them money to do with their souls' concerns, more than the grocer or butcher who takes it?"

"And yet," said Mitchell's cynical voice, "look at her! How hungry she is!"

Kirby tapped his boot with his cane. No one spoke. Only the dumb face of the rough image looking into their faces with the awful question, "What shall we do to be saved?" Only Wolfe's face, with its heavy weight of brain, its weak, uncertain mouth, its desperate eyes, out of which looked the soul of his class,—only Wolfe's face turned towards Kirby's. Mitchell laughed,—a cool, musical laugh.

"Money has spoken!" he said, seating himself lightly on a stone with the air of an amused spectator at a play. "Are you answered?"—turning to Wolfe his clear, magnetic face.

Bright and deep and cold as Arctic air, the soul of the man lay tranquil beneath. He looked at the furnace-tender as he had looked at a rare mosaic in the morning; only the man was the more amusing study of the two.

"Are you answered? Why, May, look at him! 'De profundis clamavi.'[18] Or, to quote in English, 'Hungry and thirsty, his soul faints in him.' And so Money sends back its answer into the depths through you, Kirby! Very clear the answer, too!—I think I remember reading the same words somewhere:—washing your hands in Eau de Cologne, and saying, 'I am innocent of the blood of this man. See ye to it!'"

Kirby flushed angrily.

"You quote Scripture freely."

"Do I not quote correctly? I think I remember another line, which may amend my meaning: 'Inasmuch as ye did it unto one of the least of these, ye did it unto me.' Deist? Bless you, man, I was raised on the milk of the Word. Now, Doctor, the pocket of the world having uttered its voice, what has the heart to say? You are a philanthropist, in a small way,—n'est ce pas? Here, boy, this gentleman can show you how to cut korl better,—or your destiny. Go on, May!"

"I think a mocking devil possesses you to-night," rejoined the Doctor, seriously.

He went to Wolfe and put his hand kindly on his arm. Something of a vague idea possessed the Doctor's brain that much good was to be done here by a friendly word or two: a latent genius to be warmed into life by a waited-for sun-beam. Here it was: he had brought it. So he went on complacently: —

"Do you know, boy, you have it in you to be a great sculptor, a great man?—do you understand?" (talking down to the capacity of his hearer: it is a way people have with children, and men like Wolfe)—"to live a better, stronger life than I, or Mr. Kirby here? A man may make himself anything he chooses. God has given you stronger powers than many men,—me, for instance."

May stopped, heated, glowing with his own magnanimity. And it was magnanimous. The puddler had drunk in every word, looking through the Doctor's flurry, and generous heat, and self-approval, into his will, with those slow, absorbing eyes of his.

"Make yourself what you will. It is your right."

"I know," quietly. "Will you help me?"

Mitchell laughed again. The Doctor turned now, in a passion, —

"You know, Mitchell, I have not the means. You know, if I had, it is in my heart to take this boy and educate him for"—

"The glory of God, and the glory of John May."

May did not speak for a moment; then, controlled, he said, —

"Why should one be raised, when myriads are left?—I have not the money, boy," to Wolfe, shortly.

"Money?" He said it over slowly, as one repeats the guessed answer to a riddle, doubtfully. "That is it? Money?"

"Yes, money,—that is it," said Mitchell, rising, and drawing his furred coat about him. "You've found the cure for all the world's diseases.— Come, May, find your good-humor, and come home. This damp wind chills my very bones. Come and preach your Saint-Simonian [19] doctrines to-morrow to Kirby's hands. Let them have a clear idea of the rights of the soul, and I'll venture next week they'll strike for higher wages. That will be the end of it."

"Will you send the coach-driver to this side of the mills?" asked Kirby, turning to Wolfe.

He spoke kindly: it was his habit to do so. Deborah, seeing the puddler go, crept after him. The three men waited outside. Doctor May walked up and down, chafed. Suddenly he stopped.

"Go back, Mitchell! You say the pocket and the heart of the world speak without meaning to these people. What has its head to say? Taste, culture, refinement? Go!"

Mitchell was leaning against a brick wall. He turned his head indolently, and looked into the mills. There hung about the place a thick, unclean odor. The slightest motion of his hand marked that he perceived it, and his insufferable disgust. That was all. May said nothing, only quickened his angry tramp.

"Besides," added Mitchell, giving a corollary to his answer, "it would be of no use. I am not one of them."

"You do not mean"—said May, facing him.

"Yes, I mean just that. Reform is born of need, not pity. No vital movement of the people's has worked down, for good or evil; fermented, instead, carried up the heaving, cloggy mass. Think back through history, and you will know it. What will this lowest deep—thieves, Magdalens, negroes—do with the light filtered through ponderous Church creeds, Baconian theories, Goethe schemes? Some day, out of their bitter need will be thrown up their own light-bringer,—their Jean Paul, their Cromwell, their Messiah."

"Bah!" was the Doctor's inward criticism. However, in practice, he adopted the theory; for, when, night and morning, afterwards, he prayed that power might be given these degraded souls to rise, he glowed at heart, recognizing an accomplished duty.

Wolfe and the woman had stood in the shadow of the works as the coach drove off. The Doctor had held out his hand in a frank, generous way, telling him to "take care of himself, and to remember it was his right to rise." Mitchell had simply touched his hat, as to an equal, with a quiet look of thorough recognition. Kirby had thrown Deborah some money, which she found, and clutched eagerly enough. They were gone now, all of them. The man sat down on the cinder-road, looking up into the murky sky.

" 'T be late, Hugh. Wunnot hur come?"

He shook his head doggedly, and the woman crouched out of his sight against the wall. Do you remember rare moments when a sudden light flashed over yourself, your world, God? when you stood on a mountain-peak, seeing your life as it might have been, as it is? one quick instant, when custom lost its force and every-day usage? when your friend, wife, brother, stood in a new light? your soul was bared, and the grave,—a fore-taste of the nakedness of the Judgment-Day? So it came before him, his life, that night. The slow tides of pain he had borne gathered themselves up and surged against his soul. His squalid daily life, the brutal coarseness eating into his brain, as the ashes into his skin: before, these things had been a dull aching into his consciousness; to-night, they were reality. He griped the filthy red shirt that clung, stiff with soot, about him, and tore it savagely from his arm. The flesh beneath was muddy with grease and ashes,—and the heart beneath that! And the soul? God knows.

Then flashed before his vivid poetic sense the man who had left him,—the pure face, the delicate, sinewy limbs, in harmony with all he knew of beauty or truth. In his cloudy fancy he had pictured a Something like this. He had found it in this Mitchell, even when he idly scoffed at his pain: a Man all-knowing, all-seeing, crowned by Nature, reigning,—the keen glance of his eye falling like a sceptre on other men. And yet his instinct taught him that he too—He! He looked at himself with sudden loathing, sick, wrung his hands with a cry, and then was silent. With all the phantoms of his heated, ignorant fancy, Wolfe had not been vague in his ambitions. They were practical, slowly built up before him out of his knowledge of what he could do. Through years he had day by day made this hope a real thing to himself,—a clear, projected figure of himself, as he might become.

Able to speak, to know what was best, to raise these men and women working at his side up with him: sometimes he forgot this defined hope in the frantic anguish to escape,—only to escape,—out of the wet, the pain, the ashes, somewhere, anywhere,—only for one moment of free air on a hill-side, to lie down and let his sick soul throb itself out in the sunshine. But to-night he panted for life. The savage strength of his nature was roused; his cry was fierce to God for justice.

"Look at me!" he said to Deborah, with a low, bitter laugh, striking his puny chest savagely. "What am I worth, Deb? Is it my fault that I am no better? My fault? My fault?"

He stopped, stung with a sudden remorse, seeing her hunchback shape writhing with sobs. For Deborah was crying thankless tears, according to the fashion of women.

"God forgi' me, woman! Things go harder wi' you nor me. It's a worse share."

He got up and helped her to rise; and they went doggedly down the muddy street, side by side.

"It's all wrong," he muttered, slowly,—"all wrong! I dunnot understan'. But it'll end some day."

"Come home, Hugh!" she said, coaxingly; for he had stopped, looking around bewildered.

"Home,—and back to the mill!" He went on saying this over to himself, as if he would mutter down every pain in this dull despair.

She followed him through the fog, her blue lips chattering with cold.

They reached the cellar at last. Old Wolfe had been drinking since she went out, and had crept nearer the door. The girl Janey slept heavily in the corner. He went up to her, touching softly the worn white arm with his fingers. Some bitterer thought stung him, as he stood there. He wiped the drops from his forehead, and went into the room beyond, livid, trembling. A hope, trifling, perhaps, but very dear, had died just then out of the poor puddler's life, as he looked at the sleeping, innocent girl,—some plan for the future, in which she had borne a part. He gave it up that moment, then and forever. Only a trifle, perhaps, to us: his face grew a shade paler,—that was all. But, somehow, the man's soul, as God and the angels looked down on it, never was the same afterwards.

Deborah followed him into the inner room. She carried a candle, which she placed on the floor, closing the door after her. She had seen the look on his face, as he turned away: her own grew deadly. Yet, as she came up to him, her eyes glowed. He was seated on an old chest, quiet, holding his face in his hands.

"Hugh!" she said, softly.

He did not speak.

"Hugh, did hur hear what the man said,—him with the clear voice? Did hur hear? Money, money,—that it wud do all?"

He pushed her away,—gently, but he was worn out; her rasping tone fretted him.

"Hugh!"

The candle flared a pale yellow light over the cobwebbed brick walls, and the woman standing there. He looked at her. She was young, in deadly earnest; her faded eyes, and wet, ragged figure caught from their frantic eagerness a power akin to beauty.

"Hugh, it is true! Money ull do it! Oh, Hugh, boy, listen till me! He said it true! It is money!"

"I know. Go back! I do not want you here."

"Hugh, it is t' last time. I 'll never worrit hur again."

There were tears in her voice now, but she choked them back.

"Hear till me only to-night! If one of t' witch people wud come, them we heard of t' home, and gif hur all hur wants, what then? Say, Hugh!"

"What do you mean?"

"I mean money."

Her whisper shrilled through his brain.

"If one of t' witch dwarfs wud come from t' lane moors to-night, and gif hur money, to go out,—*out*, I say,—out, lad, where t' sun shines, and t' heath grows, and t' ladies walk in silken gownds, and God stays all t' time,—where t' man lives that talked to us to-night,—Hugh knows,— Hugh could walk there like a king!"

He thought the woman mad, tried to check her, but she went on, fierce in her eager haste.

"If *I* were t' witch dwarf, if I had t' money, wud hur thank me? Wud hur take me out o' this place wid hur and Janey? I wud not come into the gran' house hur wud build, to vex hur wid t' hunch,—only at night, when t' shadows were dark, stand far off to see hur."

Mad? Yes! Are many of us mad in this way?

"Poor Deb! poor Deb!" he said, soothingly.

"It is here," she said, suddenly jerking into his hand a small roll. "I took it! I did it! Me, me!—not hur! I shall be hanged, I shall be burnt in hell, if anybody knows I took it! Out of his pocket, as he leaned against t' bricks. Hur knows?"

She thrust it into his hand, and then, her errand done, began to gather chips together to make a fire, choking down hysteric sobs.

"Has it come to this?"

That was all he said. The Welsh Wolfe blood was honest. The roll was a small green pocket-book containing one or two gold pieces, and a check for an incredible amount, as it seemed to the poor puddler. He laid it down, hiding his face again in his hands.

"Hugh, don't be angry wud me! It 's only poor Deb,—hur knows?"

He took the long skinny fingers kindly in his.

"Angry? God help me, no! Let me sleep. I am tired."

He threw himself heavily down on the wooden bench, stunned with pain and weariness. She brought some old rags to cover him.

It was late on Sunday evening before he awoke. I tell God's truth, when I say he had then no thought of keeping this money. Deborah had hid it in his pocket. He found it there. She watched him eagerly, as he took it out.

"I must gif it to him," he said, reading her face.

"Hur knows," she said with a bitter sigh of disappointment. "But it is hur right to keep it."

His right! The word struck him. Doctor May had used the same. He washed himself, and went out to find this man Mitchell. His right! Why did this chance word cling to him so obstinately? Do you hear the fierce devils whisper in his ear, as he went slowly down the darkening street?

The evening came on, slow and calm. He seated himself at the end of an alley leading into one of the larger streets. His brain was clear to-night, keen, intent, mastering. It would not start back, cowardly, from any hellish temptation, but meet it face to face. Therefore the great temptation of his life came to him veiled by no sophistry, but bold, defiant, owning its own vile name, trusting to one bold blow for victory.

He did not deceive himself. Theft! That was it. At first the word sickened him; then he grappled with it. Sitting there on a broken cart-wheel, the fading day, the noisy groups, the church-bells' tolling passed before him like a panorama, while the sharp struggle went on within. This money! He took it out, and looked at it. If he gave it back, what then? He was going to be cool about it.

People going by to church saw only a sickly mill-boy watching them quietly at the alley's mouth. They did not know that he was mad, or they would not have gone by so quietly: mad with hunger; stretching out his hands to the world, that had given so much to them, for leave to live the life God meant him to live. His soul within him was smothering to death; he wanted so much, thought so much, and *knew*—nothing. There was nothing of which he was certain, except the mill and things there. Of God and heaven he had heard so little, that they were to him what fairyland is to a child: something real, but not here; very far off. His brain, greedy, dwarfed, full of thwarted energy and unused powers, questioned these men and women going by, coldly, bitterly, that night. Was it not his right to live as they,—a pure life, a good, true-hearted life, full of beauty and kind words? He only wanted to know how to use the strength within him. His heart warmed, as he thought of it. He suffered himself to think of it longer. If he took the money?

Then he saw himself as he might be, strong, helpful, kindly. The night crept on, as this one image slowly evolved itself from the crowd of other thoughts and stood triumphant. He looked at it. As he might be! What wonder, if it blinded him to delirium,—the madness that underlies all revolution, all progress, and all fall?

You laugh at the shallow temptation? You see the error underlying its argument so clearly,—that to him a true life was one of full development rather than self-restraint? that he was deaf to the higher tone in a cry of voluntary suffering for truth's sake than in the fullest flow of spontaneous harmony? I do not plead his cause. I only want to show you the mote in my brother's eye: then you can see clearly to take it out.

The money,—there it lay on his knee, a little blotted slip of paper, nothing in itself; used to raise him out of the pit; something straight from God's hand. A thief! Well, what was it to be a thief? He met the question at last, face to face, wiping the clammy drops of sweat from his forehead. God made this money—the fresh air, too—for his children's use. He never made the difference between poor and rich. The Something who looked down on him that moment through the cool gray sky had a kindly face, he knew, — loved his children alike. Oh, he knew that!

There were times when the soft floods of color in the crimson and purple flames, or the clear depth of amber in the water below the bridge, had somehow given him a glimpse of another world than this, — of an infinite depth of beauty and of quiet somewhere, — somewhere, — a depth of quiet and rest and love. Looking up now, it became strangely real. The sun had sunk quite below the hills, but his last rays struck upward, touching the zenith. The fog had risen, and the town and river were steeped in its thick, gray damp; but overhead, the sun-touched smoke-clouds opened like a cleft ocean, — shifting, rolling seas of crimson mist, waves of billowy silver veined with blood-scarlet, inner depths unfathomable of glancing light. Wolfe's artist-eye grew drunk with color. The gates of that other world! Fading, flashing before him now! What, in that world of Beauty, Content, and Right, were the petty laws, the mine and thine, of mill-owners and mill-hands?

A consciousness of power stirred within him. He stood up. A man, — he thought, stretching out his hands, — free to work, to live, to love! Free! His right! He folded the scrap of paper in his hand. As his nervous fingers took it in, limp and blotted, so his soul took in the mean temptation, lapped it in fancied rights, in dreams of improved existences, drifting and endless as the cloud-seas of color. Clutching it, as if the tightness of his hold would strengthen his sense of possession, he went aimlessly down the street. It was his watch at the mill. He need not go, need never go again, thank God! — shaking off the thought with unspeakable loathing.

Shall I go over the history of the hours of that night? how the man wandered from one to another of his old haunts, with a half-consciousness of bidding them farewell, — lanes and alleys and back-yards where the mill-hands lodged, — noting, with a new eagerness, the filth and drunkenness, the pig-pens, the ash-heaps covered with potato-skins, the bloated, pimpled women at the doors, — with a new disgust, a new sense of sudden triumph, and, under all, a new, vague dread, unknown before, smothered down, kept under, but still there? It left him but once during the night, when, for the second time in his life, he entered a church. It was a sombre Gothic pile, where the stained light lost itself in far-retreating arches; built to meet the requirements and sympathies of a far other class than Wolfe's. Yet it touched, moved him uncontrollably. The distances, the shadows, the still, marble figures, the mass of silent kneeling worshippers, the mysterious music, thrilled, lifted his soul with a wonderful pain.

Wolfe forgot himself, forgot the new life he was going to live, the mean terror gnawing underneath. The voice of the speaker strengthened the charm; it was clear, feeling, full, strong. An old man, who had lived much, suffered much; whose brain was keenly alive, dominant; whose heart was summer-warm with charity. He taught it to-night. He held up Humanity in its grand total; showed the great world-cancer to his people. Who could show it better? He was a Christian reformer; he had studied the age thoroughly; his outlook at man had been free, world-wide, over all time. His faith stood sublime upon the Rock of Ages; his fiery zeal guided vast schemes by which the gospel was to be preached to all nations. How did he preach it to-night? In burning, light-laden words he painted the incarnate Life, Love, the universal Man: words that became reality in the lives of these people,—that lived again in beautiful words and actions, trifling, but heroic. Sin, as he defied it, was a real foe to them; their trials, temptations, were his. His words passed far over the furnace-tender's grasp, toned to suit another class of culture; they sounded in his ears a very pleasant song in an unknown tongue. He meant to cure this world-cancer with a steady eye that had never glared with hunger, and a hand that neither poverty nor strychnine-whiskey had taught to shake. In this morbid, distorted heart of the Welsh puddler he had failed.

Wolfe rose at last, and turned from the church down the street. He looked up; the night had come on foggy, damp; the golden mists had vanished, and the sky lay dull and ash-colored. He wandered again aimlessly down the street, idly wondering what had become of the cloud-sea of crimson and scarlet. The trial-day of this man's life was over, and he had lost the victory. What followed was mere drifting circumstance,—a quicker walking over the path,—that was all. Do you want to hear the end of it? You wish me to make a tragic story out of it? Why, in the police-reports of the morning paper you can find a dozen such tragedies: hints of ship-wrecks unlike any that ever befell on the high seas; hints that here a power was lost to heaven,—that there a soul went down where no tide can ebb or flow. Commonplace enough the hints are,—jocose sometimes, done up in rhyme.

Doctor May, a month after the night I have told you of, was reading to his wife at breakfast from this fourth column of the morning-paper: an unusual thing,—these police-reports not being, in general, choice reading for ladies; but it was only one item he read.

"Oh, my dear! You remember that man I told you of, that we saw at Kirby's mill?—that was arrested for robbing Mitchell? Here he is; just listen:—'Circuit Court. Judge Day. Hugh Wolfe, operative in Kirby &

John's Loudon Mills. Charge, grand larceny. Sentence, nineteen years hard labor in penitentiary.'—Scoundrel! Serves him right! After all our kindness that night! Picking Mitchell's pocket at the very time!"

His wife said something about the ingratitude of that kind of people, and then they began to talk of something else.

Nineteen years! How easy that was to read! What a simple word for Judge Day to utter! Nineteen years! Half a lifetime!

Hugh Wolfe sat on the window-ledge of his cell, looking out. His ankles were ironed. Not usual in such cases; but he had made two desperate efforts to escape. "Well," as Haley, the jailer, said, "small blame to him! Nineteen years' imprisonment was not a pleasant thing to look forward to." Haley was very good-natured about it, though Wolfe had fought him savagely.

"When he was first caught," the jailer said afterwards, in telling the story, "before the trial, the fellow was cut down at once,—laid there on that pallet like a dead man, with his hands over his eyes. Never saw a man so cut down in my life. Time of the trial, too, came the queerest dodge of any customer I ever had. Would choose no lawyer. Judge gave him one, of course. Gibson it was. He tried to prove the fellow crazy; but it wouldn't go. Thing was plain as day-light: money found on him. 'T was a hard sentence,—all the law allows; but it was for 'xample's sake. These mill-hands are gettin' onbearable. When the sentence was read, he just looked up, and said the money was his by rights, and that all the world had gone wrong. That night, after the trial, a gentleman came to see him here, name of Mitchell,—him as he stole from. Talked to him for an hour. Thought he came for curiosity, like. After he was gone, thought Wolfe was remarkable quiet, and went into his cell. Found him very low; bed all bloody. Doctor said he had been bleeding at the lungs. He was as weak as a cat; yet, if ye 'll b'lieve me, he tried to get a-past me and get out. I just carried him like a baby, and threw him on the pallet. Three days after, he tried it again: that time reached the wall. Lord help you! he fought like a tiger,—giv' some terrible blows. Fightin' for life, you see; for he can't live long, shut up in the stone crib down yonder. Got a death-cough now. 'T took two of us to bring him down that day; so I just put the irons on his feet. There he sits, in there. Goin' to-morrow, with a batch more of 'em. That woman, hunchback, tried with him,—you remember?—she's only got three years. 'Complice. But *she's* a woman, you know. He's been quiet ever since I put on irons: giv' up, I suppose. Looks white, sick-lookin'. It acts different on 'em, bein' sentenced. Most of 'em gets reckless, devilish-like. Some prays awful, and sings them vile songs of the mills, all in a breath. That woman, now, she 's desper't'. Been beggin' to see Hugh, as she calls him, for three days. I'm a-goin' to let her in. She don't go with him. Here she is in this next cell. I'm a-goin' now to let her in."

He let her in. Wolfe did not see her. She crept into a corner of the cell, and stood watching him. He was scratching the iron bars of the window with a piece of tin which he had picked up, with an idle, uncertain, vacant stare, just as a child or idiot would do.

"Tryin' to get out, old boy?" laughed Haley. "Them irons will need a crow-bar beside your tin, before you can open 'em."

Wolfe laughed, too, in a senseless way.

"I think I'll get out," he said.

"I believe his brain's touched," said Haley, when he came out.

The puddler scraped away with the tin for half an hour. Still Deborah did not speak. At last she ventured nearer, and touched his arm.

"Blood?" she said, looking at some spots on his coat with a shudder.

He looked up at her. "Why, Deb!" he said, smiling,—such a bright, boyish smile, that it went to poor Deborah's heart directly, and she sobbed and cried out loud.

"Oh, Hugh, lad! Hugh! dunnot look at me, when it wur my fault! To think I brought hur to it! And I loved hur so! Oh, lad, I dud!"

The confession, even in this wretch, came with the woman's blush through the sharp cry.

He did not seem to hear her,—scraping away diligently at the bars the bit of tin.

Was he going mad? She peered closely into his face. Something she saw there made her draw suddenly back,—something which Haley had not seen, that lay beneath the pinched, vacant look it had caught since the trial, or the curious gray shadow that rested on it. That gray shadow,—yes, she knew what that meant. She had often seen it creeping over women's faces for months, who died at last of slow hunger or consumption. That meant death, distant, lingering: but this —— Whatever it was the woman saw, or thought she saw, used as she was to crime and misery, seemed to make her sick with a new horror. Forgetting her fear of him, she caught his shoulders, and looked keenly, steadily, into his eyes.

"Hugh!" she cried, in a desperate whisper,—"oh, boy, not that! for God's sake, not *that*!"

The vacant laugh went off his face, and he answered her in a muttered word or two that drove her away. Yet the words were kindly enough. Sitting there on his pallet, she cried silently a hopeless sort of tears, but did not speak again. The man looked up furtively at her now and then. Whatever his own trouble was, her distress vexed him with a momentary sting.

It was market-day. The narrow window of the jail looked down directly on the carts and wagons drawn up in a long line, where they had unloaded. He could see, too, and hear distinctly the clink of money as it changed hands, the busy crowd of whites and blacks shoving, pushing one another, and the chaffering and swearing at the stalls. Somehow, the sound, more than anything else had done, wakened him up,—made the whole real to him. He was done with the world and the business of it. He let the tin fall, and looked out, pressing his face close to the rusty bars. How they crowded and pushed! And he,—he should never walk that pavement again! There came Neff Sanders, one of the feeders at the mill, with a basket on his arm. Sure enough, Neff was married the other week. He whistled, hoping he would look up; but he did not. He wondered if Neff remembered he was there,—if any of the boys thought of him up there, and thought that he never was to go down that old cinder-road again. Never again! He had not quite understood it before; but now he did. Not for days or years, but never!—that was it.

How clear the light fell on that stall in front of the market! and how like a picture it was, the dark-green heaps of corn, and the crimson beets, and golden melons! There was another with game: how the light flickered on that pheasant's breast, with the purplish blood dripping over the brown feathers! He could see the red shining of the drops, it was so near. In one minute he could be down there. It was just a step. So easy, as it seemed, so natural to go! Yet it could never be—not in all the thousands of years to come—that he should put his foot on that street again! He thought of himself with a sorrowful pity, as of some one else. There was a dog down in the market, walking after his master with such a stately, grave look!— only a dog, yet he could go backwards and forwards just as he pleased: he had good luck! Why, the very vilest cur, yelping there in the gutter, had not lived his life, had been free to act out whatever thought God had put into his brain; while he— No, he would not think of that! He tried to put the thought away, and to listen to a dispute between a countryman and a woman about some meat; but it would come back. He, what had he done to bear this?

Then came the sudden picture of what might have been, and now. He knew what it was to be in the penitentiary,—how it went with men there. He knew how in these long years he should slowly die, but not until soul and body had become corrupt and rotten,—how, when he came out, if he lived to come, even the lowest of the mill-hands would jeer him, — how his hands would be weak, and his brain senseless and stupid. He believed he was almost that now. He put his hand to his head, with a puzzled, weary look. It ached, his head, with thinking. He tried to quiet himself. It was only right, perhaps; he had done wrong. But was there right or wrong for such as he? What was right? And who had ever taught him? He thrust the whole matter away. A dark, cold quiet crept through his brain. It was all wrong; but let it be! It was nothing to him more than the others. Let it be!

The door grated, as Haley opened it.

"Come, my woman! Must lock up for t' night. Come, stir yerself!"

She went up and took Hugh's hand.

"Good-night, Deb," he said, carelessly.

She had not hoped he would say more; but the tired pain on her mouth just then was bitterer than death. She took his passive hand and kissed it.

"Hur 'll never see Deb again!" she ventured, her lips growing colder and more bloodless.

What did she say that for? Did he not know it? Yet he would not be impatient with poor old Deb. She had trouble of her own, as well as he.

"No, never again," he said, trying to be cheerful.

She stood just a moment, looking at him. Do you laugh at her, standing there, with her hunchback, her rags, her bleared, withered face, and the great despised love tugging at her heart?

"Come, you!" called Haley, impatiently.

She did not move.

"Hugh!" she whispered.

It was to be her last word. What was it?

"Hugh, boy, not THAT!"

He did not answer. She wrung her hands, trying to be silent, looking in his face in an agony of entreaty. He smiled again, kindly.

"It is best, Deb. I cannot bear to be hurted any more."

"Hur knows," she said, humbly.

"Tell my father good-bye; and — and kiss little Janey."

She nodded, saying nothing, looked in his face again, and went out of the door. As she went, she staggered.

"Drinkin' to-day?" broke out Haley, pushing her before him. "Where the Devil did you get it? Here, in with ye!" and he shoved her into her cell, next to Wolfe's, and shut the door.

Along the wall of her cell there was a crack low down by the floor, through which she could see the light from Wolfe's. She had discovered it days before. She hurried in now, and, kneeling down by it, listened, hoping to hear some sound. Nothing but the rasping of the tin on the bars. He was at his old amusement again. Something in the noise jarred on her ear, for she shivered as she heard it. Hugh rasped away at the bars. A dull old bit of tin, not fit to cut korl with.

He looked out of the window again. People were leaving the market now. A tall mulatto girl, following her mistress, her basket on her head, crossed the street just below, and looked up. She was laughing; but, when she caught sight of the haggard face peering out through the bars, suddenly grew grave, and hurried by. A free, firm step, a clear-cut olive face, with a scarlet turban tied on one side, dark, shining eyes, and on the head the basket poised, filled with fruit and flowers, under which the scarlet turban and bright eyes looked out half-shadowed. The picture caught his eye. It was good to see a face like that. He would try to-morrow, and cut one like it. *To-morrow!* He threw down the tin, trembling, and covered his face with his hands. When he looked up again, the daylight was gone.

Deborah, crouching near by on the other side of the wall, heard no noise. He sat on the side of the low pallet, thinking. Whatever was the mystery which the woman had seen on his face, it came out now slowly, in the dark there, and became fixed,—a something never seen on his face before. The evening was darkening fast. The market had been over for an hour; the rumbling of the carts over the pavement grew more infrequent: he listened to each, as it passed, because he thought it was to be for the last time. For the same reason, it was, I suppose, that he strained his eyes to catch a glimpse of each passer-by, wondering who they were, what kind of homes they were going to, if they had children,—listening eagerly to every chance word in the street, as if—(God be merciful to the man! what strange fancy was this?)—as if he never should hear human voices again.

It was quite dark at last. The street was a lonely one. The last passenger, he thought, was gone. No,—there was a quick step: Joe Hill, lighting the lamps. Joe was a good old chap; never passed a fellow without some joke or other. He remembered once seeing the place where he lived with his wife. "Granny Hill" the boys called her. Bedridden she was; but so kind as Joe was to her! kept the room so clean!—and the old woman, when he was there, was laughing at "some of t' lad's foolishness." The step was far down the street; but he could see him place the ladder, run up, and light the gas. A longing seized him to be spoken to once more.

"Joe!" he called, out of the grating. "Good-bye, Joe!"

The old man stopped a moment, listening uncertainly; then hurried on. The prisoner thrust his hand out of the window, and called again, louder;

but Joe was too far down the street. It was a little thing; but it hurt him, — this disappointment.

"Good-bye, Joe!" he called, sorrowfully enough.

"Be quiet!" said one of the jailers, passing the door, striking on it with his club.

Oh, that was the last, was it?

There was an inexpressible bitterness on his face, as he lay down on the bed, taking the bit of tin, which he had rasped to a tolerable degree of sharpness, in his hand, — to play with, it may be. He bared his arms, looking intently at their corded veins and sinews. Deborah, listening in the next cell, heard a slight clicking sound, often repeated. She shut her lips tightly, that she might not scream; the cold drops of sweat broke over her, in her dumb agony.

"Hur knows best," she muttered at last, fiercely clutching the boards where she lay.

If she could have seen Wolfe, there was nothing about him to frighten her. He lay quite still, his arms outstretched, looking at the pearly stream of moonlight coming into the window. I think in that one hour that came then he lived back over all the years that had gone before. I think that all the low, vile life, all his wrongs, all his starved hopes, came then, and stung him with a farewell poison that made him sick unto death. He made neither moan nor cry, only turned his worn face now and then to the pure light, that seemed so far off, as one that said, "How long, O Lord? how long?"

The hour was over at last. The moon, passing over her nightly path, slowly came nearer, and threw the light across his bed on his feet. He watched it steadily, as it crept up, inch by inch, slowly. It seemed to him to carry with it a great silence. He had been so hot and tired there always in the mills! The years had been so fierce and cruel! There was coming now quiet and coolness and sleep. His tense limbs relaxed, and settled in a calm languor. The blood ran fainter and slow from his heart. He did not think now with a savage anger of what might be and was not; he was conscious only of deep stillness creeping over him. At first he saw a sea of faces: the mill-men, — women he had known, drunken and bloated, — Janeys timid and pitiful, — poor old Debs: then they floated together like a mist, and faded away, leaving only the clear, pearly moonlight.

Whether, as the pure light crept up the stretched-out figure, it brought with it calm and peace, who shall say? His dumb soul was alone with God in judgment. A Voice may have spoken for it from far-off Calvary, "Father, forgive them, for they know not what they do!" Who dare say? Fainter and fainter the heart rose and fell, slower and slower the moon floated from behind a cloud, until, when at last its full tide of white splendor swept over the cell, it seemed to wrap and fold into a deeper stillness the dead figure that never should move again. Silence deeper than the Night! Nothing that moved, save the black, nauseous stream of blood dripping slowly from the pallet to the floor!

There was outcry and crowd enough in the cell the next day. The coroner and his jury, the local editors, Kirby himself, and boys with their hands thrust knowingly into their pockets and heads on one side, jammed into the corners. Coming and going all day. Only one woman. She came late, and outstayed them all. A Quaker, or Friend, as they call themselves. I think this woman was known by that name in heaven. A homely body, coarsely dressed in gray and white. Deborah (for Haley had let her in) took notice of her. She watched them all—sitting on the end of the pallet, holding his head in her arms—with the ferocity of a watch-dog, if any of them touched the body. There was no meekness, no sorrow, in her face; the stuff out of which murderers are made, instead. All the time Haley and the woman were laying straight the limbs and cleaning the cell, Deborah sat still, keenly watching the Quaker's face. Of all the crowd there that day, this woman alone had not spoken to her,—only once or twice had put some cordial to her lips. After they all were gone, the woman, in the same still, gentle way, brought a vase of wood-leaves and berries, and placed it by the pallet, then opened the narrow window. The fresh air blew in, and swept the woody fragrance over the dead face. Deborah looked up with a quick wonder.

"Did hur know my boy wud like it? Did hur know Hugh?"

"I know Hugh now."

The white fingers passed in a slow, pitiful way over the dead, worn face. There was a heavy shadow in the quiet eyes.

"Did hur know where they 'll bury Hugh?" said Deborah in a shrill tone, catching her arm.

This had been the question hanging on her lips all day.

"In t' town-yard? Under t' mud and ash? T' lad 'll smother, woman! He wur born on t' lane moor, where t' air is frick and strong. Take hur out, for God's sake, take hur out where t' air blows!"

The Quaker hesitated, but only for a moment. She put her strong arm around Deborah and led her to the window.

"Thee sees the hills, friend, over the river? Thee sees how the light lies warm there, and the winds of God blow all the day? I live there,—where the blue smoke is, by the trees. Look at me." She turned Deborah's face to her own, clear and earnest. "Thee will believe me? I will take Hugh and bury him there to-morrow."

Deborah did not doubt her. As the evening wore on, she leaned against the iron bars, looking at the hills that rose far off, through the thick sodden clouds, like a bright, unattainable calm. As she looked, a shadow of their solemn repose fell on her face: its fierce discontent faded into a pitiful, humble quiet. Slow, solemn tears gathered in her eyes: the poor weak eyes turned so hopelessly to the place where Hugh was to rest, the grave heights looking higher and brighter and more solemn than ever before. The Quaker watched her keenly. She came to her at last, and touched her arm.

"When thee comes back," she said, in a low, sorrowful tone, like one who speaks from a strong heart deeply moved with remorse or pity, "thee shall begin thy life again,—there on the hills. I came too late; but not for thee,—by God's help, it may be."

Not too late. Three years after, the Quaker began her work. I end my story here. At evening-time it was light. There is no need to tire you with the long years of sunshine, and fresh air, and slow, patient Christ-love, needed to make healthy and hopeful this impure body and soul. There is a homely pine house, on one of these hills, whose windows overlook broad, wooded slopes and clover-crimsoned meadows,—niched into the very place where the light is warmest, the air freest. It is the Friends' meeting-house. Once a week they sit there, in their grave, earnest way, waiting for the Spirit of Love to speak, opening their simple hearts to receive His words. There is a woman, old, deformed, who takes a humble place among them: waiting like them: in her gray dress, her worn face, pure and meek, turned now and then to the sky. A woman much loved by these silent, restful people; more silent than they, more humble, more loving. Waiting: with her eyes turned to hills higher and purer than these on which she lives,—dim and far off now, but to be reached some day. There may be in her heart some latent hope to meet there the love denied her here,—that she shall find him whom she lost, and that then she will not be all-unworthy. Who blames her? Something is lost in the passage of every soul from one eternity to the other,—something pure and beautiful, which might have been and was not: a hope, a talent, a love, over which the soul mourns, like Esau deprived of his birthright. What blame to the meek Quaker, if she took her lost hope to make the hills of heaven more fair?

Nothing remains to tell that the poor Welsh puddler once lived, but this figure of the mill-woman cut in korl. I have it here in a corner of my library. I keep it hid behind a curtain,—it is such a rough, ungainly thing. Yet there are about it touches, grand sweeps of outline, that show a master's hand. Sometimes,—to-night, for instance,—the curtain is accidentally drawn back, and I see a bare arm stretched out imploringly in the darkness, and an eager, wolfish face watching mine: a wan, woful face, through which the spirit of the dead korl-cutter looks out, with its thwarted life, its mighty hunger, its unfinished work. Its pale, vague lips seem to tremble with a terrible question. "Is this the End?" they say,— "nothing beyond?—no more?" Why, you tell me you have seen that look in the eyes of dumb brutes,—horses dying under the lash. I know.

The deep of the night is passing while I write. The gas-light wakens from the shadows here and there the objects which lie scattered through the room: only faintly, though; for they belong to the open sunlight. As I glance at them, they each recall some task or pleasure of the coming day. A half-moulded child's head; Aphrodite;[20] a bough of forest-leaves; music; work; homely fragments, in which lie the secrets of all eternal truth and beauty. Prophetic all! Only this dumb, woful face seems to belong to and end with the night. I turn to look at it. Has the power of its desperate need commanded the darkness away? While the room is yet steeped in heavy shadow, a cool, gray light suddenly touches its head like a blessing hand, and its groping arm points through the broken cloud to the far East, where, in the flickering, nebulous crimson, God has set the promise of the Dawn.

John Lamar

Atlantic Monthly, April 1862

The guard-house was, in fact, nothing but a shed in the middle of a stubblefield. It had been built for a cider-press last summer; but since Captain Dorr had gone into the army, his regiment had camped over half his plantation, and the shed was boarded up, with heavy wickets at either end, to hold whatever prisoners might fall into their hands from Floyd's forces. It was a strong point for the Federal troops, his farm,— a sort of wedge in the Rebel Cheat counties[1] of Western Virginia. Only one prisoner was in the guard-house now. The sentry, a raw boat-hand from Illinois, gaped incessantly at him through the bars, not sure if the "Secesh" were limbed and headed like other men; but the November fog was so thick that he could discern nothing but a short, squat man, in brown clothes and white hat, heavily striding to and fro. A negro was crouching outside, his knees cuddled in his arms to keep warm: a field-hand, you could be sure from the face, a grisly patch of flabby black, with a dull eluding word of something, you could not tell what, in the points of eyes,— treachery or gloom. The prisoner stopped, cursing him about something: the only answer was a lazy rub of the heels.

"Got any 'baccy, Mars' John?" he whined, in the middle of the hottest oath.

The man stopped abruptly, turning his pockets inside out.

"That 's all, Ben," he said, kindly enough. "Now begone, you black devil!"

"Dem 's um, Mars'! Goin' 'mediate,"—catching the tobacco, and lolling down full length as his master turned off again.

Dave Hall, the sentry, stared reflectively, and sat down.

"Ben? Who air you next?"—nursing his musket across his knees, baby-fashion.

Ben measured him with one eye, polished the quid in his greasy hand, and looked at it.

"Pris'ner o' war," he mumbled, finally,—contemptuously; for Dave's trousers were in rags like his own, and his chilblained toes stuck through the shoe-tops. Cheap white trash, clearly.

"Yer master's some at swearin'. Heow many, neow, hes he like you, down to Georgy?"

The boatman's bony face was gathering a woful pity. He had enlisted to free the Uncle Toms, and carry God's vengeance to the Legrees. Here they were, a pair of them.

Ben squinted another critical survey of the "miss'able Linkinite."

"How many wells hev *yer* poisoned since yer set out?" he muttered.

The sentry stopped.

"How many 'longin' to de Lamars? 'Bout as many as der 's dam' Yankees in Richmond 'baccy-houses!" [2]

Something in Dave's shrewd, whitish eye warned him off.

"Ki yi! yer white nigger, yer!" he chuckled, shuffling down the stubble.

Dave clicked his musket,—then, choking down an oath into a grim Methodist psalm, resumed his walk, looking askance at the coarse-moulded face of the prisoner peering through the bars, and the diamond studs in his shirt,—bought with human blood, doubtless. The man was the black curse of slavery itself in the flesh, in his thought somehow, and he hated him accordingly. Our men of the Northwest have enough brawny Covenanter muscle in their religion to make them good haters for opinion's sake.

Lamar, the prisoner, watched him with a lazy drollery in his sluggish black eyes. It died out into sternness, as he looked beyond the sentry. He had seen this Cheat country before; this very plantation was his grandfather's a year ago, when he had come up from Georgia here, and loitered out the summer months with his Virginia cousins, hunting. That was a pleasant summer! Something in the remembrance of it flashed into his eyes, dewy, genial; the man's leather-covered face reddened like a child's. Only a year ago,—and now— The plantation was Charley Dorr's now, who had married Ruth. This very shed he and Dorr had planned last spring, and now Charley held him a prisoner in it. The very thought of Charley Dorr warmed his heart. Why, he could thank God there were such men. True grit, every inch of his little body! There, last summer, how he had avoided Ruth until the day when he (Lamar) was going away!— then he told him he meant to try and win her. "She cared most for you always," Lamar had said, bitterly; "why have you waited so long?" "You loved her first, John, you know." That was like a man! He remembered that even that day, when his pain was breathless and sharp, the words made him know that Dorr was fit to be her husband.

Dorr was his friend. The word meant much to John Lamar. He thought less meanly of himself, when he remembered it. Charley's prisoner! An odd chance! Better that than to have met in battle. He thrust back the thought, the sweat oozing out on his face,—something within him muttering, "For Liberty! I would have killed him, so help me God!"

He had brought despatches to General Lee, that he might see Charley, and the old place, and—Ruth again; there was a gnawing hunger in his heart to see them. Fool! what was he to them? The man's face grew slowly pale, as that of a savage or an animal does, when the wound is deep and inward.

The November day was dead, sunless: since morning the sky had had only enough life in it to sweat out a few muddy drops, that froze as they fell: the cold numbed his mouth as he breathed it. This stubbly slope was where he and his grandfather had headed the deer: it was covered with hundreds of dirty, yellow tents now. Around there were hills like uncouth monsters, swathed in ice, holding up the soggy sky; shivering pine-forests; unmeaning, dreary flats; and the Cheat, coiled about the frozen sinews of the hills, limp and cold, like a cord tying a dead man's jaws. Whatever outlook of joy or worship this region had borne on its face in time gone, it turned to him to-day nothing but stagnation, a great death. He wondered idly, looking at it, (for the old Huguenot brain of the man was full of morbid fancies) if it were winter alone that had deadened color and pulse out of these full-blooded hills, or if they could know the colder horror crossing their threshold, and forgot to praise God as it came.

Over that farthest ridge the house had stood. The guard (he had been taken by a band of Snake-hunters,[3] back in the hills) had brought him past it. It was a heap of charred rafters. "Burned in the night," they said, "when the old Colonel was alone." They were very willing to show him this, as it was done by his own party, the Secession "Bush-whackers"; took him to the wood-pile to show him where his grandfather had been murdered, (there was a red mark,) and buried, his old hands above the ground. "Colonel said 't was a job fur us to pay up; so we went to the village an' hed a scrimmage,"[4]—pointing to gaps in the hedges where the dead Bush-whackers yet lay unburied. He looked at them, and at the besotted faces about him, coolly. Snake-hunters and Bush-whackers, he knew, both armies used in Virginia as tools for rapine and murder: the sooner the Devil called home his own, the better. And yet, it was not God's fault, surely, that there were such tools in the North, any more than that in the South Ben was—Ben. Something was rotten in freer States than Denmark, he thought.

One of the men went into the hedge, and brought out a child's golden ringlet as a trophy. Lamar glanced in, and saw the small face in its woolen hood, dimpled yet, though dead for days. He remembered it. Jessy Birt, the ferryman's little girl. She used to come up to the house every day for milk. He wondered for which flag *she* died. Ruth was teaching her to write. *Ruth*! Some old pain hurt him just then, nearer than even the blood of the old man or the girl crying to God from the ground. The sergeant mistook the look. "They 'll be buried," he said, gruffly. "Ye brought it on yerselves." And so led him to the Federal camp.

The afternoon grew colder, as he stood looking out of the guard-house. Snow began to whiten through the gray. He thrust out his arm through the wicket, his face kindling with childish pleasure, as he looked closer at the fairy stars and crowns on his shaggy sleeve. If Floy were here! She never had seen snow. When the flakes had melted off, he took a case out of his pocket to look at Floy. His sister,—a little girl who had no mother, nor father, nor lover, but Lamar. The man among his brother officers in Richmond was coarse, arrogant, of dogged courage, keen palate at the table, as keen eye on the turf. Sickly little Floy, down at home, knew the way to something below all this: just as they of the Rommany blood see below the muddy boulders of the streets the enchanted land of Boabdil bare beneath. Lamar polished the ivory painting with his breath, remembering that he had drunk nothing for days. A child's face, of about twelve, delicate,—a breath of fever or cold would shatter such weak beauty; big, dark eyes, (her mother was pure Castilian,) out of which her little life looked irresolute into the world, uncertain what to do there. The painter, with an unapt fancy, had clustered about the Southern face the Southern emblem, buds of the magnolia, unstained, as yet, as pearl. It angered Lamar, remembering how the creamy whiteness of the full-blown flower exhaled passion of which the crimsonest rose knew nothing,—a content, ecstasy, in animal life. Would Floy— Well, God help them both! they needed help. Three hundred souls was a heavy weight for those thin little hands to hold sway over,—to lead to hell or heaven. Up North they could have worked for her, and gained only her money. So Lamar reasoned, like a Georgian: scribbling a letter to "My Baby" on the wrapper of a news-paper,—drawing the shapes of the snow-flakes,—telling her he had reached their grandfather's plantation, but "have not seen our Cousin Ruth yet, of whom you may remember I have told you, Floy. When you grow up, I should like you to be just such a woman; so remember, my darling, if I"— He scratched the last words out: why should he hint to her that he could die? Holding his life loose in his hand, though, had brought things closer to him lately,—God and death, this war, the meaning of it all. But he would keep his brawny body between these terrible realities and Floy, yet awhile. "I want you," he wrote, "to leave the plantation, and go with your old maumer[5] to the village. It will be safer there." He was sure the letter would reach her. He had a plan to escape to-night, and he could put it into a post inside the lines. Ben was to get a small hand-saw that would open the wicket; the guards were not hard to elude. Glancing up, he saw the negro stretched by a camp-fire, listening to the gaunt boatman, who was off duty. Preaching Abolitionism, doubtless: he could hear Ben's derisive shouts of laughter. "And so, good bye, Baby Florence!" he scrawled. "I wish I could send you some of this snow, to show you what the floor of heaven is like."

While the snow fell faster without, he stopped writing, and began idly drawing a map of Georgia on the tan-bark with a stick. Here the Federal troops could effect a landing: he knew the defences at that point. If they did? He thought of these Snake-hunters who had found in the war a peculiar road for themselves downward with no gallows to stumble over, fancied he saw them skulking through the fields at Cedar Creek, closing around the house, and behind them a mass of black faces and bloody bayonets. Floy alone, and he here,—like a rat in a trap! "God keep my little girl!" he wrote, unsteadily. "God bless you, Floy!" He gasped for breath, as if he had been writing with his heart's blood. Folding up the paper, he hid it inside his shirt and began his dogged walk, calculating the chances of escape. Once out of this shed, he could baffle a blood-hound, he knew the hills so well.

His head bent down, he did not see a man who stood looking at him over the wicket. Captain Dorr. A puny little man, with thin yellow hair, and womanish face: but not the less the hero of his men,—they having found out, somehow, that muscle was not the solidest thing to travel on in war-times. Our regiments of "roughs" were not altogether crowned with laurel at Manassas! So the men built more on the old Greatheart soul in the man's blue eyes: one of those souls born and bred pure, sent to teach, that can find breath only in the free North. His hearty "Hillo!" startled Lamar.

"How are you, old fellow?" he said, unlocking the gate and coming in.

Lamar threw off his wretched thoughts, glad to do it. What need to borrow trouble? He liked a laugh,—had a lazy, jolly humor of his own. Dorr had finished drill, and come up, as he did every day, to freshen himself with an hour's talk to this warm, blundering fellow. In this dismal war-work, (though his whole soul was in that, too) it was like putting your hands to a big blaze. Dorr had no near relations; Lamar—they had played marbles together—stood to him where a younger brother might have stood. Yet, as they talked, he could not help his keen eye seeing him just as he was.

Poor John! he thought: the same uncouth-looking effort of humanity that he had been at Yale. No wonder the Northern boys jeered him, with his slothways, his mouthed English, torpid eyes, and brain shut up in that worst of mudmoulds,—belief in caste. Even now, going up and down the tan-bark, his step was dead, sodden, like that of a man in whose life God had not yet wakened the full live soul. It was wakening, though, Dorr thought. Some pain or passion was bringing the man in him out of the flesh, vigilant, alert, aspirant. A different man from Dorr.

In fact, Lamar was just beginning to think for himself, and of course his thoughts were defiant, intolerant. He did not comprehend how his companion could give his heresies such quiet welcome, and pronounce sentence of death on them so coolly. Because Dorr had gone farther up the mountain, had he the right to make him follow in the same steps? The right,—that was it. By brute force, too? Human freedom, eh? Consequently, their talks were stormy enough. To-day, however, they were on trivial matters.

"I've brought the General's order for your release at last, John. It confines you to this district, however."

Lamar shook his head.

"No parole for me! My stake outside is too heavy for me to remain a prisoner on anything but compulsion. I mean to escape, if I can. Floy has nobody but me, you know, Charley."

There was a moment's silence.

"I wish," said Dorr, half to himself, "the child was with her cousin Ruth. If she could make her a woman like herself!"

"You are kind," Lamar forced out, thinking of what might have been a year ago.

Dorr had forgotten. He had just kissed little Ruth at the door-step, coming away: thinking, as he walked up to camp, how her clear thought, narrow as it was, was making his own higher, more just; wondering if the tears on her face last night, when she got up from her knees after prayer, might not help as much in the great cause of truth as the life he was ready to give. He was so used to his little wife now, that he could look to no hour of his past life, nor of the future coming ages of event and work, where she was not present,—very flesh of his flesh, heart of his heart. A gulf lay between them and the rest of the world. It was hardly probable he could see her as a woman towards whom another man looked across the gulf, dumb, hopeless, defrauded of his right.

"She sent you some flowers, by the way, John,—the last in the yard,—and bade me be sure and bring you down with me. Your own colors, you see?—to put you in mind of home,"—pointing to the crimson asters flaked with snow.

The man smiled faintly: the smell of the flowers choked him: he laid them aside. God knows he was trying to wring out this bitter old thought: he could not look in Dorr's frank eyes while it was there. He must escape to-night: he never would come near them again, in this world, or beyond death,—never! He thought of that like a man going to drag through eternity with half his soul gone. Very well: there was man enough left in him to work honestly and bravely, and to thank God for that good pure love he yet had. He turned to Dorr with a flushed face, and began talking of Floy in hearty earnest,—glancing at Ben coming up the hill, thinking that escape depended on him.

"I ordered your man up," said Captain Dorr. "Some canting Abolitionist had him open-mouthed down there."

The negro came in, and stood in the corner, listening while they talked. A gigantic fellow, with a gladiator's muscles. Stronger than that Yankee captain, he thought,—than either of them: better breathed,—drawing the air into his brawny chest. "A man and a brother." Did the fool think he did n't know that before? He had a contempt for Dave and his like. Lamar would have told you Dave's words were true, but despised the man as a crude, unlicked bigot. Ben did the same, with no words for the idea. The negro instinct in him recognized gentle blood by any of its signs,—the transparent animal life, the reticent eye, the mastered voice: he had better men than Lamar at home to learn it from. It is a trait of serfdom, the keen eye to measure the inherent rights of a man to be master. A negro or a Catholic Irishman does not need "Sartor Resartus" to help him to see through any clothes. Ben leaned, half-asleep, against the wall, some old thoughts creeping out of their hiding-places through the torpor, like rats to the sunshine: the boatman's slang had been hot and true enough to rouse them in his brain.

"So, Ben," said his master, as he passed once, "your friend has been persuading you to exchange the cotton-fields at Cedar Creek for New-York alleys, eh?"

"Ki!" laughed Ben, "white darkey. Mind ole dad, Mars' John, as took off in der swamp? Um asked dat Linkinite ef him saw dad up Norf. Guess him 's free now. Ki! ole dad!"

"The swamp was the place for him," said Lamar. "I remember."

"Dunno," said the negro, surlily: "him 's dad, af'er all: tink him 's free now,"—and mumbled down into a monotonous drone about

"Oh yo, bredern, is yer gwine ober Jordern?"

Half-asleep, they thought,—but with dull questionings at work in his brain, some queer notions about freedom, of that unknown North, mostly mixed with his remembrance of his father, a vicious old negro, that in Pennsylvania would have worked out his salvation in the under cell of the penitentiary, but in Georgia, whipped into heroism, had betaken himself into the swamp, and never returned. Tradition among the Lamar slaves said he had got off to Ohio, of which they had as clear an idea as most of us have of heaven. At any rate, old Kite became a mystery, to be mentioned with awe at fish-bakes and barbecues. He was this uncouth wretch's father,—do you understand? The flabby-faced boy, flogged in the cotton-field for whining after his dad, or hiding away part of his flitch and molasses for months in hopes the old man would come back, was rather a comical object, you would have thought. Very different his, from the feeling with which you left your mother's grave,—though as yet we have not invented names for the emotions of those people. We 'll grant that it hurt Ben a little, however. Even the young polypus,[6] when it is torn from the old one, bleeds a drop or two, they say. As he grew up, the great North glimmered through his thought, a sort of big field,—a paradise of no work, no flogging, and white bread every day, where the old man sat and ate his fill.

The second point in Ben's history was that he fell in love. Just as you did,—with the difference, of course: though the hot sun, or the perpetual foot upon his breast, does not make our black Prometheus less fierce in his agony of hope or jealousy than you, I am afraid. It was Nan, a pale mulatto house-servant, that the field-hand took into his dull, lonesome heart to make life of, with true-love defiance of caste. I think Nan liked him very truly. She was lame and sickly, and if Ben was black and a picker, and stayed in the quarters, he was strong, like a master to her in some ways: the only thing she could call hers in the world was the love the clumsy boy gave her. White women feel in that way sometimes, and it makes them very tender to men not their equals. However, old Mrs. Lamar, before she died, gave her house-servants their free papers, and Nan was among them. So she set off, with all the finery little Floy could give her: went up into that great, dim North. She never came again.

The North swallowed up all Ben knew or felt outside of his hot, hated work, his dread of a lashing on Saturday night. All the pleasure left him was 'possum and hominy for Sunday's dinner. It did not content him. The spasmodic religion of the field-negro does not teach endurance. So it came, that the slow tide of discontent ebbing in everybody's heart towards some unreached sea set in his ignorant brooding towards that vague country which the only two who cared for him had found. If he forgot it through the dogged, sultry days, he remembered it when the overseer scourged the dull tiger-look into his eyes, or when, husking corn with the others at night, the smothered negro-soul, into which their masters dared not look, broke out in their wild, melancholy songs. Aimless, unappealing, yet no prayer goes up to God more keen in its pathos. You find, perhaps, in Beethoven's seventh symphony the secrets of your heart made manifest, and suddenly think of a Somewhere to come, where your hope waits for you with late fulfilment. Do not laugh at Ben, then, if he dully told in his song the story of all he had lost, or gave to his heaven a local habitation and a name.

From the place where he stood now, as his master and Dorr walked up and down, he could see the purplish haze beyond which the sentry had told him lay the North. The North! Just beyond the ridge. There was a pain in his head, looking at it; his nerves grew cold and rigid, as yours do when something wrings your heart sharply: for there are nerves in these black carcasses, thicker, more quickly stung to madness than yours. Yet if any savage longing, smouldering for years, was heating to madness now in his brain, there was no sign of it in his face. Vapid, with sordid content, the huge jaws munching tobacco slowly, only now and then the beady eye shot a sharp glance after Dorr. The sentry had told him the Northern army had come to set the slaves free; he watched the Federal officer keenly.

"What ails you, Ben?" said his master. "Thinking over your friend's sermon?"

Ben's stolid laugh was ready.

"Done forgot dat, Mars'. Would n't go, nohow. Since Mars' sold dat cussed Joe, gorry good times 't home. Dam' Abolitioner say we ums all goin' Norf,"—with a stealthy glance at Dorr.

"That's more than your philanthropy bargains for, Charley," laughed Lamar.

The men stopped; the negro skulked nearer, his whole sense sharpened into hearing. Dorr's clear face was clouded.

"This slave question must be kept out of the war. It puts a false face on it."

"I thought one face was what it needed," said Lamar. "You have too many slogans. Strong government, tariff, Sumter, a bit of bunting, eleven dollars a month.[7] It ought to be a vital truth that would give soul and *vim* to a body with the differing members of your army. You, with your ideal theory, and Billy Wilson with his 'Blood and Baltimore!' Try human freedom. That 's high and sharp and broad."

Ben drew a step closer.

"You are shrewd, Lamar. I am to go below all constitutions or expediency or existing rights, and tell Ben here that he is free? When once the Government accepts that doctrine, you, as a Rebel, must be let alone."

The slave was hid back in the shade.

"Dorr," said Lamar, "you know I'm a groping, ignorant fellow, but it seems to me that prating of constitutions and existing rights is surface talk; there is a broad common-sense underneath, by whose laws the world is governed, which your statesmen don't touch often. You in the North, in your dream of what shall be, shut your eyes to what is. You want a republic where every man's voice shall be heard in the council, and the majority shall rule. Granting that the free population are educated to a fitness for this,—(God forbid I should grant it with the Snake-hunters before my eyes!)—look here!"

He turned round, and drew the slave out into the light: he crouched down, gaping vacantly at them.

"There is Ben. What, in God's name, will you do with him? Keep him a slave, and chatter about self-government? Pah! The country is paying in blood for the lie, to-day. Educate him for freedom, by putting a musket in his hands? We have this mass of heathendom drifted on our shores by your will as well as mine. Try to bring them to a level with the whites by a wrench, and you'll waken out of your dream to a sharp reality. Your Northern philosophy ought to be old enough to teach you that spasms in the body-politic shake off no atom of disease,—that reform, to be enduring, must be patient, gradual, inflexible as the Great Reformer. 'The mills of God,' the old proverb says, 'grind surely.' But, Dorr, they grind exceeding slow!"

Dorr watched Lamar with an amused smile. It pleased him to see his brain waking up, eager, vehement. As for Ben, crouching there, if they talked of him like a clod, heedless that his face deepened in stupor, that his eyes had caught a strange, gloomy treachery,—we all do the same, you know.

"What is your remedy, Lamar? You have no belief in the right of Secession, I know," said Dorr.

"It 's a bad instrument for a good end. Let the white Georgian come out of his sloth, and the black will rise with him. Jefferson Davis may not intend it, but God does. When we have our Lowell, our New York, when we are a self-sustaining people instead of lazy land-princes, Ben here will have climbed the second of the great steps of Humanity. Do you laugh at us?" said Lamar, with a quiet self-reliance. "Charley, it needs only work and ambition to cut the brute away from my face, and it will leave traits very like your own. Ben's father was a Guinea fetich-worshipper; when we stand where New England does, Ben's son will be ready for his freedom."

"And while you theorize," laughed Dorr, "I hold you a prisoner, John, and Ben knows it is his right to be free. He will not wait for the grinding of the mill, I fancy."

Lamar did not smile. It was womanish in the man, when the life of great nations hung in doubt before them, to go back so constantly to little Floy sitting in the lap of her old black maumer. But he did it,—with the quick thought that to-night he must escape, that death lay in delay.

While Dorr talked, Lamar glanced significantly at Ben. The negro was not slow to understand,—with a broad grin, touching his pocket, from which projected the dull end of a hand-saw. I wonder what sudden pain made the negro rise just then, and come close to his master, touching him with a strange affection and remorse in his tired face, as though he had done him some deadly wrong.

"What is it, old fellow?" said Lamar, in his boyish way. "Homesick, eh? There's a little girl in Georgia that will be glad to see you and your master, and take precious good care of us when she gets us safe again. That's true, Ben!" laying his hand kindly on the man's shoulder, while his eyes went wandering off to the hills lying South.

"Yes, Mars'," said Ben, in a low voice, suddenly bringing a blacking-brush, and beginning to polish his master's shoes,—thinking, while he did it, of how often Mars' John had interfered with the over-seers to save him from a flogging,—(Lamar, in his lazy way, was kind to his slaves,)— thinking of little Mist' Floy with an odd tenderness and awe, as a gorilla might of a white dove: trying to think thus,—the simple, kindly nature of the negro struggling madly with something beneath, new and horrible. He understood enough of the talk of the white men to know that there was no help for him,—none. Always a slave. Neither you nor I can ever know what those words meant to him. The pale purple mist where the North lay was never to be passed. His dull eyes turned to it constantly,— with a strange look, such as the lost women might have tuned to the door, when Jesus shut it: they forever outside. There was a way to help himself? The stubby black fingers holding the brush grew cold and clammy,— noting withal, the poor wretch in his slavish way, that his master's clothes were finer than the Northern captain's, his hands whiter, and proud that it was so,—holding Lamar's foot daintily, trying to see himself in the shoe, smoothing down the trousers with a boorish, affectionate touch,—with the same fierce whisper in his ear, Would the shoes ever be cleaned again? would the foot move to-morrow?

It grew late. Lamar's supper was brought up from Captain Dorr's, and placed on the bench. He poured out a goblet of water.

"Come, Charley, let's drink. To Liberty! It is a war-cry for Satan or Michael."

They drank, laughing, while Ben stood watching. Dorr turned to go, but Lamar called him back,—stood resting his hand on his shoulder: he never thought to see him again, you know.

"Look at Ruth, yonder," said Dorr, his face lighting. "She is coming to meet us. She thought you would be with me."

Lamar looked gravely down at the low field-house and the figure at the gate. He thought he could see the small face and earnest eyes, though it was far off, and night was closing.

"She is waiting for you, Charley. Go down. Good night, old chum!"

If it cost any effort to say it, Dorr saw nothing of it.

"Good night, Lamar! I'll see you in the morning."

He lingered. His old comrade looked strangely alone and desolate.

"John!"

"What is it, Dorr?"

"If I could tell the Colonel you would take the oath? For Floy's sake."

The man's rough face reddened.

"You should know me better. Good bye."

"Well, well, you are mad. Have you no message for Ruth?"

There was a moment's silence.

"Tell her I say, God bless her!"

Dorr stopped and looked keenly in his face,—then, coming back, shook hands again, in a different way from before, speaking in a lower voice,—

"God help us all, John! Good night!"—and went slowly down the hill.

It was nearly night, and bitter cold. Lamar stood where the snow drifted in on him, looking out through the horizonless gray.

"Come out o' dem cold, Mars' John,' whined Ben, pulling at his coat.

As the night gathered, the negro was haunted with a terrified wish to be kind to his master. Something told him that the time was short. Here and there through the far night some tent-fire glowed in a cone of ruddy haze, through which the thick-falling snow shivered like flakes of light. Lamar watched only the square block of shadow where Dorr's house stood. The door opened at last, and a broad, cheerful gleam shot out red darts across the white waste without; then he saw two figures go in together. They paused a moment; he put his head against the bars, straining his eyes, and saw that the woman turned, shading her eyes with her hand, and looked up to the side of the mountain where the guard-house lay,—with a kindly look, perhaps, for the prisoner out in the cold. A kind look: that was all. The door shut on them. Forever: so, good night, Ruth!

He stood there for an hour or two, leaning his head against the muddy planks, smoking. Perhaps, in his coarse fashion, he took the trouble of his manhood back to the same God he used to pray to long ago. When he turned at last, and spoke, it was with a quiet, strong voice, like one who would fight through life in a manly way. There was a grating sound at the back of the shed: it was Ben, sawing through the wicket, the guard having lounged off to supper. Lamar watched him, noticing that the negro was unusually silent. The plank splintered, and hung loose.

"Done gone, Mars' John, now,"—leaving it, and beginning to replenish the fire.

"That's right, Ben. We'll start in the morning. That sentry at two o'clock sleeps regularly."

Ben chuckled, heaping up the sticks.

"Go on down to the camp, as usual. At two, Ben, remember! We will be free to-night, old boy!"

The black face looked up from the clogging smoke with a curious stare.

"Ki! we'll be free to-night, Mars'!"—gulping his breath.

Soon after, the sentry unlocked the gate, and he shambled off out into the night. Lamar, left alone, went closer to the fire, and worked busily at some papers he drew from his pocket: maps and schedules. He intended to write until two o'clock; but the blaze dying down, he wrapped his blanket about him, and lay down on the heaped straw, going on sleepily, in his brain, with his calculations.

The negro, in the shadow of the shed, watched him. A vague fear beset him—of the vast, white cold,—the glowering mountains,—of himself; he clung to the familiar face, like a man drifting out into an unknown sea, clutching some relic of the shore. When Lamar fell asleep, he wandered uncertainly towards the tents. The world had grown new, strange; was he Ben, picking cotton in the swamp-edge?—plunging his fingers with a shudder in the icy drifts. Down in the glowing torpor of the Santilla flats, where the Lamar plantations lay, Ben had slept off as maddening hunger for life and freedom as this of to-day; but here, with the winter air stinging every nerve to life, with the perpetual mystery of the mountains terrifying his bestial nature down, the strength of the man stood up: groping, blind, malignant, it may be; but whose fault was that? He was half-frozen: the physical pain sharpened the keen doubt conquering his thought. He sat down in the crusted snow, looking vacantly about him, a man, at last,—but wakening, like a new-born soul, into a world of unutterable solitude. Wakened dully, slowly; sitting there far into the night, pondering stupidly on his old life; crushing down and out the old parasite affection for his master, the old fears, the old weight threatening to press out his thin life; the muddy blood heating, firing with the same heroic dream that bade Tell[8] and Garibaldi[9] lift up their hands to God, and cry aloud that they were men and free: the same,—God-given, burning in the imbruted veins of a Guinea slave. To what end? May God be merciful to America while she answers the question! He sat, rubbing his cracked, bleeding feet, glancing stealthily at the southern hills. Beyond them lay all that was past; in an hour he would follow Lamar back to—what? He lifted his hands up to the sky, in his silly way sobbing hot tears. "Gor-a'mighty, Mars' Lord, I 'se tired," was all the prayer he made. The pale purple mist was gone from the North; the ridge behind which love, freedom waited, struck black across the sky, a wall of iron. He looked at it drearily. Utterly alone: he had always been alone. He got up at last, with a sigh.

"It's a big world,"—with a bitter chuckle,—"but der 's no room in it fur poor Ben."

He dragged himself through the snow to a light in a tent where a voice in a wild drone, like that he had heard at negro camp-meetings, attracted him. He did not go in: stood at the tent-door, listening. Two or three of the guard stood around, leaning on their muskets; in the vivid fire-light rose the gaunt figure of the Illinois boatman, swaying to and fro as he preached. For the men were honest, God-fearing souls, members of the same church, and Dave, in all integrity of purpose, read aloud to them,— the cry of Jeremiah against the foul splendors of the doomed city,—waving, as he spoke, his bony arm to the South. The shrill voice was that of a man wrestling with his Maker. The negro's fired brain caught the terrible meaning of the words,—found speech in it: the wide, dark night, the solemn silence of the men, were only fitting audience.

The man caught sight of the slave, and, laying down his book, began one of those strange exhortations in the manner of his sect. Slow at first, full of unutterable pity. There was room for pity. Pointing to the human brute crouching there, made once in the image of God,—the saddest wreck on His green foot-stool: to the great stealthy body, the revengeful jaws, the foreboding eyes. Soul, brains,—a man, wifeless, homeless, nationless, hawked, flung from trader to trader for a handful of dirty shinplasters. "Lord God of hosts," cried the man, lifting up his trembling hands, "lay not this sin to our charge!" There was a scar on Ben's back where the lash had buried itself: it stung now in the cold. He pulled his clothes tighter, that they should not see it; the scar and the words burned into his heart: the childish nature of the man was gone; the vague darkness in it took a shape and name. The boatman had been praying for him; the low words seemed to shake the night:—

"Hear the prayer of Thy servant, and his supplications! Is not this what Thou hast chosen: to loose the bands, to undo the heavy burdens, and let the oppressed go free? O Lord, hear! O Lord, hearken and do! Defer not for Thine own sake, O my God!"

"What shall I do?" said the slave, standing up.

The boatman paced slowly to and fro, his voice chording in its dull monotone with the smothered savage muttering in the negro's brain.

"The day of the Lord cometh; it is nigh at hand. Who can abide it? What saith the prophet Jeremiah? 'Take up a burden against the South. Cry aloud, spare not. Woe unto Babylon, for the day of her vengeance is come, the day of her visitation! Call together the archers against Babylon; camp against it round about; let none thereof escape. Recompense her: as she hath done unto my people, be it done unto her. A sword is upon Babylon: it shall break in pieces the shepherd and his flock, the man and the woman, the young man and the maid. I will render unto her the evil she hath done in my sight, saith the Lord.'"

It was the voice of God: the scar burned fiercer; the slave came forward boldly,—

"Mars'er, what shall I do?"

"Give the poor devil a musket," said one of the men. "Let him come with us, and stike a blow for freedom."

He took a knife from his belt, and threw it to him, then sauntered off to his tent.

"A blow for freedom?" mumbled Ben, taking it up.

"Let us sing to the praise of God," said the boatman, "the sixty-eighth psalm," lining it out while they sang,—the scattered men joining, partly to keep themselves awake. In old times David's harp charmed away the demon from a human heart. It roused one now, never to be laid again. A dull, droning chant, telling how the God of Vengeance rode upon the wind, swift to loose the fetters of the chained, to make desert the rebellious land; with a chorus, or refrain, in which Ben's wild, melancholy cry sounded like the wail of an avenging spirit:—

"That in the blood of enemies
Thy foot imbrued may be:
And of thy dogs dipped in the same
The tongues thou mayest see."

The meaning of that was plain; he sang it lower and more steadily each time, his body swaying in cadence, the glitter in his eye more steely.

Lamar, asleep in his prison, was wakened by the far-off plaintive song: he roused himself, leaning on one elbow, listening with a half-smile. It was Naomi they sang, he thought,—an old-fashioned Methodist air that Floy had caught from the negroes, and used to sing to him sometimes. Every night, down at home, she would come to his parlor-door to say good-night: he thought he could see the little figure now in its white night-gown, and hear the bare feet pattering on the matting. When he was alone, she would come in, and sit on his lap awhile, and kneel down before she went away, her head on his knee, to say her prayers, as she called it. Only God knew how many times he had remained alone after hearing those prayers, saved from nights of drunken debauch. He thought he felt Floy's pure little hand on his forehead now, as if she were saying her usual "Good night, Bud." He lay down to sleep again, with a genial smile on his face, listening to the hymn.

"It's the same God," he said,—"Floy's and theirs."

Outside, as he slept, a dark figure watched him. The song of the men ceased. Midnight, white and silent, covered the earth. He could hear only the slow breathing of the sleeper. Ben's black face grew ashy pale, but he did not tremble, as he crept, cat-like, up to the wicket, his blubber lips apart, the white teeth clenched.

"It's for Freedom, Mars' Lord!" he gasped, looking up to the sky, as if he expected an answer. "Gor-a'mighty, it's for Freedom!" And went in.

A belated bird swooped through the cold moonlight into the valley, and vanished in the far mountain-cliffs with a low, fearing cry, as though it had passed through Hades.

They had broken down the wicket: he saw them lay the heavy body on the lumber outside, the black figures hurrying over the snow. He laughed low, savagely, watching them. Free now! The best of them despised him; the years past of cruelty and oppression turned back, fused in a slow, deadly current of revenge and hate, against the race that had trodden him down. He felt the iron muscles of his fingers, looked close at the glittering knife he held, chuckling at the strange smell it bore. Would the Illinois boatman blame him, if it maddened him? And if Ben took the fancy to put it to his throat, what right has he to complain? Has not he also been a dweller in Babylon? He hesitated a moment in the cleft of the hill, choosing his way, exultantly. He did not watch the North now; the quiet old dream of content was gone; his thick blood throbbed and surged with passions of which you and I know nothing: he had a lost life to avenge. His native air, torrid, heavy with latent impurity, drew him back: a fitter breath than this cold snow for the animal in his body, the demon in his soul, to triumph and wallow in. He panted, thinking of the saffron hues of the Santilla flats, of the white, stately dwellings, the men that went in and out from them, quiet, dominant, — feeling the edge of his knife. It was his turn to be master now! He ploughed his way doggedly through the snow, — panting, as he went, — a hotter glow in his gloomy eyes. It was his turn for pleasure now: he would have his fill! Their wine and their gardens and ——— He did not need to choose a wife from his own color now. He stopped, thinking of little Floy, with her curls and great listening eyes, watching at the door for her brother. He had watched her climb up into his arms and kiss his cheek. She never would do that again! He laughed aloud, shrilly. By God! she should keep the kiss for other lips! Why should he not say it?

Up on the hill the night-air throbbed colder and holier. The guards stood about in the snow, silent, troubled. This was not like a death in battle: it put them in mind of home, somehow. All that the dying man said was, "Water," now and then. He had been sleeping, when struck, and never had thoroughly wakened from his dream. Captain Poole, of the Snake-hunters, had wrapped him in his own blanket, finding nothing more could be done. He went off to have the Colonel summoned now, muttering that it was "a damned shame." They put snow to Lamar's lips constantly, being hot and parched; a woman, Dorr's wife, was crouching on the round beside him, chafing his hands, keeping down her sobs for fear they would disturb him. He opened his eyes at last, and knew Dorr, who held his head.

"Unfasten my coat, Charley. What makes it so close here?"

Dorr could not speak.

"Shall I lift you up, Captain Lamar?" asked Dave Hall, who stood leaning on his rifle.

He spoke in a subdued tone, Babylon being far off for the moment. Lamar dozed again before he could answer.

"Don't try to move him, — it is too late," said Dorr, sharply.

The moonlight steeped mountain and sky in a fresh whiteness. Lamar's face, paling every moment, hardening, looked in it like some solemn work of an untaught sculptor. There was a breathless silence. Ruth, kneeling beside him, felt his hand grow slowly colder than the snow. He moaned, his voice going fast,—

"At two, Ben, old fellow! We 'll be free to-night!"

Dave, stooping to wrap the blanket, felt his hand wet: he wiped it with a shudder.

"As he hath done unto My people, be it done unto him!" he muttered, but the words did not comfort him.

Lamar moved, half-smiling.

"That's right, Floy. What is it she says? 'Now I lay me down' ——— I forget. Good night. Kiss me, Floy."

He waited,—looked up uneasily. Dorr looked at his wife: she stooped, and kissed his lips. Charley smoothed back the hair from the damp face with as tender a touch as a woman's. Was he dead? The white moonlight was not more still than the calm face.

Suddenly the night-air was shattered by a wild, revengeful laugh from the hill. The departing soul rushed back, at the sound, to life, full consciousness. Lamar started from their hold,—sat up.

"It was Ben," he said, slowly.

In that dying flash of comprehension, it may be, the wrongs of the white, man and the black stood clearer to his eyes than ours: the two lives trampled down. The stern face of the boatman bent over him: he was trying to stanch the flowing blood. Lamar looked at him: Hall saw no bitterness in the look,—a quiet, sad question rather, before which his soul lay bare. He felt the cold hand touch his shoulder, saw the pale lips move.

"Was this well done?" they said.

Before Lamar's eyes the rounded arch of gray receded, faded into dark; the negro's fierce laugh filled his ear: some woful thought at the sound wrung his soul, as it halted at the gate. It caught at the simple faith his mother taught him.

"Yea," he said aloud, "though I walk through the valley of the shadow of death, I will fear no evil: for Thou art with me."

Dorr gently drew down the uplifted hand. He was dead.

"It was a manly soul," said the Northern captain, his voice choking, as he straightened the limp hair.

"He trusted in God? A strange delusion!" muttered the boatman.

Yet he did not like that they should leave him alone with Lamar, as they did, going down for help. He paced to and fro, his rifle on his shoulder, arming his heart with strength to accomplish the vengeance of the Lord against Babylon. Yet he could not forget the murdered man sitting there in the calm moonlight, the dead face turned towards the North,—the dead face, whereon little Floy's tears should never fall. The grave, unmoving eyes seemed to the boatman to turn to him with the same awful question. "Was this well done?" they said. He thought in eternity they would rise before him, sad, unanswered. The earth, he fancied, lay whiter, colder,— the heaven farther off; the war, which had become a daily business, stood suddenly before him in all its terrible meaning. God, he thought, had met in judgment with His people. Yet he uttered no cry of vengeance against the doomed city. With the dead face before him, he bent his eyes to the ground, humble, uncertain,—speaking out of the ignorance of his own weak, human soul.

"The day of the Lord is nigh," he said; "it is at hand; and who can abide it?"

 David Gaunt

Atlantic Monthly, September 1862

Was ihr den Geist der Zeiten heisst,
Das ist im Grund der Herren eigner Geist.

—Faust

PART I

What kind of sword, do you think, was that which old Christian had in that famous fight of his with Apollyon,[1] long ago? He cut the fiend to the marrow with it, you remember, at last; though the battle went hardly with him, too, for a time. Some of his blood, Bunyan says, is on the stones of the valley to this day. That is a vague record of the combat between the man and the dragon in that strange little valley, with its perpetual evening twilight and calm, its meadows crusted with lilies, its herd-boy with his quiet song, close upon the precincts of hell. It fades back, the valley and the battle, dim enough, from the sober freshness of this summer morning. Look out of the window here, at the hubbub of the early streets, the freckled children racing past to school, the dewy shimmer of yonder willows in the sunlight, like drifts of pale green vapor. Where is Apollyon? does he put himself into flesh and blood, as then, nowadays? And the sword which Christian used, like a man, in his deed of derring-do?

Reading the quaint history, just now, I have a mind to tell you a modern story. It is not long: only how, a few months ago, a poor itinerant, and a young girl, (like these going by with baskets on their arms), who lived up in these Virginia hills, met Evil in their lives, and how it fared with them: how they thought that they were in the Valley of Humiliation, that they were Christian, and Rebellion and Infidelity Apollyon; the different ways they chose to combat him; the weapons they used. I can tell you that; but you do not know—do you?—what kind of sword old Christian used, or where it is, or whether its edge is rusted.

I must not stop to ask more, for these war-days are short, and the story might be cold before you heard it.

A brick house, burrowed into the side of a hill, with red gleams of light winking out of the windows in a jolly way into the winter's night: wishing, one might fancy, to cheer up the hearts of the freezing stables and barn and hen-house that snuggled about the square yard, trying to keep warm. The broad-backed old hill (Scofield's Hill, a famous place for papaws in summer) guards them tolerably well; but then, house and barn and hill lie up among the snowy peaks of the Virginian Alleghanies, and you know how they would chill and awe the air. People away down yonder in the river-bottoms see these peaks dim and far-shining, as though they cut through thick night; but we, up among them here, find the night wide, filled with a pale star-light that has softened for itself out of the darkness overhead a great space up towards heaven.

The snow lay deep, on this night of which I tell you,—a night somewhere near the first of January in this year. Two old men, a white and a black, who were rooting about the farm-yard from stable to fodder-rack, waded through deep drifts of it.

"Tell yer, Mars' Joe," said the negro, banging the stable-door, "dat hoss ort n't ter risk um's bones dis night. Ef yer go ter de Yankee meetin', Coly kern't tote yer."

"Well, well, Uncle Bone, that's enough," said old Scofield testily, looking through the stall-window at the horse, with a face anxious enough to show that the dangers of foundering for Coly and for the Union were of about equal importance in his mind.

A heavily built old fellow, big-jointed, dull-eyed, with a short, black pipe in his mouth, going about peering into sheds and out-houses,—the same routine he and Bone had gone through every night for thirty years,—joking, snarling, cursing, alternately. The cramped old routine, dogged, if you choose to call it so, was enough for him: you could tell that by a glance at his earnest, stolid face; you could see that it need not take Prospero's Ariel[2] forty minutes to put a girdle about this man's world: ten would do it, tie up the farm, and the dead and live Scofields, and the Democratic party, with an ideal reverence for "Firginya" under all. As for the Otherwhere, outside of Virginia, he heeded it as much as a Hindoo does the turtle on which the earth rests. For which you shall not sneer at Joe Scofield, or the Pagan. How wide is your own "sacred soil"?—the creed, government, bit of truth, other human heart, self, perhaps, to which your soul roots itself vitally,—like a cuttle-fish sucking to an inch of rock,—and drifts out palsied feelers of recognition into the ocean of God's universe, just as languid as the aforesaid Hindoo's hold upon the Kalpas[3] of emptiness underneath the turtle?

Joe Scofield sowed the fields and truck-patch,—sold the crops down in Wheeling; every year he got some little, hardly earned snugness for the house (he and Bone had been born in it, their grand-fathers had lived there together). Bone was his slave; of course, they thought, how should it be otherwise? The old man's daughter was Dode Scofield; his negro was Bone Scofield, in degree.[4] Joe went to the Methodist church on Sundays; he hurrahed for the Democratic candidate: it was a necessity for Whigs to be defeated; it was a necessity for Papists to go to hell. He had a tight grip on these truths, which were born, one might say, with his blood; his life grew out of them. So much of the world was certain,—but outside? It was rather vague there: Yankeedom was a mean-soiled country, whence came clocks, teachers, peddlers, and infidelity; and the English,—it was an American's birthright to jeer at the English.

We call this a narrow life, prate in the North of our sympathy with the universal man, don't we? And so we extend a stomachic greeting to our Spanish brother that sends us wine, and a bow from our organ of ideality to Italy for beauty incarnate in Art,—see the Georgian slave-holder only through the eyes of the cowed negro at his feet, and give a dime on Sunday to send the gospel to the heathen, who will burn forever, we think, if it never is preached to them. What of your sympathy with the universal man, when I tell you Scofield was a Rebel?

His syllogisms on this point were clear, to himself. For slavery to exist in a country where free government was put on trial was a tangible lie, that had worked a moral divorce between North and South. Slavery was the vital breath of the South; if she chose to go out and keep it, had not freemen the right to choose their own government? To bring her back by carnage was simply the old game of regal tyranny on republican cards. So his head settled it: as for his heart,—his neighbors' houses were in ashes, burned by the Yankees; his son lay dead at Manassas. He died to keep them back, did n't he? "Geordy boy," he used to call him,—worth a dozen puling girls:[5] since he died, the old man had never named his name. Scofield was a Rebel in every bitter drop of his heart's blood.

He hurried to the house to prepare to go to the Union meeting. He had a reason for going. The Federal troops held Romney[6] then, a neighboring village, and he knew many of the officers would be at this meeting. There was a party of Confederates in Blue's Gap, a mountain-fastness near by, and Scofield had heard a rumor that the Unionists would attack them to-morrow morning: he meant to try and find out the truth of it, so as to give the boys warning to be ready, and, maybe, lend them a helping hand. Only for Dode's sake, he would have been in the army long ago.

He stopped on the porch to clean his shoes, for the floor was newly scrubbed, and Miss Scofield was a tidy housekeeper, and had, besides, a temper as hot and ready to light as her father's pipe. The old man stopped now, half chuckling, peeping in at the window to see if all was clear within. But you must not think for this that Dode's temper was the bugbear of the house,—though the girl herself thought it was, and shed some of the bitterest tears of her life over it. Just a feverish blaze in the blood, caught from some old dead grandfather, that burst out now and then.

Dode, not being a genius, could not christen it morbid sensibility; but as she had a childish fashion of tracing things to commonplace causes, whenever she felt her face grow hot easily, or her throat choke up as men's do when they swear, she concluded that her liver was inactive, and her soul was tired of sitting at her Master's feet, like Mary. So she used to take longer walks before breakfast, and cry sharply, incessantly, in her heart, as the man did who was tainted with leprosy, "Lord, help me!" And the Lord always did help her.

My story is of Dode; so I must tell you that these passion-fits were the only events of her life. For the rest, she washed and sewed and ironed. If her heart and brain needed more than this, she was cheerful in spite of their hunger. Almost all of God's favorites among women, before their life-work is given them, pass through such hunger,—seasons of dull, hot inaction, fierce struggles to tame and bind to some unfitting work the power within. Generally, they are tried thus in their youth,—just as the old aspirants for knighthood were condemned to a night of solitude and prayer before the day of action. This girl was going through her probation with manly-souled bravery.

She came out on the porch now, to help her father on with his coat, and to tie his spatterdashes.[7] You could not see her in the dark, of course; but you would not wonder, if you felt her hand, or heard her speak, that the old man liked to touch her, as everybody did,—spoke to her gently: her own voice, did I say? was so earnest and rich,—hinted at unsounded depths of love and comfort, such as utter themselves in some unfashionable women's voices and eyes. Theodora, or -dosia, or some such heavy name, had been hung on her when she was born,—nobody remembered what: people always called her Dode, so as to bring her closer, as it were, and to fancy themselves akin to her.

Bone, going in, had left the door ajar, and the red firelight shone out brightly on her, where she was stooping. Nature had given her a body white, strong, and womanly,—broad, soft shoulders, for instance, hands slight and nervous, dark, slow eyes. The Devil never would have had the courage to tempt Eve, if she had looked at him with eyes as tender and honest as Dode Scofield's.

Yet, although she had so many friends, she impressed you as being a shy home-woman. That was the reason her father did not offer to take her to the meeting, though half the women in the neighborhood would be there.

"She a'n't smart, my Dode," he used to say,—" 's got no public sperrit."

He said as much to young Gaunt, the Methodist preacher, that very day, knowing that he thought of the girl as a wife, and wishing to be honest as to her weaknesses and heresies. For Dode, being the only creature in the United States who thought she came into the world to learn and not to teach, had an odd habit of trying to pick the good lesson out of everybody: the Yankees, the Rebels, the Devil himself, she thought, must have some purpose of good, if she could only get at it. God's creatures alike. She durst not bring against the foul fiend himself a "railing accusation," being as timid in judging evil as were her Master and the archangel Michael. An old-fashioned timidity, of course: people thought Dode a time-server, or "a bit daft."

"She don't take sides sharp in this war," her father said to Gaunt, "my little girl; 'n fact, she is n't keen till put her soul intill anythin' but lovin'. She 's a pore Democrat, David, an' not a strong Methody,—allays got somethin' till say fur t' other side, Papishers an' all. An' she gets religion quiet. But it 's the real thing,"—watching his hearer's face with an angry suspicion. "It 's out of a clean well, David, I say!"

"I hope so, Brother Scofield,"—doubtfully, shaking his head.

The conversation had taken place just after dinner. Scofield looked upon Gaunt as one of the saints upon earth, but he "danged him" after that once or twice to himself for doubting the girl; and when Bone, who had heard it, "guessed Mist' Dode 'd never fling herself away on sich whinin' pore-white trash," his master said nothing in reproof.

He rumpled her hair fondly, as she stood by him now on the porch.

"David Gaunt was in the house,—he had been there all the evening," she said,—a worried heat on her face. "Should not she call him to go to the meeting?"

"Jest as *you* please, Dode; jest as you please."

She should not be vexed. And yet ——— What if Gaunt did not quite appreciate his girl, see how deep-hearted she was, how heartsome a thing to look at even when she was asleep? He loved her, David did, as well as so holy a man could love anything carnal. And it would be better, if Dode were married; a chance shot might take him off any day, and then— what? She did n't know enough to teach; the farm was mortgaged; and she had no other lovers. She was cold-blooded in that sort of liking,— did not attract the men: thinking, with the scorn coarse-grained men have for reticent-hearted women, what a contrast she was to her mother. *She* was the right sort,—full-lipped, and a cooing voice for everybody, and such winning blue eyes! But, after all, Dode was the kind of woman to anchor to; it was "Get out of *my* way!" with her mother, as with all milky, blue-eyed women.

The old man fidgeted, lingered, stuffing "old Lynchburg" into his pipe, (his face was dyed saffron, and smelt of tobacco,) glad to feel, when Dode tied his fur cap, how quick and loving for him her fingers were, and that he always had deserved they should be so. He wished the child had some other protector to turn to than he, these war-times,—thinking uneasily of the probable fight at Blue's Gap, though of course he knew he never was born to be killed by a Yankee bullet. He wished she could fancy Gaunt; but if she did n't,—that was enough.

Just then Gaunt came out of the room on to the porch, and began loitering, in an uncertain way, up and down. A lean figure, with an irreso- lute step: the baggy clothes hung on his lank limbs were butternut-dyed, and patched besides: a Methodist itinerant in the mountains,—you know all that means? There was nothing irresolute or shabby in Gaunt's voice, however, as he greeted the old man,—clear, thin, nervous. Scofield looked at him wistfully.

"Dunnot drive David off, Dody," he whispered; "I think he's summat on his mind. What d' ye think 's his last whimsey? Told me he's goin' off in the mornin',—Lord knows where, nor for how long. Dody, d' ye think?— he'll be wantin' till come back for company, belike? Well, he 's one o' th' Lord's own, ef he is a bit cranky."

An odd tenderness came into the man's jaded old face. Whatever trust in God had got into his narrow heart among its bigotry, gross likings and dislikings, had come there through the agency of this David Gaunt. He felt as if he only had come into the secret place where his Maker and himself stood face to face; thought of him, therefore, with a reverence whose roots dug deep down below his coarseness, into his uncouth grop- ings after God. Outside of this,—Gaunt had come to the mountains years before, penniless, untaught, ragged, intent only on the gospel, which he preached with a keen, breathless fervor. Scofield had given him a home, clothed him, felt for him after that the condescending, curious affection which a rough barn-yard hen might feel for its adopted poult, not yet sure if it will turn out an eagle or a silly gull. It was a strange affinity between the lank-limbed, cloudy-brained enthusiast at one end of the porch and the shallow-eyed, tobacco-chewing old Scofield at the other,—but a real affinity, striking something deeper in their natures than blood-kinship. Whether Dode shared in it was doubtful; she echoed the "Poor David" in just the voice with which high-blooded women pity a weak man. Her father saw it. He had better not tell her his fancy to-night about Gaunt wishing her to be his wife.

He hallooed to him, bidding him "hap up an' come along till see what the Yankees were about.—Go in, Dode,—you sha'n't be worrit, child."

Gaunt came closer, fastening his thin coat. A lean face, sharpened by other conflicts than disease,—poetic, lonesome eyes, not manly.

"I am going," he said, looking at the girl. All the pain and struggle of years came up in that look. She knew where he was going: did she care? he thought. She knew,—he had told her, not an hour since, that he meant to lay down the Bible, and bring the kingdom of Jesus nearer in another fashion: he was going to enlist in the Federal army. It was God's cause, holy: through its success the golden year of the world would begin on earth. Gaunt took up his sword, with his eye looking awe-struck straight to God. The pillar of cloud, he thought, moved, as in the old time, before the army of freedom. She knew that when he did this, for truth's sake, he put a gulf between himself and her forever. Did she care? Did she? Would she let him go, and make no sign?

"Be quick, Gaunt," said Scofield, impatiently. "Bone hearn tell that Dougl's Palmer was in Romney to-night. He 'll be down at Blue's Gap, I reckon. He 's captain now in the Lincolnite army,—one of the hottest of the hell-hounds,—he is! Ef he comes to the house here, as he 'll likely do, I don't want till meet him."

Gaunt stood silent.

"He was Geordy's friend, father," said the girl, gulping back something in her throat.

"Geordy? Yes. I know. It 's that that hurts me," he muttered, uncertainly. "Him an' Dougl's was like brothers once, they was!"

He coughed, lit his pipe, looking in the girl's face for a long time, anxiously, as if to find a likeness in it to some other face he never should see again. He often had done this lately. At last, stooping, he kissed her mouth passionately, and shuffled down the hill, trying to whistle as he went. Kissing, through her, the boy who lay dead at Manassas: she knew that. She leaned on the railing, looking after him until a bend in the road took him out of sight. Then she turned into the house, with no thought to spare for the man watching her all this while with hungry eyes. The moon, drifting from behind a cloud, threw a sharp light on her figure, as she stood in the door-way.

"Dode!" he said. "Good bye, Dode!"

She shook hands, saying nothing,—then went in, and shut the door.

Gaunt turned away, and hurried down the hill, his heart throbbing and aching against his bony side with the breathless pain which women, and such men as he, know. Her hand was cold, as she gave it to him; some pain had chilled her blood: was it because she bade him good-bye forever, then? Was it? He knew it was not: his instincts were keen as those of the old Pythoness,[8] who read the hearts of men and nations by surface-trifles. Gaunt joined the old man, and began talking loosely and vaguely, as was his wont,—of the bad road, and the snow-water oozing through his boots,—not knowing what he said. She did not care; he would not cheat himself: when he told her tonight what he meant to do, she heard it with a cold, passive disapproval,—with that steely look in her dark eyes that shut him out from her. "You are sincere, I see; but you are not true to yourself or to God": that was all she said. She would have said the same, if he had gone with her brother. It was a sudden stab, but he forgave her: how could she know that God Himself had laid this blood-work on him, or the deathly fight his soul had waged against it? She did not know,—nor care. Who did?

The man plodded doggedly through the melting snow, with a keener sense of the cold biting through his threadbare waist-coat, of the solitude and wrong that life had given him,—his childish eyes turning to the gray depth of night, almost fierce in their questioning,—thinking what a failure his life had been. Thirty-five years of struggle with poverty and temptation! Ever since that day in the blacksmith's shop in Norfolk, when he had heard the call of the Lord to go and preach His word, had he not striven to choke down his carnal nature,—to shut his eyes to all beauty and love,—to unmake himself, by self-denial, voluntary pain? Of what use was it? To-night his whole nature rebelled against this carnage before him,—his duty; scorned it as brutal; cried out for a life as peaceful and meek as that of Jesus, (as if that were not an absurdity in a time like this,) for happiness, for this woman's love; demanded it, as though these things were its right!

The man had a genial, childish temperament, given to woo and bind him, in a thousand simple, silly ways, into a likeness of that Love that holds the world, and that gave man no higher hero-model than a trustful, happy child. It was the birthright of this haggard wretch going down the hill, to receive quick messages from God through every voice of the world,—to understand them, as few men did, by his poet's soul,—through love, or color, or music, or keen healthy pain. Very many openings for him to know God through the mask of matter. He had shut them; being a Calvinist, and a dyspeptic, (Dyspepsia is twin-tempter with Satan, you know,) sold his God-given birthright, like Esau, for a hungry, bitter mess of man's doctrine. He came to loathe the world, the abode of sin; loathed himself, the chief of sinners; mapped out a heaven in some corner of the universe, where he and the souls of his persuasion, panting with the terror of being scarcely saved, should find refuge. The God he made out of his own bigoted and sour idea, and foisted on himself and his hearers as Jesus, would not be as merciful in the Judgment as Gaunt himself would like to be,—far from it. So He did not satisfy him. Sometimes, thinking of the pure instincts thwarted in every heart,—of the noble traits in damned souls, sent hellwards by birth or barred into temptation by society, a vision flashed before him of some scheme of the universe where all matter and mind were rising, slowly, through the ages, to eternal life. "Even so in Christ should all be made alive." All matter, all mind, rising in degrees towards the Good? made order, infused by God? And God was Love. Why not trust this Love to underlie even these social riddles, then? He thrust out the Devil's whisper, barred the elect into their narrow heaven, and tried to be content.

Douglas Palmer used to say that all Gaunt needed to make him a sound Christian was education and fresh meat. Gaunt forgave it as a worldly scoff. And Palmer, just always, thought, that, if Christ was just, He would remember it was not altogether Gaunt's fault, nor that of other bigots, if they had not education nor spiritual fresh meat. Creeds are not always "good providers."

The two men had a two-miles' walk before them. They talked little, as they went. Gaunt had not told the old man that he was going into the Northern army: how could he? George's dead face was between them, whenever he thought of it. Still, Scofield was suspicious as to Gaunt's politics: he never talked to him on the subject, therefore, and to-night did not tell him of his intention to go over to Blue's Gap to warn the boys, and, if they were outnumbered, to stay and take his luck with them. He nor Dode never told Gaunt a secret: the man's brain was as leaky as a sponge.

"He don't take enough account o' honor, an' the like, but it 's for tryin' till keep his soul right," he used to say, excusingly, to Dode. "That's it! He minds me o' th' man that lived up on th' pillar, prayin'."

"The Lord never made people to live on pillars," Dode said.

The old man looked askance at Gaunt's worn face, as he trotted along beside him, thinking how pure it was. What had he to do with this foul slough we were all mired in? What if the Yankees did come, like incarnate devils, to thieve and burn and kill? This man would say "that ye resist not evil." He lived back there, pure and meek, with Jesus, in the old time. He would not dare to tell him he meant to fight with the boys in the Gap before morning. He wished he stood as near to Christ as this young man had got; he wished to God this revenge and blood-thirstiness were out of him; sometimes he felt as if a devil possessed him, since George died. The old fellow choked down a groan in the whiffs of his pipe.

Was the young man back there, in the old time, following the Nazarene? The work of blood Scofield was taking up for the moment, he took up, grappled with, tried to put his strength into. Doing this, his true life lay drained, loathsome, and bare. For the rest, he wished Dode had cared,— only a little. If one lay stabbed on some of these hills, it would be hard to think nobody cared: thinking of the old mother he had buried, years before. Yet Dode suffered: the man was generous to his heart's core,— forgot his own want in pity for her. What could it have been that pained her, as he came away? Her father had spoken of Palmer. *That?* His ruled heart leaped with a savage, healthy throb of jealousy.

Something he saw that moment made him stop short. The road led straight through the snow-covered hills to the church where the meeting was to be held. Only one man was in sight, coming towards them, on horseback. A sudden gleam of light showed him to them clearly. A small, middle-aged man, lithe, muscular, with fair hair, dressed in some shaggy dark uniform and a felt hat. Scofield stopped.

"It 's Palmer!" he said, with an oath that sounded like a cry.

The sight of the man brought George before him, living enough to wring his heart. He knocked a log off the worm-fence,[9] and stepped over into the field.

"I 'm goin', David. To think o' him turnin' traitor to Old Virginia! I'll not bide here till meet him."

"Brother!" said Gaunt, reprovingly.

"Don't hold me, Gaunt! Do you want me till curse my boy's old chum?"—his voice hoarse, choking.

"He is George's friend still"—

"I know, Gaunt, I know. God forgi' me! But—let me go, I say!"

He broke away, and went across the field.

Gaunt waited, watching the man coming slowly towards him. Could it be he whom Dode loved,—this Palmer? A doubter? an infidel? He had told her this to-day. A mere flesh-and-brain machine, made for the world, and no uses in him for heaven!

Poor Gaunt! no wonder he eyes the man with a spiteful hatred, as he waited for him, leaning against the fence. With his subtle Gallic brain, his physical spasms of languor and energy, his keen instincts that uttered themselves to the last syllable always, heedless of all decencies of custom, no wonder that the man with every feminine, unable nerve in his body rebelled against this Palmer. It was as natural as for a delicate animal to rebel against and hate and submit to man. Palmer's very horse, he thought, had caught the spirit of its master, and put down its hoofs with calm assurance of power.

Coming up at last, Gaunt listened sullenly, while the other spoke in a quiet, hearty fashion.

"They tell me you are to be one of us to-night," Palmer said, cordially. "Dyke showed me your name on the enlistment-roll: your motto after it, was it? 'For God and my right.' That 's the gist of the whole matter, David, I think, eh?"

"Yes, I'm right. I think I am. God knows I do!"—his vague eyes wandering off, playing with the horse's mane uncertainly.

Palmer read his face keenly.

"Of course you are," he said, speaking gently as he would to a woman. "I'll find a place and work for you before morning."

"So soon, Palmer?"

"Don't look at the blood and foulness of the war, boy! Keep the cause in view, every moment. We secure the right of self-government for all ages: think of that! 'God,'—His cause, you know?—and 'your right.' Have n't you warrant to take life to defend your right—from the Christ you believe in? Eh?"

"No. But I know"—Gaunt held his hand to his forehead as if it ached—"we have to come to brute force at last to conquer the right. Christianity is not enough. I've reasoned it over, and"—

"Yet you look troubled. Well, we 'll talk it over again. You 've worked your brain too hard to be clear about anything just now,"—looking down on him with the questioning pity of a surgeon examining a cancer. "I must go on now, David. I 'll meet you at the church in an hour."

"You are going to the house, Palmer?"

"Yes. Good night."

Gaunt drew back his hand, glancing at the cold, tranquil face, the mild blue eyes.

"Good night,"—following him with his eyes as he rode away.

An Anglo-Saxon, with every birth-mark of that slow, inflexible race. He would make love philosophically, Gaunt sneered. A made man. His thoughts and soul, inscrutable as they were, were as much the accretion of generations of culture and reserve as was the chalk in his bones or the glowless courage in his slow blood. It was like coming in contact with summer water to talk to him; but underneath was—what? Did Dode know? Had he taken her in, and showed her his unread heart? Dode?

How stinging cold it was!—looking up drearily into the drifting heaps of gray. What a wretched, paltry balk the world was! What a noble part he played in it!—taking out his pistol. Well, he could pull a trigger, and let out some other sinner's life; that was all the work God thought he was fit for. Thinking of Dode all the time. *He* knew her! *He* could have summered her in love, if she would but have been passive and happy! He asked no more of her than that. Poor, silent, passionate Dode! No one knew her as he knew her! What were that man's cold blue eyes telling her now at the house? It mattered nothing to him.

He went across the cornfield to the church, his thin coat flapping in the wind, looking at his rusty pistol with a shudder.

Dode shut the door. Outside lay the winter's night, snow, death, the war. She shivered, shut them out. None of her nerves enjoyed pain, as some women's do. Inside,—you call it cheap and mean, this room? Yet her father called it Dode's snuggery; he thought no little nest in the world was so clean and warm. He never forgot to leave his pipe outside, (though she coaxed him not to do it,) for fear of "silin' the air." Every evening he came in after he had put on his green dressing-gown and slippers, and she read the paper to him. It was quite a different hour of the day from all of the rest: sitting, looking stealthily around while she read, delighted to see how cozy he had made his little girl,—how pure the pearl-stained walls were, how white the matting. He never went down to Wheeling with the crops without bringing something back for the room, stinting himself to do it. Her brother had had the habit, too, since he was a boy, of bringing everything pretty or pleasant he found to his sister; he had a fancy that he was making her life bigger and more heartsome by it, and would have it all right after a while. So it ended, you see, that everything in the room had a meaning for the girl,—so many mile-stones in her father and

Geordy's lives. Besides, though Dode was no artist, had not what you call taste, other than in being clean, yet every common thing the girl touched seemed to catch her strong, soft vitality, and grow alive. Bone had bestowed upon her the antlers of a deer which he had killed,—the one great trophy of his life; (she put them over the mantel-shelf, where he could rejoice his soul over them every time he brought wood to the fire;) last fall she had hung wreaths of forest-leaves about them, and now they glowed and flashed back the snow-light, in indignant life, purple and scarlet and flame, with no thought of dying; the very water in the vases on the table turned into the silver roots of hyacinths that made the common air poetic with perfume; the rough wire-baskets filled with mould, which she hung in the windows, grew living, and welled up, and ran over into showers of moss, and trailing wreaths of ivy and cypress-vine, and a brood of the merest flakes of roses, which held the hot crimson of so many summers gone that they could laugh in the teeth of the winter outside, and did do it, until it seemed like a perfect sham and a jest.

The wood-fire was clear, just now, when Dode came in; the little room was fairly alive, palpitated crimson; in the dark corners, under the tables and chairs, the shadows tried not to be black, and glowed into a soft maroon; even the pale walls flushed, cordial and friendly. Dode was glad of it; she hated dead, ungrateful colors: grays and browns belonged to thin, stingy duty-lives, to people who are patient under life, as a perpetual imposition, and, as Bone says, "gets into heben by the skin o' their teeth." Dode's color was dark blue: you know that means in an earthly life stern truth, and a tenderness as true: she wore it to-night, as she generally did, to tell God she was alive, and thanked Him for being alive. Surely the girl was made for to-day; she never missed the work or joy of a moment here in dreaming of a yet ungiven life, as sham, lazy women do. You would think that, if you had seen her standing there in the still light, motionless, yet with latent life in every limb. There was not a dead atom in her body: something within, awake, immortal, waited, eager to speak every moment in the coming color on her cheek, the quiver of her lip, the flashing words or languor of her eye. Her auburn hair, even, at times, lightened and darkened.

She stood, now, leaning her head on the window, waiting. Was she keeping, like the fire-glow, a still, warm welcome for somebody? It was a very homely work she had been about, you will think. She had made a panful of white cream-crackers, and piled them on a gold-rimmed China plate, (the only one she had,) and brought down from the cupboard a bottle of her raspberry-cordial. Douglas Palmer and George used to like those cakes better than anything else she made: she remembered, when they were starting out to hunt, how Geordy would put his curly head over the gate and call out, "Sis! are you in a good-humor? Have some of your famous cakes for supper, that's a good girl!" Douglas Palmer was coming to-night, and she had baked them, as usual,—stopping to cry now and then, thinking of George. She could not help it, when she was alone. Her father never knew it. She had to be cheerful for herself and him too, when he was there.

Perhaps Douglas would not remember about the crackers, after all?— with the blood heating and chilling in her face, as she looked out of the window, and then at the clock,—her nervous fingers shaking, as she arranged them on the plate. She wished she had some other way of making him welcome; but what could poor Dode do? She could not talk to him, had read nothing but the Bible and Jay's "Meditations";[10] she could not show glimpses of herself, as most American women can, in natural, dramatic words. Palmer sang for her,—sometimes, Schubert's ballads, Mendelssohn: she could not understand the words, of course; she only knew that his soul seemed to escape through the music, and come to her own. She had a strange comprehension of music, inherited from the old grandfather who left her his temper,—that supernatural gift, belonging to but few souls among those who love harmony, to understand and accept its meaning. She could not play or sing; she looked often in the dog's eyes, wondering if its soul felt as dumb and full as hers; but she could not sing. If she could, what a story she would have told in a wordless way to this man who was coming! All she could do to show that he was welcome was to make crackers. Cooking is a sensual, grovelling utterance of feeling, you think? Yet, considering the drift of most women's lives, one fancies that as pure and deep love syllables itself every day in beefsteaks as once in Sapphic odes. It is a natural expression for our sex, too, somehow. Your wife may keep step with you in keen sympathy, in brain and soul; but if she does not know whether you like muffins or toast best for breakfast, her love is not the kind for this world, nor the best kind for any.

She waited, looking out at the gray road. He would not come so late?— her head beginning to ache. The room was too hot. She went into her chamber, and began to comb her hair back; it fell in rings down her pale cheeks,—her lips were crimson,—her brown eyes shone soft, expectant; she leaned her head down, smiling, thanking God for her beauty, with all her heart. Was that a step?—hurrying back. Only Coly stamping in the stable. It was eight o'clock. The woman's heart kept time to the slow ticking of the clock, with a sick thudding, growing heavier every moment.

He had been in the mountains but once since the war began. It was only George he came to see? She brought out her work and began to sew. He would not come: only George was fit to be his friend. Why should he heed her poor old father, or her?—with the undefinable awe of an unbred mind for his power and wealth of culture. And yet—something within her at the moment rose up royal—his equal. He knew her, as she might be! Between them there was something deeper than the shallow kind greeting they gave the world,—recognition. She stood nearest to him,—she only! If sometimes she had grown meanly jealous of the thorough-bred, made women, down in the town yonder, his friends, in her secret soul she knew she was his peer,—she only! And he knew it. Not that she was not weak in mind or will beside him, but she loved him, as a man can be loved but once. She loved him,—that was all!

She hardly knew if he cared for her. He told her once that he loved her; there was a half-betrothal; but that was long ago. She sat, her work fallen on her lap, going over, as women will, for the thousandth time, the simple story, what he said, and how he looked, finding in every hackneyed phrase some new, divine meaning. The same story; yet Betsey finds it new by your kitchen-fire to-night, as Gretchen read it in those wondrous pearls of Faust's!

Surely he loved her that day! though the words were surprised, half-accident: she was young, and he was poor, so there must be no more of it then. The troubles began just after, and he went into the army. She had seen him but once since, and he said nothing then, looked nothing. It is true they had not been alone, and he thought perhaps she knew all: a word once uttered for him was fixed in fate. *She* would not have thought the story old or certain, if he told it to her forever. But he was coming to-night!

Dode was one of those women subject to sudden revulsions of feeling. She remembered now, what in the hurry and glow of preparing his welcome she had crushed out of sight, that it was better he should not come,—that, if he did come, loyal and true, she must put him back, show him the great gulf that lay between them. She had strengthened herself for months to do it. It must be done to-night. It was not the division the war made, nor her father's anger, that made the bar between them. Her love would have borne that down. There was something it could not bear down. Palmer was a doubter, an infidel. What this meant to the girl, we cannot tell; her religion was not ours. People build their faith on Christ, as a rock,—a factitious aid. She found Him in her life, long ago, when she was a child, and her soul grew out from Him. He was a living Jesus to her, not a dead one. That was why she had a healthy soul. Pain was keener to her than to us; the filth, injustice, bafflings in the world,—they hurt her; she never glossed them over as "necessity," or shirked them as we do: she cried hot, weak tears, for instance, over the wrongs of the slaves about her, her old father's ignorance, her own cramped life; but she never said for these things, "Does God still live?" She saw, close to the earth, the atmosphere of the completed work, the next step upward,—the kingdom of that Jesus; the world lay in it, swathed in bands of pain and wrong and effort, growing, unconscious, to perfected humanity. She had faith in the Recompense, she thought faith would bring it right down into earth, and she tried to do it in a practical way. She did do it: a curious fact for your theology, which I go out of the way of the story to give you,—a peculiar power belonging to this hot-tempered girl,—an anomaly in psychology, but you will find it in the lives of Jung Stilling[11] and St. John. This was it: she and the people about her needed many things, temporal and spiritual: her Christ being alive, and not a dead sacrifice and example alone, whatever was needed she asked for, and it was always given her. *Always.* I say it in the full strength of meaning. I wish every human soul could understand the lesson; not many preachers would dare to teach it to them. It was a commonplace matter with her.

Now do you see what it cost her to know that Palmer was an infidel? Could she marry him? Was it a sin to love him? And yet, could *she* enter heaven, he left out? The soul of the girl that God claimed, and the Devil was scheming for, had taken up this fiery trial, and fought with it savagely. She thought she had determined; she would give him up. But—he was coming! he was coming! Why, she forgot everything in that, as if it were delirium. She hid her face in her hands. It seemed as if the world, the war, faded back, leaving this one human soul alone with herself. She sat silent, the fire charring lower into glooming red shadow. You shall not look into the passion of a woman's heart.

She rose at last, with the truth, as Gaunt had taught it to her, full before her, that it would be crime to make compact with sin or a sinner. She went out on the porch, looking no longer to the road, but up to the uncertain sky. Poor, simple Dode! So long she had hid the thought of this man in her woman's breast, clung to it for all strength, all tenderness! It stood up now before her,—Evil. Gaunt told her to-night that to love him was to turn her back on the cross, to be traitor to that blood on Calvary. Was it? She found no answer in the deadened sky, or in her own heart. She would give him up, then? She looked up, her face slowly whitening. "I love him," she said, as one who had a right to speak to God. That was all.

So, in old times, a soul from out of the darkness of His judgments faced the Almighty, secure in its own right: "Till I die I will not remove mine integrity from me."

Yet Dode was a weak woman; the trial went home to the very marrow. She stood by the wooden railing, gathering the snow off of it, putting it to her hot forehead, not knowing what she did. Her brain was dull, worn-out, she thought; it ached. She wished she could sleep, with a vacant glance at the thick snow-clouds, and turning to go in. There was a sudden step on the path,—he was coming! She would see him once more,—once! God could not deny her that! her very blood leaping into hot life.

"Theodora!" (He never called her the familiar "Dode," as the others did.) "Why, what ails you, child?"—in his quiet, cordial fashion. "Is this the welcome you give me? The very blood shivers in your hand! Your lips are blue!"—opening the door for her to go in, and watching her.

His eye was more that of a physician than a lover, she felt, and cowered down into a chair he put before the fire for her,—sheltering her face with her hands, that he might not see how white it was, and despise her. Palmer stood beside her, looking at her quietly; she had exhausted herself by some excitement, in her old fashion; he was used to these spasms of bodily languor,—a something he pitied, but could not comprehend. It was an odd symptom of the thoroughness with which her life was welded into his, that he alone knew her as weak, hysteric, needing help at times. Gaunt or her father would have told you her nerves were as strong as a ploughman's.

"Have you been in a passion, my child?"

She chafed her hands, loathing herself that she could not deaden down their shiver or the stinging pain in her head. What were these things at a time like this? Her physician was taking a different diagnosis of her disease from his first. He leaned over her, his face flushing, his voice lower, hurried.

"Were you disappointed? Did you watch—for me?"

"I watched for you, Douglas,"—trying to rise.

He took her hand and helped her up, then let it fall: he never held Dode's hand, or touched her hair, as Gaunt did.

"I watched for you,—I have something to say to you,"—steadying her voice.

"Not to-night," with a tenderness that startled one, coming from lips so thin and critical. "You are not well. You have some hard pain there, and you want to make it real. Let it sleep. You were watching for me. Let me have just that silly thought to take with me. Look up, Theodora. I want the hot color on your cheek again, and the look in your eye I saw there once, — only once. Do you remember?"

"I remember," — her face crimson, her eyes flashing with tears. "Douglas, Douglas, never speak of that to me! I dare not think of it. Let me tell you what I want to say. It will soon be over."

"I will not, Theodora," he said, coolly. "See now, child! You are not your healthy self to-night. You have been too much alone. This solitude down there in your heart is eating itself out in some morbid whim. I saw it in your eye. Better it had forced itself into anger, as usual."

She did not speak. He took her hand and seated her beside him, talked to her in the same careless, gentle way, watching her keenly.

"Did you ever know the meaning of your name? I think of it often, — *The gift of God*, — *Theodora*. Surely, if there be such an all-embracing Good, He has no more helpful gift than a woman such as you might be."

She looked up, smiling.

"Might be? That is not" —

"Lover-like? No. Yet, Dode, I think sometimes Eve might have been such a one as you, — the germ of all life. Think how you loathe death, inaction, pain; the very stem you thrust into earth catches vitality from your fingers, and grows, as for no one else."

She knew, through all, that, though his light words were spoken to soothe her, they masked a strength of feeling that she dared not palter with, a something that would die out of his nature when his faith in her died, never to live again.

"Eve fell," she said.

"So would you, alone. You are falling now, morbid, irritable. Wait until you come into the sunshine. Why, Theodora, you will not know yourself, the broad, warm, unopened nature."

His voice faltered; he stooped nearer to her, drew her hand into his own.

"There will be some June days in our lives, little one, for you and me," — his tone husky, broken, — "when this blood-work is off my hand, when I can take you. My years have been hard, bare. You know, child. You know how my body and brain have been worn out for others. I am free now. When the war is over, I will conquer a new world for you and me."

She tried to draw away from him.

"I need no more. I am contented. For the future, — God has it, Douglas."

"But my hand is on it!" he said, his eye growing hard. "And you are mine, Theodora!"

He put his hand on her head: he never had touched her before this evening: he stroked back her hair with an unsteady touch, but as if it and she belonged to him, inalienable, secure. The hot blood flushed into her cheeks, resentful. He smiled quietly.

"You will bring life to me," he whispered. "And I will bleach out this anger, these morbid shadows of the lonesome days,—sun them out with—love."

There was a sudden silence. Gaunt felt the intangible calm that hung about this man: this woman saw beneath it flashes of some depth of passion, shown reluctant even to her, the slow heat of the gloomy soul below. It frightened her, but she yielded: her will, her purpose slept, died into its languor. She loved, and she was loved,—was not that enough to know? She cared to know no more. Did Gaunt wonder what the "cold blue eyes" of this man told to the woman to-night? Nothing which his warped soul would have understood in a thousand years. The room heated, glowless, crimson: outside, the wind surged slow against the windows, like the surf of an eternal sea: she only felt that her head rested on his breast,—that his hand shook, as it traced the blue veins on her forehead: with a faint pleasure that the face was fair, for his sake, which his eyes read with a meaning hers could not bear; with a quick throb of love to her Master for this moment He had given her. Her Master! Her blood chilled. Was she denying Him? Was she setting her foot on the outskirts of hell? It mattered not. She shut her eyes wearily, closed her fingers as for life upon the hand that held hers. All strength, health for her, lay in its grasp: her own life lay weak, flaccid, morbid on his. She had chosen: she would hold to her choice.

Yet, below all, the words of Gaunt stung her incessantly. They would take effect at last. Palmer, watching her face, saw, as the slow minutes passed, the color fade back, leaving it damp and livid, her lips grow rigid, her chest heave like some tortured animal. There was some pain here deeper than her ordinary heats. It would be better to let it have way. When she raised herself, and looked at him, therefore, he made no effort to restrain her, but waited, attentive.

"I must speak, Douglas," she said. "I cannot live and bear this doubt."

"Go on," he said, gravely, facing her.

"Yes. Do not treat me as a child. It is no play for me,"—pushing her hair back from her forehead, calling fiercely in her secret soul for God to help her to go through with this bitter work He had imposed on her. "It is for life and death, Douglas."

"Go on,"—watching her.

She looked at him. A keen, practical, continent face, with small mercy for whims and shallow reasons. Whatever feeling or gloom lay beneath, a blunt man, a truth-speaker, bewildered by feints or shams. She must give a reason for what she did. The word she spoke would be written in his memory, ineffaceable. He waited. She could not speak; she looked at the small vigilant figure: it meant all that the world held for her of good.

"You must go, Douglas, and never come again."

He was silent,—his eye contracted, keen, piercing.

"There is a great gulf between us, Douglas Palmer. I dare not cross it."

He smiled.

"You mean—the war?—your father?"

She shook her head; the words balked in her throat. Why did not God help her? Was not she right? She put her hand upon his sleeve,—her face, from which all joy and color seemed to have fallen forever, upturned to his.

"Douglas, you do not believe—as I do."

He noted her look curiously, as she said it, with an odd remembrance of once when she was a child, and they had shown her for the first time a dead body, that she had turned to the sky the same look of horror and reproach she gave him now.

"I have prayed, and prayed,"—an appealing cry in every low breath. "It is of no use,—no use! God never denied me a prayer but that,—only that!"

"I do not understand. You prayed—for me?"

Her eyes, turning to his own, gave answer enough.

"I see! You prayed for me, poor child? that I could find a God in the world?"—patting the hand resting on his arm pitifully. "And it was of no use, you think? no use?"—dreamily, his eye fixed on the solemn night without.

There was a slow silence. She looked awe-struck in his face: he had forgotten her.

"I have not found Him in the world?"—the words dropping slowly from his lips, as though he questioned with the great Unknown.

She thought she saw in his face hints that his soul had once waged a direr battle than any she had known,—to know, to be. What was the end? God, and Life, and Death, what were they to him now?

He looked at her at last, recalled to her. She thought he stifled a sigh. But he put aside his account with God for another day: now it was with her.

"You think it right to leave me for this, Theodora? You think it a sin to love an unbeliever?"

"Yes, Douglas,"—but she caught his hand tighter, as she said it.

"The gulf between us is to be the difference between heaven and hell? Is that true?"

"*Is* it true?" she cried suddenly. "It is for you to say. Douglas, it is you that must choose."

"No man can force belief," he said, dryly. "You will give me up? Poor child! You cannot, Theodora!"—smoothing her head with an unutterable pity.

"I will give you up, Douglas!"

"Think how dear I have been to you, how far-off you are from everybody in the world but me. Why, I know no woman so alone or weak as you, if I should leave you!"

"I know it,"—sobbing silently.

"You will stay with me, Theodora! Is the dull heaven Gaunt prates of, with its psalms and crowns, better than my love? Will you be happier there than here?"—holding her close, that she might feel the strong throb of his heart against her own.

She shivered.

"Theodora!"

She drew away; stood alone.

"Is it better?"—sharply.

She clutched her hands tightly, then she stood calm. She would not lie.

"It is not better," she said, steadily. "If I know my own heart, nothing in the coming heaven is so dear as what I lose. But I cannot be your wife, Douglas Palmer."

His face flashed strangely.

"It is simple selfishness, then? You fear to lose your reward? What is my poor love to the eternity of happiness you trade it for?"

A proud heat flushed her face.

"You know you do not speak truly. I do not deserve the taunt."

The same curious smile glimmered over his mouth. He was silent for a moment.

"I overrate your sacrifice: it costs you little to say, like the old Pharisee, 'Stand by, I am holier than thou!' You never loved me, Theodora. Let me go down—to the land where you think all things are forgotten. What is it to you? In hell I can lift up my eyes"—

She cried out sharply, as with pain.

"I will not forsake my Master," she said. "He is real, more dear than you. I give you up."

Palmer caught her hand; there was a vague deadness in her eye that terrified him; he had not thought the girl suffered so deeply.

"See, now," she gasped quickly, looking up, as if some actual Presence stood near. "I have given up all for you! Let me die! Put my soul out! What do I care for heaven?"

Palmer bathed her face, put coridal to her lips, muttering some words to himself. "Her sins, which are many, should be forgiven; she loves much." When, long after, she sat on the low settle, quiet, he stood before her.

"I have something to say to you, Theodora. Do you understand me?"

"I understand."

"I am going. It is better I should not stay. I want you to thank God your love for your Master stood firm. I do. I believe in you: some day, through you, I may believe in Him. Do you hear me?"

She bent her head, worn-out.

"Theodora, I want to leave you one thought to take on your knees with you. Your Christ has been painted in false colors to you in this matter. I am glad that as you understand Him you are true to Him; but you are wrong."

She wrung her hands.

"If I could see that, Douglas!"

"You will see it. The selfish care of your own soul which Gaunt has taught you is a lie; his narrow heaven is a lie: my God inspires other love, other aims. What is the old tale of Jesus?—that He put His man's hands on the vilest before He blessed them? So let Him come to me,—through loving hands. Do you want to preach the gospel, as some women do, to the Thugs? I think your field is here. You shall preach it to the heart that loves you."

She shook her head drearily. He looked at her a moment, and then turned away.

"You are right. There is a great gulf between you and me, Theodora. When you are ready to cross it, come to me."

And so left her.

PART II

It was late. Palmer, unhitching his horse from the fence, mounted and rode briskly down the hill. He would lose the girl: saw the loss, faced it. Besides the love he bore her, she had made God a truth to him. He was jaded, defeated, as if some power outside of himself had taken him unexpectedly at advantage to-night, and wrung this thing from him. Life was not much to look forward to,—the stretch it had been before: study, and the war, and hard common sense,—the theatre,—card-playing. Not being a man, I cannot tell you how much his loss amounted to. I know, going down the rutted wagon-road, his mild face fell slowly into a haggard vacancy foreign to it: one or two people at the tavern where he stopped asked him if he were ill: I think, too, that he prayed once or twice to whatever God he had, looking up with dry eye and shut lips,—dumb prayers, wrung out of some depth within, such as Christian sent out of the slough, when he was like to die. But he did stop at the tavern, and there drank some brandy to steady his nerves; and he did not forget that there was an ambuscade of Rebels at Blue's Gap, and that he was to share in the attack on them at day-light: he spurred his horse, as he drew nearer Romney. Dode, being a woman, thinking love lost, sat by the fire, looking vacantly at nothing. Yet the loss was as costly to him as to her, and would be remembered as long.

He came up to the church where the meeting had been held. It was just over; the crowded room was stifling with the smoke of tobacco and tallow-candles; there was an American flag hanging over the pulpit, a man pounding on a drum at the door, and a swarm of loafers on the steps, cheering for the Union, for Jeff Davis, etc. Palmer dismounted, and made his way to the pulpit, where Dyke, a lieutenant in his company, was.

"All ready, Dyke?"

"All right, Capt'n."

Palmer lingered, listening to the talk of the men. Dyke had been an Ohio-River pilot; after the troubles began, had taken a pork-contract under Government; but was lieutenant now, as I said. It paid better than pork, he told Palmer,—a commission, especially in damp weather. Palmer did not sneer. Dykes, North and South, had quit the hog-killing for the man-killing business, with no other motive than the percentage, he knew; but he thought the rottenness lay lower than their hearts. Palmer stood looking down at the crowd: the poorer class of laborers,—their limbs cased in shaggy blouses and green baize [12] leggings,—their faces dogged, anxious as their own oxen.

" 'Bout half on 'em Secesh," whispered Jim Dyke. " 'T depends on who burned their barns fust."

Jim was recruiting to fill up some vacancies in Palmer's company. He had been tolerably successful that day; as he said, with a wink, to the Captain,—

"The twenty dollars a month on one side, an' the test-oath on t' other, brought loyalty up to the scratch."

He presented some of the recruits to Palmer: pluming himself, adjusting the bogus chains over his pink shirt.

"Hyur's Squire Pratt. Got two sons in th' army,—goin' hisself. That 's the talk! Charley Orr, show yerself! This boy's father was shot in his bed by the Bushwhackers." [13]

A mere boy, thin, consumptive, hollow-chested: a mother's-boy, Palmer saw, with fair hair and dreamy eyes. He held out his hand to him.

"Charley will fight for something better than revenge. I see it in his face."

The little fellow's eyes flashed.

"Yes, Captain."

He watched Palmer after that with the look one of the Cavaliers might have turned to a Stuart. But he began to cough presently, and slipped back to the benches where the women were. Palmer heard one of them in rusty black sob out,—"Oh, Charley! Charley!"

There was not much enthusiasm among the women; Palmer looked at them with a dreary trail of thought in his brain. They were of the raw, unclarified American type: thick-blooded, shrewish, with dish-shaped faces, inelastic limbs. They had taken the war into their whole strength, like their sisters, North and South: as women greedily do anything that promises to be an outlet for what power of brain, heart, or animal fervor they may have, over what is needed for wifehood or maternity. Theodora, he thought, angrily, looked at the war as these women did, had no poetic enthusiasm about it, did not grasp the grand abstract theory on either side. She would not accept it as a fiery, chivalric cause, as the Abolitionist did, nor as a stern necessity, like the Union-saver. The sickly Louisianian, following her son from Pickens to Richmond, besieging God for vengeance with the mad impatience of her blood, or the Puritan mother praying beside her dead hero-boy, would have called Dode cowardly and dull. So would those blue-eyed, gushing girls who lift the cup of blood to their lips with as fervid an *abandon* as ever did French *bacchante*.[14] Palmer despised them. Their sleazy lives had wanted color and substance, and they found it in a cant of patriotism, in illuminating their windows after slaughter, in dressing their tables with helmets of sugar, (after the fashion of the White House)—delicate *souvenirs de la guerre*!

But Theodora and these women had seen their door-posts slopped with blood,—that made a difference. This woman in front had found her boy's half-charred body left tied to a tree by Rebel scouts: this girl was the grandchild of Naylor, a man of seventy, — the Federal soldiers were fired at from his house one day, — the next, the old man stood dumb upon its threshold; in this world, he never would call to God for vengeance. Palmer knew these things were true. Yet Dode should not for this sink to low notions about the war. She did: she talked plain Saxon of it, and what it made of men; said no cause could sanctify a deed so vile, — nothing could be holy which turned honest men into thieves and assassins. Her notions were low to degradation, Palmer thought, with the quickening cause at his heart; they had talked of it the last time he was here. She thought they struck bottom on some eternal truth, a humanity broader than patriotism. Pah! he sickened at such whining cant! The little Captain was common-sensed to the backbone, — intolerant. He was an American, with the native taint of American conceit, but he was a man whose look was as true as his oath; therefore, talking of the war, he never glossed it over, — showed its worst phases, in Virginia and Missouri; but he accepted it, in all its horror, as a savage necessity. It was a thing that must be, while men were men, and not angels.

While he stood looking at the crowd, Nabbes, a reporter for one of the New-York papers, who was lounging in the pulpit, began to laugh at him.

"I say, Captain, you Virginia Loyalists don't go into this war with *vim*. It 's a bitter job to you."

Palmer's face reddened.

"What you say is true, thank God," — quietly.

Nabbes stuck his hands into his pockets, whistling. He shrewdly suspected Palmer was n't "sound." No patriot would go into the war with such a miserable phiz as that. Yet he fought like a tiger up in the mountains. Of course, the war was a bad business, — and the taxes — whew! Last summer things were smashed generally, and when Will (his brother) sailed in Sherman's expedition, it was a blue day enough: how his mother and the girls did carry on! (Nabbes and Will supported the family, by the way; and Nabbes, inside of his slang, billiards, etc., was a good, soft-hearted fellow.) However, the country was looking up now. There were our victories, — and his own salary was raised. Will was snug down at Port Royal,[15] — sent the girls home some confoundedly pretty jewelry; they were as busy as bees, knitting socks, and ——— What, the Devil! were we to be ridden over rough-shod by Davis and his crew? Northern brain and muscle were toughest, and let water find its own level. So he tore out a fly-leaf from the big Bible, and jotted down notes of the meeting, — "An outpouring of the loyal heart of West Virginia,"—and yawned, ready for bed, contented with the world, himself, and God.

Dyke touched Palmer's arm.

"Lor', Capt'n," he whispered, "ef thar a'n't old Scofield! 'n the back o' th' house, watchin' you. Son killed at Manassas,—George,—d' ye know?"

"I know."

"Danged ef I don't respect Secesh like them," broke out Dyke. "Ye 'll not sin his soul with a test-oath. Thar 's grit thar. Well, God help us!"

Palmer stepped down from the pulpit; but the old man, seeing him coming, turned and shouldered his way out of the crowd, his haggard face blood-red.

"What'll the old chap say to Gaunt's enlistin'?" said Dyke.

"Gaunt in? Bully for the parson!" said Squire Pratt.

"Parson 'listed?" said the reporter. "They and the women led off in this war. I 'm glad of it,—brings out the pith in 'em."

"I dunno," said Dyke, looking round. "Gaunt's name brought in a dozen; but —— It 's a dirty business, the war. I wish 'n somebody's hands hed stayed clean of it."

"It 's the Lord's work," said Pratt, with a twang, being a class-leader.

"Ye-s? So 'ud Bishop Polk say. Got a different Lord down thar? 'S likely. Henry Wise used to talk of the 'God of Virginia.'"

"Was a fellow," said Nabbes, nursing one foot, "that set me easy about my soul, and the thing. A chaplain in Congress: after we took down that bitter Mason-and-Slidell pill, it was. Prayed to Jesus to keep us safe until our vengeance on England was ripe,—to 'aid us through the patient watch and vigil long of him who treasures up a wrong.' Old boy, thinks I, if that 's Christianity, it's cheap. I 'll take stock in it. Going at half-price, I think."

"I am tired of this cant of Christians refusing to join in the war," said Palmer, impatiently. "God allows it; it helps His plans."

"Humph! So did Judas," muttered Dyke, shrewdly. "Well, I a'n't a pur-fessor myself.—Boys, come along! Drum-call time. You 're in luck. We 'll have work afore mornin',—an' darned ef you sha'n't be in it, in spite of rules!"

When the recruits went out, the meeting broke up. Palmer put on his hat, and made his way out of a side-door into the snow-covered field about the church, glancing at his watch as he went. He had but little time to spare. The Federal camp lay on a distant hill-side below Romney: through the dun winter shadows he could see points of light shifting from tent to tent; a single bugle-call had shrilled through the mountains once or twice;

the regiments ordered for the attack were under arms now, he concluded. They had a long march before them: the Gap, where the Confederate band were concealed, lay sixteen miles distant. Unless the Union troops succeeded in surprising the Rebels, the fight, Palmer knew, would be desperate; the position they held was almost impregnable,—camped behind a steep gash in the mountain: a handful of men could hold it against Dunning's whole brigade, unshielded, bare. A surprise was almost impossible in these mountains, where Rebel guerrillas lurked behind every tree, and every woman in the village-shanties was ready to risk limbs or life as a Rebel spy. Thus far, however, he thought this movement had been kept secret: even the men did not know where they were going.

Crossing the field hurriedly, he saw two men talking eagerly behind a thorn-bush. One of them, turning, came towards him, his hat slouched over his face. It was Scofield. As he came into the clear star-light, Palmer recognized the thick-set, sluggish figure and haggard face, and waited for him,—with a quick remembrance of long summer days, when he and George, boys together, had looked on this man as the wisest and strongest, sitting at his side digging worms or making yellow flies for him to fish in the Big Cacapon,—how they would have the delicate broiled trout for supper,—how Dode was a chubby little puss then, with white apron and big brown eyes, choosing to sit on his lap when they went to the table, and putting her hand slyly into his coffee. An odd thing to think of then and there! George lay stiff now, with a wooden board only at his head to tell that he once lived. The thoughts struck through Palmer's brain in the waiting moment, making his hand unsteady as he held it out to the old man.

"Uncle Scofield! Is the war to come between you and me? For George's sake! I saw him at Harper's Ferry before—before Manassas. We were no less friends then than ever before."

The old man's eyes had glared defiance at Palmer under their gray brows when he faced him, but his big bony hand kept fumbling nervously with his cravat.

"Yes, Dougl's. I did n't want to meet yer. Red an' white 's my colors,— red an' white, so help me God!"

"I know," said Palmer, quietly.

There was a silence,—the men looking steadily at each other.

"Ye saw George?" the old man said, his eyes falling.

"Yes. At Harper's Ferry. I was making my way through the Confederate lines; George took me over, risking his own life to do it, then reported himself under arrest. He did not lose his commission; your general was just"—

Scofield's face worked.

"That was like my boy! Thar's not a grandfather he hes in the country whar he 's gone to that would believe one of our blood could do a mean thing! The Scofields ar'n't well larned, but they 've true honor, Dougl's Palmer!"

Palmer's eyes lighted. Men of the old lion-breed know each other in spite of dress or heirship of opinion.

"Ye 've been to th' house to-night, boy?" said the old man, his voice softened. "Yes? That was right. Ye 've truer notions nor me. I went away so 's not till meet yer. I 'm sorry for it. George 's gone, Dougl's, but he 'd be glad till think you an' me was the same as ever,—he would!"

He held out his hand. Something worthy the name of man in each met in the grasp, that no blood spilled could foul or embitter. They walked across the field together, the old man leaning his hand on Palmer's shoulder as if for support, though he did not need it. He had been used to walk so with George. This was his boy's friend: that thought filled and warmed his heart so utterly that he forgot his hand rested on a Federal uniform. Palmer was strangely silent.

"I saw Theodora," he said at last, gravely.

Scofield started at the tone, looked at him keenly, some new thought breaking in on him, frightening, troubling him. He did not answer; they crossed the broad field, coming at last to the hill-road. The old man spoke at last, with an effort.

"You an' my little girl are friends, did you mean, Dougl's? The war did n't come between ye?"

"Nothing shall come between us,"—quietly, his eye full upon the old man's. The story of a life lay in the look.

Scofield met it questioningly, almost solemnly. It was no time for explanation. He pushed his trembling hand through his stubby gray hair.

"Well, well, Dougl's. These days is harrd. But it 'll come right! God knows all."

The road was empty now,—lay narrow and bare down the hill; the moon had set, and the snow-clouds were graying heavily the pale light above. Only the sharp call of a discordant trumpet broke the solitude and dumbness of the hills. A lonesome, foreboding night. The old man rested his hand on the fence, choking down an uncertain groan now and then, digging into the snow with his foot, while Palmer watched him.

"I must bid yer good-bye, Dougl's," he said at last. "I've a long tramp afore me to-night. Mebbe worse. May-hap I may n't see you agin; men can't hev a grip on the next hour, these days. I'm glad we 're friends. Whatever comes afore mornin', I'm glad o' that!"

"Have you no more to say to me?"

"Yes, Dougl's, — 's for my little girl, — ef so be as I should foller my boy sometime, I'd wish you 'd be friends to Dode, Dougl's. Yes! I would," — hesitating, something wet oozing from his small black eye, and losing itself in the snuffy wrinkles.

Palmer was touched. It was a hard struggle with pain that had wrung out that tear. The old man held his hand a minute, then turned to the road.

"Whichever of us sees Geordy first kin tell him t' other 's livin' a true-grit honest life, call him Yankee or Virginian, — an' that's enough said! So good bye, Dougl's!"

Palmer mounted his horse and galloped off to the camp, the old man plodding steadily down the road. When the echo of the horse's hoofs had ceased, a lean gangling figure came from out of the field-brush, and met him.

"Why, David boy! whar were ye to-night?" Scofield's voice had grown strangely tender in the last hour.

Gaunt hesitated. He had not the moral courage to tell the old man he had enlisted.

"I waited. I must air the church, — it is polluted with foul smells."

Scofield laughed to himself at David's "whimsey," but he halted, going with the young man as he strode across the field. He had a dull foreboding of the end of the night's battle: before he went to it, he clung with a womanish affection to anything belonging to his home, as this Gaunt did. He had not thought the poor young man was so dear to him, until now, as he jogged along beside him, thinking that before morning he might be lying dead at the Gap. How many people would care? David would, and Dode, and old Bone.

Gaunt hurried in, — he ought to be in camp, but he could not leave the house of God polluted all night, — opening the windows, even carrying the flag outside. The emblem of freedom, of course, — but— He hardly knew why he did it. There were flags on every Methodist chapel, almost: the sect had thrown itself into the war *con amore*. But Gaunt had fallen into that sect by mistake; his animal nature was too weak for it: as for his feeling about the church, he had just that faint shade of Pantheism innate in him that would have made a good Episcopalian. The planks of the floor were more to him than other planks; something else than sunshine had often shone in to him through the little panes,—he touched them gently; he walked softly over the rag-carpet on the aisle. The LORD was in His holy temple. With another thought close behind that, of the time when the church was built, more than a year ago; what a happy, almost jolly time they had, the members giving the timber, and making a sort of frolic of putting it up, in the afternoons after harvest. They were all in one army or the other now: some of them in Blue's Gap. He would help ferret them out in the morning. He shivered, with the old doubt tugging fiercely at his heart. Was he right? The war was one of God's great judgments, but was it *his* place to be in it? It was too late to question now.

He went up into the pulpit, taking out the Bible that lay on the shelf, lighting a candle, glancing uneasily at the old man on the steps. He never had feared to meet his eye before. He turned to the fly-leaf, holding it to the candle. What odd fancy made him want to read the uncouth, blotted words written there? He knew them well enough. "To my Dear friend, David Gaunt. May, 1860. the Lord be Betwien mee And thee. J. Scofield." It was two years since he had given it to Gaunt, just after George had been so ill with cholera, and David had nursed him through with it. Gaunt fancied that nursing had made the hearts of both son and father more tender than all his sermons. He used to pray with them in the evenings as George grew better, hardly able to keep from weeping like a woman, for George was very dear to him. Afterwards the old man came to church more regularly, and George had quit swearing, and given up card-playing. He remembered the evening when the old man gave him the Bible. He had been down in Wheeling, and when he came home brought it out to Gaunt in the old corn-field, wrapped up in his best red bandanna hand-kerchief,—his face growing red and pale. "It 's the Book, David. I thort ef you 'd use this one till preach from. Mayhap it would n't be right till take it from a sinner like me, but—I thort I 'd like it, somehow,"—showing him the fly-leaf. "I writ this,—ef it would be true,—what I writ,—'The Lord be between me and thee'?"

Gaunt passed his fingers now over the misspelled words softly as he would stroke a dead face. Then he came out, putting out the candle, and buttoning the Bible inside of his coat.

Scofield waited for him on the steps. Some trouble was in the old fellow's face, Gaunt thought, which he could not fathom. His coarse voice choked every now and then, and his eyes looked as though he never hoped to see the church or Gaunt again.

"Heh, David!" with a silly laugh. "you 'll think me humorous, boy, but I hev an odd fancy."

He stopped abruptly.

"What is it?"

"It 's lonesome here,"—looking around vaguely. "God seems near here on the hills, d' ye think? David, I 'm goin' a bit out on the road to-night, an' life 's uncertain these times. Whiles I think I might never be back to see Dode agin,—or you. David, you're nearer to Him than me; you brought me to Him, you know. S'pose,—you'll think me foolish now,—ef we said a bit prayer here afore I go; what d' ye think? Heh?"

Gaunt was startled. Somehow to-night he did not feel as if God was near on the hills, as Scofield though.

"I will,"—hesitating. "Are you going to see Dode first, before you go?"

"Dode? Don't speak of her, boy! I'm sick! Kneel down an' pray,—the Lord's Prayer,—that's enough,—mother taught me that,"—baring his gray head, while Gaunt, his worn face turned to the sky, said the old words over. "Forgive," he muttered,—"resist not evil,"—some fragments vexing his brain. "Did He mean that? David boy? Did He mean His people to trust in God to right them as He did? Pah! times is different now,"—pulling his hat over his forehead to go. "Good bye, David!"

"Where are you going?"

"I don't mind tellin' you,—you'll keep it. Bone 's bringin' a horse yonder to the road. I'm goin' to warn the boys to be ready, an' help 'em,—at the Gap, you know?"

"The Gap? Merciful God, no!" cried Gaunt. "Go back"—

The words stopped in his throat. What if he met this man there?

Scofield looked at him, bewildered.

"Thar 's no danger," he said, calmly. "Yer nerves are weak. But yer love for me 's true, David. That's sure,"—with a smile. "But I 've got to warn the boys. Good bye,"—hesitating, his face growing red. "Ye 'll mind, ef anything should happen,—what I writ in the Book,—once,—'The Lord be between me an' thee,' dead or alive? Them 's good, friendly words. Good bye! God bless you, boy!"

Gaunt wrung his hand, and watched him as he turned to the road. He saw Bone meet him, leading a horse. As the old man mounted, he turned, and seeing Gaunt, nodded cheerfully, and going down the hill began to whistle. "Ef I should never come back, he kin tell Dode I hed a light heart at th' last," he thought. But when he was out of hearing, the whistle stopped, and he put spurs to the horse.

Counting the hours, the minutes,—a turbid broil of thought in his brain, of Dode sitting alone, of George and his murderers, "stiffening his courage,"—right and wrong mixing each other inextricably together. If, now and then, a shadow crossed him of the meek Nazarene leaving this word to His followers, that, let the world do as it would, *they* should resist not evil, he thrust it back. It did not suit to-day. Hours passed. The night crept on towards morning, colder, stiller. Faint bars of gray fell on the stretch of hill-tops, broad and pallid. The shaggy peaks blanched whiter in it. You could hear from the road-bushes the chirp of a snow-bird, wakened by the tramp of his horse, or the flutter of its wings. Overhead, the stars disappeared, like flakes of fire going out; the sky came nearer, tinged with healthier blue. He could see the mountain where the Gap was, close at hand, but a few miles distant.

He had met no pickets: he believed the whole Confederate camp there was asleep. And behind him, on the road he had just passed, trailing up the side of a hill, was a wavering, stealthy line, creeping slowly nearer every minute, — the gray columns under Dunning. The old man struck the rowels into his horse, — the boys would be murdered in their sleep! The road was rutted deep: the horse, an old village hack, lumbered along, stumbling at every step. "Ef my old bones was what they used to be, I 'd best trust them," he muttered. Another hour was over; there were but two miles before him to the Gap: but the old mare panted and balked at every ditch across the road. The Federal force was near; even the tap of their drum had ceased long since; their march was as silent as a tiger's spring. Close behind, — closer every minute! He pulled the rein savagely, — why could not the dumb brute know that life and death waited on her foot? The poor beast's eye lightened. She gathered her whole strength, sprang forward, struck upon a glaze of ice, and fell. The old man dragged himself out. "Poor old Jin! ye did what ye could!" he said. He was lamed by the fall. It was no time to think of that; he hobbled on, the cold drops of sweat oozing out on his face from pain. Reaching the bridge that crosses the stream there, he glanced back. He could not see the Federal troops, but he heard the dull march of their regiments, — like some giant's tread, slow, muffled in snow. Closer, — closer every minute! His heavy boots clogged with snow; the pain exhausted even his thick lungs, — they breathed heavily; he climbed the narrow ridge of ground that ran parallel with the road, and hurried on. Half an hour more, and he would save them!

A cold, stirless air: Gaunt panted in it. Was there ever night so silent? Following his lead, came the long column, a dark, even-moving mass, shirred with steel. Sometimes he could catch glimpses of some vivid point in the bulk: a hand, moving nervously to the sword's hilt; faces, — sensual, or vapid, or royal, side by side, but sharpened alike by a high purpose, with shut jaws, and keen, side-glancing eyes.

He was in advance of them, with one other man,—Dyke. Dyke took him, as knowing the country best, and being a trustworthy guide. So this was work! True work for a man. Marching hour after hour through the solitary night, he had time to think. Dyke talked to him but little: said once, "P'raps 't was as well the parsons had wakened up, and was mixin' with other folks. Gettin' into camp 'ud show 'em original sin, he guessed. Not but what this war-work brought out good in a man. Makes 'em, or breaks 'em, ginerally." And then was silent. Gaunt caught the words. Yes,— it was better preachers should lay off the prestige of the cloth, and rough it like their Master, face to face with men. There would be fewer despicable shams among them. But *this?*—clutching the loaded pistol in his hand. Thinking of Cromwell and Hedley Vicars. Freedom! It was a nobler cause than theirs. But a Face was before him, white, thorn-crowned, bent watchful over the world. He was sent of Jesus. To do what? Preach peace by murder? What said his Master? "That *ye* resist not evil." Bah! Palmer said the doctrine of non-resistance was whining cant. As long as human nature was the same, right and wrong would be left to the arbitrament of brute force. And yet—was not Christianity a diviner breath than this passing through the ages? "Ye are the light of the world." Even the "roughs" sneered at the fighting parsons. It was too late to think now. He pushed back his thin yellow hair, his homesick eyes wandering upwards, his mouth growing dry and parched.

They were nearing the mountain now. Dawn was coming. The gray sky heated and glowed into inner deeps of rose; the fresh morning air sprang from its warm nest somewhere, and came to meet them, like some one singing a heartsome song under his breath. The faces of the columns looked more rigid, paler, in the glow: men facing death have no time for fresh morning thoughts.

They were within a few rods[16] of the Gap. As yet there was no sign of sentinel,—not even the click of a musket was heard. "They sleep like the dead," muttered Dyke. "We 'll be on them in five minutes more." Gaunt, keeping step with him, pressing up the hill, shivered. He thought he saw blood on his hands. Why, this was work! His whole body throbbed as with one pulse. Behind him, a long way, came the column; his quickened nerves felt the slow beat of their tread, like the breathing of some great animal. Crouching in a stubble-field at the road-side he saw a negro,— a horse at a little distance. It was Bone; he had followed his master: the thought passing vaguely before him without meaning. On! on! The man beside him, with his head bent, his teeth clenched, the pupils of his eyes contracted, like a cat's nearing its prey. The road lay bare before them.

"Halt!" said Dyke. "Let them come up to us."

Gaunt stopped in his shambling gait.

"Look!" hissed Dyke, — "a spy!" — as the figure of a man climbed from a ditch where he had been concealed as he ran, and darted towards the rebel camp. "We 'll miss them yet!" — firing after him with an oath. The pistol missed, — flashed in the pan. "Wet!" — dashing it on the ground. "Fire, Gaunt! — quick!"

The man looked round; he ran lamely, — a thick, burly figure, a haggard face. Gaunt's pistol fell. Dode's father! the only man that loved him!

"Damn you!" shouted Dyke, "are you going to shirk?"

Why, this *was* the work! Gaunt pulled the trigger; there was a blinding flash. The old man stood a moment on the ridge, the wind blowing his gray hair back, then staggered, and fell, — that was all.

The column, sweeping up on the double-quick, carried the young disciple of Jesus with them. The jaws of the Gap were before them, — the enemy. What difference, if he turned pale, and cried out weakly, looking back at the man that he had killed?

For a moment the silence was unbroken. The winter's dawn, with pink blushes, and restless soft sighs, was yet wakening into day. The next, the air was shattered with the thunder of the guns among the hills, shouts, curses, death-cries. The speech which this day was to utter in the years was the old vexed cry, — "How long, O Lord? how long?"

A fight, short, but desperate. Where-ever it was hottest, the men crowded after one leader, a small man, with a mild, quiet face, — Douglas Palmer. Fighting with a purpose: high, — the highest, he thought: to uphold his Government. His blows fell heavy and sure.

You know the end of the story. The Federal victory was complete. The Rebel forces were carried off prisoners to Romney. How many, on either side, were lost, as in every battle of our civil war, no one can tell: it is better, perhaps, we do not know.

The Federal column did not return in an unbroken mass as they went. There were wounded and dying among them; some vacant places. Besides, they had work to do on their road back: the Rebels had been sheltered in the farmers' houses near; the "nest must be cleaned out": every homestead but two from Romney to the Gap was laid in ashes. It was not a pleasant sight for the officers to see women and children flying half-naked and homeless through the snow, nor did they think it would strengthen the Union sentiment; but what could they do? As great atrocities as these were committed by the Rebels. The war, as Palmer said, was a savage necessity.

When the fight was nearly over, the horse which Palmer rode broke from the *mêlée* and rushed back to the road. His master did not guide him. His face was set, pale; there was a thin foam on his lips. He had felt a sabre-cut in his side in the first of the engagement, but had not heeded it: now, he was growing blind, reeling on the saddle. Every bound of the horse jarred him with pain. His sense was leaving him, he knew; he wondered dimly if he was dying. That was the end of it, was it? He hoped to God the Union cause would triumph. Theodora, — he wished Theodora and he had parted friends. The man fell heavily forward, and the horse, terrified to madness, sprang aside, on a shelving ledge on the road-side, the edge of a deep mountain-gully. It was only sand beneath the snow, and gave way as he touched it. The animal struggled frantically to regain his footing, but the whole mass slid, and horse and rider rolled senseless to the bottom. When the noon-sun struck its peering light that day down into the dark crevice, Palmer lay there, stiff and stark.

When the Federal troops had passed by that morning, Scofield felt some one lift him gently, where he had fallen. It was Bone.

"Don't yer try ter stan', Mars' Joe," he said. "I kin tote yer like a fedder. Lor' bress yer, dis is nuffin'. We 'll hev yer roun' 'n no time," — his face turning ash-colored as he talked, seeing how dark the stain was on the old man's waistcoat.

His master could not help chuckling even then.

"Bone," he gasped, "when will ye quit lyin'? Put me down, old fellow. Easy. I 'm goin' fast."

Death did not take him unawares. He had thought all day it would end in this way. But he never knew who killed him, — I am glad of that.

Bone laid him on a pile of lumber behind some bushes. He could do little, — only held his big hand over the wound with all his force, having a vague notion he could so keep in life. He did not comprehend yet that his master was dying, enough to be sorry: he had a sort of pride in being nearest to Mars' Joe in a time like this, — in having him to himself. That was right: had n't they always been together since they were boys and set rabbit-traps on the South-Branch Mountain? But there was a strange look in the old man's eyes Bone did not recognize, — a new and awful thought. Now and then the sharp crack of the musketry jarred him.

"Tink dem Yankees is gettin' de Debbil in de Gap," Bone said, consolingly. "Would yer like ter know how de fight is goin', Mars'?"

"What matters it?" mumbled the old man. "Them things is triflin', after all, — now, — now."

"Is dar anyting yer 'd like me ter git, Mars' Joe?" said Bone, through his sobs.

The thought of the dying man was darkening fast; he began to mutter about Dode, and George at Harper's Ferry, — "Give Coly a warm mash to-night, Bone."

"O Lord!" cried the negro, "ef Mist' Dode was hyur! Him 's goin', an' him's las' breff is given ter de beast! Mars' Joe," calling in his ear, "fur God's sake say um prayer!"

The man moved restlessly, half-conscious.

"I wish David was here, — to pray for me."

The negro gritted his teeth, choking down an oath.

"I wish, — I thort I 'd die at home, — allays. That bed I 've slep' in come thirty years. I wish I was in th' house."

His breath came heavy and at long intervals. Bone gave a crazed look toward the road, with a wild thought of picking his master up and carrying him home. But it was nearly over now. The old man's eyes were dull; they would never see Dode again. That very moment she stood watching for him on the porch, her face colorless from a sleepless night, thinking he had been at Romney, that every moment she would hear his "Hillo!" round the bend of the road. She did not know that could not be again. He lay now, his limbs stretched out, his grizzly old head in Bone's arms.

"Tell Dode I did n't fight. She 'll be glad o' that. Thar 's no blood on my hands." He fumbled at his pocket. "My pipe? Was it broke when I fell? Dody 'd like to keep it, mayhap. She allays lit it for me."

The moment's flash died down. He muttered once or twice, after that, — "Dode," — and "Lord Jesus," — and, then his eyes shut. That was all.

They had buried her dead out of her sight. They had no time for mourning or funeral-making now. They only left her for a day alone to hide her head from all the world in the coarse old waistcoat, where the heart that had been so big and warm for her lay dead beneath, — to hug the cold, haggard face to her breast, and smooth the gray hair. She knew what the old man had been to her — now! There was not a homely way he had of showing his unutterable pride and love for his little girl that did not wring her very soul. She had always loved him; but she knew now how much warmer and brighter his rough life might have been, if she had chosen to make it so. There was not a cross word of hers, nor an angry look, that she did not remember with a bitterness that made her sick as death. If she could but know he forgave her! It was too late. She loathed herself, her coldness, her want of love to him, — to all the world. If she could only tell him she loved him, once more! — hiding her face in his breast, wishing she could lie there as cold and still as he, whispering, continually, "Father!

Father!" Could he not hear? When they took him away, she did not cry nor faint. When trouble stabbed Dode to the quick, she was one of those people who do not ask for help, but go alone, like a hurt deer, until the wound heals or kills. This was a loss for life. Of course, this throbbing pain would grieve itself down; but in all the years to come no one would take just the place her old father had left vacant. Husband and child might be dearer, but she would never be "Dody" to any one again. She shut the loss up in her own heart. She never named him afterwards.

It was a cold winter's evening, that, after the funeral. The January wind came up with a sharp, dreary sough into the defiles of the hills, crusting over the snow-sweeps with a glaze of ice that glittered in the pearly sunlight, clear up the rugged peaks. There, at the edge of them, the snow fretted and arched and fell back in curling foam-waves with hints of delicate rose-bloom in their white shining. The trees, that had stood all winter bare and patient, lifting up their dumb arms in dreary supplication, suddenly, to-day, clothed themselves, every trunk and limb and twig, in flashing ice, that threw back into the gray air the royal greeting of a thousand splendid dyes, violet, amber, and crimson,—to show God they did not need to wait for summer days to praise Him. A cold afternoon: even the seeds hid in the mould down below the snow were chilled to the heart, and thought they surely could not live the winter out: the cows, when Bone went out drearily to feed them by himself, were watching the thin, frozen breath steaming from their nostrils with tears in their eyes, he thought.

A cold day: cold for the sick and wounded soldiers that were jolted in ambulances down the mountain-roads through its creeping hours. For the Federal troops had evacuated Romney. The Rebel forces, under Jackson, had nearly closed around the mountain-camp before they were discovered: they were twenty thousand strong. Lander's force was but a handful in comparison; he escaped with them for their lives that day, leaving the town and the hills in full possession of the Confederates.

A bleak, heartless day: coldest of all for Dode, lying on the floor of her little room. How wide and vacant the world looked to her! What could she do there? Why was she born? She must show her Master to others,— of course; but—she was alone: everybody she loved had been taken from her. She wished that she were dead. She lay there, trying to pray, now and then,—motionless, like some death in life; the gray sunlight looking in at her, in a wondering way. It was quite contented to be gray and cold, till summer came.

Out in the little kitchen, the day had warmed up wonderfully. Dode's

Aunt Perrine, a widow of thirty years' standing, had come over to "see to things durin' this murnful affliction." As she had brought her hair-trunk and bonnet-box, it was probable her stay would be indefinite. Dode was conscious of her as she would be of an attack of nettle-rash. Mrs. Perrine and her usual burying-colleague, "Mis' Browst," had gotten up a snug supper of fried oysters, and between that and the fresh relish of horror from the funeral were in a high state of enjoyment.

Aunt Perrine, having officiated as chief mourner that very morning, was not disposed to bear her honors meekly.

"It was little Jane Browst knew of sorrer. With eight gells well married,—*well* married, Jane,—deny it, ef you can,—what can you know of my feelins this day? Hyur 's Mahala's husband dead an' gone,—did you say tea or coffee, Jane?—Joseph Scofield, a good brother-in-law to me 's lives, laid in the sod this day. You may well shake yer head! But who 'll take his place to me? Dode there 's young an' 'll outgrow it. But it 's me that suffers the loss,"—with a fresh douse of tears, and a contemptuous shove of the oyster-plate to make room for her weeping head. "It 's me that 's the old 'n' withered trunk!"

Mis' Browst helped herself freely to the oysters just then.

"Not," said Aunt Perrine, with stern self-control, "that I don't submit, an' bear as a Christian ought."

She took the spoon again.

" 'N' I could wish," severely, raising her voice, " 's all others could profit likewise by this dispensation. Them as is kerried off by tantrums, 'n' consorts with Papishers 'n' the Lord knows what, might see in this a judgment, ef they would."

Mis' Browst groaned in concert.

"Ye need n't girn that away, Jane Browst," whispered Aunt Perrine, emphatically. "Dode Scofield 's a different guess sort of a gell from any Browst. Keep yer groans for yer own nest. Ef I improve the occasion while she 's young an' tender, what 's that to you? Look at home, you 'd best, I say!"

Mis' Browst was a woman of resources and English pluck. She always came out best at last, though her hair was toffy-colored and her eyes a washed-out blue, and Aunt Perrine was of the color of a mild Indian. Two of Mis' Browst's sons-in-law had been "burned out" by the Yankees; another was in the Union army: these trump-cards of misery she did now so produce and flourish and weep over that she utterly routed the enemy, reduced her to stolid silence.

"Well, well," she muttered, getting breath. "We 'll not talk of our individooal sorrers when affliction is general, Jane Browst. S'pose we hev Bone in, and hear the perticklers of the scrimmage at Blue's Gap. It 's little time I 've hed for news since,"—with a groan to close the subject finally.

Mis' Browst sighed an assent, drinking her coffee with a resigned gulp, with the firm conviction that the civil war had been designed for her especial trial and enlargement in Christian grace.

So Bone was called in from the cow-yard. His eyes were quite fiery, for the poor stupid fellow had been crying over the "warm mash" he was giving to Coly. "Him's las' words was referrin' ter yer, yer pore beast," he had said, snuffling out loud. He had stayed in the stables all day, "wishin' all old she-cats was to home, an' him an' Mist' Dode could live in peace."

However, he was rather flattered at the possession of so important a story just now, and in obedience to Aunt Perrine's nod seated himself with dignity on the lowest step of the garret-stairs, holding carefully his old felt hat, which he had decorated with streaming weepers of crape.

Dode, pressing her hands to her ears, heard only the dull drone of their voices. She shut her eyes, sometimes, and tried to fancy that she was dreaming and would waken presently,—that she would hear her father rap on the window with his cowhide, and call, "Supper, Dody dear?"—that it was a dream that Douglas Palmer was gone forever, that she had put him away. Had she been right? God knew; she was not sure.

It grew darker; the gray afternoon was wearing away with keen gusts and fitful snow-falls. Dode looked up wearily: a sharp exclamation, rasped out by Aunt Perrine, roused her.

"Dead? Dougl's dead?"

"Done gone, Mist'. I forgot dat—ter tell yer. Had somefin' else ter tink of."

"Down in the gully?"

"Saw him lyin' dar as I went ter git Flynn's cart ter—ter bring Mars' Joe, yer know,—home. Gone dead. Like he 's dar yit. Snow 'ud kiver him fast, an' de Yankees hed n't much leisure ter hunt up de missin',—yi! yi!"—with an attempt at a chuckle.

"Dougl's dead!" said Aunt Perrine. "Well!—in the midst of life— Yer not goin', Jane Browst? What 's yer hurry, woman? You 've but a step across the road. Stay to-night. Dode an' me 'll be glad of yer company. It 's better to come to the house of murnin' than the house of feastin', you know."

"You may be thankful you 've a house to cover you, Ann Perrine, an'"—

"Yes,—I know. I 'm resigned. But there 's no affliction like death.—

Bone, open the gate for Mis' Browst. Them hasps is needin' mendin', as I 've often said to Joseph,—um!"

The women kissed each other as often as women do whose kisses are—cheap, and Mis' Browst set off down the road. Bone, turning to shut the gate, felt a cold hand on his arm.

"Gor-a'mighty! Mist' Dode, what is it?"

The figure standing in the snow wrapt in a blue cloak shook as he touched it. Was she, too, struck with death? Her eyes were burning, her face white and clammy.

"Where is he, Uncle Bone? where?"

The old man understood—all.

"Gone dead, darlin',"—holding her hand in his paw, tenderly. "Don't fret, chile! Down in de Tear-coat gully. Dead, chile, dead! Don't yer understan'?"

"He is not dead," she said, quietly. "Open the gate," pulling at the broken hasp.

"Fur de Lor's sake, Mist' Dode, come in 'n' bathe yer feet 'n' go to bed! Chile, yer crazy!"

Common sense, and a flash of something behind to give it effect, spoke out of Dode's brown eyes, just then.

"Go into the stable, and bring a horse after me. The cart is broken?"

"Yes, 'm. Dat cussed Ben"—

"Bring the horse,—and some brandy, Uncle Bone."

"Danged ef yer shall kill yerself! Chile, I tell yer he 's dead. I 'll call Mist' Perrine."

Her eyes were black now, for an instant; then they softened.

"He is not dead. Come, Uncle Bone. You 're all the help I have, now."

The old man's flabby face worked. He did not say anything, but went into the stable, and presently came out, leading the horse, with fearful glances back at the windows. He soon overtook the girl going hurriedly down the road, and lifted her into the saddle.

"Chile! chile! yer kin make a fool of ole Bone, allays."

She did not speak; her face, with its straight-lidded eyes, turned to the mountain beyond which lay the Tear-coat gully. A fair face under its blue hood, even though white with pain,—an honorable face: the best a woman can know of pride and love in life spoke through it.

"Mist' Dode," whined Ben, submissively, "what are yer goin' ter do? Bring him home?"

"Yes."

"Fur de lub o' heben!"—stopping short. "A Yankee captain in de house, an' Jackson's men rampin' over de country like devils! Dey 'll burn de place ter de groun', ef dey fin' him."

"I know."

Bone groaned horribly, then went on doggedly. Fate was against him: his gray hairs were bound to go down with sorrow to the grave. He looked up at her wistfully, after a while.

"What 'll Mist' Perrine say?" he asked.

Dode's face flushed scarlet. The winter mountain night, Jackson's army, she did not fear; but the staring malicious world in the face of Aunt Perrine did make her woman's heart blench.

"It does n't matter," she said, her eyes full of tears. "I can't help that, Uncle Bone,"—putting her little hand on his shoulder, as he walked beside her. The child was so utterly alone, you know.

The road was lonely,—a mere mountain-path striking obliquely through the hills to the highway: darkening hills and sky and valleys strangely sinking into that desolate homesick mood of winter twilight. The sun was gone; one or two sad red shadows lay across the gray. Night would soon be here, and he lay stiff-cold beneath the snow. Not dead: her heart told her that imperiously from the first. But there was not one instant to lose.

"I cannot wait for you, Uncle Bone. I must go alone."

"Debbil de step! I 'll take yer 'cross fields ter Gentry's, an' ride on myself."

"You could not find him. No one could find him but me."

Something possessed the girl, other than her common self. She pushed his hand gently from the reins, and left him. Bone wrung his hands.

" 'N' de guerrillas,—'n' de rest o' de incarnate debbils!"

She knew that. Dode was no heroine,—a miserable coward. There was not a black stump of a tree by the road-side, nor the rustle of a squirrel in the trees, that did not make her heart jump and throb against her bodice. Her horse climbed the rocky path slowly. I told you the girl thought her Helper was alive, and very near. She did to-night. She thought He was beside her in this lonesome road, and knew she would be safe. She felt as if she could take hold of His very hand. It grew darker: the mountains of snow glowered wan like the dead kings in Hades; the sweeps of dark forests whispered some broken mysterious word, as she passed; sometimes, in a sudden opening, she could see on a far hill-side the red fires of a camp. She could not help the sick feeling in her throat, nor make her hand steady; but the more alone she was, the nearer He came,—the pale face of the Nazarene, who loved His mother and Mary, who took the little children in His arms before He blessed them. Nearer than ever before; so she was not afraid to tell Him, as she went, how she had suffered that day, and that she loved this man who lay dying under the snow: to ask that she might find him. A great gulf lay between them. Would *He* go with her, if she crossed it? She knew He would.

A strange peace came to the girl. She untied her hood and pushed it back, that her whole head might feel the still air. How pure it was! God was in it,—in all. The mountains, the sky, the armies yonder, her own heart, and his under the snow, rested in Him, like motes in the sunshine.

The moon, rising behind a bank of cloud, threw patches of light now and then across the path: the girl's head, as she rode through them, came into quick relief. No saint's face,—a very woman's, its pale, reserved beauty unstrung with pain, her bosom full of earthly love, but in her eyes that look which Mary must have given, when, after she thought her Lord was dead, He called her, "Mary!" and she, looking up, said, "Master!"

She had reached the highway at last. She could see where, some distance yet beyond, the gully struck black across the snow-covered fields. The road ran above it, zigzag along the hill-side. She thought, as her horse galloped up the path, she could see the very spot where Douglas was lying. Not dead,—she knew he was not dead! She came to it now. How deathly still it was! As she tied the horse to the fence, and climbed down the precipice through the snow, she was dimly conscious that the air was warmer, that the pure moonlight was about her, genial, hopeful. A startled snow-bird chirped to her, as she passed. Why, it was a happy promise! Why should it not be happy? He was not dead, and she had leave to come to him.

Yet, before she gained the level field, the pulse in her body was weak and sick, and her eyes were growing blind. She did not see him. Half covered by snow, she found his gray horse, dead, killed by the fall. Palmer was gone. The gully was covered with muddy ice; there was a split in it, and underneath, the black water curdled and frothed. Had he fallen there? Was that thing that rose and fell in the roots of the old willow his dead hand? There was a floating gleam of yellow in the water,—it looked like hair. Dode put her hand to her hot breast, shut her dry lips. He was not dead! God could not lie to her!

Stooping, she went over the ground again, an unbroken waste of white: until, close to the water's edge, she found the ginseng-weeds torn and trampled down. She never afterwards smelt their unclean, pungent odor, without a sudden pang of the smothered pain of this night coming back to her. She knelt, and found foot-marks,—one booted and spurred. She knew it: what was there he had touched that she did not know? He was alive: she did not cry out at this, or laugh, as her soul went up to God, — only thrust her hand deep into the snow where his foot had been, with a quick, fierce tenderness, blushing as she drew it back, as if she had forgotten herself, and from her heart caressed him. She heard a sound at the other side of a bend in the hill, a low drone, like somebody mumbling a hymn.

She pushed her way through the thicket: the moon did not shine there; there was a dark crevice in the hill, where some farmer's boy had built a shed. There was a fire in it, now, smouldering, as though whoever made it feared its red light would be seen by the distant pickets. Coming up to it, she stood in the door-way. Douglas Palmer lay on a heap of blankets on the ground: she could not see his face, for a lank, slothful figure was stooping over him, chafing his head. It was Gaunt. Dode went in, and knelt down beside the wounded man, — quietly: it seemed to her natural and right she should be there. Palmer's eyes were shut, his breathing heavy, uncertain; but his clothes were dried, and his side was bandaged.

"It was only a flesh-wound," said Gaunt, in his vague way, — "deep, though. I knew how to bind it. He 'll live, Douglas will."

He did not seem surprised to see the girl. Nothing could be so bizarre in the world, that his cloudy, crotchety brain did not accept it, and make a common-place matter out of it. It never occurred to him to wonder how she came there. He stood with folded arms, his bony shoulders bolstering up the board wall, watching her as she knelt, her hands on Palmer's pillow, but not touching him. Gaunt's lean face had a pitiful look, sometimes, — the look of the child he was in his heart, — hungry, wistful, as though he sought for something, which you might have, perhaps. He looked at Dode, — the child of the man that he had killed. She did not know that. When she came in, he thought of shaking hands with her, as he used to do. That could never be again, — never. *The man that he had killed?* What-ever that meant to him, his artist eye took keen note of Dode, as she knelt there, in spite of remorse or pain below: how her noble, delicate head rose from the coarse blue drapery, the dark rings of her curling hair, the pale, clear-cut face, the burning lips, the eyes whose earthly soul was for the man who lay there. He knew that, yet he never loved her so fiercely as now, — now, when her father's blood lay between them.

"Did you find him?" she asked, without looking up. "I ought to have done it. I wish I had done that. I wish I had given him his life. It was my right."

One would think she was talking in her sleep.

"Why was it your right?" he asked, quietly.

"Because I loved him."

Gaunt raised his hand to his head suddenly.

"Did you, Dode? I had a better right than that. Because I hated him."

"He never harmed you, David Gaunt,"—with as proud composure as that with which a Roman wife would defend her lord.

"I saved his life. Dode, I'm trying to do right: God knows I am. But I hated him: he took from me the only thing that would have loved me."

She looked up timidly, her face growing crimson.

"I never would have loved you, David."

"No? I 'm sorry you told me that, Dode."

That was all he said. He helped her gently, as she arranged the carpets and old blanket under the wounded man; then he went out into the fresh air, saying he did not feel well. She was glad that he was gone; Palmer moved uneasily; she wanted his first look all to herself. She pushed back his fair hair: what a broad, melancholy forehead lay under it! The man wanted something to believe in,—a God in life: you could see that in his face. She was to bring it to him: she could not keep the tears back to think that this was so. The next minute she laughed in her childish fashion, as she put the brandy to his lips, and the color came to his face. He had been physician before; now it was her turn to master and rule. He looked up at last, into her eyes, bewildered,—his face struggling to gather sense, distinctness. When he spoke, though, it was in his quiet old voice.

"I have been asleep. Where is Gaunt? He dressed my side."

"He is out, sitting on the hill-side."

"And you are here, Theodora?"

"Yes, Douglas."

He was silent. He was weak from loss of blood, but his thoughts were sharp, clear as never before. The years that were gone of his life seemed clogged into one bulk; how hungry they had been, hard, cruel! He never had felt it as now, while he lay helpless, his sultry look reading the woman's eyes bent on his. They were pure and restful; love and home waited in them; something beyond,—a peace he could not yet comprehend. But his life was not for him,—he remembered that; the girl was nothing to him now: he was not fool enough to taunt himself with false hopes. She came there out of pity: any woman would do as much for a wounded man. He would never fool himself to be so balked again. The loss cut too deep. So he forced his face to be cool and critical, while poor Dode waited, innocently wondering that he did not welcome her, pity her now that her father was dead, forgetting that he knew nothing of that. For him, he looked at the fire, wondering if the Rebel scouts could see it,—thinking it would not be many days before Lander would dislodge Jackson,—trying to think of anything rather than himself, and the beautiful woman kneeling there.

Her eyes filled with tears at last, when he did not speak, and she turned away. The blood rushed to Palmer's face: surely that was more than pity! But he would not tempt her,—he would never vex her soul as he had done before: if she had come to him, as a sister might, because she thought he was dying, he would not taunt her with the old love she had for him.

"I think I can stand up," he said, cheerfully; "lend me your arm, Theodora."

Dode's arm was strong-nerved as well as fair; she helped him rise, and stood beside him as he went to the door, for he walked unsteadily. He took his hand from her shoulder instantly,—did not look at her: followed with his eye the black line of the fretted hills, the glimmer of the distant watch-fires. The path to the West lay through the Rebel camps.

"It is a long trail out of danger," he said, smiling.

"You are going? I thought you needed rest."

Calm, icy enough now: he was indifferent to her. She knew how to keep the pain down until he was gone.

"Rest? Yes. Where did you mean I should find it?"—facing her, sudden and keen. "Where am I to be sheltered? In your home, Theodora?"

"I thought that. I see now that it was a foolish hope, Douglas."

"How did you hope it? What brought you here?"—his voice thick, tremulous with passion. "Were you going to take me in as a Sister of Charity might some wounded dog? Are pity and gratitude all that is left between you and me?"

She did not answer,—her face pale, unmoving in the moonlight, quietly turned to his. These mad heats did not touch her.

"You may be cold enough to palter with fire that has burned you, Theodora. I am not."

She did not speak.

"Sooner than have gone to you for sisterly help and comfort, such as you gave just now, I would have frozen in the snow, and been less cold. Unless you break down the bar you put between us, I never want to see your face again,—never, living or dead! I want no sham farce of friendship between us, benefits given or received: your hand touching mine as it might touch Bone's or David Gaunt's; your voice cooing in my ear as it did just now, cool and friendly. It maddened me. Rest can scarcely come from you to me, now."

"I understand you. I am to go back, then? It was a long road,—and cold, Douglas."

He stopped abruptly, looked at her steadily.

"Do not taunt me, child! I am a blunt man: what words say, they mean, to me. Do you love me, Theodora?"

She did not speak, drawn back from him in the opposite shadow of the door-way. He leaned forward, his breath coming hurried, low.

"Are you cold? See how shaggy this great cloak is,—is it wide enough for you and me? Will you come to me, Theodora?"

"I did come to you. Look! you put me back: 'There shall be no benefits given or received between us.'"

"How did you come?"—gravely, as a man should speak to a woman, childish trifling thrust aside. "How did you mean to take me home? As a pure, God-fearing woman should the man she loved? Into your heart, into your holiest thought? to gather strength from my strength, to make my power your power, your God my God? to be one with me? Was it so you came?"

He waited a minute. How cold and lonely the night was! How near rest and home came to him in this woman standing there! Would he lose them? One moment more would tell. When he spoke again, his voice was lower, feeble.

"There is a great gulf between you and me, Theodora. I know that. Will you cross it? Will you come to me?"

She came to him. He gathered her into his arms as he might a little child, never to be cold again; he felt her full heart throb passionately against his own; he took from her burning lips the first pure, womanly kiss: she was all his. But when he turned her head, there was a quick upward glance of her eyes, he knew not whether of appeal or thanks. There was a Something in the world more near and real to her than he; he loved her the better for it: yet until he found that Unknown God, they were not one.

It was an uncertain step broke the silence, cracking the crusted snow.

"Why, Gaunt!" said Palmer, "what are you doing in the cold? Come to the fire, boy!"

He could afford to speak cordially, heartily, out of the great warmth in his own breast. Theodora was heaping shavings on the ashes. Gaunt took them from her.

"Let me do it," he muttered. "I 'd like to make your whole life warm, Dode,—your life, and—any one's you love."

Dode's face flushed with a happy smile. Even David never would think of her as alone again. Poor David! She never before had thought how guileless he was,—how pitiful and solitary his life.

"Come home with us," she said, eagerly, holding out her hand.

He drew back, wiping the sweat from his face.

"You cannot see what is on my hand. I can't touch you, Dode. Never again. Let me alone."

"She is right, Gaunt," said Palmer. "You stay here at the risk of your life. Come to the house. Theodora can hide us; and if they discover us, we can protect her together."

Gaunt smiled faintly.

"I must make my way to Springfield to-morrow. My work is there,— my new work, Palmer."

Palmer looked troubled.

"I wish you had not taken it up. This war may be needed to conquer a way for the day of peace and good-will among men; but you, who profess to be a seer and actor in that day, have only one work: to make it real to us now on earth, as your Master did, in the old time."

Gaunt did not speak,—fumbled among the chips at the fire. He raised himself at last.

"I 'm trying to do what 's right," he said, in a subdued voice. "I have n't had a pleasant life,—but it will come right at last, maybe."

"It will come right, David!" said the girl.

His face lighted: her cheery voice sounded like a welcome ringing through his future years. It was a good omen, coming from her whom he had wronged.

"Are you going now, Gaunt?" asked Palmer, seeing him button his thin coat. "Take my blanket,—nay, you shall. As soon as I am strong enough, I 'll find you at Springfield."

He wished he could hearten the poor unnerved soul, somehow.

Gaunt stopped outside, looking at them,—some uncertain thought coming and going in his face.

"I 'll speak it out, whatever you may think. Dode, I 've done you a deadly hurt. Don't ask me what it is,—God knows. I 'd like, before I go, to show you I love you in a pure, honorable way, you and your husband"—

The words choked in his throat; he stopped abruptly.

"Whatever you do, it will be honorable, David," said Palmer, gently.

"I think—God might take it as expiation,"—holding his hand to his head.

He did not speak again for a little while, then he said,—

"I will never see these old Virginian hills again. I am going West; they will let me nurse in one of the hospitals;—that will be better than this that is on my hand."

Whatever intolerable pain lay in these words, he smothered it down, kept his voice steady.

"Do you understand, Douglas Palmer? I will never see you again. Nor Dode. You love this woman; so did I,—as well as you. Let me make her your wife before I go,—here, under this sky, with God looking down on us. Will you? I shall be happier to know that I have done it."

He waited while Douglas spoke eagerly to the girl, and then said,—

"Theodora, for God's sake don't refuse! I have hurt you,—the marks of it you and I will carry to the grave. Let me think you forgive me before I go. Grant me this one request."

Did she guess the hurt he had done her? Through all her fright and blushes, the woman in her spoke out nobly.

"I do not wish to know how you have wronged me. Whatever it be, it was innocently done. God will forgive you, and I do. There shall be peace between us, David."

But she did not offer to touch his hand again: stood there, white and trembling.

"It shall be as you say," said Palmer.

So they were married, Douglas and Dode, in the wide winter night. A few short words, that struck the very depths of their being, to make them one: simple words, wrung out of the man's thin lips with what suffering only he knew.

"Those whom God hath joined together let no man put asunder." Thus he shut himself out from her forever. But the prayer for a blessing on them, came from as pure a heart as any child's that lives. He bade them good-bye, cheerfully, when he had finished, and turned away, but came back presently, and said good-night again, looking in their faces steadily, then took his solitary way across the hills. They never saw him again.

Bone, who had secured two horses by love or money or—confiscation, had stood mutely in the background, gulping down his opinion of this extraordinary scene. He did not offer it now, only suggested it was "high time to be movin'," and when he was left alone, trudging through the snow, contented himself with smoothing his felt hat, and a breathless, "Ef dis nigger on'y knew what Mist' Perrine *would* say!"

A June day. These old Virginia hills have sucked in the winter's ice and snow, and throbbed it out again for the blue heaven to see in a whole summer's wealth of trees quivering with the luxury of being, in wreathed mosses, and bedded fern: the very blood that fell on them speaks in fair, grateful flowers to Him who doeth all things well. Some healthy hearts, like the hills, you know, accept pain, and utter it again in fresher-blooded peace and life and love. The evening sunshine lingers on Dode's little house to-day; the brown walls have the same cheery whim in life as the soul of their mistress, and catch the last ray of light,—will not let it go. Bone, smoking his pipe at the garden-gate, looks at the house with drowsy complacency. He calls it all "Mist' Dode's snuggery," now: he does not know that the rich, full-toned vigor of her happiness is the germ of all this life and beauty. But he does know that the sun never seemed so warm, the air so pure, as this summer,—that about the quiet farm and homestead there is a genial atmosphere of peace: the wounded soldiers who come there often to be cured grow strong and calm in it; the war seems far-off to them; they have come somehow a step nearer the inner heaven. Bone rejoices in showing off the wonders of the place to them, in matching Coly's shiny sides against the "Government beastesses," in talking of the giant red beets, or crumpled green cauliflower, breaking the rich garden-mould. "Yer've no sich cherries nor taters nor raspberries as dem in de Norf, I'll bet!" Even the crimson trumpet-flower on the wall is "a *Virginny* creeper, Sah!" But Bone learns something from them in exchange. He does not boast so often now of being "ole Mars' Joe's man,"—sits and thinks profoundly, till he goes to sleep. "Not of leavin' yer, Mist' Dode. I know what free darkies is, up dar; but dar's somefin' in a fellah's 'longin' ter hisself, af'er all!" Dode only smiles at his deep cogitations, as he weeds the garden-beds, or fodders the stock. She is a half-Abolitionist herself, and then she knows her State will soon be free.

So Dode, with deeper-lit eyes, and fresher rose in her cheek, stands in the door this summer evening waiting for her husband. She cannot see him often; he has yet the work to do which he calls just and holy. But he is coming now. It is very quiet; she can hear her own heart beat slow and full; the warm air holds moveless the delicate scent of the clover; the bees hum her a drowsy good-night, as they pass; the locusts in the lindens have just begun to sing themselves to sleep; but the glowless crimson in the West holds her thought the longest. She loves, understands color: it speaks to her of the Day waiting just behind this. Her eyes fill with tears, she knows not why: her life seems rounded, complete, wrapt in a great peace; the grave at Manassas, and that planted with moss on the hill yonder, are in it: they only make her joy in living more tender and holy.

He has come now; stops to look at his wife's face, as though its fairness and meaning were new to him always. There is no look in her eyes he loves so well to see as that which tells her Master is near her. Sometimes she thinks he too— But she knows that "according to her faith it shall be unto her." They are alone to-night; even Bone is asleep. But in the midst of a crowd, they who love each other are alone together: as the first man and woman stood face to face in the great silent world, with God looking down, and only their love between them.

The same June evening lights the windows of a Western hospital. There is not a fresh meadow-scented breath it gives that does not bring to some sick brain a thought of home, in a New-England village, or a Georgia rice-field. The windows are open; the pure light creeping into poisoned rooms carries with it a Sabbath peace, they think. One man stops in his hurried work, and looking out, grows cool in its tranquil calm. So the sun used to set in old Virginia, he thinks. A tall, slab-sided man, in the dress of a hospital-nurse: a worn face, but quick, sensitive; the patients like it better than any other: it looks as if the man had buried great pain in his life, and come now into its Indian-summer days. The eyes are childish, eager, ready to laugh as cry,—the voice warm, chordant,—the touch of the hand unutterably tender.

A busy life, not one moment idle; but the man grows strong in it,— a healthy servant, doing a healthy work. The patients are glad when he comes to their ward in turn. How the windows open, and the fresh air comes in! how the lazy nurses find a masterful will over them! how full of innermost life he is! how real his God seems to him!

He looks from the window now, his thought having time to close upon himself. He holds up his busy, solitary life to God, with a happy smile. He goes back to that bitter past, shrinking; but he knows its meaning now. As the warm evening wanes into coolness and gray, the one unspoken pain of his life comes back, and whitens his cheerful face. There is blood on his hands. He sees the old man's gray hairs blown again by the wind, sees him stagger and fall. Gaunt covers his bony face with his hands, but he cannot shut it out. Yet he is learning to look back on even that with healthy, hope-ful eyes. He reads over again each day the misspelled words in the Bible,— thinking that the old man's haggard face looks down on him with the old kindly, forgiving smile. What if his blood be on his hands? He looks up now through the gathering night, into the land where spirits wait for us, as one who meets a friend's face, saying,—

"Let it be true what you have writ,—'The *Lord* be between me and thee,' forever!"

 Blind Tom

Atlantic Monthly, November 1862

Only a germ in a withered flower,
That the rain will bring out—sometime.

Sometime in the year 1850, a tobacco-planter in Southern Georgia (Perry H. Oliver by name) bought a likely negro woman with some other field-hands. She was stout, tough-muscled, willing, promised to be a remunerative servant; her baby, however, a boy a few months old, was only thrown in as a makeweight to the bargain, or rather because Mr. Oliver would not consent to separate mother and child. Charity only could have induced him to take the picaninny, in fact, for he was but a lump of black flesh, born blind, and with the vacant grin of idiocy, they thought, already stamped on his face. The two slaves were purchased, I believe, from a trader: it has been impossible, therefore, for me to ascertain where Tom was born, or when. Georgia field-hands are not accurate as Jews in preserving their genealogy; *they* do not anticipate a Messiah. A white man, you know, has that vague hope unconsciously latent in him, that he is, or shall give birth to, the great man of his race, a helper, a provider for the world's hunger: so he grows jealous with his blood; the dead grandfather may have presaged the possible son; besides, it is a debt he owes to this coming Saul to tell him whence he came. There are some classes, free and slave, out of whom society has crushed this hope: they have no clan, no family-names among them, therefore. This idiot-boy, chosen by God to be anointed with the holy chrism, is only "Tom,"—"Blind Tom," they call him in all the Southern States, with a kind cadence always, being proud and fond of him; and yet—nothing but Tom? That is pitiful. Just a mushroom-growth,—unkinned, unexpected, not hoped for, for generations, owning no name to purify and honor and give away when he is dead. His mother, at work to-day in the Oliver plantations, can never comprehend why her boy is famous; this gift of God to him means nothing to her. Nothing to him, either, which is saddest of all; he is unconscious, wears his crown as an idiot might. Whose fault is that? Deeper than slavery the evil lies.

Mr. Oliver did his duty well to the boy, being an observant and thoroughly kind master. The plantation was large, heartsome, faced the sun, swarmed with little black urchins, with plenty to eat, and nothing to do.

All that Tom required, as he fattened out of baby- into boyhood, was room in which to be warm, on the grass-patch, or by the kitchen-fires, to be stupid, flabby, sleepy,—kicked and petted alternately by the other hands. He had a habit of crawling up on the porches and verandas of the mansion and squatting there in the sun, waiting for a kind word or touch from those who went in and out. He seldom failed to receive it. Southerners know nothing of the physical shiver of aversion with which even the Abolitionists of the North touch the negro: so Tom, through his very helplessness, came to be a sort of pet in the family, a play-mate, occasionally, of Mr. Oliver's own infant children. The boy, creeping about day after day in the hot light, was as repugnant an object as the lizards in the neighboring swamp, and promised to be of as little use to his master. He was of the lowest negro type, from which only field-hands can be made,—coal-black, with protruding heels, the ape-jaw, blubber-lips constantly open, the sightless eyes closed, and the head thrown far back on the shoulders, lying on the back, in fact, a habit which he still retains, and which adds to the imbecile character of the face. Until he was seven years of age, Tom was regarded on the plantation as an idiot, not unjustly; for at the present time his judgment and reason rank but as those of a child four years old. He showed a dog-like affection for some members of the household,—a son of Mr. Oliver's especially,—and a keen, nervous sensitiveness to the slightest blame or praise from them,—possessed, too, a low animal irritability of temper, giving way to inarticulate yelps of passion when provoked. That is all, so far; we find no other outgrowth of intellect or soul from the boy: just the same record as that of thousands of imbecile negro-children. Generations of heathendom and slavery have dredged the inherited brains and temperaments of such children tolerably clean of all traces of power or purity,—palsied the brain, brutalized the nature. Tom apparently fared no better than his fellows.

It was not until 1857 that those phenomenal powers latent in the boy were suddenly developed, which stamped him the anomaly he is to-day.

One night, sometime in the summer of that year, Mr. Oliver's family were wakened by the sound of music in the drawing-room: not only the simple airs, but the most difficult exercises usually played by his daughters, were repeated again and again, the touch of the musician being timid, but singularly true and delicate. Going down, they found Tom, who had been left asleep in the hall, seated at the piano in an ecstasy of delight, breaking out at the end of each successful fugue into shouts of laughter, kicking his heels and clapping his hands. This was the first time he had touched the piano.

Naturally, Tom became a nine-days' wonder on the plantation. He was brought in as an after-dinner's amusement; visitors asked for him as the show of the place. There was hardly a conception, however, in the minds of those who heard him, of how deep the cause for wonder lay. The planters' wives and daughters of the neighborhood were not people who would be apt to comprehend music as a science, or to use it as a language; they only saw in the little negro, therefore, a remarkable facility for repeating the airs they drummed on their pianos,—in a different manner from theirs, it is true,—which bewildered them. They noticed, too, that, however the child's fingers fell on the keys, cadences followed, broken, wandering, yet of startling beauty and pathos. The house-servants, looking in through the open doors at the little black figure perched up before the instrument, while unknown, wild harmony drifted through the evening air, had a better conception of him. He was possessed; some ghost spoke through him: which is a fair enough definition of genius for a Georgian slave to offer.

Mr. Oliver, as we said, was indulgent. Tom was allowed to have constant access to the piano; in truth, he could not live without it; when deprived of music now, actual physical debility followed: the gnawing Something had found its food at last. No attempt was made, however, to give him any scientific musical teaching; nor—I wish it distinctly borne in mind—has he ever at any time received such instruction.

The planter began to wonder what kind of a creature this was which he had bought, flesh and soul. In what part of the unsightly baby-carcass had been stowed away these old airs, forgotten by every one else, and some of them never heard by the child but once, but which he now reproduced, every note intact, and with whatever quirk or quiddity of style belonged to the person who originally had sung or played them? Stranger still the harmonies which he had never heard, had learned from no man. The sluggish breath of the old house, being enchanted, grew into quaint and delicate whims of music, never the same, changing every day. Never glad: uncertain, sad minors always, vexing the content of the hearer,—one inarticulate, unanswered question of pain in all, making them one. Even the vulgarest listener was troubled, hardly knowing why,—how sorry Tom's music was!

At last the time came when the door was to be opened, when some listener, not vulgar, recognizing the child as God made him, induced his master to remove him from the plantation. Something ought to be done for him; the world ought not to be cheated of this pleasure; besides—the money that could be made! So Mr. Oliver, with a kindly feeling for Tom, proud, too, of this agreeable monster which his plantation had grown, and sensible that it was a more fruitful source of revenue than tobacco-fields, set out with the boy, literally to seek their fortune.

The first exhibition of him was given, I think, in Savannah, Georgia; thence he was taken to Charleston, Richmond, to all the principal cities and towns in the Southern States.

This was in 1858. From that time until the present Tom has lived constantly an open life, petted, feted, his real talent befogged by exaggeration, and so pampered and coddled that one might suppose the only purpose was to corrupt and wear it out. For these reasons this statement is purposely guarded, restricted to plain, known facts.

No sooner had Tom been brought before the public than the pretensions put forward by his master commanded the scrutiny of both scientific and musical skeptics. His capacities were subjected to rigorous tests. Fortunately for the boy: for, so tried,—harshly, it is true, yet skilfully,—they not only bore the trial, but acknowledged the touch as skilful; every day new powers were developed, until he reached his limit, beyond which it is not probable he will ever pass. That limit, however, establishes him as an anomaly in musical science.

Physically, and in animal temperament, this negro ranks next to the lowest Guinea type: with strong appetites and gross bodily health, except in one particular, which will be mentioned hereafter. In the every-day apparent intellect, in reason or judgment, he is but one degree above an idiot,—incapable of comprehending the simplest conversation on ordinary topics, amused or enraged with trifles such as would affect a child of three years old. On the other side, his affections are alive, even vehement, delicate in their instinct as a dog's or an infant's; he will detect the step of any one dear to him in a crowd, and burst into tears, if not kindly spoken to.

His memory is so accurate that he can repeat, without the loss of a syllable, a discourse of fifteen minutes in length, of which he does not understand a word. Songs, too, in French or German, after a single hearing, he renders not only literally in words, but in notes, style, and expression. His voice, however, is discordant, and of small compass.

In music, this boy of twelve years, born blind, utterly ignorant of a note, ignorant of every phase of so-called musical science, interprets severely classical composers with a clearness of conception in which he excels, and a skill in mechanism equal to that of our second-rate artists. His concerts usually include any themes selected by the audience from the higher grades of Italian or German opera. His comprehension of the meaning of music, as a prophetic or historical voice which few souls utter and fewer understand, is clear and vivid: he renders it thus, with whatever mastery of the mere material part he may possess, fingering, dramatic effects, etc.: these are but means to him, not an end, as with most artists. One could fancy that Tom was never traitor to the intent or soul of the theme. What God or the Devil meant to say by this or that harmony, what the soul of one man cried aloud to another in it, this boy knows, and is to that a faithful witness. His deaf, uninstructed soul has never been tampered with by art-critics who know the body well enough of music, but nothing of the living creature within. The world is full of these vulgar souls that palter with eternal Nature and the eternal Arts, blind to the Word who dwells among us therein. Tom, or the dæmon in Tom, was not one of them.

With regard to his command of the instrument, two points have been especially noted by musicians: the unusual frequency of occurrence of *tours de force* in his playing, and the scientific precision of his manner of touch. For example, in a progression of augmented chords, his mode of fingering is invariably that of the schools, not that which would seem most natural to a blind child never taught to place a finger. Even when seated with his back to the piano, and made to play in that position, (a favorite feat in his concerts,) the touch is always scientifically accurate.

The peculiar power which Tom possesses, however, is one which requires no scientific knowledge of music in his audiences to appreciate. Placed at the instrument with any musician, he plays a perfect bass accompaniment to the treble of music *heard for the first time as he plays*. Then taking the seat vacated by the other performer, he instantly gives the entire piece, intact in brilliancy and symmetry, not a note lost or misplaced. The selections of music by which this power of Tom's was tested, two years ago, were sometimes fourteen and sixteen pages in length; on one occasion, at an exhibition at the White House, after a long concert, he was tried with two pieces, — one thirteen, the other twenty pages long, and was successful.

We know of no parallel case to this in musical history. Grimm tells us, as one of the most remarkable manifestations of Mozart's infant genius, that at the age of nine he was required to give an accompaniment to an aria which he had never heard before, and without notes. There were false accords in the first attempt, he acknowledges; but the second was pure. When the music to which Tom plays *secondo* is strictly classical, he sometimes balks for an instant in passages; to do otherwise would argue a creative power equal to that of the master composers; but when any chordant harmony runs through it, (on which the glowing negro soul can seize, you know,) there are no "false accords," as with the infant Mozart. I wish to draw especial attention to this power of the boy, not only because it is, so far as I know, unmatched in the development of any musical talent, but because, considered in the context of his entire intellectual structure, it involves a curious problem. The mere repetition of music heard but once, even when, as in Tom's case, it is given with such incredible fidelity, and after the lapse of years, demands only a command of mechanical skill, and an abnormal condition of the power of memory; but to play *secondo* to music never heard or seen implies the comprehension of the full drift of the symphony in its current,—a capacity to creat, in short. Yet such attempts as Tom has made to dictate music for publication do not sustain any such inference. They are only a few light marches, gallops, etc., simple and plaintive enough, but with easily detected traces of remembered harmonies: very different from the strange, weird improvisations of every day. One would fancy that the mere attempt to bring this mysterious genius within him in bodily presence before the outer world woke, too, the idiotic nature to utter its reproachful, unable cry. Nor is this the only bar by which poor Tom's soul is put in mind of its foul bestial prison. After any too prolonged effort, such as those I have alluded to, his whole bodily frame gives way, and a complete exhaustion of the brain follows, accompanied with epileptic spasms. The trial at the White House, mentioned before, was successful, but was followed by days of illness.

Being a slave, Tom never was taken into a Free State; for the same reason his master refused advantageous offers from European managers. The highest points North at which his concerts were given were Baltimore and the upper Virginia towns. I heard him sometime in 1860. He remained a week or two in the town, playing every night.

The concerts were unique enough. They were given in a great barn of a room, gaudy with hot, soot-stained frescoes, chandeliers, walls splotched with gilt. The audience was large, always; such as a provincial town affords: not the purest bench of musical criticism before which to bring poor Tom. Beaux and belles, siftings of old country families, whose grandfathers trapped and traded and married with the Indians,—the savage thickening of whose blood told itself in high cheek-bones, flashing jewelry, champagne-bibbing, a comprehension of the tom-tom music of schottisches and polkas; money-made men and their wives, cooped up by respectability, taking concerts when they were given in town, taking the White Sulphur or Cape May in summer, taking beef for dinner, taking the pork-trade in winter,—*toute la vie en programme*; the *débris* of a town, the roughs, the boys, school-children,—Tom was nearly as well worth a quarter as the negro-minstrels; here and there a pair of reserved, home-sick eyes, a peculiar, reticent face, some whey-skinned ward-teacher's, perhaps, or some German cobbler's, but hints of a hungry soul, to whom Beethoven and Mendelssohn knew how to preach an unerring gospel. The stage was broad, planked, with a drop-curtain behind,—the Doge marrying the sea, I believe; in front, a piano and chair.

Presently, Mr. Oliver, a well-natured looking man, (one thought of that,) came forward, leading and coaxing along a little black boy, dressed in white linen, somewhat fat and stubborn in build. Tom was not in a good humor that night; the evening before had refused to play altogether; so his master perspired anxiously before he could get him placed in rule before the audience, and repeat his own little speech, which sounded like a Georgia after-dinner gossip. The boy's head, as I said, rested on his back, his mouth wide open constantly; his great blubber lips and shining teeth, therefore, were all you saw when he faced you. He required to be petted and bought like any other weak-minded child. The concert was a mixture of music, whining, coaxing, and promised candy and cake.

He seated himself at last before the piano, a full half-yard distant, stretching out his arms full-length, like an ape clawing for food,—his feet, when not on the pedals, squirming and twisting incessantly,—answering some joke of his master's with a loud "Yha! yha!" Nothing indexes the brain like the laugh; this was idiotic.

"Now, Tom, boy, something we like from Verdi."

The head fell farther back, the claws began to work, and those of his harmonies which you would have chosen as the purest exponents of passion began to float through the room. Selections from Weber, Beethoven, and others whom I have forgotten, followed. At the close of each piece, Tom, without waiting for the audience, would himself applaud violently, kicking, pounding his hands together, turning always to his master for the approving pat on the head. Songs, recitations such as I have described, filled up the first part of the evening; then a musician from the audience went upon the stage to put the boy's powers to the final test. Songs and intricate symphonies were given, which it was most improbable the boy could ever have heard; he remained standing, utterly motionless, until they were finished, and for a moment or two after,—then, seating himself, gave them without the break of a note. Others followed, more difficult, in which he played the bass accompaniment in the manner I have described, repeating instantly the treble. The child looked dull, wearied, during this part of the trial, and his master, perceiving it, announced the exhibition closed, when the musician (who was a citizen of the town, by-the-way) drew out a thick roll of score, which he explained to be a Fantasia of his own composition, never published.

"*This* it was impossible the boy could have heard; there could be no trick of memory in this; and on this trial," triumphantly, "Tom would fail."

The manuscript was some fourteen pages long,—variations on an inanimate theme. Mr. Oliver refused to submit the boy's brain to so cruel a test; some of the audience, even, interfered; but the musician insisted, and took his place. Tom sat beside him,—his head rolling nervously from side to side,—struck the opening cadence; and then, from the first note to the last, gave the *secondo* triumphantly. Jumping up, he fairly shoved the man from his seat, and proceeded to play the treble with more brilliancy and power than its composer. When he struck the last octave, he sprang up, yelling with delight:—

"Um 's got him, Massa! um 's got him!" cheering and rolling about the stage.

The cheers of the audience—for the boys especially did not wait to clap—excited him the more. It was an hour before his master could quiet his hysteric agitation.

That feature of the concerts which was the most painful I have not touched upon: the moments when his master was talking, and Tom was left to himself,—when a weary despair seemed to settled down on the distorted face, and the stubby little black fingers, wandering over the keys, spoke for Tom's own caged soul within. Never, by any chance, a merry, childish laugh of music in the broken cadences; tender or wild, a defiant outcry, a tired sigh breaking down into silence. Whatever wearied voice it took, the same bitter, hopeless soul spoke through all: "Bless me, even me, also, O my Father!" A something that took all the pain and pathos of the world into its weak, pitiful cry.

Some beautiful caged spirit, one could not but know, struggled for breath under that brutal form and idiotic brain. I wonder when it will be free. Not in this life: the bars are too heavy.

You cannot help Tom, either; all the war is between you. He was in Richmond in May. But (do you hate the moral to a story?) in your own kitchen, in your own back-alley, there are spirits as beautiful, caged in forms as bestial, that you *could* set free, if you pleased. Don't call it bad taste in me to speak for them. You know they are more to be pitied than Tom,—for they are dumb.

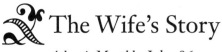
The Wife's Story

Atlantic Monthly, July 1864

I will tell you the story of my life, since you ask it; for, though the meaning of the life of any woman of my character would be the same, I believe, the facts of mine, being sharp and compressed, may make it, perhaps, more apparent. It will be enough for me to give you the history of one day, — that of our first coming to Newport; for it seems to me as if it held and spoke out plainly whatever gist and significance there was in all the years for me. I know many people hold the theory, that once in every life God puts the stuff of which He has made the man or woman to the test, gives the soul a chance of a conscious fight with that other Power to win or lose itself, once for all. I do not know: it seems but just that one should be so left, untrammelled, to choose between heaven and hell: but who can shake off trammels, — make themselves naked of their birth and education? I know on that day when the face of my fate changed, I myself was conscious of no inward master-struggle: the great Life above and Life below pressed no closer on me, seemed to wait on no word of mine. It was a busy, vulgar day enough: each passing moment occupied me thoroughly. I did not look through them for either God or Death; and as for the deed I did, I had been drifting to that all my life: it began when I was a pampered, thin-blooded baby, learning the alphabet from blocks on my mother's lap; then years followed, succulent to satiety for my hungry brain and stimulated tastes; a taint of hereditary selfishness played its part, and so the end came. Yet I know that on that day I entered the gate through which there is no returning: for, believe me, there are such ways and gates in life; every day, I see more clearly how far and how immovably the paths into those other worlds abut into this, and I know that I, for one, have gone in, and the door is closed behind me. There is no going back for me into that long-ago time. Only He who led me here knows how humbly and through what pain I dared to believe this, and dare to believe that He did lead me, — that it was by no giddy, blear-sighted free-will of my own that I arrived where I stand to-day.

It was about eighteen months after my marriage that we came to Newport. But let me go back a few weeks to one evening when my husband first told me of the failure of the house in which his property was invested; for it was then, I think, that the terror and the temptation which had beset my married life first took a definite shape and hold on me.

It was a cool September evening, I remember: a saffronish umber stain behind the low Hudson hills all that was left of the day's fresh and harvest-scented heat; the trails of black smoke from the boats against the sky, the close-shut cottages on the other shore, the very red cows coming slowly up from the meadow-pool, looking lonesome and cold in the sharp, blue air. In the library, however, there was a glow of warmth and light, as usual where Doctor Manning sat. He had been opening the evening's mail, and laid the last letter on the table, taking off his glasses in his slow, deliberate way.

"It is as we feared," turning to me. "It's quite gone, Hester, quite. I'll have to begin at the beginning again. It would have been better I had not trusted the whole to Knopps,—yes."

I said nothing: the news was not altogether unexpected. He took off his wig, and rubbed his head slowly, his eyes fixed on my face with some anxious, steady inquiry, which his tones did not express.

"I'll go back to Newport. Rob's there. I'll get a school again. You did not know I taught there when I was a young man?"

"No."

I knew nothing of my husband's youth. Miss Monchard, his ward, who was in the room, did, however; and after waiting for me a moment to go on, she said, cheerfully,—

"The boys will be men now, Sir. Friends ready waiting. And different sort of friends from any we have here, eh?"

He laughed.

"Yes, Jacky, you're right. Yes. They've all turned out well, even those Arndts. Jim Arndt used to trot you on his knee on the school-house steps, when you were a baby. But he *was* a wild chap. He's in the sugar-trade, Rob writes me. But they'll always be boys to me, Jacky,—boys."

His head dropped, with a smile still on his mouth, and he began fingering his scanty beard, as was his habit in his fits of silent musing. Jacqueline looked at him satisfied, then turned to me. I do not know what she saw upon my face, but she turned hastily away.

"It's a town with a real character of its own, Newport, Mrs. Manning," —trying to make her coarse bass voice gentle. "You'll understand it better than I. New-York houses, now, even these on the Hudson, hint at nothing but a satisfied animal necessity. But there, with the queer dead streets, like a bit of the old-time world, and the big salt sea"— She began to stammer, as usual, and grow confused. "It's like looking out of some far-gone, drowsy old day of the Colonies, and yet feeling life and eternity fresh and near to you."

I only smiled civilly, by way of answer. Jacqueline always tried me. She was Western-born, I a New-Englander; and every trait about her, from the freedom with which she hurled out her opinions to the very setting-down of her broad foot, jarred on me as a something boorish and reckless. Her face grew red now.

"I don't say what I want exactly," she hesitated. "I only hoped you'd like the town, that it would reconcile— There's crabs there," desperately turning to Teddy, who was playing a furtive game of marbles under the table, and grabbing him by the foot. "Come here till I tell you about the crabs."

I remember that I got up and went out of the low window on to the porch, looking down at the quiet dun shadows and the slope of yellowed grass leading to the river, while Jacky and the boy kept up a hurly-burly conversation about soldier-crabs that tore each other's legs off, and purple and pink sea-roses that ate raw meat, and sea-spiders like specks of blood in the rocks. My husband laughed once or twice, helping Jacky out with her natural history. I think it was the sound of that cheery, mellow laugh of his that fermented every bitter drop in my heart, and brought clearly before me for the first time the idea of the course which I afterwards followed. I thrust it back then, as if it had been a sneer of the Devil's at all I held good and pure. What was there in the world good and pure for me but the man sitting yonder, and the thought that I was his wife? And yet— I had an unquiet brain, of moderate power, perhaps, but which had been forced and harried and dragged into exertion every moment of my life, according to the custom with women in the States from which I came. Every meanest hint of a talent in me had been nursed, every taste purged, by the rules of my father's clique of friends. The chance of this was all over,—had been escaping since my marriage-day. Now I clearly saw the life opening before me. What would taste or talent be worth in the coarse struggle we were about to begin for bread and butter? "Surely, we have lost something beyond money," I thought, looking behind into the room, where my husband was quietly going back to the Arndts in quest of food for reflection, and Jacky prosed on about sea-anemones. I caught a glimpse of my sallow face in the mirror: it was full of a fierce disgust. Was their indifference to this loss a mere torpid ignorance of the actual brain- and soul-wants it would bring on us, or did they really look at life and accept its hard circumstances from some strange standing-ground of which I knew nothing? I had not become acclimated to the atmosphere of my husband's family in the year and a half that I had been his wife. He had been married before; there were five children, beginning at Robert, the young preacher at Newport, and ending with Teddy, beating the drum with his fists yonder on the table; all of them, like their father, Western-born, with big, square-built frames, and grave, downright-looking faces; simple-hearted, and much given, the whole party, to bursts of hearty laughter, and a habit of perpetually joking with each other. There might be more in them than this, but I had not found it: I doubted much if it were worth the finding. I came from a town in Massachusetts, where, as in most New-England villages, there was more mental power than was needed for the work that was to be done, and which reacted constantly on itself in a way which my husband called unwholesome; it was no wonder, therefore, that these people seemed to me but clogs of flesh, the mere hands by which the manual work of the world's progress was to be accomplished. I had hinted this to Doctor Manning one day, but he only replied by the dry, sad smile with which it had become his habit of late to listen to my speculations. It had cost me no pain thus to label and set aside his children: but for himself it was different; he was my husband. He was the only thing in the world which I had never weighed and valued to estimate how much it was worth to me: some feeling I could not define had kept me from it until now. But I did it that evening: I remember how the cool river-air blew in the window-curtain, and I held it back, looking steadily in at the thick-set, middle-aged figure of the man sitting there, in the lamp-light, dressed in rough gray: peering at the leather-colored skin, the nervous features of the square face, at the scanty fringe of iron-gray whisker, and the curly wig which he had bought after we were married, thinking to please me, at the brown eyes, with the gentle reticent look in them belonging to a man or beast who is thorough "game"; taking the whole countenance as the metre of the man; going sharply over the salient points of our life together, measuring myself by him, as if to know—what? to know what it would cost me to lose him. God be merciful to me, what thought was this? Oh, the wrench in heart and brain that came then! A man who has done a murder may feel as I did while I stood for the next half-hour looking at the red lights of the boats going up and down the Hudson, in the darkening fog.

After a while Teddy came waddling out on the porch, in his usual uncouth fashion, and began pulling at my cape.

"You're getting cold, mother. Come in. Come!"

I remember how I choked as I tried to answer him, and, patting his gilt-buttoned coat, took the fat chapped little hands in mine, kissing them at last. I was so hungry for affection that night! I would have clung to a dog that had been kind to me. I thought of the first day Doctor Manning had brought him to me, in this same comical little jacket, by the way, and the strangely tender tone in which he had said,—"This is your mother, boy. He's as rough as a bear, Hetty, but he won't give you trouble or pain. Nothing shall give you pain, if I"— Then he stopped. I never heard that man make a promise. If he had come out instead of Teddy on the porch that night, and had spoken once in the old tone, calling me "Hetty," God knows how different all that came after would have been. The motherless boy, holding himself up by my knees, was more sturdy than I that night, and self-reliant: never could have known, in his most helpless baby-days, the need with which I, an adult woman, craved a cheering word, and a little petting.

Jacqueline came behind me and pinned a woollen shawl around my neck, patting my shoulders in her cozy, comfortable fashion.

"None of your dark river-fogs at Newport," she laughed. "The sea-air has the sweep of half the world to gather cold and freshness in, and it makes even your bones alive. Your very sleep is twice as much sleep there as anywhere else."

Jacky's rough voice was like the cuckoo's: it always prophesied pleasant weather. She went in again now, and sat down on her little sewing-chair. The low, rolling fogs outside, and the sharp September wind rattling the bare branches of the orchard-trees and the bushes on the lawn, only made the solid home-look of comfort within warmer and brighter. There was a wood-fire kindled on the library-hearth, and its glow picked out red flushes of light on the heavy brown curtains, and the white bust of Psyche,[1] and a chubby plaster angel looking down. Jacky, rocking and sewing, her red mouth pursed up, half whistling, suited the picture, somehow, I could not but feel, mere lump and matter though she might be. There was something fresh and spicy about her. I never had been impressed so justly by her as on that night. Rough, perhaps, but it was a pure rough-ness: everything about the girl had been clean since she was born, you felt, from the paint of the house where she lived to the prayer her nurse had taught her. Her skin was white and ruddy, her blue eyes clear and full of honesty, her brown curls crisp and unoiled. She could not reason, maybe; but she was straightforward and comfortable: every bone in her roly-poly little figure forgot to be a bone, and went into easy cushions of dimpled flesh. If ever Jacky died and went into a more spiritual world, she would be sure to take with her much of the warmth and spring and vigor of this. She had drawn her chair close to Doctor Manning's, where the flickering light touched the soft woollen folds of her dress and the bit of crimson ribbon at her throat. He liked bright colors, like most men of his age. It was a pretty picture.

I turned and looked down at the river again, shivering,—trying to think of the place and all we were leaving. I did not wonder that it cost the others little to give up the house: it meant but little to them. Doctor Manning had bought it just before we were married, being then a square chocolate-colored farm-house, and we had worked our own whims on it to make it into a home, thrusting out a stout-pillared big porch at one side, and one or two snug little bay-windows from my sewing-room. There was a sunny slope of clover down to the river, a dusky old apple and plum orchard at the left, and Mary's kitchen-garden on the right, with a purblind old pea-cock strutting through the paths, showing its green and gold. Not much in all this: nothing to please Jacky's artist and poet sense, if she had any. But— I held on to the porch-railings now, drumming with my fingers, as I thought of it. It was all the childhood *I* ever had known. He brought me there the day we were married, and until August—six months—we had been there alone. I could hear his old nag Tinder neighing now, in the stable where we used to go every evening to feed and rub him down: for I went with Daniel, as I called him, then, everywhere, even to consult his mason or farm-hands. He used to stand joking with them a minute after the business was over, in an unwonted fashion for him, and then scramble into the buggy beside me, and drive off, his fresh, bright eye turned to the landscape as if enjoying it for the first time.

"God bless you, Hetty!" he used to say, "this is putting new blood into my veins."

Generally, in those long rides, I used to succeed in coaxing him imperceptibly back to talk of his life in South America,—not only that I liked to hear this new phase of wild adventuring life, but my own blood would glow and freshen to see the fierce dare-devil look come back into the eye, and the shut teeth of the grave, laconic old Doctor. People did not know the man I had married,—no; and I would draw in closer to his shaggy coat, and spur him on to his years of trading in the West, and later in this State. He had a curious epigrammatic way of talking that I have noticed in a less degree in many Western men: coming at the marrow and meaning of a scene or person in his narration with a sheer subtilized common-sense, a tough appreciation of fact beyond theory, and of its deeper, juster significance, and a dramatic aptness for expression. Added to all this, my husband's life had been compacted, crowded with incident; it had sad-dened and silenced his nature abnormally; this was the first break: a going back to what he might have been, such as his children were now.

"I never talked to any one before, Hetty," he said thoughtfully once, as we were driving along, after a few moments' silence. "I feel as if I had got breath, this late in the day, that I never expected, for whatever thought was in me,—and—whatever love."

He turned away his face, crimson at this. He was as strangely reticent and tender on some points as a woman. So seldom he put his love into words! That time I remember how the tears suddenly blinded me, when I heard him, and my fingers grew unsteady, holding the reins. I was so happy and proud. But I said nothing: he would not have liked it.

Of one time in his life Doctor Manning had never talked to me: of his earlier youth; when he was married before. He was not a man of whom you could ask questions; yet I had hinted an inquiry once or twice in his presence, but only by a change of color and a strange vague restlessness had he shown that he understood my drift of meaning. Soon after that, his eldest son, Robert, came to see his father's new wife, and stayed with us a day or two. He was a short, thickly built young man, with heavy jaws and black hair and eyes,—keen eyes, I soon felt, that were weighing and analyzing me as justly, but more shrewdly than ever his father had done. The night before he went away he came up to the porch-step where I sat, and said abruptly,—

"I am satisfied, and happy to go now."

"I am glad of that," I said earnestly; for the tenderness of the son to the father had touched me.

"Yes. You cannot know the dread I had of seeing you. I knew the risk he ran in laying his happiness in any woman's hands at his hour of life. But it was hard he never should know a home and love like other men,"— his voice unsteady, and with an appealing look.

"He never shall need it, I said, quietly.

"You think not?"—his eyes on the ground. "At all events,"—after a pause,—"he is resting like a child now: it will not be easy to startle him to any harsh reality, and," looking up, "I hope God may deal with you, Mrs. Manning, as you deal with my father. Forgive me," as I began to speak, "you do not know what this is to me. It makes me rough, I know. I never yet have forgiven the woman that"— His mother? He caught the look, stopped, pushed his hair back, caught his breath. "One thing let me say," after a moment's silence. "You do not know my father. If he wakens to find his wife is not what he thinks her, it will be too late for me to warn you then. He has been hurt sore and deeply in his life. Your chance is but once."

I did not reply to Robert Manning, nor was I offended: there was too much solemnity in his coarseness. The man's affection for his father was as part of his life-blood, I believed.

My husband came to me when he saw Robert go, and loosened my hands from my face. I clung to him as I never did before.

"What is this hurt he talks of in your life, Daniel? Will I be enough to take it out? Will I?"

He laughed, a low, constrained laugh, holding my shoulders as if I were a bit of a child.

"God knows you are enough, Hetty. I never thought He'd send me this. Rob has been talking to you? He"—

"He is bitter."

"He loves me,—poor Rob!"

"Tell me of those people that hurt you, as he says."

It was a prurient, morbid curiosity that had seized me. A sort of shiver ran over his frame.

"Eh, what, Hetty?"—in a low voice. "Let that go, let that go,"—standing silent a moment, looking down. "Why would we bring them back, and hack over the old dead faults? Had *she* no pain to bear? We could n't find that out to speak for her. But God knows it."

I might have known how my question would have ended; for, always, he covered over the ill-doing of others with a nervous haste, with the charity of a man himself sharply sensitive to pain.

"It is healthful to go back to past pain," I said, half dissatisfied.

"Is it so?"—doubtfully, as he turned away with me. "I don't know, child. Now and then He has to punish us, or cut out a cancer maybe. But for going back to gloat over the cure or the whip-lash— No; it will keep us busy enough to find good air and food, every minute for itself"; and, with a ruddy, genial smile, he had stooped and kissed my forehead.

A year had passed since that night. I was standing on the same porch, but I was alone now. My husband sat a few feet from me in his old easy-chair, but no gulf could have parted us so wide and deeply. Robert Manning had said I would have but one chance. Well, I had had it, and it was gone. So I stood there, looking quietly at him and Jacky and the boy. The child had pushed his father's wig off, and his bare head with its thin iron-gray hair fell forward on his breast, resting on Teddy's sleeping cheek. I saw now how broad and sad the forehead was,—the quiet dignity on the whole face. Yet it had been such a simple-hearted thing to do,— to buy that wig to please me! One of those little follies the like of which would never come again.

I went in and sat down as usual, apart, throwing aside from my neck the shawl which Jacky had pinned there, loathing anything she had touched, so real and sharp was the thought about her become, as if the evening's fog and cold had lent it a venomous life. They had made a quiet cozy picture before, which had bitterly brought back our first married days, but it was broken up now. The Doctor's three boys came lumbering in, with muddy shoes, game-bags, and the usual fiery faces and loud jokes after their day's sport. Jacky threw down her sewing, and went out to see the squirrels drawn, and the Doctor smoothed Teddy's hair, looking after them with a pleased smile. One of the rarest sparkles of our daily life! It was a year since Doctor Manning had brought his children home. They filled the house. Musing on the past now, and trying to look at that year calmly, while I sat by the fire, my husband would fade back in the picture into an unmeaning lay-figure. Was this my fault? Could I help it, if God had made me with a different, clearer insight into life and its uses than these people with their sound beef and muscle, their uncouth rejoicing in being alive? There was work enough in them: a broad-fisted grappling with the day's task or obstacle, a drinking of its pain or success into their slow brains, but nowhere the metre to note the soul's changes, nor the eye to speculate on them. "No," my husband had said to me one day, "we Western people have the mass of this country's appointed work to do, so we are content that God should underlie the hypotheses. We waste no strength in guesses at the reason why."

I remember how intolerably the days of that year dragged even in memory, as I sat there trying to judge them fairly,—how other years of my life thrust them aside, persistently, as foreign, alien to me. These others were to me home,—the thoughts that had held me nearest the divine life: I went back to them, my eyes wet, and my heart sick under my weak lungs. The little village of Concord, away up yonder, where I was born,—I was glad to have been born there: thinking how man not only had learned there to stand self-poised and found himself God, but Nature herself seemed there to stop and reflect on her own beauty, and so root deeper in the inner centre. The slow-dropping river, the thoughtful hills, the very dust-colored fern that covers its fields, which might grow in Hades, so breathless and crisp it is, came back to me with a glamour of quiet that night. The soul had space to grow there! remembering how its doors of thought stood wider open to welcome truth than anywhere else on earth. "The only object in life is to grow." It was my father's,—Margaret Fuller's motto. I had been nursed on it, I might say. There had been a time when I had dreamed of attaining Margaret's stature; and as I thought of that, some old subtle flame stirred in me with a keen delight. New to me, almost; for, since my baby was born, my soul as well as my body had been weak and nauseated. It had been so sharp a disappointment! I had intended my child should be reared in New England: what I had lacked in gifts and opportunities he should possess: there was not a step of his progress which I had not mapped out. But the child was a girl, a weazen-faced little mortal, crying night and day like any other animal. It was an animal, wearing out in me the strength needed by-and-by for its mental training. I sent it to a nurse in the country. Her father had met the woman carrying it out to the wagon, and took it in his arms. "Eh? eh? is it so, little lass?" I heard him say. For days after that he looked paler, and his face had a quiet, settled look, as if he had tested the world and was done with it. The days of Tinder and the paddock and the drives were long gone then. I do not remember that after this he ever called me Hetty. But he was cheerful as ever with the boys, and, the week after, Jacky came.

Why did I think of all this now? Some latent, unconscious jar of thought brought suddenly before me a scene of many years before, a damp spring morning in Paris, when I had gone to Rosa Bonheur's[2] studio, just out of the city, to see her "Horse-Fair": the moist smell of jonquils; the drifting light clouds above the Seine, like patches of wool; but most, the peculiar life that seemed to impregnate the place itself, holding her, as it were, to her own precise niche and work in the world, — the sharply managed lights, the skins, trappings, her disguises on the walls, the stables outside, and the finished work before us, instinct with vigor and an observation as patient as keen. I remembered how some one had quoted her as saying, "Any woman can be a wife or mother, but this is my work alone."

I, too, had my gift: but one. But again the quick shiver of ecstasy ran through me; — it was my power, my wand with which to touch the world, my *"Vollmachtsbrief zum Glücke"*:[3] was I to give it unused back to God? I could sing: not that only; I could compose music, — the highest soul-utterance. I remember clutching my hands up to my throat, as if holding safe the power that should release me, suffer me to grow again, and looking across the oil-lamp on the table at my husband. I *had* been called, then, — set apart to a mission; it was a true atom of the creative power that had fired my brain; my birth had placed me on a fitting plane of self-development, and I had thrust it all aside — for what? A mess of weakest pottage, — a little love, silly rides behind Tinker, petting and paltering such as other women's souls grew imbecile without. It was the consciousness of this that had grown slowly on me in the year just gone; I had put my husband from me day by day because of it; it had reached its intolerable climax to-night. Well, it was fact: no fancy. My nature was differently built from others: I could look now at my husband, and see the naked truth about us both. Two middle-aged people, with inharmonious intellects: tastes and habits jarring at every step, clenched together only by faith in a vague whim or fever of the blood called love. Better apart: we were too old for fevers. If I remained with Doctor Manning, my *rôle* was outlined plain to the end: years of cooking, stitching, scraping together of cents: it was the fate of thousands of married women without means, to grovel every year nearer the animal life, to grow niggardly and common. Better apart.

As I thought that, he laid Teddy down, and came towards me, — the usual uncertain, anxious half-smile on his face with which he regarded me.

"I am sure they will all like my old home, now, lads and all. I'm glad of that. Sure of all but you, Hester. But you say nothing."

"The loss is great."

I shut my lips firmly, and leaned back, for he had put his hard hand gently on my shoulder. It made me turn faint, with some weakness that must have come down to me from my infant days, so meaningless was it. I did not hear his answer; for with the same passionate feebleness I caught the sleeve of his dressing-gown in my fingers, and began smoothing it. It was the first thing I had ever made for him. I remembered how proud I was the evening he put it on. He was looking down steadily at me with his grave, reasonable eyes, and speaking when I looked up.

"I have been knocked up and down so perpetually in my own life: that may be the reason the change did not trouble me as it ought. It makes one feel as if outside matters were but just the tithes of mint and cumin, — a hurly-burly like that which I've lived in. I am sorry. I thought you would grieve least of all, Hester. You are stronger-brained than we Mannings, eh? I was sure the life meant so much more to you than food or raiment."

"What do you mean by the life? Have I found it here, Daniel?"

"No, Hester?"

"I want work fit for me," I said, almost fiercely. "God made me for a good, high purpose."

"I know," cheerfully. "We 'll find it, dear: no man's work is kept back from him. We 'll find it together."

But under the cheerfulness there was a sad quiet, as of one who has lost something forever, and tries to hide the loss from himself. There was a moment's silence, then I got up, and pushed him down into my chair. I took the gray head in my arms, leaned it on my shoulder, held the thin bits of hair in my hand.

"Why, why, child!"

"Call me Hetty, Daniel. I'd like to think that name belonged to me yet."

"Surely, dear. Why! but—this is just the old times again, Hetty! You'll be bringing me my slippers again."

"Yes, I will."

I went to the cupboard, and brought them, sitting down on the floor as he put them on. Another of the old foolish tricks gone long ago. There was a look on his face which had not been there this many a day. He had such a credulous heart, so easy to waken into happiness. I took his wrist in my bony hands, to raise myself; the muscles were like steel, the cording veins throbbing with health; there was an indescribable rest in the touch.

"Daniel," I said, looking him full in the face, "I'd like to have no mission in God's world. I'd like to give up my soul, and forget everything but you."

He did not answer. I think now that he understood me then and before far better than I dreamed. He only put his hand on mine with an unutterable tenderness. I could read nothing on his face but a grave common-sense. Presently he unbuttoned my sleeves and the close collar about my throat to let the cool damp blow on me.

"Yes," I said, "it 's a fever, Daniel. In the blood. That is all,—with me. I decided that long ago. It will not last long." And I laughed.

"Come," he said, quietly. "I am going to write to Rob now, about our plans. You can help me."

I followed him, and sat down by the table. "There is something in the man stronger than the woman," I thought, doggedly, "inside of blood and muscle." Yet the very galling of that consciousness set me more firmly in the mind to be again free.

A month after that we came to Newport. It was not an idle month. Jacky had proposed a review of my husband's and his sons' clothes, and day after day I had sat by the window looking out on the sluggish Hudson, a hank of patent thread about my neck, stitching patches on the stiff, half-worn trousers. "It becomes us to take care of the pence now," she would say, and go on with her everlasting whistling, La-la. It rasped on my brain like the chirp of the partridge outside in the cedar-hedge. When she would go out of the room sometimes, I would hold my hand to my head, and wonder if it was for this in reality God had made me.

Yet I had my own secret. The work of my life, before I was married, had been the score of an opera. I got it out now by stealth, at night, putting my pen to it here and there, with the controlled fever with which a man might lay his hand on a dear dead face, if he knew the touch would bring it back to life. Was there any waking that dead life of mine? At that time, in New

York, M. Vaux was trying the experiment of an English opera in one of the minor theatres. I sent the score to him. It did not trouble me, that, if produced, its first effect would be tried on an uncultured caste of hearers: if the leaven was pure, what matter where it began to work? and no poet or artist was ever more sincere in the belief that the divine power spoke through him than I. I thought, that, if I remained with Doctor Manning as his wife, this venture mattered little: if I shook myself free, and, taking up my mission, came before the public as a singer, it would open the way for me. For my plan had grown defined and practical to me now.

M. Vaux had left his family at Newport after the season was over. I was to meet him there when we went down, and hear his decision on the score. I met him one day on Broadway, and hinted my vague desire of making my voice also available.

"To sing? did you say sing, Mrs. Manning? go on the stage?"—pawing his chin with one hand.

He was a short, puffy little man, with a bullet head at half-cock in the air, producing a general effect of nostrils on you.

"Sing, eh?" he mumbled, once or twice.

Before this I had been Mrs. Manning, throwing off an opera-score as a careless whim, one of the class to whom he and his like presented arms: he surveyed me now with the eye of a stock-raiser buying a new mule, and set the next evening as the time when I should "drop in at his house and give him a trill or two. —Keeping dark before the old man yet, eh?" with a wink. I went in the next day, but he declined to pronounce judgment until we came to Newport.

I remember my husband met me at the gate when I returned, and lifted me from the little pony-carriage.

"I'm so glad my girl is taking her drives again,"—his face in a glow,— "coming back with the old red cheeks, too. They're a sort of hint of all the good years coming. We 're far off from being old people yet, Hetty." And so went beside me slowly up the garden-walk, his hands clasped behind him, stopping to look now and then at his favorite purple and crimson hollyhocks.

I looked at him askance, as we went through the evening shadows. There was something grand in the quiet of the face, growing old with the depth of sadness and endurance subdued in it: the kindly smile over all. I had brought the smile there. But it would not be for long: and I remember how the stalk of gilly-flower I held snapped in my hand, and its spicy odor made me throw it down. I have loathed it ever since. Was my life to be wasted in calling a smile to an old man's face? My husband and M. Vaux were different men; but, on the other side, they were gates to me of different lives: here, a sordid slavery of work; there,—something in me glowed warm and triumphant,—fame and an accomplished deed in life!

Surely these mawkish home-ties were fast loosing their hold on me, I thought, as we went in. I asked no questions as to my husband's plans; no one spoke to me of them. In the few days before our departure I roped up chairs, packed china in straw, sorted clothes into trunks, working harder than the others, and then creeping off alone would hum an air from the score, thanking God for giving me this thoroughly pure, holy message to utter in the world. It was the redemption of my soul from these vulgar taints: it was a sort of mortgage I held on the eternal truth and life. Yet, when no one told me of their plans, when I saw they all held some secret back from me, watching me constantly and furtively, when Jacky buzzed about my husband all day, whispering, laughing, cooking his favorite omelet for breakfast, bringing his slippers at night,—it was like so many sharp stings through stupor. "It's the woman's flesh of me!" I used to say bitterly, when I would have been glad to meanly creep after them, to cuddle Teddy up in my arms, or to lean my head on his father's knees. "I can live it down. I have 'a manly soul.'" For it was part of my creed that Nature was something given us to be lived down in fulfilling our mission.

We went by the evening's boat to Newport. I saw M. Vaux in the outer cabin, as we passed through: he nodded familiarly when Doctor Manning's back was turned, without removing his cigar.

It was stifling below, with the smell of frying meat and numerous breaths. We went on deck, my husband drawing a bench around to shelter me from the keen wind across the bow, and wrapping my flannel hood closer to my throat when we drifted out within scent of salt water. It was a night that waited and listened: the sea silent and threatening, a few yellow, dogged, low breakers running in at long intervals; now and then a rasping gurgle of wind from shore, as of one who held his breath; some thin, brown clouds ragged along the edges of the cold sky, ready for flight.

I sat there thinking how well the meaning of the sea suited my soul that night. It was no work of God's praising Him continually: it was the eternal protest and outcry against Fate,—chained, helpless, unappealing. Let the mountains and the sunshine and the green fields chant an anthem, if they would; but for this solitary sea, with its inarticulate cry, surely all the pain and impatience of the world's six thousand years had gone down and found a voice in that. Having thus cleared to myself the significance of the sea in Nature, I was trying to define its exact effect upon my own temperament, (a favorite mental exercise of my father's,) when my husband touched my shoulder.

"I'll go down and smoke a bit, Hetty dear, and leave you with Jacky. She's as good guard as a troop of horse."

Jacky nodded vehemently once or twice from where she stood, followed him with her eyes as he went down the steps, anxiously, and then stood gravely silent. She was but a lump of "woman's flesh," that was clear, and I doubted if there was any soul inside to live it down. Her face was red and her eyes shining with the sea-wind. She had been at the stern with the boys, making a riot about the porpoises rolling under the boat; in the engine-room with Teddy; had tried to drag me to the deck-railing to watch the unsteady shimmer of some pale-blue sea-weed under the water, which the wheel threw up in silver flashes, or to see how, before the sun went down, we floated over almost motionless stretches of pale tea-colored water, holding, it seemed, little curdling pools of light far below in their depths on depths of shivering brown and dull red mosses.

"Ach-h! I 'm glad I 'm alive to-night!" she had said, gritting her teeth in her Dutch fashion.

But some new demon had possession of her brain now: she stood working with her shawl uncertainly, a trifle pale, watching me. She came to me at last, and stood balancing herself first on her heels and then her toes, biting her lip as if doubtful how to begin.

"I wish we had the baby along!" came with a gruff burst, finally. "God bless its little soul! I went out to see it on Saturday. It would do Uncle Daniel good. He needs something fresh and hearty, bread-and-butter-like, or a baby. You did not notice him this evening particularly, Mrs. Manning, eh?" anxiously.

"No."

"Nothing— Well, no matter. I'm fanciful, maybe. There's an old saying in the family about him, some Doctor's prophecy, and it makes me over-watchful, likely."

She waited for a question. I asked none. There was a dull throb of pain in my heart, but I thrust it down. The girl waited a few moments, debating with herself: I could read the struggle on her face: then she looked up straight into my eyes, her small white teeth showing determined as a steel-trap.

"It's quiet here, Mrs. Manning, and will be for a bit, and there's a story I'd like to tell you. It would do me good, if it were off my mind. Perhaps you, too," with a sharp glance.

"Go on."

She put her hand into her pocket and pulled out a broken morocco case.

"Look here. This tells the whole of the story, almost,"—holding it where the light from the cabin-window fell on it.

It was the daguerreotype of a woman: one of those faces that grow out of a torpid, cunning, sensual life; apparently marked, too, by some strange disease, the skin white, and hanging loose from the flesh. I pushed it away. Jacqueline polished it with her palm.

"She was an opium-eater, you see? The eyes have that rigid staring, like Death looking into life. You pushed it from you, Mrs. Manning?"— shutting it. "Yet I know a man who cherished that living face tenderly in his bosom for fifteen long years, and never opened his lips to say to God once that it was hard to bear: faugh!" and she flung the case into the water. "I only kept it to show you. She, the foul vampire, sucked his youth away. I think it was but the husk of life that was left him when she died;—and we are making that mean and poor enough,"—in a lower voice. "Yet that man"—more firmly—"has a stronger brain and fresher heart than you or I are fit to comprehend, Mrs. Manning. One would think God meant that the last of his life, after that gone, should be a warm Indian-summer day, opening broad and happily into the life He is keeping for him,—would you not?"

"Who is the man?"—my lips growing cold.

"Your husband."

"I thought so. You did well to tell me that story."

She looked from me, her color coming and going.

"It was hard to do it. You are an older woman than I. But I thought it was needed."

I looked up at the hard-set, chubby little face, beyond at the far yellow night-line of sea, listened to the low choke, choke, of the water in the wheels.

"I wish you would leave me. Let me be alone awhile."

She went to the other end of the deck, where she could keep me in sight. It was so dull, that throb of the water, playing some old tune that would not vary! The sea stretched out in such blank, featureless reaches!

To nestle down into this man's heart and life! To make his last years that warm Indian-summer day! I could do it! I! What utter rest there were in that!

Yet was this power within me to rot and waste? My nature, all the habit and teaching of the years gone, dragged me back, held up my Self before me, bade me look at that. A whiff of tobacco-scented breathing made me look up. M. Vaux was leaning on the deck-railing, his legs crossed, surveying me critically through his half-shut eyes.

"Well, 'm, glad of the chance t' tell you. Henz and Doctor Howe thought so well of that little thing of yours that we 've put it in rehearsal,— bring it out Monday week. 'N' 've concluded you can try the part of Marian[4] in it. Not much in that,—one aria you can make something of, but begin easy, hey?"

"I have concluded to give up that scheme, Monsieur."

"Tut! tut! No such thing. Why, you 've a master-talent,—that is, with cultivation, cultivation. A fine gift, Madam. Belongs to the public. Why," tapping his yellow teeth with his cane-head, "it's shutting up a bird in a cage, to smother a voice like yours. Must have training,—yes, yes, 'll see to that; 'n' there are tricks and bits of stage-effect; but you 'll catch 'em,—soon enough. There's other little matters," with a furtive glance at my square shoulders and bony figure, "necessary to success. But you 'll understand."

I saw how anxious the man was that I should accede to the proposal. I had not overrated my genius, then?

"If the thing's to be done, let it be done quickly. I'm going to run back to town to-morrow night, and you 'd best go with me, and go in rehearsal at once. You can break it to your people to-morrow. I'll meet you in the boat,—that is," with an unwilling hesitation, "if you decide to go."

Jacky approached us.

"I will let you know," I said; and as he walked away, the water began its dull throb, throb, again, that lasted all night long.

All night long! Other people may approach the crisis of their fate with senses and faculties all on guard and alert; but with me, although I knew the next day would witness my choice for life, I believe that heavy thud of the water was the most real thought, trying my brain beyond endurance. I tried to reason coolly in the night about M. Vaux and his scheme: both vulgar, degrading in outside appearance,—I felt that, to the quick, keenly enough; but inside lay a career, utterance for myself,—and I had been dumb and choking so long!

A beam of light from the cabin-chandelier struck just then sharply across Doctor Manning's face, where he lay asleep in his berth. There was an unusual look in it, as Jacky had said, now that I looked closely: a blueness about the mouth, and a contraction of the nostrils. Was it a hint of any secret disease, that she had looked so terrified, and even the boys had kept such a sidelong scrutiny over him all day? I sat up. If I could go to him, put my hands about his head, cling to him, let my young strength and life ooze into his to atone for all he had lost in those old days! There was passion and power of love under my stiff-muscled fingers and hard calculating brain, such as these people with their hot blood knew nothing of. It *was* passion, a weak fever of the flesh. I drew the sheet over me, and lay down again.

The morning was stiflingly hot. I remember the crowd of porters, drays, etc., jostling on the wharf: the narrow street: Monsieur passing me, as we turned into it, and muttering, "By six this afternoon I must know your decision": Robert's grave, inquiring face, when he first met his father, and saw his changed look. The rooms he had taken for us were but partially furnished, carpetless, the sun staring in through dirty windows, blue and yellow paper on the walls. He went out with Dr. Manning for a walk; the boys scattered off noisily to the sea-side. I went to work making a sort of lounge for Teddy to sleep on, out of some blocks of wood and staves of an old barrel, and so passed the time until noon. Then I sat down to mend the weekly heap of boys' socks, half-washed and leather-stained. Out of the window where I sat I looked down into the muddy back-yard of the boarding-house, where an Irishwoman was washing and gossiping with the cook cleaning fish over the ash-heap. *This* was what Life held for me now, was it? When the door was opened, a strong whiff of dinner filled the room. Two o'clock came.

"I will not go down to dinner," I said to Jacqueline, when the cracked bell rang. "I will go out and find Doctor Manning on the cliffs. I may have something to say to him."

But when she was gone, I darned on at the unclean socks. Somehow the future faced me in my work and surroundings. But I did not think of it as a whole. The actual dignity and beauty of life, God's truth itself, may have grown dim to me, behind a faint body and tired fingers; but let the hard-worked woman who is without that sin throw the first stone at me. I got up at last, folded the stockings, and put them away; then pinned on my bonnet and shawl. Teddy was sitting on the stairs, half asleep. I stopped to kiss him.

"You'll be back soon, mother?"—hugging me close about the neck.

"Good bye, Bud! Bring your father his pipe to-night, as he likes you to do,—and every night."

I strained him close to my breast again; he had a warm, honest little heart of his own; he would be such a man as his father. I gasped, set him down: I dared not kiss him after I thought of that: and went out of the hall, stumbling over the boarders' hats and greasy oil-cloth. Without, the air had that yellow stirless calm peculiar to Newport, which gives to the sea and landscape the effect of those French pictures glassed in tinted crystal. There were but few passengers on the street. I wondered if any of them held his fate in his hand as I did mine that day. Before I reached the cliffs the afternoon was passing away rapidly; the heated pavements under my feet growing cooler, and barred with long gray shadows; a sea-breeze blowing tattered sand-colored clouds inland; the bell of the steamer rang out sharply down at the quiet little wharf. In half an hour she would sail. M. Vaux was on board, awaiting me. I had but little time to spare.

I turned and crept slowly along the road to where the grassy street opened on the cliffs, and sat down on the brown rocks. I could see my husband on the sands with Robert, pacing to and fro; the scent of their cigars almost reached me where I sat. I must see him once more. The bell of the boat rang again; but I sat still, breaking off bits of the salt crust from the rock, hardly looking up to see if her steam was up. I was going. I knew she would not sail until I was on board. And I must see him again; he would call me Hetty, maybe: that would be something to remember. It was very quiet. The bare, ghastly cliffs formed a sort of crescent, on which I sat; far below, the sea rolled in, over the white sand, in heavy ashen sweeps: in one horn of the crescent the quaint old town nestled, its smoky breath sleepily giving good-night to the clear pink air; in the other stood the sullen fort, the flag flapping sharply against the sky. The picture cut itself vividly on my brain. The two black figures came slowly towards me, across the sands, seeing me at last. I would not tell him I was going: I could write from New York: I thought, my courage giving way. What a hard, just face Robert Manning had! What money I made should go to the support of my child: Robert should not think me derelict in every duty. Then I tried to get up to meet them, but leaned back more heavily on the rocks, twisting my fingers in a tuft of salt hay that grew there.

I heard Robert say something about "jaded" and "overworked," as he looked at me, throwing away his cigar; his father answered in a whisper, which made the young man's face soften, and when they came near, he called me "mother," for the first time. Into the face of the man beside him I did not look: I thought I never could look again. There was a small rip in the sleeve of his great-coat: I remember I saw it, and wondered feebly if Jacky would attend to it,—if my child, when she was a woman, would be careful and tender with her father. Meantime my husband was talking in his cheerfullest, heartiest voice.

"Coming here makes me feel as if the old boy-time had come back, Hetty. Rob and I have been planning out our new life, and the sea and the fresh air and the very houses seemed to join in the talk, and help me on as they used to do then. I'll begin all new: just as then. Only now" —

He put his hand on my shawl with a motion that had infinite meaning and affection in it. The little steamer at the wharf swayed and rocked. Her freight was nearly all on deck: I had but a few moments more, — that is, if I meant to be free.

"We are going down to the hotel for a few minutes, — business, Hetty," he said. "Will you wait for us here? or are you afraid to be alone?"

"No, I'm not afraid to be alone. It is better for me."

"Good bye, then. Come, Rob."

I did not say good-bye. Even then, I think I did not know what I had resolved. I thrust my fingers deeper into the wet tuft of grass, heard the long dash of the breakers on the beach, looked at the square black figure of Robert Manning as it went slowly up the sandy road into the street. At the other, taller and more bent, beside it, I did not once look. I wiped the clammy moisture off my face and throat.

"It's the woman's flesh of me," I said. "There is better stuff in me than that. I will go now, and fulfil my calling."

On the wharf, as I went creeping along, I met Monsieur. He offered me his fat little arm, with smiles and congratulations, and handed me hurriedly over the plank on to the deck. In a moment the steamer was puffing out of harbor.

I was to play Marian in my own opera. God had given me a power of head-work, skill for a certain mission, and I was going to perform it. The vast, vague substance on which I was to act was brought before me to-night, palpable, — the world, posterity, time; how did I call it? But, somehow, it was not what I had dreamed of since my babyhood up yonder in Concord. Nothing was vast or vague. I was looking into a little glass in a black-painted frame, and saw the same Mrs. Manning, with the same high cheek-bones, the yellow mole on the upper lip, the sorrowful brown eyes: dressed in tulle now, though, the angular arms and shoulders bare, and coated with chalk, a pat of rouge laid on each cheek: under the tulle-body the same old half-sickness; the same throbbing back-tooth threatening to ache. The room was small, triangular: a striped, reddish cotton carpet on the floor, a door with a brass handle, my bandbox open on a chair, a basin with soapy water, soiled towels, two dripping tallow-candles: in short, a dressing-room in a theatre. Outside, wheels, pulleys, pasteboard castles, trees, chairs, more bony women, more chalk, more tulle. Monsieur in a greasy green dressing-gown odorous of tobacco, swearing at a boy with blear eyes,—a scene-shifter. The orchestra tuning beyond the foot-lights: how vilely the first violin slurred over that second passage! "Life's Prophecy," I called it; and that "Vision of Heaven," the trombonist came in always false on the bass, because, as Monsieur said, he had always two brandy-slings too much. Beyond was "the world," passive, to be acted upon; the parquet,—ranged seats of young men with the flash-stamp on them from their thick noses to the broad-checked trousers; the dress-circle,—young girls with their eyes and brains full-facing their attendant sweethearts, and a side-giggle for the stage; crude faces in the gallery, tamed faces lower down; gray and red and black and tow-colored heads full of myriad teeming thoughts of business, work, pleasure, outside of this: treble and tenor notes wandering through them, dying almost ere born; touching what soul behind the dress and brain-work? and touching it how? Ah, well! "I am going to fulfil my mission." I said that, again and again, as I stood waiting. "Now. This is it. I take it up." But my blood would not be made to thrill.

"This wart must be covered," said a walking-lady in red paper-muslin, touching the mole on my lip with Meen Fun. M. Vaux tapped at the door,—a sly, oily smile on his mouth.

"We are honored to-night. Be prepared, my dear Madam, for surprises in your audience. Your husband is in the house,—and his son, Robert Manning."

I put up my hands in the vain effort to cover the bare neck and shoulders,—then, going back into the dressing-room, sat down, without a word. I remember how the two tallow-candles flared and sputtered, as I sat staring at them; how on the other side of the brass-handled door the play went on, the pulleys creaked, and the trombones grated, and the other women in tulle and chalk capered and sang, and that at last the stuffy voice of the call-boy outside cried, "Marian, on," and it was my time to fulfil my mission. I remember how broad a gap the green floor of the stage made to the shining tin foot-lights; how the thousand brassy, mocking eyes were centred on the lean figure that moved forward; how I heard a weak quaver going up, and knew it to be my own voice: I remember nothing more until the scene was ended: the test and last scene of the opera it had been: and as the curtain fell, it was stopped by a faint, dismal hiss that grew slowly louder and more venomous, was mingled with laughs and jeers from the gallery, and the play was damned. I stood with my white gauze and bony body and rouge behind a pasteboard flower-vase, and looked out at the laughing mob of faces. This was the world; I had done my best head-work for it, and even these plebeian brains had found it unfit for use, and tossed it aside. I waited there a moment, and then passing Monsieur, whose puffy face was purple with disappointment and rage, went into the dressing-room.

"What wonder?" I heard him demand in French. "It was so coarse a theft! But I hoped the catch-dresses would pass it off."

I wrapped a flannel cloak over my airy robes, and went out, down the crooked back-stairs into the street. I had no money; if I went back to the hotel where I had been stopping, it would be as a beggar.

I waited outside of the theatre by an old woman's candy-stand for the crowd to hustle past, holding myself up by her chair-back. She was nodding, for it was past midnight, but opened her red eyes to lift a little child on her knees who had been asleep at her feet.

"Come, Puss, the play's out, it's time for you an' Granny to be snug at home."

I laughed. Why, there was not one of these women or men crowding by, the very black beggar holding your horse, who had not a home, a child to touch, to love them,—not one. And I—I had my Self. I had developed that.

I pulled the cloak closer about me and went down the pavement. The street was thronged with street-cars stopping for the play-goers, hacks, and omnibuses; the gas flamed in red and green letters over the house-fronts; the crowd laughed and swayed and hummed snatches of songs, as they went by. I saw one or two husbands drawing the wrappings tighter about their wives' throats, for the air was sharp. My husband had seen my shoulders to-night,—so had they all, covered with chalk. There were children, too, cuddling close to their mothers' sides in the carriages. I wondered if my child would ever know it had a mother. So I went slowly down the street. I never saw the sky so dark and steely a blue as it was that night: if there had been one star in it, I think it would have looked softer, more pitying somehow, when I looked up. Knowing all that I had done, I yet cannot but feel a pity for the wretch I was that night. If the home I had desolated, the man and child I had abandoned, had chosen their revenge, they could not have asked that the woman's flesh and soul should rise in me with a hunger so mad as this.

At the corner of the street, a group from the crowd had stopped at the door of a drug-shop; they were anxious, curious, whispering back to those behind them. Some woman fainting, perhaps, or some one ill. I could not pass the lock of carriages at the crossing, and stopped, looking into the green light of the window-bottles. In a moment I caught my own name, "Manning," from a policeman who came out, and a word or two added.

The crowd drew back with a sudden breath of horror; but I passed them, and went in. It was a large shop: the lustres, marble soda-fountains, and glittering shelves of bottles dazzled me at first, but I saw presently two or three men, from whom the crowd had shrunk away, standing at the far end of the shop. Something lay on the counter among them, — a large, black figure, the arm hanging down, the feet crossed. It did not move. I do not know how long I stood there, it might be hours, or minutes, and it did not move. But I knew, the first moment I looked at it, that it never would move again. They worked with him, the three men, not speaking a word. The waistcoat and shirt were open; there was a single drop of blood on the neck, where they had tried to open a vein. After a while the physician drew back, and put his hand gently on the shoulder of the shorter, stouter of the other two men.

"My friend," he said, compassionately.

Robert Manning did not seem to hear him. He had knelt on the floor and hid his face in the hand that hung down still and cold. The druggist, a pale, little person, drew the doctor aside.

"What is it, now? Apoplexy?" his face full of pity.

"No. Brought on by nervous excitement, — heart, you know. Threatened a long time, his son says. His wife, the woman who" —

The policeman had been eying my dress under the cloak for some time.

"Hi! *You*'d best move on," he whispered. "This a'n't no place for the likes of you."

I stood still a moment, looking at the brawny black figure lying on the counter. The old days of Tinder and the paddock, — I don't know why I thought of them. It did not move: it never would move again. Dead. I had murdered him. I! I got my fingers in my oily hair, and pulled at it. "Hetty, Hetty Manning," I said, "good bye! Good bye, Daniel!" I remember hearing myself laugh as I left the shop-door; then I went down the street.

When I was far down the Bowery, an old thought came feebly up in my brain. It was how the water had choked, choked, all that night long in the wheel of the boat. When I thought of that, I waited to think. Then I turned and went to the bay, beyond Castle Garden.

The rain, drip, dripping on a cottage-roof: on branches, too, near at hand, that rustled and struck now and then against the little window-shutters, in a fashion just dreary enough to make one nestle closer into the warm bed, and peep out into the shadowy chamber, with the cozy little fire burning hotly in the grate. Patter, patter: gurgling down the spouts:

slacking for a minute, threatening to stop and let you sleep in a usual, soundless, vulgar way, as on other nights: then at it again, drip, drip, more monotonous, cheerfuller in its dreariness than ever. Thunder, too: growling off in the hills, where the night and rain found no snug little bed-room to make brighter by their besieging: greenish-white jets of lightning in the cracks of the shutters, making the night-lamp on the toilet-table and the fire suddenly go out and kindle up fiercely again.

This for a long time: hours or not, why should one try to know? A little bed, with crimson curtains, cool white pillows: a soft bed, where the aching limbs rested afresh with every turn. After a while, a comfortable, dumpling little figure in a loose wrapper, popping out of some great chair's depths by the fire and stirring some posset[5] on the hearth: smelling at a medicine-bottle: coming to the bed-side, putting a fat hand on one's forehead: a start, a nervous kiss, a shaky little laugh or two, as she fumbles about, saying, "Hush-h!" and a sudden disappearing behind the curtains. A grave, pale face looking steadily down, as if afraid to believe, until the dear eyes fill with tears, and the head, with its old wig, is dropped, and I and God only know what his soul is saying.

"My husband!"

"Hetty!"

"Is it you?—Daniel?"

He lifted me in his arms farther up on the pillow, smoothing the blankets about me, trying to speak, but only choking, in a ridiculous fashion.

"And the opera, and the drug-shop, and"—

I held my hand to my head.

"The truth is," said Jacky, bobbing out from behind the curtains, her eyes suspiciously red and shiny, "I'm afraid you've had some bad dreams, dear. Just take a teaspoonful of this, that's a good soul! You've been ill, you see. Brain-fever, and what not. The very day we came to Newport. Uncle Daniel and Robert found you on the cliff."

"When we came from the hotel, you remember?" still pulling the blanket up, his lip unsteady.

"You'll choke her; what a nurse you are, to be sure, Uncle Dan! And the woman's feet as bare"—

"There, there, Jacky! I know,"—submissively, twitching at my night-cap, and then gathering my head into his arms until I could hear how his heart throbbed under the strong chest. "My wife! Hetty! Hetty!" he whispered.

I knew he was thanking God for giving me to him again. *I* dared not think of God, or him: God, that had given me another chance.

I lay there until morning, weak and limp, on his arm, touching it now and then to be sure it was alive, an actual flesh-and-blood arm,—that I was not a murderer. Weak as any baby: and it seemed to me—it comes to me yet as a great truth—that God had let me be born again: that He, who gave a new life to the thief in his last foul breath, had given me, too, another chance to try again. Jacky, who was the most arbitrary of nurses, coiled herself up on the foot of the bed, and kept her unwinking eyes sharp on us to enforce silence. Never were eyes more healthful and friendly, I thought, feebly. But I tried all the time to press my poor head in closer to my husband's breast: I was barely free from that vacuum of death and crime, and in there were the strength and life that were to save me; I knew that. God, who had brought me to this, alone knew how I received it: whether it was a true wife that lay on Daniel Manning's bosom that night; how I loathed the self I had worshipped so long; how the misused, diseased body and soul were alive with love for him, craved a week's, a day's life to give themselves utterly to him, to creep closer to him and the Father that he knew so simply and so well. I heard him once in the night, when he thought I was asleep, say to himself something of the wife who had been restored to him, who "was dead and is alive again, was lost and is found." But how true those words were he can never know.

I fell asleep towards morning, and when I woke, it was with a clear head and stronger eye to comprehend my new chance in life. The room had a pure, fresh, daylight look, snug and tidy; a clear fire crackled on the clean hearth; Jacky herself had her most invigorating of morning faces, going off at the least hint of a joke into redness and smiles. It rained still, but the curtains were drawn back, and I could see through the gray wet what a pleasant slope of meadow there was outside, clumped over with horse-chestnuts and sycamores, down to a narrow creek. The water was fogged over now with drifting mist, but beyond I caught glimpses of low wooded hills, and far to the left the pale flush of the sea running in on the sand. My husband was watching me eagerly as I looked out.

"I do not know where I am, Daniel."

"No, of course you don't,"—rubbing his forehead, as he always did when he was especially pleased. "There's so much to tell you, Hetty dear! We're beginning all new again, you see."

"You 'll not tell a word, until she's had her breakfast," said Jacky, dogmatically, coming with her white basin of cool water.

Oh, the remembrance of that plunge of cold on the hot skin, of the towel's smelling of lavender, of the hard-brushed hair, of the dainty little tray, with its smoking cup of fragrant, amber tea, and delicatest slice of crips toast! Truly, the woman's flesh of me, having been triumphant so long, goes back with infinite relish to that first meal, and the two bright faces bent over me. And then came Teddy, slying to the pillow-side, watching my pale face and thin hands with an awe-struck gaze, and carrying off the tea and toast to finish by the hearth.

"You can't see much for the rain, mother," anxiously. "Not the orchard, nor the stable,—but there *is* a stable, and hay, and eggs every morning, only the gray hen's trying to set, if you'll believe it. And old Mary's in the kitchen, and we've got even Tinder and our old peacock from the Hudson."

"Eat your toast now, Captain," said his father, putting his arm about me again.

"Yes, Hetty, it's a bit of a farm—ten or fifteen acres. Our cozery: yours and mine, dear. It's Rob's surprise,"—with the awkward laugh a man gives, when, if he were a woman, the tears would come.

"Rob?"

"Yes. He had it ready. I knew it before we left New York, but we wanted to surprise you. The boys all put in a little. They're good boys. I've hardly deserved it of them,"—pulling at the quilt-fringe. "I've been a glum, unsociable old dog. I might have made their lives cheerfuller. They're going West: Bill and John to Chicago, and Jem to St. Louis: just waiting for you to be better."

"I am sorry."

I was sorry. The thought of their earnest, honest, downright faces came to me now with a new meaning, somehow: I could enter into their life now: it was an eager affection I was ready to give them, that they could not understand: I had wakened up, so thirsty for love, and to love.

"Yes, Rob did it,"—lingering on the name tenderly. "It's a snug home for us: we'll have to rough it outside a little, but we're not old yet, Hetty, eh?" turning up my face. "I have my old school in town again. We have everything we want now, to begin afresh."

I did not answer; nor, through the day, when Jacky and the boys, one after another, would say anxiously, as one does to a sick person, "Is there anything you need, mother?" did I utter a wish. I dared not: I knew all that I had done: and if God never gave me *that* gift again, I never should ask for it. But I saw them watching me more uneasily, and towards evening caught part of Jacky's talk with Doctor Manning.

"I tell you I will. I'll risk the fever," impatiently. "It's that she wants. I can see it in her eyes. Heaven save you, Uncle Dan, you're not a woman!"

And in a moment she brought my baby and laid it in my breast. It was only when its little hand touched me that I surely knew God had forgiven me.

It ceased raining in the evening: the clouds cleared off, red and heavy. Rob had come up from town, and took his father's place beside me, but he and Jacky brought their chairs close, so we had a quiet evening all together. Their way of talking, of politics or religion or even news, was so healthy and alive, warm-blooded! And I entered into it with so keen a relish! It was such an earnest, heartsome world I had come into, out of myself! Once, when Jacqueline was giving me a drink, she said,—

"I wish you'd tell us what you dreamed in all these days, dear."

Robert glanced at me keenly.

"No, Jacky," he said, his face flushing.

I looked him full in the eyes: from that moment I had a curious reliance and trust in his shrewd, just, kindly nature, and in his religion, a something below that. If I were dying, I should be glad if Robert Manning would pray for me. I should think his prayers would be heard.

"I will not forget what I dreamed, Robert," I said.

"No, mother. I know."

After that, awhile, I was talking to him of the home he had prepared for his father and me.

"I wanted you just to start anew, with Teddy and the baby, here," he said, lightly.

"And Jacky," I added, looking up at the bright, chubby face.

It grew suddenly crimson, then colorless, then the tears came. There was a strange silence.

"Rob," she whispered, hiding her head sheepishly, "Rob says no."

"Yes, Rob says no," putting his hand on her crisp curls. "He wants you. And mother, here, will tell you a woman has no better work in life than the one she has taken up: to make herself a visible Providence to her husband and child."

I kissed Jacky again and again, but I said nothing. He went away just after that. When he shook hands, I held up the baby to be kissed. He played with it a minute, and then put it down.

"God bless the baby," he said, "and its mother," more earnestly.

Then he and Jacky went out and left me alone with my husband and my child.

# Out of the Sea

Atlantic Monthly, May 1865

A raw, gusty afternoon: one of the last dragging breaths of a nor'easter, which swept, in the beginning of November, from the Atlantic coast to the base of the Alleghanies. It lasted a week, and brought the winter, — for autumn had lingered unusually late that year; the fat bottom-lands of Pennsylvania, yet green, deadened into swamps, as it passed over them: summery, gay bits of lakes among the hills glazed over with muddy ice; the forests had been kept warm between the western mountains, and held thus late even their summer's strength and darker autumn tints, but the fierce ploughing winds of this storm and its cutting sleet left them a mass of broken boughs and rotted leaves. In fact, the sun had loitered so long, with a friendly look back-turned into these inland States, that people forgot that the summer had gone, and skies and air and fields were merry-making together, when they lent their color and vitality to these few bleak days, and then suddenly found that they had entertained winter unawares.

Down on the lee coast of New Jersey, however, where the sea and wind spend the year making ready for their winter's work of shipwreck, this storm, though grayer and colder there than elsewhere, toned into the days and nights as a something entirely matter-of-course and consonant. In summer it would have been at home there. Its aspect was different, also, as I said. But little rain fell here; the wind lashed the ocean into fury along the coast, and then rolled in long, melancholy howls into the stretches of barren sand and interminable pine forests; the horizon contracted, though at all times it is narrower than anywhere else, the dome of the sky wider, — clouds and atmosphere forming the scenery, and the land but a round, flat standing-place: but now the sun went out; the air grew livid, as though death were coming through it; solid masses of gray, wet mist moved, slower than the wind, from point to point, like gigantic ghosts gathering to the call of the murderous sea.

"Yonder go the shades of Ossian's[1] heroes," said Mary Defourchet to her companion, pointing through the darkening air.

They were driving carefully in an old-fashioned gig, in one of the lulls of the storm, along the edge of a pine wood, early in the afternoon. The old Doctor,—for it was MacAulay, (Dennis,) from over in Monmouth County, she was with,—the old man did not answer, having enough to do to guide his mare, the sleet drove so in his eyes. Besides, he was gruffer than usual this afternoon, looking with the trained eyes of an old water-dog out to the yellow line of the sea to the north. Miss Defourchet pulled the oil-skin cloth closer about her knees, and held her tongue; she relished the excitement of this fierce fighting the wind, though; it suited the nervous tension which her mind had undergone lately.

It was a queer, lonesome country, this lee coast,—never so solitary as now, perhaps; older than the rest of the world, she fancied,—so many of Nature's voices, both of bird and vegetable, had been entirely lost out of it: no wonder it had grown unfruitful, and older and dumber and sad, listening for ages to the unremorseful, cruel cries of the sea; these dead bodies, too, washed up every year on its beaches, must haunt it, though it was not guilty. She began to say something of this to Doctor Dennis, tired of being silent.

"Your country seems to me always to shut itself out from the world," she said; "from the time I enter that desolate region on its border of dwarf oaks and gloomy fires of the charcoal-burners, I think of the old leper and his cry of 'Unclean! unclean!'"

MacAulay glanced anxiously at her, trying to keep pace with her meaning.

"It's a lonesome place enough," he said, slowly. "There be but the two or three farm-keepers; and the places go from father to son, father to son. The linen and carpet-mats in that house you 're in now come down from the times before Washington. Stay-at-home, quiet people,—only the men that follow the water, in each generation. There be but little to be made from these flats of white sand. Yes, quiet enough: the beasts of prey are n't scaret out of these pine forests yet. I heard the cry of a panther the other night only, coming from Tom's River: close by the road it was: sharp and sorrowful, like a lost child.—As for ghosts," he continued, after a thoughtful pause, "I don't know any that would have reason for walking, without it was Captain Kidd. His treasure 's buried along-shore here."

"Ay?" said Mary, looking up shrewdly into his face.

"Yes," he answered, shaking his head slowly, and measuring his whip with one eye. "Along here, many 's the Spanish half-dollar I 've picked up myself among the kelp. They do say they 're from a galleon that went ashore come next August thirty years ago, but I don't know that."

"And the people in the hamlet?" questioned Mary, nodding to a group of scattered, low-roofed houses.

"Clam-fishers, the maist o' them. There be quite a many wrackers, but they live farther on, towards Barnegat. But a wrack draws them, like buzzards to a carcass."

Miss Defourchet's black eye kindled, as if at the prospect of a good tragedy.

"Did you ever see a wreck going down?" she asked, eagerly.

"Yes,"—shutting his grim lips tighter.

"That emigrant ship last fall? Seven hundred and thirty souls lost, they told me."

"I was not here to know, thank God," shortly.

"It would be a sensation for a life-time,"—cuddling back into her seat, with no hopes of a story from the old Doctor.

MacAulay sat up stiffer, his stern gray eye scanning the ocean-line again, as the mare turned into the more open plains of sand sloping down to the sea. It was up-hill work with him, talking to this young lady. He was afraid of a woman who had lectured in public, nursed in the hospitals, whose blood seemed always at fever heat, and whose æsthetic taste could seek the point of view from which to observe a calamity so horrible as the emigrant ship going down with her load of lives. "She 's been fed on books too much," he thought. "It 's the trouble with young women nowadays." On the other hand, for himself, he had lost sight of the current of present knowledges,—he was aware of that, finding how few topics in common there were between them; but it troubled the self-reliant old fellow but little. Since he left Yale, where he and this girl's uncle, Doctor Bowdler, had been chums together, he had lived in this out-of-the-way corner of the world, and many of the rough ways of speaking and acting of the people had clung to him, as their red mud to his shoes. As he grew older, he did not care to brush either off.

Miss Defourchet had been a weight on his mind for a week or more. Her guardian, Doctor Bowdler, had sent her down to board in one of the farm-houses. "The sea-air will do her good, physically," he said in a note to his old chum, with whom he always had kept up a lingering intercourse; "she 's been over-worked lately,—sick soldiers, you know. Mary went into the war *con amore*, like all women, or other happy people who are blind of one eye. Besides, she is to be married about Christmas, and before she begins life in earnest it would do her good to face something real. Nothing like living by the sea, and with those homely, thorough-blood Quakers, for bringing people to their simple, natural selves. By the way, you have heard of Dr. Birkenshead, whom she marries? though he is a surgeon,—not exactly in your profession. A surprisingly young man to have gained his reputation. I 'm glad Mary marries a man of so much mark; she has pulled alone so long, she needs a master." So MacAulay had taken pains to drive the young lady out, as to-day, and took a general fatherly sort of charge of her, for his old friend's sake.

Doctor Bowdler had frankly told his niece his reasons for wishing her to go down to the sea-shore. They nettled her more than she chose to show. She was over thirty, an eager humanitarian, had taught the freedmen at Port Royal, gone to Gettysburg and Antietam with sanitary stores, — surely, she did not need to be told that she had yet to begin life in earnest! But she was not sorry for the chance to rest and think. After she married she would be taken from the quiet Quaker society in Philadelphia, in which she always had moved, to one that would put her personal and mental powers to a sharp proof; for Birkenshead, by right of his professional fame, and a curiously attractive personal eccentricity, had gradually become the nucleus of one of the best and most brilliant circles in the country, men and women alike distinguished for their wit and skill in extracting the finest tones from life while they lived. The quiet Quaker girl was secretly on her mettle, — secretly, too, a little afraid. The truth was, she knew Doctor Birkenshead only in the glare of public life; her love for him was, as yet, only a delicate intellectual appreciation that gave her a keen delight. She was anxious that in his own world he should not be ashamed of her. She was glad he was to share this breathing-space with her; they could see each other unmasked. Doctor Bowdler and he were coming down from New York on Ben Van Note's lumber-schooner. It was due yesterday, but had not yet arrived.

"You are sure," MacAulay said to her, as they rode along, "that they will come with Ben?"

"Quite sure. They preferred it to the cars for the novelty of the thing, and the storm lulled the day they were to sail. Could the schooner make this inlet in a sea like that?"

Doctor Dennis, stooping to arrange the harness, pretended not to hear her.

"Ben, at least," he thought, "knows that to near the bar to-day means death."

"One would think," he added aloud, "that Dick Bowdler's gray hairs and thirty years of preaching would have sobered his love of adventure. He was a foolhardy chap at college."

Miss Defourchet's glance grew troubled, as she looked out at the gathering gloom and the crisp bits of yellow foam blown up to the carriage-wheels. Doctor Dennis turned the mare's head, thus hiding the sea from them; but its cry sounded for miles inland to-day,—an awful, inarticulate roar. All else was solemn silence. The great salt marshes rolled away on one side of the road, lush and rank,—one solitary dead tree rising from them, with a fish-hawk's uncouth nest lumbering its black trunk; they were still as the grave; even the ill-boding bird was gone long ago, and kept no more its lonely vigil on the dead limb over wind and wave. She glanced uneasily from side to side: high up on the beach lay fragments of old wrecks; burnt spars of vessels drifted ashore to tell, in their dumb way, of captain and crew washed, in one quick moment, by this muddy water of the Atlantic, into that sea far off whence no voyager has come back to bring the tidings. Land and sea seemed to her to hint at this thing,—this awful sea, cold and dark beyond. What did the dark mystery in the cry of the surf mean but that? That was the only sound. The heavy silence without grew intolerable to her: it foreboded evil. The cold, yellow light of day lingered long. Over-head, cloud after cloud rose from the far watery horizon, and drove swiftly and silently inland, bellying dark as it went, carrying the storm. As the horse's hoofs struck hard on the beach, a bird rose out of the marsh and trailed through the air, its long legs dragging behind it, and a blaze of light feathers on its breast catching a dull glow in the fading evening.

"The blue heron flies low," said the Doctor. "That means a heavier storm. It scents a wreck as keenly as a Barnegat pirate." [2]

"It is fishing, maybe?" said Mary, trying to rouse herself.

"It's no a canny fisher that," shaking his head. "The fish you 'd find in its nest come from the deep waters, where heron never flew. Well, they do say," in answer to her look of inquiry, "that on stormy nights it sits on the beach with a phosphoric light under its wing, and so draws them to shore."

"How soon will the storm be on us?" after a pause.

"In not less than two hours. Keep your heart up, child. Ben Van Note is no fool. He 'd keep clear of Squan Beach as he would of hell's mouth, such a night as this is going to be. Your friends are all safe. We 'll drive home as soon as we 've been at the store to see if the mail 's brought you a letter."

He tucked in his hairy overcoat about his long legs, and tried to talk cheerfully as they drove along, seeing how pale she was.

"The store" for these two counties was a large, one-roomed frame building on the edge of the great pine woods, painted bright pink, with a wooden blue lady, the old figure-head of some sloop, over the door. The stoop outside was filled with hogsheads and boxes; inside was the usual stock of calicoes, china-ware, molasses-barrels, and books; the post-office, a high desk, on which lay half a dozen letters. By the dingy little windows, on which the rain was now beating sharply, four or five dirty sailors and clam-diggers were gathered, lounging on the counter and kegs, while one read a newspaper aloud slowly. They stopped to look at Miss Defourchet, when she came in, and waited by the door for the Doctor. The gloomy air and forlorn-looking shop contrasted and threw into bright relief her pretty, delicate little figure, and the dainty carriage-dress she wore. All the daylight that was in the store seemed at once to cling to and caress the rare beauty of the small face, with its eager blue eyes and dark brown curls. There was one woman in the store, sitting on a beer-cask, a small, sharp-set old wife, who drew her muddy shoes up under her petticoats out of Mary's way, but did not look at her. Miss Defourchet belonged to a family to whom the ease that money gives and a certain epicureanism of taste were natural. She stood there wondering, not unkindly, what these poor creatures did with their lives, and their dull, cloddish days; what could they know of the keen pains, the pleasures, the ambitions, or loves, that ennobled wealthier souls?

"This be yer papper, Doctor," said one; "but we 've not just yet finished it."

"All right, boys; Jem Dexter can leave it to-night, as he goes by. Any mail for me, Joe? But you 're waiting, Mother Phebe?"—turning with a sudden gentleness to the old woman near Mary.

"Yes, I be. But it don't matter. Joseph, serve the Doctor,"—beating a tattoo on the counter with her restless hands.

The Doctor did not turn to take his letters, however, nor seem to heed the wind which was rising fitfully each moment without, but leaned leisurely on the counter.

"Did you expect a letter to-day?"—in the same subdued voice.

She gave a scared look at the men by the window, and then in a whisper,—

"From my son, Derrick,—yes. The folks here take Derrick for a joke,—an' me. But I 'm expectin'. He said he 'd come, thee sees?"

"So he did."

"Well, there 's none from Derrick to-day, Mother Phebe," said the burly storekeeper, taking his stubby pipe out of his mouth.

She caught her breath.

"Thee looked carefully, Joseph?"

He nodded. She began to unbutton a patched cotton umbrella,—her lips moving as people's do sometimes in the beginning of second childhood.

"I 'll go home, then. I 'll be back mail-day, Wednesday, Joseph. Four days that is, — Wednesday."

"Lookee here now, Gran!" positively, laying down the pipe to give effect to his words; "you 're killin' yerself, you are. Keep a-trottin' here all winter, an' what sort of a report of yerself 'll yer make to Derrick by spring? When that 'ere letter comes, if come it do, I 've said I 'd put on my cut an' run up with it. See there!" — pulling out her thin calico skirt before the Doctor, — "soaked, she is."

"Thee 's kind, Joseph, but thee don't know," — drawing her frock back with a certain dignity. "When my boy's handwrite comes, I must be here. I learned writin' on purpose that I might read it first," — turning to Mary.

"How long has your boy been gone?" asked Miss Defourchet, heedless of Joseph's warning "Hush-h!"

"Twenty years, come February," eagerly volunteered one or two voices by the window. "She's never heerd a word in that time, an' she never misses a mail-day, but she 's expectin'," added one, with a coarse laugh.

"None o' that, Sam Venners," said Joe, sharply. "If so be as Dirk said he 'd come, be it half-a-hunder' years, he 'll stan' to 't. I knowed Dirk. Many 's the clam we toed out o' th' inlet yonner. He 's not the sort to hang round, gnawin' out the old folk's meat-pot, as some I cud name. He" —

"I 'll go, if thee 'll let me apast," said the old woman, humbly curtsying to the men, who now jammed up the doorway.

"It 's a cussed shame, Venners," said Joe, when she was out. "Why can't yer humor the old gran a bit? She 's the chicken-heartedest woman ever I knowed," explanatory to Miss Defourchet, "an' these ten years she 's been mad-like, waitin' for that hang-dog son of hers to come back."

Mary followed her out on the stoop, where she stood, her ragged green umbrella up, her sharp little face turned anxiously to the far sea-line.

"Bad! bad!" she muttered, looking at Mary.

"The storm? Yes. But you ought not to be out in such weather," kindly, putting her furred hand on the skinny arm.

The woman smiled, — a sweet, good-humored smile it was, in spite of her meagre, hungry old face.

"Why, look there, young woman," — pulling up her sleeve, and showing the knotted tendons and thick muscles of her arm. "I 'm pretty tough, thee sees. There 's not a boatman in Ocean County could pull an oar with me when I was a gell, an' I 'm tough yet," — hooking her sleeve again.

The smile haunted Miss Defourchet; where had she seen it before?

"Was Derrick strongly built?" — idly wishing to recall it.

"Thee 's a stranger; maybe thee has met my boy?"—turning on her sharply. "No, that 's silly,"—the sad vagueness coming back into the faded eyes. After a pause,—"Derrick, thee said? He was short, the lad was,—but with legs and arms as tender and supple as a wild-cat's. I loss much of my strength when he was born; it was wonderful, for a woman, before; I giv it to him. I 'm glad of that! I thank God that I giv it to him!"—her voice sinking, and growing wilder and faster. "Why! why!"

Mary took her hand, half-scared, looking in at the store-door, wishing Doctor Dennis would come.

The old woman tottered and sat down on the lower rung of a ladder standing there. Mary could see now how the long sickness of the hope deferred had touched the poor creature's brain, gentle and loving at first. She pushed the wet yellow sun-bonnet back from the gray hair; she thought she had never seen such unutterable pathos or tragedy as in this little cramped figure, and this old face, turned forever watching to the sea.

"Thee does n't know; how should thee?"—gently, but not looking at her. "Thee never had a son; an' when thee has, it will be born in wedlock. Thee 's rich, an' well taught. I was jess a clam-fisher, an' knowed nothin' but my baby. His father was a gentleman: come in spring, an' gone in th' fall, an' that was the last of him. That hurt a bit, but I had Derrick. *Oh, Derrick! Derrick!*"—whispering, rocking herself to and fro as if she held a baby, cooing over the uncouth name with an awful longing and tenderness in the sound.

Miss Defourchet was silent. Something in all this awed her; she did not understand it.

"I mind," she wandered on, "when the day's work was done, I 'd hold him in my arms,—so,—and his sleepy little face would turn up to mine. I seemed to begin to loss him after he was a baby,"—with an old, worn sigh. "He went with other boys. The Weirs and Hallets took him up; they were town-bred people, an' he soon got other notions from mine, an' talked of things I 'd heerd nothin' of. I was very proud of my Derrick; but I knowed I 'd loss him all the same. I did washin' an' ironin' by nights to keep him dressed like the others,—an' kep' myself out o' their way, not to shame him with his mother."

"And was he ashamed of you?" said Mary, her face growing hot.

"Thee did not know my little boy,"—the old woman stood up, drawing herself to her full height. "His wee body was too full of pluck an' good love to be shamed by his mother. I mind the day I come on them suddint, by the bridge, where they were standin', him an' two o' the Hallets. I was carryin' a basket of herrings. The Hallets they flushed up, an' looked at him to see what he 'd do; for they never named his mother to him, I heerd. The road was deep with mud; an' as I stood a bit to balance myself, keepin' my head turned from him, before I knew aught, my boy had me in his arms, an' carried me t' other side. I 'm not a heavy weight, thee sees, but his face was all aglow with the laugh.

"'There you are, dear,' he says, puttin' me down, the wind blowin' his brown hair.

"One of the Hallets brought my basket over then, an' touched his hat as if I 'd been a lady. That was the last time my boy had his arms about me: next week he went away. That night I heerd him in his room in the loft, here an' there, here an' there, as if he could n't sleep, an' so for many nights, comin' down in the mornin' with his eyes red an' swollen, but full of the laugh an' joke as always. The Hallets were with him constant, those days. Judge Hallet, their father, were goin' across seas, Derrick said. So one night, I 'd got his tea ready, an' were waitin' for him by the fire, knittin',—when he come in an' stood by the mantel-shelf, lookin' down at me, steady. He had on his Sunday suit of blue, Jim Devines giv him.

"'Where be yer other clothes, my son?' I said.

"'They're not clean,' says he. 'I 've been haulin' marl[3] for Springer this week. He paid me to-night; the money 's in the kitchen-cupboard.'

"I looked up at that, for it was work I 'd never put him to.

"'It 'll buy thee new shoes,' said I.

"'I did it for you, mother,' he says, suddint, puttin' his hand over his eyes. 'I wish things were different with you.'

"'Yes, Derrick.'

"I went on with my knittin'; for I never talked much to him, for the shame of my bad words, since he 'd learned better. But I wondered what he meant; for wages was high that winter, an' I was doin' well.

"'If ever,' he says, speakin' low an' faster, 'if ever I do anything that gives you pain, you 'll know it was for love of you I did it. Not for myself, God knows! To make things different for you.'

"'Yes, Derrick,' I says, knittin' on, for I did n't understan' thin. Afterwards I did. The room was dark, an' it were dead quiet for a bit; then the lad moved to the door.

"'Where be thee goin', Derrick?' I said.

"He come back an' leaned on my chair.

"'Let me tell you when I come back,' he said. 'You 'll wait for me?' stoopin' down an' kissin' me.

"I noticed that, for he did not like to kiss,—Derrick. An' his lips were hot an' dry.

"'Yes, I'll wait, my son,' I said. 'Thee 'll not be gone long?'

"He did not answer that, but kissed me again, an' went out quickly.

"I sat an' waited long that night, an' searched till mornin'. There's been a many nights an' days since, but I've never found him. The Hallets all went that night, an' I heerd Derrick went as waiter-boy, so 's to get across seas. It's twenty years now. But I think he'll come,"—looking up with a laugh.

Miss Defourchet started; where had she known this woman? The sudden flicker of a smile, followed by a quick contraction of the eyelids and mouth, was peculiar and curiously sensitive and sad; somewhere, in a picture maybe, she had seen the same.

Doctor Dennis, who had waited purposely, came out now on the stoop. Miss Defourchet looked up. The darkness had gathered while they stood there; the pine woods, close at the right, began to lower distant and shapeless; now and then the wind flapped a raw dash of rain in their faces, and then was suddenly still. Behind them, two or three tallow candles, just lighted in the store, sputtered dismal circles of dingy glare in the damp fog; in front, a vague slope of wet night, in which she knew lay the road and the salt marshes; and far beyond, distinct, the sea-line next the sky, a great yellow phosphorescent belt, apparently higher than their heads. Nearer, unseen, the night-tide was sent in: it came with a regular muffled throb that shook the ground. Doctor Dennis went down, and groped about his horse, adjusting the harness.

"The poor beast is soaked to the marrow: it's a dull night: d' ye hear how full the air is of noises?"

"It be the sea makin' ready," said Joe, in a whisper, as if it were a sentient thing and could hear. He touched the old woman on the arm and beckoned her inside to one of the candles.

"There be a scrap of a letter come for you; but keep quiet. Ben Van Note's scrawl of a handwrite, think."

The letters were large enough,—printed, in fact: she read it but once.

"Your Dirk come Aboord the Chief at New York. I knowed him by a mark on his wrist—the time jim hallet cut him you mind. he is aged and Differentt name. I kep close. we sail today and Ill Breng him Ashor tomorrer nite plese God. be on Handd."

She folded the letter, crease by crease, and put it quietly in her pocket. Joe watched her curiously.

"D' Ben say when the Chief ud run in?"

"To-night."

"Bah-h! there be n't a vessel within miles of this coast,—without a gale drives 'm in."

She did not seem to hear him: was feeling her wet petticoats and sleeves. She would shame Derrick, after all, with this patched, muddy frock! She had worked so long to buy the black silk gown and white neckercher that was folded in the bureau-drawer to wear the day he 'd come back!

"When he come back!"

Then, for the first time, she realized what she was thinking about. *Coming to-night!*

Presently Miss Defourchet went to her where she was sitting on a box in the dark and rain.

"Are you sick?" said she, putting her hand out.

"Oh, no, dear!" softly, putting the fingers in her own, close to her breast, crying and sobbing quietly. "Thee hand be a'most as soft as a baby's foot," after a while, fancying the little chap was creeping into her bosom again, thumping with his fat feet and fists as he used to do. Her very blood used to grow wild and hot when he did that, she loved him so. And her heart to-night was just as warm and light as then. He was coming back, her boy: maybe he was poor and sick, a worn-out man; but in a few hours he would be here, and lay his tired head on her breast, and be a baby again.

Joe went down to the Doctor with a lantern.

"Van Note meant to run in the Chief to-night,"—in an anxious, inquiring whisper.

"He 's not an idiot!"

"No,—but, bein' near, the wind may drive 'em on the bar. Look yonder."

"See that, too, Joe?" said bow-legged Phil, from Tom's River, who was up that night.

"That yellow line has never been in the sky since the night the James Frazier—*Ach-h! it 's come!*"

He had stooped to help Doctor Dennis with his harness, but now fell forward, clapping his hands to his ears. A terrible darkness swept over them; the whole air was filled with a fierce, risping crackle; then came a sharp concussion, that seemed to tear the earth asunder. Miss Defourchet cried aloud: no one answered her. In a few moments the darkness slowly lifted, leaving the old yellow lights and fogs on sea and land. The men stood motionless as when the tornado passed, Doctor Dennis leaning on his old mare, having thrown one arm about her as if to protect her, his stern face awed.

"There 's where it went," said Joe, coolly, drawing his hands from his pockets, and pointing to a black gap in the pine woods. "The best farms in this Jersey country lie back o' that. I told you there was death in the pot, but I did n't think it ud 'a' come this fashion."

"When will the storm be on us?" asked Mary, trembling.

Joe laughed sardonically.

"Have n't ye hed enough of it?"

"There will be no rain after a gust like that," said MacAulay. "I' ll try and get you home now. It has done its worst. It will take years to wipe out the woe this night has worked."

The wind had fallen into a dead silence, frightened at itself. And now the sudden, awful thunder of the sea broke on them, shaking the sandy soil on which they stood.

"Thank God that Van Note is so trusty a sailor as you say!" said Mary, buttoning her furs closer to her throat. "They 're back in a safe harbor, I doubt not."

Joe and Doctor Dennis exchanged significant glances as they stood by the mare, and then looked again out to sea.

"Best get her home," said Joe, in a whisper.

Doctor Dennis nodded, and they made haste to bring the gig up to the horse-block.

Old Phebe Trull had been standing stirless since the gust passed. She drew a long breath when Mary touched her, telling her to come home with them.

"That was a sharp blow. I 'm an old Barnegat woman, an' I 've known no such cutters as that. But he 'll come. I 'm expectin' my boy to-night, young woman. I 'm goin' to the beach now to wait for him,—for Derrick."

In spite of the queer old face peering out from the yellow sun-bonnet, with its flabby wrinkles and nut-cracker jaws, there was a fine, delicate meaning in the smile with which she waved her hand down to the stormy beach.

"What 's that?" said Doctor Dennis, starting up, and holding his hand behind his ear. His sandy face grew pale.

"I heard nothing," said Mary.

The next moment she caught a dull thud in the watery distance, as if some pulse of the night had throbbed feverishly.

Bow-legged Phil started to his feet.

"It 's the gun of the Chief! Van Note 's goin' down!" he cried, with a horrible oath, and hobbled off, followed by the other men.

"His little brother Benny be on her," said Joe. "May God have mercy on their souls!"

He had climbed like a cat to the rafters, and thrown down two or three cables and anchors, and, putting them over his shoulders, started soberly for the beach, stopping to look at Miss Defourchet, crouched on the floor of the store.

"You 'd best see after her, Doctor. Ropes is all we can do for 'em. No boat ud live in that sea, goin' out."

Going down through the clammy fog, his feet sinking in the marsh with the weight he carried, he could see red lights in the mist, gathering towards shore.

"It 's the wrackers goin' down to be ready for mornin'."

And in a few moments stood beside them a half-dozen brawny men, with their legs and chests bare. The beach on which they stood glared white in the yellow light, giving the effect of a landscape in Polar seas. One or two solitary headlands loomed gloomily up, covered with snow. In front, the waters at the edge of the sea broke at their feet in long, solemn, monotonous swells, that reverberated like thunder,—a death-song for the work going on in the chaos beyond.

"Thar 's no use doin' anything out thar," said one of the men, nodding gloomily to a black speck in the foaming hell. "She be on the bar this ten minutes, an' she 's a mean-built craft, that Chief."

"Could n't a boat run out from the inlet?" timidly ventured an eager, blue-eyed little fellow.

"No, Snap," said Joe, letting his anchor fall, and clearing his throat. "Well, there be the end of old Ben, hey? Be yer never tired, yer cruel devil?" turning with a sudden fierceness to the sly foam creeping lazily about his feet.

There was a long silence.

"Bowlegs tried it, but his scow stud still, an' the breakers came atop as if it war a clam-shell. He war n't five yards from shore. His Ben 's aboard."

Another peal of a gun from the schooner broke through the dark and storm.

"God! I be sick o' sittin' on shor', an' watchin' men drownin' like rats on a raft," said Joe, wiping the foam from his thick lips, and trotting up and down the sand, keeping his back to the vessel.

Some of the men sat down, their hands clasped about their knees, looking gravely out.

"What cud we do, Joey?" said one. "Thar be Hannah an' the children;

we kin give Hannah a lift. But as for Ben, it 's no use thinkin' about Ben no more."

The little clam-digger Snap was kindling a fire out of the old half-burnt wrecks of vessels.

"It 's too late to give 'em warnin'," he said; "but it 'll let 'em see we 're watchin' 'em at the last. One ud like friends at the last."

The fire lighted up the shore, throwing long bars of hot, greenish flame up the fog.

"Who be them, Joe?" whispered a wrecker, as two dim figures came down through the marsh.

"She hev a sweetheart aboord. Don't watch her."

The men got up, and moved away, leaving Miss Defourchet alone with Doctor Dennis. She stood so quiet, her eyes glued on the dull, shaking shadow yonder on the bar, that he thought she did not care. Two figures came round from the inlet to where the water shoaled, pulling a narrow skiff.

"Hillo!" shouted Doctor Dennis. "Be you mad?"

The stouter of the figures hobbled up. It was Bowlegs. His voice was deadened in the cold of the fog, but he wiped the hot sweat from his face.

"In God's name, be thar none of ye ull bear a hand with me? Ud ye sit here an' see 'em drown? Benny 's thar,—my Ben."

Joe shook his head.

"My best friend be there," said the old Doctor. "But what can ye do? Your boat will be paper in that sea, Phil."

"That 's so," droned out one or two of the wreckers, dully nodding.

"Curses on ye for cowards, then!" cried Bowlegs, as he plunged into the surf, and righted his boat. "Look who 's my mate, shame on ye!"

His mate shoved the skiff out with an oar into the seething breakers, turning to do it, and showed them, by the far-reaching fire-light, old Phebe Trull, stripped to her red woollen chemise and flannel petticoat, her yellow, muscular arms and chest bare. Her peaked old face was set, and her faded blue eye aflame. She did not hear the cry of horror from the wreckers.

"Ye 've a better pull than any white-liver of 'em, from Tom's to Barnegat," gasped Bowlegs, struggling against the surf.

She was wrestling for life with Death itself; but the quiet, tender smile did not leave her face.

"My God! ef I cud pull as when I was a gell!" she muttered. "Derrick, I 'm comin'! I 'm comin', boy!"

The salt spray wet their little fire of logs, beside which Snap sat crying,—put it out at last, leaving a heap of black cinders. The night fell heavier and cold; boat and schooner alike were long lost and gone in outer darkness. As they wandered up and down, chilled and hopeless, they could not see each other's faces,—only the patch of white sand at their feet. When they shouted, no gun or cry answered them again. All was silence, save the awful beat of the surf upon the shore, going on forever with its count, count of the hours until the time when the sea shall at last give up its dead.

Ben Van Note did not run the Chief in near shore purposely; but the fog was dense, and Ben was a better sailor than pilot. He took the wheel himself about an hour before they struck,—the two or three other men at their work on deck, with haggard, anxious faces, and silent: it is not the manner of these Jersey coast-men to chatter in heavy weather.

Philbrick, Doctor Bowdler's boy, lounged beside Ben, twisting a greasy lantern: "a town-bred fellow," Ben said; "put him in mind of young, rank cheese."

"You 'd best keep a sharp eye, Van Note," he said; "this is a dirty bit of water, and you 've two great men aboard: one patcher of the body, t' other of the soul."

"I vally my own neck more than either," growled Ben, and after a while forced himself to add, "*He* 's no backbone,—the little fellow with your master, I mean."

"Umph!" superciliously. "I 'd like to see the 'little fellow' making neat bits out of that carcass of yours! His dainty white fingers carve off a fellow's legs and arms, caring no more than if they were painting flowers. He is a neat flower-painter, Dr. Birkenshead; moulds in clay, too."

He stared as Van Note burst into a coarse guffaw.

"Flower-painter, eh? Well, well, young man. You 'd best go below. It 's dirtier water than you think."

Doctors Bowdler and Birkenshead were down in the little cabin, reading by the dull light of a coal-oil lamp. When the vessel began to toss so furiously, the elder man rose and paced fussily to and fro, rubbing his fingers through his iron-gray hair. His companion was too much engrossed by his paper to heed him. He had a small, elegantly shaped figure,—the famous surgeon,—a dark face, drawn by a few heavy lines; looking at it, you felt, that, in spite of his womanish delicacies of habit, which lay open to all, never apologized for, he was a man whom you could not approach familiarly, though he were your brother born. He stopped reading presently, slowly folding the newspaper straight, and laying it down.

"That is a delicious blunder of the Administration," with a little gurgling laugh of thorough relish. "You remember La Rochefoucauld's[4] aphorism, 'One is never so easily deceived as when one seeks to deceive others'?"

Doctor Bowdler looked uncomfortable.

"A selfish French Philister, La Rochefoucauld!" he blurted out. "I feel as if I had been steeped in meanness and vulgarity all my life, when I read him."

"He knew men," said the other, coolly, resetting a pocket set of chessmen on the board where they had been playing,—"Frenchmen," shortly.

"Doctor Birkenshead," after a pause, "you appear to have no sympathies with either side, in this struggle for the nation's life. You neither attack nor defend our government."

"In plain English, I have no patriotism? Well, to be honest, I don't comprehend how any earnest seeker for truth can have. If my country has truth, so far she nourishes me, and I am grateful; if not,—why, the air is no purer nor the government more worthy of reverence because I chanced to be born here."

"Why, Sir," said the Doctor, stopping short and growing red, "you could apply such an argument as that to a man's feeling for his wife or child or mother!"

"So you could," looking closely at the queen to see the carving.

Doctor Bowdler looked at him searchingly, and then began his angry walk again in silence. What was the use of answering? No wonder a man who talked in that way was famed in this country and in Europe for his coolness and skill in cutting up living bodies. And yet—remorsefully, looking furtively at him—Birkenshead was not a hard fellow, after all. There was that pauper-hospital of his; and he had known him turn sick when operating on children, and damn the people who brought them to him.

Doctor Bowdler was a little in dread of this future husband of his niece, feeling there was a great gulf between them intellectually, the surgeon having a rare power in a line of life of which he knew nothing. Besides, he could not understand him,—not his homely, keen little face even. The eyes held their own thought, and never answered yours; but on the mouth there was a forlorn depression sometimes, like that of a man who, in spite of his fame, felt himself alone and neglected. It rested there now, as he idly fingered the chessmen.

"Mary will kiss it away in time, maybe,"—doubting, as he said it, whether Mary did not come nearer the man's head than his heart. He stopped, looking out of the hole by the ladder that served the purpose of a window.

"It grows blacker every minute. I shall begin to repent tempting you on such a harebrained expedition, Doctor."

"No. This Van Note seems a cautious sailor enough," carelessly.

"Yes. He's on his own ground, too. We ought to run into Squan Inlet by morning. Did you speak?"

Birkenshead shook his head; the Doctor noticed, however, that his hand had suddenly stopped moving the chess-men; he rested his chin in the other.

"Some case he has left worries him," he thought. "He's not the man to relish this wild-goose chase of mine. It's bad enough for Mary to jar against his quiet tastes with her reforming whims, without my"—

"I would regret bringing you here," he said aloud, "if I did not think you would find a novelty in this shore and people. This coast is hardly 'canny,' as MacAulay would say. It came, literally, out of the sea. Sometime, ages ago, it belonged to the bed of the ocean, and it never has reconciled itself to the life of the land; its Flora is different from that of the boundaries; if you dig a few feet into its marl, you find layers of shells belonging to deep soundings, sharks' teeth and bones, and the like. The people, too, have a 'marvellously fishy and ancient smell.'"

The little man at the table suddenly rose, pushing the chessmen from him.

"What is there to wonder at?"—with a hoarse, unnatural laugh. "That's Nature. You cannot make fat pastures out of sea-sand, any more than a thorough-blood *gentilhomme* out of a clam-digger. The shark's teeth will show, do what you will." He pulled at his whiskers nervously, went to the window, motioning Doctor Bowdler roughly aside. "Let me see what the night is doing."

The old gentleman stared in a grave surprise. What had he said to startle Birkenshead so utterly out of himself? The color had left his face at the first mention of this beach; his very voice was changed, coarse and thick, as if some other man had broken out through him. At that moment, while Doctor Bowdler stood feebly adjusting his watch-chain, and eying his companion's back, like one who has found a panther in a domestic cat, and knows not when he will spring, the tornado struck the ocean a few feet from their side, cleaving a path for itself into deep watery walls. There was an instant's reeling and intense darkness, then the old Doctor tried to gather himself up, bruised and sick, from the companion-way, where he had been thrown.

"Better lie still," said Birkenshead, in the gentle voice with which he was used to calm a patient.

The old gentleman managed to sit up on the floor. By the dull glare of the cabin-lantern he could see the surgeon sitting on the lower rung of the ladder, leaning forward, holding his head in his hands.

"Strike a light, can't you, Birkenshead? What has happened? Bah! this is horrible! I have swallowed the sea-water! Hear it swash against the sides of the boat! Is the boat going to pieces?"

"And there met us 'a tempestuous wind called Euroclydon,'"[5] said Birkenshead, looking up with a curious smile.

"Did there?"—rubbing his shoulder. "I've kept clear of the sea so far, and I think in future— Hark! what's that?" as through the darkness and the thunderous surge of the water, and the short, fierce calls of the men on board, came a low shivering crack, distinct as a human whisper. "What is it, Birkenshead?" impatiently, when the other made no answer.

"The schooner has struck the bar. She is going to pieces."

The words recalled the old servant of Christ from his insane fright to himself.

"That means death! does it not?"

"Yes."

The two men stood silent,—Doctor Bowdler with his head bent and eyes closed. He looked up presently.

"Let us go on deck now and see what we can do,"—turning cheerfully.

"No, there are too many there already."

There was an old tin life-preserver hanging on a hook by the door; the surgeon climbed up to get it, and began buckling it about the old man in spite of his remonstrances. The timbers groaned and strained, the boat trembled like some great beast in its death-agony, settled heavily, and then the beams on one side of them parted. They stood on a shelving plank floor, snapped off two feet from them, the yellow sky overhead, and the breakers crunching their footing away.

"O God!" cried Bowdler, when he looked out at the sea. He was not a brave man; and he could not see it, when he looked; there was but a horror of great darkness, a thunder of sound, and a chilly creeping of salt-water up his legs, as if the great monster licked his victim with his lifeless tongue. Straight in front of them, at the very edge of the horizon, he thought the little clam-digger's fire opened a tunnel of greenish light into the night, "dull and melancholy as a scene in Hades." They saw the men sitting around the blaze with their hands clasped about their knees, the woman's figure alone, and watching.

"Mary!" cried the old man, in the shrill extremity of his agony.

His companion shivered.

"Take this from me, boy!" cried Doctor Bowdler, trying to tear off the life-preserver. "It's a chance. I 've neither wife nor child to care if I live or die. You're young; life 's beginning for you. I 've done with it. Ugh! this water is deadly cold. Take it, I say."

"No," said the other, quietly restraining him.

"Can you swim?"

"In this sea?"—with a half-smile, and a glance at the tossing breakers.

"You 'll swim? Promise me you 'll swim! And if I come to shore and see Mary?"

Birkenshead had regained the reticent tone habitual to him.

"Tell her, I wish I had loved her better. She will understand. I see the use of love in this last hour."

"Is there any one else?"

"There used to be some one. Twenty years ago I said I would come, and I 'm coming now."

"I don't hear you."

Birkenshead laughed at his own thought, whatever it was. The devil who had tempted him might have found in the laugh an outcry more bitter than any agony of common men.

The planks beneath their feet sank inch by inch. They were shut off from the larboard side of the vessel. For a time they had heard oaths and cries from the other men, but now all was silent.

"There is no help coming from shore,"—(the old man's voice was weakening,)—"and this footing is giving way."

"Yes, it's going. Lash your arms to me by your braces, Doctor. I can help you for a few moments."

So saying, Birkenshead tore off his own coat and waistcoat; but as he turned, the coming breaker dashed over their heads, he heard a faint gasp, and when his eyes were clear of the salt, he saw the old man's gray hair in the midst of a sinking wave.

"I wish I could have saved him," he said,—then made his way as best he could by feet and hands to a bulk of timber standing out of the water, and sitting down there, clutched his hands about his knees, very much as he used to do when he was a clam-digger and watched the other boys bringing in their hauls.

"Twenty years ago I said I 'd come, and I 'm coming," he went on repeating.

Derrick Trull was no coward, as boy or man, but he made no effort to save himself; the slimy water washed him about like a wet rag. He was alone now, if never before in those twenty years; his world of beautiful, cultured, graceful words and sights and deeds was not here, it was utterly gone out; there was no God here, that he thought of; he was quite alone: so, in sight of this lee coast, the old love in that life dead years ago roused, and the mean crime dragged on through every day since gnawed all the manliness and courage out of him.

She would be asleep now, old Phebe Trull, — in the room off the brick kitchen, her wan limbs curled up under her check nightgown, her pipe and noggin of tea on the oven-shelf; he could smell the damp, musty odor of the slopsink near by. What if he could reach shore? What if he were to steal up to her bed and waken her?

"It's Derrick, back, mother," he would say. How the old creature would skirl and cry over her son Derrick! — Derrick! he hated the name. It belonged to that time of degradation and stinting and foulness.

Doctor Birkenshead lifted himself up. Pish! the old fish-wife had long since forgotten her scapegrace son, — thought him dead. *He was dead.* He wondered — and this while every swash of the salt-water brought death closer up to his lips — if Miss Defourchet had seen "Mother Phebe." Doubtless she had, and had made a sketch of her to show him; — but no, she was not a picturesque pauper, — vulgar, simply. The water came up closer; the cold of it, and the extremity of peril, or, maybe, this old gnawing at the heart, more virulent than either, soon drew the strength out of his body: close study and high living had made the joints less supple than Derrick Trull's: he lay there limp and unable, — his brain alert, but fickle. It put the watery death out of sight, and brought his familiar every-day life about him: the dissecting-room; curious cases that had puzzled him; drawing-rooms, beautiful women; he sang airs from the operas, sad, broken little snatches, in a deep, mellow voice, finely trained, — fragments of a litany to the Virgin. Birkenshead's love of beauty was a hungry monomania; his brain was filled with memories of the pictures of the Ideal Mother and her Son. One by one they came to him now, the holy woman-type which for ages supplied to the world that tenderness and pity which the Church had stripped from God. Even in his delirium the man of fastidious instincts knew this was what he craved; even now he remembered other living mothers he had known, delicate, nobly born women, looking on their babes with eyes full of all gracious and pure thoughts. With the sharp contrast of a dream came the old clam-digger, barefoot in the mud, her basket of soiled clothes on her shoulder, — her son Derrick, a vulgar lad, aping gentility, behind her. Closer and closer came the waters;

a shark's gray hide glittered a few feet from him. Death, sure of his prey, nibbled and played with it; in a little while he lay supine and unconscious.

Reason came back to him like an electric shock; for all the parts of Dr. Birkenshead's organization were instinctive, nervous, like a woman's. When it came, the transient delirium had passed; he was his cool, observant self. He lay on the wet floor of a yawl skiff, his head resting on a man's leg; the man was rowing with even, powerful strokes, and he could feel rather than see in the darkness a figure steering. He was saved. His heart burned with a sudden glorious glow of joy, and genial, boyish zest of life,—one of the excesses of his nature. He tried to speak, but his tongue was stiff, his throat dry; he could have caressed the man's slimy sleeve that touched his cheek, he was so glad to live. The boatman was in no humor for caresses; he drew his labored breath sharply, fighting the waves, rasping out a sullen oath when they baffled him. The little surgeon had tact enough to keep silent; he did not care to talk, either. Life rose before him a splendid possibility, as never before. From the silent figure at the helm came neither word nor motion. Presently a bleak morning wind mingled with the fierce, incessant nor'easter; the three in the yawl, all sea-bred, knew the difference.

"Night ull break soon," said Bowlegs.

It did break in an hour or two into a ghastly gray dawn, bitter cold,—the slanting bars of sharp light from beyond the sea-line falling on the bare coast, on a headland of which moved some black, uneasy figures.

"Th' wrackers be thar."

There was no answer.

"Starboard! Hoy, Mother Phebe!"

She swayed her arms round, her head still fallen on her breast. Doctor Birkenshead, from his half-shut eyes, could see beside him the half-naked, withered old body, in its dripping flannel clothes. God! it had come, then, the time to choose! It was she who had saved him! she was here,—alive!

"Mother!" he cried, trying to rise.

But the word died in his dry throat; his body, stiff and icy cold, refused to move.

"What ails ye?" growled the man, looking at her. "Be ye giv' out so near land? We 've had a jolly seinin' together," laughing savagely, "ef we did miss the fish we went for, an' brought in this herrin'."

"Thee little brother's safe, Bowlegs," said the old woman, in a feeble, far-off voice. "My boy ull bring him to shore."

The boatman gulped back his breath; it sounded like a cry, but he laughed it down.

"You think yer Derrick ull make shore, eh? Well, I don't think that ar way o' Ben. Ben 's gone under. It 's not often the water gets a ten-year-older like that. I raised him. It was I sent him with Van Note this run. That makes it pleasanter now!" The words were grating out stern and sharp.

"Thee knows Derrick said he 'd come," the woman said simply.

She stooped with an effort, after a while, and, thrusting her hand under Doctor Birkenshead's shirt, felt his chest.

"It 's a mere patchin' of a body. He 's warm yet. Maybe," looking closely into the face, "he 'd have seen my boy aboord, an' could say which way he tuk. A drop of raw liquor ull bring him round."

Phil glanced contemptuously at the surgeon's fine linen, and the dia-mond *solitaire* on the small, white hand.

"It 's not likely that chap ud know the deck-hands. It 's the man Doctor Dennis was expectin'."

"Ay?" vaguely.

She kept her hand on the feebly beating heart, chafing it. He lay there, looking her straight in the eyes; in hers—dull with the love and waiting of a life—there was no instinct of recognition. The kind, simple, blue eyes, that had watched his baby limbs grow and strengthen in her arms! How gray the hair was! but its bit of curl was in it yet. The same dear old face that he used to hurry home at night to see! Nobody had loved him but this woman,—never; if he could but struggle up and get his head on her breast! How he used to lie there when he was a big boy, listening to the same old stories night after night,—the same old stories! Something homely and warm and true was waking in him to-night that had been dead for years and years; this was no matter of æsthetics or taste, it was real, *real*. He wondered if people felt in this way who had homes, or those simple folk who loved the Lord.

Inch by inch, with hard, slow pulls, they were gaining shore. Mary De-fourchet was there. If he came to her as the clam-digger's bastard son, owning the lie he had practised half his life,—what then? He had fought hard for his place in the world, for the ease and culture of his life,—most of all, for the society of thorough-bred and refined men, his own kindred. What would they say to Derrick Trull, and the mother he had kept smoth-ered up so long? All this with his eyes fixed on hers. The cost was counted. It was to give up wife and place and fame,—all he had earned. It had not been cheaply earned. All Doctor Birkenshead's habits and intellect, the million nervous whims of a sensitive man, rebelled against the sacrifice. Nothing to battle them down but—what?

"Be ye hurt, Mother Phebe? What d' yer hold yer breath for?"

She evaded him with a sickly smile.

"We 're gainin', Bowlegs. It 's but a few minutes till we make shore. He 'll be there, if—if he be ever to come."

"Yes, Gran," with a look of pity.

The wind stood still; it held its breath, as though with her it waited. The man strained against the tide till the veins in his brawny neck stood out purple. On the bald shore, the dim figures gathered in a cluster, eagerly watching. Old Phebe leaned forward, shading her eyes with her hand, peering from misty headland to headland with bated breath. A faint cheer reached them from land.

"Does thee know the voices, Bowlegs?"—in a dry whisper.

"It be the wreckers."

"Oh!—Derrick," after a pause, "would be too weak to cheer; he 'd be worn with the swimmin'. Thee must listen sharp. Did they cry my name out? as if there was some'ut for me?"

"No, Mother," gruffly. "But don't ye lose heart after twenty years' waitin'."

"I 'll not."

As he pulled, the boatman looked over at her steadily.

"I never knowed what this was for ye, till now I 've loss Ben," he said, gently. "It 's as if you 'd been lossin' him every day these twenty years."

She did not hear him; her eyes, straining, scanned the shore; she seemed to grow blind as they came nearer; passed her wet sleeve over them again and again.

"Thee look for me, Bowlegs," she said, weakly.

The yawl grated on the shallow waters of the bar; the crowd rushed down to the edge of the shore, the black figures coming out distinct now, half a dozen of the wreckers going into the surf and dragging the boat up on the beach. She turned her head out to sea, catching his arm with both hands.

"Be there any strange face to shore? Thee did n't know him. A little face, full o' th' laugh an' joke, an' brown curls blown by the wind."

"The salt 's in my eyes. I can't rightly see, Mother Phebe."

The surgeon saw Doctor Bowdler waiting, pale and haggard, his fat little arms outstretched: the sea had spared him by some whim, then. When the men lifted him out, another familiar face looked down on him: it was Mary. She had run into the surf with them, and held his head in her arms.

"I love you! I love you!" she sobbed, kissing his hand.

"There be a fire up by the bathing houses, an' hot coffee," said old Doctor Dennis, with a kindly, shrewd glance at the famous surgeon. "Miss Defourchet and Snap made it for you. *She* knew."

Birkenshead, keeping her hand, turned to the forlorn figure standing shivering alone, holding both palms pressed to her temples, her gray hair and clothes dripping.

"Thee don't tell me that he 's here, Bowlegs," she said. "There might be some things the wrackers hes found up in the bathin'-houses. There might,—in the bathin'-houses. It's the last day,—it 's twenty year"—

Doctor Birkenshead looked down at the beautiful flushed face pressed close to his side, then pushed it slowly from him. He went over to where the old woman stood, and kneeled beside her in the sand, drawing her down to him.

"Mother," he said, "it 's Derrick, mother. Don't you know your boy?"

With the words the boy's true spirit seemed to come back to him,— Derrick Trull again, who went with such a hot, indignant heart to win money and place for the old mother at home. He buried his head in her knees, as she crouched over him, silent, passing her hands quickly and lightly over his face.

"God forgive me!" he cried. "Take my head in your arms, mother, as you used to do. Nobody has loved me as you did. Mother! mother!"

Phebe Trull did not speak one word. She drew her son's head close into her trembling old arms, and held it there motionless. It was an old way she had of caressing him.

Doctor Dennis drew the eager, wondering crowd away from them.

"I don't understand," said Doctor Bowdler, excitedly.

"I do," said his niece, and, sitting down in the sand, looked out steadfastly to sea.—

Bow-legged Phil drove the anchor into the beach, and pulled it idly out again.

"I 've some'ut here for you, Phil," said Joe, gravely. "The water washed it up."

The fellow's teeth chattered as he took it.

"Well, ye know what it is?" fiercely. "Only a bit of a Scotch cap,"— holding it up on his fist. "I bought it down at Port Monmouth, Saturday, for him. I was a-goin' to take him home this week up to the old folks in Connecticut. I kin take *that* instead, an' tell 'em whar our Benny is."

"That 's so," said Joe, his eye twinkling as he looked over Phil's shoulder.

A fat little hand slapped the said shoulder, and "Hillo, Bowlegs!" came in a small shout in his ear. Phil turned, looked at the boy from head to foot, gulped down one or two heavy breaths.

"Hi! you young vagabond, you!" he said, and went suddenly back to his anchor, keeping his head down on his breast for a long while. —

He had piled up the sand at her back to make her a seat while they waited for the wagons. Now he sat on her skirts, holding her hands to warm them. He had almost forgotten Mary and the Doctor. Nature or instinct, call it what you will, some subtle whim of blood called love, brought the old clam-digger nearer to him than all the rest of the world. He held the bony fingers tight, looked for an old ring she used to wear, tried to joke to bring out the flicker of a smile on her mouth, leaned near to catch her breath. He remembered how curiously sweet it used to be, like new milk.

The dawn opened clear and dark blue; the sun yet waited below the stormy sea. Though they sat there a long while, she was strangely quiet, — did not seem so much afraid of him as she used to be when he began to rise above her, — held his hand, with a bright, contented face, and said little else than "My boy! my boy!" under her breath. Her eyes followed every movement of his face with an insatiate hunger; yet the hesitation and quiet in her motions and voice were unnatural. He asked her once or twice if she were ill.

"Wait a bit, an' I'll tell thee, Derrick," she said. "Thee must remember I'm not as young as I was then," with a smile. "Thee must speak fast, my son. I'd like to hear of thee gran' home, if thee's willin'."

He told her, as he would to please a child, of the place and fame and wealth he had won; but it had not the effect he expected. Before he had finished, the look in her eyes grew vague and distant. Some thought in the poor clam-digger's soul made these things but of little moment. She interrupted him.

"There be one yonner that loves my boy. I'd like to speak a word to her before— Call her, Derrick."

He rose and beckoned to Miss Defourchet. When she came near, and saw the old woman's face, she hurried, and, stooping down quickly, took her head in her arms.

"Derrick has come back to you," she said. "Will you let him bring me with him to call you mother?"

"Mary?"

She did not look at him. Old Phebe pushed her back with a searching look.

"Is it true love you'll give my boy?"

"I'll try." In a lower voice, — "I never loved him so well as when he came back to you."

The old woman was silent a long time.

"Thee 's right. It was good for Derrick to come back to me. I don't know what that big world be like where thee an' Derrick 's been. The sea keeps talkin' of it, I used to think; it 's kep' moanin' with the cries of it. But the true love at home be worth it all. I knowed that always. I kep' it for my boy. He went from it, but it brought him back. Out of the sea it brought him back."

He knew this was not his mother's usual habit of speech. Some great truth seemed coming closer to the old fish-wife, lifting her forever out of her baser self. She leaned on the girl beside her, knowing her, in spite of blood and education, to be no truer woman than herself. The inscrutable meaning of the eyes deepened. The fine, sad smile came on the face, and grew fixed there. She was glad he had come,—that was all. Mary was a woman; her insight was quicker.

"Where are you hurt?" she said, softly.

"Hush! don't fret the boy. It was the pullin' last night, think. I 'm not as strong as when I was a gell."

They sat there, watching the dawn break into morning. Over the sea the sky opened into deeps of silence and light. The surf rolled in, in long, low, grand breakers, like riders to a battle-field, tossing back their gleaming white plumes of spray when they touched the shore. But the wind lulled as though something more solemn waited on the land than the sea's rage or the quiet of the clouds.

"Does thee mind, Derrick," said his mother, with a low laugh, "how thee used to play with this curl ahint my ear? When thee was a bit baby, thee begun it. I 've kep' it ever since. It be right gray now."

"Yes, mother."

He had crept closer to her now. In the last half-hour his eyes had grown clearer. He dared not look away from her. Joe and Bowlegs had drawn near, and Doctor Bowdler. They stood silent, with their hats off. Doctor Bowdler felt her pulse, but her son did not touch it. His own hand was cold and clammy; his heart sick with a nameless dread. Was he, then, just too late?

"Yes, I did. I kep' it for thee, Derrick. I always knowed thee 'd come,"— in a lower voice. "There 's that dress, too. I 'd like thee to 've seen me in that; but"—

"Take her hands in yours," whispered Mary.

"Is it thee, my son?"—with a smile. After a long pause,—"I kep' it, an' I kep' true love for thee, Derrick. God brought thee back for 't, I think.

It be the best, after all. He 'll bring thee to me for 't at th' last, my boy, —
my boy!"

As the faint voice lingered and died upon the words, the morning sun
shone out in clear, calm glory over the still figures on the beach. The
others had crept away, and left the three alone with God and His great
angel, in whose vast presence there is no life save Love, no future save
Love's wide eternity.

The Harmonists

Atlantic Monthly, May 1866

My brother Josiah I call a successful man,—very successful, though only an attorney in a manufacturing town. But he fixed his goal, and reached it. He belongs to the ruling class,—men with slow, measuring eyes and bull-dog jaws,—men who know their own capacity to an atom's weight, and who go through life with moderate, inflexible, unrepenting steps. He looks askance at me when I cross his path; he is in the great market making his way: I learned long ago that there was no place there for me. Yet I like to look in, out of the odd little corner into which I have been shoved,—to look in at the great play, never beginning and never ending, of bargain and sale, for which all the world's but a stage; to see how men like my brother have been busy, since God blessed all things he had made, in dragging them down to the trade level, and stamping price-marks on them. Josiah looks at me grimly, as I said. Jog as methodically as I will from desk to bed and back to desk again, he suspects some outlaw blood under the gray head of the fagged-out old clerk. He indulges in his pictures, his bronzes: I have my high office-stool, and a bedroom in the fifth story of a cheap hotel. Yet he suspects me of having forced a way out of the actual common-sense world by sheer force of whims and vagaries, and to have pre-empted a home-stead for myself in some dream-land, where neither he nor the tax-gatherer can enter.

"It won't do," he said to-day, when I was there (for I use his books now and then). "Old Père Bonhours,[1] you're poring over? Put it down, and come take some clam soup. Much those fellows knew about life! Zachary! Zachary! you have kept company with shadows these forty years, until you have grown peaked and gaunt yourself. When will you go to work and be a live man?"

I knew we were going to have the daily drill which Josiah gave to his ideas; so I rolled the book up to take with me, while he rubbed his spectacles angrily, and went on.

"I tell you, the world 's a great property-exchanging machine, where everything has its weight and value; a great, inexorable machine,—and whoever tries to shirk his work in it will be crushed! Crushed! Think of your old friend Knowles!"

I began to hurry on my old over-coat; I never had but two or three friends, and I could not hear their names from Josiah's mouth. But he was not quick to see when he had hurt people.

"Why, the poet,"—more sententious than before,—"the poet sells his song; he knows that the airiest visions must resolve into trade-laws. You cannot escape from them. I see your wrinkled old face, red as a boy's, over the newspapers sometimes. There was the daring of that Rebel Jackson,[2] Frémont's[3] proclamation, Shaw's[4] death; you claimed those things as heroic, prophetic. They were mere facts tending to solve the great problem of Capital vs. Labor. There was one work for which the breath was put into our nostrils,—to grow, and make the world grow by giving and taking. Give and take; and the wisest man gives the least and gains the most."

I left him as soon as I could escape. I respect Josiah: his advice would be invaluable to any man; but I am content that we should live apart,—quite content. I went down to Yorke's for my solitary chop. The old prophet Solomon somewhere talks of the conies[5] or ants as "a feeble folk who prepare their meat in the summer." I joke to myself about that sometimes, thinking I should claim kindred with them; for, looking back over the sixty years of Zack Humphreys's life, they seem to me to have pretty much gone in preparing the bread and meat from day to day. I see but little result of all the efforts of that time beyond that solitary chop; and a few facts and hopes, may be, gathered outside of the market, which, Josiah says, absorb all of the real world. All day, sitting here at my desk in Wirt's old counting-house, these notions of Josiah's have dogged me. These sums that I jotted down, the solid comforts they typified, the homes, the knowledge, the travel they would buy,—these were, then, the real gist of this thing we called life, were they? The great charities money had given to the world,—Christ's Gospel preached by it.—Did it cover all, then? Did it?

What a wholesome (or unwholesome) scorn of barter Knowles had! The old fellow never collected a debt; and, by the way, as seldom paid one. The "dirty dollar" came between him and very few people. Yet the heart in his great mass of flesh beat fiercely for an honor higher than that known to most men. I have sat here all the afternoon, staring out at the winter sky, scratching down a figure now and then, and idly going back to the time when I was a younger man than now, but even then with neither wife nor child, and no home beyond an eating-house; thinking how I caught old Knowles's zest for things which lay beyond trade-laws; how eager I grew in the search of them; how he inoculated me with Abolitionism, Communism, every other fever that threatened to destroy the commercial status of the world, and substitute a single-eyed regard for human rights. It occurred to me, too, that some of those odd, one-sided facts, which it used to please me to gather then,—queer bits of men's history, not to be judged by Josiah's rules,—it might please others to hear. What if I wrote them down these winter evenings? Nothing in them rare or strange; but they lay outside of the market, and were true.

Not one of them which did not bring back Knowles, with his unwieldy heat and bluster. He found a flavor and meaning in the least of these hints of mine, gloating over the largess given and received in the world, for which money had no value. His bones used to straighten, and his eye glitter under the flabby brow, at the recital of any brave, true deed, as if it had been his own; as if, but for some mischance back yonder in his youth, it might have been given to even this poor old fellow to strike a great, ringing blow on Fate's anvil before he died,—to give his place in the life-boat to a more useful man,—to help buy with his life the slave's freedom.

Let me tell you the story of our acquaintance. Josiah, even, would hold the apology good for claiming so much of your time for this old dreamer of dreams, since I may give you a bit of useful knowledge in the telling about a place and people here in the States utterly different from any other, yet almost unknown, and, so far as I know, undescribed. When I first met Knowles it was in an obscure country town in Pennsylvania, as he was on his way across the mountains with his son. I was ill in the little tavern where he stopped; and, he being a physician, we were thrown together,—I a raw country lad, and he fresh from the outer world, of which I knew nothing,—a man of a muscular, vigorous type even then. But what he did for me, or the relation we bore to each other, is of no import here.

One or two things about him puzzled me. "Why do you not bring your boy to this room?" I asked, one day.

His yellow face colored with angry surprise. "Antony? What do you know of Antony?"

"I have watched you with him," I said, "on the road yonder. He 's a sturdy, manly little fellow, of whom any man would be proud. But you are not proud of him. In this indifference of yours to the world, you include him. I 've seen you thrust him off into the ditch when he caught at your hand, and let him struggle on by himself."

He laughed. "Right! Talk of love, family affection! I have tried it. Why should my son be more to me than any other man's son, but for an extended selfishness? I have cut loose all nearer ties than those which hold all men as brothers, and Antony comes no closer than any other."

"I 've watched you coming home sometimes," I said, coolly. "One night you carried the little chap, as he was sound asleep. It was dark; but I saw you sit by the pond yonder, thinking no one saw you, caressing him, kissing his face, his soiled little hands, his very feet, as fierce and tender as a woman."

Knowles got up, pacing about, disturbed and angry; he was like a woman in other ways, nervous, given to sudden heats of passion,—was leaky with his own secrets. "Don't talk to me of Antony! I know no child, no wife, nor any brother, except my brother-man."

He went trotting up and down the room, then sat down with his back to me. It was night, and the room was dimly lighted by the smoky flame of a lard lamp. The solitary old man told me his story. Let me be more chary with his pain than he was; enough to say that his wife was yet living, but lost to him. Her boy Antony came into the room just when his father had ceased speaking,—a stout little chap of four years, with Knowles's ungainly build, and square, honest face, but with large, hazel, melancholy eyes. He crept up on my bed, and, lying across the foot, went to sleep.

Knowles glanced at him,—looked away, his face darkening. "Sir," he said, "I have thrust away all arbitrary ties of family. The true life,"—his eye dilating, as if some great thought had come into his brain,—"the true life is one where no marriage exists,—where the soul acknowledges only the pure impersonal love to God and our brother-man, and enters into peace. It can so enter, even here, by dint of long contemplation and a simple pastoral work for the body."

This was new talk in that country tavern: I said nothing.

"I 'm not dreaming dreams," raising his voice. "I have a real plan for you and me, lad. I have found the Utopia of the prophets and poets, an actual place, here in Pennsylvania. We will go there together, shut out the trade-world, and devote ourselves with these lofty enthusiasts to a life of purity, celebacy, meditation,—helpful and loving to the great Humanity."

I was but a lad; my way in life had not been smooth. While he talked on in this strain my blood began to glow. "What of Tony?" I interrupted, after a while.

"The boy?" not looking at the little heap at the foot of the bed. "They will take him in, probably. Children are adopted by the society; they receive education free from the personal taints given by father and mother."

"Yes," not very clear as to what he meant.

The moon began to fleck the bare floor with patches of light and shadow, bringing into relief the broad chest of the man beside me, the big, motionless head dropped forward, and the flabby yellow face set with a terrible, lifelong gravity. His scheme was no joke to him. Whatever soul lay inside of this gross animal body had been tortured nigh to death, and this plan was its desperate chance at a fresh life. Watching me askance as I tried to cover the boy with the blankets, he began the history of this new Utopia, making it blunt and practical as words could compass, to convince me that he was no dreamer of dreams. I will try to recall the facts as he stated them that night; they form a curious story at all times.

In 1805, a man named George Rapp, in Würtemberg, became possessed with the idea of founding a new and pure social system,—sowing a mere seed at first, but with the hope, doubtless, of planting a universal truth thereby which should some day affect all humanity. His scheme differed from Comte's[6] or Saint-Simon's,[7] in that it professed to go back to the old patriarchal form for its mode of government, establishing under that, however, a complete community of interest. Unlike other communist reformers, too, Rapp did not look through his own class for men of equal intelligence and culture with himself of whom to make converts, but, gathering several hundred of the peasants from the neighborhood, he managed to imbue them with an absolute faith in his divine mission, and emigrated with them to the backwoods of Pennsylvania, in Butler County. After about ten years they removed to the banks of the Wabash, in Indiana; then, in 1825, returned to Pennsylvania, and settled finally in Beaver County, some sixteen miles below Pittsburg, calling their village Economy.

"A great man, as I conceive him, this Rapp," said Knowles. "His own property, which was large, was surrendered to the society at its foundation, and this to the least particular, not reserving for his own use even the library or gallery of paintings pertaining to his family; nor did the articles of association allow any exclusive advantage to accrue to him or his heirs from the profits of the community. He held his office as spiritual and temporal head, not by election of the people, but assumed it as by Divine commission, as Moses and Aaron held theirs; and not only did the power of the man over his followers enable him to hold this autocratic authority during a long life, unimpaired, but such was the skill with which his decrees were framed that after his death this authority was reaffirmed by the highest legal tribunal of the country.[8] With all his faith in his divine mission, too, he had a clear insight into all the crookedness and weakness of the natures he was trying to elevate. He knew that these dogged, weak

Germans needed coercion to make them fit for ultimate freedom; he held the power of an apostle over them, therefore, with as pure purpose, it's my belief, as any apostle that went before him. The superstitious element lay ready in them for him to work upon. I find no fault with him for working it."

"How?" I asked.

Knowles hesitated. "When their stupidity blocked any of his plans for their advancement, he told them that, unless they consented, their names should be blotted out from the Book of Life,—which was but a coarse way of stating a great truth, after all; telling them, too, that God must be an unjust Judge should he mete out happiness or misery to them without consulting him,—that his power over their fate stretched over this life and the next,—which, considering the limitless influence of a strong mind over a weak one, was not so false, either."

Rapp's society, Knowles stated, did not consist altogether of this class, however. A few men of education and enthusiasm had joined him, and carried out his plans with integrity. The articles of association were founded in a strict sense of justice; members entering the society relinquished all claim to any property, much or little, of which they might be possessed, receiving thereafter common maintenance, education, profit, with the others; should they at any time thereafter choose to leave, they received the sum deposited without interest. A suit had just been decided in the Supreme Court of Pennsylvania[9] which had elicited this point.

Knowles, more and more eager, went on to describe the settlement as it had been pictured to him; the quaint, quiet village on the shores of "the Beautiful River," the rolling hills of woodland, the quiet valleys over which their flocks wandered, the simple pastoral work in which all joined; the day begun and ended with music;—even the rich, soft tints of the fresh Western sky about them were not forgotten, nor the picturesque dresses of the silent, primitive people.

"A home in which to forget all pain and sore, boy," ended the old man, gulping down a sigh, and then falling into a heavy silence.

It was long before I broke it. "They do not marry?"

"No," anxiously, as if I had reached the core of the truth in this matter at last. "It was their founder's scheme, as I believe, to lift them above all taint of human passion,—to bring them by pure work, solitude, and contact with a beautiful nature into a state of being where neither earthly love, nor hate, nor ambition can enter,—a sphere of infinite freedom, and infinite love for Him and all His creatures."

There was no doubting the fire of rapt enthusiasm in his eye, rising and looking out across the moonlit fields as if already he saw the pleasant hills of Beulah.[10]

"Thank God for George Rapp! he has found a home where a man can stand alone,"—stretching out his arms as if he would have torn out whatever vestige of human love tugged at his sick old heart, his eye hunting out Tony as he spoke.

The boy, startled from his sleep, muttered, and groped as a baby will for its mother's breast or hand. No hand met the poor little fingers, and they fell on the pillow empty, the child going to sleep again with a forlorn little cry. Knowles watched him, the thick lips under his moustache growing white.

"I purpose," he said, "that next week you and I shall go to these people, and, if possible, become members of their community,—cut loose from all these narrow notions of home and family, and learn to stand upright and free under God's heaven. The very air breathed by these noble enthusiasts will give us strength and lofty thoughts. Think it over, Humphreys."

"Yes."

He moved to the door,—held it open uncertainly. "I 'll leave the boy here to-night. He got into a foolish habit of sleeping in my arms when he was a baby; it 's time he was broke of it."

"Very well."

"He must learn to stand alone, eh?" anxiously. "Good night";—and in a moment I heard his heavy steps on the stairs, stopping, then going on faster, as if afraid of his own resolution.

In the middle of the night I was wakened by somebody fumbling for Tony at my side,—"Afraid the child would prove troublesome,"—and saw him go off with the boy like a mite in his arms, growling caresses like a lioness who has recovered her whelp. I say lioness, for, with all his weight of flesh and coarseness, Knowles left the impression on your mind of a sensitive, nervous woman.

Late one spring afternoon, a month after that, Knowles and I stood on one of the hills overlooking the communist village of Economy. I was weak and dizzy from illness and a long journey; the intense quiet of the landscape before me affected me like a strain of solemn music. Knowles had infected me with his eager hope. Nature was about to take me to her great mother's bosom, for the first time. Life was to give me the repose I asked, satisfy all the needs of my soul: here was the foretaste. The quaint little hamlet literally slept on the river-bank; not a living creature was visible on the three grass-grown streets; many of the high-gabled brick houses, even at that date of the colony, were closed and vacant, their inmates having dropped from the quiet of this life into an even deeper sleep, and having been silently transferred to rest under the flat grass of the apple-orchards, according to the habit of the society. From the other houses, however, pale rifts of smoke wavered across the cold blue sky; great apple and peach orchards swept up the hills back of the town, quite out of sight. They were in blossom, I remember, and covered the green of the hills with a veil of delicate pink. A bleak wind, as we stood there, brought their perfume towards us, and ruffled the broad, dark river into sudden ripples of cut silver: beyond that, motion there was none. Looking curiously down into the town, I could distinguish a great, barn-like church, a public laundry, bakery, apiary, and one or two other buildings, like factories, but all empty, apparently, and deserted. After all, was this some quaint German village brought hither in an enchanted sleep, and dropped down in the New World? About the houses were silent, trim little gardens, set round with yew and box cut in monstrous shapes, and filled with plants of which this soil knew nothing. Up a path from the woods, too, came at last some curious figures, in a dress belonging to the last century.

Knowles had no idea, like mine, of being bewitched; he rubbed his hands in a smothered excitement. "We too shall be Arcadians!" he burst out. "Humphreys!" anxiously, as we plodded down the hill, "we must be careful, very careful, my boy. These are greatly innocent and pure natures with which we have come in contact; the world must have grown vague and dim to them long ago, wrapped in their high communings. We must leave all worldly words and thoughts outside, as a snake drops his skin. No talk of money here, lad. It would be as well, too, not to mention any family ties, such as wife or child: such bonds must seem to this lofty human brotherhood debasing and gross."

So saying, and dropping Tony's hand in order that the child even might stand alone, we came into the village street; Knowles growing red with eagerness as one of the odd figures came towards us. "Careful, Zachary!" in a hoarse whisper. "It all depends on this first day whether we are accepted or not. Remember their purity of thought, their forms gathered from the patriarchs and apostles!"

I had a vague remembrance of a washing of feet, practised in those days; of calf-killing and open tents for strangers; so stood perplexed while the brother approached and stood there, like an animate lager-bier barrel, dressed in flannel, with a round hat on top. *"Was brauchen Sie?"* [11] he grumbled.

I don't know in what words Knowles's tremulous tones conveyed the idea that we were strangers, going on to state that we were also world-weary, and—

"Ach! want der supper," he said, his face brightening, and, turning, he jogged on, elephant-like, before, muttering something about himself. "Bin Yosef, an keepit der tavern,"[12]—to the door of which, one of the silent brick dwellings, he speedily brought us; and, summoning some "Christina" in a subdued bellow from the bowels of the cellar, went into the neat bar-room, and swallowed two glasses of wine to revive himself, dropping exhausted, apparently, into a chair.

Christina, an old dried-up woman, in the quaint, daintily clean dress of blue, emerged from the cellar-door, bringing with her a savory smell of frying ham and eggs. She glanced at us with suspicious blue eyes, and then, with "*Ach! der Liebling! mein schöner Schatz!*"[13] caught up Tony to her shrivelled breast in a sudden surprise, and, going back to the door, called "Fredrika!" Another old woman, dried, withered, with pale blue eyes, appeared, and the two, hastily shoving us chairs, took Tony between them, chattering in delighted undertones, patting his fat cheeks, his hands, feeling his clothes, straightening his leg, and laughing at the miniature muscles.

Knowles stared dumbly.

"You will haf der supper, hein?" said the first old woman, recollecting herself and coming forward, her thin jaws yet reddened. "Der ham? Shickens? It is so long as I haf seen a little shild," apologetically.

I assented to the ham and chicken proposition, answering for myself and Tony at least. As they went down the stairs, they looked wistfully at him. I nodded, and, picking him up, they carried him with them. I could presently distinguish his shrill little tones, and half a dozen women's voices, caressing, laughing with him. Yet it hurt me somehow to notice that these voices were all old, subdued; none of them could ever hold a baby on her lap, and call it hers. Joseph roused himself, came suddenly in with a great pitcher of domestic wine, out again, and back with ginger-cakes and apples,—"Till der supper be cookin'," with an encouraging nod,—and then went back to his chair, and presently snored aloud. In a few minutes, however, we were summoned to the table.

Knowles ate nothing, and looked vaguely over the great smoking dishes, which Tony and I proved to be marvels of cookery. "Doubtless," he said, "some of these people have not yet overcome this grosser taste; we have yet seen but the dregs of the society; many years of Rapp's culture would be needed to spiritualize German boors."

The old women, who moved gently about, listened keenly, trying to understand why he did not eat. It troubled them.

"We haf five meals a day in der society," said Christina, catching a vague notion of his meaning. "Many as finds it not enough puts cheese and cakes on a shelf at der bed-head, if dey gets faint in de night."

"Do you get faint in the night?" I asked.

"Most times I does," simply.

Knowles burst in with a snort of disgust, and left the table. When I joined him on the stoop he had recovered his temper and eagerness, even laughing at Joseph, who was plying him in vain with his wine.

"I was a fool, Humphreys. These are the flesh of the thing; we 'll find the brain presently. But it was a sharp disappointment. Stay here an hour, until I find the directors of the society,—pure, great thinkers, I doubt not, on whom Rapp's mantle has fallen. They will welcome our souls, as these good creatures have our bodies. Yonder is Rapp's house, they tell me. Follow me in an hour."

As he struck into one of the narrow paths across the grassy street, I saw groups of the colonists coming in from their field-work through the twilight, the dress of the women looking not unpicturesque, with the tight flannel gown and broad-rimmed straw hat. But they were all old, I saw as they passed; their faces were alike faded and tired; and whether dull or intelligent, each had a curious vacancy in its look. Not one passed without a greeting more or less eager for Tony, whom Christina held on her knees, on the steps of the stoop.

"It is so long as I haf not seen a baby," she said, again turning her thin old face round.

I found her pleased to be questioned about the society.

"I haf one, two, dree kinder when we come mit Father Rapp," she said. "Dey is dead in Harmony; since den I just cooken in der tavern. Father Rapp say the world shall end in five years when we come in der society, den I shall see mein shilds again. But I wait, and it haf not yet end."

I thought she stifled a quick sigh.

"And your husband?"

She hesitated. "John Volz was my man, in Germany. He lives in yonder house, mit ein ander[14] family. We are in families of seven."

"Husbands and wives were separated, then?"

"Father Rapp said it must to be. He knows."

There was a long pause, and then, lowering her voice, and glancing cautiously around, she added hurriedly, "Frederick Rapp was his brother: he would not leave his wife."

"Well, and then?"

The two old women looked at each other, warningly, but Christina, being on the full tide of confidence, answered at last in a whisper, "Father Rapp did hold a counsel mit five others."

"And his brother?"

"He was killed. He did never see his child."

"But," I resumed, breaking the long silence that followed, "your women do not care to go back to their husbands? They dwell in purer thoughts than earthly love?"

"Hein?" said the woman with a vacant face.

"Were you married?"—to Fredrika, who sat stiffly knitting a blue woollen sock.

"Nein," vacantly counting the stitches. "Das ist not gut, Father Rapp says. He knows."

"*She* war not troth-plight even," interrupted the other eagerly, with a contemptuous nod, indicating by a quick motion a broken nose, which might have hindered Fredrika's chances of matrimony. "There is Rachel," pointing to a bent figure in a neighboring garden; "she was to marry in the summer, and in spring her man came mit Father Rapp. He was a sickly man."

"And she followed him?"

"Ya. He is dead."

"And Rachel?"

"*Ya wohl!* There she is," as the figure came down the street, passing us.

It was only a bent old Dutchwoman, with a pale face and fixed, tearless eyes, that smiled kindly at sight of the child; but I have never seen in any tragedy, since, the something which moved me so suddenly and deeply in that quiet face and smile. I followed her with my eyes, and then turned to the women. Even the stupid knitter had dropped her work, and met my look with a vague pity and awe in her face.

"It was not gut she could not marry. It is many years, but she does at no time forget," she mumbled, taking up her stocking again. Something above her daily life had struck a quick response from even her, but it was gone now.

Christina eagerly continued: "And there is—" (naming a woman, one of the directors.) "She would be troth-plight, if Father Rapp had not said it must not be. So they do be lovers these a many years, and every night he does play beneath her window until she falls asleep."

When I did not answer, the two women began to talk together in undertones, examining the cut of Tony's little clothes, speculating as to their price, and so forth. I rose and shook myself. Why! here in the new life, in Arcadia, was there the world,—old love and hunger to be mothers, and the veriest gossip? But these were women: I would seek the men with Knowles. Leaving the child, I crossed the darkening streets to the house which I had seen him enter. I found him in a well-furnished room, sitting at a table, in council with half a dozen men in the old-time garb of the Communists. If their clothes were relics of other times, however, their shrewd, keen faces were wide awake and alive to the present. Knowles's alone was lowering and black.

"These are the directors of the society," he said to me aloud, as I entered. "Their reception of us is hardly what I expected," nodding me to a seat.

They looked at me with a quiet, business-like scrutiny.

"I hardly comprehend what welcome you anticipated," said one, coolly. "Many persons offer to become members of our fraternity; but it is, we honestly tell you, difficult to obtain admission. It is chiefly an association to make money: the amount contributed by each new-comer ought, in justice, to bear some proportion to the advantage he obtains."

"Money? I had not viewed the society in that light," stammered Knowles.

"You probably," said the other, with a dry smile, "are not aware how successful a corporation ours has been. At Harmony, we owned thirty thousand acres; here, four thousand. We have steam-mills, distilleries, carry on manufactures of wool, silk, and cotton. Exclusive of our stocks, our annual profit, clear of expense, is over two hundred thousand dollars. There are few enterprises by which money is to be made into which our capital does not find its way."

Knowles sat dumb as the other proceeded, numbering, alertly as a broker, shares in railroad stocks, coal-mines, banks.

"You see how we live," he concluded; "the society's lands are self-supporting,—feed and clothe us amply. What profits accrue are amassed, intact."

"To what end?" I broke in. "You have no children to inherit your wealth. It buys you neither place nor power nor pleasure in the world."

The director looked at me with a cold rebuke in his eyes. "It is not surprising that many should desire to enter a partnership into which they bring nothing, and which is so lucrative," he said.

"I had no intention of coming empty-handed," said Knowles in a subdued voice. "But this financial point of view never occurred to me."

The other rose with a look of pity, and led us out through the great ware-rooms, where their silks and cottons were stored in chests, out to the stables to inspect stock, and so forth. But before we had proceeded far, I missed Knowles, who had trotted on before with a stunned air of perplexity. When I went back to the tavern, late that night, I found him asleep on the bed, one burly arm around his boy. The next morning he was up betimes, and at work investigating the real condition of the Harmonists. They treated him with respect, for, outside of what Josiah called his vagaries, Knowles was shrewd and honest.

Tony and I wandered about the drowsy village and meadows, looking at the queer old gardens, dusky with long-forgotten plants, or sometimes at their gallery of paintings, chief among which was one of West's [15] larger efforts.

It was not until the close of the second day that Knowles spoke openly to me. Whatever the disappointment had cost him, he told nothing of it,—grew graver, perhaps, but discussed the chances in the stock market with the directors,—ate Christina's suppers, watching the poor withered women and the gross men with a perplexed look of pity.

"They are but common minds and common bodies, perhaps," he said one evening, as we sat in our corner, after a long, quiet scrutiny of them: "in any case, their lives would have been meagre and insignificant, and yet, Humphreys, yet even that little possibility seems to have been here palsied and balked. I hope George Rapp cannot look back and see what his scheme has done for these people."

"You were mistaken in it, then?"

His dark face reddened gloomily. "You see what they are. Yet Rapp, whatever complaints these people may make of him, I believe to have been an enthusiast, who sacrificed his property to establish a pure, great reform in society. But human nature! human nature is as crooked to drive as a pig tied by a string. Why, these Arcadians, sir, have made a god of their stomachs, and such of them as have escaped that spend their lives in amassing dollar after dollar to hoard in their common chest."

I suggested that Rapp and he left them nothing else to do. "You shut them out both from a home and from the world; love, ambition, politics, are dead words to them. What can they do but eat and grub?"

"Think! Go back into Nature's heart, and, with contemplation, bear fruit of noble thoughts unto eternal life!" But he hesitated; his enthusiasm hung fire strangely.

After a while,—"Well, well, Zachary," with a laugh, "we 'd better go back into the world, and take up our work again. Josiah is partly right, may be. There are a thousand fibres of love and trade and mutual help which bind us to our fellow-man, and if we try to slip out of our place and loose any of them, our own souls suffer the loss by so much life withdrawn. It is as well not to live altogether outside of the market; nor—to escape from this," lifting Tony up on his knee, and beginning a rough romp with him. But I saw his face work strangely as he threw the boy up in the air, and when he caught him, he strained him to his burly breast until the child cried out. "Tut! tut! What now, you young ruffian? Come, shoes off, and to bed; we 'll have a little respite from you. I say, Humphreys, do you see the hungry look with which the old women follow the child? God help them! I wonder if it will be made right for them in another world!" An hour after, I heard him still pacing the floor up stairs, crooning some old nursery song to put the boy to sleep.

I visited the Harmonists again not many months ago; the village and orchards lie as sleepily among the quiet hills as ever. There are more houses closed, more grass on the streets. A few more of the simple, honest folk have crept into their beds under the apple-trees, from which they will not rise in the night to eat, or to make money,—Christina among the rest. I was glad she was gone where it was sunny and bright, and where she would not have to grow tired for the sight of "a little shild." There have been but few additions, if any, to the society in the last twenty years. They still retain the peculiar dress which they wore when they left Würtemberg: the men wearing the common German peasant habit; the women, a light, narrow flannel gown, with wide sleeves and a bright-colored silk handker-chief crossed over the breast, the whole surmounted by a straw hat, with a rim of immense width. They do not carry on the manufactures of silk or woollen now, which were Rapp's boast; they have "struck oil" instead, and are among the most successful and skilful land-owners in Pennsylvania in the search for that uncertain source of wealth.

The "Economite Wells" are on the Upper Alleghany, nearly opposite Tidionte.[16] In later years, I believe, children have been brought into the society to be cared for by the women.

It needs no second-sight to discern the end of Rapp's scheme. His single strength sustained the colony during his life, and since his death one or two strong wills have kept it from crumbling to pieces, converting the whole machinery of his system into a powerful money-making agent. These men are the hand by which it keeps its hold on the world,—or the market, perhaps I should say. They are intelligent and able; honorable too, we are glad to know, for the sake of the quiet creatures drowsing away their little remnant of life, fat and contented, driving their ploughs through the fields, or smoking on the stoops of the village houses when evening comes. I wonder if they ever cast a furtive glance at the world and life from which Rapp's will so early shut them out? When they finish smoking, one by one, the great revenues of the society will probably fall into the hands of two or three active survivors, and be merged into the small currents of trade, according to the rapid sequence which always follows the accretion of large properties in this country.

Rapp is remembered, already, even by the people whom he meant to serve, only as a harsh and tyrannical ruler, and his very scheme will not only prove futile, but be forgotten very soon after Fredrika and Joseph have drank their last cup of home-made wine, and gone to sleep under the trees in the apple-orchard.

# The Story of Christine

Peterson's Magazine, September 1866

"Dutch Christine," as all the town called her, is one of the properties of my childhood. Perhaps that may have led me to overrate the interest
of her story when I thought it would be worth telling to you; for you,
all of you, know the curious glamour that hangs about any remembrance
of the time when we were children; when we begin to look back to it—
a sort of mystery and far-off charm impossible to define in words to our
grown-up selves, and just as impossible to convey to others.

Christine was an old Hollander, stiff, lean, and angular, whom I oftenest
saw in a certain corner of a back-pew in the old Baptist church at home. It
was a country church, built on the far outskirts of a Pennsylvanian village,
just where the drowsy noise of the weed-grown street dulled down into
the silence of hills and valleys; a square, wooden affair, with unshuttered
windows, bare pulpit of red cherry wood, and straight-backed, uncarpeted
pews—all the barer, and straighter, and harder to sit quiet in, for the sweep
of meadow outside, and the wood of sycamores rustling and cool in the
summer sunshine; that is, harder for me, a girl of twelve, with a heavy
superfluity of legs and arms always restlessly in somebody's way.

But about the church. There were three pewter lamps, I recollect, which
hung from the ceiling; and I used to watch the shadow of the rope, by
which they were suspended, as it crept up the white-washed wall. When
it crossed the third window it was time for the "finally;" and I took a
fresh breath and courage to stiffen myself up into another last stretch of
patience. After that, I knew, came the exhortation, and then the welcome
bustle of rising for the doxology and blessing—welcome especially to me,
sandwiched, hot and perspiring as I was, between my aunts Hubbard and
Cunningham; two portly old ladies they were, heads of the ruling families in Scottsville. Couldn't any one see, at a glance, that they belonged to
the good old stock? It hinted itself in the high Roman noses, ridden by
gold spectacles; in the stiff, black satin gowns; in the "Hubbard underlip,"
somewhat long and narrow of its kind; in the polite complaisance with
which their fat bodies slowly rustled up and down, affably worshiping their
Maker. Somewhat perceptible, I should hope, the difference between us

and the flashy new-comers to Scottsville! But to go back. Sunday was, of all days, the barest and hardest to me; my aunts (outside of blood) were good-natured, ignorant, comfortable people enough, delighting to feed you when you were well, and dose you when sick; and performing both these duties indiscriminately to me during week-days; but on Sundays crowding all the moral instruction needed into the shape of a few vivid pictures of my past short-comings, and the future "worm that dieth not, and fire that is not quenched." As with too many children who study the shorter catechism, fear of hell was my religion; and as I was most religious on a Sunday—not even the inevitable pot-peach pie of that day could make it tolerable. The height of my discomfort was reached, I think, in church, about the time of the exhortation. At the first mention of "impenitent brethren," therefore, I began peering beyond the wall of black satin on either side to catch a glimpse of Christine. I had so odd an affection and curiosity for the old Dutchwoman, that the sight of her was sure to put everything else out of my head. She had her especial seat near the door, where she sat bolt upright through the long sermon, her long, wrinkled face and pleasant blue eyes turned to the old doctor, as if fire and brimstone never entered into her thoughts. I don't believe they did; and if she did not quite understand his long syllogism, I am sure nothing worse took their place, in her childish brain, than a calculation of how many pounds of my aunt's rags would go to the yard of carpet; or how her own sage or summer savory would turn out this fall; for Christine made her scanty living by sewing homemade carpets, dyeing old dresses and skirts, and furnishing herbs to the house-keepers. For herself, everything about her was dyed, except, indeed, the gray hair that was smoothly parted under a white cap; but the purple ribbon on the cap and straw bonnet; the stuff gown; the bit of a yellow silk shawl folded crosswise on her breast; the knit mittens—all had gone through the vat, and came out fresh and tidy as old Christine herself. Her very fingers were purple, and smelled faintly pungent of logwood. Out of all Holland, though, you would not find an old woman as clean, or neat to stiffness, as this one who sat there, Sunday after Sunday, her hymn-book wrapped in an unfolded snow-white handkerchief held in both hands, and a bit of tansy and June pinks between her finger and thumb. She had pots of both in her window; so all the year it was just the same—always a bit of tansy and June pinks. After sermon, Christine stood still in her pew until my aunts went by, dropping a little jerk of a courtesy to them, and receiving a gracious nod in return, patting me on the head with a slow, kindly smile. I never could understand then the peculiar tie that bound the old Hollander to the Hubbard family; on her part it smacked of the blind submission of a slave to his master; and with those of them who were old enough to remember the generation past, there was a curious anxiety to be kind to her, as if some wrong lay between them yet unatoned, but not unrepented. From my earliest remembrance I understood that, in some unexplained way, Christine belonged to us; that we owed her an unusual care and consideration.

Every day her dinner was sent to her from aunt Hubbard's table, sliced and chosen of the best; it was one of my childish rewards to be allowed to carry it down to her. On rare Sundays, too, I took her by the hand, and went home with her to lunch before the afternoon service. Somehow, holding her hand, and jogging alongside down the shady lane, I forgot that "there was a dreadful hell;" the vulgarity I had caught in the last week in a great boarding-school seemed to slip off, and I was, more than at any other time, only a happy child. Christine was fond of talking, and very few people but children cared to listen to her simple stories of Holland, and of the saints and their dealings with the Low Dutch—for she had been a Roman Catholic long ago; and good Baptist as she was now, she had come out of that dark wood with some glittering cobwebs of superstition hanging about her, very beautiful, and surely not harmful. At any rate, Sunday suddenly cleared up for me into a good, heartsome day, which, if not holy, was happy and innocent, when the old woman quickened her pace as eager as I, with a "Now, *Kindchen*, for the plum-tart, and then little Peterkin and the Christ-child," which was my favorite of all the stories. Perhaps the pleasure was as coarse which I took in the story as in the tart; yet there have been dark days in my life when I have looked back to remember how little Peterkin was led out of the wood. "Be sure," was always Christine's moral, "dem as holds fast to the good Lord's hand is brought through. But it's hard to shake off the sin at de other side. It stings—I tell you, Kindchen, *it stings*," with a curious earnestness in her eyes, usually as blue and shining as a bit of delft. Long afterward I understood her moral, and what it meant to her.

After we had jogged down the lane some quarter of a mile, we would come to Christine's house, a queer triangular affair, built of logs, and set in the midst of an lot, also three-sided, in which grew herbs of all sorts, pinks, holly-hocks, and half a dozen gnarled old apple-trees. Inside, the house was like no other that ever I had seen; it was an ark of wonders to me, from the great clock in the corner, to the queer Dutch cabinet filled with odd needle-books; glass perfume bottles, with a sad, faint breath of dead fragrance about them; samplers of marvelous needle-work; yellow scraps of old Dutch news-papers. These were all in the front room, where the little fire-place was set in the corner of the triangle, with its miniature mantle-piece over it, on which stood the black-and-red tea-tray, and a polished nautilus shell; down below, a green rag hearth-rug, and the cat asleep on it. Outside of this was the diminutive kitchen, three-sided like the rest, with its floors and tins shining; up stairs, Christine's bed-room, the door of which she never unlocked, even to me. "There are things there that belong not to this place," she said to me once. Whatever had been the trouble and guilt of her life, she kept its traces there, it may be. But the walls of the odd little house were the source of my most constant delight. Instead of papering, the old body white-washed them, and with the aid of the indigo-box and rag, garlanded them with blue bouquets and festoons, which she grew tired of, and renewed every week or two. What am I prosing about the walls, and clock, and samplers, of the old house for? I have made you sleepy, maybe, already—but one forgets themselves going back to a childish story. Besides, the old creature loved me, and I, giving her back, childlike, her affection with a liberal interest of zeal and demonstration of it, helped, unconsciously, to make some of her last years happier—and I am glad to remember that now.

I was gone from Scottsville for several years. When I came back, almost a woman, I had lost all hold on the course of events there. Going up the long village street in the heavy stage-coach, I watched eagerly from the window to see the changes as I passed; the narrow stoops that had given place to fashionable, open fronts; the new hotel with its transparency in front; the increased buzz and stir everywhere; the village was fast being spoiled into a town. But one place had grown stiller and older than before; Christine's little house, of which I caught a glimpse as we passed the lane. The doors and windows were closed; the herbs were grown up in the garden like a wilderness of weeds; the fruit from the old trees lay rotten on the ground.

"Dead?" I said, after a few minutes to the driver, nodding back at the house, something choking in my throat.

"Christine? No, *she's* not dead. It's not so that you've not heard, Miss Lotty? Your folks must be slow about news-giving."

That was all the answer he gave me. There are two classes in every village, those who tell the news, and those who hear it; John Frisk was one of the latter; but I thought from his quieted face afterward that some fate of unusual severity had fallen on my old friend. But I never guessed the truth.

That evening, seated about aunt Hubbard's well-filled tea-table, I caught the first silence to ask, "Where was Christine? She ought to have been here to welcome me." There was a sudden hush, as if I had struck a rough chord, I even saw little Patty, on the other side of the lamp, turn white as though sick and faint; no one replied. I looked at aunt Hubbard, her fingers were unsteady as she tried to adjust the urn. "Something is wrong," I said. "Will no one tell me?"

"Hush, Charlotte!" said my aunt. "Christine is in her house. I have not seen her for a year. No one has seen her."

When they all began to talk again, as if trying to recover the cheerful tone my question had disturbed, my aunt leaned over and whispered a word in my ear that drove the blood to my heart with a sudden chill. A fate had fallen on my poor, old friend so different from, and so surpassing all others in its pain and horror, that from the beginning of the world it has been set apart as the especial curse of God. That night I heard the strange story of Christine, which I am going to tell you.

One hot day in a summer, some fifty years back, the good ship Wunderbar, with her well-known figure-head of a black swan, lay ready to set sail at the harbor of Amsterdam. She was a jaunty little brig, and a favorite on the wharves, being a fast as well as lucky sailer. Emigration was not so common then as now; but whenever any of the Amsterdam people did voyage to the far off Americas, they chose the Wunderbar to go in, much as they disliked her captain, Jan Velt.

Jan stood now on the wharf, leaning against a heap of barrels, his unlit pipe in his thick lips. One would not wonder, looking at his face, that he was the most unpopular young boor who had followed the water from that Stadt; and Jan probably knew it himself, the angry scorn and sneer had so deepened and hardened in his small, bead-like eyes and heavy jaws. Yet Jan was a well-built young fellow, and handsome, so far as mere flesh and blood went in an animal fashion; at least so many of the burghers' daughters thought, casting a side-long glance at him as they went by, their blue and scarlet cloth petticoats brightening in and out of the dull row of shops that faced the water. No young man in their class could plenish a house for this wife like old Velt's son—they did not forget that, either.

Jan was a bit of a fop, also, in his clumsy, boorish way. The ship was *voll roobl*,[1] as the men had it, loaded to the water's edge, her three cabin passengers on board, the steerage crowded to its limit. Nothing remained but to hoist anchor, and break a bottle to the good ship's voyage; but Jan had hastily donned his Sunday suit of blue, and stood lingering on the wharf, fingering the gold hoop that hung from one ear, and chewing the end of his pipe-stem.

His eye brightened cunningly after awhile, as he caught a glimpse of two women coming down the church steps, burghers, it was evident by the embroidery on their bodice-sleeves in lieu of fur, but wealthy burghers, as every portion of the dress showed. Jan started up from his lazy lounge and hastily followed them, his eyes set like a pointer's who has run the game near to the death. "All the better that the Hagedohn woman is with her!" he muttered, panting as he went. "She will be the more apt to fall into the trap. One or two lucky hits farther, Madam Christine, and I will have paid you all I owe!" At the end of the Platz he overtook them. Christine was a pretty girl of sixteen then, a good type of the higher order of Dutch beauty, such as seldom comes to our shores, of rare delicacy in its tints and lines. "Her skin," my aunt Hubbard used to say, "was like a child's, milky-white, and just such a soft rose in the cheeks, and her hands as tender and small as a baby's." This day that Jan Velt pursued her, her dress heightened, perhaps, her natural fairness; a bodice of dark-blue velvet, trimmed with silver bells, with its dainty lace rippling about shoulders and arms; a petticoat of fine crimson levantine,[2] short enough to show the white embroidered stockings, and the pointed shoes with their tiny ruby clasps above the instep; her hair, a pale golden, parted in wavy lines on her forehead, and held in a peaked silver net, with a light fringe of blue and silver edging the front, and falling on the neck behind.

Now Christine had shared in the town's antipathy to Jan Velt. She carried the dislike into deed, in fact, for it had made her reject the handsome young *capitaine* a month or two ago, with as much unnecessary scorn as her vain little head thought becoming to bestow. After that event, however, not all the town combined had half the patience or charity for Jan Velt as shone in Christine's blue eyes, which was only human nature after all. She turned to meet him now, all the more quickly for the warning whisper of her companion, her pretty face a little flushed, and tossing her dimpled chin. "People will call me *handfest* with the Herr if I bid him a civil good-by? So, well! I have not often heeded Amsterdam gossips, and that you should know, Margaret." So she perversely halted until he crossed the street, and held out her hand to him. She never had granted that unusual sign of intimacy before; and Jan, glancing at the other girl's hot and angry face, understood the reason for it; but that mattered little to him. So they walked slowly down the side-path together, still tending to the wharves. How the morning's walk came about Christine could never fairly tell, nor why she was so easily led, one step after another, by a man whom, at bottom, she despised. She was young, giddy, and vain, to begin with. Very few of the Amsterdam gossips whom she so derided knew of the devotion of the rich, young captain to her; and she was not at all unwilling it should be known, especially as Justus Hainer, whose *lieber Schatz*[3] she knew she was, was watching her with blank, amazed face from his shop window. "Well enough to let him see other folks value me," thought the little moth Christine, fluttering nearer and nearer to the fire. "He will come to think he picked me up too lightly, like a wayside weed." Then this poor Jan was so heart-broken at his disappointment; he thought she looked quite pale and worn; and she never would see him again in all probability; this voyage was to be his last, he said; the ship and its cargo were already disposed of to a merchant in New York, and he himself meant to turn landsman, and settle in that far distant country. She looked at him with the awe and pity in her eyes with which we now look at some bold venturer into the unknown horrors of African deserts. Poor Jan! Before he came back, if he ever *did* come back, she would be Frau Hainer, fat, red-faced, a cap like—ach! Meanwhile, what earthly harm could there be in a few friendly words of good-by? Mere grains of comfort, as he said. The three walked on together, Margaret's face redder with each step, and angrier than before; but the blue-eyed woman, like all blue-eyed women, had her own way. In one point she was disappointed, however. Jan Velt did not lead her to the Spazier Platz, where the city gossips most did congregate. On the contrary, the by-streets, through which they passed, were faced by the back parts of the great warehouses, and on the whole way there was scarcely a face she knew. "It was to be quieter," he said. The sun was near its setting, too, and something in the lengthened shadows, and tolling of the evening bell touched a light wave of feeling, and lent a half sadness to the thought of this farewell she had to say. "It was harder to say than she thought. She wished she could please him in some trifle before he went! She who had made his whole life desolate!"

So when the last tones of the bell died away with a clang, and the soft notes of the great organ began to fill the air like mellowed thunder, she stood irresolute at the end of a small alley that opened on the wharf, half smiling, looking down at her pretty-pointed toe, ready to yield to his entreaty, whatever it might be.

"Are you mad, Christine?" said her companion. "What will your father say? And Hainer?" lowering her voice. "For me, I will have nothing to do in such a madcap frolic."

"But I am sure you will, pretty Margaret," said the smooth-tongued Jan. "It is no mad-cap frolic, but a civil, friendly act, such as no maiden in the Stadt would refuse. Only to come on board my house, swinging in the water yonder, for an hour, and see how a sailor lives. Do you think, of all women, I would tempt Christine to do what might seem unmaidenly?"

She knows how I esteem her," in a lowered tone, that brought the bright blood up to her cheek.

"Margaret is right," she said, hastily. "I ought not to go."

"Besides," continued Jan, as if she had not spoken; "talking of your father, my eyesight deceived me if he was not among the merchants whom I left in the cabin, examining some curious specimens of this new crimson glass. In the shape of cordial-cups, my specimens are."

Christine laughed. "It is likely," she said. "Even we women have heard of your liqueurs, Jan. Now, Margaret, it seems to me this alters the case. If we shall meet my father, and some of his old cronies there, with Herr Velt, doubtless?" turning to Jan.

"Assuredly," he eagerly rejoined; "my father superintends the clearing of each cargo, as you know."

She poised her foot again, glanced from it up to the soft, pearly sky, with one crimson cloud scudding to the north, then to the white sails of the ship floating lightly on the breast of the heaving waves. "How pretty she is!" her blue eye looking knowingly at jib and foresail, as became a sea-trader's daughter. "If her cabin is as well worth seeing as—" and then hesitated.

Jan had some reasonable pretext for his invitation; the girls knew that, in his rough way, he had a taste for pictures, ornaments, such trifles and curiosities as could be picked up in distant countries by a watchful trader. His store of these things were on board of the vessel going with him to his new home; there were ivory basso-relievos from Florence, corals, gems, wonderful wreaths made of feathers and fish-scales, from the far-off Madeiras—what not to tempt a silly girl?

"There is but little time left to decide," at last said Christine, after long pleading from Jan. "What say you, Margaret? It will be but an hour's absence from home; and if we meet my father there. We will be back before the sun goes down?" to Jan.

"Surely."

"I'll not let you go alone," grumbled Margaret. She had not been forgotten in Jan's flattery. "I see you are bent on the fool's errand."

In twenty minutes more the two girls were on deck. They had come on board with so little notice from the crew, that Margaret, thinking it over afterward, concluded their coming had been expected and prepared for. The cabin, to which Jan led them, was apart from the main one, and so full of the curiosities he had promised, that the girls, for half an hour, forgot to examine whether the voices on the other side of the door were, in truth, as he said, those of their fathers and friends.

The ship, they thought, rocked unsteadily at anchor. There was an odd sound of grating ropes and chains; but they suspected no evil—why should they? What time passed they hardly knew, until the waning light in the little sky-light caused Margaret to start. "We must go," she said, hurriedly. "It is late. Do you not feel how cold the evening grows?"

Jan did not interpose; drew aside, indeed, and allowed the two girls to make their way on deck alone, growing a thought paler beneath his red whiskers. When they reached the deck, Stadt and wharf, and busy little fleet of sloops and schooners had vanished like a dream; the cold air was the gust from the ebbing side; the crimson cloud lay far behind them; and around was the dreary, sullen waste of water, with but a slow, murky vapor to tell of their lost home. The ship ploughed her way steadily away from it; it faded, appeared again a mere spot on the horizon's edge. They were far out at sea.

It is nearly a century ago, this time of which we write; deeds were done habitually then, and made legal in this good city of Brotherly Love, which the just and merciful grandchildren of good old Quakers would hardly credit of their ancestors. Let me tell you of one. At the lower end of Market, then called High street, stood a large, low-built building, used as a hotel, much frequented by Western merchants, who crossed the mountains, once a year on horseback, to make their purchases. It was much repaired to, also, by sea-traders and captains, as a sort of head-quarters of commerce. In a front room, barred off from the public tap by a green curtain, one night in early winter of the year of which we write, two men were sitting by a square table, on which lay writing materials, a beer-pot, one or two broken tobacco-pipes, and a flaring tallow-candle, by the light of which all was seen. The older of the two was a tall, thin man, with beaked nose and grinding lips, dressed in brown, short-clothes, and long, black silk stockings—a dress which even then looked oddly old-fashioned. The other was a younger man, with a coarser, but no less shrewd face, habited in the working dress of a sailor—the captain of the good ship Wunderbar, just in after a favorable run of four months. "I am especially fortunate to have met you, captain," said the older of the pair. "Your commodity is not often to be met with of a quality worth buying, but this article you assure me—"

"You shall see for yourself, Herr," replied Velt. "But one word, however. It would be better if I had some idea with whom I had made this bargain in case that—if—"

"I understand—you are right, undoubtedly. I am a Western farmer. Our law forbids our holding such negroes as are yet slaves in Pennsylvania, after the age of twenty-eight; and by this law I lose, next year, both house and field hands, and, of course, must supply their place. That of redemptioners⁴ are the next most available service I could command; but I hardly hoped to meet with the good fortune which has already resulted from our accidental encounter."

"You'll like the woman," said Jan, rising and pacing the room. "She's strongly-built, though she looks frail. She'll do for a field or house hand. It's not likely she'll come back to Philadelphia?"

The old man smiled. It was not a pleasant smile. "It is a six weeks' journey on horse-back for a woman," he said. "No, it's not likely." He looked up, as if to ask some question; probably one of curiosity, but checked himself.

"You shall see her to-morrow," said Jan. "Meanwhile, it may be as well to have this ready," and, sitting down, began to fill up a redemption paper. (One word of explanation. At the time of which we write, the custom of buying redemptionists still prevailed. Any person paying to the master of a vessel the passage-money of emigrants, bought the service of such emigrants until the debt was discharged—a transaction apparently fair and just. But when we consider that the unfortunate wretches were publicly sold to the highest bidder, with no choice of their own as to the purchaser; that being sold, it was permissible for their owner to transfer them, at his own option, to whomsoever he pleased; that the ignorance even of the language of his new country, placed the serf entirely in the power of the master in a condition of absolute slavery. The story I am telling is a true one, with but slight alteration of names and places; merely hint at facts, which, filled in with the habits and customs of the time, would make a volume.)

The two men had been talking in a sort of mongrel dialect of mixed Dutch and German, helped now and then by an English word, which Jan suddenly changed altogether to English as a stranger entered the room, and after idling about a moment or two, began pacing thoughtfully up and down, his head bent on his breast, apparently neither heeding nor seeing Velt or Hubbard—for the old man was my grandfather, I shame to say. Jan, glowering up from his paper, gave a grunt of annoyance as the stranger passed him, giving one sharp glance from under a heavy pair of iron-gray brows.

"Who is it?" said my grandfather.

"No need to lower your voice," said Velt, roughly; "the fellow has no English. He came over in my ship, a surgeon from Hamburgh, they say.

I'll teach him Jan Velt is not to be spied upon and meddled with before I have done with him."

Apparently the stranger did not understand English, for by neither word or look did he give a sign of having comprehended Velt; but continued his slow, even walk until the men had finished their whispered conference, and Jan had left the room. He stopped then, looking out of the little dingy window at the rain, for it was a stormy night; then, coming up to where Hubbard sat, broke out with a round English oath, "You have a thorough-bred sharper there in that Jan Velt! I know him, Mynherr! I came in his brig—four months crawling over the water, and I learned to know him in that time, I'll warrant you!"

My grandfather coolly went on assorting his papers as he raised his eyes, and surveyed the stranger from head to foot. "Ah?" was his reply.

The rebuff acted like magic on the other. His passion seemed to cool instantly, and he returned the glance with one as penetrating. After a minutes scrutiny he bowed distantly with a quiet air of one used to exert authority. "Pardon, Mynherr! I fancied the character of those with whom you dealt concerned you?"

"Why should it?" said my grandfather, in the same unmoved tone.

The stranger smiled dryly. "True! Why should it? Enough of the good capitaine, then," with the slight motion of the hand of one who disposes of something finally. "My object in addressing you was not, in fact, to discuss Jan Velt, but to ask a question. Would you transfer this purchase you have made to me, after Velt's departure, for a like sum as that you paid for it? I cannot offer you more, unfortunately." His color rose at this.

"The bargain is not yet completed," said the other, civilly. "Jan made me the offer this evening. I am to see the wench to-morrow. But if she proves to be as good an investment as he promised, I see no reason why I should give up my claim, even for an advance of price."

"I cannot offer that, I—" The man was embarrassed, seemed to be attempting to control some strong emotion. "My want of money cripples me, or I would make it a dangerous matter for any one to tamper with the girl—compounding of felony, in fact. If the cursed laws of Holland were low enough for a poor man to lay his hand on, Jan Velt should be rotting in the hold of his own vessel bound for Amsterdam now, instead of filling his pockets with the price of flesh and blood."

Whether my grandfather suspected that he was putting his fingers into a bit of villainy, and wanted to wash them in ignorance before-hand, I know not; but he rose hastily, saying, as he thrust the papers in his breast-pocket,

"I know nothing about the woman, I tell you. Jan told me he disposed of one this morning. You seem heated, sir. It is a mere business transaction, and calls for no such display of feeling. I wish you good-night."

As he left the room, he looked at the man more attentively; a middle-aged man he was used to describe him, thick-set, and below the ordinary height, with a face marked by strong passions; his clothes, rich in texture, but thread-bare from use. "I did not believe the man's purpose, with regard to the wench, was good as my own," he said, afterward. "For me, my care was to procure a good farm-hand at the lowest cost; who or what she was, or how Velt came by her, mattered nothing to me. The man, Petrelli—he was an Italian by descent—hung about the tavern all that night. I saw he had made up his mind not to be baffled; and he was not, as the event proved. Jan showed me the girl the next day. She was a lithe, toughly-built wench, though worn down and weakened by a long illness, he told me—so I took her. I had some doubts about her, I confess, she appeared half-idiotic, giving but little sign of sense other than fear of Velt. Petrelli came in while I was there, and her face cleared a little. I could not understand what they said, for he spoke rapidly to her in French, which, to my surprise, she understood; but I noted that he assumed a fatherly manner to her, patting her on the head, and looking kindly at her through his spectacles. The girl was in filthy rags when I bought her." Thus my grandfather looked at the matter through cool, trading eyes.

When the interview of which he speaks was over, and the girl was left alone in the garret in which they had seen her, she sat down by the table and began playing with some beans that lay there, ranging them in lines and hollow squares. She was a silly, dull-witted thing at best, and the pain she had borne in these last four months had stunned, instead of rousing her. My grandfather was not far wrong when he suspected idiocy lay not far from this sort of torpor. She looked down at the coarse flannel petticoat she wore, and foul linen, with a heavy sob, such as children give.

"Christine!" Jan stood before her. She nodded, and fingered her beans nervously. The beauty she had once was nearly lost; her skin haggard; her nose and chin peaked and sharp. Jan viewed her critically. "It will come back," he thought. "A little kindness and good feeding would bring it back. Christine! It is your last chance. Do you understand what that man came for an hour ago?"

"Yes, I understand. You told me, Jan," patting the palms of her hands together as they lay on her knee.

"Come, none of that!" roughly. "You'd nearly spoiled the bargain by some such senseless trick. You have had four months to think this matter over, and it's time we were done with tears and mad capers. The bargain's not completed; the money's not paid. I can rue, even now. Do you see what I mean, Christine? I can save you from going with this man."

She said nothing, sat staring at him with her faded face.

"Do you care whether you go or not?"

"What is it to me where I go?" she cried, starting to her feet. "What matters it? What matters it?" She pushed her hair back with both hands, cried sharply two or three times; cowed suddenly down on catching sight of his face, like a whipped dog before his master.

"See now, be reasonable, Christine," he said, sitting down. "I had this in my mind from the day you flouted and sneered at me, asking you to be my wife. I knew who was my rival."

"It was Hainer," she said, dully. "I am *handfest* with Hainer. "Ach! if he were to see these clothes!" with a shiver.

Jan concealed a smile. "Now you talk as a pretty maiden ought; for Hainer, you are done with him. He could not find you, if he would. There are but two ways to choose. Go with that man, to work in his fields, or be his scullion-maid, or be my wife, and wear finer linen and softer fur than any Ritter's dame in Holland. Think of the eardrops of chased gold I showed you, the combs studded with emeralds."

Christine was weak and vain, but she had a real sense of womanly honor, and, at heart, a sincere love for her old lover, and an animal and moral antipathy to this wretch before her. Besides, she did not think it so hopeless a fate, the going West, as Jan knew it to be. "I can write," she thought; "and if it were in the bottom of the sea, Hainer would find a way to come to me."

Something of this she hinted to Velt, taunting him withal, woman-like, until his rage was thoroughly aroused. He got up, leaning his knuckles on the table, his jaws growing pale. "You have said enough. The little devil is not dead in you yet, I see. Very well. You shall cry if your new master be not a harder slave-driver than Jan Velt would have been to his wife. My wife you shall never be."

The girl gave a half silly, half desperate laugh, which made Jan a trifle more quiet and livid. "To-morrow you go with him—but one thing before I leave you. You count on this Petrelli to send back news of you to Amsterdam? I have blocked your way there, my pretty Fraulein; I have made known my own story. There is not a *Meisterin* in Amsterdam but would pull her skirts back if you passed her now, lest they might touch Jan Velt's *frei Liebchen*."

She buried her face in her hands with a low moan, and he left her.

Velt's parting stab sunk deeper than any former cruelty, hurt the woman more vitally. It struck not only at her honor and her love for the far-off Hainer, who, in his shop at home, despised her as a wanton light o' love; but there was no remembrance of her home, no girlish vanity that it did not touch to mildew and kill.

"There was nothing," she said afterward, telling her story to my aunt Hubbard, who, in her ignorant way, pitied her—"nothing for me to catch and live for. Nothing back, nothing forward but shame—shame! My name was foul in the streets of my own home; my clothes were greasy rags; my very skin was thick with the dirt of the kitchen-work of your father; and so my heart got foul and dead, too, I think. And then—"

She always stopped there. It was not until many years afterward that she told thus much of her story. When my grandfather brought her home, she appeared but an unusually stupid, inanimate Dutchwoman, and was at once transferred to the lowest department of the scullery-work in a large establishment. The petty martyrdom of such a life is easily imagined, and not pleasant to describe. The farm was large; the work heavy; the servants, both field and house-hands, were negroes just nearing their time of freedom, accustomed to the rule of a harsh master—for a year they were the girl's sole associates. In that time she managed to send a letter to her father, and another to Hainer, neither of which ever reached their destination. Months—a year passed, and then the last spark of hope or spirit from her old life died out.

"I take shame to myself," my aunt Hubbard said, fanning herself gravely, "that I did not know the poor creature's story—her fate might have been different. But you know, my dear, one cannot know the private histories of all one's servants, and I was but a mere chit of a girl at home. I knew the kitchen was a hot, dirty, stifling place, and used to pity the one white girl among so many blacks. But she seemed duller than any of them—a half idiot, in fact; so that I was the more surprised when Petrelli, who was by that time respectably, even richly clothed, and had the appearance of a man well-born, though nobody in Scottsville knew anything about him, appeared in town, and after one or two interviews with my father, offered to pay the sum yet due on the girl's service, for the purpose, he said, of making her his wife. Your grandfather very promptly refused the offer; he doubted the man's motives. I don't know if he were right; young people did not judge their elders in those days—but so it was. However, one morning soon after that, the man Petrelli and Christine were both missing; and, as it proved, he had absconded with her; the inference is, that whatever feeling he had for her was genuine of its kind. The wretched girl was hopeless, I suppose, and willing to serve any one for the wages of a kind word now and then. Petrelli had money, and a position as surgeon on a government vessel. He dressed her as she loved to be dressed, and took her with him, as his wife, wherever he went; to China, the African coast, South America, and many places of which I scarcely know the name."

"To Holland?"

"Not to Holland. Her beauty came back to her, I judge, with the easy life and Petrelli's care. But at some place in those heathen countries she contracted this disease, which has broken out in her blood so late. It was in New Orleans that Petrelli deserted her, about four years after he took her away. She lived by pawning her clothes a few months, and then worked and begged her way up to us. It was not a pleasant home," (my aunt's sallow face reddened,) "but it was the best she knew; and your grand-father being dead, sister Cunningham and myself did the best we could for her, and established her in the little house, you know. That is the story of Christine."

I listened with my chin in my hand. "Who pronounced Christine's disease leprosy?" My aunt Hubbard bridled, and her upper lip, with its fringe of mustache, grew stiffer. "My son John. You will not doubt the authority, I presume, Charlotte? He says it is the nearest approach to Asiatic leprosy possible in this climate. In all his practice he has known nothing like it; for precaution, therefore, Christine has been, in a manner, tabooed by the village. Her meals are sent to the enclosure, and there received by a little black girl who remains with her, and who seems to have no fear of the disease."

Thus far my aunt. Now, as Dr. John Hubbard's practice had been limited to the village of Scottsville, where Asiatic pestilences were not likely to walk abroad at noonday, I took the liberty of, secretly, very much doubt-ing this pronunciamento. That evening, after nightfall, therefore, I quietly went out of the back gate down the lane, and, unseen by any one, dived under the locked turn-stile, and into Christine's little yard. The herbs and ground-ivy had overgrown the beds and walks. I pushed my way through them, and opening the unlatched door, not without a slight tremor at heart, entered. The poor, old creature lay in bed, the coarse linen sheets as whitely bleached as ever, a frilled cap nearly covering the thin jaws, and gray hair. She was asleep when I came in, her withered hands lying outside of the quilt; the little black girl nodding by the fire, which burned cheer-fully; and on the clean-swept hearth lay Christine's old gray cat. Poor Tony, the little nurse, had a careful, kind soul in her black body. Well for this victim of village stupidity, or she would have died on their hands long before. Even now I cannot rightly define the true nature of her disease. I have never seen nor read of anything to which its symptoms precisely corresponded. It was a whitish, cutaneous affection, not mortal, and, so far as my experience was concerned, certainly not contagious; for I continued my clandestine visits to her for some months without danger. When she died, early in the winter, it was, I believe, from the exhaustion consequent upon long worn-out nerves, than from any definite ailment. I am aware this is a most undramatic end to my story; it is true, however, and in most true lives death shifts the scene when the actors have but half played out their parts. The last curtain falls, it may be, upon an accomplished justice far on in the next life. We never see it.

The poor, old woman had lost almost all memory of the years gone since she left Holland. In Tony's sayings and doings she took a vivid, childish interest. My own was a face she liked to see; but outside, back of that small life, she went straight to the days of her beauty and queenship in the burgher's gay circles in Amsterdam. It was pitiful to hear. Sometimes she woke weakly to a consciousness of all that had passed since then. "I ought to have trusted to Hainer," she would say; "there was my sin. Ah, Kindchen! have faith in them that love you." At the last, this thought of her old lover grew dominant, kept her brain restless and wandering; it was the truest action her heart had ever known in its life; and so it went back to that, coming nearer to the world where all things are true and real. "It is many years," she would say, "for Hainer to wait to hear from me. I was sold into slavery. I was not true to him; but I loved him." To indulge this uneasy wish, I wrote to Justus Hainer, Amsterdam, without a hope of receiving a reply—yet in the mere fancy that the man might receive it. I told Christine's story, instead of taking down the incoherent messages which she dictated.

In due course of time an answer did come, however. Justus Hainer was married, the father of eight children, and had prospered mightily in his business—the chief fact which he seemed to wish to impress upon our minds in the whole letter. He expressed a portly, dignified interest in "the poor creature," however, enclosing a very decent donation to make her latter days more easy; enlarged upon the facts of his own career, especially his removal from the lower Strazze with his shop, and his election to the town council of burghers; sent a daguerreotype of himself in his official robes, and fastened in the back of the case another, a little colored drawing on paper, taken the year Christine left Amsterdam.

"It may please her to look at it," he said. I gave that to Christine; the money I returned; and the picture of the fat, swelling dignitary, quietly threw into the fire. About Madam Hainer and the eight I also kept my own counsel.

So the poor old soul, as childish as the day she left Amsterdam, used to look at the yellow hair and staring blue eyes of the lover, dead long ago. "I was *handfest* with Hainer," she would say, proudly. I was a romantic girl, then; so, when she died, I put it in her coffin. They had much ado in Scottsville to bury her, with safety to themselves, and much horror at finding I had shared Tony's watch so often. It is an unpleasant remembrance, I will not dwell on it. Christine was buried in her own little garden. I planted her June pinks and tansy over her, and under them, wrapped in her dyed shroud, she sleeps well as if she had been Madam Hainer. The house fell to pieces from neglect. The people of Scottsville yet point to it, and tell the story of "our leper" with a justifiable pride, marred by a secret regret that Tony and I did not add to their glory by catching the disease and dying in the odor of that Eastern horror.

 # In the Market

Peterson's Magazine, January 1868

I remember a story which I would like to tell to young girls — girls, especially, who belong to that miserable border land between wealth and poverty, whose citizens struggle to meet the demands of the one state out of the necessities of the other. I hope that none but the class for whom it is written may read it. I think I remember enough of their guild language to make it intelligible to them; but to others it would, perhaps, be worse than meaningless. I have a man's reverence for them; I dower them with all the beauty of both the child and the woman.

There is a weekly concert given in a quiet hall in Philadelphia, to which I often go, not more for the music than for the rest in the softly-tinted colors of the room, the gray lights of the winter's afternoon, and the numberless fresh, beautiful girl-faces that hem me in on every side. It reminds me of the chamber of Peace, whose wide windows opened toward the morning; the atmosphere is redolent with purity and innocence. Nor do their fantastic vanities of dress break the charm; nor the silly little jests and light-hearted laughter; nor the perpetual whisper about the Proteus-hero "he!" "he!" nor the shy conscious blushes as they pass the cordon of young men outside. Nature is always pure.

But there is a phrase which I have heard used about them all, which I have heard themselves use, which is not pure; and because I do reverence them, I chose it as the title of this story, hoping that it would carry the same meaning to them as to me.

CHAPTER I

"Check, and — mate! You will have no chance for revenge either, Miss Porter, I am going west to-morrow;" and Mr. Bohme dropped the cheap chess-men into their box, one by one.

"And to Paris in November?" she added. "Our games are over."

Mr. Bohme pushed a pawn down into place with a quick, furtive glance after Clara Porter's tall, light figure, as she moved indolently away, pausing by the piano. She never touched it unless she had something to say through it. He held his hand suspended, therefore, his eyes half closing with a curious eagerness, as she stood with her thin, nervous fingers on the keys. One might have fancied that it was a trial-moment of their lives, and he was waiting for her to interpret it. She only struck a single note, however; struck it again, and went on mechanically to the window, while it vibrated through the room.

John Bohme looked puzzled a moment; then he laughed, rubbing his smooth-shaven chin. "One might question fate itself with such a despairing, perplexed cry as that," he said.

"It is the defeated who question fate; and I lost the game, you know," with an indifferent smile on her childish lips, that caused Mr. Bohme to look more puzzled than before.

Outwardly, she was nipping the dead leaves carefully from a fuschia; inwardly, she was summoning up her future, and staring it in the face. This large, heavily-built man, lounging on the sofa, dressed in gray from head to foot, a burning-red stone on his finger, half-shut, controlled gray eyes moving furtively, had been as a glimpse to her of a new, unknown world of thought and feeling. She had never been out of the little manufacturing town where he found her. These careless allusions of his to art, music, literature, to the great under schemes of politics, of which she knew nothing—what were they but gleams from the region to which she of right belonged? Her blood had burned, her brain throbbed as he talked to her daily. It was a careless, commonplace matter to him to enter great libraries, or to take passage for the western prairies, for England, or for Spain; to her it would be scarcely less a change than for her freed soul to shake off the husk of its cramping body.

There is an old belief that, through the constellation of Orion, there are hints given of unattainable spheres beyond the known heavens—regions for which astronomy has neither names nor rules. Such glimpses of a beyond, to which we deem ourselves not alien, come to us all some time in life.

If John Bohme would take her with him as his wife? If she had but two years chance of the culture which had been given to him, and then was suffered to put her hands to his work, she could keep pace with him! Her wide pupils dilated; the firm jaws under her shell-tinted oval chin set like a vice. If she married John Bohme there might not be between them a throb of passion or affection, but there would be a keen intellectual appreciation, and an intense, nervous strain to keep step. There would not be a power or a capability left undeveloped in either. Men and women had started in the race of marriage with meaner bonds than that.

She gathered the dead leaves in her hand and let them fall on the open window, watching the wind whirl them away. A sharp lance of light fell across the delicately-moulded head, the transparent temple, and the blue, liquid eyes. Mr. Bohme twirled the knight in his hand more slowly. How did this dainty Ariel of a woman be born of such surroundings? It was like finding a picturesque bit of color in a gutter.

If he took her out of the gutter? He was motionless and grave.

"You will return here when you come from the west?"

"I do not know."

She broke a branch of pendant drops of color—purple, and scarlet, and gleaming white. The door opened, and her father thrust his head into the room—a squat, pallid, overworked man, with a stench of onions and strong tobacco hanging about him.

"Hillo, Cal!" he said, and went on. Mason Porter, her brother, passed the open door, gave a knowing wink, and stuck his thumb into his gandy waistcoat. The girl became a shade paler, and hung the fuschias in her bosom.

There was no divorcing her from her surroundings. Bohme stifled a sigh.

"I will not return. I would like to reach Paris in time for the opening of the chambers."

"True, I had forgotten."

He held out his hand, looking down at her half kindly, half shrewdly from his heavy, gray height. "So the ships hail and sail apart, eh? I will not return for years to this country, probably."

She smiled. "What is the old form on bills of lading? 'May God give to the good ships a safe harbor.'"

"I was mistaken," thought Bohme. "She cared nothing for me." He went down the street with a cowed, defeated look, behind the smoke of his segar.

Another girl came into the parlor where Clara stood. It was a tawdrish, square room, the patched carpet of glaring colors, that "would wear;" the wall-paper of dingy yellow and purple: a half-open door showed the dirty dining-room, which the family, about a square table, gulped down their supper in the stale odors of long-ago beef and cabbage.

"He is gone, Clara?" The speaker had a peculiarly quiet, unobtrusive voice.

"Yes."

"I am sorry," taking the cold fingers in her own.

"It was not the man I cared for. But the chance of escape."

The soft, gray eyes of the other girl blanched at the word, but she said nothing.

"They are at supper? I may as well face them all at once," and with a long, shivering breath she passed her elder sister, and entered the room. There was a little stir of expectation when she came in. They all knew that Bohme was going that day. Would he come to the point with Cal, or not? Jess, and Joe, and Roy giggled and nudged each other in the elbows; but with the elder sisters the day for jesting had gone by. There were two besides Margaret, the one who had followed her—girls whose cheeks betrayed, in the blabby lining of the jaws, the first tell-tale marks of creeping age. Clara felt their hard, eager eyes on her as she entered; but it was her mother's that she dreaded to meet. There was a strange sympathy between the white-robed, spiritual-looking girl, and the thin, jaded, red-skinned woman, who, in a greasy gown, presided over the supper which she had cooked; she knew how the hungry, blue eyes, so like her own, would falter and dull when they saw that she had "missed her chance." She sat undisturbed until the meal was nearly over; then her father looked up at her.

"Bohme came to bid you farewell, Clara?"

"Yes, father."

"Will he come back to Lenox?"

"No, I think not."

He pushed back his chair hastily, took up his hat and went out; she heard him give a stifled sigh as he shut the door. The Porters were not an intentionally vulgar family. Nobody taunted Clara because she had not "played her cards" better; there was an awkward, grave silence. When they had finished, Jane and little Jess whisked the greasy plates out into the kitchen, and began to clatter and wash them amid a steam of hot water and loud talking; the other older worn-out sister sat down in the unswept room with a heaped basket of stockings to darn. Clara half rose, glancing from kitchen and basket to the soiled, patched table-cloth, and the two or three anxious faces bent over it, a new and bitter disgust seized her with her life. It was meager and barren. She saw her mother at the moment draw two or three papers from her pocket with a frightened glance at Mason, and stopped with her hand on her chair. When there were any danger of pain to Mrs. Porter, Clara was sure to be near enough to ward it off. The girls dreaded Mason's anger. Their father's discontent, when he felt it, was shown to his wife alone; but Mason had only within the year been made a partner in the business, and with the boastfulness of youth suffered his sisters to feel that they were partially dependent on him. It was unendurably galling to them.

"What are those, mother"? he said, sharply. "The monthly bills you gave me on Monday; and some of them are yet unpaid?", in a lower voice.

"Yes, my son," her fingers trembling nervously about the papers. "But these are for shoes—Jessie's and Jane's; and Clara's winter dress. I am sorry, Mason."

"So am I," with an angry laugh, that vanished in a frown. "Mother, this is growing too serious a matter; you should have some mercy on father, if my sisters have none. I tell you truth, there has not been a dollar some days this week in the store. The whole concern will go by the board, what with the tight times in trade, and the incessant drain from the house. The old man's head has been kept to the grind-stone this forty years! And if there were any chance of a change—any chance!"

"You mean," said Clara, with white lips, "if some of us would marry?"

"Now, Clara, there is no need of temper—it won't pay bills. God knows I do all I can, and so does my father, to keep you girls in idleness and plenty. It's only natural that you should do as other women—go to homes of your own. But if you don't, you might be reasonably grateful and not meet a fellow with abuse."

He turned and went out, slamming the door after him. A dead silence fell upon the weaker animals left behind.

Jane whimpered feebly. "I nursed Mason when he was a sickly baby, and he begrudges me the pittance that I eat." Another muttered, "Father never complained."

The mother's heart sided with the accused. "You are unjust to Mason. He works hard; he denies himself many luxuries common to boys of his age. You know he loves you, and is proud of you all. But he sees that the burden of such a large family is crushing your father's life out. I see it! I have known it this many a day!" She hid her colorless face in her hands.

"Mother!" cried Clara. Margaret put her quiet hand on her arm, but without effect. "Mother, there is something to be said for us. Is it our will that we are a burden? God knows how vacant and intolerable the days are. Is there no work for us beyond dish-washing and stocking-mending? You say the bread I eat is taking my father's life to earn. Is it easy for me or my sisters to eat it, knowing that? How can we help it? How can we be independent? There is Joe, who was a baby but yesterday, can earn his own living how."

"Joe is a boy; he is intended to buffet with the world."

"There's nothing worse in the world to buffet than poverty—we have that here; and his hands are not tied as ours." Clara, according to her wont, was growing hysterical. Her mother rose, soothingly.

"Clara, my child, what would you or your sisters do with your hands? Why should they not be 'tied?' Surely a daughter of mine is not driven to manual labor—that is, outside of her father's roof. If you marry, now—you are so attractive, your father hoped you would marry well. If you had married Mr. Bohme, it would have been a settlement for you, and a chance for your sisters. As it is—" with a downward, despairing movement of her hands, "I see no prospect. There are but one or two young men in Lenox—and so many girls in the market."

Clara went up to her mother, resting her hands on her shoulders, and looking her in the eyes. There was, as I said, a curious likeness between the one blue-eyed woman, withered and weary, and the other, delicate and young. "Mother," she said, "is that all that marriage means? Is that all it meant to you?"

The faded face quailed a moment; but she had been taught in the hard school of necessity for forty years. "No, Clara; I loved your father. But times were different then, money was more easily made—the price of living was just half what it is now. It is as well to look at facts, you know. Now the west had drained the eastern States of young men, and girls have not the liberty of choice they had then. They must marry as they can."

"Or starve!"

"Your father taught me the philosophy of the question."

"And we learn it for ourselves."

She went up to her own room, followed by Margaret. The two girls were going to a little *fete* that evening. In the town where they lived Clara had pre-eminence as a brilliant woman. She would have won the term in a wider field, perhaps; but in Lenox it had, probably, hindered her marriage. The commonplace mill-owners or farmers of the neighborhood, did not understand her fitful moods; and her quiet retorts seemed always to contain a covert meaning, known only to herself. They were afraid of her. She dressed herself with care this evening. "I am on exhibition—in the market!" she said, bitterly, to Margaret.

There was a good deal of beauty among the Porter sisters; but it was the beauty compatible with ill-health—chalky-whiteness of skin, a hectic flush, a nervous glitter of the eye. They had inherited strong constitutions; but the digestion of one was wrong, the liver of another, and the nerves of all. Had they been machines, some expert would have pronounced that the rust and decay came from want of use. But they were women, and like other American women. None of them, if we except Clara, had any decided talent, not even a love of books or music. They read such semi-religious novels as they could borrow; they did the work at home; turned and returned their old dresses; kept up a system of mild visiting. What unused brain or nerve-power there was in them, escaped (for it will escape) in perpetual headaches and hysterics.

"If they were well married!" their mother would cry, with a sore heart. It was the only open door she saw for them. She forgot that entrance through it had not given herself comfort or rest.

Margaret was the exception; she was, perhaps, the homeliest and most attractive among them. She was young and thoroughly healthy. There was a curious look of cleanness in her fresh, clear skin and eyes. You felt that her heart was both light and honest. She was a small, round-limbed girl, fond of wearing crisp, white muslins, though they were, of necessity, coarse; fond of skating on the pond in winter, and digging in the garden in summer—a tomboy, the elder girls called her; but her mother knew no one was so quiet and tender in sickness as Margaret. She was quiet and tender now, looking at Clara, when she turned from her, with as awe-struck a face as if it were a mortal sickness that ailed her.

CHAPTER II

If mother, or older sisters, could have seen Margaret that evening, they would have found in her a new revelation, hardly measurable by their rules. She was walking with George Goddard, in Mrs. Ford's old-fashioned garden. Nothing, surely, unusual in that; they had sat, side-by-side, in the widow Trimlett's school, "tripped" in the spelling-class, played snow-ball with each other in those winters just as they skated together in these latter ones. They strolled along in a careless, inconsequent way, as they might have done when children, stopping by the currant-bushes for Margaret to pluck a handful of the fruit. The juice stained her white hand like wine; Goddard took it in his own, looked at it with flushed face and quickened breath. It was plain that the Margaret of to-day was no more to him, his old play-mate than the moonlight which drew around them a solitude of dreams was the ordinary dull light that shone on his cot-bed when he was a boy. He drew her to a seat under a walnut-tree, where the lights and music from the house came to them faintly. There they sat silent, or speaking at long intervals. But the old dream went on through words or silence—the dream that brought a new light to the girl's eyes, and a new strength to every hope or ambition of the boy.

"It is all idle, George," Margaret said, at last, raising her voice; "it is time to give it up." Her voice showed that the words cost her much; they were as simple and unconventional about their love as they had been in their old games.

"You have told me that so often, Margaret."

"But we are girl and boy no longer, George. It is time we looked at facts as they are."

"I think I have done that," said George Goddard, standing up, his features sinking easily into stern, grave lines. "I have worked my way steadily up, from the day I went into the office as errand-boy until I have mastered my profession. They were hard times—harder than you know. I think it was not ambition that urged me on."

She was silent. "You thrust off the chance of our marriage from year to year," he continued, after a pause; "and now, forever. You don't know what it is you put away from both of us, Margaret." He drew his hand slowly over his wet forehead.

She was silent. The "chance" she lost was different from Clara's, and cost her more. "I think I know," she said, at last; and, after awhile, in a stronger tone, "I will not put a burden on you that no man should bear, George. If you were unincumbered, I would not be afraid—we could make a home for ourselves, but—"

His face grew clouded. "I know—my mother and Lizzie. But I can work harder to give myself this comfort."

It was not easy for any young girl to be persistently the one to put love and romance aside, and bring up dollars and cents. But the resolute little girl was a true lover—she did it. "Your first duty is to them, George; you could not work harder than you do; your salary will not be increased for years; and, as you know, it barely suffices to maintain them. I will not make debt and poverty certain to you at the beginning of your life. We must give it up."

"And you, Margaret?" turning suddenly to clasp her hands. "Will your life be happier than mine? Nothing can take the place of the love we have had for each other; you have no resource more than I."

There was a little bitterness in her quiet smile. "No. Love and religion are the only resources for women."

Steps were heard approaching. "I am not a boy!" he exclaimed, passionately; "I will not be put aside by a word. I need you, Margaret. You will be mine in spite of reason."

She smiled again, and they went out into the path; but she knew that he, too, saw reason—and that, through all their pain or rebellion, it would prevail with them both at last.

Little Margaret found the *fete* tiresome, for the first time in her life. She waited for Clara, who came to her about an hour afterward, her cheeks flushed, her eyes brilliant in their sunken, discolored sockets.

"You are pale, Maggy. I thought you were a little body made of leather, that never knew pain nor ache. Going home? Yes," in a shrill, excited tone, drawing a crimson hood over her head. "The brightest hour must end," looking at her companion, the cheeks hotter, the eyes more hard and bright.

Mr. Geasly, a short, obese man of about fifty, rolled uneasily on his feet, wiping his blotched, and just now delighted face. "I am glad to have made the time happy to you. I have not always been so successful, though. You know what your presence is to me—*couleur de rose*, eh? Tinging the hours—what is it the poets say?" and then, as if in defiance of Margaret's astonished glance, he put his hand familiarly on her sister's arm. "A word with you, Clara?" drawing her aside, and whispering ostentatiously. He walked home beside her, the slight, proud figure inclining away from him, Margaret fancied with loathing.

She remembered, with a sudden sinking of the heart, the fatherly petting which the repulsive old bachelor had been wont to bestow on Clara since her childhood; but this was a different phase of liking. He was a man who owned one of the mills near the town—he had formerly been a puddler in it. As he gained money, he had acquired neither culture nor refinement: only had added avarice to his former vulgarity. He left them at the gate. Margaret saw, with a shiver, that he took her sister's hand and pressed it to his foul lips.

Clara passed rapidly into the house, and, without giving Margaret time to speak to her, entered the room where her mother sat stooping over her sewing. "It is late, mother," going up to her rapidly, putting her cold hands over the aching eyes. "It is midnight."

"But I must finish."

"Mother!" without hearing her, "I must make a change in my life." She pushed her hair back feverishly, holding her forehead. "There are times when I think I am going mad; and to-day has been one of them."

Her mother dropped the coat she was mending, and looked at her, trembling and pale. There was a strange power in Clara's eyes which she did not understand.

"Surely, in this great world, there is somewhere a place for me!" stretching out her arms vaguely.

"You don't want to go for a missionary, Clara," feebly.

"I don't know any class that want a missionary more than American girls such as I am. I want to be anything that will justify my right to live. If I could teach."

"I don't see how that could be," anxiously, "even if your father would consent. You are not competent to teach anything thoroughly, and then, where is there a place? The school here is filled, and it is the same everywhere; the country is overrun with female teachers. Why, in Massachusetts alone there is a surplus of twenty thousand unmarried women. Teaching and sewing are the only means open to them of earning their living. So you see that's folly, Clara."

"I could sew."

"Your health wouldn't bear the confinement. Besides, you've no right to lower the position of your sisters. No one of our class would marry a sempstress. Why, look at George Goddard's sister—she undertook machine-work for two years, and it developed that spinal complaint. She's a burden now on George for life."

"I can go out as a servant."

"Clara, you are not yourself to-night and talk foolishly. You shall not leave your father's house until you go into one of your own. Content yourself, my child. You have your little crosses to bear, but God meant you to be patient."

"I doubt that," said Clara, boldly, "God never meant any creature he made to cumber the earth uselessly. These rules of custom that face me, turn where I will, are not of his making. He never meant that marriage should be the only means by which a woman should gain her food and clothes, and provide for her old age. See how it ends; or, failing in that, dwindle down into the withered parasite lives which Jane and Sarah endure in legal prostitution. You blush at the words on my lips, mother. But we are in the market—in the market." She left the room hastily.

"These words seem to have taken a morbid hold on Clara," said Mrs. Porter, beginning to cry.

"But, mother," said Margaret, "there are other ways open for women to earn their own living?"

"They can be clerks, type-setters, and the like: but only in the two or three eastern cities, and even there a woman is looked upon with suspicion who takes up a profession or an unusual occupation. She unsexes herself, you see, my dear. A woman's mission is to marry and bear children."

"If she loves. But suppose she cannot marry where she loves?" asked little Margaret, her eyes growing dim, "must she sit idle all her life?"

"She—she may meet some one whom she can love. It is not modest nor womanly to engage in trade or barter, just like a man, my dear. Any woman loses caste who does it."

Margaret went slowly up to bed.

She did not meet Clara until the next morning, when she encountered her on the upper landing. Clara wore a dark, plain dress, and was strangely pale and grave, with dark marks about her lips and eyes, as if the blood had settled heavily. She kissed Margaret gently. "I have left Mr. Geasly with father, Maggy." Margaret gave a sob of pain, which her own sacrifice had never drawn from her. "You mean—"

"I could not sink into the life which Jane leads, dear. There was but one door of escape from it—I will marry him."

She went into her own room and closed the door. Margaret stood with one hand on the balaster a long time, her breath coming heavy and slow. "I think I will find another door," she said.

CHAPTER III

Another six months after this, Dr. Eveart, the old physician, who had ushered the people of Lenox in and out of life for the last twenty years, received a visit in his office from a neat little girl, with peculiarly bright eyes and firm, cherry mouth.

"Margaret? Margaret Porter?" putting on his spectacles. "Well, my dear? Is it Jane who wants the blue pills, or Sarah?"

"Neither. It is a little business of my own, Doctor," blushing.

He took off his spectacles again. "Then it is fancy. Nothing ails you, Maggy. Let well alone. You dig and potter in that yard of yours too much to give me the chance of tinkering on you."

"It is about my digging I came to speak with you. I want to extend it to that lot of yours sloping down to the creek."

"What? Eh?"

"Doctor," her lips began to tremble, "I am going to do something for myself in the world. Don't laugh at me."

"I mean to make my own living," without seeming to hear him. "It seems to me the world is full of pleasure and comfort to be had for money;

and God did not put the power into woman's head to make the money for no use."

"Oh! ho!" leaning forward and looking at her curiously. "You are going to teach?"

"No. I'm not well educated; I've no accomplishments; and, indeed, I don't care for books at all," laughing.

"What have you in your brain then, Maggy?"

She hesitated, growing serious. "Phrenologists say that the faculty of saving money is different from that of making it. I cannot save, because I haven't it. But I think I could make it better than most men I know."

"How, for instance? Do you mean to plant turnips or radishes on my lot?"

"No," gravely. "Turnips and radishes yield a small profit, and I could not work them without help. I mean to plant herbs."

"Eh?"

"Medicinal herbs. They will command a ready sale in the large laboratories in Philadelphia, if they are properly raised. I wrote for information as to the prices given, and then I studied the method of culture. Two acres have been made to yield two thousand dollars a year."

"The deuce they have! They would not yield you two thousand cents."

"Why?"

"Well—you're a woman."

Margaret laughed.

"Why don't you marry, child?"

"Perhaps I may, some day. But marriage I can't force into my life."

"And money you can. What does Porter say to this, eh? Or that young cub of a brother of yours?"

"I don't think Mason is a cub. They are very angry." She grew pale, and moved restlessly.

"You will make a dead failure."

"Perhaps I shall, the first year. But I will try the second."

"And you want me to give you the ground? I have it in use."

Her color rose. "I did not want you to give it to me. I have heard the rent you receive for it in pasture, and I will give you double. It is not much, or I could not do it," laying some notes on the table.

He counted them over carefully. "That is the exact amount. Now put it in your pocket. Don't do business like a woman. I did not ask you for rent in advance; but I'll take it from you at the proper time. Where did you get the money, by-the-by?"

"Made it by sewing."

"Why don't you make more by sewing, then? It is a more feminine way. Who ever heard of a lady turning huckster?" watching her narrowly.

"It is a more feminine way, and consequently poorly paid." He laughed. "Well, well, you shall have the ground. How is that sister of yours, Mrs. Geasly? Marriage has not strengthened her in any way, I'm afraid."

"Clara was always dyspeptic," said Margaret, quietly.

"So! So! But I like the clannish spirit of the girl," he added, after she was gone.

The old doctor was right in his foreboding. Margaret's acre did not yield her two thousand, nor twenty cents, in the first year. Rain came when she wanted sun, and sun when the plants were dried and baked with heat; she had not sown lightly enough; she had burned up the ground with guano. The anger and astonishment with which her family had seen her begin broke out in a torrent of wrath and sneers from Mason, of cool contempt from her sisters; her father was gloomily silent, thinking her whole action a covert reproach upon himself. This last cut Margaret to the quick. Society, too, was ready with its witticisms and jeers; George Goddard, struggling hard, in spite of himself, to approve her as courageous and true-hearted, secretly was angry that his pure, shy little Daisy, as he loved to call her, should be brought before the town as a strong-minded reformer.

Margaret cried half the night, but worked cheerfully by day. It did not need any strength of mind to plant seeds, to hoe, or to weed; even Clara, driving by wearily in her carriage, thought the girl never had looked so fresh and pretty as with her heat, coarse dress and flushed cheeks. When the first year failed, she want to her needle again and sewed until the rent of the second was earned. People began to tire of her and her whim as a topic; they ceased to notice her; scarcely knew that more misfortunes and want of experience caused her to barely clear expenses in the end of her second trial. At home she was no longer opposed. Margaret had a strong, quiet will—and the strong will, not love or authority, always govern the family; just as out in the world it goes into the fortress and sits down master, while genius stands knocking at the door.

At the end of the third year money came to Margaret—enough money to conquer some of the comfort and pleasure of the world of which she had talked. When the monthly bills were sometimes found paid before they were demanded; when the sewing was taken out of her mother's basket and sent off to the sempstress; when the girls had new dresses, and

Mason a gorgeous shirt-pin, they began to think that Margaret's whim had some substance in it.

About the fourth year, she was so successful that her friends all came to her with advice; thought she could find a better market by trying different firms; counseled her to invest her money here and there. When she took it to hire more ground, however, and employed help, (woman's help,) they shook their heads doubtfully. She was going beyond her depth. She would ruin the enterprise; and really it was a very pretty scheme, an easy way of making money; they wondered nobody had thought of it before! One or two tried it, and undersold Margaret, to the indignation of Mason, who found her undertaking coming up, side-by-side, in importance with his own business, and began to take an equal pride in it. But the other experiments proved failures. The girl was a hard student and began to master her business; her herbs were free from dust and mixture. She sent only the best quality into the market; they brought the highest price, and the demand increased steadily year by year.

"Why don't you marry, child?" the old doctor asked her from time to time.

"Perhaps I may," she said, at first; but afterward, as the years slipped by, she would only smile and begin to talk of poppy or snake-root. For George Goddard, at his mother's death, had gone away with his sister, and did not return, nor even made a sign of remembrance. "I am his little Daisy no longer," Margaret said, with a quiet, sorrowful smile.

CHAPTER IV

Eight years had passed since Margaret began work before Goddard came back. His sister was dead; the last of their little patrimony had been exhausted in traveling with her in search of health. He had obtained an office which could enable him to reside in Lenox, traveling at intervals through the State.

All Lenox was ready for him, with its gossip and half-expressed condolence at having "lost his chance with his school-boy love."

"Miss Porter," so went the talk, "bade fair to be one of the wealthiest citizens of the village, and was to be bought at a merely nominal price, and she had a singularly good judgment and the soil required for her purpose. She had gone into enterprises unheard of among the people of Lenox; set out a vineyard on the back of Starr's Hill; drained a bit of swamp in the meadow, and planted cranberries. They are better than oil!" exclaimed farmer Thornly. "The girl has a wonderful knack about planting and sowing; if she'd put in a broomstick, it'd grow, as the saying goes. I tell my girls, what's to hinder? Why shouldn't a woman grow grapes as well as gilliflowers"?

"Where are the other sisters"? asked Goddard.

"Well, Jane and Sarah went with Margaret to Philadelphia, and there she gave them a start at a trimming-store; and Barr, who saw them other week, says they're fat and portly, got a house of their own, and have lost all their sour, bitter little ways. Jessie, she's book-keeper for them. Mason's married, you know, and Joe's grown so there's nobody at home but Margaret with the old folks, and that pretty little Bey. She's going to marry our young parson, the talk goes."

"*She* is not in trade?" laughed Goddard, bitterly.

Thornly stroked his chin thoughtfully. "Well, George—now I don't know about Margaret. It's made a great difference in them Porter girls to have some business of their own in the world; and it's made their chances for marriage better. That poor Clary—she's a miserable, sickly creetur. Old Geasly's a hard man—niggardly with his hands, and worse with his wife. You ought to call round and see the old folks and Margaret, George."

George was restless and nervous until he had obeyed the old man's advice. He tried to reconcile Margaret, as she doubtless had become a hard, keen-faced, prematurely-old woman, with the rosy, resolute little girl who had put him from her, though with her whole soul called him back through her brown eyes; aye, and held him from her. In the evening he went up to the Porter-farm, for they had moved out of the village. It was a quiet, home-like old farm-house which he found, with a slope of grass in front, shaded by old trees. The room into which he was ushered was a large, simply-furnished parlor, with a few good engravings on the walls: new books, flowers, the countless little signs of culture and ease in the daily life scattered about. Old Mr. Porter sat reading, his wife was trimming some flowers on the window-ledge. Goddard had a theory that all old people should be idle. The look of grave, simple content on the faces of this gray-haired man and woman, their easily moved smile, justified his fancy. "They have a breathing time to look back and learn what lesson life had for them," he thought. "And Margaret has given them that, at whatever sacrifice of herself."

Her mother had gone out to summon her, and a moment afterward, a light, elastic boot-step came over the porch, and Margaret stood before him. At first Goddard was conscious only of a dull impression that time had not moved; that it was his Daisy of long-ago, whose brown eyes met his, and whose color went and came with every word. Then the change grew perceptible; there was a free, unconstrained grace in thought and language which the conscious, awkward girl had not possessed; her features were cut out from the unmeaningness of youth, delicate and refined. There was a careless gayety in her tone, and ready laugh; a certain repose in pose and gesture, which is peculiar to those sure of their position and errand in the world.

He had intended to remain but a few moments; but the evening was gone before he remembered his resolve. Margaret sang for him; she had a sweet and true voice, adapted to ballad-music—and she had spared neither time nor money in educating it. He noticed, too, that she was lavishly fastidious in the details of her dress. She always had liked soft, rich clothing, and now indulged her whims. The fault, if fault it were, pleased him. He found the conversation becoming more and more a narrative of his eight years of foreign life. Margaret was the best of listeners, and had a habit of leading her companions into their best talking-ground, and leaving them there to make their own happiness; yet he fancied that a secret, deeper feeling made her silent and reticent with him.

He rose at last—they were alone in the room. It hardly seemed to him courteous to ignore, as they apparently had done, her novel way of life.

"I find you changed, Miss Porter," looking beyond her rather than into the frank eyes that met his. "You have the quiet manner, now, of one born to an inheritance."

"Then it is false manner," quickly. "Talent, or skill, such as some women possess, is a heritage; but I have only the ordinary faculties of common sense and perseverance. Any woman has enough power given her to stand alone, if need be."

Now George Goddard had his due, manly prerogative of superior sense and conservatism; he had begun with the intention of entering his protest against the radical folly of her whole life; but in the face of her changed home and changed self, he could not pronounce it to be folly. Besides, the light was faint, the scent of the roses stole in at the open window, the white-robed woman, whose beautiful face was upturned to his, had been dear to him all his life. He did not commence his argument on work and wages.

"To stand alone?" he repeated. "Is there need that you should stand alone, Margaret? I have waited long and faithfully. You are far dearer to me now than on the day when you put me away from you."

She tried to tell him there was no need, and that she, too, had been true and faithful; but she said nothing, only put her hand in his, and blushed and sobbed a little, like any other foolish woman.

Margaret never gave up her business. The Goddard mansion stands in the midst of the most productive tracts in Pennsylvania, which she superintends. Her husband's position in the political world draws constantly about them men and women of strong and affluent natures, among whom Margaret is honored and recognized as she deserves, and as every woman requires to be, for her healthy development. Her household is better managed, and her cooking and sewing more thoroughly done, because she can afford to employ skillful-brained servants, and does not spend her strength in the desperate, incompetent endeavors of a maid-of-all-work. A beautiful, gracious lady, now that white hairs are beginning to glisten in the brown, as she was in her earlier youth. Her daughters have each been given a trade or profession, which they can use if the necessity ever comes for them to make their own living. The one burden in her life is the perpetual presence of her sister, Clara, and her half dozen of children, who were left dependent upon herself and George Goddard by Geasly's sudden, insolvent death. Clara alternately bemoans her fate, indulges in outbreaks of temper, and rails at society.

"One is tempted," she cries, "to go back to Fourier, or St.-Simon, for a true solution of the social enigma. The war has made thousands of women helpless and penniless at the very time when the price of living is doubled. They cannot all teach nor sew, nor become shop-girls; and they and their children must live. Yet if a woman attempts a man's business, hear the outcry that follows her! What am I to do with my girls? If Nan were a boy, I'd have her taught engraving; she has an artist's eye and delicate fingers. But she shall not unsex herself; she is very pretty."

"And may marry well. Why do you not finish your sentence, Clara?" said Margaret, indignantly. "And the idea that a good marriage was the one stroke of business by which she was to make her living, has been instilled into Nelly until, from the age of sixteen, a boy could not approach her without being regarded as a possible husband. Surely there are other and worse ways of unsexing a woman than the use of a burin." [1]

"May God help poor women!" sighed Clara.

"May He rather show them how to help themselves."

"You found an open door easily. But we cannot all plant herbs and cranberries."

"No; but there is no prison from which there is not a means of escape."

# Earthen Pitchers

Scribner's Monthly, November 1873–April 1874

CHAPTER I

"We'll drive?" said young Chalkley, anxiously, halting on the steps of the Continental Hotel. He had Mr. Burgess, the English magazinist, in charge. "Oh, drive, of course!" beckoning to a hackman. If heaven had but willed him in this crisis of fate a buggy of his own—a team of any sort! This Londoner, no doubt, dwelt in an atmosphere of rank where coroneted chariots and footmen were every-day matters. It is true, Chalkley hired a trotting-horse for an hour per day, and he would willingly have mounted Burgess upon it, and run behind, like an Egyptian donkey boy, if the thing had been practicable. As it was, he had to call a hack.

"Tut, no," said Burgess, "I vote to walk."

"Why, certainly," with a reassured little giggle. "Why, I forgot what tremendous fellows you English are with your constitutionals, and so on." He looked doubtfully down as they walked, at the little wiry man beside him, with his foxy face and red beard. Certainly, this was not his ideal of bluff John Bull; but none the less did he feel that the New World was on trial to-night before the Old. Elsewhere, this judge could inspect its institutions and politics; but Parr Chalkley felt it had fallen to his lot to present its social aspects.

"Here you have the Quaker element," waving his hand up the broad street, asleep at that early hour of the evening, the red brick fronts and marble steps distinct in the moonlight. "Arch street. Nobody, of course, in society lives north of Market street. We have our distinctions of rank here, Mr. Burgess, as in older countries. Still, it is possible to visit in some houses in Arch."

"Is Miss Derby's one of them?"

"No, no!" laughing. "Society never heard of Miss Derby. I take you there just as I should to the Museum yonder. Both places are—well, irregular; but you'll find some curious animals in them. I know what *you* want," complacently. "You want our idiosyncrasies. Our good society is just a repetition of what you have at home."

Mr. Burgess's eyes twinkled. "Yes, well-bred people are the same the world over," he said, politely, "and family parties are apt to be monotonous, as you say."

"As for mountains and rivers," continued Parr, loftily, "I never thrust them at any foreigner. They may have that hobby, or they may not. Nature, in my opinion, is a bore." (He said "in me ahpinion is a barr.")

"No, but really you know!" protested Burgess. "Your scenery is very nice indeed. It lacks the charm of history of course—what one might call the sauce of Age. But it serves the better as a background for my articles. We, Dickens, Kingsley and the rest of us, have used up all the back-grounds: Europe, the Nile, Australia. I think I've had a very lucky 'find' here. I mean to produce some very pretty effects in my papers with your Rocky Mountains, Yosemite and all those, eh? This is Miss Derby's street?" as they turned a corner. "It looks respectable. Nothing Bohemian [1] here."

"Oh, there are no Bohemians in Philadelphia," energetically; "there is no room for them. No more than for cheap weeds in these grass plats. No, no, sir. You must not think of Jenny—of Miss Derby as anything but a very respectable girl. Yes, and a very sweet girl too," he added, but with a quaver as though knowing that he put Society at defiance.

"But clever?" Burgess's red-rimmed eyes were twinkling again. "Now come. American ladies are all oppressively clever, you know. 'Have you read my last tragedy?' says one. Another thinks it more a woman's work to dissect babies than to suckle them. The very school-girls attack you with their views of John Stuart Mill; and this Miss Derby, still in her teens you say, lives alone, and has her 'Saturday evenings.'"

"Don't know," said Parr, turning his whitish eyes full on Burgess; "I never thought Jenny Derby clever." He was stolidly perplexed. Undoubtedly his companion was not what he had been taught to think well-bred. "'Read her last tragedy'? Why it's the Lambs he means, where he stayed in New York!" thought Parr with the look of an amazed ox. But—"It must be a shock," he said gently, a moment after, "to plunge into our social chaos after the culture and refinement of England." He hoped, however, that Burgess would see how little he, a Philadelphian of the Philadelphians, had to do with social chaoses. He was going to London in the fall, and had planned that his new friend should introduce him into the very arcana of fashion. Burgess, meanwhile, was eyeing the big young fellow shrewdly; the heavy features, complexion like a girl's, fair Dundreary [2] whiskers, foppish clothes, the rose in his buttonhole, skittish walk: all good points for a comic picture of a Philadelphian for his book. Since he came to this country he usually sketched his host's face on his thumb-nail whenever he was invited out to dine, and so was accumulating a good stock of figures to front his "backgrounds." The truth was, Burgess, being the son of a green-grocer at home, knew nothing of society beyond the acquaintance of a few men in inferior clubs, and had to make the best of his chance while he was here.

"No, Jenny Derby's not clever," maundered Parr, going back, as was his habit, to pick up a subject and wring more talk out of it. "She's knocked around a good deal for her age, though old Derby was cranky; they lived in Italy when she was a little thing, and he went into spiritualism and then into Italian freedom; seeker after truth—American Patriot—all that sort of thing. Jenny, it seems, was a pet with some people worth knowing: Mrs. Browning, Mazzini, and so on. Four or five years later Derby was sent from here to Germany on some Reform Committee: Peace—Colonization, heaven knows what, and takes her with him, and they lunch with that bishop and dine with this duke—all humanitarians."

"Tolerably sharp practice in the old man."

"Not at all. Derby was not sharp. Derby," deliberately, "was as little sharp as any man I know. But it gave Jenny a chance to see life, and she made deuced good use of her eyes. It's astonishing the use she always makes of them!" growing animated. "Now that girl's on two or three papers. Writes book notices, and a woman's column. And that European experience of hers is all her material. Same thing over and over; roast, hash, and ragout; you have it again week after week, and, 'pon my word, you don't recognize it."

"I know that kind of woman. And these receptions?"

"Oh, they don't deserve such a large name as that. The old man left her in a Quaker boarding-house when he died, and they give her the use of a vacant room there. So she says to one friend and another, 'Don't come here through the week: you only are in my way. Come on Saturday evening. That's your Sabbath, and mine.' Newspaper people, you understand. So we go, to see Jenny, or each other. Sometimes she gives us tea, and dry toast; sometimes a supper from Augustin's, if she's in funds; but you never know what's coming. Oh, it's very nice indeed. Here we are," turning up the marble steps of one of the interminable red houses and ringing the bell.

They entered a long hall, bare but for the gas flaring and the flying Naiads on the old wall paper: passing up a flight or two of stairs, and into a room, wide, high, and softly lighted. Burgess's little eyes glanced here and there. Floor bare and stained in imitation of walnut, tables covered with warm-colored cloth, scattered about, with men at them, playing chess, and smoking, and women sewing. The whole affair was notably unlike any social gathering which Burgess had ever seen, to which women were admitted, and smacked much more of the club than the drawing-room. Yet men and women were quiet, low-voiced, and, if they had not been so eager and interested, would have satisfied his notions of good-breeding.

"Why these *are* pictures," he cried, with an involuntary start, going up to the wall. "But what a combination! A Gérôme,[3] a Bonheur,[4] and—surely I am not mistaken—this is a Meissonier?"[5]

"I'm sure I don't know. I'll ask. This is only a tea-and-toast night. I see the cups yonder."

"She has the walls the proper tint for them, too. But how can a woman earn enough money by scribbling for the daily journals to buy such pictures as these?"

"She does not buy them," said a school-girl in an ill-fitting blue merino, who was looking at the Meissonier. She turned to Burgess, thinking he had asked her the question. "These are part of the Lingard collection which was brought to town for sale."

Burgess bowed respectfully. "And Miss Derby hires them for her reception?"

"No. Mr. Lingard imports them twice a year, and he hangs the best here on private view. The critics and press reporters are sure to see them to-night. Lingard had the walls stained for her. It pays him. ''Tis Monsieur Puff, my lord, coming round the corner,'" she quoted, laughing and glancing up at Chalkley.

"And Miss Derby allows her walls to be used as advertisements?" He spoke to Parr, but the little girl replied:

"If it makes them pleasant to her guests, why not? She is a penniless little wretch, not able to put on wall paper. She allows Mr. Chalkley here to pay for that wood fire, and every pianist to bring his own instrument. It is a sort of neutral ground this, for artists and their critics to meet. There is John Shively, the publisher, coming in at the door. He will tell you in five minutes more how many millions he is worth. There are half a dozen other kings here, in sugar or cotton. What would they care for Jane Derby or her dry toast and tea if they did not know that they would see better pictures and hear better music here than in any house in town?"

Burgess turned to Parr: "Yet you told me this woman was neither clever nor sharp?"

Chalkley stood between the two, red, bulky, stammering. The little girl laughed good-humoredly, and held out both her fat hands deprecatingly: "Don't go any farther, Mr. Burgess. I am Jenny Derby. I thought you knew." Seeing his embarrassment she covered it adroitly by leading him to the fire. "Here is a seat from which you can take notes. I advised Mr. Chalkley to bring you here. Among these odds and ends of American society you may find a point or two for your book or lecture on us, whichever it is to be."

"Neither, I assure you. Yet I might take you as the typical American girl, I suppose, Miss Derby?" staring at her through his half-shut red eyelashes.

"By no means," quietly. "I am outside of all orthodox lines. But women can go on to man's ground with safety further here than in England. Kit, pray give your chair to Mr. Chalkley. I want you." She spoke to a man who sat by the fire playing with a dog. He rose leisurely, without looking at the newcomers, and followed her.

Mr. Burgess looked after her eagerly. "I don't wonder I mistook her for a school-girl. She has the unformed figure and manner of a girl of fifteen; but there's a cool *aplomb* about her, and a speculation in those gray eyes that show she has seen a good deal of the world."

"Ah, that she has! I knew you would admire her!"

"She has seen more than you, Chalkley," smiling. "But what a hospitality! 'You came to caricature us. So to your business.'"

"'Pon my soul," cried Chalkley, with sudden candor, "I'm afraid she was in the right, Mr. Burgess. She's the honestest creature alive. She is just as blunt about your faults as her own."

"Who comes here?" hastily turning the subject.

Parr shrugged his big shoulders. "Shively, the publisher. A new man. Advertised himself into a fortune, and now he's trying to advertise himself into society. I can't present you. I don't know him," as he stood before them.

But Shively smiled on him benignly from his lank and bony height. From his shining shoes to his long hatchet-faced head with its curling ruffle of red whiskers and hair, he was one smile, affable, patronizing, aggressively innocent. Parr turned off with a distant bow, while Shively held out both hands to the Englishman.

"Mr. Burgess! Let me name myself! John Shively. You may have heard of my publications. Small things, small things! But they help me to aid my fellow-creatures, and for what else, in God's name, are we here? But you!—I know you well, Mr. Burgess—through your works. We are old friends. Comrades in spirit, I may say, without being sentimental."

"I do not doubt it, Mr. Shively."

"And so you are going to write us up? Ah, you young fellows, you must each have your fling at us Americans. But we have grown more pachy-dermatous than in the days of Mrs. Trollope and Dickens. Seriously," Mr. Shively growing suddenly grave, "the better men of the two nations have lately, as I may say, struck hands and brought their countries into accord. My friend, the Earl of Dundas, remarked when he was dining with me the other day: 'We are but one clan, after all, Shively.' The Prince of Wales, (and a fine young fellow he is, by the way,) made a casual observa-tion to me, when he was here, tending to the same effect. I do what *I* can to foster that brotherhood of feeling between America and all other nations. I had a Russian prince at my house yesterday, quite a cultivated man, too. It was really surprising to see how well informed he was on many subjects. You must come up and see my little place, by the way, Mr. Burgess. Only worth your notice as an example of what industry may do for a man who begins penniless in this country. Why the parlor curtains alone stood me in twelve thousand, and that in gold, sir. My wife will have nothing but point lace for her pillow slips. These women have their whims you know, so I indulge her. Little points like that in your book will whet your readers' appetite for heavier statistics. And I began as an errand boy. Yes, sir. An er-rand boy."

"So I have heard."

"Ah, indeed? Well, John Shively is tolerably well known, and he never denied his origin. I strive to uplift the class from which I came, Mr. Burgess. My employés have a bank of their own, and a private graveyard on my grounds where they can be buried as comfortably as though they were millionaries. Ah yes! little things, but they help our fellow creatures, and what else in God's name are we here for? Those fellows, the press reporters, look upon me as a godsend. 'You and your benefactions keep us in items, Mr. Shively,' they often say," drawing down his glossy shirt-cuffs.

"Who are these women, if I may ask?" interrupted Burgess, glancing around.

"Ah, women? None from our old families, Mr. Burgess. None of the class to which my young friend Parr Chalkley belongs. I do not bring my daughter here, as you perceive. Though little Miss Derby is very nice— very nice! And these persons are all respectable. Ah yes, quite so. Those Quaker ladies with white hair are old Anti-Slavery leaders. That young female in the corner, short, aggressive, you see, is a lecturer, I think; but really one cannot be familiar with all orders in a society so uncertain and chaotic as ours. That lovely creature with the mass of reddish hair tumbling about her shoulders is the famous actress, Devereux; fine woman, Mr. Burgess."

Mr. Burgess lifted his eye-glass. "Yes, she is," he said, after a critical pause. "But how does a busy man like yourself spare time to come here?"

Shively held up his white pulpy hand to his mouth. "*Entre nous*, it *is* business. I find this kind of people, artists, editors, and the like much cheaper when you take them unawares out of their offices—off guard, as one might say. Just now I want a series of articles written, half scientific, half popular, for which I am willing to pay liberally. I know but one young fellow capable of doing it, and of course I'll try to get him on as easy terms as possible. I came to find him to-night, but he is not here. A most brilliant young scamp, moody and unreliable, like all your men of genius."

"Who is he? I have heard of him, no doubt."

"Ah yes. One of the most promising men of the day, Niel Goddard. Is it possible Miss Derby hears me? She turned as I named him. *She* would advise him against my offer. She has notably a sharp eye for the pennies. Harte, where is your comrade, Goddard, now?"

Burgess turned quickly. Of Harte, he had heard—a figure painter, beginning to be known in Europe as here for the delicacy of his touch as well as the subtle grace of his meaning. He was a solid, squat, good-natured looking fellow, wearing spectacles, and with black brows which met over his nose.

"Not in town. He is down on the coast, somewhere, studying the effect of sunset on the neap tide, for a marine he is going to paint."

"Absurd! He is not going to waste his time in painting?"

"If Niel Goddard chose to take brush and palette seriously in hand," said Harte, with some heat, "none of us could touch him. But he is lazy. That inevitable *vis inertiæ* of genius, you know."

"Now Harte," said Shively, as he turned away, "has no genius whatever. But the most indomitable endurance! Son of a butcher, sir! Chose the canvas instead of a meat-block, and has starved and drudged and worked his way for ten years, until he has done some neat things."

"You will wake up some day and find in Harte a great painter," said Burgess. "We begin to know him in England."

"But if you could see Goddard's studies! Just a line, here and there. But when you come to talk of power!—"

"What has Goddard done? Written or painted?"

"Done? done? Oh, if you put it that way, but little as yet, sir. Like all real artists, his studies will be severe. But as for promise, I know no man in America to equal him."

CHAPTER II

Miss Derby, followed by the big fair-haired man whom she called Kit, went into a little ante-room or closet where a girl not so young as herself was kneeling before an open fire, toasting thin slices of bread already thoroughly dried. Jenny broke a bit critically. "Too brown," she said sharply. "And one slice must *not* lie on another; not for an instant. I don't want to give them soggy dough. The refreshment is cheap," smiling up at Kit, "but it must be perfect of its kind. Now this tea. It was a Christmas gift from Mr. Theris; not a pound of the like in the country. People talk of it when they go away, and that attracts notice. Pays me, you see? These Japanese cups I picked up in a London pawn shop. The man did not know their value. They look like a bubble cut in half. You drop a pinch of the tea in each. Pour on your water, and cover with the other half. Now taste, Kit."

"It seems poor stuff, to tell you the truth. Besides, it's only half a mouthful, Jenny."

"I can't give this lot of people what you'd call a square meal," tartly. "Sometimes I do give them a supper that costs a quarter's salary—though I get it cheaper than other people, by giving the caterer a puff, and besides he takes back from me whatever terrapin or croquettes are left."

"Why do you go to such expense, Jenny? I cannot understand why you bring these people here, any how. This is not like our supper parties down in Delaware, where we all go because we like each other," glancing to the open door.

"I do it because it pays me, you may be sure of that. In town they talk of me as a sharp woman pushing into a man's place. People come here and they know me always afterward as Jenny Derby: a genial, warm-hearted little thing that needs help. And they're all ready to help. You see?"

Christopher stood lazily pulling the dog's ears for a minute; then he laughed. "I see that you are about as genial and warm-hearted as most other women, Jenny. But I can fancy you at forty, hoarding your money in an old tea-pot like our grandmother Shaw, and caring for nothing so much as the hoarding. You have her blood in you, so take care."

She looked at him steadily for a moment. "I believe you're right," she said suddenly; then crossed the room to the fire. "That is enough, Miss

Croft. Much obliged, I'm sure. You need not wait any longer. No, she's not a servant," to Kit's look of inquiry. "She's a wood engraver. I got work for her in the offices, and she's glad to pay me in this way."

"It saves you a burned face, at least;" drily. "Hers was purple."

"Yes: and the servants would waste the bread and have to be paid besides. As for her face, it don't matter to her. Now if it was that Devereux woman, yonder, it would be of some importance; her face is worth a capital of a million. It brings her in an interest of five thousand per week."

She went back to the larger room, and her cousin followed leisurely, and sat down by the window, through which a patch of moonlight fell. The dog kept close beside him; it was the only one of Jenny's companions who had made friends with the Delaware farmer, or with whom he felt at home. He had an awed admiration for all literary folk, or artists. The man who had written a book or painted a picture, vaguely ranked in his mind, with Cæsar or the Muses, or Michael Angelo, or any of those dim Presences to whom he had been introduced in his college days, but had lost sight of since in the hurry of raising early peaches and Chester County pigs. But he was disappointed now that he was brought face to face with these makers of the lightning which illumined the world. *Was* this genius? It sounded to him like gossip smelling rankly of paint and ink. Was it in this fashion that the wits in Dick Steele's time met at White's, and drank and talked? After all, had Jenny got into the real Holy of Holies of literature? Were these the Simon-pure masters in intellect, or only shrewd hucksters of brain work? The talk and laughter about him seemed to him all sham and unmeaning, though in reality there was unusual heartiness and jest in it. People out of all cliques and ranks met at Miss Derby's, and there was a certain newly wakened expression with both curiosity and humor in their eyes, as though each was testing the other unknown specimens of humanity in this newly discovered atmosphere.

Miss Derby herself stood near him with the Englishman, to whom she pointed out one after another her guests. "Those two prettily dressed ladies by the door belong to a class you don't know yet in England, women correspondents of the newspapers. I too!" nodding and touching her breast, "I write letters from Paris for the *Day-book*, and from Rome for the *Progress*. They furnish me the news items, and it is quite easy to dress them up. There are two New York journalists, both of them from the West. Western men are never as authors worth a penny, but they are at the head of the newspaper profession everywhere. What journalism wants is common sense, and that is the genius of the West."

"Miss Derby is like other American ladies," Burgess said to Parr when she had gone to some other part of the room. "She does not talk, she orates."

"That is because of her business. I have always remarked that women who write for the press have that snappy didactic manner. If they tell you what's o'clock, they must needs make an epigram out of it."

It was Sturm who said this: languidly, as became the cynical philosophic turn of mind for which he was noted: a character which had grown on him of late years, since his bald head, shallow face, and waxed moustache seemed to require it. (Sturm was then, and indeed is still, musical critic for the *Review*.)

"I am glad I came here to-night," replied Mr. Burgess. "I get a pretty fair idea, I fancy, of your professors of literature and art, with a good deal of the radical social element besides: one looks for radicalism in Philadelphia."

"If literature and art," enunciated Sturm slowly, "be trades, you are right. The time was, sir, when to be an author was to be a prophet, priest, and king. A man wrote a book, however poor, as the oracles spoke, from some divine impulse within. Now the book, the poem, or the article is manufactured and offered by these—these venders," glancing around, "just as a clown turns a summersault or plays a fresh prank—for the sake of a few pennies."

"You're right; by George you're right!" chuckled Shively, "I've said as much in the office a dozen times! Why my writers—on books or papers—have as keen noses for their copyrights or salaries as the poorest mechanic in the bindery. You're right, Sturm."

"They don't understand, probably, why the fountain of Helicon[6] should bubble without charge either for mankind or for Mr. Shively," said Sturm drily. "It's the demand," turning to Burgess, "the steady sale of literary work that has coarsened its quality. When a man used to give five years to the elaboration of the idea which he offered to the public, he fancied some of the real water of life sparkled in it: but these tradespeople in ink are like men who keep drinking booths at a fair. They stir up their drinks in an hour. What do they care whether they sell nectar, or bitter beer, or ginger-pop, so that the pressing thirst of the crowd is satisfied and they get their cursed money?"

Nobody appreciated this tirade but Shively, who chuckled through it continuously, rubbing his thick gold chain between his fat thumb and finger. "Yes, sir. I've known a dozen painters and authors who talked of being true to art, and meant to do some great work, and they all took to daubing pot-boilers of landscapes for the auction-shops, or scribbling skits of stories and articles for the newspapers and magazines. Pegasus[7] is greedy for his oats, nowadays, and I can always tell when he is ready to lay his wings by and hire out to do carting by the day. No talk of Art then, but— how much a column, Mr. Shively?' "

Miss Derby, who stood near them, sheltering her flushed face from the fire, interposed, "I know one man whom you concede to have a real genius, Mr. Shively, as his birthright; but I heard you propose to buy him to-night for a very small mess of pottage indeed."

"Oh, Goddard? Yes, I've no doubt Goddard will make his mark some day. Hit the public a downright blow between the eyes. But in the meanwhile he might as well turn an honest penny by writing up my popular scientific summary. Ah, going, Mr. Burgess? I see our friends are dropping off. I'll accompany you. Good night, Miss Derby. You'll not prejudice Mr. Goddard against my offer?"

"I shall not interfere," said Jenny.

People began to come up to say good night to her. Whether they bowed or shook hands, Kit, whose lazy blue eyes saw every thing, observed that there was none of that fantastic deferential homage which men always pay to a young and pretty girl, but instead, a certain air of cordial comradeship as though Miss Derby were a hearty good fellow.

"They don't quite slap her on the back: but very near it," he thought, as she stood joking with Sturm and the others.

She evidently liked the comradeship. Her cheeks burned and her eyes sparkled as the last one turned lingering away. "That's Stillwell, Kit; I went out with him on that exploring expedition a year ago to visit the Indian country. Old Doctor Swan and his wife were in command. Semi-political you see. I got an appointment as artist to the expedition. With that and my letters for the *Progress* I cleared three hundred dollars, besides expenses. After we came home, the Stillwell woman and I hired two good nags and rode through every county in Maryland, picking up adventures and land scapes and characters for our writing. You don't approve of that I see, Kit?"

"We wanted you to spend that summer on the coast with us, Jenny," he said evasively. "Why do you prefer such knight errantry to living among your father's people? None of them know you but me, and I've had to force myself on you here."

She leaned forward and touched him on the arm. Because of the very manliness of the girl a touch from her had all the force of a caress from sweet fondling women. "I don't know that they are all like you, Kit. Besides what *matériel* could I find in Delaware? I must have capital, grist to grind. I am making my bread and butter."

"I suppose you have chosen the right way," hesitatingly. "A woman with genius—"

Jenny laughed: a hearty laugh enough, yet there was a pathetic ring about it. "Bah! I have none of that, if even there be such a thing. I have not even a woman's ordinary skill in saying pretty nothings about nothing. I know just what I am."

The room was large and lonely: she sat in front of the firelight which flashed and darkened over her face, and showed it relaxed, and older than when nerved and heated by excitement. "No, Kit: circumstances pushed me among literary people and put a pen in my hand. I have covered up my real character in a reputation for wit and fancy just as I hide the bare walls with those pictures, which don't belong to me. It is shop-work with me. I read this book and that to find a style. I scour the country for ideas and facts as capital. Yet I write successful poetry. It tells. If I were older and had enough money saved I think I'd go into trade. I could make a fortune at that." It certainly was a very shrewd face which met Kit's, from the sharp chin to the broad, low, white brow.

"I know nothing about either poetry or trade," he said gravely. "I suppose you must be born fit for one, and make yourself fit for the other. But I must go to business. I came to-night to bring you a message from Mr. Goddard."

"Yes." She rose suddenly and began putting the chairs in their places.

"He has been in Lewes for nearly a month now. He brought me your letter of introduction the day he arrived."

"In Lewes? His business was in Georgetown."

"Yes; he told me all about that business. He's franker than I'd be under the circumstances."

Finding that he stopped, Miss Derby came back and stood leaning on the low mantel-shelf looking down at him. Her cousin, glancing up from the dog, found her apparently more attractive than before, for he watched her attentively.

"Do you think he will succeed?" she said.

"I've no doubt of it. The property has lain unclaimed since George Goddard's death, waiting for this nephew to present himself. It was supposed that he was in the West; but he will have no difficulty in proving himself to be the person."

"No. His father came from Iowa ten years ago. Is the property large?" after a pause.

"It will make him comfortable—not rich. I don't have the faith in those late peaches most people do. The whole farm's stocked with late peaches. The house is as good as any in Sussex County."

"Niel Goddard ought to be a rich man. His temperament requires ease and luxury for its development. I think, too—" she hesitated—"he would be a happier man if he were able to—to marry."

"Very likely," with a gravity for which there seemed no adequate cause. "He bade me bring you home with me, Jenny. There were some knotty points in the will which he thought your shrewd wit could help him with. My mother will expect you. The will is registered at Georgetown. I went up with him twice to look at it—Why, what is the matter?"

"Oh, I could not go, Kit. Your mother is a stranger, and—"

"You are not afraid to go junketing over the whole United States with a troop of strangers, and yet you blush and are frightened and tremble at the thought of meeting my mother. Why, Jenny?" taking her hand tenderly, for behind her smile and blush he could see the tears in her eyes. He certainly never had thought his cousin pretty before. It occurred to him for the first time now that he would like to take her in his arms and kiss her.

"Oh," she fluttered, how *could* I go, Christopher?" She went to the window on pretense of closing the curtains, and lingered shyly in the moonlight. Then she said sharply, without turning: "Only been to Georgetown twice, and now it's a month? What does Mr. Goddard find in Lewes to keep him there? Is he really studying the tides, as Mr. Harte said?"

"I think it probable. I heard Audrey expounding them learnedly the other day. She puts implicit faith in his wisdom, and deals it about to us second-hand."

"Audrey?"

Miss Derby stood quite quiet with her hands covering her eyes for a long time as she always did when she was planning the plot of a story. When she turned and came back it was with her ordinary cool, collected expression. "I am very glad that Mr. Goddard has such a chance of success about his farm; but I could not go down to advise him about the will, Christopher. Tell him so. I shall see you in the morning?" as, without pressing the matter further, he rose to go.

"Yes; I shall take the noon train."

"Why do you never bring Audrey, as you call her, to town? I should make her welcome, I'm sure."

"Audrey?" Looking about him with a smile. "I could not imagine Audrey here. Oh, no, that would never do."

"Too coarse a setting for your jewel?" with an answering smile. "She is a very beautiful woman then?"

Christopher hesitated. "I do not know. I think not. I really never considered before whether she was a pretty girl or not. But one cannot think of Audrey away from the sea."

"Oh! You men are fanciful about women. About womanly women, that is," with a bitter laugh. She had gone with him a step or two outside of the door, and after shaking hands, stood looking after him as he went down the stairway, nodding and smiling good-night as he looked back.

When he was gone, she crossed the halls hastily to her own chamber, locked the door, and stirred the clear anthracite fire. Her boots stood on the rug. They were short, broad and heavily soled; her gloves lay on the table. She took them up, looking at her thick and somewhat stumpy fingers. Stillwell, when they were out roughing it on the Prairies, used to say to her, "You are built for use and not for show, Jenny."

She had not minded it a bit in Stillwell, and had never liked him a whit the less. But in Niel Goddard's eyes, she *was* "a womanly woman." She thought of that now, holding the glove, and playing with it softly as she looked in the fire, as she might with a baby's hand. "I'm sharp, and a screw[8] to all the world, even to Kit who sees everybody in the pleasantest light," she thought. "But Niel—."

Even to herself she did not say what she well knew; that in his big, blue, dreamy eyes her muddy skin was fair, her thin lips soft, her jet black eyes liquid and passionate as any tenderest sweetheart's among women. Men who wished to stand well with Jenny were wont to talk to her of the strength of her articles; "quite as masculine as if they had been done by a man." Niel laughed at all she wrote. "You precious little dunce!" he said often. Just as though she were a stupid child both silly and dear. Jane, remembering it now as she undressed herself, saw in the glass her hard eyes grow dewy and tender. But she saw too that they were hard eyes; and that her lips were thin and her breast flat. "Even Nature," she said to herself, "forgot that I was a woman. Niel never does."

Even alone as she was, the hidden woman in her answered to his name; flat breast and thin lips grew hot: she turned quickly from the glass too happy and ashamed to meet her own eyes.

"Audrey? What is Audrey to me? When would she give up for him what I have given up?" she said.

Presently she took down a japanned box filled with papers, neatly tied with red tape. Seating herself with a business air she took from among them copies of George Goddard's will, and of one or two deeds relating to the Stone-post farm. For Miss Derby had privately been down to Sussex county a year ago on this business. It was she indeed who had unearthed the fact that Niel Goddard was the missing heir, and sent him down. She went over the papers now carefully line by line: then took out another, a legal opinion from a high authority—"for which he charged a pretty penny!" she muttered. But it was clear and decisive. The Stone-post farm belonged to the oldest living son of James Goddard. It had been left fifty years ago to Elizabeth Goddard and her heirs. But Elizabeth had married a Cortrell and gone to the West Indies on ill terms with her family and her whereabouts had never been discovered. The old man, George, who died last year, had made provision that the property should return to her heirs, should they present themselves. Failing that, James Goddard and his children came next in succession. Niel was James Goddard's only living child.

Miss Derby folded the papers carefully in the same creases. Her thoughts ran in this wise, done into plain English; "Niel Goddard might think her or all women tender-eyed and soft-lipped, but he would dawdle through life until he was gray, and never ask one of them to marry him, as long as he had no money. With money, he would be on fire to marry tomorrow. He was the heir to this property, provided none of Elizabeth Goddard's descendants were living. But Elizabeth Goddard's only daughter had married a Derby and Jane Derby's father was her son. He had been used in his vague whimsical way to talk of family estates to which it might be worth while to trace his claim. But with his usual slip-shod habit he had never traced it. His daughter had no whimsical slip-shod habit. Her claim was made out, ready in the japanned box. She never meant to present it. Niel himself never knew of it.

"It will be so sweet to take all from him—all!" She pushed the papers into the box as she thought this and stood up, her hands on the lid, her face lifted and glowing. For the moment it was a rare face worth study. It would content her to be a beggar and fed by his hand!

A few moments later, however, she arranged the papers of her claim more carefully, placed the case in her travelling bag and shut it with a snap.

I'll go down to Lewes with Kit tomorrow," she thought. "It can do no harm to see how matters stand," nodding significantly as she put the satchel away.

CHAPTER III

The morning, after Miss Derby and Kit had reached the cars, proved to be warm. The fire was suffered to die out in the stove, and the windows were opened that the few lazy travelers might feel the soft October air which always differs from the soft air of spring because it seems to carry with it the strength and vitality of the whole of summer. Whether because of this air or of some subtile influence in her errand, Jenny had an odd sense that everybody but herself was out for a holiday. The road hurried out from the walling streets of brick and marble into pretty glimpses of villas, with Greek fronts and Gothic stables and henneries; and beyond them out again into breezy slopes of stubble-fields, copper-colored, blackened in patches by the early frost; with a blaze here and there in the dark lines of fence of orange butterfly-weed or the maroon velvet of the sumach. There were stretches of miles of peach orchards, too, when they had entered Delaware, the late pale green fruit clinging to the leaf-less boughs, dry and luscious, waiting to be plucked. A farm-house now and then showed itself on a sunny hillside, wide and pleasant and open-doored; a dog asleep on the porch, or fat brown cows huddled down in the muddy, lush meadow by the creek, would look up leisurely as the train went by, and drop their heads drowsily again. The few passengers in the car were peach farmers who had been up to close their accounts with their agents. The leisurely year was before them until the few busy weeks of harvest came again; why should they be in a hurry? The whole world was quiet and bright and still.

"The very sunshine is yellow and does not move," said Jenny, shuffling her feet impatiently. "When we stop at a station every black and white lounger there is as glad to see you, Kit, as if you were the one friend of their souls, and they had no other business in life but to sit on the fence and watch for you."

"I know them all," quietly.

"Have they no work to do?" sharply. "Can all Delaware afford to go to sleep?" She had brought the items in her satchel out of which the next foreign letters were to be constructed; and even as she watched the people about her, she was dotting down notes for her woman's column of the next week. "I left word at the office to telegraph me in case a steamer comes in," she said, with a little importance, conscious of filling a place in the world unknown to Kit or Delaware.

As the still morning widened into stiller noon, however, she put away her note-book. She began to wish she too had gone out on a holiday. Her backbone felt heavy; shooting fibers of pain went through her legs, her arms, over the back of her head. It was only the neuralgia which she had every day; it never relaxed its grip of her; but she took time to think of it now, and of the doctor's warning stories of other newspaper people who had suddenly collapsed and dropped from overwork. When they reached Georgetown, she looked eagerly over the sleeping, sunny hills. One day, in a home among some of them, she too could rest. Kit, turning around as the train stopped, saw the rare bright and tender look again filling her eyes.

"Can you see Mr. Goddard's farm from here?" she asked.

"I don't know. I have never been there."

She was glad that he had not. Niel had not allowed any one to cross the threshold of his new home. He was waiting for her to come. It would be in keeping with his usual fancies. She felt as if she could taste the delight now of wandering over it step by step with him.

"Audrey," said her cousin, "thought it dead and unmeaning. But she would find that fault with any inland place."

"Miss Swenson has seen the farm then?"

"Yes. Mr. Goddard drove her over to look at it as soon as his title was secure."

"Secure!" she cried in a loud, uncadenced voice. "Unless the Cortrells who have a prior claim should appear, you mean. No doubt," she added presently. "Miss Swenson could give him valuable advice in the management of his property."

He laughed. "Audrey? She's not a capable woman like you, Jenny. She has no opinions. She never advised any body in her life. Not even herself," he added to himself. "Mr. Goddard," with a quizzical amusement in his heavy good-natured face, "professes to have unearthed some marvelous talent in her. But I fancy there's nothing in it."

The remainder of the afternoon was passed almost in silence. Jane, with her hand over her eyes, pretended to sleep. The sun was going down as they approached Lewes. When the clearing and thinning of the sky, and the salt gusts of wind over the low flats showed that they neared the sea, she grew nervous and irritable. She had quite forgotten the kinsfolk she was going to meet. The end of her journey was to her only Goddard and this Audrey.

At the next station above Lewes the train stopped for a moment; as it began its leisurely journey again Miss Derby heard a light footstep coming up the car behind her. She started and reddened like a schoolgirl. "Mr. Goddard—it's Niel coming!" just as a small hand tapped on Kit's hat.

"So Graff, you brought her? I knew you would. That lumbering, honest way of yours conquers the women. No, don't rise, I can stand. Ta ta ta!—well, if you insist—thanks." He sank in his light luxurious way into the seat opposite Jenny; so light and luxurious and dainty that for the glimmer of a moment the dirty plush seat appeared purple and royal. Graff, nodding good-naturedly, went out of the car, feeling snubbed, unreasonably enough, and heavy and earthy from his slow brain to his big feet.

"And now!"—said Goddard.

He leaned forward, putting the tips of his fingers on her satchel. His little body always seemed weighted too heavily with his soul, and now his small face was on fire with eagerness. The womanish, sensitive chin trembled. The red, curling hair waved impatiently back from his broad forehead to his neck. The large blue eyes were luminous, fixed on hers. From any other man words of irrepressible passion would have followed such a look.

"I thought you would come and see how I was," said Mr. Goddard. "I know those souls which are like a rock to be built upon. Some day," thoughtfully, "I mean to place and define the different uses of friends. Those who serve us as the dull earth, and make us sure of our footing; those who give us water once, and no more, and those who lift—lift us!" with a quick glance at the clear sky. "*Tu es Petrus*, eh, Jenny? You may have the subject—nice little essay for the *Atlantic*—humorous, under-vein of pathos—or boil it down into a social-topic editorial. But how do you think I am looking? That demon of sleeplessness is routed; you can tell that by my complexion and the white of my eye. It's all owing to this place; no medicine. Nature and Man are asleep here together. You walk through this unalterable, waiting calm day after day, until you fancy that somewhere in the clear, bright air the fountain of life and youth which De Leon sought surely will open before you."

"You look as though you had found it," said Jenny, gently. "And the sailor clothes—why one would think they had been invented for you, Nicl."

"Don't laugh at me," gaily picking at the blue flannel shirt and tarpaulin hat. "I sloughed off the cheviot clothes[9] because they smelled of cigars and wines and printer's ink. Audrey knows nothing of these things, and I don't wish that she should." He paused a moment uncertainly. "Jenny"—leaning forward again, "there was once a younger son who sat all his life in the ashes, and he set off one day to seek his fortune by the sea, and he found—"

"Audrey. I know." Miss Derby looked jaded with her long journey, but she smiled pleasantly. "You shall tell me all about her presently. As to the other part of the fortune—the farm turns out very well, Kit tells me. A snug income, not enough to give you a thorough-bred to ride or Château Lafitte to drink every day; but snug."

"It saves me," gravely, "from the necessity of selling whatever original power I have for mere food and clothes. That's enough!" in his usual light, half-ecstatic tone. "That means freedom! Love! Thorough-bred horses indeed? Why I shall 'walk on thrones. I shall out-Anthony Anthony!'"

"How much a year does it bring in, Niel?"

"How much? Always 'how much?' Oh, Jenny come, let us go look for De Leon's fountain; you need it. Here we are at Lewes." He rose gaily and preceded her to the platform. "You've a carry-all here, Graff? What a careful fellow you are! Just take Miss Derby's trunk and satchel up in it and I'll walk with her. Thanks. Now,—" drawing her arm in his with an air of thorough enjoyment when they were alone on the grassy road, in the melancholy twilight. Far off the lights of the village burned red in the gray cold; white dunes of sand which to her unpracticed eye appeared interminable, stretched drearily toward the sea, whose sullen roar was rising with the evening wind. Goddard's face, turned slowly from side to side, seemed to gather the meaning of it all.

"Do you feel the silence—the infinite rest?" he said. "Out on the prairies or the Western cañons there is a calm, but it is different. That is the sleep of Nature before it has been called on for its strength; an infant giant or god in his cradle. But this is a place which has tried all agitation and work, and found it vain. Lewes is an old settlement, full of wealth and stir in the colonial times. Old legends hang about it of a tropical trade with the West Indies, of spicy breezes in the streets where stately ladies in brocade paced to church with a guard of black slaves. Now in its old age it has shaken off such frivolities, and fallen into a perpetual calm Even the railroad, as you see, passes on one side and will not waken it."

They had reached the uneven street now, and were passing between the old solid stone houses, fenced by their double doors and windows against the winter storms; the quaint gardens smothered and hidden by old English ivy and hedges of box. Pale whiffs of smoke rose from the chimneys into the cold evening air; there was no other sign of life; the grass-grown streets, full of signs of long opulence, were abandoned to the damp fog coming up from the sea, and to a houseless dog that ran about without barking.

Miss Derby's eye glanced about contemptuously. "Is it possible for you to content yourself here, Niel? I see no signs of work; not even a blacksmith or shoemaker's shop. How can these people progress?"

"They don't progress, thank God!" cried Goddard. "There's not a news-paper in the town; their ideas of literature have halted back in the Elizabethan era. What is our work at any rate?" pushing his thin fingers through the mass of red hair until in Jane's eyes it resembled a halo. "To grub for money, in order to wear fine clothes—or buy better pictures than our neighbors. A man of culture here is content to use the furniture of his grandfather, and dress in the same fashion. He needs so little money that he has leisure to study himself and his place in the legion of souls. His poor neighbor 'progs'[10] instead of working, fishes, hunts crabs for one day in the week, and rests and tastes life in the other six. Do you see the cannon used to fence in the gutter? There are four others laid in the street to command the bay, all grown over with grass and lichen. A hundred or so years ago the town was bombarded and the pilots and fishermen sit in the sun now on these cannons, day by day, and watch for the besieging ships to come again. I tell you, Jenny," solemnly, "this calm, this tardiness of thought—this drowse has had a most wholesome effect on me. I mean to condense the whole idea into a picture or probably a story; but whichever it is, it will be my great work."

Miss Derby stopped and faced him in the dull twilight. When she spoke again it was with a forced smile.

"And this woman—Audrey—what is she to you?"

Goddard threw up his hands querulously: "Tut, tut! You bring the town with you, Jenny, with your sharp incisive questions. How can I tell what she is to me? Say that you go out and see the sea and the mountains for the first time, can you map and paint and label them out for your parlor at home? I cannot map out Audrey Swenson for you. To be with her is for any man to breathe a new and alien air."

"Don't be vexed with me, Niel," for his face wore the scowl which marked that his sensitive soul had been disturbed. Everybody knew Goddard's sensitive soul, and humored his insolence and ill-temper, knowing that they proceeded from the eccentricities of genius. He beamed forgiveness instantly on Jenny's submission. "Seriously, the girl," he said, loftily, "has had an inspiring effect on me. I find that my development requires me to come in contact with wealthy, original souls, from time to time, and so be lifted into fresh levels. Just as a child's body demands different food at different times, while it is growing. You shall see Audrey to-morrow. I planned that we should spend the evening with her and her uncle. Ah!

here is your cousin's house, and Graff waiting at the door. No; I'll not come in. Good night."

CHAPTER IV

The Swensons, of whom Audrey was the last representative, had been a Swedish colonial family of higher rank and wealth than any in Southern Delaware. Before going the next day to their house (where she thought, doubtless, the ancient stately grace still held sway), Jane gave many an anxious thought to her dress and demeanor. Her father had been originally a shoe-maker; and though that was a secret known only to a few, it gave Miss Derby a double share of the usual American uneasiness about wealth and dress and position. In the afternoon she went down to the sea to clear her brain for this state supper with the heiress. It was a walk of two or three miles, but she reached the beach before the sun was down. She had brought paper and pencil, meaning to jot down a few ideas on the situation of the Papacy. But the ideas did not come. The town lay asleep behind her; at her left hand the Delaware Bay lapsed without a sound into the ocean; countless white sails hidden during the high wind behind the breakwater, were flitting out noiselessly to their far off havens; at her other side sand-hill beyond hill stretched bleakly from the sea landward. Despite the chilly salt air, and the pink sky, there was a mysterious ghost-like silence and meaning about her which the moan of the sea did not disturb, and which would not fit into Jane's patchworked items for the *Review*. It annoyed her, as anything always did which lay outside of her own shrewd comprehension. She was relieved by seeing something human and tangible on the sea-beach—a boy catching blue mackerel with a squid. Jane sat down on one of the sand-hills to watch him; the small, black figure coming into bold relief between her and the sky, like a fine sepia drawing. This, at least, she could comprehend; and it was a pretty picturesque sight. The lad, who had a curiously free, lithe movement, paced slowly along the beach, as he rolled the line into a coil on one arm, then darted breast-high into the breaker. The glittering lead was thrown like a lasso far out into the still water; then he walked backward with head thrown back, and high, quick steps up the beach, drawing in the cord, hand over hand. At the end flapped a large shining fish. Jane, as pleased as though she had caught it herself, jumped up to go towards him when she perceived that her boy was a girl in a white flannel bathing suit. Just then Goddard, who had followed her, came up and stretched himself lazily on the sand.

"That fishwoman yonder has such a long, loping step that I took her for a boy, Niel. What magnificent build and freedom of action she has for a woman! Her feet scarcely make a dint in the sand."

"Sit still. She does not see us."

The girl came towards them, glancing at the sun to know the time. The truth was she had gone out to catch something to eat. No fish, no supper. As she neared them, Pike, one of the incorrigible proggers of the village, came creeping up, smelling of whiskey and tobacco, from a heap of kelp and clam shells. She held up the mackerel. "Is it a ten-pounder, Pike," anxiously. "I want it to be a ten-pounder."

"Dunno. Know you owe me de price of dat ar, Misses," hauling his hat over one eye.

She let the fish slip to the ground. "I don't know what you mean. Why, I caught it."

"Jess so. Ef you had'nt caught it, you'd hev bought one off of me. Why, God bless you, de Lord gib you de money an' me de fish. When you goes a fishin' you is robbin' ol'e Pike of his sheer of bread an' butter; dar's all about it."

The girl stood frightened and anxious staring at him.

"That seems fair," she said at last, putting her hand reluctantly to a pocket in her breast. "How much should I have paid you for it, Pike?"

He named a price and she paid him.

"But, my good girl, this is idiotic," cried Jane, getting up indignantly. "How can you let yourself be so swindled? I can't bear to see money wasted by anybody."

"You think he cheated me, then?" looking angrily after the slouching Pike. "You should n't laugh, Mr. Goddard. It is no laughing matter. I have been saving for months to buy a fall dress, and now I shall not have enough to do it. Well, no matter!" shaking off her irritation with a laughing shrug. "I forgot my slippers on the beach; I'll run for them."

Goddard did not offer to run for them, but watched her go with kindling eye. "That white woolen hangs about her like the drapery of an antique statue! Do you see how noble and grave and innocent she is from head to foot? Do you see how she finishes and gives the key-note to this landscape, to its strength and untainted freshness? Audrey—"

"That Audrey?" cried Jane. "Why, that girl is stupid! She is an imbecile. You can't mean it, Neil?"

Goddard combed his beard with his fingers reflectively. "Yes, that is Audrey. I believe she *is* what one would call lacking in intelligence on some points. 'Imbecile' would be going too far, perhaps. But what of that?

In old times they did not ask from the oracle, through whom the divine message came, any special shrewdness of her own."

"And how do you expect the divine message through this—this very remarkable fishwoman?"

"By her comprehension of music," coolly. "When Audrey Swenson has studied (and she has bent herself to dry, hard work like an artist), there will be no interpreter through harmony with such power as hers in the world."

"Ah, Niel! you have found so many lodes of gold that turned out to be nothing but poor quartz!" There was a pain and passion in Jane's sharp voice which made Mr. Goddard turn. His soul, as everybody knew, responded, like an Æolian harp, to every touch of emotion. His eyes, fixed on hers in silence for a moment, caught a subtle fire from them and burned tender and brilliant.

"I never said," he said in a low voice over which he had momentarily lost the control, "that divine messages came to the world through *you*. Your message is just a word or two of home and of womanly love. And I fancy sometimes it was sent only to me. Am I right, Jenny?" His face in his earnestness came close to hers. He took her short, thick hand in his delicate fingers; but dropped it again quickly. The fiery spirit in his veins rose to meet the heat in hers, and his womanish heart ached in pity for her jealous pain, but he really could not bear to see a young girl with a paw shaped like a man's.

A moment before, the gray dunes of sand had stretched dreary and blank before Jane to the drearier, blanker sea. Now they shone like hills of gold in the yellow light. The waves plashed in little glad pools at her feet. Waves and beach and the vast sunset sky bending over were waiting breathless with her, listening for the words which her lover would say.

He *was* her lover? He lay in the warm, light sand, his chin resting in his hand, reading her face with the beatified, rapt look of some old star-gazer finding the secret of his future in the skies. No one but a lover could discover such meanings in her round, freckled visage. Now Niel Goddard, undersized though he was, was to her an exceptionally masculine, manly man; clear-minded too: while he usually bore down difficulties and swept people before him with a series of gusts of magnetic energy, the wind one felt was never unclean or malarious. Outside of his genius Jane had a keen pride in him as her own. He was her own! For years he had been wont thus to gaze in her face: there was a subtle fine kinship between them which in a crowd made them one by a touch or glance: there was not a secret or plan of his life which he had not brought to her: he had half finished a play once of which their exquisite sympathy and happy love had been the *motif.* He had never in so many words asked her to marry him: simply, as Miss Derby reasoned, because he had not the money. Now, he had it. It was hers, it is true, but it would soon be hers again of his free gift. So she waited, trembling with expectation. Mr. Goddard watched the fever heat and redden her cheeks with pleasure. It was contagious enough to excite him agreeably, and what a benefit, he thought, her love for him had been to Jenny! How it rarefied and ennobled an else commonplace character! His love for her too; how it calmed his nerves, and brought him *en rapport* with sea and sky and even the salt invigorating wind! No matter what rain fell, Goddard's cup was always ready and up. He enjoyed a dinner set out with artistic china and æsthetic cooking with just as much *goût* as this scene of his long-lived drama with Jenny and his share of their mutual fine-spun passion.

But he did not ask her to marry him, then.

"How wet those clouds are against the sun! One can almost feel the damp winds shut up in them!" he said, looking about him lazily. "We have lost Audrey. But her cousin Kit is with her, down on the sands."

"Until lately," Miss Derby said with a sudden keen watchfulness of him, "I inferred that Miss Swenson was engaged to her cousin."

Goddard looked at them attentively a moment. "I don't know, I'm sure. A love affair loses its rare flavor of interest to me, as soon as the public is called in to see it and appraise it. There is no poem like the intangible accord of two spirits hymning their way through life together with a secret harmony of which no one knows but themselves and God. But when they make it a vulgar matter of engagements and wedding-rings, a community in clothes and marketing — pah! The flavor is gone for me, as I said."

Miss Derby rose. "I don't know any thing about hymning souls," bitterly. The tears came into the poor girl's eyes as she glanced down at the noble head lifted from the sand to look after the pair on the beach. How often she had thought of the keen delight of mending the clothes of this red-haired young Apollo, of marketing for him, saving the ten-cents and quarters for him, which he earned so slowly and flung about so recklessly! Her love was no intangible hymning. She was impatient to put it into matters which could be touched, tasted, handled. A pot or pan which had cooked anything for him, was as a sacred vessel in her eyes; she had an old hat-band which he had thrown aside long ago hanging next to her soft, hot bosom now.

"If Audrey should marry that unmannered lout, Graff," continued Goddard, reflectively, "there is an end of *her*. In a dozen years she will be a tailoress and a cook for him and his children. It is intolerable!" rising, his fine features red with excitement. "I tell you, Jane, not one human being in a million is born into the world with such largess with her for mankind, as that girl!"

"You had better marry her yourself, Niel, and preserve the largess for mankind," said Miss Derby, suddenly.

He did not take his eyes from Audrey's distant figure. "Marry her? Marry Audrey? I had not thought of that," he said quietly after a long pause. "No, I never thought of that before."

CHAPTER V

Christopher Graff had gone to find his cousin Audrey with a purpose. What the purpose was she discovered in the first half dozen words, and walked more slowly in order to fling pebbles at her ease into the surf and to listen: People made such a habit of advising and lecturing Audrey, her ignorance and blunders were so great, in matters which were commonplace to all other girls, that she turned as readily to hear the advice and lecturing as a plant lifts its leaf to the rain when it is dry.

"You know I have been out in the world more than you, Audrey. I can compare this man by other men. Besides, you have no perception of human nature. Never had; not the slightest."

"Very likely not, Christopher," laughing.

"Besides—what does he mean? In Delaware, or among civilized people anywhere, when a gentleman waits upon a lady as he has done on you he means love and a proposal and marriage. Now he—"

"But I don't wish to marry Mr. Goddard. It is no disappointment to me. I did not even think of it," gravely.

"That has nothing to do with his conduct. It is all of a piece! He's an artist you say. Where are his pictures? Jane calls him a great writer; but he has not colored paper with ink in Lewes. That's what he is!" stopping wrathfully by a pond of salt water, and pointing down to the bloated little angel fish at the bottom. "In front you see his wings outspread ready to fly. But it all ends in a miserable wriggle."

"It is not like you to be coarse, or ill-tempered, Christopher," she said looking up at him anxiously.

"Because I cannot see you tampered with, Audrey." He put his hand on her shoulder as they walked, as though she were a child and going to fall. She might be dull, but she saw that the big man, ordinarily so good-humored, looking down at her, was now greatly moved, and forced himself to be calm.

"Now he has taken it into his cracked brain to convince you that you are like himself, and possess some exceptional power. What folly is that! You play very nicely, no doubt, though the piano is but a poor tinkling thing to my notion. And as for your singing, candidly, Audrey, I've heard one or two women in the choir at Georgetown whose voices were stronger than yours. More volume in them, eh? I wish you could go up to Georgetown some Sunday, and you'd see for yourself. But Goddard would persuade you to give years of your life to studying those cursed Do Re Mis, and, then he'd bring you out on the stage of a theater. *You*, in a theater! What do you think of that?"

"I have never thought of the theater." She had stopped and was looking across the gray sand, not at Neil, her companion noted shrewdly, but far out to sea, as if behind that darkening horizon she had once found some secret of her life, and was searching for it again.

"To think of you—*you* in that tinsel, and bedaubed with paint, men reeking with liquor and tobacco flinging you bouquets! It was to-day Goddard broached the subject to me. He had much to say of the sympathetic quality of your voice, and its timbre, as if I cared for the damnable musical slang. Audrey," turning on her so as to put his burly body between her and the sea, "I must have the right to protect you from such meddling. A fellow like that," with a contemptuous nod towards Goddard, "such a wasp of a man as that only amuses me. If he struck me I believe I could laugh. But when he begins to finger and play with you as if you were his pet fiddle, and talk of your power and your future, it maddens me almost as if he had put his hand on your person. You know what I want, Audrey!" abruptly.

"Oh, yes. You wish me to marry you at once, Kit." She had clasped her hands behind her head, and stood looking past him. Goddard regarding her as a statue would have been thrilled anew by the noble, grave, innocence of the figure. But she was no statue to Graff.

"I wish you'd look at me, Audrey," irritably. "You have a bad habit of putting your hands over your head, and looking off in that way as if your concerns were elsewhere, and you had nothing to do with people. It's hardly civil, to my notion. Yes. Why shouldn't we be married now? We have talked of it since we were children. You surely cannot doubt my love for you?' his coarse, steady voice shaken more than she had ever known it before.

"No, I don't doubt you in any way,' energetically. "I trust nobody as I do you." She laid her large white hand on his exactly as a man might do.

"Not even this Goddard?"

"I don't know whether I trust him at all or not. There are times when I think of him just as you do, but at others—"

"Why should you think of him at all?" his hands on her shoulders. "Good God! Audrey, don't you belong to me? Hasn't all Sussex county talked for years of how you were to be my wife when you were grown? Have you forgotten that I built the addition to the house for you? Why, there's even the new heifer waiting for you to name."

"Yes, I know all that."

"And here at the eleventh hour comes this Goddard with his talk of pianos. I am expected to sit down in the chimney corner, while my wife sets off on a wild-goose chase through the world with her gift for humanity." He stopped hot and red, but she made no reply. "Now, perhaps," he resumed, coaxingly, "you are afraid of the work and responsibility at the head of a large farm? You shall not be a drudge, like these farmers' wives, Audrey. Mother will manage for you. And I'll have plenty of help in peach season, and you'll soon learn to can and dry peaches. It's really not difficult, either canning or drying. Mother says you have quite a nice talent for preserves now. Well?" after a breathless pause, "won't you answer me, Audrey? Just tell me exactly what you think of it."

But she did not answer him directly.

"I knew long ago," she said at last, "that if Audrey Swenson was not a musician, she was as poor material as ever a woman was made out of. As for canning or preserving or the heifers, they're nice enough. But I don't really often think about them. I'm afraid, Kit," with a quizzical laugh, the vexed tears ready to rise to her eyes, "I've no real genius for either housekeeping or love. But Mr. Goddard," going back to the first idea with a dogged, persistent nod, as she walked on, "told me nothing new about myself. I knew all that long ago—long ago."

CHAPTER VI

Meanwhile, the wet clouds against the sun had blown away; the tide was running out, and the light striking direct upon the flattened sea, two-thirds of the world seemed a vast plain of rippling, transparent yellow. The strip that was left was weird and dreary. The gray stretch of sand, Cape Henlopen[11] light-house rising out of it, glittering and white, at the back of all the smoke of the village hanging blue in the cold air. Graff, as they walked, looked down at his companion anxiously, and cleared his throat once or twice.

"I hope you're enjoying this view, Audrey?" At least she should not suppose Goddard's was the only soul alive to Nature's beauties. "Now there's a very pretty effect on the top of those rollers, d'ye see? I don't know that I ever saw a better yellow than that—a kind of a corn-color. On the whole, I believe I'd as lief look at the sea as at a landscape, though of course, one misses the houses and people. A human being must have something human, you know." He was very well satisfied with this little intellectual effort: he was used to look at the sea in the light of blue fish and sheepshead, but now that he chose to consider it æsthetically, he thought he had put the question as neatly as though, like Goddard, he had been in the habit of making pilgrimages to Concord to sit at the feet of the Yankee Gamaliel,[12] Emerson. Miss Swenson was pleased, too, apparently, for her eye ran over him from head to foot, and she smiled a queer, slow smile peculiar to herself, that had in it something inexpressibly tender and loyal.

"So I am to name the house and the heifer? Heifer first, then. Now— let me see—" They walked on deliberating together. Miss Derby, as they came near, noted this slow, fine smile of the other woman and her movements, as leisurely as those of a deer at ease in its own covert. Audrey, she was sure, had never felt one throb of love in her soul or passion in her body. While she—she and Goddard, at least, had grasped life *in medias res* half an hour ago. They approached, they had almost touched, the imminent moment of their lives: all these long years of repressed fire and longing would have culminated in a few words, as they sat on the sand, if it had not been for this girl, whose every thought was single and cool, and alien to theirs. As for Audrey, she hardly observed the awkward constraint of her companions. To talk of love, in no wise embarrassed her. She was very fond of Kit, of course. Everybody was fond of Kit; marriage with him simply meant to live a little nearer to his good nature, to have a share in his house, heifers, and peach-canning.

Her eyes suddenly kindled: "Why here are all the guests, and here is the supper! Why not cook it now?" This was something at least with zest in it.

"Capital!" cried Niel, who had had enough of emotional entertainment for the day, and felt chowder to be a relief.

"Gather the wood, then; and you, Kit, go to the house for bread, butter, and coffee. You know as well as I do what is wanted." Mr. Graff muttered irritably, for he had rather made a point to himself of this supper, and the effect which the Swenson china and old plate would have on Jane.

"It's not the thing at all which Miss Derby has a right to expect from you," following Audrey as she flew here and there, gathering dried sea-grass and bits of wreck. "A regular tea at least—"

"Oh, Kit, go!"

"If I do go, you must promise to call properly on her to-morrow. Wear that summer silk. It's not made as I saw them in town, but Jane's not particular as to fashion. But as for this absurd bathing rig—"

Jane, meanwhile, with the envy and jealous rage which belongs to women of her caliber, and which is so often kindled by a matter of hats and petticoats, watched the bathing rig: watched Niel Goddard's rapt scrutiny of it and every motion of its wearer, as he lay idle on the sand, the fire gone out in his cigar.

" 'Fleet-footed Atalanta [13] skims across the plain,' he murmured, his eyes passing critically over Audrey, from the wavy masses of reddish-brown hair to the delicate blue-veined feet.

"It would have been more to the purpose if Atalanta had sent for her stockings," Miss Derby replied.

He laughed. "Jenny," flinging away his cigar, "I mean to give serious thought to that idea of yours, about making Audrey my wife. It strikes me as if you had drawn up the curtain from a landscape with which I was long familiar. A woman of absolute, original power is really, after all, what I need. It would be a daily cordial to give me life. Of course, I never should have burthened myself with work for the support of a wife. What I am I have dedicated to art. But the farm would clear away the money difficulty—"

"O, yes. The farm—it all arranges itself very comfortably." She got up as she spoke and fell to gathering sea-weed; but Niel did not follow her stumpy figure with his eyes.

"Though in fact, Jenny," he reflected, "has a narrow intense power of affection, as valuable in its way as grace of body or attractive features. That old, ever recurring domestic type of woman! There it comes again, even in a scribbler for the press who lives by her wits! Well, well! I wonder if it is not the best for a man to have about him, after all?"

CHAPTER VII

The fish was not made into chowder; Audrey broiled it a golden brown over the hot coals; Goddard, who had the palate of an epicure, and the deft fingers of a cook, seasoned it. He was as pleased as a baby with a toy at the sight of the old damask cloth which Graff had brought and pinned down on the sand with half a dozen pieces of the famous Swenson china. But Jane, stunned as she was at the wreck of her life which she foresaw, could not help scolding at Audrey's folly in risking such priceless pottery. Her dread of Goddard's fickleness was not as overwhelming, however, as it would have been had she not known him so long.

"He has had such fancies and fevers a dozen times," she thought, as she stood, pale and jaded, watching him fluttering and beaming down on Audrey and the coffee-pot, radiant as a winged Mercury just lighted on the earth. "There was that pious Madame La Rouche, hippopotamus of a woman as she was; his taste for six months ran into devotion and fatness, and that silly Quaker girl with her beetles last summer; and the jolly burlesque actress afterward. It was always the good in them that he loved— some good—that *I* had not. His taste is so pure!" and the poor young woman groaned almost audibly. "It will be the same after we are married, I suppose. Though he always comes back to me as he would to a comfortable old coat that he liked." As she buttered the biscuit, which was her share of the work, she set herself again as she had done every day for so many years, to find out how she was to strain her nature to match it with his. It was, she felt, the bare stalk of corn with its one or two ears stretching itself to mate with the great blossoming tree which flung wide its branches to catch every breeze.

"If he had been like Kit Graff? If I could have just canned peaches or buttered biscuit for him and satisfied him with that and—" She did not say "love," only looked across the fire at the handsome little man until the water stood in her eyes with the hunger of them. It was for him, Jenny Derby with her dull intellect and sharp perception had worked half her life to be *Bohémienne* and *littérateuse*, and groped and stretched after the æsthetic tastes and fancies so real to him, but to her such airy, unconquerable nothings.

After all, the little feast was gay and hearty enough. Goddard and Audrey, like two children out on a frolic, cooked and told stories, and sang by turns: Graff after consoling himself with observing that Goddard actually wore No. 4 boots, and that no sensible woman could care for such a little gadfly, ate his supper comfortably. Besides, the sea air had made them all hungry, except Miss Derby, who tasted nothing but talked more than anyone, her cheeks colorless and eyes burning. When the supper was over she got up and walked about.

"You will make a picture of it, you say, Niel?" shivering and glancing about her. "I never want to see the picture, then, I'm sure. These gray sands and the eternal wash of water and the dull red blotch of fire with your three faces behind it—it is all unreal and ghastly to me. As if some final crisis for one of us was coming to-night, and these common things had taken on the life, and, somehow, had a prophetic meaning."

"I think I know what you mean," said Audrey, eagerly. "I have seen it when death came suddenly. The very walls and trees had a prophecy of evil. My grandmother," turning earnestly to Goddard, "had the second sight. Many a time when she was spinning, she said that she held in her hand instead of thread the bride's dress or shroud it was to be. Miss Derby is the same. She touched the shroud just now."

"Miss Derby," irritably, "has nerves, and you are a silly, superstitious child, I'm afraid. Do sit down, Jane, and talk common sense. You do not know how real such things are to people on the sea coast."

"We live nearer to Nature; so it is natural that she should take part with us and make some sign when we are about to die." Audrey tried to joke the matter away, but she was ill at ease, and watched Miss Derby anxiously.

"I had no intention of playing seeress or medium," said Jenny tartly. But she still went to and fro; she could not be quiet; every nerve was strung and rasped. Audrey, before night fell, had wrapped a waterproof cloak about her. It was her head rising out of this mass of black drapery, and lighted by the dull burning fire that Jane saw instead of any spirit; its rare sweetness and power made her draw her breath more quickly; what must it be then to Goddard? The poor girl did not need second sight to tell her the crisis of life was coming to her to-night; and the sands and sky and wash of water seemed to wait and listen with her.

Graff cleared his throat once or twice. "There are some queer beliefs hung around Henlopen Cape," he said, ponderously. "I don't make much account of them, though Audrey does. These old pilots and fishermen have so much time on their hands that they spend it in seeing ghosts. They'll tell you that the old Swensons and Rodneys keep guard over the Cape to this day. By the way," hesitating a little, "there was an odd thing happened to me a year or two ago. I set one of my men, a stout mulatto (Henry it was, Audrey) to ploughing a certain pasture land, one morning. Presently he came to me, his yellow skin actually spotted with his fright. A man on horseback, with flowing gray hair, and sword in hand, had suddenly stood before him and commanded him to stop. His dress, as the lad described it, was that of an officer in the Continental uniform. On going to the place I found the fellow had, without knowing it, ploughed up the grave where a hundred years ago Colonel Dagmar Graff had been laid—not to rest, as it seems, but to keep watch," forcing an uneasy laugh. "There's the fact. I don't pretend to explain it. Of course Henry had never heard of Colonel Graff."

There was an uncomfortable silence. Usually, Goddard would have relished a well authenticated ghost-story as he would a good cigar, but now he was busied with the effect on Audrey. In his opinion, if she had fault, it was that of indifference. Very few subjects interested her; but to-night she was roused and excited by these trifles. "Not," thought Goddard, shrewdly, "that she cares for these dead Graffs, but this lonely coast and sea have come to be the reallest thing in the world to her, and she fancies through these superstitions she will get at their secrets."

Graff had beckoned one of his men who was in waiting, to carry home the basket, and now began to throw sand on the fire. "Time for home and bed," he said, hiding a yawn. They strolled slowly all together down the beach. The sun had long gone down. Inland was an unbroken, sullen darkness, except where the five gigantic white hills of sand loomed in spectral procession. A low moon hung over the sea in the far horizon, hardly strong enough to throw their shadows upon the beach. The sea was to-night simply an unknown dark and cold; the waves flowed out of it to their feet and ebbed into it again unseen but for an instant flash of dappled light on the wet sand as each died away.

"The old settlers at the Cape will tell you these sands are alive," said Audrey, with a good deal of embarrassment. "These great mountains rise out of the sea year after year, and march steadily southward. No one knows whence they came, or why they move. It is a thing which I suppose nobody could explain," she added gravely.

"Any geography would give you the reason for it," retorted Jane sharply. "In the Landes of Gascony thse dunes are—"

"These are very different, of course, as Audrey says, from any European hills," interrupted Graff, gruffly. "Where do they come from?—there's the question. Do you see those green twigs at the top of that first hill? That is not grass, but the highest branches of a pine forest under which Audrey and I have played many a day. Fourteen feet and a half these hills move southward every year; not an inch more or less. Do you think there's no intelligence in that? But they have their object," dropping his tone, "and they are following it, as sure and certain as death; and no man can stop them."

Miss Derby was hurrying on with her scientific explanation, but Goddard checked her by an amused look. "What is their purpose?" he said gently.

"It may be only a foolish tale to you," Audrey said, "but it is a fact that these mysterious hills were not always here. The story is that shipwrecks were once so common on the coast that the people grew hardened, and would risk nothing to save the crews. One ship was suffered to go down within sight of land when a single boat could have rescued the men on board. A man named Cortrell was the only one who saw it, and he sat quiet, too selfish to venture to their help. One of the sailors, who was washed ashore, lived long enough, the story goes, to pray that the vengeance of God might pursue this man from out of the sea until there should be not one drop of his blood, or trace that he had lived, left on the earth; he swore too that he would not sleep in his grave until this vengeance was fulfilled."

"Well?"

"That is the legend; the facts are that these dunes did rise out of the sea that very year, and have gone down the coast until every hearth-stone of the Cortrells is buried out of sight. The old man's two sons went down at sea: he was lost in a quicksand, it is supposed; for he went out one day and never returned. Only his whip and a sunken spot in the sand showed where the sea had stretched its fingers inland to claim him."

"The rest of the story may be true, too," said Graff, "for all ship-wrecked sailors were buried hereabout in the sand, and here—you see the result." He stopped and pointed to the side of a white hillock, whence pro-truded a broken coffin and some glistening polished bones. "Hide them as you will, the wind uncovers them. The sailors are keeping watch still."

"What beastly inhumanity! The town of Lewes ought to look for the fate of the Cortrells," said Goddard, with a shudder. "Come away, Audrey."

"The whole tradition has taken a curious meaning here," said Audrey. "They say that the sea stretches out its hands to punish selfishness. Sand or wave creeps over every man's life who lives for himself alone. He is sure to die by the one or the other."

They had reached the Graff house now, and paused at the gate to bid good night to Jane. Kit went in with her, as bound by hospitality. "Mr. Goddard will leave you safely at home, Audrey," he said with an air of ownership. When he entered the house he found, much to his relief, that Jane had gone to her own room. She was watching from the windows the two dark figures passing down the road. They did not turn to the Swen-son house, but went back to the beach. After a moment, Jane, wrapping a cloak about her, followed them.

## CHAPTER VIII

"Certainly," said Audrey. "I will go down to the sands for a while. Unless," bluntly, "your being with me would annoy Miss Derby. I will not do that. Going or not going, is of no importance to me."

Of no importance? Niel Goddard looked at her. The grapes out of reach became desirable. At that moment he first felt a real love for her. It was real, though purely of the Goddard kind.

"There is no reason why it should matter anything to Jane," he said quietly.

"None?" Yea was yea to Audrey Swenson, and nay, nay. Her large blue eyes rested on him steadily for a minute as they walked on together. After that some impalpable veil which she had let fall between them was gone.

There is so little to tell of these two who were going down together, and of Jane following behind, that I am tempted to give up the story. But after all what is all life but the history of some man and some woman—lovers, or husband and wife, or mother and child, with a background of sea sand or farm-house or city street, trying to catch hands—to find in each other something which they lack in themselves or in God? Marriage seldom makes a break in the story. Sometimes the knife or pistol interferes to put a vulgar, bloody, cluttered end to the fine tragedy or comedy, and then it becomes public.

The mist was heavy, and not only hid Jane, but carried their voices toward her. No scruples had she about eaves-dropping; her notions of honor were never accurate nor neat. Fighting for her life as she was just now, all the world for her had gone down into those two shadows in the mist—the woman's a little taller than the man's, and held carefully apart; for Audrey had an odd habit of walking free, and alone. "If she once touches hands with him, that will be the sign it is all over," thought Jane, guessing at even the personal whims of the woman who had taken her place. She knew well—no guessing there—all that would go in that other and smaller shadow, into the marriage. Just now, when she loved him best, she held up his faults and *minauderies* [14] and jeered at them savagely. "If she knew him as I do, she would not care for him; she is not a fool!" she said. She knew by the merest drift of a word the current of their talk; for Niel, like all "brilliant conversationalists" was apt to repeat himself. "Now he is telling her about his mother; every woman cries when he tells about his mother; now he is on his struggles to keep art out of trade; he makes the common run of women think he could feed himself on fame and his aspirations without market-money. Aspirations, indeed! Though it does seem as if his soul kept his body alive," said Jane, faithful in her rage, with a choke and sob in her throat. "And now—now he is letting silence speak for him." One of his maxims was, that "with souls nearest akin to our own, intuition took the place of words." She knew all his maxims as she did her alphabet; they were a sort of alphabet to her, in fact.

Dropping the cloak-hood from her ears, Jane came closer to catch their words more distinctly. They had stopped below a headland on the beach. She was hidden in its shadow; between them lay a patch of wet sand. The moon was bright enough for her to see Goddard's face. She knew it in all its moods, but never had seen it kindled with such resolve and intentness as now. But could she have heard their words she would have found that this was assuredly on Audrey's part no love-making.

"What I want from you," deliberately as if she were buying sugar from a grocer, "is to tell me what my voice, touch, and knowledge of music are worth. These are only my tools, to be sure, but I must know whether they are good tools or not. I never met anybody before who could tell me."

"It would need five years, at least, of severe study to give you such power of expression as would content you."

She nodded gravely. "I thought it would be longer. Well, I can give that."

"You would not be a very young girl at the end of five years," essayed Goddard, after a cautious pause. "It is the very time of life which most women give to dreams and fancy, and to—love."

She was looking at him anxiously, with precisely the practical air that she might have worn had she doubted that the sugar was good. "I'm not sure;" thoughtfully, "but I don't think that I know what dreams and love are, as other women do."

Niel Goddard was no sensualist, but he drew his breath faster as his eye ran over the delicate yet strong hand and arm which the cloak left bare. The swelling throat, the erect head of the girl, held at a level with his own, were unique, in his knowledge of women, in their beauty and power. Nature, he remembered, made no mistakes. Cleopatra in soul or body was not better fitted for the subtile communion of spirit, the kindling of passion, than this cold, unawakened child. "I don't believe," she continued with a grave simplicity, "that God made me to be a wife or mother."

"You think," said Goddard, as grave as she, "that instead, he has given you a message to deliver?"

She turned sharply. "Who told you that I thought that? I never did. I never put that into words." She was greatly shaken, and finally, without recovering herself, walked hastily away from him. He followed her, speaking as though she had not answered him at all.

"You are not sure of your means of expression in music. But are you sure of what you want to say?"

"Yes. I know that. I do know that. If I were not sure of that—what would become of me?"

Goddard stopped to consider. He began to comprehend how this one idea possessed this lonely woman, almost to insanity. She had always been so simple in words and manner that he had begun to think her ignorant of her exceptional power, and shallow in feeling, to deficiency. Now, he feared to meddle, to suggest an idea to her, as though he had been about to thrust his rough hand into the chorded strings of a harp. If his words should be coarse, jar against this belief, offend her!

"In your message is it only the sky or sea you must interpret? Has no other woman a share in it? No man?"

She laughed. Her secret was shut down by this time quite out of sight— no glimpse of emotion in the steady blue eye. Outside of her secret, the world was still but a cheerful holiday ground to Audrey. "What could I have to say for humanity? Humanity for me means my uncle and Kit."

"And me?" carelessly.

"And you." Surely he detected a pale pink on her face that had not been there before. There was a sudden silence, too, which they found it difficult to break.

Miss Derby, unable to hear what they said, had had time to decide upon a plan of action. There was something in Goddard's manner different from anything she had ever seen there with the women who had been the objects of his fervent shortlived friendships. "All other women have petted Niel. This is the first one whom he could protect," she thought shrewdly. The danger, therefore, was real.

But Jane tapped her thin breast, under which a paper rustled. "He will never marry her while he is a poor man. And the Stonepost Farm is mine— mine."

Nothing was easier than to join them; to prevent Goddard, by her mere presence, from betraying his feeling, and when they were alone together to show him the paper,—"in a light, joking way," she resolved, "as if it would be impossible for me to interfere with his good fortune. It is precisely the absurd romantic kind of generosity which Niel would appreciate. He will believe afterward in this girl's 'largesse for mankind' just as entirely; he will pay homage to her hair and eyes and genius, for a week or two, but he will never make her his wife while I own the Stonepost Farm. Market-money *versus* Aspiration! I know which will win." With bitter tears in her eyes she buttoned her cloak, looking for a dry path, for the sand on which she stood was uncomfortably wet and clammy, but seeing none, struck boldly across the sunken space between herself and him. The next moment she looked down. Was it mud on which she walked? It gave way quickly to her tread, but closed and clung about her shoes. Her feet sank deeper with each step; the weight of the wet sand, if sand it were, grew heavy on them as though it were glue. Before she was one-third of the way across her ankles were not strong enough to drag them out.

"Niel! Niel!" she cried.

"Miss Derby has followed us," Audrey exclaimed, and hurried to meet her. Goddard came slowly after her with an impatient shrug, muttering something about being spied upon perpetually. Audrey stopped.

"She does not move," turning to him startled, "and this is near—"

"I cannot move," cried Jane. "It feels as if some one were dragging my feet down."

"So like a woman!" muttered Goddard. "She has run open-eyed into a swamp, and cries to be taken out of it." But Audrey caught him by the shoulder breathlessly.

"Stop! Let me see where we are," turning her pale face from side to side. "The lighthouse to the left. Symme's pond at our back. Merciful God! she is in the quicksand!"

Goddard shook her off. "Let me go. Keep still, Jenny. Don't struggle, I'm coming. Let go my arm, I say!" But Audrey held him in a grip like iron.

"No, I'll not let you go. You don't understand. Three men have been lost in that quicksand, with the whole village looking on. There's no help possible. You would only sink with her."

"Yes, I am heavier than she, that's true," wiping the cold sweat from his face. "But, good God! I can't stand here and see Jenny Derby die! You don't know what she has been to me, woman! Let me go. I can die with her." He shook her off, and shivering and quaking stretched out his hands to Jane, who stood quite motionless, hearing every word that was spoken, but uttering neither word nor cry. "It was natural that the other woman should hold him back. But he loves me! *Me.*" The thought flashed through her like a fiery heat of triumph. For herself she suffered no physical pain. It was incredible that she could be in imminent danger. Her feet and ankles were buried in the sand, which had now closed firmly about them. She was not conscious of the slow, steady sinking.

Audrey had loosed her hold. "But you will not go," she said, as an older person speaks to a younger. "I do not mean that she shall die. There must be a way. We shall find one. I am going for Kit and the people. Stand here, Mr. Goddard. Just here. You can give her great comfort and strength by speaking to her. But if you go to her you only cause her to sink faster. Remember that." She disappeared swift as a shadow.

Goddard held out his arms across the dull gray space. "I could not bear the agony of seeing her die!" glancing up to heaven in a confidential way, and wiping the cold sweat from his face. Then he called to her: "If I cannot devise a way to save you, I will come, and we will die together, Jenny."

"Yes, Niel," she said quietly. Her head fell upon her breast. In her ordinary moods Jane would have struggled against dying, tried medicines and doctors with all the alertness and shrewdness of her small body and small mind, but death had taken her by the throat when she was in a manner lifted above her usual self by passion and jealousy. She was calm to heroism. It seemed to her a simple and natural thing that this man whom she loved should come to die with her.

As for Goddard, he stood still. Ten steps would bring him at any minute beside her, on to the swaying shadow which the moon made of her figure on the fatal glistening flat of sand. Death seemed to him at that moment a drink divine. Surrounded by the somber majesty of the night, in the vast silence of sea and shore, going like a young god to the side of this faithful creature who loved him with dog-like affection—it was to pass the dark portals as a hero or a king! Indeed, the first line of a poem descriptive of the sacrifice he meant to make rushed into his heated brain.

Meanwhile, with his hands outstretched the wind blowing back his hair from his white, set face, instinct with all its noble meanings, he was a very fair type of a hero.

CHAPTER IX

Goddard, after awhile, recovering from his rapt contemplation of death, was conscious of a crowd of people ringed about the quicksand. There was but little noise: the most of them being horrified into silence. Kit Graff's big, burly figure was nearest to him. "Tut! tut!" was all that Kit could find to say, now that the crisis which poor Jenny had foreseen was upon her. Goddard turned from him disgusted.

"You might as well have brought one of his own oxen," he thundered to Audrey. The little man's fiery indignation was always ready to blaze forth recklessly at any hint of cowardice or lack of feeling.

The moon was up now; sea and quicksand, the whispering groups of women and arguing men, stood out clear against its ghastly pallor to Goddard's eye as a black picture on a white ground—one of Fuseli's terrible outlines. In the midst, with the treacherous pitfall around her, underneath which lay death and the grave, Jane crouched on the ground a black tumbled heap. Her heroism had evaporated; she struggled and cried and shrieked and threw herself to and fro as any other poor unreasoning animal would do, sucked into the jaws of death inch by inch. How far her body had really sunken it was impossible to tell owing to her crouching position.

But now that she had wakened to the fear of death for herself, she was suddenly conscious that it might come to Goddard. She stopped short in her cries for help (which had been so shrill and piteous as to drive the blood to the heart of every man there) the moment she heard his loud protestation of his resolve to die with her, and listened intently. Then she stood up and called out to them with a certain tone of authority.

"You men, I'll not cry for you to help me again. I don't want to vex any of my friends. But I'll pay any man well that will come to save me. And I'll pay you double if you will keep Mr. Goddard back. For God's sake keep him back."

The moonlight showed her her Apollo, poised vehement, as though ready to spring to her from the heights of heaven. She could see the upturned flash of his blue eyes, the moonlight was so bright; see even the intaglio which dangled from his watch-chain over his blue sailor shirt; and she remembered, poor Jane, how she had gone without meat and butter for a year, to buy and send it to him anonymously. "He thought old Shively sent it; and that pleased him better," she thought, looking at him with a queer, tender smile, even while the dead weight on her legs tugged cold and heavy, as though her feet were in truth already in the grave. So that he were pleased, what did it matter who had had the credit?

The hum of voices began to grow dull to her ears; the black encircling line of figures swam and swayed like a mist; only Goddard stood out distinct. If she died he would suffer so! It seemed to her but little matter whether she lived or died if he could be kept safe in his youth and brilliance and power. And yet an hour ago she had intended, in her mean, selfish spite, to rob him of his inheritance, to keep him from marrying the woman she thought he loved. She stretched out her hands to him. If she could but creep into some corner of the world, and watch him from there, happy with any woman, even with Audrey! What! was poor Jane Derby to be the wife of such a man!

It was but a little while that she was thus driven in on herself by the hold of death, but it first taught her what love was, as it does many a woman and man. After that the very cold and pain and physical nervous shock conquered her, and she fell into a sort of stupor.

The villagers, during those few minutes, had great difficulty in keeping Goddard back. He was quite sincere in his efforts to dash across the sand and perish with her. However, they held him, while they laid plans for her rescue, and discussed the situation with that deliberative zeal about to-morrow's work peculiar to people in Delaware and Jersey.

"I do allow," said Pike, "that she could have been got out of any other sands or swamp than this by means of ropes and drags such as Mr. Graff there is preparing. But not out of this. No sir. It's noted dangerous, this quicksand is."

Audrey, who was the only woman who was not weeping, and who did not join the men in their talk, came up now to Graff. "I thought or heard of a way, long ago, that seems worth trying. If she had thin, stout planks, such as the staves of a hogshead, and could drive them into the sand about her, in a circle—sloping in, you understand, until they met below her feet—the sand in which she stood would then be motionless and we could easily drag her out of it."

There was the usual civil, doubting pause with which men receive a practical suggestion from women. Then Pike nodded. "Seems to be somethin' in that, Mr. Graff, provided we had the staves. But staves don't lie loose around hyar on the beach. Nor axes to drive 'em. Before we'd bring 'em, that poor young creature 'll be drawed out of sight."

"The difficulty would be," said Graff, "that she is not strong enough to drive the staves sufficiently deep. But—we'll go for them, boys," nodding to a group of young men. After they were gone the others went on talking.

"Who is this young woman? Derby? Don't know the name. Don't belong to Sussex county." Audrey paid no heed to those whisperings going about, until one question made her prick up her ears.

"Is she got any Cortrell blood? I'd like to know that. If she has there's no chance for her. The sea'll never give up its old grudge agin the Cortrells."

"It is not possible that she should have any Cortrell blood in her veins?" going up anxiously to Goddard as he stood gloomily apart, his eyes closed to keep out the death scene in which he could not share. "Her foreboding to-night was strange. Women with the second-sight always have those clear gray eyes. What do you think, eh?"

Audrey's shudder, her evident belief in the superstition itself threw Goddard quite out of his agony, just as a switch puts a train off one track on to another. He stared at her as Hamlet at the murdered Dane. "Her grandfather or aunt or somebody *was* a Cortrell! I remember now hearing her once talk of them."

"Now," said Graff to the men, who, like himself carried a lot of these planks on their backs, "Lay them here. Stand out of the way, if you please, Mr. Goddard. You're the strongest, Joe. When I call out to you, 'steady!' you're to throw the planks to me, one at a time."

"Where are you going?" Audrey stepped in front of him. Her face more than her hand barred his way.

"Stand aside, child. There's no time to lose. She's not able to drive the staves, but I am, I fancy. I can reach her safe enough, and when I reach her we're safe enough, too." Goddard wondered why the man, if he did propose to play the hero, could not shape his sentences more grammatically and dramatically.

"This is *my* errand," stepping forward and thrusting Graff aside, "I am ready, God knows, to risk or give my life for her."

"Very likely," said Graff, cooly, "you can find another axe and follow if you like. You can't have this one. I don't reckon you're much of a pile-driver, though," looking down contemptuously on the thin little man dilated with heroic resolve. "You understand, boys? Heft me the planks as I call for them. Bye-bye, child," looking down at Audrey for an instant, and then turning quickly away.

"You must not go, Kit," and down went her voice to a whisper, — "*She is a Cortrell.*"

Graff unquestionably lost color. "The devil!" stopping short, axe in hand. "So she is. I remember now. Well," drawing breath, "no matter." He turned to the quicksand again. But as he passed Audrey he laid his hand on her shoulder, and looking at her steadily, said, "Good-bye, child," once more.

CHAPTER X

Audrey's plan for getting out of a quicksand, like the invention of a sewing machine, or the best passages of Shakespeare, was so simple and admirable a matter, when done, so undeniably the only way in which the thing could properly be done, that nobody found much in it to applaud.

"It was lucky," Pike said, his hands in the waistband of his trousers, "that Miss Swenson hit on it 'arly in the evenin'. But of course it was the right way. Some on us would have hit on it afore long."

Mr. Goddard bestowed a word of praise on her. "Very nice in you to remember that idea," coming up to where she stood like a ghost watching Graff's steady driving of the piles. Goddard was quite secure of Jane's rescue, and was his own buoyant self again, sauntering from group to group, enjoying their queer idioms and traits. One could have sworn that his fanciful blue suit of clothes was newer than the one he wore half an hour ago, and surely his reddish mustache was freshly waxed. "Very *apropos*, your remembrance, I'm sure, and fortunate for poor Jane. But really you must not fill your brain with facts. It would be like choking up a vase of old Dresden[15] with matches, burned and unburned, as I have seen done."

"'Old Dresden?' Oh yes, certainly, certainly," said Audrey, staring at the two dark figures in the quicksand. Goddard, finding she was deaf to all sounds but the axe, wandered off up the beach and stood alone with an awe-struck face surveying the awful plane of water and the sky above, muttering to himself, "The heavens declare the glory of God. Day unto day uttereth speech, and night unto night showeth knowledge."[16] The words so expressed his own emotion that the tears rose to his eyes, and he quite forgot the dying Jane, who loved him, and the living Audrey, whom he loved.

Graff had time to think of both. Driving the piles was slow work, and the remembrance of the Cortrell blood of his companion dragged him down harder than the invisible jaws of the sand below. Jenny kept him from any serious thoughts of death by an incessant nagging of questions and orders how to work. If it had not been for that, he would have liked to pray silently in this extreme and sore strait, for Kit was a steady churchgoing Methodist. Jane had not looked at the question of death at all from a religious point of view; the top of her head was remarkably flat. She observed Goddard going off to Audrey as soon as Graff reached her; she felt with an humble, dull misery, that it would have helped to keep her soul alive, and eased the deathly cold in her back if he had stayed on the bank, but what did it matter for her? It was all miserable. Even if she were saved she could not use the experience in her newspaper letters. There was something so ridiculous in being swallowed in a quicksand. "But Goddard would have died for me if they had not kept him back," she said at last, looking after him.

"No doubt, no doubt. Goddard's a very clever fellow. Another stave, Joe," hallooed Kit.

"I wish he would go home out of this night-air. His bronchial tubes are affected; he forgets he's not used to out-door work like these rough men here. *I* can't see the use of driving those planks in slanting," turning to him snappishly. "It's a mistake. Drive them straight. You're so slow, too. Do you think there's any chance for me?"

"We'll hope so at any rate. Try and keep up, Jenny," cheerfully. But for himself he had very little hope. He knew he could drive a pile with any man, but not when the Cortrell blood and the sea were both against him.

Hammer, hammer away. The moon had set, but the men had kindled fires on the bank, and the fierce red glow flushed out now and then through the gray mist. They had not spoken for a long time.

"That pounding," said Jane at last with a feeble cackle of a laugh, "sounds as if you were making our coffins."

"Umph!" muttered Graff. "It would be more to the purpose if you'd sing a hymn, Jane, or say a prayer."

"I don't sing hymns. But if I die, when he marries Audrey, Kit, I want you to tell him that I said I hoped God would bless him."

Graff stopped. "Don't talk like a fool. Do you think Audrey would marry that—that cock-sparrow?"

She did not answer him, and looking around he saw that she had fallen and lay at his feet. "Jane! Jenny!" He was not sure whether she had fainted or was dead. "And I spoke like a brute to her!" he said. But death and the chance that Audrey would marry Goddard were too near at hand for him to choose his words or stop his pounding.

CHAPTER XI

Jane was quite cold and white when Graff at last dragged her out and carried her to the side of one of the sand-hills. The crowd gathered about her. Audrey began to breathe in her mouth.

"Lay her down, Christopher. Just here," said his mother who had arrived with a black woman and a wheelbarrow of necessaries. She was a little light woman in black alpaca, with a curl of gray hair dangling at each cheek from a side-comb; one of those executive and legislative females who, if she had been in Eve's place, would have had flannels, and a patent medicine, and a code of morals in half an hour wherewith to defy death and put Satan to the right-about.

"Lay her on this settle.[17] Now take it up, you men. Tut, tut! She's sopping wet to the hips. She'll have a pretty cold!"

"It's not likely to end in a cold," said Audrey, "the sea has had a hold on her, and she has the Cortrell blood."

"I don't know that the Cortrells ever had more rheumatism than other folks," dryly. "Don't be absurd, child. Kit, do you go home at once and take a hot bath and get to bed."

"You are coming, Audrey?" anxiously. "Then I will, mother. I'll drink some boneset tea,[18] too." For Kit, like many other brawny heroes, would follow duty to the cannon's mouth, but liked to be coddled and plastered and dosed for every twinge of a sick stomach.

A miscellaneous group formed their escort. "That ar Goddard's a tremendous fellow, Mrs. Graff," said Pike. "We could hardly hold him from rushin' to the young woman, to die with her. It 'ud have brought the tears to yer eyes to hear him cryin', 'Let me sheer her fate! let me sheer her fate!'"

Mrs. Graff's restless black eyes were on Audrey in an instant. "No doubt, you thought that very fine, child, eh?"

"What more can a man do than to die for his friend? said Audrey gravely.

"Don't know," returned Kit's mother, "when a woman's in a scrape it's the business of a man to take her out of it, just as it is to hold an umbrella over her, or to earn her bread and butter and clothes. So I've taught my boy, at any rate, and I'm glad to see he remembered his training to-night. Do you think he would have dared come home to me if he had left Jenny in the lurch?"

But Audrey, apparently, attached no more credit to Kit's night work than to any ordinary stave-driving. She turned her head carefully from him and stooped over Jane. "Her eyes are open, Aunt Ann," she said.

"Of course her eyes are open. Three quinine pills will bring her right. Take Kit's arm, child. He looks shaky." But Audrey drew off and walked in her usual lonely, free fashion, her hands clasped behind her. Aunt Ann had superintended motherless little Audrey through measles and whooping-cough, and so up to the age of love, and was now engineering her into a marriage with Kit. "A shiftless, good-natured creature who would waste a year's income in a month. But dear me! the boy would not care for his life without her," she said. She was fond of the girl besides, and she really had a broad motherly bosom, if her chin was sharp. But the two women were ill at ease together, always. Audrey usually stood off as she did now, and eyed her in her sober absorbing fashion, feeling herself big and young and useless beside the energetic little woman. A block of unhewn stone, if stone could feel, might have just such a sense of uncouthness and out-of-place-ness beside a sharp little steel chisel tip-tapping and boring into it.

Audrey was conscious suddenly that Goddard was beside her, and dropped behind to walk with him, with a brilliant smile of welcome, at sight of which Jane, Kit, and his mother all pricked up their ears.

"She is better," said Audrey, nodding to the settle.

"Oh, yes," indifferently. "My head," pressing both hands over it, "has been oppressed too much. I want relief. Let me hear you talk."

She nodded, but walked on so silently that he doubted if she had understood him. The night, after the moon had gone down, was dark. They had left the fires behind them, but a sudden flash of auroral light showed their faces to each other and the dark, scattered figures trooping silently along the beach, the dunes rising in a procession of gigantic white shadows against the vague darkness.

"We look like the damned upon the shores of that last sea," said Goddard, determined to make small talk out of the vastness and terror, as he could not shift the scene. "The sky is dead and the sea is dead, and those are but the ghosts of hills, too." Another glimmer of light showed him that Audrey was not looking at sea or sky; her head was bent on her breast, her face thoughtful. He started forward.

"I read it in your eyes! You have learned a new lesson to-night. You can never say again that nature suffices to you! Some heroic thought, some human being has touched you closer than ever you were touched before! Audrey?" He took her hand, and when the light died out she had not yet withdrawn it. Kit, turning from them in sullen, dumb rage, saw by the same flash Jane's eyes fixed on the clasped hands, and heard a faint sigh.

"What a gesticulating talent your friend Goddard has, my dear," observed Mrs. Graff, calmly. "He ought to turn it to account on the stage. Too much hand wringing there for every day use."

"The man is well enough, mother," said Kit, sharply; he would like to have knocked him down with the axe he held, but he could not tolerate woman's pin-sticking revenges. "He is going to make a great name as an artist, I have heard."

"I should suppose his virtues lay in the future," retorted his mother coldly.

CHAPTER XII

"I hope, Audrey," said Mrs. Graff, as they halted at the gate of the Swenson House, "that you'll go to bed at once. I would advise a Dover's powder [19] also, and hot water bottles for your feet."

"Yes, Aunt Ann."

"Dover's powder?" grunted Audrey's uncle, as she pushed open the door of the sitting-room. "What is that female quack doing abroad at this time of night? It is Ann Graff, isn't it?"

"She is taking home a sick woman."

"The Lord have mercy on the sick woman then." Audrey made no reply. She let her Aunt Ann and the night's events drop at once, having no fondness for waving red rags in anybody's face. In fact, it was what Audrey did *not* say that gave people the odd sense of security and faith in both her depth and height.

Doctor Swenson trotted over to a book-case, wrapping his faded dressing-gown about him with a shrill little chuckle. "Your Aunt Ann is not content with drenching people with magnesia, and pills, and potassium, she dabbles in spiritual pharmacy. She comes to me with a story of one who has fallen from grace into a state of despair, when I know all that ails the man is too much salt pork; and of another who sees visions like St. Teresa, and all that she or St. Teresa needed was a husband and a baby. Did you see my slippers anywhere? I began to look for them to go up to bed, and took up my violin, and now it is quite late. No, Audrey, you need not dispute the point; there is not a trait nor a passion in a man's character, as you sentimentalists call them, that cannot be resolved into an overplus of carbon, or ozone, or a lack of phosphorus. Did I ever explain this theory to you before?" anxiously. "Of course I have, though. I'm a bore to everybody with it, I suppose. Now, Audrey, you are fond of what they call Nature. You look at the clouds or the river, and have what you deem immortal longings. It is nothing but the matter in the trees, or rain, or growing corn attracting similar matter in your body. Lime calls to lime, and oxygen to oxygen. When you or Kit die you will be so much salts, so much phosphates, so much gaseous matter; that's all, nothing more." The little man stood see-sawing in his gray stocking feet, a candle in one hand, the other grasping his flowered gown, his round cheeks and blue eyes on fire with delight under the wig pulled askew.

Audrey laughed. "You are an amiable ghoul! Go to bed, uncle."

"I cannot sleep. Neither can you, I'll wager. Now you think it's love or remorse keeps you awake? It's electricity. Why, the sea and sky are alive to-night with it. If I were a sentimentalist like you I should say they were angry—had been disappointed of their prey."

"So they were. One of the Cortrells—" She stopped, and laughed. What could the great forces of Nature have to do with poor scribbling Jane, with her shrewd brain and lumpy body?

"Cortrell, eh?" eagerly snuffing the candle with his fingers. "Now, do you know there's a great deal of reason in those old superstitions? Sea and sand are made of the same matter as ourselves, so how can we tell how much of the same knowledge they have? You're not sick, my dear? Your nose is pinched, and there are dark rings about your eyes. Liver all right, Audrey?" He took her hand in his, and Audrey was glad to let it lie there, though the pudgy fingers were stained with snuff and candle-wick. She had a curious longing to-night, for the mother she had never known, and could almost have laid her head against the flowered gown, and cried.

Instead, she only laughed when he stroked her hand fondly.

"Some lime and phosphate is worth a good deal more to you than others. Eh, Uncle Tom?"

"I've made such a poor substitute for your mother, child. That's the trouble. Susan would have known how to manage about your lessons, and falling in love, and diet, and all that. I could only make you sound in your music. As to your knowledge of counterpoint, I'm satisfied there, quite satisfied. Suppose we try—?" taking down his violin, and opening the old, fine piano that seemed oddly out of place on the bare floor with its strip of rag-carpet.

"Not to-night. You must really go to sleep." She lighted the candle again, found the slippers, and kissed him good-night. She did not know what ailed her to-night; even his petting she could not bear. Of the usual nervous, sickly megrims of girls, Audrey, with her light strong frame, and fair firm flesh, rose-tinted and healthy as a baby's, knew nothing; but now a kind touch made her shiver, and, as he opened his door to nod good-night again, her blue eyes filled with tears. Was it only the electricity, as her uncle said? She took up the violin to play the sonata with which she often quieted the old man to sleep, but the notes seemed to have caught the fierce foreboding temper of the night, and shrieked fitfully. The girl listened as though a living being was talking to her, laid down the violin, and, paler than was her wont to be, went out to the garden, which, darkened with the quaint box of the old colony town, sloped down to the sands.

If these were the dead sea, and sky of Hades, as Goddard said, they had taken life in the last hour, and, as it seemed to Audrey, the life of a vengeful, malignant purpose. The long stretch of beach and dunes had drawn back into a gray melancholy twilight, and the sea thrust itself into sight, solid and black, yellow flashes of phosphoric light upon the incoming waves, like the fiery crest of Milton's Satan as he rose from the undermost darkness. It muttered with an ominous thunder. Audrey had learned its voices since she was a child, but this was unknown to her. To the north and west, hedging in and driving on the sea, pale columns of auroral light followed each other through the darkness. She went through the gate aimlessly, over the sand, her grave, steady face turned towards them as though some one called her. The village was lost in the fog and silence, the light was out in her uncle's window; she remembered, hardly knowing that she remembered it, that he and Kit, and even her aunt, Ann Graff, were asleep. She was glad that all the world was asleep, and she alone was left to receive the message. Audrey had been abroad in all seasons; in nights when the storms had driven sea-faring men in-doors; when she was a child, frightened at the wind or crash of the waves on the shore, she yet had gone, dragged, as it were, against her will. Now, it seemed to her, she had grown to the age of sea and woods: they had received her into their company: she was one with them. She knew in sun or storm, summer or winter, she must go when they called her, to know what was this word they would have her speak for them. She never had found it. It came near her, often, in sight as in sound, in a nor'-easter whistling through the rigging, in the fretted brown seeds upon a fern leaf, in the glint of sun through the tan-colored bay water upon the kelp below. It was so real a thing to her, they were such actual companions, that she talked of them to no one, just as a man does not talk of the wife whose head lies on his bosom to mere passers-by. Aunt Ann, had she ever sounded the girl's brain, would have called her an idiot, and Kit would not have taken an undeniably mad woman to be his wife. But Audrey kept silent, and looked on their blindness with an amused wonder. "Can they not hear the sea? Does not the sun shine on them as on me? Are these things not as real to them as a Dover's powder, or a box of canned peaches?"

The voice she could almost hear, the uncomprehended message was never as near her to-night. It was as though all the world sang a lofty hymn, in which there was one word lacking left for her to supply. It seemed to her that all nature came close and pressed upon her to give her knowledge of it. She stooped and buried her hands in the warm sand, she touched the thick bay-leaves as she passed; the wet sou'-wester flapped dashes of spray in her face. The cries of the sea grew shriller, as it sent in a heavier tide from its far off caverns; the northern lights, to the north, crossed the unbroken night unceasingly like a troop of pale and vengeful ghosts.

She wandered down the beach; she would have penetrated into the heart of this eternal world if she could; its mysteries, its vastness, its infinite, inaccessible repose, even in this transient outcry, reached through her flesh to something within which awoke and answered again. Her blood grew heavy in her veins, vain tears rushed to her eyes. The longing, the hope, which belong to those who are akin with Nature, for which no man has ever found words, oppressed and choked her, "And I," she said, looking up and around her, as one who seeks a familiar face, "I, too!"

She would find words for this unknown hope; her message had been close to her to-night. Some day she would reach it.

A curious change came upon Audrey from that moment. The forces that had appealed to her might be incomprehensible to others, but their effect upon her was plain and practical enough. She had heard a heavenly call and she would not slight it. Messages of high meaning were given to a few men to deliver to the world, as of old to the prophets; they wrote or painted, or cut them out of stone. Audrey knew that she had no utterance but in song. "It may be but a poor work that is given to me to do; but it is mine," she said humbly.

She sat down on one of the sand-hills overlooking the sea. Strains of simple, powerful harmony were heard, unknown before by her; whether she sang them or not she did not know. If she could make audible to the world the meaning of this night to her? How angry storm and prophetic sea, the malignant wind, and the gracious, comforting earth to its smallest green leaf, summoned alike the unwilling soul to the work which God had given it, and forbade it to accept any other. If she could find fit utterance for even so much as this, her life were cheaply given.

Morning had broken before she entered the garden again. The box hedges drenched with rain were hung with spiders' webs, and in the early light her cow was fretting in the stable to be sent down to the salt-marsh pastures; they belted the beach with rich browns and purples, covered yet by mist; a biting wind drove the pink clouds from the brightening west to the dark sky overhead; a covey of white sail fled further behind the wall of the breakwater; a flock of kingbirds preparing to go southward whirred from a clump of cedars past her feet. Audrey and they were old friends; their black beads of eyes, full of a courage greater than that of any living creature were fixed on her with a friendly meaning. Wherever she turned, from the vast, red plane of the sea, with the sandpiper hopping along the white-wash of the tide, to the wet poppies and gillyflowers of the beds beside her, all things seemed waiting, glad, questioning, having accepted her as their own. She went down and threw herself into the sea, floated out to deep water; the waves light and buoyant caressing her with fine supporting touches. To Audrey it had the solemnity of a baptism. She came out with a glad bound of her blood from heart to limbs. Beyond the brilliant sky line lay the world where she must work; she felt the touch of sun and wind as a benediction; even the man she loved, (and in her secret soul Audrey knew she loved him,) would surely bid her God speed.

## CHAPTER XIII

Mr. Goddard was awake with the dawn that day. He usually hit upon all his plans for life before breakfast; it was the enervating, deliberative evening that shook his faith in them and had postponed them all, an unlaid meddlesome mob of ghosts, to the present time. This nipping east wind and bright sunshine strengthened his resolution. He would marry Miss Swenson. He lay in his feather-bed at the hotel, looking at the smouldering wood-fire in the stove, and out of the window at the glittering bay and the silent ships, with their bare masts behind the dark bar of the breakwater. He wished that lazy negro would come and kindle the fire; he was glad that he had not been born into one of the indolent, tropical races; the Anglo-Saxon—what if he should go and get a boat and take Audrey out into some of those hushed, dusky coves and there ask her to marry him? Whereupon he sprang out of bed. Before his boots were on he was in a fever of love, and zeal, and energy from head to foot; he could have died, or even worked for her just then, provided fate had been there to hit the nail on its momentary head. But would there be any necessity for working? The farm was good for an easy income, rented on shares. Jenny could tell him how much, no doubt; and the farm was his absolutely, unless some heir of that mythical Elizabeth Cortrell turned up. He was shaving as these meditations passed through his mind, and stopped, razor in hand. No danger of such an infernal chance as that, surely? The fine poetic eyes stared thoughtfully at themselves and the lathered chin in the glass awhile; then he finished shaving gravely. "I'll go and talk to Jane about it first," he said, nodding to himself.

"Bail out that boat," he called, as he went out of the tavern door, to a bare-legged youth who sat on one of the cannon, meditatively throwing pebbles into a skiff on the shore. "I want it in five minutes." He hurried off, leaving the boy to look after him, stunned for a moment by such fiery heat, and then to resume his pebble-throwing with increased thoughtfulness.

Miss Derby was up and dressed; none of Mrs. Graff's household tarried in bed, well or ill.

Goddard took both her hands in his, and looked fondly into her eyes. He was an affectionate fellow, as everybody knew; his aged mother declared he was the tenderest son ever mother had; and his brother, who supported them both, fancied he found Niel more sympathetic than even a wife would have been. His sympathies were alive to-day as the flock of migrating birds outside, fluttering here and there through the world to find a nest and home.

"You are quite well, Jane?" he said. "You look remarkably well after your terrible night, except for the hollows under your eyes. It was a terrible night to me, I assure you. Looking on and comprehending your danger, I suffered, of course, as you could not do. I feel every nerve frightfully shaken. But I have a plan. I wish to consult you. We'll go and take a row along the beach. You'll go, Jane?"

"Oh, yes; I'll go, Niel." There was an odd submission and humility in her sharp tones which startled him, but he said nothing. He could attend to poor Jane and her case after a while, when his own affairs were settled.

"You shall not go out of the house without a cup of hot coffee and a roll," said Mrs. Graff, coming in as Jane was buttoning her sacque. "Sea, indeed. The sea is there year in and year out, and did any body ever see me bathing or punting about in it, or making a magazine article out of it? Drink the coffee, and be back in half an hour at the farthest, mind."

Jane made no reply, but followed Goddard. She would have followed him as a servant to the ends of the earth, and asked no wages of love, or even notice. She had gone down into the grave last night and shaken hands with death, and it had taught her the actual truth of things—what this man, this red-headed god was to her, must always be to her, and that she was nothing to him. She knew he was going to tell her that he meant to marry Audrey Swenson, and that by a word she could prevent it. She went up to her chamber for a few minutes; and when she came back she carried a little Japanned case in her hand, inside of which was her own title to the Stone-post farm.

"Going to dredge for specimens?" glancing at the case. "I did not know any of your tastes ran into weeds or fishes, Jane; but I shall require all your attention to-day. I will carry the case, though."

"No!" hiding it jealously under her arm.

Mr. Goddard was unusually silent as they walked down the drowsy village street. His boots were unblacked, the clay of the night before yet stained his fanciful sailor clothes, and he had forgotten to trim his curling, red beard. Such signs were open letters to Jane. In his ordinary friendships and loves he was finical and dainty. "This is a reality to him," thought Jane.

Down the long board-path; past the quaint old houses with their double doors and windows to fend off the fierce wind; their walls green with ivy, and roofs gray with lichen, while the gardens, filled with old-fashioned prince's feathers and asters, crimsoned and purpled in patches, in the sun; Jane with a dreary sense of humor, thought of herself as of some criminal going to his death, with no chance of reprieve. For so many years the world had meant for her only this little man, walking beside her in his baggy, blue flannel shirt and trousers, and in five minutes more they would be done with each other for ever. Yet it was Jane who, with that reticence with which an ordinary woman is born, armored as an armadillo with his scales, kept up the flow of small talk. She pointed out the beds of oyster-shells on the sands, accumulated by the Indians centuries ago. "They seem of more interest to me than the sand or the sea, because human beings touched them," she said. "Here is a broken stone-hammer which, I suppose, some young chief wore in his belt, and the bone needle with which his squaw mended his moccasin!

Goddard looked at them and stopped. "Yes, the hammer and needle are here, while they are but lime and clay, and their loves and hates are remembered no more. Yet, no doubt, Jane, their love was deep and real as ours now-a-days."

Jane dropped the needle. "Very likely," she said dryly, and walked on.

She showed him presently a ship's cabin perched close to the sidewalk, with half a dozen children swarming in and out. "There is Peggotty's[20] house, Niel." But Goddard was one of the school of later critics who smile patronizingly on Dickens. "Burlesque sailors and old mawthers[21] are neither Nature nor Art," he said loftily, "Wait until I have settled down in my new life here and I will write you a story, which will stir the blood of the nation, I fancy. Lewes shall suffice for scenery."

She hurried on. This new life? She had not been mistaken, then? She walked more slowly past an old, weather-beaten house, looking curiously over the garden-fence; Goddard could see nothing worth notice except an enormous turtle's shell, which was turned over and filled with verbenas. But Jane, beyond the gaudy blooms, saw a baby who had crawled out and fallen asleep on the lower door-step, one fat, muddy leg sunken in the soft grass.

"What the deuce is in that to bring the water to her eyes?" Goddard asked himself impatiently as they walked on. "Jane has the most disagreeable habit of unearthing a misery at shorter notice than any woman I ever saw."

Past the high grave-yard, looking down upon the quiet street out of the height of its eternal silence; past the bald, bare hotel with its many windows staring down at the bay, waiting hopelessly for the quiet to be broken; past the solemn group of pilots with their skins and breeches alike of leather color, seated on the old cannon, waiting for the bombardment of their grandfathers to be renewed, down to the edge of the rippling water. Jane wondered vaguely to herself how these things would look when she came back; if, after she had heard those few words of his, anything in the world would seem as it had done before.

Goddard found the boy preparing to go down and bail out the boat; he swore with impatience, snatched the sponge and tin dipper from him, and in a few moments called to Jane to come on, while the pilots and fishermen smiled at each other at his energy, and nodded significantly over their pipes.

"Now, thank God, we are rid of them!" he exclaimed, drawing a long breath, as the boat floated out into the bright ripples of the bay. "Do you, know, Jane, human beings oppress me lately? They rob me of myself,— each a little. I begin to feel like a mirror which has reflected a crowd of people, and is nothing in itself. That is one reason I feel that a strong personality close to mine would serve to nourish and shield me from these outside influences."

"You know best what you need, Niel."

They drifted down the shore until they were opposite to the Swenson house. Its open windows could be seen behind the cedars. Through one of them they could see a little man in his shirt-sleeves, with a high beaver hat, playing on the violin as anxiously as though he played to save a life. It was Dr. Swenson, who had stopped digging his potatoes to give Audrey an idea from Beethoven's Seventh Symphony, which he thought she had never observed. She stood beside him, attentive, her eyes apparently fixed on the far sea-line, as she did not notice the boat.

Jane was glad at that moment; glad of the simplicity and power of this figure in the window, draped in black; of the delicate, proud head, the royal yet confiding eyes. Were not all these goods for Niel? Ought he not to have the best the world could offer? But—

"She is there, Jane," whispered Niel, with a sort of gasp, and did not speak again for a long time.

"I wonder," said Jane, "if her poor uncle was digging potatoes for his breakfast. Mrs. Graff tells me that Audrey is no better manager than the dog or cat. They fare miserably." She could not resist this thrust of a needle, though she had spent half of the night praying God to bless them both in their marriage.

"I should fancy Audrey would be a poor caterer," said Niel, with a happy indulgent laugh. His face glowed as he stood in the prow, sheltering his eyes to catch a last glimpse of her; his eyes were radiant; the sun brought out the fine red lights in his heavy hair. To Jane he had the strength of a man, and the tenderness and pure fire of a young girl. When she thought of his marriage with Audrey it was like a poem,—a saga of the loves of the Norse youths and maidens in old times, when drops of the blood of the gods ran in their veins. What she said was:—

"Kit's mother tells me that she had but little education and knows nothing of home duties; she can actually neither sew a seam nor cook a beefsteak. You see yourself how she flings money about."

"You must teach her, then, Jane. You will always be a welcome visitor at the Stone-post Farm,—be sure of that. I shall not give up my friends for my wife. Audrey will have no little jealousies either; her mind is too largely built for that."

"You wish me to come as a guest to that farm?" said Jane slowly. She was stooping over the side, and letting the water pass through her fingers. "Your guest and Audrey Swenson's?"

"Yes, Jane; certainly. It will be pleasant for you in peach-season, when you are off the paper. And I really would take more holidays, Jenny," tenderly. "I cannot bear to think of you moiling[22] over proofs and cooking those hashes of letters, when I shall be one of the 'Lords High Proprietors' of the soil, as the old Delaware records would have had it."

That word or two of kindness saved him. Jane's brain had been gathering up a bitter store against him. Why should she spare him? He cast her away as indifferently as he would a half-burned cigar. He was going to take this woman to his breast in order that they might take their ease for the rest of their lives on her money—her farm. But, at this first careless, affectionate touch of interest in her, her face relaxed. She said quietly, "Newspaper work is tiresome in summer, that is true; but it is my work, Niel, after all. I suppose I'll die in the harness."

They drifted on and on. Goddard, all fire and zeal about his love, appeared quite content to spend the morning in dreaming about it, and to leave its realization until afternoon. Jane, stiff little martinet always over herself, tried to turn away from the sea and from him, and to go back to the old newspaper work, the office, to her receptions, and Parr Chalkley and Sturm and Shively. How wretched a sham it all was! The tasteless tea and the chaffy toast; the huckster notions of art and authorship! The morning was sunny, the sea air full of vitality; but Jane, in that half-hour, felt that she was no longer a young woman. Nothing was left to her in life but the newspaper jobbery, and to fight off neuralgia from back and head. She went wearily back to think of the Indian woman, who, hundreds of years ago, sat in the sand yonder by the heap of shells. She wondered if her one chance of love was lost to her—and was that bone needle as wearying to take up again as the pen in her ink-stand at home would be to-morrow?

"You can command a view of the sea from the porch at the Farm,—did I tell you, Jane? I was just thinking that may save Audrey an attack of calenture."[23]

She did not speak for a moment. "You have quite determined on this marriage, Niel?"

"Why, no. Certainly not until I have your advice. Why, that is what I brought you here for. But I have regarded this step seriously. It is no sudden whim with me. Audrey is necessary to me. I feel as though Providence had designedly planned her for my support and comfort. There is a fund of original power about her which—other women exhaust, drain me; but she would be as a fountain of life ready to my hand." He waited a moment for a reply, but Jane was looking down through the pale, brown water at the shadows of the ripples on the sand below. "Well," with an embarrassed laugh, "you know I told you she had largesse for mankind, so you cannot blame me if I try to claim it all for myself."

"No. Push out into deeper water, Niel. These shimmering shadows blind me."

"I feel,"—after a few vigorous strokes which shot the boat out beyond the breakers,—"I feel, Jenny, at times an intolerable solitude about me, a lack, a want of something which I have never had in life. Do you understand what I mean?"

"Yes, I understand."

"God knows whether love will satisfy this longing, but I hope it will."

Jane spoke at last, after her silence had made him look curiously at her. "If you had not the Farm—"

His face sank into blank disappointment, but he answered firmly, "I could not marry without the Farm. I am no more fit to earn beefsteaks than Audrey to cook them."

On and on over the rolling water, each time coming nearer to shore. Oh, to stay out for ever! To leave farm, Audrey, newspapers, all questions of genius or of money behind, and to drift on with that one face before her. But after that flash of blinding passion, thought, cool, keen, comprehensive, came to Jane's shrewd brain. She held in her hand the proof which made her owner of the farm; if she showed it Goddard would never marry Audrey; it was possible, even probable, that he might marry her. It was no slight thing, too, for her to throw from her the ownership of the farm even if she never married. It was the only chance of comfort for age;

happiness she had done with to-day, but there would be a certain pleasure in managing crops, in rearing cattle, in saving pennies from the sale of milk and butter. Even in this hour of her great pain and loss, the idea of these occupations came to Jane with a sense of compensation as strong as literature was hateful to her. If she made the sacrifice, she at least knew its worth. Her black, penetrating eyes were fixed on his.

"Niel, if you had not this farm,—if you could not marry her—?" But she did not need to wait for an answer. The color left his face, intolerable pain showed itself through his eyes, his contracted features, his quivering chin. "God knows best. I would bear it as best I could."

She stood up, unconscious, so strongly was she moved, that the boat rocked to and fro with her.

"You do love her then?"

"I never loved woman before, Jane."

She made no answer except a commonplace, "Very well," and sat down again.

"What *are* you thinking of?" he asked irritably, after a while. "You do not take much interest in my affairs it seems to me, Jane."

"Yes," she said slowly. "I was thinking, Niel, that nothing ought to stand in the way of your happiness."

"Nothing is going to stand in its way that I know of."

"Is this the deep sea-water here? How many fathoms deep?"

"How should I know? I am not nautical beyond my clothes. Deep enough if you fall overboard to hold you where you will never touch shore again."

"I think you are mistaken, we are not off the bar. The swell would soon carry anything in from here. Push out further."

"As you please," moodily. It was selfish in Jane to chatter about trifles when his whole future was at stake.

"If I should throw anything in here," she said when they had reached the darker green beyond, "it would never come back?"

"Not till the sea gives up its dead. What is that you are going to sacrifice?" trying civilly to be interested. "Your specimens? That's a pity."

"There is nothing in the box of any value except to me," holding it uncertainly in her hand, and looking down into the water.

"If you were a mother burying your child, you could not look more wretched, Jane," laughing.

She turned and looked at him quickly. "*My child?*" she said.

She let the case fall into the water, which closed over it with a dull gurgle. "It is not such women as I who have children to bury. Let us go back now, Niel. It is time you were with Audrey."

## CHAPTER XIV

When Goddard had reached Miss Swenson's house, and found her alone, he was not long in unfolding his errand. An hour or two of dreaming of the future as her husband, made him feel secure as an already married man, and it seemed to him there was little more to do than to mention the matter to her, that she might immediately begin to dream with him of the joy and development in store for both. The manner of mentioning it had not, it is true, been without its force. There was always a certain strength and exaltation in Goddard's statement of his plans, which affected his hearers, and usually carried them with him. When he began to make a balloon at school, which was to convey him both to New York and to glory, most of the other boys were ready to go up with him; and though they were men now, and knew it was never finished, but rotted in an outhouse, they remembered him still as a fellow of fine invention, and likely even now to do something in the balloon way. No man could write a more slashing leading article. Year before last he carried half Philadelphia with him in his radical notions of municipal election reform; last year he became conservative, and then so persuasive was his eloquence, that all his followers sank back again contented into the embrace of stock-jobbers, repeaters and ward politicians. It was no wonder that Audrey Swenson was startled and moved by his fiery love-making. But he began to think presently that her answer lingered a long time on the way. She had walked from him to the open window. He had leisure to contemplate the free, light figure in relief against the lowering afternoon light. If he ever chose to be a sculptor, (and he had begun two or three very remarkable things in that way,) here was a model ready to his hand. As she stood poised on the beach yesterday, for instance, the mackerel line just flung! By George, the very thing! What would your impossible young Mohawks or imaginary Cleopatras be to that as a bit of American art; or, if he finished the novel he had planned, she should be the principal figure; or, if he wrote poems, she could set them to music—free, simple, outspoken music like herself. But he must draw consent now from the sweet, shy creature. He was about to rise when she turned toward him. Sweet and shy enough, probably, but had the Swensons been Swedish kings instead of Swedish sailors she could not have held her suitor from her with more grave stateliness.

"I never have had lovers, Mr. Goddard; I have to consider before I give you an answer as to how I ought to give it."

"There is no need to speak any words at all. I need you, Audrey; come to me!" He held out both hands passionately.

Audrey surveyed them tranquilly. There was a gleam of fun in her steady, soft eyes. "Yes, you told me that you needed me for many purposes. I do not at all understand how that can be. But," with sudden gravity, "supposing it were true, if I loved you, if your need of me was as great as that of the dead for life, I could not go to you. I say this to you so strongly," after a momentary pause, "because I want you not to hurt yourself by thinking that I should have decided differently with a different man. I can never marry."

With an ordinary woman all this would have been the prelude to a coy acceptance; but Goddard knew this was no ordinary woman. The man at bottom was genuine. His manner changed on the instant. He was frank, outspoken, straight-forward as she.

"You propose to give your life to your art?"

"Yes; my art," hurriedly, "is all there is of me."

"The best of you, I grant," eagerly. "But not all." They had suddenly shifted from the question of love to the freemasonry of those who stand on the ground of a common idea. "Half of your nature will lie fallow. Besides, what do you know to teach by your art? What experience have you of life? Why none at all, Audrey; you have not even loved."

"No;" yet, as she stopped, the sudden warm blood rushed to her face and throat and bosom. Like a spark on tinder, the blush set Goddard on fire.

"Let me be your teacher then," in his low, passionate tones. "I will make you know what love is, and you shall utter it again to charm the world if you will." Unfortunately for his cause, he laid his hand upon her arm. Audrey drew hastily back, straightening the black sleeve. Goddard, who was wont to sit like Apollo, crowned by the Muses, among the literary women of New York and Philadelphia, was to her at that moment simply a presuming, disagreeable, little man, whose breath was rank with tobacco.

"I shall never marry," quietly. "Nothing can make that possible."

Goddard started and turned away from her. He showed signs of pain by shivers and uncertain motions as a hurt animal would do. He stood looking down on the sea a long time before he said, "I am sorry to have annoyed you. But I loved you; I have never loved a woman before, and I never shall again."

Audrey's innocent blue eyes filled, as she watched him go out for his hat and gloves. She had never seen such hopeless woe as his sensitive face bore.

"Will you bid me a farewell in your own way?" coming back, and pausing by her chair.

She got up eagerly, and went to the piano, struck the keys once again, and then stopped. "There is nothing for me to say to you. How can I play?"

To her amazement, his countenance was at once irradiated. "But this is the feeling of a true artist! On such an idea Mozart, Beethoven, Mendelssohn built their divine work—the necessity of utterance. They wrote no score for a royalty of filthy dollars. You did right to reject me. Let me be sacrificed to art. Better so! better so!"

He paced up and down, rubbing his wrists like a nervous woman, while Audrey eyed him with a cold surprise.

He stopped before her at last, his thin face red with enthusiasm. "Ah, God! that I had your devotion, your integrity to your work! I shall think of you and your beauty and power as set apart hereafter from human touch. My love was a mistake, but I shall take with me this great thought to refresh me. Thank God there are sometimes such thoughts to refresh me!" He looked at her from head to foot in a hazy, rapt way. "Nature," he said earnestly, "could have created no more perfect type of the vestal virgin to dedicate to Art, and I will help to dedicate it."

"Eh? What's that? What's the matter, Mr. Goddard?" cried the Doctor bustling in, half awake from his afternoon nap.

"Nothing, sir, nothing," abstractedly. "But I have this moment thought of a plan which concerns Miss Swenson's future life. I must go and elaborate it. Good-bye," holding out his hand to her. "I shall take the next train. Trust all to me. Don't make a step without my advice in this matter. As soon as my arrangements are perfected you shall hear from me."

"What ails that young man, Audrey?"

"How can I tell?" dryly, closing the piano.

"What the deuce has he to do with your future life? Vestal virgin, eh? His talk has had no Catholic tendency? No mention of nunneries, eh?"

"No, sir. He was in great trouble a few minutes ago. But it certainly seems to have quite evaporated," as she rose and went out.

CHAPTER XV

A couple of hours later Goddard, bustling into the little railway station, in and out of which an engine was puffing sleepily, ran against Kit.

"Going up to town, Graff?" airily.

"Yes." But he waited to buy his ticket and count the change before finishing the sentence. His only defense for his heavy bucolic self against this tricksy little Ariel in marvelous attire was a stiff formality. "I am going up with Miss Derby, Mr. Goddard. Probably you know better than I why she limits her visit to Lewes to one day."

"Jane going? Now that is lucky. So am I; so am I! You need not go up with her, my dear boy. Not the slightest necessity. I'll take charge of Jane."

"I shall escort my cousin home again," drily.

"Certainly," cried Goddard. "Delighted to have you of the company. Well, I'll go in the car and hunt Jenny up if you'll buy my ticket and check my trunk," tossing him his porte-monnaie, and disappearing in the car.

Jane sat alone. She was dressed with scrupulous plainness; the shabby alpaca and unbecoming hat with its flat bows had given her the sort of dismal comfort which a widow takes in the blackness of her new veil. A book, and newspaper, and box of gum-drops, which Kit had provided for the journey, lay on her lap, while her eyes were closed. Niel glanced at the colorless fat face.

"Why, Jenny! homesick for the office?"

"You here! Niel?"

"Yes, to be sure. Don't look so wild. Did I waken you? You look ready to cry. Lucky I chanced on this train, isn't it?" dropping into the seat beside her. He had doffed his sailor shirt and trousers, and wore the carefully unpretending clothes fit for Chestnut street.

"Why have you left—left your friend?" Jane could not force the name to her tongue.

"Audrey? Oh, Jane! I have the most capital plan! It occurred to me this afternoon, and every moment some detail arranges itself. I want to smooth the way for her in the world—like the messengers who ran before the king, you remember, eh? Prepare the way. You must help, too, a little later. I know every prima donna and tenore that has sung in this country. They'll furnish introductory letters to whatever master I select for her in Europe. Two or three years of study, with such hints as I shall give her as to changes in public taste;—then she comes home—our influence can command every musical critic in New York, and Boston, and at home—you furnish the popular squibs, anecdotes, etc., etc.,—first nights, a packed jury of our own choosing,—oh! success is certain! No such true artist has ever sung on American boards."

Jane sat up erect. "You mean your wife to appear in opera?"

"Wife! Why, didn't you know? She would not marry me. It all seems so long ago, what with packing and so on, that I had really forgotten to tell you. No. She is vowed to her art. Audrey Swenson is an uncommonly sensible woman, Jane. And heroic. The woman who refuses marriage to devote herself to any art, is a daughter of the gods, divinely taller than the rest of her sex. Why, what's the matter? Are you ill, Jane? Is the car—?"

"The motion has made her dizzy, that is all," said Graff, quietly, from where he sat, unnoticed, opposite. He brought her a glass of water, and fanned her with a handkerchief smelling of a horrible sachet powder, a queer twinkle in his eye whenever he glanced toward Goddard. "You do not choose your subjects carefully enough," he remarked as he took his seat again, and turned his back to them.

Goddard sat silent for a long time. Could it be the loss of him that had so chilled and aged Jenny in a few days? Did the child care for him then so much? Jane was really a year older than himself, but he thought of her as quite a tender baby, and felt his heart ache to pain with her suffering. After all, it was pleasant to be coming back to the club, and the gossip of studios and newspaper offices, and to Christian clothes for himself, and to women who did *not* wear bathing suits in mid-day. Jenny meant all these things to him. He could not understand why she sat so stiff and immovable beside him. She did not seem at all relieved that he had not married Audrey, and was coming back to her. "For really Jenny is quite as necessary to me as my pipe, or old dressing-gown, or any other comfort. The woman I marry must marry her too, I suppose."

Just as he reached this sage conclusion the train rushed into a fresh cut in the road, the high banks of dripping clay over-topping the cars at either side. And then—Heaven knows how it all came about! It was the one experience which Goddard never described, and which Jane never used as material. It was a grating sound and a convulsive shriek or two of the engine, and then a blinding crash and darkness. When light and consciousness came to Goddard, he was quite assured that he was dead. A weight seemed to have been taken from his brain, which turned back as from an airy height, to look at life again.

He was lying on the muddy roadside, his head in a woman's arms. There was a horrible smell of cinders and burning wood. Opening his eyes at last, he saw the crowd far off, the green branches of a sycamore rustling between him and the sky, and close beside him Jane Derby's homely, familiar face.

"I am not dead, then?"

She shook her head, the tears coming too fast for her to speak. How strangely dear the ugly face showed itself to him at that!

The crowd came and went; there was a wild uproar and confusion; dust and soot whirled past in clouds; the engines shrieking; shapeless masses, covered with coats, carried by on boards; but, through all, the steady eyes of the woman never moved from his, and her hand chafed his head. Eyes and hands were dragging him back to life, he felt, by some power stronger than magnetism. "O God, I want to live!" he cried, to help her, if he could. How he hated the grave then, as never before! It was then, halting on the precipice of death, that Niel Goddard thought how steadily these eyes had always turned towards him; and the fingers (he could not help laughing inwardly to remember how thick and pudgy they were!) had love in their very touch. Who, besides, of all his hosts of followers and admirers in the life he had almost let slip from him, was true to him as this woman? Not one. What was there, besides her love, secure and stable for him to build the future on? "*Tu es Petrus*, Jenny." This old, poor joke came back to his memory, and his lips moved with it, but made no sound.

"Did you speak, Niel?" she whispered, bending her head.

"Stoop closer, Jenny. Is it so that women bring back to life the men they love? Stay!" passionately holding her down with a grip like that of a dead man. "It is you who have given me life to-day Jenny. There is nothing for me to come back to in that life but you."

"Ah, Niel!" disengaging herself with a laugh more sorrowful than any sigh, "there are all the Audreys past, and all the Audreys to come. What am I?"

"You are the only living being who loves me! Don't desert me. This is no sudden fancy, as the others were,—I've loved you a good many years. There's no happiness for either of us," after a little pause, during which he looked up thoughtfully into the tree overhead, "unless we are husband and wife. What do you say, Jenny?"

She laid his head back on the grass quickly, and stood up, trembling violently, "I shall say nothing now. Your brain is dizzy; the shock—thinking you were dead—and finding nobody but me under the tree—oh, I know how it was! I know. To-morrow—"

"You are growing ungrammatical, Jenny," smiling. "Very well; leave it until to-morrow," closing his eyes wearily. "By the way, where is Graff?"

"Yonder, helping the passengers out of the car. He carried you out."

Goddard raised himself on his elbow. Graff, with one or two others, stood on a ledge of the cut, lifting the bodies, both dead and living, that were handed to him over the heaps of *débris*. Goddard watched him for a moment, and then gave a sudden exclamation, for a sharp explosion took place just at the entrance to the cut, and a cloud of fiery white steam rushed up from some neglected boiler over Graff's body and head. He stood one instant, and then toppled and fell, like a log, into the ruins.

"He is gone!" cried Goddard.

"Are you hurt? Did the steam reach you?" said Jenny.

CHAPTER XVI

"Eight hours of Gluck; no wonder your head aches." The old doctor, perceiving Audrey leave the piano, followed her, anxious and fussing, out into the garden.

"It is not headache, nor is it Gluck," she said, looking about, as if searching for something. A light, cold mist, almost amounting to rain, was chilling the air. She bared her head and shook her hair loose in it.

"Not enough breakfast then?" chirped the old man, after feeling her pulse. "You usually are a hearty eater, Audrey; that encouraged me as to your chances of success as an artist. The mill must have grist, my dear. Your great musicians have been men of strong physique,—kept the divine fire in the head burning with plenty of either beef or beer in the stomach. What do you expect to achieve on a soft-boiled egg? Go, take a walk on the sands and come back hungry, and after supper you can go to Gluck with some chance of comprehension."

Was it, then, only a lack of beef that made the day seem so empty? Audrey went alone to the garden gate, and stood with her hands clasped over her head, in her old habit, when dull or ill at ease.

It had been a day of hard, faithful work; yet when she looked for the recompense it did not come.

All music was unmeaning to her; her own voice, harsh and unable. The truth was, Audrey, like every worker mastering his tools, found them master her for the moment. Was Art, then, nothing but technical rules; a sequence of facts inexorable and material as a mathematical problem? She went out of doors, as other women come to their firesides, for the cheer and comfort of her real home, but it was not there. Mother Nature had no word for her child to-day. Nature, living, eternal, restful, was not there. Nothing was there but heaps of grains of sand, and a vast wash of water. If sea or shore had other meaning, she was blind and deaf to it.

Now the loss of this subtle, cheery greeting which Audrey was wont to receive as soon as she went out from the house, chilled and disheartened her as none of us, probably, can comprehend. She walked on down the beach. The driving mist crossed the field of the sea like solid walls advancing from horizon to horizon.

"Fine weather for the late ploughing!" said an incisive voice behind her. "What on earth, Audrey Swenson, are you doing without a water-proof?"

"I'll bring it at once, Aunt Ann," said Audrey, who always conceded every step of the way in advance to Mrs. Graff.

"What ails you, child?" looking curiously in her eyes. "You're either sick or you're unhappy, and there is no use in denying it."

"Uncle Tom says too much music and too little beef accounts for my ailment," laughed Audrey.

"Very likely. Though I never approved of girls eating meat. It ruins the complexion. You ought to have spent the day with me. I was putting up tomatoes, canning catsup and soy. Of course, you don't know how to make good soy?"

"I'm afraid not."

"Now," after a moment's angry pause, in which Aunt Ann was striving to control her temper, "don't you think it would be more to the purpose if you would spend part of the day in my kitchen or sewingroom, than wandering on this beach in all kinds of weather? How can you ever govern or manage a house without knowledge of this kind?"

It was impossible to irritate Audrey. "But I shall not have a house to manage," she said smiling.

"Why, you are a woman. You cannot shirk your real work for any whim. Nobody can do that, and not suffer for it in the long run. There's Pike going down to the breakwater. The lazy scamp engaged to bring me my blue fish for salting down, last week, and not one have I seen. They are all alike, these fellows," and off she went, her feet leaving hollows in the sand with every firm, swift step.

The world about her seemed dumber and more unmeaning after that. For the first time in her life, Audrey doubted. The something which spoke to her in sun or sea was intangible; might be but the dream of a dream, or as her uncle said, only the attraction of matter for matter; but tomatoes and salt fish, and a comfortable, well ordered household, these were realities. What, if she had made a mistake? What, if, though there were such a voice, she had no power to comprehend or interpret it? She might spend years in hard work such as this of to-day, and find herself a poor, unable failure after all. And yet— As she turned to go home, she looked toward the far sea-line, behind which the ships, phantom-like, were going down. So they went down year after year. There was a great unknown world of men and women beyond, which she had meant to reach some day. The welcome and the friends waiting for her there had grown real things to her in her lonely fancies. Surely there was there some one for whom fish and tomatoes and household drudgery were not the best of life? She had something to say to such a one—something which ached and pained in her breast now. It would give her a share in their joy or their sorrow. Some day she would be able to utter it clearly.

Until that day nothing should turn her from her work.

At that moment she perceived half a dozen of men hurrying from the little station on the beach down the road. As they came near they consulted for a moment, and then one or two left the others and came towards her. They were in trouble, she saw, and it was usual for people in trouble in the town to come to Audrey or her uncle.

"Well, what is it, Ben?"

"There's been an accident on the train up to town this morning, Miss Swenson, and there is a car just run in with some of the dead and wounded. Mr. Graff—"

But she threw out her hand to silence him, and turning, walked swiftly away.

"She might ha' stayed to hear the rest on't," grumbled Pike, who had built a good deal on her behavior when she heard the news for his evening's gossip.

"She couldn't bear it. She was stunned," said good-humored Ben. "She's gone straight to Mrs. Graff's house. They're cousins, you know."

Dead? Kit dead? How heavy this shawl about her head was! She dropped it on the sand as she went, but the weight on her breast was still heavy to suffocation. What was her fantastic dream of voices and mother Nature now? Here was reality—torn bodies and shattered cars, and coffins, and Kit—

Why it was only yesterday he had been planning his whole life out for her, and she had laughed at it and at him. Now it was over and gone. She suddenly saw his face and hands as she had seen them last night as he carried Jane out from the quicksand, big, and red, and covered with mud.

"He's a good fellow—a good fellow!" she said, and then stopped, shocked at herself. Any of these men would have said as much for Kit. Had she, a woman, nothing tenderer to give to her old play-mate? He had always loved her so faithfully, too. If he were dead, perhaps he would know why—

She had reached the gate of the Graff house. A crowd of dark, whispering figures stood about it, but made way for her. A lamp, lighted hastily, flared and smoked without its chimney on the hall table, and Audrey thought, as one thinks of absurd trifles in the face of sudden horror, how her aunt Ann's head would wildly shake at the sight of it.

The parlor was vacant; the door from it open into Mrs. Graff's chamber beyond; by the gray, dreary twilight in the row of square windows, she could see a large figure on the bed, covered with blankets, the face hidden in white bandages. The silence of death was in the room.

Death? She looked about her quickly. There was the bare floor, the chairs with the von Graff coat of arms worked in dingy chenille, Kit's portrait when he was a red-cheeked baby in laces. Kit and she had been every day in this room together, ever since that portrait was painted.

Old Doctor Dorn, who saw her from the bed-chamber, came out. "Be calm, Miss Swenson," he whispered, heavily. "Do not disturb his last moments by any outcry. He has asked for you."

"He is alive, then?"

"Well, yes," with doubtful solemnity; "he still lives. But come in. He has asked for you. It is always my opinion that the wishes of the dying should be gratified, when it is feasible."

Aunt Ann's voice, shriller than usual, through excessive pain, was heard at the moment. "What do you want with her, my son? She's down wandering on the beach, I suppose. Let your mother nurse you. She's a poor, do-less creature; she never cared for you as she ought."

Kit's voice was feeble and hoarse. "On the beach! I shall die before she comes!"

Audrey went in, passing quickly before the doctor. Mrs. Graff would have moved from where she stood by his side, but Audrey, with her large, firm hands on the little woman's shoulders, pushed her gently down.

"Not your place," she said, humbly, and knelt down by the bed. "I am here, Kit."

He put his hand out feebly, and she took it in hers.

The evening darkened: they brought a lamp, and placed it where the light fell on him. The crowd without (a quiet grave crowd, being sea-coast people) disappeared one by one across the sands. Doctor Swenson and his compeer, the village physician, shabby and ponderous as his saddle-bags, which lay on the table, sat side by side by the foot-board. Mrs. Graff stooped over her boy silently, wetting bandages; but still Audrey knelt motionless, her hand immovable in his.

Once when he spoke, they all leaned forward to listen. "It's all for you, if I die, Audrey. My farm. Mother's provided for. I only cared for it for you."

"It would appear to me to be proper," whispered Doctor Dorn, "to send for a lawyer, and let him make his will." But Audrey, with an imperative gesture, commanded silence.

"Audrey!"

"I am here."

"I must speak to you alone."

They drew back, and Audrey stooped closer to catch the broken whisper. "I've been selfish," said poor Kit; "but you were all I had. The other young men had cared for a dozen girls; but I loved you since we were little together. I want you to forget that I worried you for your love, if I die. I want you to forget me, and be happy. If there is anybody else, Audrey—." He stopped. The big hand grew cold in hers.

"There's nobody else," and Audrey, with that queer, loyal smile of hers, held his hand tighter.

"There will be. You never loved me as a wife ought to love her husband. When he comes, and you marry him, be sure that I am glad of it. It was just you I cared for—to make you happy, that was all."

He held her fingers tightly, but did not speak again. Presently she knew by his breathing that he was asleep; his hand fell from hers. Mrs. Graff stole gently up, caught her by the shoulder, and drew her out of the room.

"Audrey, did my boy ask you to marry him now?"

"No."

"You must do it then. He is dying; he has but a few hours to live, and you see how every thought is for you. You surely will not refuse him any comfort you can give him?"

"Marry him? Marry him?"

"Good God! the girl is stone! Any woman would be proud of my boy's love. You can make his last hour happy, and you will not do it; yet you love him, Audrey Swenson?"

"I love Kit, yes." She walked to the window. There was the look of a caged animal in her blue eyes. To go out—out—if but for a moment to the sea and free air, and leave this death and breathless pressure behind!

"Then why not marry him? It would be but the saying of a word or two. You will not be bound to him but an hour—."

"And who the deuce authorized you to say that?" demanded Dr. Swenson, shrilly, at her back. "The boy is in no more danger of dying than you, Ann Graff. It's all that old humbug, Dorn," he growled. "Don't let it fret you, Audrey, and do you go back to your bandages, Ann, and you'll have your darling about in a week."

"He'll live?" Mrs. Graff rose, and staggered to the door. "Live," she muttered again, as she went in.

"Yes, and better for him he had died," ejaculated the old man. "A pretty mess you would have made of your life, Audrey, if I had not come in. To marry that man!"

Audrey raised her head indignantly. "Why should I not marry him? Any woman might be proud of his love."

" 'Yes, yes,' so his mother says. Hen and chick crow alike. Kit's well enough, good, honest creature; but not the sort of man to interfere with your career as an artist. To begin with, he is a beggar. Gives you his farm indeed! It is not his to give, as I happen to know. The law suit which was settled yesterday in Wilmington, concerning lands held as crown gifts by the heirs, will take from him the best part of his property. A very homœopathic portion of it will be left."

"Kit," said Audrey calmly, after the first twinge of pity, "is not a man dependent on property. He can earn his living in a dozen ways."

"He could before this accident."

She turned on him quickly. "You told me he was safe? How is he hurt?"

"Better he had died in my opinion. The man is blind for life."

It was a long time before Audrey answered him. She stood still by the window.

"He has nothing left then? Nothing?" she said.

Her uncle replied, but she did not seem to hear his answer. She was looking down at the sea and at the shore, as one who goes from them inland to see them no more.

She turned at last, and opening the door went up to Kit's bed. His mother, who was alone with him, with one quick look at her face, drew back and left her there.

"Kit," she said, taking his hand again in hers; "Kit."

"Yes, my darling."

"Your mother has told you, you will live?"

"Yes, she has told me."

"Would it make your life worth more, if I should come and share it with you?"

"*Audrey!*" he tried to stretch out his hands to her, and vainly strove to open the closed eyes.

"I will come, then," she said quietly, and, stooping over him, kissed for the first time the poor scorched lips.

## CHAPTER XVII

Goddard did not repent the next day of his resolution to marry Jenny, or, if he did, he found it easier to drift lazily into marriage, than once in, to get out of the current. Jane, on the other hand, had too much tact to startle him by her happiness, or by the necessity of any change in his habits or manners. Matters jogged on as usual for a month or two, when they found that nothing interfered with their being married at once. Jenny had her new winter dresses ready, and Goddard decided that he could begin his new book with better chances of success in the quiet of the Delaware farm-house, with Jane to keep off society.

One evening, therefore, when Jenny had her usual Saturday reception, Goddard mentioned in a casual way to their most intimate friends that Miss Derby and he had been married the day before, and everybody was quick enough to take the cue, and to express neither superfluous surprise nor congratulation.

Mr. Burgess, indeed, noted the incident eagerly, as an illustration of the habit of young girls in American society to drop casually into a church, and be married while out on a morning stroll.

Parr Chalkley, who would have had a lingering flirtation with Jenny, had she belonged to the proper set in Philadelphia, sent her the next day a wedding present of a jeweled dressing case, which Goddard appropriated and used ever after. Shively the publisher, too, hearing of the matter, presented Jenny with a paid up policy of her husband's life, for ten thousand dollars which she put carefully away.

But eight years have passed since then, and there appears to be little risk for the insurance companies. Goddard has grown fat and scant o' breath. His wife and their three boys live on the farm the year round, which, under Jenny's management has increased in both acres and quality, until it now yields a larger income than any other in the county. Jenny herself has softened and brightened into a genial, gentle and handsome middle age. Her gowns are turned and re-turned until they are too ragged to give away, and her boys are taught to wear the coarsest cloth and eat the plainest food, but the keen delight of her life is to see Goddard in the finest of linen, and to prepare little surprises for him of gifts of choice jewelry or rare old editions. He always spends the peach season at the farm, bringing a party of clever fellows down from town; but in winter he remains in Philadelphia, as it is necessary for him to be near libraries, and to receive a weekly mail from Europe, in the preparation of the great treatise on Modern Art which he is going to write. Jenny sold an acre or two to enable him to go to the Vienna Exposition, as, she said, that would aid him so materially in his studies, to that especial end. A party of young journalists, musicians, etc., went over to New York to see him off. None of them mentioned to Mrs. Goddard that Miss Roberts, the noted painter of *la nature morte*,²⁴ was on the Scotia. She is Niel's last intimate friend; Mrs. Goddard does not usually share in these pure and platonic friendships. However, all the world knows that Niel's thirsty soul requires such spiritual refreshment occasionally, and society is not niggardly, now-a-days; it knows how to regard with liberal eye the needs and frailties of genius. If Jane does not share in its magnanimous view of the young women who run after her brilliant husband, she, at least, has enough of her old tact and good sense to laugh at them secretly, knowing they cannot touch her hold on him.

She drives over to Lewes now and then, to give her advice to her cousin Kit and his wife, for, since her Aunt Ann became too old to move about, the household affairs, Jane fancies, need supervision from an experienced eye. She went over last October to see if the canning, pickling, etc., had been properly attended to, and found they had all been forgotten until too late.

"One can so easily buy those things," said Audrey, calmly. "I suppose I shall always be a bad housekeeper, Mrs. Goddard."

Audrey is always calm; and what enrages Jane still more, her big, handsome husband (there is no handsomer man in Sussex county than Kit Graff), whatever she may do or leave undone, follows her with the same contented, adoring eyes; for Kit, after a few years of partial blindness recovered his sight, and by dint of hard work and shrewd management was able to buy back a large share of his property. During these years, while he was both blind and helpless, his wife supported the family by giving music lessons to all the children in the neighborhood. Her old uncle opposed her bitterly, and made a queer speech in Jane's hearing.

"Don't make a market of your birthright," he said, "hide it, bury it in a napkin if you will. You sold yourself, but don't sell that for your own selfish ends, or God will punish you."

"My birthright is to love," said Audrey, and laid her hand on her husband's arm.

Jane always thought the old man half crazy before that, and was not particularly grieved to hear, soon afterwards, that he was dead. "People with such odd notions," she said, "were better in some other sphere and society than this. Not take your talent into the market, indeed! What were we commanded to do with them, except to trade, and to trade for usury, too?"

Her sharp little speeches and sarcasms trouble Audrey no more than the buzzing of wasps in the window-pane. Jane, who likes almost everybody (though she loves nobody but her husband) does not like Kit Graff's wife, and would only be glad of a ground for quarreling with her. But people can only quarrel on trifles, and Audrey takes no heed of trifles. Meanwhile she goads Jane to desperation. She works hard to make money, and lets it slip from her like water. She knows nothing of "good society," yet her manner is so simple and rare that even Jane pays her unwilling homage. She cares nothing for dress, but her plain clothes hang upon her like the bathing rig of old, with the grand grace of the drapery of an antique statue. No wife could be more loving and cheerful with Kit. Yet, unconsciously, she gives you the impression that she has her own home and her own people elsewhere, and will be gone to them presently.

After Jane had paid them her last visit, Graff went with Audrey and their little girl down to the beach to watch the tide come in. He seemed glad to be rid of the closeness of the air in-doors, and of Jane's gossip, and to rejoice in his own fashion in the sun and sea.

"The thermometer is at 78," he says. "Audrey, that is very good for this time of year. These are fine swells, too. Watch for the big tenth one, little sweetheart."

But Audrey ties the child's shoe indifferently. The sun is heat to her now, and the sea, water.

Presently, when evening begins to gather, and the sunset colors the sky and the pools in the marshes behind them, blood-red, and the sea washes into their feet, dark and heavy, with subdued cries and moans, as though all the love and unappeased longing of the world had gone down into it, and sought to find speech in it, Audrey takes up the child, and begins to hush it on her breast, singing a little cradle song, a simple chant with which she was always crooning it to sleep. It is so hopeful, so joyful, so full of the unutterable brooding tenderness of mother's love, that Kit, who cares little for music, finds his heart swell and his eyes dim.

"Your uncle and that Goddard," he observes, "used to think you had a pretty talent for music, Audrey. You were going to teach the whole world by your songs, I remember. But that little tune is all you ever made, eh?"

"That is all."

"And nobody ever heard it but Baby and me. However, it's very pretty, very pretty. And it was lucky your uncle taught you as thoroughly as he did. Your scales and notes helped us over a rough place. They served their purpose very well, though your voice is quite gone with teaching."

He got up presently, and strolled up the beach.

When he was out of sight, a flock of king-birds flew up from the hedges of bay bushes, and lighted near her, turning on her their bright black eyes with a curious look of inquiry. When was it they had looked at her so before?

For one brief moment the tossing waves, the sand dunes, the marshes put on their dear old familiar faces. Old meanings, old voices came close to her as ghosts in the sunlight. The blood rushed to her face, her blue eyes lighted. She buried her hands in the warm white sand. She held the long salt grass to her cheeks. She seemed to have come home to them again. "Child," they said to her, as the statues to Mignon,[25] "where hast thou stayed so long?"

It seemed to her that she must answer them. She began to sing, she knew not what. But the tones were discordant, the voice was cracked. Then she knew that whatever power she might have had was quite wasted and gone. She would never hear again the voice that once had called to her.

She rose then, and, taking up her child, went to the house, still looking in its face. Kit joined her, and was dully conscious that she had been troubled. "You're not vexed at what I said down there, eh?" he asked. "You're not really sorry, that you leave nothing to the world but that little song?"

"I leave my child," said Audrey; repeating after awhile, "I leave my child."

Her husband, at least, was sure that she made no moan over that which might have been and was not.

# Dolly

Scribner's Monthly, November 1874

Just before young Fanning went to Rome—six or seven years ago—he showed me his sketch-book.

"I have been up among the Moravians[1] all summer in Bethlehem, Pennsylvania," he said. "It's the only place where one can catch a flavor of age in this cursedly new country."

The little fellow, from his yellow Dundreary whiskers to his dainty gaiters, was a mere exaggeration of his mother's æsthetic sensibilities. If Nature had thrown in to boot a little back-bone, or stomach, or passions, it would have been better; but, no matter. As things were, one was not surprised the country jarred on him. The old Moravian town had apparently contented him; he had made studies of the bridge and the quaint Eagle Hotel, and the fortress-like Brother and Sister and Gemein Houses,[2] which the first settlers built in the wilderness of solid stone, and which stand now unaltered in the village street, solid enough to last for ages. He had the gray massive piles in crayons, and in water colors and in oils, with the yellow harvest sky behind them, or a thunder cloud, or the pale pink of spring dawn. Here was a bit of the buttress with wild ivy flaming red over it; there was a dim interior of a stone corridor, and an old woman, cloaked, with velvet slippers and a blue handkerchief on her head, sat on a high-backed bench, fingering the dusty strings of an old violin which she had just taken from its case.

"That," he said, "is one of the old Sisters, Frau Baum. The Moravian missionaries come home to these Houses when their work is done, and find shelter and repose. Life in them is but a long, calm twilight. That violin was unearthed one day from some closet where it had been buried almost a hundred years. If it had been knocking about the world in that time, just think of the thousands of waltzes and dances and song tunes it would have given to people! It would have been worn out, or at least have been common and unclean. But there it lay, with all its music, sacred and dumb, unwakened within it. I like to think of that."

I could not follow the young man's fantastic talk. "These Houses seem to have had a secret enchantment of some kind for you," I said, turning over the loose sheets; and just as I spoke I guessed that I had found the enchantment. I took up a carefully-finished picture of the door of the Sister-House, a deep-arched cut in the stone. In it, as in a frame, was a young girl looking back with a laughing good-bye before she disappeared in the darkness. There was another sketch of the same young woman standing in the graveyard, her hands clasped, her eyes bent thoughtfully on the rows of flat gray stones at her feet.

"A portrait, George?"

"Yes." He hesitated. "The niece of old Sister Baum. She is nothing but a child—has lived her sixteen years in that old house, just as pure as a flower that never felt the outside air. Did you ever see innocence or unselfishness shine so transparent in any face? Dolly—that is her name—Dorothea. That is a poor picture enough; the real Dolly, with the shimmer of yellow hair about her face, is fairer than one of Correggio's Madonnas."

I thought Dolly much less insipid than any of those virgins, who, surely, were only immaculate from sheer lack of ideas. There were inexhaustible resources of honesty and friendliness, and sweet temper, in this soft, pink-tinted face.

"Your Dorothea could bear the outside air," I suggested.

"She will never be tried, I hope," suddenly shutting the portfolio with a scowl. "Surroundings make a life, as a background a picture. This little girl will not leave the Sister-House until—until I come back for her."

He went on to convince me and himself of the wisdom of marrying her. The ordinary run of American girls were necessarily tainted by the publicity of their training and free manners. This girl had been reared in a seclusion equal to that of a French convent, etc., etc. The Fannings, mother and son, belonged to that class of Bostonians who stood on a level above consideration of wealth, conventionality, or even birth. I thought that there was every probability that Dolly's history, as it had begun like a story in a cheap magazine, would end in the same romantic groove. Mrs. Fanning was precisely the woman to rejoice in her daughter-in-law's picturesque antecedents, more than in a dower of Pennsylvania Central stock, and would go through society making out of Moravians, and old Sisters, and Gemein Houses a halo for this glorified Madonna.

George Fanning had been gone for a year, however, when, being on a visit to Bethlehem, I heard mention of an auction sale of some old chairs and crockery belonging to a Sister Baum, who had died the week before; certain lovers of rococo furniture bewailing an ancient clock, which had brought twenty-five cents, and a priceless harpsichord sold for firewood. Dolly, I learned, had been carried off by a cousin, living in Pennsylvania, who "charged herself with the girl's keep." She was, they assured me, "a helpful young woman, a good housekeeper, and the best hand with children!"—which is more than could be predicated on sight of any pictured Madonna of Southern Europe.

Dolly and her fortunes had died out of my remembrance, when, a couple of years later, I landed from an old-fashioned stage-coach, with a dozen other passengers, late at night, at the door of a pretentious inn in a country town in the Alleghanies. It was raining hard outside; cross women in waterproofs, whining little boys in knickerbockers, lunch baskets, screaming babies in crushed, white plumed hats, umbrellas and gaping leather valises, were huddled in one damp mass in the whitewashed parlor, a kerosene lamp flaring on the mantel-shelf, and a lady-boarder, with red chignon, calmly playing "Twilight Dews" on the piano.

Suddenly, enter to us—Dolly. Her marvelous hair was not in a frouzy halo, but tucked up in a comb. She was ready, bright-eyed, low-voiced; she wore an apron with the pocket full of keys. I knew her the moment she opened the door. She went quickly, quietly, to one and another.

"Yes, madam, the rooms are ready. Yes, the fire is burning quite clear. And you are all back already? Where are the dear children? Let the baby come to Dolly. I shall have time to put her to sleep presently. Ah, how wet you are!" loading herself with dripping cloaks and overshoes. "Come up stairs at once, it is so comfortable—it is almost too warm there. I shall bring your supper up myself as soon as you are dry."

One of the men asked if she were the chambermaid. She might have been the chambermaid—these were all menial things that she did. But she carried quiet and comfort about with her, and we were wet and shivering. What Dolly's social rank was did not matter to us nor to her. Fanning had not overdrawn the rarity or fine quality of her beauty. Her eyes were dark and blue, and as full of light as any mediæval saint's—but I protest they seemed most beautiful to me when she brought me a cup of hot tea, or went tugging up the stairs, with the driver's lame and dirty boy in her arms.

George Fanning was of our party: he had come up to the mountains for the troutfishing. He happened to enter the hall, dripping, in his oil-skin coat, as she came down again, a tray of dishes in her hand. I do not believe he really ever would have gone back to Bethlehem to find his Madonna; but this was not the less terrible shock to him. She held out one hand eagerly. Many people had been kind to Dolly, and George was only one of the many. He had been well? *She* had been well, and was very comfortable—oh, as comfortable as could be! There was a good deal to do. She had not time to be idle or melancholy—and she went on to see that his chocolate was properly made.

George looked ghastly—nauseated. He went to the other hotel that night, but said nothing. He was too well-bred to make his moan over his dead illusions for the benefit of the public. One could not but wish, maliciously, that he would come back to see "how many tunes, waltzes, dances, and lullabies" his musical instrument was giving to the very common world about her. The landlord and his wife had adopted her—she took the part of the daughter of the house. "Dolly" was known to the public of three counties. Nobody called her a heroine or a mediæval saint, but the public,—teamsters, and traders, and tourists,—were only so many human beings whom the modest, friendly girl had fed or cared for when they were hungry or tired. Each man and woman fancied they alone had discovered how blue and soft was her eye, how delicate and gentle her voice; their thought of the little Moravian was always modest and friendly.

There was a good deal of gossip in the inn about a young farmer whom Dolly was going to marry, but George Fanning was spared that. He went up the mountains the next day through the pelting storm, "after trout," he said.

Two winters later P. T. Barnum brought his traveling museum to Philadelphia. Attached to the show was a hippodrome,[3] in which young girls ran chariot and hurdle races, driving three and four spirited horses abreast. George Fanning took my boys and their mother to look at the horses and audience, a queer phase of American life. In the midst of a headlong race I heard the little man give a groan and mutter, "Good God! has she fallen to that?"

Following his eye to the arena I saw Dolly in flowing robes of spangled blue, standing in a gilt chariot, driving three horses abreast at a frightful speed. Her eyes were flashing, her soft cheeks burning; her yellow hair floated behind her. It was for the moment Boanerges[4] rushing to victory; the next the poor creature had disappeared behind the curtain. With some confused thoughts of the best way to appeal to unrepentant Magdalenes I followed her there when the crowd had dispersed. She had taken off her butterfly attire, and in a gray suit and sober bonnet, was walking composedly toward her cheap boarding-house, holding a little boy by the hand. She turned on me, beaming.

"To think of meeting me! Every day some old friend found her out. It was so pleasant! This was Joe, her boy, and the baby was at home. A girl—yes. So good to have it a girl. *He* was in Nebraska—had gone out to find them a home. This riding was a little trick of hers. He had written about a wonderful bit of ground to be had for four hundred dollars, and Mr. Barnum just then offered fifty dollars a week for chariot drivers. In two months—there was the money, you see. Such a surprise for him!" All this with flushes and wet eyes, and a thousand little bursts and thrills of delighted laughter.

The appeal to poor lost creatures or unrepentant Magdalenes seemed strangely inappropriate just then. Yet George Fanning's brain was full of such thoughts, as he went night after night to watch her drive her horses. What the angels' thoughts were, keeping record overhead—how can we tell? Yet they surely would keep watch over hippodromes and country inns, as well as over the saintly seclusion of ancient nunneries or Sister-Houses! But Dolly, flashing by, probably never thought of men or angels; she only felt she was doing the natural and right thing for her to do, just as she had felt when she served the guests with hot tea in the country inn. She only saw "him," away off in Nebraska, and little Joe, and the baby in its cradle, and plenty of friendly people all about her.

I heard of Dolly's husband the other day. He is a judge—governor, for aught I know, in Nebraska. "His wife," says my informant, "is a lovely, genuine woman, of singularly quiet, gentle manner. Husband and children and the people about her fill up every moment of her life." George Fanning heard the story and said nothing, but I observed him showing a picture that evening to his wife of a faded old woman in the Moravian Sister-House, and heard him tell her of some instrument of marvelous sweetness that lay buried there until it crumbled to pieces—"died with all its music in it."

Something in the picture and the story seemed to please his æsthetic sensibilities.

# The Yares of Black Mountain

Lippincott's Magazine, 1875

"Old fort!"

The shackly little train jolted into the middle of an unploughed field and stopped. The railway was at an end. A group of Northern summer-tourists, with satchels and waterproofs in shawl-straps, came out of the car and looked about them. They had fallen together at Richmond, and by the time they had reached this out-of-the-way corner of North Carolina were the best of boon-companions, and wondered why they had never found each other out in the world before. Yet, according to American habit, it was a mere chance whether the acquaintance strengthened into lifelong friendship or ended with a nod in the next five minutes.

It bade fair just now to take the latter turn.

Nesbitt, who had been in consultation with one or two men ploughing at the side of the station, came hurrying up: "Civilization stops here, it appears. Thirty miles' staging to Asheville, and after that carts and mules. The mails come, like the weather, at the will of Providence. I think I shall explore no farther. When does your train go back, conductor?"

"The scenery disappoints me," said Miss Cook, bridging her nose with her eye-glasses. "It lacks the element of grandeur."

"You'll find it lacking more than that beyond," said a Detroit man who had come down to speculate in lumber. "Nothing but mountains, and balsam timber as spongy as punk.[1] A snake couldn't get his living out of ten acres of it."

Across the field was a two-roomed wooden house, over which a huge board was mounted whereon was scrawled with tar, "Dinner and BAR-ROOM." They all went, stumbling over the lumpy meadow, toward it. Miss Cook, who was always good-humored except on æsthetic questions, carried the baby's satchel with her own.

"Shall you go on?" she asked the baby's mother. "The conductor says the mountains are inaccessible to women."

"Of course. Why he has slept every night since we came on to high land."

"I doubt very much whether the cloud-effects will be as good as in the White Mountains. The sky is too warm." This was said thoughtfully.

"He has one stomach-tooth almost through. The balsam-air will be such a tonic! We'll go up if it is on foot, won't we, Charley?" And she buried her face in the roll of blanket.

There was a fine odor of burnt beans and whisky in the hot little parlor of the house, with its ragged horsehair chairs and a fly-blown print of the "Death of Robert E. Lee" on the wall. On the other side of the hall was the bar-room, where a couple of red-faced majors in homespun trousers and shirts were treating the conductor. It was a domestic-looking bar-room after all, in spite of red noses and whisky: there were one or two geraniums in the window, and a big gray cat lay asleep beside them on the sill.

One of the majors came to Baby's mother in the parlor. "There is a rocking-chair in the—the opposite apartment," he said, "and the air will be better there for the child. A very fine child, madam! very fine, indeed!"

She said yes, it was, and followed him. He gave Baby a sprig of geranium, bowed and went out, while the other men began to discuss a Methodist camp-meeting, and the barkeeper shoved a newspaper over his bottles and worked anxiously at his daybook. The other passengers all went to dinner, but Nesbitt was back at her side in five minutes.

"I'm glad you stayed here," he said. "There is a bare wooden table set in a shed out yonder, and a stove alongside where the cooking goes on. You would not have wanted to taste food for a month if you had seen the fat pork and cornbread which they are shoveling down with iron forks. Now, if I thought—if we were going to rough it in the mountains—camp-fire, venison, trout cooked by ourselves, and all that sort of thing, I'd be with you. But this civilized beastliness I don't like—never did. I'll take this train back, and strike the trunk-line at Charlotte, and try Texas for my summer holiday. I must be off at once."

"Good-bye, then, Mr. Nesbitt. I am sorry you are not going: you've been so kind to Charley."

"Not at all. Good-bye, madam. God bless you, little chap!" stopping to put his finger in the baby's thin hand. He was quite sure the little woman in black would never bring her child back from the mountains.

"I'm glad he's gone," said Miss Cook, coming in from the shed. "It's absurd, the row American men make about their eating away from home. They want Delmonico's table set at every railway-station."

"You will go on up the mountain, then?"

"Yes. I've only three weeks' vacation, and I can get farther from my usual rut, both as to scenery and people, here than anywhere else. I've been writing on political economy lately, and my brain needs complete change of idea. You 'know how it is yourself.'"

"No, I—" She unlocked her satchel, and as she took out Baby's powder looked furtively at Miss Cook. This tight little person, buckled snugly into a water-proof suit, her delicate face set off by a brown hat and feather, talking political economy and slang in a breath, was a new specimen of human nature to her.

She gave the powder, and then the two women went out and deposited themselves and their wraps in a red stage which waited at the door. A fat, jolly-faced woman, proprietor of the shed and cooking-stove, ran out with a bottle of warm milk for the child, the Carolinian majors and barkeeper took off their hats, the Detroit man nodded with his on his head, and with a crack of the whip the stage rolled away with them. It lurched on its leather springs, and luffed and righted precisely like a ship in a chopping sea, and threw them forward against each other and back into dusty depths of curled hair, until even the baby laughed aloud.

Miss Cook took out her notebook and pencil, but found it impossible to write. "There is nothing to make note of, either," she said after an hour or two. "It is the loneliest entrance to a mountain-region I ever saw. These glassless huts we see now and then, and ruins of cabins, make it all the more forlorn. I saw a woman ploughing with an ox just now on the hillside, where it was so steep I thought woman, plough and ox would roll down together.—Is there no business, no stir of any sort, in this country?" she called sharply to the driver, who had got down and looked in at the door at that minute.

"I don't know," he said leisurely. "Come to think on't, it's powerful quiet ginerally."

"No mining—mills?"

"Thar war mica-mines. But ther given over. An' thar war a railroad. But that's given over too. I was a-goin' to ask you ladies ef you'd wish to git out an' see whar the traveler was murdered last May, up the stream a bit. I kin show you jest whar the blood is yet; which, they do say, was discovered by the wild dogs a-gnawin' at the ground."

The baby's mother held it closer, with her lips unusually pale. "No, thank you," she said cheerfully. "Probably we can see it as we come back."

"Well, jest as *you* please," he replied, gathering up the reins with a dis-contented air. "Thar's been no murder in the mountings for five years, an' 'tisn't likely there'll be another."

A few miles farther on he stopped to water his horses at a hill-spring. "Thar's a house yonder, ef you ladies like to rest an hour," he said, nodding benignantly.

"But the mail?—you carry the mail?"

"Oh, the mail won't trouble itself," taking out his pipe and filling it. "That thar child needs rest, I reckon."

The two women hurried up the stony field to the large log hut, where the mistress and a dozen black-haired children stood waiting for them.

"Something to eat?" cried Miss Cook. "Yes indeed, my good soul; and the sooner the better. Finely-cut face, that," sketching it rapidly while the hostess hurried in and out. "Gallic. These mountaineers were all originally either French Huguenots or Germans. It would be picturesque, dirt and all, under a Norman peasant's coif and red umbrella, but in a dirty calico wrapper—bah!"

The house also was dirty and bare, but the table was set with fried chicken, rice, honey and delicious butter.

"And how—how much are we to pay for all this?" said Miss Cook before sitting down.

"If ten cents each would not be too much?" hesitated the woman.

Miss Cook nodded: her very porte-monnaie gave a click of delight in her pocket. "I heard that these people were miserably poor!" she muttered rapturously. "Don't look so shocked. If you earned your bread by your brains, as I do, you'd want as much bread for a penny as possible."

The sky began to darken before they rose from the table, and, looking out through the cut in the wall which served for a window, they saw that the rain was already falling heavily. A girl of sixteen, who had been spinning in the corner, drew her wheel in front of the window: the square of light threw her delicately-lined face and heavy yellow hair into relief. She watched the baby with friendly smiles as she spun, giving it a bit of white wool to hold.

"What a queer tribe we have fallen among!" said Miss Cook in scarcely lowered tones. "I never saw a spinning-wheel before, except Gretchen's in *Faust*; and there is a great hand-loom. Why it was only Tuesday I crossed Desbrosses Ferry, and I am already two centuries back from New York. Very incurious, too, do you observe? The women don't even glance at the shape of our hats, and nobody has asked us a question as to our business here. People who live in the mountains or by the sea generally lack the vulgar curiosity of the ordinary country farmer."

"Do they? I did not know. These are the kindest people *I* ever met," said the little woman in black with unwonted emphasis.

"Oh, they expect to make something out of you. Travelers are the rarest of game in this region, I imagine," observed Miss Cook carelessly, and then stopped abruptly with a qualm of conscience, remarking for the first time the widow's cap which her companion wore. These people had perhaps been quicker than she in guessing the story of the little woman—that the child, dying as it seemed, was all that was left to her, and that this journey to the balsam mountains was the last desperate hope for its life.

She looked with a fresh interest at the thin, anxious face, the shabby black clothes, and then out of the window to where the high peaks of the Black Range were dimly visible like cones of sepia on the gray horizon. She had read a paper in some magazine on the inhospitable region yonder, walled by the clouds. It was "almost unexplored, although so near the seaboard cities"; the "haunt of beasts of prey"; the natives were "but little raised above the condition of Digger Indians." All this had whetted Miss Cook's appetite. She was tired of New York and New Yorkers, and of the daily grinding them up into newspaper correspondence wherewith to earn her bread. To become an explorer, to adventure into the lairs of bears and wolves, at so cheap a cost as an excursion ticket over the Air-Line Railroad, was a rare chance for her. As it rained now, she gathered her feet and skirts up on the chair-rungs from the dirty floor and confided some of these thoughts to her companion, who only said absently, "She did not know. Doctor Beasly—perhaps Miss Cook had heard of Doctor Beasly?—had said Charley must have mountain-air, and that the balsams were tonics in themselves. She did not suppose the Diggers or animals would hurt *her*."

The truth was, the little woman had been fighting Death long (and vainly, as it proved) over a sick bed. She knew his terrors there well enough: she had learned to follow his creeping, remorseless fingers on clammy skin and wasted body, and to hear his coming footsteps in the flagging beats of a pulse. She had that dry, sapless, submissive look which a woman gains in long nursing—a woman that nurses a patient who holds part of her own life and is carrying it with him, step by step, into the grave. The grave had closed over this woman's dead, and all that he had taken with him from her: even to herself she did not dare to speak of him as yet. The puny little boy on her arms was the only real thing in life to her. There was a chance in these mountains of keeping him—a bare chance. As for wild beasts or wild people, she had thought of them no more than the shadows on the road which passed with every wind.

The rain beat more heavily on the roof: the driver presented himself at the door, dripping. "Ef we don't go on, night'll catch us before we make Alexander's," he said. "Give me that little feller under my coat. I'll kerry him to the stage."

Miss Cook shivered in the chilly wind that rushed through the open door. "Who would believe that the streets in New York were broiling at 105° this minute?"

"That baby's not wrapped warm enough for a night like this," said the woman of the house, and forthwith dragged out of a wooden box a red flannel petticoat, ragged but clean, and pinned it snugly about him.

"She'll charge you a pretty price for it," whispered Miss Cook; "and it's only a rag."

"No, no," laughed the woman, when the widow drew out her portemonnaie. "Joe kin bring it back some day. That's all right."

"You seem as touched by that as though it were some great sacrifice," said Miss Cook tartly after they were settled again in the stage.

"It was all she had." Adding after a pause, "I have been living in New York for five years. My baby was born there, and—and I had trouble. But we came strangers, and were always strangers. I knew nobody but the doctor. I came to look upon the milkman and baker who stopped at the door as friends. People are in such a hurry there. They have not time to be friendly."

"You are a Southerner? You are coming back to your old home?"

"No, I never was in the South before."

The stage tossed and jolted, the rain pelted against the windows. Miss Cook snored and wakened with jumps, and the baby slept tranquilly. There was a certain purity in the cold damp air that eased his breathing, and the red petticoat was snug and warm. The touch of it seemed to warm his mother too. The kind little act of giving it was something new to her. It seemed as if in the North she too had been in a driving hurry of pain and work since her birth, and had never had time to be friendly. If life here was barbarous, it was at ease, unmoving, kindly. She could take time to breathe.

It was late in the night when the stage began to shiver, like the one-horse shay in its last gasp of dissolution, over the cobble-stoned streets of the little hill-village of Asheville. It drew up in front of an inn with wooden porches sheltered by great trees: there were lights burning inside, and glimpses of supper waiting, and a steam of frying chicken and coffee pervading the storm. One or two men hurried out from the office with umbrellas, and a pretty white-aproned young girl welcomed them at the door.

"Supper is ready," she said. "Yours shall be sent to your room, madam. We have had a fire kindled there on account of the baby."

"Why, how *could* you know Charley was coming?" cried the widow breathlessly.

"Oh, a week ago, madam. While you stopped at Morganton. The conductor of the Salisbury train sent on a note, and afterward the clergyman at Linville. We have been warned to take good care of you," smiling brightly.

The baby's mother said nothing until she was seated in her room before a wood-fire which crackled and blazed cheerfully. The baby lay on her lap, its face red with heat and comfort.

"Since I left Richmond one conductor has passed me on to another," she said solemnly to Miss Cook. "The baby was ill at Linville, and the train was stopped for an hour, and the ladies of the village came to help me. And now these people. It is just as though I were coming among old friends."

"Pshaw! They think you have money. These Southerners are impoverished by the war, and they have an idea that every Northern traveler is overloaded with wealth, and is fair game."

"The war? I had forgotten that. One would forgive them if they were churlish and bitter."

The woman was a weak creature evidently, and inclined to drivel. Miss Cook went off to bed, first jotting down in her notebook some of the young girl's queer mistakes in accent, and a joke on her yellow dress and red ribbons. They would be useful hereafter in summing up her estimate of the people. The girl and the widow meantime had grown into good friends in undressing the boy together. When his mother lay down at last beside him the firelight threw a bright glow over the bed, and the pretty young face came again to the door to nod good-night.

It was only a hotel, and outside a strange country and strange people surrounded her. But she could not rid herself of the impression that she had come home to her own friends.

The sun rose in a blue dappled sky, but before he was fairly above the bank of wet clouds Miss Cook was out, note-book in hand. She had sketched the outline of the mountains that walled in the table-land on which the village stood; had felt the tears rise to her eyes as the purple shadow about Mount Pisgah flamed into sudden splendor (for her tears and emotions responded quickly to a beautiful sight or sound); she had discovered the grassy public square in which a cow grazed and a woman was leisurely driving a steer that drew a cart; she had visited four emporiums of trade—little low-ceiled rooms which fronted on the square, walled with calicoes and barrels of sugar, and hung overhead with brown crockery and tin cups; she had helped two mountaineers trade their bag of flour for shoes; had talked to the fat post-master through the open pane of his window, to the negro women milking in the sheds, to a gallant Confederate colonel hoeing his corn in a field, to a hunter bringing in a late lot of peltry from the Smoky Range. As they talked she portioned out the facts as material for a letter in the *Herald*. The quaint decaying houses, the swarming blacks, the whole drowsy life of the village set high in the chilled sunshine and bound by its glittering belt of rivers and rampart of misty mountain-heights, were sketched in a sharp effective bit of word-painting in her mind.

She trotted back to the Eagle Hotel to put it on paper; then to breakfast; then off again to look up schools, churches and editors.

Late in the afternoon, tramping along a steep hill-path, she caught sight of two women in a skiff on a lonely stream below. It was the baby's mother and the pretty girl from the inn. No human being was in sight; the low sunlight struck luminous bars of light between the trunks of the hemlocks into the water beneath the boat as it swung lazily in the current; long tangled vines of sweet-brier and the red trumpet-creeper hung from the trees into the water; the baby lay sound asleep on a heap of shawls at his mother's feet, while she dipped the oars gently now and then to keep in the middle of the stream.

"How lazy you look!" called Miss Cook. "You might have been made out of the earth of these sleepy hills. Here, come ashore. D'ye see the work I've done?" fluttering a sheaf of notes. "I've just been at the jail. A den! an outrage on the civilization of the nineteenth century! Men have been branded here since the war. Criminals in this State are actually secured in iron cages like wild beasts! I shall use that fact effectively in my book on the *Causes of the Decadence of the South*: one chapter shall be given to 'The Social and Moral Condition of North Carolina.'"

"You will need so many facts!" ejaculated the little woman, awestruck, yet pityingly. "It will take all your summer's holiday to gather them up."

Miss Cook laughed with cool superiority: "Why, child, I have them all now—got them this morning. Oh, I can evolve the whole state of society from half a dozen items. I have the faculty of generalizing, you see. No," folding up her papers decisively, "I've done the mountains and mountaineers. Between slavery and want of railroads, humanity has reached its extremest conditions here. I should not learn that fact any better if I stayed a week."

"You are not going back?"

"Back? Emphatically, yes. I go to Georgia to-morrow morning. This orange I have sucked dry."

Miss Cook posted to the hotel, and passed the night in making sketches to illustrate her article from a bundle of photographic views which she found in possession of the landlady.

Looking out of the parlor-window next morning, she saw half the inmates of the house gathered about a cart drawn by two oxen in which sat the widow and Charley. A couple of sacks of flour lay at her feet, and a middle-aged man, a giant as to height and build, dressed in butternut homespun, cracked his long whip at the flies.

"Where can she be going?" asked Miss Cook of a young woman from Georgia whom she had been pumping dry of facts all the morning. The Georgian wore a yellow dress with a coarse frill about her swarthy neck: she sat at the piano and played "Love's Chidings."

The man, she said, was Jonathan Yare, a hunter in the Black Mountains. Her brother had told her his terrible history. Her brother had once penetrated into the mountains as far as the hut where the Yares lived, some thirty miles from here. Beyond that there were no human beings: the mountains were given up to wild beasts. As for these Yares, they had lived in the wilderness for three generations, and, by all accounts, like the beasts.

Miss Cook rushed out: political economist and author though she might be, she had a gossip's keen enjoyment in a piece of bad news. "Do you know these hunters?" she whispered. "They have a terrible history: they live like wild beasts."

The little woman's color left her. Her head filled instantly with visions of the Ku-Klux[2] and the Lowery gang. "I never asked what they were," she gasped. "I only wanted to take Charley among the balsams."

The man looked back at this moment, and seeing that the valise and box and baby's bottle of milk were in the cart, cracked his long whip over the near ox, and the next moment the widow and her baby were jolting up the rocky hill-street, abandoned to the tender mercies of the middle-aged man in butternut and his gang.

Nobody need laugh if we say that she felt a spasm of fear. When Death laid his hand on her child she had taken him up and fled to these mountains without a second thought, as the women in the times of the apostles carried their dead and dying to be cured by miraculous aid. But she was a woman like the rest of us, used to jog along the conventional paths to church, to market, to the shops; her only quarrels with the departed

David had been about his unorthodox habits in business and politics; and she never could be easy until she was sure that her neighbors liked her new bonnet. What would her neighbors—any neighbor—David himself, have said at seeing her in league with this desperate character, going into frightful solitudes "inaccessible to women"?

The man spoke to her once or twice, but she answered with an inaudible little chirp, after which he fell into silence, neither whistling nor speaking to his oxen, as she noticed.

She could not help observing how unusually clear the light about her was from the thinness of the air, although the sun was out of sight in a covered, foreboding sky, and black ragged fragments of cloud from some approaching thunderstorm were driven now and then across the horizon. The road, if road you chose to call it, crept along beside the little crystal-clear Swannanoa River, and persisted in staying beside it, sliding over hills of boulders, fording rushing mountain-streams and dank snaky swamps, digging its way along the side of sheer precipices, rather than desert its companion. The baby's mother suddenly became conscious that the river was a companion to whom she had been talking and listening for an hour or two. It was narrow, deep, and clear as the air above it: it flowed with a low soothing sound in which there came to her somehow an assurance of security and good-will. But she was bewildered by the multitudes of trailing vines: they hedged in the river; they covered the banks, and threw long clutching branches into the water: they crept out on projecting trees on either side and leaped across the stream, bridging it with arches of wreaths and floating tendrils. There were the dark waving plumes of the American ivy, the red cornucopias of the trumpet-creeper, morning-glories with great white blossoms, the passion-flower trailing its mysterious purple emblems through the mud beneath the oxen's feet,—all creeping or turning in some way toward the river. Surely there were some airy affections, some subtle friendlinesses, among these dumb living creatures! They all seemed alive to her, though she was a prosaic woman, who had read little beyond her cookery-book and Bible. It was as though she had come unbidden into Nature's household and interrupted the inmates talking together. The vines tangled in masses under the hunter's feet; every tree was covered with them, every fence-post or stump; the black thick stems interlaced up the trunks and on top, falling over in a green tent-like crown. The Carolina rose stretched in masses for miles along the road—the very earth seemed to blush with it: here and there a late rhododendron hung out its scarlet banner. The tupelo thrust its white fingers out of the shadow like a maiden's hand, and threw out into the air the very fragrance of the lilies-of-the-valley which used to grow in the garden she made when she was a little girl. The silence was absolute, except when a pheasant rose with a whirr or a mocking-bird sounded its melancholy defiant call in the depths of the forest. Long habit of grief had left her heart tender and its senses keen: these things, which were but game or specimens for the naturalist, were God's creatures to her, and came close to her. Charley woke, and looking up saw her smiling down on him with warm cheeks. She did not know the name of a plant or tree or bird, but she felt the friendliness and welcome of the hills, just as she used to be comforted and lifted nearer to God by distant church music, although she could not hear a word of the hymn.

Leaving the road, they entered deep silent gorges, and followed the bed of mountain-streams through cañons walled in by gray frowning rocks, over which the sky bent more darkly each moment. At last there was a break in the gorge. About her was a world of gigantic mountains. There was no sign of human habitation—nothing but interminable forests that climbed the heights, and, failing half-way, left them bare to pierce the clouds.

She had started on this journey with a vague notion of reaching some higher land where balsam trees grew, the air about which would be wholesome for Charley. She had penetrated to the highest summits of the Appalachian Range, the nursery or breeding-place from which descend the Blue Ridge, the Alleghanies, the Nantahela—all the great mountain-bulwarks that wall the continent on its eastern coast. The mighty peaks rose into the sky beyond her sight, while the gathering storm-clouds clung to their sides, surging and eddying with the wind. How petty and short-lived was wind or storm! She looked up at those fixed, awful heights, forgetting even the child on her knee. It was as if God had taken her into one of the secret places where He dwelt apart.

She came to herself suddenly, finding that the cart had stopped and the driver was standing beside examining the baby's milk.

"I reckon," he said, "it's sour, and the little chap's hungry. I'll get some fresh, an' you kin look at the mountings."

He went into the laurel, and with a peculiar whistle brought some of the wild cattle to him, and proceeded to milk one of the cows, returning with a cupful of foaming warm milk. Now, one of the Lowery gang would hardly go to milking cows, she thought; and there was something in the man's steady grave eyes that looked as if he too understood the meaning of the "mountings." They jogged on in silence.

Half an hour later the clouds closed about them and the rain fell heavily. The cart was dragged through the bed of a mountain-stream, and then stopped in front of a low log house built into a ledge of the mountain. A room on either side opened into a passage, through which a wagon might be driven, and where the rain and wind swept unchecked. An old woman stood in it looking up the stream. Her gray hair hung about her sallow face, her dress was a dirty calico, her feet were bare. Behind her was the kitchen, a large forlorn space scarcely enclosed by the log and mud walls. A pig ran unnoticed past her into it. Another woman, tall and gaunt, was fording the stream: she was dripping wet, and carried a spade. Surely, thought the baby's mother, human nature could reach no lower depths of squalor and ignorance than these.

"Mother," said Jonathan Yare, "here is a friend that has come with her baby to stay with us a while."

The old woman turned and instantly held out her arms for the child. "Come in—come to the fire," she said cordially. "I am glad Jonathan brought you to us."

If a princess had been so taken by surprise, her courtly breeding could not have stood her in better stead.

She took the baby and its mother into a snug boarded room with half a dozen pictures from the illustrated papers on the walls, and a fire of great logs smouldering on the hearth. When they were warmed and dry they went into the kitchen. Supper was ready, and two or three six-foot mountaineers stood by the table.

"We are waiting for father," said the woman who had carried the spade. Both men and women had peculiar voices. One could never grow used to hearing such gentle tones from such great sons of Anak. At the same moment an old man of eighty, whose gigantic build dwarfed all of his sons, came into the doorway. His eyes were closed, and he groped with his staff. The widow, as soon as she saw his face, went directly up to him and took his hand.

"My name is Denby," she said. "I brought my baby here to be cured. He is all I have, sir."

"You did right to come." She guided his hand to Charley's, and he felt his skin, muscles and pulse, asking questions with shrewder insight than any physician had done. Then he led her to the table. "Boys, Mistress Denby will like to sit beside me, I think," he said.

She had an odd feeling that she had been adopted by some ancient knight, although the old man beside her wore trousers covered with patch on patch that left his hairy ankles and feet bare. Before the meal was over another strange impression deepened on her. She saw that these people were clothed and fed as the very poorest poor; she doubted whether one of them could read or write; they talked little, and only of the trivial happenings of the day—the corn or the ox that had gone lame; but she could not rid herself of the conviction that she had now, as never in her life, come into the best of good company. Nature does not always ennoble her familiars. Country-people usually are just as uneasy and vulgar in their cheap and ignorant efforts at display or fashion as townsmen. But these mountaineers were absolutely unconscious that such things were. A man was a man to them—a woman, a woman. They had never perhaps heard either estimated by their money or house or clothes. The Yares were, in fact, a family born with exceptionally strong intellects and clean, fine instincts: they had been left to develop both in utter solitude and without education, and the result as to manner was the grave self-control of Indians and a truthful directness and simplicity of thought and speech which seemed to grow out of and express the great calm Nature about them as did the trees or the flowing water.

Little Mrs. Denby was conscious of this in half an hour. These were the first human beings whom she had ever met between whom and herself there came absolutely no bar of accident—no circumstance of social position or clothes or education: they were the first who could go straight to something in her beneath all these things. She soon forgot (what they had never known) how poor they were in all these accidents.

After that Charley and his mother were adopted into the family. At night, when the child was asleep, the old hunter always sat with her and his wife beside the fire, telling stories of bear-hunts, of fights with panthers, of the mysterious Rattlesnake Valley, near which no hunter ventures. He had been born in this house, and passed the whole of his eighty years in the mountains of the Black Range. One night, noticing the scars which his encounters with bears had left on him, she said, "It is no wonder that the townspeople in Asheville talked to me of the 'terrible history of the Yares.'"

The old man smiled quietly, but did not answer. When he had gone to bed his wife said with great feeling, "It was not their fights with wolves and bears that turned the people at Asheville agen the name of my boys and their father. They were the only men anigh hyar that stood out fur the Union from first to last. They couldn't turn agen the old flag, you see, Mistress Denby."

"They should have gone into the Federal army and helped to free the slaves," cried the widow with rising color, for she had been a violent abolitionist in her day.

"Waal, we never put much vally on the blacks, that's the truth. We couldn't argy or jedge whether slavery war wholesomest for them or not. It was out of our sight. My lads, bein' known as extraordinar' strong men an' powerful bear-fighters, hed two or three offers to join Kirk's Loyal Rangers in Tennessee. But they couldn't shed the blood of their old neighbors."

"Then they fought on neither side? Their old neighbors most probably called them cowards."

"Nobody would say that of the Yares," the woman said simply. "But when they wouldn't go into the Confederit army, they was driv out—four of them, Jonathan first—from under this roof, an' for five years they lay out on the mounting. It began this a-way: Some of the Union troops, they came up to the Unaka Range, and found the house whar the Grangers lived—hunters like us. The soldiers followed the two Granger lads who was in the rebel army, an' had slipped home on furlough to see their mother. Waal, they shot the lads, catchin' them out in the barnyard, which was to be expected, p'raps; an' when their ole father came runnin' out they killed him too. His wife, seein' that, hid the baby (as they called him, though he was nigh onto eight year old) under a loose board of the floor. But he, gettin' scart, runs out and calls, 'Gentlemen, I surrender,' jest like a man. He fell with nine bullets in his breast. His mother sees it all. There never was a woman so interrupted as that pore woman that day. She comes up to us, travelin' night an' day, talkin' continual under her breath of the lads and her ole man's gray hair lyin' in a pool of blood. She's never hed her right mind sence. When Jonathan heard that from her, he said, 'Mother, not even for the Union will I join in sech work as this agen my friends.' He knowed ony the few folks on the mountings, but he keered for them as if they war his brothers. Yet they turned agen him at the warnin' of a day, and hunted him as if he was a wild beast. He's forgot that now. But his sister, she's never forgot it for him agen them. Jonathan's trouble made a different woman of Nancy."

But Mrs. Denby had felt but little interest in the gaunt, silent Nancy.

"You say they hunted your sons through the mountains?"

"Jest as if they war wolves. But the boys knowed the mountings. Thars hundreds of caves and gullies thar whar no man ever ventered but them. Three times a week Nancy went—she war a young girl then: she went up into Old Craggy and the Black miles and miles to app'inted places to kerry pervisions. I've seen her git out of her bed to go (fur she hed her aches and pains like other wimmen), and take that pack on her back, when the gorges war sheeted with snow and ice, an' ef she missed her footin' no man on arth could know whar she died."

"But five years of idleness for your sons—"

The old woman's high features flushed. "You don't understan', Mistress Denby," she said calmly. "My sons' work in them years was to protect an' guide the rebel deserters home through the mountings—people at the North don't know, likely, what crowds of them thar war—an' to bring the Union prisoners escaped from Salisbury and Andersonville safe to the Federal lines in Tennessee. One of the boys would be to Salisbury in disguise, an' the others would take them from him and run them into the mountings, an' keep 'em thar, bringin' them hyar when they could at night fur a meal's good victuals. About midnight they used to come. Nancy an' me, we'd hear a stone flung into the river yonder—seems es ef I stop listenin' fur that stone—an' we'd find them pore starved critters standin' in the dark outside with Jonathan. In ten minutes we'd have supper ready— keepin' the fire up every night—an' they'd eat an' sleep, an' be off before dawn. Hundreds of them hev slep' in this very room, sayin' it was as ef they'd come back to their homes out of hell. They looked as ef they'd been thar, raally."

"In *this* room?" Mrs. Denby stood up trembling. Her husband had been in Salisbury[3] at the same time as Albert Richardson,[4] and had escaped. He might have slept in this very bed where his child lay. These people might have saved him from death. But Mrs. Yare did not notice her agitation.

"Thar was one winter when Major Gee sent guards from Salisbury to watch the mounting-passes, 'specially about this house, knowin' my boys' work. Then they couldn't come anigh: thar was nigh a year I couldn't hear from them ef they were alive or dead. I'd hear shots, an' the guards 'ud tell me it was 'another damned refugee gone'—p'raps one of my boys. I'd set by that door all night, lookin' up to the clouds coverin' the mounting, wonderin' ef my lads was safe an' well up thar or lyin' dead an' unburied. I'd think ef I could only see one of my lads for jest once—jest once!" The firelight flashed up over her tall, erect figure. She was standing, and held her arm over her bony breast as if the old pain were intolerable even now. She said quietly after a while, "But I didn't begrudge them to their work. One night—the soldiers were jest yonder: you could see the camp-fire in the fog—thar war the stone knockin' in the stream. I says, 'Nancy, which is it?' She says, 'It's Charley's throw. Someut ails Jonathan.' An' Charley hed come to say his brother war dyin' in a cave two mile up: they'd kerried him thar. I found my lad thar, worn to a shadder, an' with some disease no yerbs could tech. Wall, fur a week we came an' went to him, past the guard who war sent to shoot him down when found like a dog; an' thar he was lyin' within call, an' the snow an' sleet driftin' about him. One day Nancy was dumb all day—not a word. I said to father, 'Let her alone: she's a-studyin' powerful. Let her alone.' 'Mother,' she says at night, 'I've been thinkin' about Jonathan. He must hev a house to cover him, or he'll die.' 'Yes, Nancy, but what house?' 'I'll show you,' says she. "You bide hyar quiet with father. The guard is used to seein' me come an' go with the cattle.' She took an axe an' went out, an' didn't come home till mornin'. In three days she hed cut down logs an' built a hut, six feet by ten, among the laurels yonder, haulin' an' liftin' them logs herself, an' floored it, an' kivered it with brush, an' brought him to it; an' thar she stayed an' nursed him. The snow fell heavy an' hid it. Yes, it seems impossible for a woman. But not many's got my Nancy's build," proudly. "One day, when Jonathan was growin' better, Colonel Barker rode up: he war a Confederit. 'Mrs. Yare,' says he, 'thar's word come your boys hev been seen hyarbouts, an' the home guard's on its way up.' An' then he tuk to talkin' cattle an' the like with father, an' turned his back on me. An' I went out an' give the signal. An' in ten minutes Nancy came in with the milk-pail as the guard rode up. I knowed the boys war safe. Waal, they sarched the laurel for hours, an' late in the afternoon they came in. 'Colonel,' says they, 'look a-here!' So we went out, an' thar war the house. 'Who built this?' says he. 'I did,' says Nancy, thinkin' the ownin' to it was death. The tears stood in his eyes. 'God help us all!' says he. 'Men, don't touch a log of it.' But they tore it to the ground when he was gone, an' took Nancy down to Asheville, an' kep her in the jail thar for a month, threatenin' to send her to Salisbury ef she'd not tell whar the boys war. They might hev hung her: of course she'd not hev told. But it wore her—it wore her. She'd be a prettier girl now," thoughtfully, "ony for what she's gone through for her brothers. Then they arrested father an' took him to Richmond, to Libby Prison. As soon as Nancy heard that, she sent for the commandant of the post. 'Give me,' she says, 'a written agreement that my father shall be released when his four sons come into Richmond, and let me go.' So they did it."

"And the boys went?"

"Of course. They reported themselves at Asheville, hopin' that would release their father sooner. But they hed to be forwarded to Salisbury, an' held there until he was brought on."

"They were in that prison, there?"

"Yes. But they was well treated, bein' wanted for soldiers. It was in the last year, when the men war desertin' and the drafts war of no use. On the fourth day the lads war brought into the guard-house before the officers.

" 'Mr. Yare,' says the major very pleasantly. 'I believe you an' your brothers are reputed to be unusually daring men.'

" 'That I don't know,' says Jonathan.

" 'You hev certainly mistaken the object of the war and your duty. At any rate, you hev incurred ten times more risk an' danger in fighting for refugees than you would have done in the army. We have determined to overlook all the offences of your family, and to permit you to bear arms in our service.'

" 'I will never bear arms in the Confederit service,' says Jonathan quietly. You know he's a quiet man, an' slow.

"A little man, a young captain, standing by, says in a heat, 'Bah! Why do you waste words with such fellows? The best use to make of the whole lot is to order them out to be shot.'

" 'I agree with you, Mac,' says the colonel. 'It's poor policy, at this stage of the game, to tax the commissariat and put arms into the hands of un-willing soldiers.—But'—then he stopped for a minute—'you have no right to answer for your brothers, Yare,' he said. 'I give you half an hour,' taking out his watch. 'You can consult together. Such of you as are willing to go into the ranks can do so at once: the others—shall be dealt with as Captain M'Intyre suggests.'

"They took the lads back into the inside room. When the half hour was up, all but five minutes, they saw a company drawn up in a hollow square outside. They were led out thar, facing them, an' thar war the officers. It was a sunshiny, clar day, an' Jonathan said he couldn't help but think of the mountings an' his father an' me.

"Charley, he spoke first. 'Jonathan is the oldest,' he says. 'He will answer for us all.'

" 'You will go into the service?' says the major.

" 'No,' said Jonathan, 'we never will.'

"The major made a sign. My lads walked down and the soldiers pre-sented arms. The major was lookin' curiously at Jonathan. 'This is not cowardice,' said he. 'Why will you not go into the ranks? I believe, in my soul, you are a Union man!"

"Jonathan says he looked quick at the guns leveled at him, and couldn't keep his breath from comin' hard.

" 'Yes,' he says out loud. 'By God, I am a Union man!'

"Captain McIntyre pushed his sword down with a clatter and turned away. 'I never saw pluck like that before,' he said.

" 'Corporal,' said the major, 'take these men back to jail.'

"Two weeks after that Lee surrendered, an' my lads came home."

The women talked often in this way. Mrs. Denby urged them again and again to come out of their solitude to the North. "There are hundreds of men there," she said, "of influence and distinction whose lives your sons have saved at the peril of their own. Here they will always pass their days in hard drudgery and surrounded by danger."

The mother shook her head, but it was Nancy who answered in her gentle, pathetic voice: "The Yares hev lived on the Old Black for three generations, Mistress Denby. It wouldn't do to kerry us down into towns. It must be powerful lonesome in them flat countries, with nothing but people about you. The mountings is company always, you see."

The little townswoman tried to picture to herself these mountaineers actually in the houses of the men whom they had rescued from death — these slow-speaking giants clad in cheap Bowery clothes, ignorant of art, music, books, bric-à-brac, politics. She understood that they would be lonesome, and that the mountains and they were company for each other.

She lived in their hut all summer. Her baby grew strong and rosy, and the mountains gave to her also their good-will and comfort.

 Marcia

Harper's New Monthly Magazine, November 1876

One winter morning a few years ago the mail brought me a roll of MS. (with one stamp too many, as if to bribe the post to care for so precious a thing) and a letter. Every publisher, editor, or even the obscurest of writers receives such packages so often as to know them at a glance. Half a dozen poems and a story—a blur of sunsets, duchesses, violets, bad French, and worse English; not a solid grain of common-sense, not a hint of reality or even of possibility, in the whole of it. The letter—truth in every word: formal, hard, practical, and the meaning of it a woman's cry for bread for her hungry children. Each woman who writes such a letter fancies she is the first, that its pathos will move hard-hearted editors, and that the extent of her need will supply the lack of wit, wisdom, or even grammar in her verses or story. Such appeals pour in literally by the thousand every year to every publishing office. The sickly daughter of a poor family; the wife of a drunken husband; a widow; children that must be fed and clothed. What was the critic's honest opinion of her work? how much would it bring in dollars and cents? etc., etc.

I did not open the letter that day. When we reach middle age we have learned, through rough experiences, how many tragedies there are in our street or under our own roof which will be none the better for our handling, and are apt, selfishly, to try to escape the hearing of them.

This letter, however, when I opened it next morning, proved to be not of a tragical sort. The writer was "not dependent on her pen for support"; she "had vowed herself to literature"; she "was resolved to assist in the Progress of humanity." Scarcely had I laid down the letter when I was told that she waited below to see me. The card she sent up was a bit of the fly-leaf of a book, cut oblong with scissors, and the name—Miss Barr— written in imitation of engraving. Her back was toward me when I came down, and I had time to read the same sham stylishness written all over her thin little person. The sleazy black silk was looped in the prevailing fashion, a sweeping white plume drooped from the cheap hat, and on her hands were washed cotton gloves.

Instead of the wizened features of the "dead beat" which I expected, she turned to me a child's face: an ugly face, I believe other women called it, but one of the most innocent and honest in the world. Her brown eyes met yours eagerly, full of a joyous good-fellowship for every thing and every body alive. She poured out her story, too, in a light-hearted way, and in the lowest, friendliest of voices. To see the girl was to be her ally. "People will do any thing for me—but publish my manuscripts," she said.

She came from Mississippi; had been the only white child on a poor plantation on the banks of the Yazoo. "I have only had such teaching as my mother could give: she had but two years with a governess. We had no books nor newspapers, except an occasional copy of a magazine sent to us by friends in the North." Her mother was the one central figure in the world to her then. In our after-intercourse she talked of her continually. "She is a little woman—less than I; but she has one of the finest minds in the world," she would cry. "The sight of any thing beautiful or the sound of music sways her as the wind does a reed. But she never was twenty miles from the plantation; she has read nothing, knows nothing. My father thinks women are like mares—only useful to bring forth children. My mother's children all died in babyhood but me. There she has lived all her life, with the swamp on one side and the forest of live-oak on the other: nothing to do, nothing to think of. Oh, it was frightful! With a mind like hers, any woman would go mad, with that eternal forest and swamp, and the graves of her dead babies just in sight! She rubbed snuff a good deal to quiet herself, but of late years she has taken opium."

"And you?"

"I left her. I hoped to do something for us both. My mind is not of as high order as hers, but it is very different from that of most women. I shall succeed some day," in the most matter-of-fact tones. "As soon as I knew that I was a poet I determined to come to Philadelphia and go straight to real publishers and real editors. In my country nobody had ever seen a man who had written a book. Ever since I came here I find how hard it is to find out any thing about the business of authorship. Medicine, or law, or blacksmithing—every body knows the workings of those trades, but people with pens in their hands keep the secret of their craft like Freemasons," laughing.

"You came alone?"

"Quite alone. I hired a little room over a baker's shop in Pine Street. They are a very decent couple, the baker and his wife. I board myself, and send out my manuscripts. They always come back to me."

"Where do you send them?"

"Oh, everywhere. I can show you printed forms of rejection from every magazine and literary newspaper in the country," opening and shutting again a black sachel on her lap. "I have written three novels, and sent them to the ——s' and ——s'. They sent them back as unavailable. But they never read them. I trick them this a-way: I put a loose blue thread between the third and fourth pages of the manuscript, and it is always there when it comes back." Her voice broke a little, but she winked her brown eyes and laughed bravely.

"How long have you been here?"

"Three years."

"Impossible! You are but a child."

"I am twenty. I had an article published once in a Sunday paper," producing a slip about two inches long.

Three years, and only that little grain of success! She had supported herself meanwhile, as I learned afterward, by sewing men's socks for a firm in Germantown.

"You are ready to give up now?"

"No; not if it were ten years instead of three."

Yet I can swear there was not a drop of New England blood in her little body. One was certain, against all reason, that she would succeed. When even such puny creatures as this takes the world by the throat in that fashion, they are sure to conquer it.

Her books and poems must, I think, have seemed unique to any editor. The spelling was atrocious; the errors of grammar in every line beyond remedy. The lowest pupil in our public schools would have detected her ignorance on the first page. There was, too, in all she said or wrote an occasional gross indecency, such as a child might show: her life on the plantation explained it. Like Juliet, she spoke the language of her nurse. But even Shakespeare's nurse and Juliet would not be allowed nowadays to chatter at will in the pages of a family magazine.

But in all her ignorance, mistakes, and weaknesses there was no trace of imitation. She plagiarized nobody. There was none of the usual talk of countesses, heather, larks, or emotions of which she knew nothing. She painted over and over again her own home on the Yazoo: the hot still sunshine, the silence of noon, the swamp, the slimy living things in the stagnant ponds, the semi-tropical forest, the house and negro quarters, with all their dirt and dreary monotony. It was a picture which remained in the mind strong and vivid as a desert by Gérôme [1] or a moor by Boughton. [2]

There could be but one kind of advice to give her—to put away pen and ink, and for three years at least devote herself to hard study. She would, of course, have none of such counsel. The popular belief in the wings of genius, which can carry it over hard work and all such obstacles as ignorance of grammar or even the spelling-book, found in her a marked example. Work was for commonplace talent, not for those whose veins were full of the divine ichor.

Meanwhile she went on sewing socks, and sending off her great yellow envelopes, with stamps to bring them back.

"Stamps and paper count up so fast!" she said, with a laugh, into which had grown a pitiful quaver. She would take not a penny of aid. "I shall not starve. When the time has come for me to know that I have failed, I can go back to my own country and live like the other women there."

Meanwhile her case very nearly reached starvation. I remember few things more pathetic than the damp, forlorn little figure in a shabby water-proof, black sachel in hand, which used to come to my door through the snows and drenching rains that winter. Her shoes were broken, and her hands shriveled blue with cold. But a plated gilt chain or a scarlet ribbon used to flaunt somewhere over the meagre, scant poverty. Sometimes she brought news with her. She had work given her—to collect a column of jokes for a Sunday paper, by which she made three dollars a week. But she lost it from trying to insert her own matter, which could not well be reckoned as funny sayings. One day she came flushed with excitement. Somebody had taken her through the Academy of Design and a private gallery of engravings then on exhibition. She had a keen, just eye for form and color, and the feeling of a true artist for both.

"That is what I could have done," she said, after keeping silence a long while. "But what chance had I? I never even saw a picture at home, except those which were cut out of illustrated papers. There seemed to be no way for me but to write."

It was suggested to her that she might find the other way even now. Painting, designing, wood-engraving, were expressions for a woman's mind, even though, like her own, it was "one of the finest in the world."

She did not smile. "It is too late," she said. "I will go on as I have begun. But it is a pity my mother and I had not known of such things."

After that her light-hearted courage seemed to give way. She persevered, but it was with dogged, indomitable resolution, and little hope.

One day in the spring I was summoned to see a visitor on business. I found a tall, lank young man stalking up and down the room, the most noticeable point about him the shock of red hair and whisker falling over his neck and greasy coat collar. The face was that of an ignorant, small-minded man. But it was candid and not sensual.

He came straight toward me. "Is Marcia Barr here?"

"No; she has been gone for an hour."

He damned his luck in a white heat of rage, which must, I thought, have required some time to kindle. Indeed, I found he had been pacing up and down the street half the morning, having seen her come in. She had gone out by a side door.

"I caught a glimpse of her half a mile off. I have come to Philadelphia three times this year to find her. Good God! how rank poor she is! Where does she live?"

I could not tell him, as Marcia had long ago left the baker's, and changed her quarters every month.

"And I reckon I'll have to wait until she comes hyah again. Tell her it's Zack Biron, the overseer's son, on—on business."

He was not long in unveiling his business, which any woman would soon have guessed. He had come to bring Marcia home and marry her. He had always "wanted her," and the old colonel, her father, had promised he should marry her provided he could bring her back from her mad flight. The colonel was dead, and he was now "runnin' the plantation for ole madam. She's no better than a walkin' corpse, with that damned drug she chews. She can't keep still now: walks, walks incessant about the place, with her eyes set an' the skin clingin' to her bones. I couldn't 'a borne it, I ashuah you, but for the sake of findin' Marcia."

Two months passed, in which he haunted the house. But Marcia did not come. She had begun to frequent newspaper offices, and occasionally was given a trifling bit of work by the managers of the reporting corps—a description of the dresses at a Männerchor ball to write, or a puff of some coming play, etc. She came at last to tell me of what she had done.

"It is miserable work. I would rather sew the heels of stockings; but the stocking looms have stopped, and I must live a little longer, at any rate. I think I have something to say, if people only would hear it."

I told her of Biron and his chase for her.

"I saw him outside the window the last time I was here. That was the reason I went out by the side street. I knew he was looking for me. You will not tell him I have been here?"

"But, Marcia, the man seems honest and kindly—"

"If he found me," in the same quiet tone, "he would marry me and take me back to the plantation."

"And you are not ready to give up?"

"No, I will not give up. I shall get into the right groove at last," with the infectious little laugh which nobody could resist.

The water-proof cloak was worn down quite into the cotton by this time, and the straw hat had been darned around the ragged edge. But there was a cheap red rose in it. Her cheek-bones showed high, and her eyes shone out of black hollows.

"No, I have no cough, and I don't need medicine," she said, irritably, when questioned. "I have had plenty of offers of help. But I'd rather steal than take alms." She rose hastily and buttoned her cloak.

"This man Biron waits only a word to come to you. He is faithful as a dog."

She nodded carelessly. Biron, or a return to her old home, held no part in her world, it was plain to see.

I was out of the city for several months. A few weeks after my return I saw in the evening paper one day, in the usual list of crimes and casualties, an item headed "*Pitiable Case.*—A young woman named Burr was arrested yesterday on charge of theft, and taken to the Central Station. About eleven o'clock the other women in the cell where she was confined perceiving that she lay on a bench breathing in a stertorous manner, summoned Lieutenant Pardy, who found life to be almost extinct. A physician was called, who discovered that the woman had swallowed some poisonous drug. With her first breath of returning consciousness she protested her innocence of the charge. She appears to have been in an extreme state of want. But little hope is entertained of her recovery. Miss Burr is favorably known, we believe, as a writer of some ability for the daily press."

In spite of the difference of name, it must be Marcia.

When we reached the Central Station we were told that her discharge was already procured. She had friends who knew what wires to work. In the outer room were half a dozen young men, reporters, a foreman of a printing-room, and one or two women, dramatic or musical critics. There is as eager an *esprit de corps* among that class of journalists as among actors. They were all talking loudly, and zealous in defense of "little Marty," as they called her, whom they declared to be "a dunce so far as head went, but pure and guileless as a child."

"I knew she was devilishly hard up," said one, "but never suspected she was starving. She would not borrow a dollar, she had that pride in her."

Marcia was still in the cell, lying on an iron stretcher. The Mississippian, Biron, was with her, kneeling on the floor in his shirt sleeves, chafing her hand. He had taken off his coat to wrap about her.

"I've a good Quaker nurse and a room ready for her at the Continental the minute she can be moved," he whispered. "Look a-here!" turning down the poor bit of lace and red ribbon at her throat, his big hairy hand shaking. "Them bones is a'most through the skin! The doctor says it's hunger—hunger! And *I* was eatin' three solid meals a day—like a beast!"

Hunger had almost done its work. There was but a feeble flicker of life left in the emaciated little body; not enough to know or speak to us when at last she opened her dull eyes.

"None o' them folks need consarn themselves any furder about her," said Biron, savagely. "She'll come home to her own now, thank God, and be done with rubbishy book-makers. Mrs. Biron will live like a lady."

Two or three weeks later, the most splendid of hired phaetons stopped at my door, and Mr. and Mrs. Biron sent up their cards. Mr. Biron was glowing with happiness. It asserted itself offensively somehow in the very jingling of his watch chain and tie of his cravat.

"We return immediately to the plantation," he said, grandiloquently. "I reckon largely on the effect of her native air in restorin' Mrs. Biron to health."

Marcia was magnificent in silk and plumes, the costliest that her owner's money could buy. Her little face was pale, however, and she looked nobody in the eye.

"We leave for the South to-morrow," she said, calmly, "and I shall not return to Philadelphia. I have no wish to return."

"Shall I sent you books or papers, Marcia?"

"No, I thank you; nothing."

When they rose to go, her husband said, "Mrs. Biron has some—rubbish she wishes to leave with you. Hyah!" calling out of the window. "You nigger, bring that thah bag!"

It was the old black sachel. Marcia took it in her white-gloved hands, half opened it, shut it quickly, came up closer.

"These are my manuscripts," she said. "Will you burn them for me? All: do not leave a line, a word. I could not do it."

I took the sachel, and they departed. Mr. Biron was vehement in his protestations of friendship and invitations to visit the plantation. But Marcia did not say a word, even of farewell.

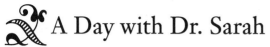

A Day with Dr. Sarah

Harper's New Monthly Magazine, September 1878

A dozen ladies were taking luncheon with Mrs. Harry Epps, of Murray Hill. That little matron's luncheons are always ideal woman's parties. This especial morning, for example.

There was plenty of space and sunshine in the pretty pale-tinted rooms. No great pictures nor distracting array of bric-à-brac. Nobody wanted to climb into regions of high art, or to admire—the day was too warm. There were flowers instead, flowers every where; a vine waving in at the bay-window. From the other windows you could hear the rustle of the trees of Central Park, and catch glimpses of slopes of grass there, of a clump of dark cedars at the base of a sunny hill, of a hedge of wistaria—a mass of snaky black arms holding up purple blooms.

Inside there was a clear feminine softness in the very atmosphere; the dishes on the table were feebly sweetish in flavor, and so was the talk. There was much good feeling and culture shown in the conversation of these delicate, low-voiced women; but an idea, naked and freshly born into the world, would have been as out of place if dragged into sight at Mrs. Epps's luncheon table as a man, or a greasy joint,[1] or the Archangel Michael with his flaming sword.

At least that was Doctor Sarah Coyt's[2] opinion as she sat in moody silence, listening to the soft ripple of talk about her. If there was one thing of which Doctor Sarah had a full supply, it was ideas. She kept a stock of them, as David did of pebbles, and was perpetually slinging them at the head of one Goliath of custom or another. The aged giants were hard to kill; indeed, her best friends hinted that her pebbles were only mud. But she fired them with desperate courage—there was no doubt of that. She had fought her way into her profession, and out of the Christian Church, and now she had clinched with Law, Religion, and Society in a hand-to-hand fight because of their treatment of woman.

When Maria Epps introduced Doctor Coyt to her friends, they felt a shock as from an electric battery, and then they all roused into pleasurable excitement. It was such a treat to see this famous creature face to face!

"I do like this sort of thing, mamma," said Margaret Whyte to her mother. "You know I went to see Jem Maco as the prize-fighter in *As you Like it*, and this woman is accounted a kind of intellectual Heenan or Morrissey[3] by the newspapers. So nice in Maria to bring her!"

"It must be true that Maria Epps is going to join the woman's rights people," said her mother, thoughtfully. "She is always aiming at the *bizarre*. You remember she was the first to drive three ponies *à la Russe* in the Park; and she went to those Moody[4] meetings. But I did *not* think she would carry her freaks as far as this."

But they were all courteous to Doctor Sarah. The courtesy, indeed, became oppressive. The very air grew clammy and heavy; all the ease, the pleasant repose, had faded out of it. The man, the greasy joint, were upon the stage now.

Visibly, Doctor Sarah was only a thin little woman in purple silk, sitting painfully erect on a straight-backed chair, her eyes glancing from one woman to another as though she were an officer, and they troops about to be drilled. Her features were delicate though worn, her eyes were sincere, sad brown eyes naturally, but they had learned a fierce trick of challenge in the rough-and-tumble fight which she had chosen to make of life. She had not said a word as yet except about her drive and the dust, but something in the flat, quivering nostril made every woman stand on guard. They felt that they were no longer Maria Epps's chance guests, lazily sipping chocolate; they were human beings—to be, to do, and to suffer.

Mrs. Epps took some pains to draw Doctor Sarah out, just as she had been careful that nobody should miss the flavor of the new salad. A novelty always gave *goût* to a luncheon or dinner.

"This talk of pictures and music must seem horribly trivial to you, doctor," she said. "We are such mere butterflies, compared to a woman with a great object in life."

Doctor Sarah smiled good-humoredly. "I find great help in music," she said, "and I paint pictures—poor ones, but they help me too. Nature and art give me a better insight into the needs of my sex."

"Doctor Coyt's object, you know," explained Mrs. Epps, beaming around the table, "is to emancipate woman."

There was a low murmur of polite assent. Mrs. Marmaduke Huff raised her eyeglasses, and courteously inspected Doctor Sarah with a gentle wonder, precisely as she had done the devil-fish that morning in the Aquarium.

"I have never had the pleasure of meeting a woman of your—your party before," said pretty Miss Purcell, softly.

"Oh, I saw several of them in London," cried Mrs. Hipple, who dressed hideously and drank beer since she came home, and fancied herself wholly

English. "It is quite a favorite *fad* with some very respectable people over there."

Then there was a sudden embarrassed pause, for every body expected Doctor Coyt to begin to defend her *fad*. But she sat silent, looking at a bit of honeysuckle which had crept in at the window. The angry red burned up into her thin cheek. Why should these people look at her as though she were the woman with the iron jaw, or some other such monster? No doubt they thought she had holes in her stockings, and went swaggering about at grog-shops. Why, her home was more womanly and fanciful than this, and she herself—

"I was in hopes, madam," said Miss Purcell, gently, "that you would give us some insight into your plans. It is we, after all, whom you should convert."

"I am no proselyter," said Doctor Sarah, with an acrid smile. She felt, as she often did, that the cause was hopeless. These frothy creatures to comprehend its great principles! Even suppose they had suffrage, what would they know of politics, of their fellow-men outside of a ball-room, or even of the money which they squandered?

In which the soured woman made the mistake which we all make when we judge of a chimpanzee, not being of chimpanzee blood. This Maria Epps, with the baby-face, had manipulated half a dozen bills through Congress last session. There was not a party wire which she did not know how to work. She had matters in train now to get Epps a foreign mission. There was not a shrewder dealer in stocks in New York than the little blonde widow, Mrs. Huff, on the other side of the table. She had made a snug fortune for herself since Marmaduke died, and had given the boys a fair start in the tobacco trade. While, as for the classes outside of society, that good Fanny Purcell had spent more time last winter in the prisons and hospitals than Doctor Sarah had done in a lifetime. Yet they all wore dresses which framed them into pictures, and they haunted curio shops, cackling about old Satsuma ware.

When they found that Doctor Sarah would not consent to be exhibited that afternoon, they went away one by one.

"Now, dear Maria," said Miss Purcell, as she kissed her hostess outside of the drawing-room door, "don't allow yourself to be entangled with that dreadful woman's set. Infidels, free-lovers—"

"Sarah Coyt is as chaste and clean-minded a woman as there is in New York," said Mrs. Epps, tartly. "Do have some charity with your religion, Fanny." Mrs. Huff hurried Fanny away.

"It is only one of Maria's political manœuvres," she said, as she seated herself in her phaeton. "Some of these woman's rights people have influence which she needs to gain Major Epps his appointment. The house will be overrun with radicals until she has secured her point, and then—Oh, we all know Maria!"

Mrs. Epps meanwhile went darting about, re-arranging the flowers, while Doctor Sarah, in her aggressive purple gown, sat bolt-up-right, watching her with a quizzical smile. Maria reminded her of a dragon-fly, with its little flutter and shine and buzz, with its poisoned sting underneath, too. She was too hard on Maria, being, like most radicals, intolerant. The little woman inside of her finesse had a hot heart and hot temper; she was just now vehemently minded to side with Doctor Sarah, because the other women had snubbed her.

"I am glad they are all gone before the business meeting commenced," she said. "You asked all the leaders of the cause to be here this afternoon?"

"Yes."

"And you go down to Washington to-night to plead the cause before a Congressional committee? Alone?"

"Yes."

"Wouldn't it be better to have a deputation—for effect, now?"

"No," she said, sharply. "I am in earnest in this matter. Who else is? I've given up my profession for it. There's not another woman in the field who gives more than half her time and energy to the cause." She talked on as if to herself, her black brows contracted, her nostrils drawn in, her eyes fixed in a fierce abstraction. "There's always an obstacle. This one must make her living by writing slipshod novels or lecturing, that one has a baby, another a dead lover to mope over. Some of our leaders have taken up the cause to gain notoriety, and some for even meaner purposes," glaring suspiciously at Maria.

"Oh dear, yes, I suppose so," said that arch little hypocrite. "And you are going to meet the committee to-morrow?" her head on one side, scanning Doctor Sarah critically. "Might I hint?—your mind is so engrossed with high matters—but you must pay some attention to your costume. I know the chairman, Colonel Hoyt, very well. A pretty woman, well dressed, can do as she pleases with him. All men are influenced by dress when women are in question. You're not offended?—it's only poor little me. But I would suggest now black velvet with a hint of scarlet. So much depends on it! I would not spare the scarlet, either."

"Yes. I did not know how much depended on it," said Doctor Sarah, smiling. It was a bitter smile. *She* had not taken up the cause to make money or notoriety out of it. Many of her colleagues laughed and fought for it as for a jolly. She never laughed. She was in as desperate earnest as ever was Luther or Patrick Henry. The newspapers all over the country jeered at her; her own sex held her off at arms-length: being a womanish woman, every jeer and snub had cut deep. But her sex, she had thought, were in as perilous a strait as was ever church or slave. She would give up every thing for them. And now that her cause was coming to a final issue, the verdict depended on a gown and its trimmings!

Two or three of the defenders of the cause had arrived by this time, and were talking apart with Maria; they held Doctor Sarah in a certain reverent awe. She never fraternized with the rest of her party, never accepted invitations to women's clubs, or posed at their public dinners.

"She is more like a wonderful machine than a human being," whispered one of her colleagues. "She makes no friends, leans on nobody, cares for nothing but the cause. Eh? Where is she going now?" For Doctor Sarah had suddenly crossed the room, and was stooping over a table. Mrs. Epps joined her, curiously. The doctor's long nervous fingers were fidgeting over a dish of mignonette and sweet-peas.

"My old-fashioned 'bow-pot,'" said Maria, smiling.

"Yes; the perfume brought me over to it. I have not seen the flowers together for many years. I used to know a man who always kept a pot of them in his room."

"It was a man that arranged these—the Reverend Matthew Niles. A poor clergyman whom we knew in Maryland. I have him up for a week's vacation, and to fit him out with some new clothes. A good creature!"

A half-quizzical, half-sad smile flickered over Doctor Sarah's sharp face. "Matthew was arranging dishes of peas and mignonette still, eh? A beggar for Major Epps's old clothes? Sentimental, effeminate, boneless creature! And I used to tremble and turn cold when the pretty fellow spoke to me. I suppose that was the disease of love. Well, I had it pretty thoroughly then," she thought. She pulled out a pea and held it to her nose. Her blood ran cold now, and her fingers shook. She could have struck them, with a rage of contempt. Why, it was twenty years ago! She had cast the man off as her inferior when she was a girl, and she had been growing ever since. What subtle physical power had this limping creature still upon her which shook her in this way? "It is my youth—my youth, which takes hold of me in him," thought the doctor, stiffening herself in her purple silk; and marching over to the table, she called for the report of the meeting in Boston.

Surely she had tested this folly of marriage, and knew what it was worth! For the doctor, as the female pioneer of the cause in the West, had married

Simon Coyt, the male pioneer, and it had not been a successful partnership. Mental qualities had balanced exactly; yet now that Simon was dead, his widow had not the slightest wish to meet him again any where on the other side of the grave.

Friend Eli Sowerby was on his feet. He was a practical, zealous little man. "We have made a wise choice in selecting Sarah Coyt to lay this matter before the committee. Yet it would be proper, in my judgment, if she would state briefly the arguments by which she will support it, that we may know precisely how she will represent us."

"I shall be guided by the suggestions of the moment in the bulk of my remarks," said the doctor; "but I can give you the principal points which I mean to make. It is only fair you should know to what I bind you."

She stood up, her hands resting on the back of a chair. She always spoke with fluency and decision, and she knew her arguments now by heart. Her thin body after a while began to glow with fiery exaltation. She rose on tiptoe, flourished her lean arms. At last the battle was at hand. She was going out alone to fight it. She was going out, like David, in the face of the conflicting hosts, her nation looking on. (Only David took his sling in the name of the Lord, and she unslung hers in the name of Sarah Coyt.)

"The American is just, reasonable in the hearing of every cause but this," she shouted, shrilly, wondering to herself at the same time what thumping noise that was in the hall, and why Mrs. Epps did not quiet it. "A woman," more vehemently, "is, first of all, a citizen. She loves, marries, by accident, but she is a citizen by inalienable right. It is her highest—"

The thumping was evidently made by a crutch. The doctor had the physician's instinct. Still gesticulating, her eye wandered to the door to see the cripple who should enter.

"She holds a legal place in the social body as a wife—a mother. But as a citizen—"

It was a child—a half-starved, shabbily dressed girl who came limping in.

"You render her—a nullity. Will nobody give that child a chair?"

The child tripped and fell headlong.

"All right," said Eli, picking her up. "Go on, doctor."

But the doctor already had the child in her lap, and was fingering her leg. "I was only about to say that the duties of a woman to the state far outweighed those which she owed as wife and mother, the latter being comparatively selfish, partial, and trivial. This child has had an attack of paraplegia, and it never has been attended to."

"What has paraplegia to do with woman's suffrage?" said Eli.

"Whose child is she? There has been the grossest neglect," continued Doctor Sarah, sharply. She rose and walked out of the room in her usual decisive fashion, the little girl in her arms. She never had entire control of herself when she had a child in her arms. When she was in the dining-room she sat down, uncovered the withered limb, and patted the thin watchful face on her breast.

"What is your name, my dear?"

"Winny Niles."

"Matthew's daughter? She might have been my child," thought Doctor Sarah. It was not her old fancy for the silly young clergyman which brought that change slowly in the expression of her sharp features as she sat holding the girl. It was the remembrance of the dead-born baby which had never lain there. The breast had been full of milk then, but the dead little lips had never touched it, and the breast had shrivelled slowly and grown hard. As Sarah held the child closer to it she remembered how hard it was, as became the mongrel creature which the newspapers called an Advanced Female.

"Bah! They know nothing about us," she broke out, hugging Winny. "You poor, patient little soul, has nothing been done for you? What has your father been about?"

"Papa has only his salary, and he helps the poor a great deal," said Winny, with dignity.

"The poor! And his child looking in this fashion! Idiot!" muttered the doctor. "Well, your mother—where was she?"

"She is dead."

A sudden heat overspread Sarah's face; she was not sorry that this woman was dead, yet assuredly she did not wish to take her place. "How many are there of you?" she said, gently.

"Four—the two boys and baby and me."

"A baby and boys," thought Sarah. "And their father as fit to govern them as a moon-calf. Well, it's none of my business. That is your father's step coming up the stairs," she said, aloud, putting the child hurriedly down. A Venetian mirror hung near them. The little doctor glanced in it quickly; there was in it a wiry, muddy-skinned, high-nosed woman in purple silk. She saw suddenly beside her a vision of a shy, rose-tinted girl, watching a young divinity student as he arranged mignonette in a pot, and she laughed to herself with a keen sense of absurdity.

The door opened, and the Reverend Matthew stood on the threshold, plump, neat, precise, from the tip of his low shoes to the folds of his lawn cravat. Above the folds of the cravat was an apple-cheeked face, full of mild good humor and feeble obstinacy. Coming up the stairs, he had met the retiring delegates to the meeting, and Mrs. Epps, who told him who was with Winny. He heard the name of the great reformer with a little conscious chuckle.

"Doctor Sarah Coyt? Tut! tut! Now, would you believe it, Mrs. Epps, that that lady was an old flame of mine? Fact! A callow fancy—calf-love, you know; had not cut my wisdom-teeth. Sarah Fetridge, she was then. But I have watched her course since with interest, in consequence. With reprobation, of course, but still with interest. I never have any thing to do with that kind of people, but I should like to see her, I confess. *Doctor* Coyt, eh? Tut! tut! Poor creature!"

Then he opened the door, and looked at her with an amused, curious smile.

"Ah, Matthew, how do you do?" Doctor Sarah nodded curtly. "Haven't seen you for twenty years, I believe. We've both grown old, eh?" holding out her hand. It shook; she could not quiet it. His was cool and soft and limp. How well she remembered the touch of it!

"On the contrary," he said, civilly, "I don't know when I have seen a woman as well preserved."

She winced. She had seen hideous caricatures of herself in illustrated papers, and laughed; why should she care when this man of all men called her "well preserved?" But she did care. The hot tears of mortification came in spite of herself to her eyes. What did it mean? Why did she quake as if with ague since he came into the room? She had no regard, no respect, for the man; he was weak, ridiculous—

Mr. Niles, who had a shrewd knack of observing trifles, saw her agitation, and began to quake in his turn. She remembered the past. She would begin to hint at love's young dream. What if she should propose to him? There was nothing which these unsexed women would not do.

Mrs. Epps came in at the moment, and he turned to her with a sense of escape. Maria began to chatter, glancing curiously at them both. She fancied that the doctor's sudden interest in Winny was explained by her old love affair with her father. But Maria was wrong. Nature adapts women to be either wives or mothers; the best of one class are not often the best of the other. Doctor Sarah, with her thin lips and broad forehead, had very few of the qualities which go to make a happy marriage; but she was a born mother. Besides, she had reached the age when the motherly instinct is strongest in any woman. She might have married Matthew now, not from love, but a protective pity—to take care of him. It was the age when Maintenon married Louis, and Margaret Fuller the Italian lad.[5]

She sat silent while Mrs. Epps and the clergyman talked of the weather, and then rose abruptly and tied on her hat; then she came up to him. A mild alarm gathered in his face: he stood on guard.

"About this child of yours, Matthew? I'm a physician, you know."

"So I have understood," repressing a smile. She eyed him a moment in silence. "Whether I deserve the name or not," she said, calmly, "matters nothing. I know enough to assure you that the child's disease is curable if taken in time, but that, if neglected much longer, she will be a helpless invalid for life. I have given up practice. But I should like to examine her again. I have taken a fancy to the little thing. Will you bring her to my house on Tuesday?"

Mr. Niles hesitated: he blushed, stammered. "Mrs.—Doctor—Coyt, I must consider the matter. I am mother and father both to the children, and, to be candid," gathering courage, "I doubt whether my wife would have risked Winny's case in the hands of so—so irregular a practitioner."

The doctor smiled—a smile which lasted a trifle too long. "I understand. I am sorry. I had taken a fancy to the child," she repeated. "Goodmorning." Mrs. Epps followed her down the stairs.

"Don't mind it, doctor. He is a bigoted little man," she said, soothingly.

"Oh, it's nothing!" Doctor Sarah replied, hurriedly. "The objection really came from his wife. Many mothers used to object to me as a practitioner because I never had a child."

When Mr. Niles and his little girl took their seats in the train that evening to return to his parish in Maryland, he saw Doctor Sarah at the other end of the car. The Rev. Mr. Abbott, one of the leaders of his Church, came in, and, much to Matthew's surprise, stopped to speak to her, and did it with marked deference. He took a seat presently beside Matthew.

"That is Sarah Coyt," he whispered. "The little woman with the strong, fine face."

"Oh yes," said Mr. Niles, giggling, "I know. One of the strong-minded sister-hood."

"She has an exceptionally clear head for business, if that is what you mean," replied Mr. Abbott. "Rides the suffrage hobby hard, I believe; but childless women must have some such outlet. But she has amassed a considerable fortune by her business tact."

"Indeed?" said Matthew, gravely. He looked at Sarah with altered eyes. He had a respectful awe of any body who could make money.

The train rolled swiftly on. Doctor Sarah talked to Eli, who accompanied her as far as Philadelphia, of her argument on the sixteenth amendment, but her eyes under her veil scanned deliberately her old lover and his child. How miserably poor they must be! Matthew did not wear now the new suit which Mrs. Epps had given him, and the child's clothes, her hair, her manner, all showed the lack of a mother's care.

"But it is no business of mine," she said.

"I leave the cause in thy hands," said Eli, parting with her at Philadelphia. "The eyes of the country will be upon thee to-morrow."

Evening was falling. The train rolled smoothly on in the soft twilight through the drowsy Maryland villages, with negroes lounging in crowds about the stations, through rich pastures crimson with clover, and the old apple orchards; over long bridges, with stretches of gray lapping water beneath, and here and there a filmy sail moving dim and spectral in the faint shine of the rising moon.

Doctor Sarah pointed them out to Matthew, who now sat behind her. "Surely a ghost sits at the rudder yonder. It might be Charon coming for us in his boat," she said.

Matthew smiled. Women were all silly and fantastic alike! But it was a kindly smile. The little man's affectionate heart smote him for his rudeness. She had meant kindness, and he had snubbed her brutally. She could not be a bad woman, when Mr. Abbott thought so well of her. He was glad when Winny went over and sat down by her. The lonely, neglected child had understood the meaning in the woman's eyes. Presently she fell asleep, and Sarah put her arm about her and drew her down on to her shoulder. Then Matthew came over to them, and the doctor nodded and smiled and pointed out Charon and his boat. After all it was comfortable to be in accord with his old friend again. It was a friendly world! That little Mrs. Epps, now, was a good Christian soul, though she had her whims. Matthew, although conscious that he was the only entirely sane person in the world, felt to-night a sense of the beauty and good-will and happiness in it as never before. Usually his little mind was kept acerb and restless by the stringent want of money. But this evening he needed nothing. He looked at the nodding passengers in the silent car with a good-humored smile, and then at the sleeping valley flooded now with the light of the risen moon. It was the time when, if he had been at home, he would have had prayers with the children. He always had the feeling, as they knelt, that their mother was near them. "The Lord is our shepherd," said the devout little man, silently. "He leadeth us beside the still waters."

The valley before him wavered giddily; there was a deafening roar, a hot rush of vapor, and then he was lying in the wet grass, the moon going out in darkness.

Doctor Sarah was unhurt. She gathered her legs and arms out of the mass of struggling bodies, and then, without a word, began to tug at Winny. The child did not move. Doctor Sarah presently caught at the arm of a burly fellow who was shouting out terrified oaths and questions.

"Try and compose yourself," she said, grimly. "We have run into a freight train, and half of us are killed. Take hold of this child. She is a cripple."

"Cripple? God help us! She's done for, then. I believe I'm not hurt," shaking himself. He drew Winny out with exceeding gentleness, and carried her to the field, followed by Sarah. "It's too late, ma'am," as he laid her down.

The doctor's practiced hands were at work. "No; she is alive, but her other leg is broken. What village is that?" For the people from the next station were crowding about the train.

It proved to be Matthew's parish. In half an hour he was carried to his own house by some of his parishioners, who seemed very fond of the little man. He was conscious, and the physicians could find no external injury.

"It is the steam which he has swallowed," said Doctor Sarah. "Bring the other children to him. It will be too late in a few minutes."

It was such a bare little house! Her keen eye took note of every mark of poverty even while she stirred a draught for the dying man. The village doctors were busy with Winny.

"It is a compound fracture," one of them said. "A case for months."

"Have these children no kinsfolk?" demanded Sarah.

"None. Poor Mr. Niles has scratched along as he could for them alone."

"And what is to become of them now, God only knows!" groaned a despondent fat mother in Israel, who held the bandages.

"The Lord will provide. He always does," said the village doctor.

The boys, ugly, manly little fellows, were brought in, terrified and half asleep. Doctor Sarah carried the baby in its night-gown, and laid her on the bed beside Matthew. But he was scarcely conscious now. "Is that you, Dot?" he said. "Papa can't romp this morning." Presently he passed his hand gropingly over her face. "Poor little Dot! O God! who is there to take care of them?"

Sarah hesitated. She remembered the cause to which she had given her life. She had been in earnest when she gave it. Then she stooped and took his hand. "I am here, Matthew," she said, quietly.

The Congressional committee met, according to appointment, and waited in vain for Doctor Sarah.

Friend Eli Sowerby was naturally indignant when he heard of it. "There is always an obstacle in the way with women," he said. "But why must it always be a man or a baby?"

# Anne

Harper's New Monthly Magazine, April 1889

It was a strange thing, the like of which had never before happened to Anne. In her matter-of-fact, orderly life mysterious impressions were rare. She tried to account for it afterward by remembering that she had fallen asleep out-of-doors. And out-of-doors, where there is the hot sun and the sea and the teeming earth and tireless winds, there are perhaps great forces at work, both good and evil, mighty creatures of God going to and fro, who do not enter into the little wooden or brick boxes in which we cage ourselves. One of these, it may be, had made her its sport for the time.

Anne, when she fell asleep, was sitting in a hammock on a veranda of the house nearest to the water. The wet bright sea-air blew about her. She had some red roses in her hands, and she crushed them up under her cheek to catch the perfume, thinking drowsily that the colors of the roses and cheek were the same. For she had had great beauty ever since she was a baby, and felt it, as she did her blood, from her feet to her head, and triumphed and was happy in it. She had a wonderful voice too. She was silent now, being nearly asleep. But the air was so cold and pure, and the scent of the roses so strong in the sunshine, and she was so alive and throbbing with youth and beauty, that it seemed to her that she was singing so that all the world could hear, and that her voice rose—rose up and up into the very sky.

Was that George whom she saw through her half-shut eyes coming across the lawn? And Theresa with him? She started, with a sharp wrench at her heart.

But what was Theresa to George? Ugly, stupid, and older than he, a woman who had nothing to win him—but money. *She* had not cheeks like rose leaves, nor youth, nor a voice that could sing at heaven's gate. Anne curled herself, smiling, down to sleep again. A soft warm touch fell on her lips.

"George!"

The blood stopped in her veins; she trembled even in her sleep. A hand was laid on her arm.

"Bless grashus, Mrs. Palmer! hyah's dat coal man wants he's money. I's been huntin' you low an' high, an' you a-sleepin' out'n dohs!"

Anne staggered to her feet.

"Mother," called a stout young man from the tan-bark path below, "I must catch this train. Jenny will bring baby over for tea. I wish you would explain the dampers in that kitchen range to her."

The wet air still blew in straight from the hazy sea horizon; the crushed red roses lay on the floor.

But she—

There was a pier-glass[1] in the room beside her. Going up to it, she saw a stout woman of fifty with grizzled hair and a big nose. Her cheeks were yellow.

She began to sing. Nothing came from her mouth but a discordant yawp. She remembered that her voice left her at eighteen, after she had that trouble with her larynx. She put her trembling hand up to her lips.

George had never kissed them. He had married Theresa more than thirty years ago. George Forbes was now a famous author.

Her fingers still lay upon her lips. "I thought that he—" she whispered, with a shudder of shame through all of her stout old body.

But below, underneath that, her soul flamed with rapture. Something within her cried out, "*I* am here—Anne! I am beautiful and young. If this old throat were different, my voice would ring through earth and heaven."

"Mrs. Palmer, de coal man—"

"Yes, I am coming, Jane." She took her account-book from her orderly work-basket and went down to the kitchen.

When she came back she found her daughter Susan at work at the sewing-machine. Mrs. Palmer stopped beside her, a wistful smile on her face. Susan was so young: she would certainly take an interest in this thing which had moved her so deeply. Surely some force outside of nature had been thrust into her life just now, and turned it back to its beginnings!

"I fell asleep out on the porch awhile ago, Susy," she said, "and I dreamed that I was sixteen again. It was very vivid. I cannot even now shake off the impression that I am young and beautiful and in love."

"Ah, yes! poor dear papa!" Susy said, with a sigh, snipping her thread. She wished to say something more, something appropriate and sympathetic, about this ancient love of her parents; but it really seemed a little ridiculous, and besides, she was in a hurry to finish the ruffle. Jasper was coming up for tea.

Mrs. Palmer hesitated, and then went on into her own room. She felt chilled and defeated. She had thought Susy would take an interest, but—Of course she could not explain to her that it was not of her poor dear papa that she had dreamed. After all, was it quite decent in a middle-aged respectable woman to have such a dream? Her sallow jaws reddened as she shut herself in. She had been very foolish to tell Susy about it at all.

Mrs. Nancy Palmer was always uncomfortably in awe of the hard common-sense of her children. They were both Palmers. When James was a baby he had looked up one day from her breast with his calm attentive eyes, and she had quailed before them. "I never shall be as old as he is already," she had thought. But as they grew up they loved their mother dearly. Her passionate devotion to them would have touched hearts of stone, and the Palmers were not at all stony-hearted, but kindly, good-humored folk, like their father.

The neighborhood respected Mrs. Palmer as a woman of masculine intellect because, after her husband's death, she had managed the plantation with remarkable energy and success. She had followed his exact, methodical habits in peach-growing and in the management of house, had cleared the property of debt, and then had invested in Western lands so shrewdly as to make herself and the children rich.

But James and Susan were always secretly amused at the deference paid to their mother by the good Delaware planters. She was the dearest woman in the world, but as to a business head—

All her peach crops, her Dakota speculations, and the bank stock which was the solid fruit thereof went for nothing as proofs to them of adult good sense. They were only dear mamma's lucky hits. How could a woman have a practical head who grew so bored with the pleasant church sociables, and refused absolutely to go to the delightful Literary Circle? who would listen to a hand-organ with tears in her eyes, and who had once actually gone all the way up to Philadelphia to hear an Italian stroller² named Salvini?

Neither of them could understand such childish outbreaks. Give a Palmer a good peach farm, a comfortable house, and half a dozen servants to worry him, and his lines of life were full. Why should their mother be uneasy inside of these lines?

That she was uneasy to-day, Susy soon perceived. A letter came from Pierce and Wall, her consignees in Philadelphia; but Mrs. Palmer threw it down unopened, though she had shipped three hundred crates of Morris Whites last Monday.

She was usually a most careful house-keeper, keeping a sharp eye on the careless negroes, but she disappeared for hours this afternoon, although Jasper Tyrrell was coming for tea, and Jane was sure to make a greasy mess of the terrapin if left to herself.

Jasper certainly had paid marked attention to Susy lately, but she knew that he was a cool, prudent young fellow, who would look at the matter on every side before he committed himself. The Tyrrells were an old, exclusive family, who would exact perfection from a bride coming among them, from her theology to her tea biscuit.

"A trifle of less importance than messy terrapin has often disgusted a man," thought Susy, her blue eyes dim with impatience.

Just before sunset Mrs. Palmer came up the road, her hands full of brilliant maple leaves. Susy hurried to meet and kiss her; for the Palmers were a demonstrative family, who expressed their affection by a perpetual petting and buzzing about each other. The entire household would shudder with anxiety if a draught blew on mamma's neck, and fall into an agony of apprehension if the baby had a cold in its head. Mrs. Palmer, for some reason, found that this habit of incessant watchfulness bore her just now.

"No, my shoes are *not* damp, Susy. No, I did not need a shawl. I am not in my dotage, child, that I cannot walk out without being wrapped up like an Esquimau. One would think I was on the verge of the grave."

"Oh, no, but you are not young, darling mamma. You are just at the age when rheumatisms and lumbagoes and such things set in if one is not careful. Where have you been?"

"I took a walk in the woods."

"Woods! No wonder your shoulders are damp. Come in directly, dear. Four grains of quinine and a hot lemonade going to bed. Walking in the woods! Really, now, that is something I cannot understand,"—smiling at her mother as though she were a very small child indeed. "Now I can walk any distance to church, or to shop, or for any reasonable motive, but to go wandering about in the swampy woods for no earthly purpose—I'll press those leaves for you," checking herself.

"No; I do not like to see pressed leaves and grasses about in vases. It is like making ornaments of hair cut from a dead body. When summer is dead, let it die." She threw down the leaves impatiently, and the wind whirled them away.

"How queer mamma and the people of that generation are—so little self-control!" thought Susy. "It is nearly time for Mr. Tyrrell to be here," she said aloud. "Can Jane season the terrapin?"

"Oh, I suppose so," said Mrs. Palmer, indifferently, taking up a book.

She was indifferent and abstracted all evening. Peter clattered the dishes as he waited at the supper-table, and the tea was lukewarm. Jasper was luke-warm too, silent and critical.

James's wife, Jenny, had come over for supper, and finding her mother-in-law so absent and inattentive, poured forth her anecdotes of baby to Mr. Tyrrell. Jenny, like most young mothers, gave forth inexhaustibly theories concerning the sleep, diet, and digestion of infants. Jasper, bored and uneasy, shuffled in his chair. He had always thought Mrs. Palmer was charming as a hostess, full of tact, in fine rapport with every one. Couldn't she see how this woman was bedevilling him with her croup and her flannels? She was apparently blind and deaf to it all.

Mrs. Palmer's vacant eyes were turned out of the window. Susy glanced at her with indignation. Was mamma deranged?

How petty the pursuits of these children were! thought the older woman, regarding them as from a height. How cautious and finical Tyrrell was in his love-making! Susy too—six months ago she had carefully inquired into Jasper's income.

Tea biscuit and flannels and condensed milk! At seventeen *her* horizon had not been so cramped and shut in. How wide and beautiful the world had been! Nature had known her and talked to her, and in all music there had been a word for her, alone and apart. How true she had been to her friends! how she had hated her enemies! how, when love came to her—Mrs. Palmer felt a sudden chill shiver through her limbs. She sat silent until they rose from table. Then she hurried to her own room. She did not make a light. She told herself that she was absurdly nervous, and bathed her face and wrists in cold water. But she could not strike a light. This creature within her, this Anne, vivid and beautiful and loving, was she to face the glass and see the old yellow-skinned woman?

She ought to think of that old long-ago self as dead.

But it was not dead.

"If I had married the man I loved," this something within her cried, "I should have had my true life. He would have understood me."

How ridiculous and wicked it all was!

"I was a loyal, loving wife to Job Palmer," she told herself, resolutely lighting the lamp and facing the stout figure in the glass with its puffy black silk gown. "My life went down with his into the grave."

But there was a flash in the gray pleading eyes which met her in the glass that gave her the lie.

They were Anne's eyes, and Anne had never been Job Palmer's wife.

Mrs. Palmer did not go down again that night. A wood fire blazed on her hearth, and she put on her wrapper and drew her easy-chair in front of it, with the little table beside her on which lay her Bible and prayer-book and à Kempis.[3] This quiet hour was usually the happiest of the day. James and Jenny always came in to kiss her good-bye, and Susy regularly crept in when the house was quiet to read a chapter with her mother and to tuck her snugly into bed.

But to-night she locked her door. She wanted to be alone. She tried to read, but pushed the books away, and turning out the light, threw herself upon the bed. Not à Kempis nor any holy saint could follow her into the solitudes into which her soul had gone. Could God Himself understand how intolerable this old clumsy body had grown to her?

She remembered that when she had been ill with nervous prostration two years ago she had in an hour suddenly grown eighty years old. Now the blood of sixteen was in her veins. Why should this soul within her thus dash her poor brain from verge to verge of its narrow range of life?

The morbid fancies of the night brought her by morning to an odd resolution. She would go away. Why should she not go away? She had done her full duty to husband, children, and property. Why should she not begin somewhere else, live out her own life? Why should she not have her chance for the few years left? Music and art and the companionship of thinkers and scholars. Mrs. Palmer's face grew pale as she named these things so long forbidden to her.

It was now dawn. She hastily put on a travelling dress, and placed a few necessary articles and her check-book in a satchel.

"Carry this to the station," she said to Peter, who, half asleep, was making up the fires.

"Gwine to Philadelphy, Mis' Palmer? Does Miss Susy know?"

"No. Tell her I have been suddenly called away."

As she walked to the station she smiled to think how Susy would explain her sudden journey by the letter from Pierce and Wall, and would look to find whether she had taken her overshoes and chamois jacket. "I hate overshoes, and I would like to tear that jacket into bits!" she thought as she took her seat in the car. She was going to escape from it all. She would no longer be happed[4] and dosed and watched like a decrepit old crone. She was an affectionate mother, but it actually did not occur to her that she was leaving Susy and James and the baby. She was possessed with a frenzy of delight in escaping. The train moved. She was free! She could be herself now at last!

It could be easily arranged. She would withdraw her certificates and government bonds from the vaults of the trust company in Philadelphia. The children had their own property secure.

Where should she go? To Rome? Venice? No. There were so many Americans trotting about Europe. She must be rid of them all. Now there was Egypt and the Nile. Or if another expedition were going to Iceland? Up there in the awful North among the glaciers and geysers, and sagas and Runic relics, one would be in another world, and forget Morris Whites[5] and church sociables and the wiggling village gossip.

"There are people in this country who live in a high pure atmosphere of thought, who never descend to gossip or money-making," she thought, remembering the lofty strains of George Forbes's last poem. "If I had been his wife I too might have thought great thoughts and lived a noble life."

She tried angrily to thrust away this idea. She did not mean to be a traitor to her husband, whom she had loved well and long.

But the passion of her youth maddened her. Job had been a good commonplace man. But this other was a Seer, a Dictator of thought to the world.

The train rolled into Broad Street station. Mrs. Palmer went to the Trust company and withdrew her bonds. She never before had come up to the city alone; Susy always accompanied her to "take care of dear mamma." Susy, who had provincial ideas as to "what people in our position should do," always took her to the most fashionable hotel, and ordered a dinner the cost of which weighed upon her conscience for months afterward. Mrs. Palmer now went to a cheap little café in a back street, and ate a chop with the keen delight of a runaway dog gnawing a stolen bone. A cold rain began to fall, and she was damp and chilled when she returned to the station.

Where should she go? Italy—the Nile— Heavens! there were the Crotons from Dover getting out of the train! She must go somewhere at once to hide herself; afterward she could decide on her course. A queue of people were at the ticket window. She placed herself in line.

"Boston?" said the agent.

She nodded. In five minutes she was seated in a parlor car, and thundering across the bridge above the great abattoir. She looked down on the cattle in their sheds. "I do wonder if Peter will give Rosy her warm mash to-night?" she thought, uneasily.

There were but three seats occupied in the car. Two men and a lady entered together and sat near to Mrs. Palmer, so that she could not but hear their talk, which at first ran upon draughts.

"You might open your window, Corvill," said one of the men, "if Mrs. Ames is not afraid of neuralgia."

Corvill? Ames? Mrs. Palmer half rose from her seat. Why, Corvill was the name of the great figure-painter! She had an etching of his "Hagar." She never looked into that woman's face without a wrench at her heart. All human pain and longing spoke in it as they did in George Forbes's poems. Mrs. Ames, she had heard, was chairman of the Woman's National Society for the Examination of Prisons. Mrs. Palmer had read her exposé of the abominations of the lessee system—words burning with a fiery zeal for humanity. There had been a symposium in Philadelphia, she remembered, of noted authors and artists this week.

No doubt these were two of those famous folk. Mrs. Palmer drew nearer, feeling as if she were creeping up to the base of Mount Olympus. This was what happened when one cut loose from Morris Whites and terrapin and that weary Jane and Peter! The Immortals were outside, and she had come into their company.

"Oh, open the window!" said Mrs. Ames, who had a hoarse voice which came in bass gusts and snorts out of a mouth mustached like a man's. "Let's have some air! The sight of those emigrants huddled in the station nauseated me. Women and babies all skin and bone and rags."

Now Mrs. Palmer had just emptied her purse and almost cried over that wretched group. That sick baby's cry would wring any woman's heart, she thought. Could it be that this great philanthropist had pity only for the misery of the masses? But the man who painted "Hagar" surely would be pitiful and tender?

"Sorry they annoyed you," he was saying. "Some very good subjects among them. I made two sketches," pulling out a note-book. "That half-starved woman near the door—see? —eh? Fine slope in the chin and jaw. I wanted a dying baby for my 'Exiles,' too. I caught the very effect I wanted. Sick child."

Mrs. Palmer turned her revolving chair away. It was a trifling disappointment, but it hurt her. She was in that strained, feverish mood when trifles hurt sharply. These were mere hucksters of art and humanity. They did not belong to the high pure level on which stood great interpreters of the truth—such, for instance, as George Forbes. The little quake which always passed through her at this man's name was increased by a shiver from the damp wind blowing upon her. She sneezed twice.

Mrs. Ames stared at her insolently, and turned her back, fearing that she might be asked to put down the window.

Mr. Corvill was talking about the decoration of the car. "Not bad at all," he said. "There is great tenderness in the color of that ceiling, and just look at the lines of the chairs! They are full of feeling."

Mrs. Palmer listened, bewildered. But now they were looking at the landscape. If he found feeling in the legs of a chair, what new meanings would he not discover in that vast stretch of lonely marsh with the narrow black lagoons creeping across it?

"Nice effect," said Mr. Corvill—"the lichen on that barn against the green. I find little worth using in the fall this year, however. Too much umber in the coloring."

Could it be, she thought, that these people had made a trade of art and humanity until they had lost the perception of their highest meanings?

"I should think," continued Corvill, turning to the other man, "you could find *matériel* for some verses in these flats. Ulalume, or The Land of Dolor. Something in that line. Eh, Forbes?"

Forbes! Her breath stopped. That fat hunched man with the greasy black whiskers and gaudy chain! Yes, that was his voice; but had it always that tone of vulgar swagger?

"I've stopped verse-writing," he said. "Poetry's a drug in the market. My infernal publishers shut down on it five years ago."

He turned, and she then saw his face—the thin hard lips, the calculating eye.

Was this man "George"? Or had that George ever lived except in her fancy?

"Mr. Forbes." She rose. The very life in her seemed to stop; her knees shook. But habit is strong. She bowed as she named him, and stood there, smiling, the courteous, thorough-bred old lady whose charm young Tyrrell had recognized. Some power in the pathetic gray eyes startled Forbes and brought him to his feet.

"I think I knew you long ago," she said. "If it is you—?"

"Forbes is my name, ma'am. Lord bless me! you can't be— Something familiar in your eyes. You remind me of Judge Sinclair's daughter Fanny."

"Anne was my name."

"Anne. To be sure. I knew it was Nanny or Fanny. I ought to remember, for I was spoons on you myself for a week or two. You know you were reckoned the best catch in the county, eh? Sit down, ma'am, sit down; people of our weight aren't built for standing."

"Is—your wife with you?"

"You refer to the first Mrs. Forbes—Theresa Stone? I have been married twice since her decease. I am now a widower." He put his hand to his mouth and coughed, glancing at the crape on his hat. His breath crossed her face. It reeked of heavy feeding and night orgies; for Forbes, though avaricious, had gross appetites.

Suddenly Job Palmer stood before her, with his fine clear-cut face and reasonable eyes. He knew little outside of his farm perhaps; but how clean was his soul! How he had loved her!

The car at that moment swayed violently from side to side; the lamps went out. "Hello!" shouted Forbes. "Something wrong! We must get out of this!" rushing to the door. She braced herself against her chair.

In the outside darkness the rushing of steam was heard, and shrieks of women in mortal agony. A huge weight fell on the car, crushing in the roof. Mrs. Palmer was jammed between two beams, but unhurt. A heavy rain was falling.

"I shall not be burned to death, at any rate," she thought, and then fortunately became insensible.

In half an hour she was cut out and laid on the bank, wet and half frozen, but with whole bones. She tried to rise, but could not; every joint ached with rheumatism; her gown was in tatters, the mud was deep under her, and the rain pelted down. She saw the fire burning on her hearth at home, and the easy-chair in front of it, and the Bible and à Kempis.

Some men with lanterns came up and bent over her.

"Great God, mother!" one of them cried. It was James, who had been on the same train, going to New York.

The next day she was safely laid in her own bed. The fire was burning brightly, and Susy was keeping guard that she might sleep. Jenny had just brought a delicious bowl of soup and fed it to her, and baby had climbed up on the bed to hug her, and fallen asleep there. She held him in her arm. James came in on tiptoe, and bent anxiously over her. She saw them all through her half-shut eyes.

"My own—flesh of my flesh!" she thought, and thanked God from her soul for the love that held her warm and safe.

As she dozed, Susy and James bent over her. "Where could she have been going?" said Susy.

"To New York; no doubt to make a better contract than the one she has with Pierce and Wall—to make a few more dollars for us. Or, an investment: her bonds were all in her satchel. Poor dear unselfish soul! Don't worry her with questions, Susy—don't speak of it."

"No, I will not, Jim," said Susy, wiping her eyes. "But if she only had taken her chamois jacket!"

James himself, when his mother was quite well, remarked one day, "We had a famous fellow-traveller in that train to New York—Forbes, the author."

"A most disagreeable, underbred person!" said Mrs. Palmer, vehemently. "I would not have you notice such people, James—a mere shopman of literature!"

Susy married Jasper Tyrrell that winter. They live in the homestead now, and Mrs. Palmer has four or five grandchildren about her, whom she spoils to her heart's content. She still dabbles a little in mining speculations; but since her accident on the cars she is troubled with rheumatism, and leaves the management of the farm and house to Jasper and Susy. She has a quiet, luxurious, happy life, being petted like a baby by all of the Palmers. Yet sometimes in the midst of all this comfort and sunshine a chance note of music or the sound of the restless wind will bring an expression into her eyes which her children do not understand, as if some creature unknown to them looked out of them.

At such times Mrs. Palmer will say to herself, "Poor Anne!" as of somebody whom she once knew that is dead.

Is she dead? she feebly wonders; and if she is dead here, will she ever live again?

Essays

# Men's Rights

Putnam's Magazine, February 1869

I have always had a perverse inclination to the other side of the question, especially if there was little to be said for it. One hates to be smothered even under truth. What if all the world, as well as our senses, say that the shield is silver? One wants the more to creep round to that solitary, dark corner yonder, and look out of the eyes of the one poor ghost who says that it is gold.

For instance: this question of Woman's Wrongs, or Woman's Needs, as I prefer to call it. It is a truth so self-evident, so weighty, that it is too late for argument about it. It finds tacit, terrible words of its own in the envious, hungry eyes of the lean women crowding in the evenings into the doors of slop-shops and arsenals; in that other mob of women, born pure as you or I, who, later in the night, stand at the street-corners, waiting—waiting; in every fresh sweet girl who carries her soul and body into the market for a husband. It is a tragedy more real to me than any other in life.

But its reality oppresses us sometimes: takes away our breath like the pêle-mêle bloodiness of Hamlet. Is there no wholesome comedy left in the world? One's heart is so sore looking at women, that it is a relief to turn to the tyrants—men, who are accused with all this misery, to find if they have not a word to plead on their side. I have a friend, a sensible young fellow, with homely practical ideas to suit his life, who fancies that men are in danger, in their turn, of losing some of their rights. His fancy has the more weight, because I think he represents the moderate and cool men, who leave the talking about this matter to those who flatter and sneer at us, or drive the women-leaders of the Rights movement into most unmanly rages by petting, and offering paper, supposing them to be refractory babies.

My neighbor, John, has neither gifts nor graces by which he will probably influence his age. He has no mania for leaving footprints on the sands of any time. He is like the majority of young men in the Middle States, mediocre in intellect, but well-meaning and industrious, hoping to make a moderate fortune, become a good citizen, husband, and father, and go through life creditably and honestly. Next week he is going into business for himself, in a small way, down on the wharf.

"So far, good," he says. "Where men are concerned, life is plain walking enough. If a man is my enemy, I knock him down, or he knocks me; if he is my friend, I give him a helping shoulder when I can, lend him money when he is hard-up, am civil to his women-folks, and, without any tears or effusion, I feel a hard tug within me when he dies. But it is the women: they have made the old landmarks marsh under our feet. I suppose it is unreasonable and the old masculine tyranny in me, but I would like to know in what relation I am to stand to them? What is my wife to be to me, or I to my wife?"

It is a state of transition with women, I tell him.

"Transition? Yes, truly! Since I began to listen to the story of their wrongs, the world is turned topsy-turvy. I'm morally sea-sick. But how long is this transition to last? Whose fault is it that it lasts so long?"

As John is one of those who come in with the mob at the end of a reform, I advise him to shut his ears to the tumult, and attend only to his business down on the wharf. But how can he shut his ears? The very air is filled with the protests of women, from France, England, and every city and village about us. Battle-cries from the stronger, groans from the weak; "outraged souls," as they style themselves, "cheated, manacled, with divine and stifled powers." No wonder that John, who is easily convinced by noise, feels, he says, like Dante looking down the ruined sweep, and believes, conscience-stricken, that these multitudinous souls are really pursued only by the cruelty of man's will.

> "On this side, and on that, above, below
> It drives them: hope of rest to solace them
> Is none, nor e'en of milder pang."

What is it they want? What is it they do *not* want? There is a savage reality in some of their needs. Suffrage, they cry; emancipation from a bondage as old as the world; equal wages and property-rights; work to save them from prostitution; and—God help us!—food for them and their children. When I hear these cries, and the wild, contradictory remedies with which they vainly rush to each other, it brings back a passage from an old book of mine.

> "And the name of the Slough was Despond: here, therefore, they wallowed for a while.
> "Then said Helpful: 'Why did you not look for the steps?'
> "'I fled the other way,' said Christian."[1]

For there never was a slough in which there were not stepping-stones, if we looked for them with common sense and a little faith in God. That is my experience.

Our grandmothers seem to have had firm ground under their feet. There is an old lady, on the other side of the fire, a keen-eyed, stiff little body, with broad, pure satin ribbon about her high cap, and a thick ring of Guinea gold on her finger—her troth-ring when she was seventeen. Girls were betrothed once then, she tells me. When she talks of her formal courtship, of the miracles of chenille-work done between the half-yearly solemn tasks of storing away pork and preserves, of the old-fashioned reverence for old age, of the mild mental intoxication provided for women in "Faber on the Prophecies," or "The Children of the Abbey," [2] I have glimpses of a life which, though narrow, was contented, clean, and decent.

What workwomen saw belonged to them then, they did without reluctance, without slighting, and without braggadocio. Is it so with us now?

But Eliza tells me, we have liberalized all that. The enfranchisement of her sex is at hand. Eliza is John's sister. I see a great many girls like her nowadays. She has pale, striking features, a skin like dough, gray, thoughtful eyes; her chest is flat; her movements and whole bearing are full of unrest, and hint subtly at suppressed power. Women are not intimate with her, though she is generous and large-natured as a lion or a fine dog, and men do not understand her. Perhaps only one ever will, and him she should marry.

The girls of her clique belong to the class who have more culture than money; but they struggle less than their mothers did to keep up appearances; even make jokes about their poverty, and parade it. They are musical or literary; some of them make specialities of bugs or German philosophy; most of them have written rejected poems for the magazines; and, although they may have just left school, I hear them, in the evenings, discussing with the men Bismarck's policy, or Herbert Spencer, or Renan,[3] with light, authoritative touches of comprehension, that leave the old lady and me behind them breathless. Whether they condemn a philosophy, or dismiss a lover, or arrange their paniers and chignons, it is done with the same careless air of *aplomb* and superiority. They would have me think that woman's brain, after its so long imprisonment, is like the vapory genie who escaped from the fisherman's iron box, in the story; there is nothing on earth or sea which it cannot cover and conquer. They are girls who do not marry early, as a rule.

John has another sister, Nelly, whom her sister deems far below the true status of women—a rosy, dimpled little dot, who is just yawning through her last year of school, with her hands full of books, and both eyes on "the beaux."

Since she was born, Nell has been brimming over with inviting little coquetries; and for my life I can see no harm in them; they are just as pure as the cooing of the birds in Spring waiting to be chosen by their mates, or the perfume of the flowers by which they silently woo one another.

The girls grow satirical when they talk of their grandmother and the lot of woman in her days. They look back upon the chenille, and pork, and preserving-work, as the butterfly on the grub from which it has escaped. They were examining some old ivory miniatures last night, and were annoyed, I saw, to find the features of these last-century women as refined as their own, and the vehicles of as subtle and strong minds. "Strange," said Eliza, as she put them away, "that they could have been contented with a life of serfdom—mere wives and mothers and house-keepers! The mental hunger of women of this age, is the trait that separates them from all others."

That last sentence seemed to me to touch the germ of the whole matter. Suffrage, or work, any of the popular cries among us, are but so many expressions of this same mental hunger or unused power.

Unused, and therefore unwholesome power. And, following, comes directly into view one marked trait about the women of the present time, as men see them, particularly those who live in large cities—a trait of which they hear but seldom. Men who flatter them, laugh coarsely at it among themselves; and men like John, to whom there is nothing on earth so worthy of reverence as a good, pure woman, look on it astonished and incredulous. He thinks secretly a great deal about the woman whom he will marry, and wonders where and how he will find her. He is awkward and shy when with them, fearing to hurt them by contact with his rough nature, believing them all to be pure and good and tender. This matter of which I speak concerns him deeply, and the men like him. But it is fitter that I, being a woman, should speak of it than he.

The most salient and apparent change in women, in the last few years (I do not say the deepest), is not advance in intelligence, marked as that may be; it is the growth in impurity. It is simply a transient effect of this roused and ungratified brain-power. The ordinary London or New York woman is too far advanced in the "progress of the age" to find employment for her awakened imagination or reason in housekeeping or in gossip; too little to turn to art or science or even downright hard business. In self-defence, then, she listens to lascivious music, or looks at the living pictures of the ballet, where her passions at least are daintily played upon. She reads, or writes, as the case may be, novels in which few of the men are honest, and none of the women virtuous, or, advancing a step farther, she finds that but a mean and ignoble life for a woman which is sacrificed to the children whom God has given her; and, on aesthetic principles, quietly does her share in building up the temples to murder, that openly face us in our most crowded streets.

I begin with an extreme case? Perhaps so. Yet hunger is not choice in its food, and there is reason to doubt whether the ordinary aliment of all women in literature or art, now, is a whit more pure and wholesome than that of men, coarse as we declare their appetites to be.

There is a class of subjects, the name of which would bring the red to the old lady's cheek yonder, but with which it is the fashion of the day to make young girls thoroughly conversant. There is no need to send Nelly out of the room now, no matter what topic the matrons may discuss. The *terra incognita* of our grandmothers is well-trodden ground to her at sixteen.

How can it be otherwise?

She finds not only men, but women, whose names are tainted, among the leaders of fashionable society; she sits beside her mother, and sees her smiling at the bald indecency of the opera-bouffe without a blush; she hears the "social evil" coolly discussed as a social necessity. It is no wonder, then, that, night after night, Nelly herself may be seen, with back and bosom half-bared, whirling and perspiring in Dick French's arms, while her mother looks placidly on. If I hint my disgust, I am told severely, that to the pure all things are pure, and that the obscene play and the waltz that sets Dick French's blood on fire, if looked on aesthetically, are, to women, refined and innocent pleasures.

I doubt if any man believes this. If, for lack of pure occupation for their brains and senses, women of society bring this offal to pollute their daily lives, they need not suppose that any affected ignorance or aesthetic sunlight will hide the real nature of the substance from the men about them. Dick French, worn *roué* that he is, has joined the school of the critic of the *Saturday Review*. He asserts that all women are represented by these. He hints that he understands the lures that these *décolleté* belles put forth.

"It's cursed hard on a fellow," he says. "The extravagance of these women won't allow a man to marry; yet they tempt him to do it with all the arts of the worst of the demi-monde." Then he and his compeers adjust their eye-glasses, and lean against doorways, criticising the paces of the delicate young girls who are whirled past, as a trader might the slaves in the market.

French goes too far. My little Nelly is not in the market; she has her secret innocent dream of true-love and marriage some day, hid away in her heart. There is not one of French's crew whom she would marry. When she unclothes herself immodestly and surrenders her person to their touch, she has no ulterior purpose beyond the intoxicating pleasure of the moment. Custom has made her eyes familiar with indecency—worm away the defensive instinct of purity with which every woman is born; but that is the worst that can be said of her. Yet, if her own blood be such ice, that the exposure of her person has no power to bring a blush to her cheek, does it matter nothing to her that pleased, unclean eyes rest on her, that half of the men who look on her mistake her motives and pity the degradation she undergoes in her effort to please them?

I use coarse language. The times are coarse. The state of society which can make a Swinburne possible, can bear a few plain words without detriment to its modesty. It is true that the evil is as yet confined to our large cities. God forbid that the fashionable fast girl of New York or Chicago should be received as the typical woman of America. She bears the same proportion to the women of the States that the feverish outbreak on the face does to the whole healthy, sweet-blooded body. But this society assumes to stand foremost in refinement and culture, and cannot object to have its claims tested. Besides, the feverish taint will spread.

Men, I think, have some claim to be heard in this matter. The most debased among them will hold one thing sacred—the honor of his wife. He has a right to demand that it come to him untainted. Dull and plain fellow as is John, he has a right to claim from the woman whom he marries, and from the mother who rears her, that she shall not have been put in the market to parade her shape like an animal; that she shall not have had her person handled by every *roué* who frequents the ball-room; that he shall not receive her hackneyed and brazen from flirtations; and that her mind shall be clean as her body.

This is a return to old-fashioned prudery. Yes. If the aesthetic culture of to-day demands the exploration of such foul fields by our young girls; and if, on the other hand, the necessity for wider careers for woman is to render motherhood the rare luxury which it has become in New England, let us, in the name of the good, pure God, go humbly back to the stagnation of our grandmothers!

I know quite well the answer ready for me. It is not *women* who have first tainted society and literature; it is not weak, starving, ill-paid women who are to blame for this Gehenna of prostitution that underlies our social fabric.

I do not think that the guilt of man has any thing to do with the responsibility of women. To our own master we stand or fall. We have always claimed to be the moral element in humanity. The claim was never made so loudly as it is now by our spokes-women. "Her right," says one of the most earnest, "is to be ministered unto in carnal things; her province is to minister in spiritual things." Another portrays venality disappearing from the courts, bribery from the halls of legislation, trickery from trade, so soon as her pure foot shall be admitted over the thresholds. "Evil shrinks away abashed before the steps of the ideal woman."

But the real? Men have a right, claims like these are made, to demand their proof. We who boast of white garments, must show them white. How can we ask for the ten talents to be given to us, when we grow less and less able to hold that one talent of purity committed to our keeping? Here is a reform more urgent than any which will follow suffrage: yet women shut their eyes to the bare facts, and hurry by.

There are other rights of men, which it would be worth our while to consider for our own sake. They are unfortunate in their manner of presenting them, it may be. It is too late for John, either to ignore his sister Eliza altogether, or to call her "a fair one," and try to tie up these very keen eyes of hers by any flimsy web of sentiment. It would suit the present posture of affairs better, perhaps, if he clapped her on the shoulder, and begged her, like a good fellow, to be done with complaining and haranguing, and look at the matter rationally, as one man with another. She has begun her argument with the peroration. The beginning of every reform has been this outcry, unrest, groping, passionate demand; but that is only the trumpet-call, the real struggle comes afterward. It is time the struggle began. So long as we cite our wrongs, and plead for standing-room in the world, we gain that tender, valueless sympathy, so readily given, because we are women: but as soon as we attempt to put our feet on the man's preempted ground, we must prove our right to every inch by the hard logic of work well done. Our stakes must be driven as deep as his before we can take his long-held territory from him. That is but fair.

To begin at the beginning: I would ask Eliza, Is it just to lay upon man the whole blame of what she calls the serfdom of woman? With but rare exceptions, she declares, they have been, in every nation, domestic slaves or petted playthings; debarred from a share in the legislation of governments, which they were taxed to support; debarred from a share in the world's work which would have made them as independent, in mind and body, as was man. Hence both mind and body are enfeebled, and marriage has become the sole approved means of earning subsistence.

I suppose it is right that all reformers must be purblind in a measure; if they only see the head of the nail they're driving, they strike the harder blows. Those words—domestic slaves and petted toys—have a ring about them which Eliza likes. She has repeated them so often that they seem to her to cover the whole ground of argument, from Sarah in Abraham's tent to the days of Mary Wollstonecraft. They seem to me as blatant as most popular cries. The condition of women in savage nations does not touch the matter with us. The larger brute makes his weaker mate grind his corn, and carry his load, in obedience to the only law he knows—that of physical force. It has been a different instinct which has hitherto assigned woman her place by the fireside in civilized countries.

Eliza calls it an unjust instinct and fraught with evil. "Man is and has always been the enemy of women," cries one of these female reformers, in a sort of unintelligible rage, which the mention of a man always rouses in her. I do not want to argue that point. It is not of importance as concerns the justice now due to women who is to blame for her past position. Only, if we were told the history of any race—who, for three thousand years, had lived in daily intercourse with another, with a chance for the same culture, with the same language, seated side by side in perfect social equality, and yet who had remained in a state of subjection, debarred from rights which they held to be theirs, we would be apt to decide, sharply enough, either that the rights were not fitted for them by nature, or that their cowardice and hesitation to grasp them deserved the serfdom. There have been women-judges, soldiers, merchants, in every country and in every time; women who were leaders in the state or in war or in trade; and the readiness with which their ground was ceded to them, the applause with which their slightest merit was welcomed, prove how easily climbed was the path they trod, and how accessible to every woman, if she had chosen to climb it.

It was not altogether the fault of the obdurate rock that it hid for so many years the rifts of manhood from the boy Theseus,[4] but his own flaccid muscles and uncertain will, which failed to overturn it. When the time to use them had come, the rock was put aside, and the golden sandals and magic sword lay beneath which were to make his path easy and clear for him. My word for it, being a real hero, and needing them for real work, he did not vent his disgust at his own weakness in rage, and kicks against the stubborn stone.

Again. Eliza, as the woman of the nineteenth century, naturally magnifies her office. It is so easy to include in one fell swoop of pity and condemnation all women who have gone before, to satirize them as pretty, half-souled lumps of matter; unable, blind to the God-given rights of which they were deprived; subject to the flatteries and wrongs of all Euphuistic tyrants, from licentious Solomon to unfortunate Doctor Todd.

But—to go to the gist and marrow of the matter—what is the real difference between Eliza and her despised great-grandmother? The women of no age have lagged far behind the men in the mental culture belonging to that age. Yet there *was* a space between the foremost man and woman in the days of "Sidney's sister, Pembroke's mother," and there is a like space now.

It is hardly fair for Eliza to flaunt in the mild faces of these ghostly ancestresses of hers, the strength which she owes to the advance of her time—an advance in which men have assuredly been the pioneers.

Putting aside this advantage, then, as irrelative, the difference between the women of the two eras is in the work which offers itself to them, not in their ability or faithfulness to their work.

The wife of the farmer in Cheshire, in County Cork, or in our own dark and bloody Kentucky ground, found as much exercise for practical knowledge, for governing power, for skilful hands and ready brain among her cows, linen-looms, or mules, as the shrewd New York girl of to-day, setting types or measuring yards of muslin. If Eliza had ever chanced to meet one of those old French women of the salons, at whom and at whose feeble imitations she rails, as at painted, useless butterflies, she would have found a new revelation in human nature to her—a something for which, beside the apparent outward graces, there had been required a variety of acquirement, a severity of mental training, an insight into human nature, and an infinite tact in the use of all her capital, which would have made up a dozen of the crude, half-taught young women who rush before the American public as its voluntary guides and instructors,—women who were true artists in their vocation, and, though they never, perhaps, lifted a pen save to write the idlest and charmingest of notes, left broad, deep traces in the world's history, became a fifth estate, with an influence as powerful and more subtle than any other.

There is a great class of women who do not belong to any rank or age, upon whom the seventh and flaming vial of Eliza's wrath is poured—women of whom my coquettish dumpling Nell is the embryo type. They look at us from every phase of art or literature, their loving, lovable faces surrounded by every halo which the hand of genius can lighten and color:

Miranda, Juliet, Rose, Bradwardine,[5] Thackeray's Amelia,[6] all of Dickens' heroines, the whole mob of perfect and silly Madonnas, are but so many exponents of the man's ideal woman, — the woman who, with accidentally more or less brain (it matters little whether less or more), lives solely in and for man; whose eyes may look outside of her home, and her hands there be moderately helpful; but who in that home lives and moves and has her being. When she comes to die, if her husband and children alone rise up and call her blessed, that is enough. She has well done a great work, and had an exceeding great reward.

Eliza, that terrible iconoclast, is sick of this stupid idol; she means to tear the pink-and-white doll down from her throne in the hearts of men, and set up the woman whom the times demand; clear-eyed, large-brained, large-hearted, fitted by nature and training to be either seeress, orator, sea-captain, or clerk in a cooperative grocery.

But men, Eliza, are mulish. They will treat you precisely as the Chinese would if you were a missionary: receive your new spiritual Deity with all politeness, with uplifted hands and gaping eyes of admiration, and the go home, and plump down on their knees before their own private little god behind the kitchen-door. The Domestic Woman has been on the throne so long, you understand? It is sheer regard for her that has made royalty itself respectable in England for half a life-time.

She is a great stumbling-block in your way, I know. She promulgates the idea that you, who talk of Woman's Rights, belong to a class of long-haired men and Bloomer-trousered women, who have lost all faith in God or George Washington, and are bent on forcing her into a cold-water pack, and marrying her daughter to the first convenient mulatto. She knows a woman who writes a book by as inevitable marks as Satan by his betraying hoof and tail: the uncombed hair, slippers down at the heel, slovenly house, and children going to perdition; There is no deceiving her on that point. During the war she was loyal, or a rebel, according to her geographical locality or the faith of her husband, though far more bitter than he. When he was killed, she and her daughters (whom she had failed to launch in the one respectable career, that of marriage), joined the great army of sewing-women, and are measurably comfortable in the meantime, as starving with the needle in one's hand is a thoroughly womanly and anti-"strong-minded" exit.

The gods themselves cannot fight against stupidity, says Eliza, and prays with all her soul that the Domestic Woman may die out, and leave no successors. But she won't die out; she won't be weeded out; she will spring up, generation after generation, like the many-headed, sweet, toothsome

clover; and there are men who, till time shall he no more, will go on pre-
ferring the clover to the stateliest tree that shades the ground—obstinate
fellows, of whom my friend John is one. He is a radical: he urges that
every career shall be opened to Eliza, with unlimited freedom of choice—
the way to the polls also; yet when he marries, it will doubtless be one of
the old-fashioned, dependent, dull women.

When Eliza has reformed a little farther, she may be clearer-sighted,
and see the uses in this familiar dear type of woman and the world-old
relations she holds. But Eliza and her class are like workmen cutting a
tunnel; just now they see nothing but the hill before them which they attack with such sounding blows: this road they make for human progress
is a necessity, they know; all civilization stands still for them to finish
it. When it is done, and they have gone farther up the heights, they will
find perhaps how wide this world is, and that there is place and need and
welcome in it, not only for this great path of progress, but for the quiet
ground that is fruitful, and for the still, well-ordered homes, whose memory lies deeper in a man's heart through life, and works greater changes
there, than visions of any shadowy mansions in a heaven which he has
never seen.

To speak plainly, I believe that the old type of the woman, whose real
life comes to her through the love of home, husband, and children, is ir-
revocably fixed by nature, in the hearts of all men and the majority of
women, as the highest and best, and that the chief obstacle in the way of
obtaining new work and wider careers for us now, is the mistake of our
spokeswomen in ridiculing that old figure, and in declaring such work and
careers incompatible with it. The quiet, retiring home-wife and home-
mother, with her strength or her silliness, all men have tried and tested,
but this new creature, who has no blush, whether her words are heard by
one or a thousand, vociferously claiming to be man's equal, politically and
in mental stature, and his superior spiritually, is, justly or not, a something
utterly distasteful to the masculine mind. It forgets that the women who
have been most *efficient* in help to the last century, have been personally
unknown to the crowd. It reasons the matter out briefly enough. "If this is
to be the result of making my daughter a clerk or engraver or physician, let
her, in God's name, stay at home, and take the only chance for women—
get a husband, if she can."

And the daughter, in whose heart, after all, the strongest cord throbs
at the thought of husband and child, is afraid, for that reason, to render
herself distasteful to men, hesitates to throw away her chance, and stays at
home, a heavy burden perhaps, both brain and body diseased from idle-

ness, and work waiting for her without. If the husband does not come soon, the innocent dream of true love and marriage begins to fade out; she feels herself the one too many, at home and abroad, a mistake in life — the solitary one of God's creatures who has neither use nor tie, and is in the world on sufferance. So she marries, if she can, any body that she can. She has a vague feeling that she is guilty of legal prostitution. But it would be so sweet to have a place as other women, a home and a baby of one's own! So the bargain and sale goes on.

There is a fatal flaw in the working of the social machine; here are the workers, and there the work. Yet the prejudice of men keeps them apart. A woman who chooses to work believes that she must lose caste, the chance of marriage, be ridiculed and underpaid. And for this prejudice against the new position for women, the noisy vehemence and unwise boasts of the leading reformers, is, I fear, responsible.

Yet mistaken though they may be in minor points, no woman ought to have for them one word that is not grateful. They are pioneers in the hardest and noblest work of the age in this country, next to the abolition of slavery. If they suppose that it is a new path that is needed for woman, rather than a widening of the old one, it is an error which time and nature will set right.

The facts of the case are so plain that the weakest girl can understand them. The number and the helplessness of our sex have become a drag in the country. There is a large surplus, in every state, of women who have no man on whom to lean for support. The old prescribed methods, of sewing and teaching, will not provide one eighth of them with food; and they must live. That is the urgent and immediate necessity. More work, and more wages.

Suffrage and property-laws are of secondary importance.

Whether the necessity for new occupations for woman is an outgrowth of these circumstances solely, or also a demand of her enlarged mental power, matters very little; the problem to be solved is whether the old idea of woman is to be displaced by them. Sneer as the reformer will at the "fireside angel" or the "sanctity of home," these catch-words are hints of an almost universal and vital reality of feeling, whose opposition is the great intangible difficulty in her way to-day. Look closely for a moment or two, and see how this acts.

Eliza is almost past the age for marriage. There is a strong inbred truth in the girl that has hindered her from marrying for a settlement. There are two or three servants employed in the house, so that she has no work to do beyond making her own dresses and hats. Her father is an old, gray-headed man, who has reached that age when he should have time to take breath, after his long life's work, before he goes hence and is seen no more. But he has not time; he works harder than ever. There are two girls besides Eliza and Nelly, and they must be dressed and maintained in a certain style, to make suitable marriages. He goes early to work and comes back late, feeble and anxious, while they are stitching at the old dresses and hats, to make them look like new ones (for they help him all they can), and then go out to dance the German, or make that husband-market in any other customary way. But they do no more than this, for fear of losing caste, though there is no one of them who has not a stronger brain and sounder body than either father or brother. Some day the old man will die, on whom they have been content to rest this heavy weight till the last. There is an insurance on his life of a few thousand dollars; and on that, I suppose, they will eke out an anxious, scanty living, half-starving indoors to keep up the miserable show of gentility, cherishing every lingering, poor remnant of beauty, in the hope of making even yet that approved disposition of themselves, balked at every turn by the want of a few dollars, their natural tastes stifled and ungratified, their natural power left unused to gnaw and torture them within to the end.

But with Eliza's progressive ideas, she cannot be cowed by the fear of losing caste? Not altogether; her difficulty is of another kind. She is what is called a capable woman—shrewd, quick-sighted cool and prompt in action, thoroughly fitted for trade; if she had been born a boy, she would, by this time, have made for herself a steady-growing business, and been known in the stock-market as a live man. But she has the mania of all intelligent girls for becoming a teacher of the public. She writes poems, sapped out of Emerson and Walt Whitman; argues for suffrage in season and out, giving weak dilutions of Mrs. Dall's[7] powerful, downright logic. She is in doubt whether to begin lecturing, or to go on the stage and restore the legitimate drama. But to open a bookstore, or to learn the fur-business as a clerk!

As an almost invariable rule, the young woman, nowadays, who feels within herself a hunger for some other work than that of her hands, believes herself qualified, by right of that hunger, for the very highest work. She must leap into the pulpit or the rostrum, or not leap at all—forgetting the innumerable trades, head-and-hand crafts that lie beneath, in which the majority of men find ample fields for all their observation, skill, and ingenuity. She forgets that the spirit of God filled Bezaleel to enable him to devise cunning works in gold and silver and brass, as much as it did Aaron, who spoke well for Him. She is dazzled by the stately journey of such a life as Lucretia Mott's,[8] and the great triumph that came to close that work to which she was called, and does not understand that they only labor worthily who confine themselves to the labor for which they are qualified, whether it be that of freeing a people or of blacking boots.

I feel how unfitted I am to give an opinion on a subject to which such women as Caroline Dall have nobly devoted years of research and labor; yet I cannot but fear that, in their struggle to lift their sex up to a higher ground, they will place us where we are not yet ready to stand. Why should women, for example, be urged to press into the pulpit as into the other learned professions? The humblest among us is called of God to preach His gospel in action; but preaching it in words is another thing. It is taking a portion of the water of life and passing it through the conduit of our own individual thought and character. It is not a mere pious intention to do good, or a few years' drudgery over Hebrew and Greek or Articles and Confessions, that can justify a man in elevating himself as an exponent of divine truth. One needs only to listen to the dull platitudes that fall so far wide of the wants of the age, to the differing acrid dogmatisms, to the truisms, old and sapless and dry, which are dealt out to us Sunday after Sunday, from too many pulpits, to feel the truth of this. If the most cultured and enlightened class of men in the cities are, as a rule, *not* members of the Christian church, if the highest successes in the cause of universal brotherhood of late years have been achieved under the name of Humanity instead of Jesus, it is because there is too much of this kind of preaching; because earnest and thoughtful men have been turned away from that Helper whose teaching solves the problem of this time as of every other, by the shallow verbiage in the pulpit of many of the men who, in their home-lives, are not unfitted to be His ministers.

I confess that I, for one, will be sorry when women are admitted into the paid ministry. Not that to some of them, as to some men, the message may not come which will burn in the soul until it be delivered, or life teach some individual lesson which may be fit for the healing of other souls. When that is the case, they will speak. God's true messengers, in all ages, have found utterance. But the salary, and the respectable position attached to the professional salvation of soul, would, under present circumstances, be more of a temptation to ordinary women than it has even proved to men; and a woman would be less likely to forget herself in the pulpit, be more apt to be swayed by a love of approbation than her brother, and so lower the standard of the Christian religion even more than he has done.

I may be wrong in this. But as man has been so ready to rush with hasty steps into this sacred office, only to show so often his own weakness and to bring it into disrepute, let us not be in haste to follow him.

I would be less eager than Eliza, too, to claim what she vehemently terms her natural and inalienable right of suffrage. It galls her beyond endurance, on election-day, to watch ignorant, drunken boors—Dutch Jake and Irish Jim—crowding to the polls, while she is forced to sit at home, passive and useless. It seems to me that if Eliza's motive is the good of her country, she might be contented to stay away from the ballot-box, if she must take with her the wives of Jake and Jim, invariably more ignorant than their husbands of politics. It does not anger me so much that "women, negroes, and idiots" are together debarred the use of the ballot, so long as neither women, negroes, nor idiots, are, as a mass, fitted to use it intelligently.

Of what avail would it be to throw heavier weights of ignorance headlong into the political scale, only for a few skilful hands to arrange and manipulate, precisely as they are doing now? When the right of suffrage is restricted to all by a certain amount of education, and thus the intelligent mind of the country made its dominant power instead of the gross matter-weight of sex and color, women and negroes may contentedly take their share in the government, both to its benefit and their own. My sympathies, I confess, are in no case so much with the prominent women of the country who aim at higher work, and whose every step wins prompter notice because they are women, so much as with the great mass of ordinary dull wives and young girls who are stumbling about in the slough because they cannot see the steps the fifty thousand sewing-hands in New York; the seventy thousand intelligent women in New England, for whom there are literally no husbands, for whom Mrs. Stowe urges domestic service; but more than all, the countless young, educated girls in struggling families, through the whole country, whose brothers are healthily and happily at work; while they are indoors, their brains idle, morbid, discontented, shut into this narrow cell by the rules of respectable gentility, waiting for the husband, who may never come.

If I had as many daughters as those with whom the Lord rewarded Job, and twice his wealth, they should each one have some head-or-hand craft by which, if need were, they could earn their own living. So far at least, like him, I would give them inheritance among their brethren.

Here, in one house, is a brother who has quietly set aside all thought of marriage for himself, for the sake of two sisters, who are dependent upon him—a generous, noble act, though common enough. The girls accept it from "Charley" with selfish indifference, as a matter of course; and Charley's generosity does not hinder him from gradually sliding into loose old-bachelor ways, and seeking in haunts of which they have never heard even the names, amusement and excitement, of which, if he had a wife and children, he would never have felt the need.

Take Mrs. A——, for instance, a book-keeper's wife, a woman with a better head for business than her husband. He has a salary of $800, out of which a family of five are to be fed, clothed, and educated. Two of the boys are scholarly, clear-brained fellows, whom it was poor A——'s one dream of ambition to educate thoroughly and give a fair chance in life. They have both begun to learn a trade, as, being boys, they must do something to help keep the wolf from the door. Their mother has made a slave of herself; is a lean, haggard woman in middle age; has done her own work of cooking, sewing, nursing, to save the scanty eight hundred dollars. Was that the best she could have done?

"Is there no advice you can give me?" writes a young girl. "I have enough of money on which to live. I never yet have seen the man whom I wished to marry. I am as intelligent and well-taught as my brothers. Would they be content to occupy their lives with a round of visiting, in a small country-town, with purposeless, unused study or fancy-work? I cannot write essays or tales; I have nothing especial to say in them. I don't succeed in teaching; I am not naturally benevolent or fond of children. Yet I think there is some strength in me. Did God make me for nothing? Surely, somewhere in the world, there is work for me to do!"

The work for her and for all of us to do is under our feet, in our hands. There are the steps out of the slough, which we will not see. Women all stand waiting for some grand movement to be made, which is to give them relief: suffrage to be granted, medical schools to be opened, Vassar Colleges established in every State, cooperative housekeeping to be inaugurated, and the myriad of house-worries taken off their hands. The only help for each woman who wants work lies in herself. She lives, perhaps, in some small inland town. There is no opening for a teacher, if she even is thorough enough for one; sewing pays poorly; she has sent articles to the *Atlantic* and *Harper*, and never heard of them again. Very likely. How many men are fitted for teachers, or tailors, or authors?

What can she do? or rather, what does some turn of mind or expertness of hands hint that she could best learn to do? What would she turn to if she were a man? To trade or farming, engraving, printing, stenography, dealing in drugs or cutlery, making chairs or photographs, raising bees or hanging paper? Whatever it be, let her begin it now, as quietly as she can, and in as humble a fashion as is necessary, learning that trade as a man would do. Miss Penny,[9] in a book published this year, gives five hundred suitable employments for women. I would reduce the number to three hundred and sixty, as those easily practicable, and in which women in England and this country have actually been engaged.[10]

"But what would people say?"

I do not think the question a weak one. I understand the shrinking soreness of heart with which a woman cowers before the tumult of wonder and sarcasm and jeers which she supposes will hail her appearance before the public.

It will depend entirely upon yourself what they will say. If you are quiet, straightforward, and in earnest, most probably they will say very little about you. The world is quick to recognize a true motive or a sensible act, and receive it as a matter of course. The higher the order of people to whom you belong, the less likely they are to be prejudiced by your action. The higher you stand, therefore, the easier and the more incumbent upon you is the duty that lies before you.

There is no use in railing against a prejudice; it must be lived down. Every woman who pursues an unusual work, steadily and faithfully, and shows that she can remain as modest, gentle, and tender as when she plied the needle or cooked the home-dinner, is doing a real service for her sex, very different from vague, frenzied citations of the Bible and Constitution to prove woman the equal of man.

It is just in this step of your course that Man's Right opposes you. There is one hard fact which we women are apt to shirk, but which we must face after all, and that is, that in the pitiless economics of nations the question is not the worker but the value of the work. Wages are given for the wages' worth, not for sentiment. If the wheat you bring into market is poor, your pay will be poor; and it is sheer folly for you to point to your pale face, or to boast of first-rate grain raised in another country by one of your family. How can that make yours worth another penny in the pound?

Before you take man's work from him, you must prove that you can do it as well as he. In that proof lies your great obstacle. Offer yourself as a clerk or apprentice to any business in your own town; if you have capital, embark in any business, and the chances are that you will have a fair field to try your chance. But after that, you will be measured strictly by the same rules that determine the value of men as laborers; and it is but just to them that you should be. If you accept work as a makeshift, a means to an end, giving it as little service as may be, it is right you should be pushed aside by those whose heart is in it. Art may be as truly worshipped in a carpenter's shop or laundry-room as in the sculptor's *atelier*, and however humble the offering may be, she is as jealous of service in one place as the other.

"Young girls," says a New York editor, "who take up the business of printing hoping to be freed from it by marriage, or widows who mean to make it serve only until their sons are able to support them, cannot be expected to turn out as thorough work as men, whose business it is to be for life." That they do not, is proved by the re-employment of men by some of the largest printing establishments, in spite of their desire to free themselves from the trammels of the printers' union by the service of females.

It is enough to dishearten any advocate for women's claim to wider work, to see the listlessness and impatience with which such work is too often done when found. Look at the incivility and indifference of the female-clerk, compared to the man who stands behind the counter with her!

"But that is to be his business; some day he hopes to be a partner; he is making capital for himself out of your good-will."

Precisely. Why should it not be her business? Why should she not become an active as well as passive helpmeet for her husband? Suppose Mrs. A—— puts her skill in drawing to account as a designer or watch-engraver; or that good housekeeper, Mrs. B——, employed fifty women, instead of one, in canning fruit; or Mrs. C——, in place of her bit of kitchen-garden, hired an acre in addition, and cleared one or two thousand a-year in raising herbs for the drug-market—all employing competent servants to do their cooking and sewing: would they not benefit both husband and children, as much by remaining, as they are now, maids of all work?

"But we are always underpaid," urges the trembling coward on the brink, afraid to make the plunge. This is but measurably true. As a rule, when the work is proved to be equal to a man's there is no difference in the wages. When Rosa Bonheur,[11] or Jean Ingelow,[12] or Fanny Kemble,[13] bring their wares into market, the question of sex does not suggest itself with that of payment. In cases where it does suggest itself, the remedy is in your own hands. Make your work equal to a man's, and then exact his rate of payment. Take not a penny less—because you are a woman. However weak you may be, you owe this much service to all other women. It is another right of the man that we should not underbid him in the market, and one which we will willingly cede to him.

After all, this reform, like any other, will not be builded like Solomon's temple of old, with silence and devout aspirations; there is squabbling and dirt and mortar flying enough to make us think that the foundations of the world are broken up. But when the work is done and the rubbish cleared away, the world will be just as it was; there will only be a more comfortable dwelling in it, a house with higher roof and wider windows than served our grandmothers. The sky above it and the human beings who found the larger dwelling in their improved circumstances necessary and pleasant, will be substantially the same.

My friend John may possess his anxious soul in patience. There are women, as well as men, who will remain unmarried, or who, married, seem to be sent with a general rather than especial mission—a "Thus saith the Lord" to deliver to all the people rather to one or two of His little children. Why should they not fulfil their errand? Why should not the way be made clear for them? But, taking us altogether, we are shaped very much as were all the generations of women who have gone before us; and in this very fashioning of both our bodies and minds show that the best and highest duties in life are those of wife and mother. We are not moving, as yet, *en masse* upon the polls or the retail-trade; nor are we demolishing our little kitchen-stoves which we bought when we were married, to plunge into the vast conglomerated cooking partnership. A good thing, no doubt, when it is a necessity; but these universal schemes, wherein every dish of potatoes and turnips is to be dipped out of a general pot instead of being cooked to suit Will's or Tom's particular taste; wherein every woman finds herself a mother, not to her own especial baby, but spiritually to the whole of the rest of mankind, are chilly—very chilly to the weaker among us.

John may choose his wife, and be very sure that she will find her little home as dear, will spoil her husband, and overrate her baby as much as any woman from Eve down.

And if he gives her *all* the work for which her brain and hands are fitted, he will find her a less morbid, sickly wife, less likely to gloat over Offenbach, and brood over possible new elective affinities for herself; he will find her, in every sense, more helpful, and more certain to place him and her baby where they ought to be, next in her duty to her God.

A Faded Leaf of History

Atlantic Monthly, January 1873

One quiet, snowy afternoon this winter, I found in a dark corner of one of the oldest libraries in the country a curious pamphlet. It fell into my hands like a bit of old age and darkness itself. The pages were coffee-colored and worn thin and ragged at the edges, like rotting leaves in fall; they had grown clammy to the touch, too, from the grasp of so many dead years. There was a peculiar smell about the book which it had carried down from the days when young William Penn went up and down the clay-paths of his village of Philadelphia, stopping to watch the settlers fishing in the clear ponds or to speak to the gangs of yellow-painted Indians coming in with peltry from the adjacent forest.

The leaves were scribbled over with the name of John,—"John," in a cramped, childish hand. His father's book, no doubt, and the writing a bit of boyish mischief. Outside now, in the street, the boys were pelting each other with snowballs, just as this John had done in the clay-paths. But for nearly two hundred years his bones had been crumbled into lime and his flesh gone back into grass and roots. Yet here he was, a boy still; here was the old pamphlet and the scrawl in yellowing ink, with the smell about it still.

Printed by Rainier Janssen, 1698. I turned over the leaves, expecting to find a sermon preached before Andros, "for the conversion of Sadducees," or some "Report of the Condition of the Principalities of New Netherland, or New Sweden, for the Use of the Lord's High Proprietors thereof" (for of such precious dead dust this library is full); but I found, instead, wrapped in weighty sentences and backed by the gravest and most ponderous testimony, the story of a baby, "a Sucking Child six Months old." It was like a live seed in the hand of a mummy. The story of a baby and a boy and an aged man, in "the devouring Waves of the Sea; and also among the cruel devouring Jaws of inhuman Canibals." There were, it is true, other divers persons in the company, by one of whom the book is written. But the divers persons seemed to me to be only part of that endless caravan of ghosts that has been crossing the world since the beginning; they never can be anything but ghosts to us. If only to find a human interest in them, one would rather they had been devoured by inhuman cannibals than not. But a baby and a boy and an aged man!

All that afternoon, through the dingy windows of the old building, I could see the snow falling soft and steadily, covering the countless roofs of the city, and fancying the multitude of comfortable happy homes which these white roofs hid and the sweet-tempered, gracious women there, with their children close about their knees. I thought I would like to bring this little live baby back to the others, with its strange, pathetic story, out of the buried years where it has been hidden with dead people so long, and give it a place and home among us all again.

I only premise that I have left the facts of the history unaltered, even in the names; and that I believe them to be, in every particular, true.

On the 22d of August, 1696, this baby, a puny, fretful boy, was carried down the street of Port Royal, Jamaica, and on board the "barkentine" Reformation, bound for Pennsylvania; a Province which, as you remember, Du Chastellux,[1] a hundred years later, described as a most savage country which he was compelled to cross on his way to the burgh of Philadelphia, on its border. To this savage country our baby was bound. He had by way of body-guard, his mother, a gentle Quaker lady; his father, Jonathan Dickenson, a wealthy planter, on his way to increase his wealth in Penn's new settlement; three negro men, four negro women, and an Indian named Venus, all slaves of the said Dickenson; the captain, his boy, seven seamen, and two passengers. Besides this defence, the baby's ship was escorted by thirteen sail of merchantmen under convoy of an armed frigate. For these were the days when, to the righteous man, terror walked abroad, in the light and the darkness. The green, quiet coasts were but the lurking-places of savages, and the green, restless seas more treacherous with pirates. Kidd had not yet buried his treasure, but was prowling up and down the eastern seas, gathering it from every luckless vessel that fell in his way. The captain, Kirle, debarred from fighting by cowardice, and the Quaker Dickenson, forbidden by principle, appear to have set out upon their perilous journey, resolved to defend themselves by suspicion, pure and simple. They looked for treachery behind every bush and billow; the only chance of safety lay, they maintained, in holding every white man to be an assassin and every red man a cannibal until they were proved otherwise.

The boy was hired by Captain Kirle to wait upon him. His name was John Hilliard, and he was precisely what any of these good-humored, mischievous fellows outside would have been, hired on a brigantine two centuries ago; disposed to shirk his work in order to stand gaping at black

Ben fishing, or to rub up secretly his old cutlass for the behoof of Kidd, or the French when they should come, while the Indian Venus stood by looking on, with the baby in her arms.

The aged man is invariably set down as chief of the company, though the captain held all the power and the Quaker all the money. But white hair and a devout life gave an actual social rank in those days, obsolete now, and Robert Barrow was known as a man of God all along the coast-settlements from Massachusetts to Ashley River,[2] among whites and Indians. Years before, in Yorkshire, his inward testimony (he being a Friend) had bidden him go preach in this wilderness. He asked of God, it is said, rather to die; but was not disobedient to the heavenly call, and came and labored faithfully. He was now returning from the West Indies, where he had carried his message a year ago.

The wind set fair for the first day or two; the sun was warm. Even the grim Quaker Dickenson might have thought the white-sailed fleet a pretty sight scudding over the rolling green plain, if he could have spared time to his jealous eyes from scanning the horizon for pirates. Our baby, too, saw little of sun or sea; for being but a sickly baby, with hardly vitality enough to live from day to day, it was kept below, smothered in the finest of linens and the softest of paduasoy.[3]

One morning when the fog lifted, Dickenson's watch for danger was rewarded. They had lost their way in the night; the fleet was gone, the dead blue slopes of water rolled up to the horizon on every side and were met by the dead blue sky, without the break of a single sail or the flicker of a flying bird. For fifteen days they beat about without any apparent aim other than to escape the enemies whom they hourly expected to leap out from behind the sky line. On the sixteenth day, friendly signs were made to them from shore. "A fire made a great Smoak, and People beckoned to us to putt on Shoar," but Kirle and Dickenson, seized with fresh fright, put about and made off as for their lives, until nine o'clock that night, when seeing two signal-lights, doubtless from some of their own convoy, they cried out, "The French! the French!" and tacked back again as fast as might be. The next day, Kirle being disabled by a jibbing boom, Dickenson brought his own terrors into command, and for two or three days whisked the unfortunate barkentine up and down the coast, afraid of both sea and shore, until finally, one night, he run her aground on a sand-bar on the Florida reefs. Wondering much at this "judgment of God," Dickenson went to work. Indeed, to do him justice, he seems to have been always ready enough to use his burly strength and small wit, trusting to them to carry him through the world wherein his soul was beleaguered by many inscrutable judgments of God and the universal treachery of his brother-man.

The crew abandoned the ship in a heavy storm. A fire was kindled in the bight of a sand-hill and protected as well as might be with sails and palmetto branches; and to this, Dickenson, with "Great trembling and Pain of Hartt," carried his baby in his own arms and laid it in its mother's breast. Its little body was pitiful to see from leanness, and a great fever was upon it. Robert Barrow, the crippled captain, and a sick passenger shared the child's shelter. "Whereupon two Canibals appeared, naked, but for a breech-cloth of plaited straw, with Countenances bloody and furious, and foaming at the Mouth"; but on being given tobacco, retreated inland to alarm the tribe. The ship's company gathered together and sat down to wait their return, expecting cruelty, says Dickenson, and dreadful death. Christianity was now to be brought face to face with heathenness, which fact our author seems to have recognized under all his terror. "We began by putting our trust in the Lord, hoping for no Mercy from these bloody-minded Creatures; having too few guns to use except to enrage them, a Motion arose among us to deceive them by calling ourselves Spaniards, that Nation having some influence over them"; to which lie all consented, except Robert Barrow. It is curious to observe how these early Christians met the Indians with the same weapons of distrust and fraud which have proved so effective with us in civilizing them since.

In two or three hours the savages appeared in great numbers, bloody and furious, and in their chronic state of foaming at the mouth. "They rushed in upon us, shouting 'Nickalees? Nickalees?' (Un Ingles.) To which we replied 'Espania.' But they cried the more fiercely 'No Espania, Nicka-lees!' and being greatly enraged thereat, seized upon all Trunks and Chests and our cloathes upon our Backs, leaving us each only a pair of old Breeches, except Robert Barrow, my wife, and child from whom they took nothing." The king, or Cassekey, as Dickenson calls him, distinguished by a horse-tail fastened to his belt behind, took possession of their money and buried it, at which the good Quaker spares not his prayers for punishment on all pagan robbers, quite blind to the poetic justice of the burial, as the money had been made on land stolen from the savages. The said Cassekey also set up his abode in their tent; kept all his tribe away from the woman and child and aged man; kindled fires; caused, as a delicate attention, the only hog remaining on the wreck to be killed and brought to them for a midnight meal; and, in short, comported himself so hospitably, and with such kindly consideration toward the broad-brimmed Quaker, that we are inclined to account him the better bred fellow of the two, in spite of his scant costume of horse-tail and belt of straw. As for the robbery of the ship's cargo, no doubt the Cassekey had progressed far enough in civilization to know that to the victors belong the spoils. Florida, for two years, had been stricken down from coast to coast by a deadly famine, and in all probability these cannibals returned thanks to whatever God they had for this windfall of food and clothes devoutly as our forefathers were doing at the other end of the country for the homes which they had taken by force. There is a good deal of kinship among us in circumstances after all, as well as in blood. The chief undoubtedly recognized a brother in Dickenson, every whit as tricky as himself, and would fain, savage as he was, have proved him to be something better; for, after having protected them for several days, he came into their tent and gravely and with authority set himself to asking the old question, "Nickalees?"

"To which, when we denied, he directed his Speech to the Aged Man, who would not conceal the Truth, but answered in Simplicity, 'Yes.' Then he cried in Wrath 'Totus Nickalees!' and went out from us. But returned in great fury with his men and stripped all Cloathes from us."

However, the clothes were returned, and the chief persuaded them to hasten on to his own village. Dickenson, suspecting foul play as usual, insisted on going to Santa Lucia.[4] There, the Indian told him, they would meet fierce savages and undoubtedly have their throats cut, which kindly warning was quite enough to drive the Quaker to Santa Lucia headlong. He was sure of the worst designs on the part of the cannibal, from a strange glance which he fixed upon the baby as he drove them before him to his village, saying with a treacherous laugh, that after they had gone there for a purpose he had, they might go to Santa Lucia as they would.

It was a bleak, chilly afternoon as they toiled mile after mile along the beach, the Quaker woman far behind the others with her baby in her arms, carrying it, as she thought, to its death. Overhead, flocks of dark-winged grakles swooped across the lowering sky, uttering from time to time their harsh foreboding cry; shoreward, as far as the eye could see, the sand stretched in interminable yellow ridges, blackened here and there by tufts of dead palmetto-trees; while on the other side the sea had wrapped itself in a threatening silence and darkness. A line of white foam crept out of it from horizon to horizon, dumb and treacherous, and licked the mother's feet as she dragged herself heavily after the others.

From time to time the Indian steathily peered over her shoulder, looking at the child's thin face as it slept upon her breast. As evening closed in, they came to a broad arm of the sea thrust inland through the beach, and halted at the edge. Beyond it, in the darkness, they could distinguish the yet darker shapes of the wigwams, and savages gathered about two or three enormous fires that threw long red lines of glare into the sea-fog. "As we stood there for many Hour's Time," says Jonathan Dickenson, "we were assured these Dreadful Fires were prepared for us."

Of all the sad little company that stand out against the far-off dimness of the past, in that long watch upon the beach, the low-voiced, sweet-tempered Quaker lady comes nearest and is the most real to us. The sailors had chosen a life of peril years ago; her husband, with all his suspicious bigotry, had, when pushed to extremes, an admirable tough courage with which to face the dangers of sea and night and death; and the white-headed old man, who stood apart and calm, had received, as much as Elijah of old, a Divine word to speak in the wilderness, and the life in it would sustain him through death. But Mary Dickenson was only a gentle, commonplace woman, whose life had been spent on a quiet farm, whose highest ambition was to take care of her snug little house, and all of whose brighter thoughts or romance or passion began and ended in this staid Quaker and the baby that was a part of them both. It was only six months ago that this first-born child had been laid in her arms; and as she lay on the white bed looking out on the spring dawning day after day, her husband sat beside her telling her again and again of the house he had made ready for her in Penn's new settlement. She never tired of hearing of it. Some picture of this far-off home must have come to the poor girl as she stood now in the night, the sea-water creeping up to her naked feet, looking at the fires built, as she believed, for her child.

Toward midnight a canoe came from the opposite side, into which the chief put Barrow, Dickenson, the child, and its mother. Their worst fears being thus confirmed, they crossed in silence, holding each other by the hand, the poor baby moaning now and then. It had indeed been born tired into the world, and had gone moaning its weak life out ever since.

Landing on the farther beach, the crowd of waiting Indians fled from them as if frightened, and halted in the darkness beyond the fires. But the Cassekey dragged them on toward a wigwam, taking Mary and the child before the others. "Herein," says her husband, "was the Wife of the Canibal, and some old Women sitting in a Cabbin made of Sticks about a Foot high, and covered with a Matt. He made signs for us to sitt down on the Ground, which we did. The Cassekey's Wife looking at my Child and having her own Child in her lapp, putt it away to another Woman, and rose upp and would not bee denied, but would have my Child. She took it and suckled it at her Breast, feeling it from Top to Toe, and viewing it with a sad Countenance."

The starving baby, being thus warmed and fed, stretched its little arms and legs out on the savage breast comfortably and fell into a happy sleep, while its mother sat apart and looked on.

"An Indian did kindly bring to her a Fish upon a Palmetto Leaf and set it down before her; but the Pain and Thoughts within her were so great that she could not eat."

The rest of the crew having been brought over, the chief set himself to work and speedily had a wigwam built, in which mats were spread, and the shipwrecked people, instead of being killed and eaten, went to sleep just as the moon rose, and the Indians began "a Consert of hideous Noises," whether of welcome or worship they could not tell.

Dickenson and his band remained in this Indian village for several days, endeavoring all the time to escape, in spite of the kind treatment of the chief, who appears to have shared all that he had with them. The Quaker kept a constant, fearful watch, lest there might be death in the pot. When the Cassekey found they were resolved to go, he set out for the wreck, bringing back a boat which was given to them, with butter, sugar, a rundlet of wine, and chocolate; to Mary and the child he also gave everything which he thought would be useful to them. This friend in the wilderness appeared sorry to part with them, but Dickenson was blind both to friendship and sorrow, and obstinately took the direction against which the chief warned him, suspecting treachery, "though we found afterward that his counsell was good."

Robert Barrow, Mary, and the child, with two sick men, went in a canoe along the coast, keeping the crew in sight, who, with the boy, travelled on foot, sometimes singing as they marched. So they began the long and terrible journey, the later horrors of which I dare not give in the words here set down. The first weeks were painful and disheartening, although they still had food. Their chief discomfort arose from the extreme cold at night and the tortures from the sand-flies and mosquitoes on their exposed bodies, which they tried to remedy by covering themselves with sand, but found sleep impossible.

At last, however, they met the fiercer savages of whom the chief had warned them, and practised upon them the same device of calling themselves Spaniards. By this time, one would suppose, even Dickenson's dull eyes would have seen the fatal idiocy of the lie. "Crying out 'Nickalees No Espanier,' they rushed upon us, rending the few Cloathes from us that we had; they took all from my Wife, even tearing her Hair out, to get at the Lace, wherewith it was knotted." They were then dragged furiously into canoes and rowed to the village, being stoned and shot at as they went. The child was stripped, while one savage filled its mouth with sand.

But at that the chief's wife came quickly to Mary and protected her from the sight of all, and took the sand out of the child's mouth, entreating it very tenderly, whereon the mass of savages fell back, muttering and angry.

The same woman brought the poor naked lady to her wigwam, quieted her, found some raw deerskins, and showed her how to cover herself and the baby with them.

The tribe among which they now were had borne the famine for two years; their emaciated and hunger-bitten faces gave fiercer light to their gloomy, treacherous eyes. Their sole food was fish and palmetto-berries, both of which were scant. Nothing could have been more unwelcome than the advent of this crowd of whites, bringing more hungry mouths to fill; and, indeed, there is little reason to doubt that the first intention was to put them all to death. But, after the second day, Dickenson relates that the chief "looked pleasantly upon my Wife and Child"; instead of the fish entrails and filthy water in which the fish had been cooked which had been given to the prisoners, he brought clams to Mary, and kneeling in the sand showed her how to roast them. The Indian women, too, carried off the baby, knowing that its mother had no milk for it, and handed it about from one to the other, putting away their own children that they might give it their food. At which the child, that, when it had been wrapped in fine flannel and embroidery had been always nigh to death, began to grow fat and rosy, to crow and laugh as it had never done before, and kick its little legs sturdily about under their bit of raw skin covering. Mother Nature had taken the child home, that was all, and was breathing new lusty life into it, out of the bare ground and open sky, the sun and wind, and the breasts of these her children; but its father saw in the change only another inexplicable miracle of God. Nor does he seem to have seen that it was the child and its mother who had been a protection and shield to the whole crew and saved them through this their most perilous strait.

I feel as if I must stop here with the story half told. Dickenson's narrative, when I finished it, left behind it a fresh, sweet cheerfulness, as if one had been actually touching the living baby with its fair little body and milky breath; but if I were to try to reproduce the history of the famished men and women of the crew during the months that followed, I should but convey to you a dull and dreary horror.

You yourselves can imagine what the journey on foot along the bleak coast in winter, through tribe after tribe of hostile savages, must have been to delicately nurtured men and women, naked but for a piece of raw deerskin, and utterly without food save for the few nauseous berries or offal rejected by the Indians. In their ignorance of the coast they wandered farther and farther out of their way into those morasses which an old writer calls "the refuge of all unclean birds and the breeding-fields of all reptiles." Once a tidal wave swept down into a vast marsh where they had built their fire, and air and ground slowly darkened with the swarming living creatures, whirring, creeping about them through the night, and uttering gloomy, dissonant cries. Many of these strange companions and some savages found their way to the hill of oyster-shells where the crew fled, and remained there for the two days and nights in which the flood lasted.

Our baby accepted all fellow-travellers cheerfully; made them welcome, indeed. Savage or slave or beast were his friends alike, his laugh and outstretched hands were ready for them all. The aged man, too, Dickenson tells us, remained hopeful and calm, even when the slow-coming touch of death had begun to chill and stiffen him, and in the presence of the cannibals assuring his companions cheerfully of his faith that they would yet reach home in safety. Even in that strange, forced halt, when Mary Dickenson could do nothing but stand still and watch the sea closing about them, creeping up and up like a visible death, the old man's prayers and the baby's laugh must have kept the thought of her far home very near and warm to her.

They escaped the sea to fall into worse dangers. Disease was added to starvation. One by one strong men dropped exhausted by the way, and were left unburied, while the others crept feebly on; stout Jonathan Dickenson taking as his charge the old man, now almost a helpless burden. Mary, who, underneath her gentle, timid ways, seems to have had a gallant heart in her little body, carried her baby to the last, until the milk in her breast was quite dried and her eyes grew blind, and she too fell one day beside a poor negress who, with her unborn child, lay frozen and dead, saying that she was tired, and that the time had come for her too to go. Dickenson lifted her and struggled on.

The child was taken by the negroes and sailors. It makes a mother's heart ache even now to read how these coarse, famished men, often fighting like wild animals with each other, staggering under weakness and bodily pain, carried the heavy baby, never complaining of its weight, thinking, it may be, of some child of their own whom they would never see or touch again.

I can understand better the mystery of that Divine Childhood that was once in the world, when I hear how these poor slaves, unasked, gave of their dying strength to this child; how, in tribes through which no white man had ever travelled alive, it was passed from one savage mother to the other, tenderly handled, nursed at their breasts; how a gentler, kindlier spirit seemed to come from the presence of the baby and its mother to the crew; so that, while at first they had cursed and fought their way along, they grew at the last helpful and tender with each other, often going back, when to go back was death, for the comrade who dropped by the way, and bringing him on until they too lay down, and were at rest together.

It was through the baby that deliverance came to them at last. The story that a white woman and a beautiful child had been wandering all winter through the deadly swamps was carried from one tribe to another until it reached the Spanish fort at St. Augustine. One day therefore, when near their last extremity, they "saw a Perre-augoe[5] approaching by sea filled with soldiers, bearing a letter signifying the governor of St. Augustine's greatt Care for our Preservation, of what Nation soever we were." The journey, however, had to be made on foot; and it was more than two weeks before Dickenson, the old man, Mary and the child, and the last of the crew, reached St. Augustine.

"We came thereto," he says, "about two hours before Night, and were directed to the governor's house, where we were led up a pair of stairs, at the Head whereof stood the governor, who ordered my Wife to be conducted to his Wife's Apartment."

There is something in the picture of poor Mary, after her months of starvation and nakedness, coming into a lady's chamber again, "where was a Fire and Bath and Cloathes," which has a curious pathos in it to a woman.

Robert Barrow and Dickenson were given clothes, and a plentiful supper set before them.

St. Augustine was then a collection of a few old houses grouped about the fort; only a garrison, in fact, half supported by the king of Spain and half by the Church of Rome. Its three hundred male inhabitants were either soldiers or priests, dependent for supplies of money, clothing, or bread upon Havana; and as the famine had lasted for two years, and it was then three since a vessel had reached them from any place whatever, their poverty was extreme. They were all, too, the "false Catholicks and hireling Priests" whom, beyond all others, Dickenson distrusted and hated. Yet the grim Quaker's hand seems to tremble as he writes down the record of their exceeding kindness; of how they welcomed them, looking, as they did, like naked furious beasts, and cared for them as if they were their brothers. The governor of the fort clothed the crew warmly, and out of his own great penury fed them abundantly. He was a reserved and silent man, with a grave courtesy and odd gentle care for the woman and child that makes him quite real to us. Dickenson does not even give his name. Yet it is worth much to us to know that a brother of us all lived on that solitary Florida coast two centuries ago, whether he was pagan, Protestant, or priest.

When they had rested for some time, the governor furnished canoes and an escort to take them to Carolina, — a costly outfit in those days, — whereupon Dickenson, stating that he was a man of substance, insisted upon returning some of the charges to which the governor and people had been put as soon as he reached Carolina. But the Spaniard smiled and refused the offer, saying whatever he did was done for God's sake. When the day came that they must go, "he walked down to see us embark, and taking our Farewel, he embraced some of us, and wished us well saying that *We should forget him when we got amongst our own nation*; and I also added that *If we forgot him, God would not forget him*, and thus we parted."

The mischievous boy, John Hilliard, was found to have hidden in the woods until the crew were gone, and remained ever after in the garrison with the grave Spaniards, with whom he was a favorite.

The voyage to Carolina occupied the month of December, being made in open canoes, which kept close to the shore, the crew disembarking and encamping each night. Dickenson tells with open-eyed wonder how the Spaniards kept their holiday of Christmas in the open boat and through a driving northeast storm; praying, and then tinkling a piece of iron for music and singing, and also begging gifts from the Indians, who begged from them in their turn; and what one gave to the other, that they gave back again. Our baby at least, let us hope, had Christmas feeling enough to understand the laughing and hymn-singing in the face of the storm.

At the lonely little hamlet of Charleston (a few farms cut out of the edge of the wilderness) the adventurers were received with eagerness; even the Spanish escort were exalted into heroes, and entertained and rewarded by the gentlemen of the town. Here too Dickenson and Kirle sent back generous gifts to the soldiers of St. Augustine, and a token of remembrance to their friend, the governor. After two months' halt, "on the eighteenth of the first month, called March," they embarked for Pennsylvania, and on a bright cold morning in April came in sight of their new home of Philadelphia. The river was gay with a dozen sail, and as many brightly painted Indian pirogues darting here and there; a ledge of green banks rose from the water's edge dark with gigantic hemlocks, and pierced with the caves in which many of the settlers yet lived; while between the bank and the forest were one or two streets of mud-huts and of curious low stone houses sparkling with mica, among which broad-brimmed Friends went up and down.

The stern Quaker had come to his own life and to his own people again; the very sun had a familiar home look for the first time in his journey. We can believe that he rejoiced in his own solid, enduring way; gave thanks that he had escaped the judgments of God, and closed his righteous gates thereafter on aught that was alien or savage.

The aged man rejoiced in a different way; for being carried carefully to the shore by many friends, they knowing that he was soon to leave them, he put out his hand, ready to embrace them in much love, and in a tender frame of spirit, saying gladly that the Lord had answered his desire, and brought him home to lay his bones among them. From the windows of the dusky library, I can see the spot now, where, after his long journey, he rested for a happy day or two, looking upon the dear familiar faces and waving trees and the sunny April sky, and then gladly and cheerfully bade them farewell and went onward.

Mary had come at last to the pleasant home that had been waiting so long for her, and there, no doubt, she nursed her baby, and clothed him in soft fooleries again, and, let us hope, out of the fulness of her soul, not only prayed, but, Quaker as she was, sang idle joyous songs, when her husband was out of hearing.

But the baby, who knew nothing of the judgments or mercy of God, and who could neither pray nor sing, only had learned in these desperate straits to grow strong and happy in the touch of sun and wind, and to hold out its arms to friend or foe, slave or savage, sure of a welcome, and so came closer to God than any of them all.

Jonathan Dickenson became a power in the new principality; there are vague traditions of his strict rule as mayor, his stately equipages and vast estates. No doubt, if I chose to search among the old musty records, I could find the history of his son. But I do not choose; I will not believe that he ever grew to be a man, or died.

He will always be to us simply a baby; a live, laughing baby, sent by his Master to the desolate places of the earth with the old message of Divine love and universal brotherhood to his children; and I like to believe too, that as he lay in the arms of his savage foster-mothers, taking life from their life, Christ so took him into his own arms and blessed him.

The Middle-Aged Woman

Scribner's Monthly Magazine, July 1875

Choose any artist that you know—the one with the kindliest nature and the finest perceptions—and ask him to give you his idea of the genius of the commonplace, and my word for it, he paints you a middle-aged woman. The thing, he will say, proves itself. Here is a creature jogging on leisurely at midday in the sight of all men along a well-tramped road. The mists of dawn are far behind her; she has not yet reached the shadows of evening. The softness and blushes, and shy, sparkling glances of the girl she was, have long been absorbed into muddy thick skin, sodden outlines, rational eyes. There are crows' feet at either temple, and yellowish blotches on the flesh below the soggy under-jaw. Her chestnut-brown hair used to warm and glitter in the sun, and after a few years it will make a white crown upon her head, a sacred halo to her children; but just now it is stiff with a greasy hair dye, and is of an unclean and indescribable hue.

Young girls, with that misty dawn about them, may lack both beauty and wit; but there is a charm in their fresh untainted homeliness, in the ardor of their foolishness. They pour forth their thoughts in silly school essays, and they seem to run no deeper than roses and moonlight and eternal friendships. They talk all day long about their lovers and pretty finery, and we listen with delight to it all, and do not ask for common sense any more than we would in the chatter of the swallows building their nests. It is the fresh morning air which blows about them and revives us. It is because they "bear white shields of expectation."

But the middle-aged woman expects nothing; she has proved, gauged it all. She does not carry a white shield, that we all can see, but a basket of undarned stockings. Her talk is of butter and cures for catarrh, and if she adverts to roses, it is to tell you the secret of her success in raising them and the manure which they prefer.

What can any artist, with either pen or pencil, make of this bare ordinary shape? Shakespeare himself, driven to the limning of her, can only

> Let husbands know
> Their wives have sense like them; they see, and smell,
> And have their palates, both for sweet and sour." [1]

The average American husband does not lack such practical knowledge of his wife. There may have been an uncertain glamour about her in the days when she stood, half child, half woman, trying to unbar with her soft pink-tinted hand certain doors of life. It may gather around her again in old age, when the dreadful prophetic shadow begins to fall upon her gray head. But in middle-age she is the unromantic center of an unromantic world of daily dinners, anxieties about children, and worries about cooks and chambermaid. Underneath all this the husband may have a dateless love, even passion for his wife, just as he has a stone foundation for the house he lives in. But he does not drag his friends down to the cellar every day to examine his foundation; and he does not pose at his wife's feet in public, or write verses in her honor. When his affection takes that form of chills and fever there is a strong probability that poses and verses will some day be tested in a divorce suit.

It is certain, however, that this woman, just at the age when the poet and novelist will have none of her, is the fittest subject for the student of human nature. After thirty her whims have hardened into prejudices, her foibles into character. There she is unmistakably, domestic machine, fool, saint. The features of the landscape are surely best seen at high noon. If the misty romance is gone from her it is because she grapples now with the real pain and joy and devils that beset life. Dolly at sixteen finds herself neglected at a ball, and writes in her diary of relentless destiny, of intolerable loneliness. At forty she finds herself a widow, penniless, with half a dozen children, and goes out bravely to get machine-sewing to do. At sixteen she weeps poetic tears over the fate of the lost Pleiad,[2] some day she will lay her little baby in the grave and go on with her work, carrying a cheerful face through the house "for the sake of father and the boys;" only at night, when she misses the little hand fumbling at her breast, daring to cry her bitter tears out upon her pillow, when none but God can see or hear.

Whoever would gain a clear idea of the condition of American society, too, must take the middle-aged woman as the index. The generation of gray-headed grandmothers are carrying out of the world its old-fashioned prejudices; the young woman is in an uneasy transition stage, not quite sure whether she would rather next week write a book, be married, or perform a capital operation in surgery.

But take a woman of forty anywhere in the States, and you have an embodied history and prophecy of the social condition of the country, practical and minute as you can find nowhere else except in a daily newspaper.

If you have a curiosity, for example, to inspect the development of woman from the fifteenth century until now, there is no need of materialized spirits to make up the panorama. For the beginning, take a horse or mule, and penetrate for a hundred miles or two the mountains of North Carolina, making friends as you go with the farmers' wives. There is her biography written, page after page, clearer than type. If you want white villanage, go into the hovels in the Nantahela range, where your hostess shall give you corn-cakes and fried opposum (which you eat with your fingers), and rye coffee poured into a gourd. This matron has, therefore, no dishes to wash and no beds to make, as by an ingenious contrivance the boards of the floor are lifted at night, disclosing a trench filled with straw, in which the whole family kennel. Life is reduced for her to the simple elements of child-bearing and eating as necessities, and the luxury of wearing a hoop-skirt (which invariably hangs on the wall) under the calico rag yclept[3] a dress.

Down in the gorges cut by the Okonalufta you will find a house made of a dozen log huts squatted together with open passageways between, through which a cart could be driven. Pigs and chickens run riot through these passages in summer, and bears in winter come down at night and peer curiously into them. My friend, Mistress Pitloe, is the head of this household. Her loom, heavy and home-made, with logs for beams, stands in one of the passages. The indigo-dyed cloth, which she, her husband and sons, all wear, was sheared in the wool, carded, spun, woven, and sewed by herself. She is a tall, raw-boned woman of fifty, scrupulously clean, with grizzled hair drawn back from the dark, clear-cut face, which betrays her French Huguenot descent. Squire Pitloe (Colonel in the war) is the wealthiest farmer in the country, a knowing politician, as politics go there. His son edits "The Haywood County Times." In Pennsylvania his wife would drive her old horses and family carriage into town, and in her seeded black silk preside as chairman of committees on jelly or pianos at the State fair. But Mistress Pitloe, as she is called, has not left the farm for five years; her chances for reading consists of the Bible and a yellow pile of Baptist tracts which lie on the chest of drawers. They belonged to her father, she tells you, but she never has had time to read them.

Her house has not a glass window in it; the walls inside show the bare logs with the mud chunking; empty boxes serve for chairs; but she has hung white homespun netting from ceiling to floor; the delicate cleanliness everywhere, the very smell of the drying herbs overhead, somehow convince you that you are in the house of a chaste wife and careful mother.

She goes afield every day with the Squire and the farm-hands (both white and black) to plow or hoe corn, and hurries back to help the negro cook with the dinner. When it is served, she sits down with her husband and sons, but only to wait on them; she eats with the servants, and is held in effect their social companion and equal. Yet, if you talk with her for an hour, you find her more keen-witted and just than any man of the household; she will give you shrewd hints of the real condition of the freed slaves or polygamous Cherokees about her—a condition her husband has hardly yet suspected to exist. But it has not yet occurred to her that emancipation waits for her. She is no more inclined to question the limitations which make a beast of burden of her, than she is to quarrel with the monotonous hill-ranges, clad in the funereal black of the balsam, that have shut her in since her birth.

I tremble to think of the consequences should Mrs. Fanning, or any other emancipated Bostonian, be tempted next summer to penetrate this prison-house of nature, and share the fried chicken and corn bread of Squire Pitloe at his boarding rate of one dollar per week. How her freed soul would yearn to carry back Mistress Pitloe, and produce her in the parlors of the Radical Club as she might a bone of the Megalosaurus, or any other relic of an extinct era!

But I am tolerably sure that grave, slow-spoken Mistress Pitloe would put this lady, or any other reformer, outside of her gates in two days' time. To her, and to her like, an unusual idea of any sort has always something in it of indecent and devilish.

Could any contrast be stronger in Mrs. Fanning's eyes than that of this obscure, gray-headed drudge, and brilliant little Mrs. Pettit, whose thoughts and opinions everybody has heard, but who is only known in the flesh to a small coterie in New York? She is too diffident to appear in public as lecturer or even reader, and too unconventional to tolerate the fashionable mobs of society. People who have been stirred by her trenchant editorials, or have felt the tears rise and their hearts soften at the pathos of her poems, manage with difficulty to penetrate to her home, and are amazed to find a little roly-poly, rose-tinted, merry dot of a woman, busied with orphan asylums, or crèches for babies, or any other business which will bring children about her. Her husband is Professor J. Pettit, well known to the scientific world; he confesses that for much of the research in German libraries, and all the statistics of his great work on "The Political History of European Peoples," we are indebted to his wife, who felt it her duty to be his helpmate in that work as much as in preparing the delicious game suppers in which his soul delights.

During the last two years, as all the writing world knows, Mrs. Pettit has had charge of one of the leading monthly periodicals of the country, the popular author whose name weights it as editor being only a figurehead for the public eye. She has a little closet of an office in the publishing house, where she sits for five hours each day in close-fitting gown of brown serge, grappling with the heap of manuscripts that grows with every mail. There is probably no subject or fact known to modern thought with which she is not thus brought in contact in the course of the year. At 4 P.M. she locks her office door, and goes home, and there is not a more picturesque, or better-dressed woman, or daintier dinner in New York, than those which welcome her husband, and her boys an hour later. Her sons are very proud of their little mother; there is nothing which she does not know, they will tell you, though perhaps babies and pottery are her strong points. She is infallible in questions of teething, and doles out the most advanced theories of hygiene to young mothers. Collectors of rare china, or Japanese bronzes, take their specimens to her for a final verdict; indeed, one can hardly tell whether her touch is more affectionate and tender when handling a new-born baby or an old cracked tea-pot.

But, after all, Mrs. Pettit, pen in hand in her office, and Mistress Pitloe holding the plow, have only taken different handles of the same electric battery. As far as each is able, she is making life healthfuller and cheerfuller, and nearer to God for her husband and children and neighbors, whether these last mean a few half-breed Indians or the hundred thousand readers of a magazine. It is precisely the same work as that of countless other unpicturesque, middle-aged women, from Maine woods to Pennsylvania villages, or California ranches—the great, decent, religious, unknown majority, never to be interviewed, or published in any shape, out of whose daily lives grow the modesties, the strength, the virtue of American homes, the safety of our future.

Such women, whether they be wives of millionaires or laborers, always make real again in the world the one poetic ideal of a middle-aged woman —Bunyan's Christiana, who set out with her little ones along the weary way from the City of Destruction to the dark flood which barred heaven from them. It is worth while for wives and mothers, even now in 1875, to read of her daily work—how she urged her boys, and carried her babies in her arms, and did not fall into the Slough of Despond, as her husband had done, and never forgot to take Mercy along with her. How one day her task was to face Apollyon, and the next, to "cure Matthew of stomach-gripes from eating green apples." How there gathered about her, in the course of the long, painful journey, children's children and friends, and the poor, the lame, and the blind, and walked with her, and were a joyous, happy company, until the end came. There is nothing to me more pathetic in any history than the words which tell of how one day the messenger came to this gray-haired woman to say that her work as wife and mother at last was done. Then she called her children about her, and was gladdened in that last hour to see that they had kept their garments so white; and after she had put them in the care of her old friends, she went down with a beckon of farewell into the dark river, beyond which the gate stood open where her Lord waited for her, and the husband of her youth, and was seen no more.

"And at her departure her children wept. But Greatheart[4] played upon the well-tuned cymbal and the harp for joy."

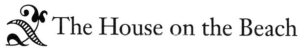

The House on the Beach

Lippincott's Magazine, January 1876

"What is that black mass yonder, far up the beach, just at the edge of the breakers?"

The fisherman to whom we put the question drew in his squid-line, hand over hand, without turning his head, having given the same answer for half a dozen years to summer tourists: "Wreck. Steamer. Creole."

"Were there many lives lost?"

"It's likely. This is the worst bit of coast in the country. The Creole was a three-decker," looking at it reflectively. "Lot of good timber there."

As we turned our field-glasses to the black lump hunched out of the water, like a great sea-monster creeping up on the sand, we saw still farther up the coast a small house perched on a headland, with a flag flying in the gray mist, and pointed it out to the Jerseyman, who nodded: "That there wooden shed is the United States signal station;" adding, after a pause, "Life-saving service down stairs."

"Old Probabilities! The house he lives in!"

"Life-boats!"

Visions of the mysterious old prophet who utters his oracles through the morning paper, of wrecks and storms, and of heroic men carrying lines through the night to sinking ships, filled our brains. Townspeople out for their summer holiday have keen appetites for the romantic and extraordinary, and manufacture them (as sugar from beets) out of the scantiest materials. We turned our backs on the fisherman and his squid-line. The signal station and the hull of the lost vessel were only a shed and timber to him. How can any man be alive to the significance of a wreck and fluttering flag which he sees twenty times a day? Noah, no doubt, after a year in the ark, came to look upon it as so much gopher-wood, and appreciated it as a good job of joinery rather than a divine symbol.

We believe, however, that our readers will find in the wrecked Creole and the wooden shed, and the practical facts concerning them, matter suggestive enough to hold them a little space. They fill a yet unwritten page in the history of our government, and of great and admirable work done by it, of which the nation at large has been given but partial knowledge.

Or, if we choose to look more deeply into things, we may find in the old hulk and commonplace building hints as significant of the Infinite Order and Power underlying all ordinary things, and of our relations to it, as in the long-ago Deluge and the ark riding over it.

The little wooden house stands upon a lonely stretch of coast in Ocean County, New Jersey. Several miles of low barren marshes and sands gray with poverty-grass on the north separate it from Manasquan Inlet and the pine woods and scattered farm-houses which lie along its shore, while half a mile below, on the south, is the head of Barnegat Bay, a deep, narrow estuary which runs into and along the Jersey coast for more than half its extent, leaving outside a strip of sandy beach, never more than a mile wide. All kinds of sea fish and fowl take refuge in this bay and the interminable reedy marshes, and for a few weeks in the snipe- and duck-season sportsmen from New York find their way to "Shattuck's" and the houses of other old water-dogs along the bay. But during the rest of the year the wooden shed and its occupants are left to the companionship of the sea and the winds.

The little building (with a gigantic "No. 10" whitewashed outside) stands close to the breakers, just above high-water mark in winter. It is divided into two large rooms, upper and lower, with a tiny kitchen in the rear and an equally comfortless bedroom overhead. The doors of the lower room (which, like those of a barn, fill the whole end of the house) being closed, we sought for Old Probabilities up stairs, and found very little at first sight to gratify curiosity or any craving for mystery. There was a large wooden room, with walls and floor of unpainted boards, the ceiling hung with brilliantly colored flags, a telegraphic apparatus, one or two desks, books, writing materials—a scientific working-room, in short, with its implements in that order which implied that only men had used them.

There were in 1874 one hundred and eight such signal stations as this, modest, inexpensive little offices, established over the United States, from the low sea-coast plains to the topmost peak of the Rocky Mountains.

If we were accurate chroniclers, we should have to go back to Aristotle and the Chaldeans to show the origin and purpose of these little offices, just as Carlyle[1] has to unearth Ulfila the Mœsogoth[2] to explain a word he uses to his butter-man. The world is so new, after all, and things so inextricably tangled up in it! In this case, as it is the sun and wind and rain which are the connecting links, it is easy enough to bring past ages close to us. The Chaldeans, building their great embankments or raiding upon Job's herds, are no longer a myth to us when we remember that they were wet by the rain and anxious about the weather and their crops, just as we are; in fact, they felt such matters so keenly, and were so little able to cope with these unknown forces, that they made gods of them, and then, beyond prayers and sacrifices, troubled themselves no further about the matter. Even the shrewd, observant Hebrews, living out of doors, a race of shepherds and herdsmen, never looked for any rational cause for wind or storm, but regarded them, if not as gods, as the messengers of God, subject to no rules. It was He who at His will covered the heavens with clouds, who prepared rain, who cast forth hoar-frost like ashes: the stormy wind fulfilled His word. Men searched into the construction of their own minds, busied themselves with subtle philosophies, with arts and sciences, conquered the principles of Form and Color, and made not wholly un-successful efforts to solve the mystery of the sun and stars; but it was not until 340 B.C. that any notice was taken of the every-day matters of wind and heat and rain.

Aristotle, the Gradgrind of philosophers, first noted down the known facts on this subject in his work *On Meteors*. His theories and deductions were necessarily erroneous, but he struck the foundation of all science, the collection of known facts. Theophrastus,[3] one of his pupils, made a compilation of prognostics concerning rain, wind and storm, and there investigation ceased for ages. For nearly two thousand years the citizens of the world rose every morning to rejoice in fair weather or be wet by showers, to see their crops destroyed by frost or their ships by winds, and never made a single attempt to discover any scientific reason or rules in the matter—apparently did not suspect that there was any cause or effect behind these daily occurrences. They accounted for wind or rain as our grandfathers did for a sudden death, by the "visitation of God." In fact, Nature—which is the expression of Law most inexorable and minute—was the very last place where mankind looked to find law at all.

About two hundred and thirty years ago Torricelli discovered that the atmosphere, the space surrounding the earth, which seemed more intan-gible than a dream, had weight and substance, and invented the barometer, the tiny tube and drop of mercury by which it could be seized and held and weighed as accurately as a pound of lead. As soon as this invisible air was proved to be matter, the whole force of scientific inquiry was di-rected toward it. The thermometer, by which its heat or cold could be measured—the hygrometer, which weighed, literally by a hair, its moisture or dryness—were the results of the research of comparatively a few years. Somewhat later came the curious instrument which measures its velocity. As soon as it was thus made practicable for any intelligent observer to handle, weigh and test every quality of the air, it became evident that wind and storm, even the terrible cyclone, were not irresponsible forces, carrying health or death to and fro where they listed, but the result of plain, immutable laws. It was an American in this our Quaker City who reduced the wind to a commonplace effect of a most ordinary cause. Franklin, one winter's day passing with a lighted candle out of a warm room into a cold one, saw that as he held it above his head the flame was blown outward before him: when he held it near the floor, the flame was blown into the room. The shrewd observer stood in the doorway, instead of hurrying out, as most of us would have done, to save the wasting candle. The warm air in the heated room, he conjectured, was expanded by the heat, consequently it rose as high as it could, and made a way for itself out of the room at the upper part of the doorway, while the heavier cold air from without rushed in below to fill the vacated space. What if he took the equatorial regions or great tracts of arid desert for the heated room? The air over them, subjected by the heat to constant rarefaction, must rise, must overflow above, and must force the colder air from the surrounding regions in below. Two sheets of air will thus set in vertically on both sides, rise, and again separate above. Here was an explanation of the great, steady, uninterrupted aërial currents which, at the rate of from fifteen to eighteen miles per hour, sweep the surface of the Atlantic and Pacific oceans. The candle, no doubt, was wasted, but the secret of the trade-winds was discovered.

The idea was correct as far as it went. It did not go very far, it is true. It had not taken into account the earth's rotation, whose force, according to Herschel, "gives at least one-half of their average momentum to all the winds which occur over the whole world;" nor the infinite variation in the movements of the atmosphere which we call winds, caused by the change in the sun's motion, by the differing amounts of vapor held in them, by the physical configuration of the earth below, by the vicinity of the sea or arid deserts, and by the passage of storms or electric currents.

The science of meteorology, especially as regards wind, is as yet searching for general principles, which can only be deduced from countless facts. We do not now, like Saint Paul, talk of the wind Euroclydon as of a special agent of God, but describe it by stating that it is an aërial ascending current over the Mediterranean, produced by the heated sands of Africa and Arabia. We can even measure its heat at 200° Fahrenheit, and its velocity at fifty-four miles per hour. But it attacks us just as unexpectedly as it did the apostle, and brings disease and death to Naples or Palermo to-day just as surely as it did to Cambyses.[4] The popular verdict on the matter would no doubt be that when meteorologists can not only describe the sirocco, but give warning of its coming, their science will justify its claim to consideration. The common sense of mankind always demands as a royalty from every science daily practical benefits to the mass of men and women. It is not enough for meteorologists to have proved that the atmosphere varies in weight, in temperature or velocity of motion according to fixed rules, or to be able to explain why no rain falls on a certain portion of the coast of Portugal, while a like coast-exposure in England is incessantly drenched; or to have determined beyond a doubt that precisely as the ocean of water, under the influence of the moon and wind, ebbs and flows and has its succession of storms or calms, the ocean of air in which we are enveloped answers to the influence of the sun in great tidal movements, and has also its vast steadily moving waves of cold or heat or moisture. These discoveries of general truths must be brought to bear directly on men's daily life before they will have fulfilled their true purpose. It would seem as if nothing were more easy than to bring them so to bear. Meteorology, more intimately perhaps than any other science, concerns our ordinary affairs. The health of mankind, navigation, agriculture, commerce, the hourly business and needs of every man, from the merchant sending out his cargo and the consumptive waiting for death in the east wind, to the laundress hanging out the family wash, are ruled by that most mysterious, most uncurbed of powers, the weather. We may rub along through life with scanty knowledge of the history of dead nations or the philosophy of living ones, but heat and cold, the climate of the coming winter, yesterday's rainfall or to-morrow's frost, are matters which take hold of every one of us and affect us every hour of the day. Now, to bring the known general truths of this science to practical rules, or to base upon them predictions of storms or changes in the weather during any future period, requires, as Sir John Herschel[5] stated twelve years ago, "patient, incessant and laborious observations, carried on in every region of the globe." One reason why this is required is the perpetually shifting conditions of heat, wind and storm. A man who sat down to work a mathematical problem in the days of Job, if there was such a man, found its result just the same as the school-boy does to-day: figures not only never lie, but never alter. But the man who solves an equation of which the winds and water are members finds that the sum to be added varies with every hour. There are, so far as is yet known, no regularly recurring cycles of weather on which to base predictions: the conditions of heat and wind and moisture are never precisely the same at any given point. Hence the necessity, if we would give the science stability and bring it to bear on our daily life, of educated, skilled observers at different points to collect and report simultaneously the daily details of the present conditions.

It is this daily detail of fact which the United States government supplies through the little stations of observation one of which we have stumbled into on the Jersey beach. Americans, indeed, have from the first taken hold of this science with a most characteristic effort to reduce it to practical uses, to bring it at once to bear on the well-being at least of farmers and navigators. Dove[6] had no sooner published his chart of isothermal lines and charts, showing the temperature throughout the world of each month, and also of abnormal temperatures, than our government issued the *Army Meteorological Register* for the United States, which for accuracy and fullness had never been equaled. In these the temperature and rainfall for each month of the year were shown. The forecasts of the weather now published daily in this country, and which come so directly home to every man's business that Old Probabilities is a real personage to us all, have been given in England for several years under the supervision of Admiral Fitzroy.

But it is high time now that we should come back to our little wooden house on the beach, and tell what we know of its occupants and uses. The courteous gentleman (in a blue flannel suit for "roughing it") who sits at the telegraphic wires is Sergeant G——, belonging to the Signal Service Department of the army. Instruction in this department is given at Fort Whipple, Va. One hundred officers besides Sergeant G—— are now in charge of stations, with 139 privates as assistants. The average force at Fort Whipple is 140 men. These men are, in point of fact, soldiers liable to be called into active service in the field: their duty there, however, is not fighting, but signaling and telegraphy—a duty quite as dangerous as the bearing of arms. Fresh recruits for this service are divided into those capable of receiving instruction only in field duty and those for "full service," which includes, with military signaling and telegraphy, the taking of meteoric observations, the collating and publication of such observations, and the deduction from them of correct results. Passing two examinations successfully in the latter course, the signal-service soldier is detailed for duty at a post as assistant, and after six months' satisfactory service is returned to Fort Whipple for the special instruction given to observer-sergeants. When qualified for this work he is detailed, as a vacancy occurs, for actual service.

Having thus discovered how our friend the sergeant came into his post, we looked about to see what he had to do there. The brilliantly-colored flags overhead drew the eye first. These flags serve the purpose of an international language on the high seas, where no other language is practicable. Twenty thousand distinct messages can be sent by them. Rogers's[7] system has been adopted by the United States Navy, the Lighthouse Board, the United States Coast Survey and the principal lines of steamers. Each flag represents a number, and four flags can be hoisted at once on the staff. With the flags there is given a book containing the meaning of each number. Thus, a wrecked ship cries silently to the shore, "Send a lifeboat" by flags 3, 8, 9, or says that she is sinking by 6, 3, 2; or a vessel under full sail hails another by 8, 6, 0, or bids her "*bon voyage*" with 8, 9, 7. Owing to the difficulty of distinguishing colors in cloudy days or when the flags will not fly, other systems of signaling are used: that of cones similar to umbrellas being considered in the English service one of the most efficient, a different arrangement of cones on the staff representing the nine numerals. Men may convert themselves into cones in an emergency by raising or letting fall their arms, and two men thus give any signal necessary. As the flags, however, belong more especially to Sergeant G——'s duty on the field of battle or to exceptional cases of storm and danger, we pass them by to examine into his daily round of duty. Outside, a queer little house of lattice-work perched on a headland shelters the thermometers and barometers: on a still higher point directly over the foaming breakers is the anemometer, the little instrument which measures the swiftness of the fiercest cyclone as easily as the lightest spring breeze. It consists of four brass cups shaped to catch the wind, and attached to the ends of two horizontal iron rods, which cross each other and are supported in the middle by a long pole on which they turn freely. The cups revolve with just one-third of the wind's velocity, and make five hundred revolutions whilst a mile of wind passes over them. A register of these revolutions is made by machinery similar to a gas-meter. The popular idea, by the way, of the speed of the wind runs very far beyond the truth: we are apt to say of a racer that he goes like the wind, when the fact is the horse of a good strain of blood leaves the laggard tempest far behind: the ordinary winds of every day travel only five miles an hour, a breeze of sixteen and a quarter miles an hour being strong enough to cause great discomfort in town or field: thirty-three miles is dangerous at sea, and sixty-five miles a violent hurricane, sweeping all before it.

Our friend the sergeant examines seven times a day at stated periods the condition of the atmosphere as to heat, weight and moisture, the velocity of the wind, the kind, amount and speed of the clouds, and measures the rainfall and the ocean swell: all these observations are recorded, and three are daily reported to headquarters at Washington. In these telegrams a cipher is used — as much, we presume, to ensure accuracy in the figures as for purposes of secrecy. In this cipher the fickle winds are given the names of women with a covert sarcasm quite out of place in the respectable old weather-prophet whom every housewife consults before the day's work begins. Thus, when the telegraph operator receives the mysterious message, "Francisco Emily alone barge churning did frosty guarding hungry," how is he to know that it means "San Francisco Evening. Rep. Barom. 29.40, Ther. 61, Humidity 18 per cent., Velocity of wind 41 mile per hour, 840 pounds pressure, Cirro-stratus. N.W. $\frac{1}{4}$ to $\frac{2}{4}$, Cumulo-stratus East, Rainfall 2.80 inch."?

Besides these simultaneous reports from the one hundred and eight United States stations which are telegraphed to the central office at Washington, there are received there daily three hundred and eighty-three volunteer reports from every part of the country, these being the system of meteorological observations under control of the Smithsonian Institution for twenty-four years, and given in charge to the Signal Service Bureau in 1874. In addition to these, again, are simultaneous reports from Russia, Turkey, Austria, Belgium, Denmark, France, England, Algiers, Italy, the Netherlands, Norway, Spain, Portugal, Switzerland, Canada — in all two hundred and fourteen. When we add together, therefore, the

United States Signal Service reports,	*108*
Volunteer reports,	*383*
International reports,	*214*
Reports of medical corps of army,	*123*

we have a grand total of eight hundred and twenty-eight daily simultaneous reports received at the central office, where Brigadier-General Albert J. Myer and his brevet aide, Captain H. W. Howgate (or, if you choose, Old Probabilities himself), wait to scan through these many watchful eyes the heavens around the world and utter incessant prophecies and warnings. Besides the regular observations, report is also made of casual phenomena — lightning, auroras, time of first and last frosts, etc., etc.

The history of the Signal Service Bureau and the establishment of these stations and telegraph-lines, bringing the whole country under the instant oversight of one intelligent observer, would, if it were briefly written, be full of points of dramatic interest. As yet it must be gathered out of acts of Congress and official reports. The service has now existed for fourteen years, but is still without that full recognition by Congress which would ensure its permanency. "With interests depending on its daily work as great as can by any possibility rest upon any other branch of the service, it is yet regarded as an experiment, an offshoot of regular army service existing on sufferance, liable at any moment to be hindered in its operations, if not totally abolished." The benefit of this daily work, however, affects too nearly and constantly the mass of the people to allow much danger of its final extinction. What the real value of this practical work is can be gathered not only from the dry statistics of annual reports, but from the increased confidence placed in it by the people, the unscientific working majority.

The help given to farmers should rank perhaps first in estimating the value of this work. At midnight of each day the midnight forecast is telegraphed to twenty centres of distribution, located strictly with regard to the agricultural population. The telegrams, as soon as received, are printed by signal-service men, rapidly enveloped in wrappers already stamped and addressed, and sent by the swiftest conveyance to every post-office which can be reached before 2 P.M. of the same day, and when received are displayed on bulletin-boards. The average time elapsing from the moment when the bulletin leaves the central office until it reaches every post-office from Maine to Florida is ten hours. In 1874, 6286 of these farmers' bulletins were issued, and when we consider that by each one of them reliable information as to the chances of success or failure in planting or reaping was given, we gain some idea of the directness and force of the work of this bureau.

The river reports of the office include not only regular daily observations of the changing depths of the great water-highways, but forecasts of coming floods or sudden rises and falls of the river-levels. Before the great floods in the Mississippi Valley in 1874 the warnings given by this means, and which could have been given by no other, saved an incalculable amount of property and human life. Bulletins are also issued regarding approaching freezing of our canals in the winter months, and have enabled shippers to avoid the accidents common heretofore when enormous quantities of grain, etc. in transit have been detained by this means, to the serious disturbance of the market.

Cautionary day and night signals are displayed at the principal ports and harbors when dangerous winds or storms are anticipated. In one year 762 of these warning signals were displayed, and 561 were verified by storms of destructive winds which otherwise would not have been foreseen. In not a single instance during the last two years has a great storm reached, without warning from the office, the lakes or seaports of the country. The amount of shipping, property and life thus saved to the country is simply incalculable.

Tri-daily deductions or probabilities of the weather, wind and storms, with part of the data on which they rest, are published in all the principal papers of the country, and each man and woman can testify as to their use of them. Who now goes to be married or to bury his dead or to begin a journey without consulting the two oracular lines in italics at the head of the leading column? They have come to take part in our domestic lives. The people would miss politics or the markets or literature out of the paper with less regret than Probabilities should the service be discontinued.

Besides this practical labor, there is the publication of nine daily charts on which are inscribed 2160 readings of different instruments, giving an accurate view of the general meteoric condition; monthly charts and charts condensing the results of years of observation; records furnished for the study of scientific men more comprehensive and regular than can be offered by any similar institution in any country.

A special bit of history comes to light respecting our little wooden shed at the head of Barnegat Bay. An act of Congress approved March, 1873, authorized the establishment of signal stations at lighthouses or life-saving stations along dangerous coasts, and the connection of the same by telegraphs, thirty thousand dollars being appropriated for that end. In consequence, signal stations were established on the Massachusetts coast, from Norfolk, Va., to Cape Hatteras, and more closely along this dangerous Ice-shore of New Jersey, and telegraphlines were laid connecting them with each other and also with the central office. The plan for the future is to net the whole coast—the lake, Atlantic and Pacific shores—with these stations and telegraph-wires. By this means information of coming storms can be conveyed by signal to vessels, or of wrecks, by telegraph, to other life-saving stations: the close watch kept upon the ocean-swell and currents will give warning inland of approaching changes in the weather; for it is a singular fact that the ocean-swell communicates this intelligence more quickly than the barometer, in quite another sense than the poet's

> Every wave has tales to tell
> Of storms far out at sea.

Our little station belongs to the advanced guard of this proposed line which is to encircle the coast, the whole work of establishing these stations and telegraph-lines having been done by Sergeant G—— and his comrades. Indeed, when we look at all the work done by our blue-coated friend, steady, unintermitting attention to duty by day and night year after year, his steady, unintermitting attention to duty by day and night year after year, his comfortless quarters in the wooden shed on the lonely beach, and the almost absolute solitude for an educated man during many months of the year, we begin to think his station not the least honorable among the soldiers of the republic. Almost any man, set down on the battle-field, one the magnetic fury of combat blazing in the air, would rise to the height of the moment and prove himself manly. But to be faithful to petty tasks hour after hour, through all kinds of privation and weather, for years, is quite a different matter.

The reports of the chief officer give us a hint of some of the privations borne by the observer-sergeants, educated young fellows like our friend. In 1872 the chief ordered one of these men to establish a station on the western coast of Alaska and on the island of St. Paul in Behring Sea, which was done, the observer continuing for a year in that farthest outpost. His record of frozen fogs which wrap the island like a pall, of cyclones from the Asian seas that lash its rocky coast, of vast masses of electric clouds seen nowhere else which sweep incessantly over it toward the Pole, reads more like the story of a nightmare dream than a scientific statement.

In the next spring the chief ordered another sergeant to found a station on Mount Mitchell, the highest mountain-peak east of the Mississippi. Professor Mitchell discovered and measured this mountain about twenty years ago. While taking meteorological observations upon it he was overtaken by a storm, lost his way, and was dashed to pieces over one of its terrible precipices. Several years after his death the government, suddenly recognizing his right to some acknowledgment from science, ordered his body to be disinterred and buried on the topmost peak of the mountain. It was a work of weeks, the body in its coffin being carried by the hardy mountaineers up almost impassable heights. But it reached the top at last, and lies there in the sky above all human life, with the mountain for a monument. One is startled by such a pathetic whim of poetic justice in a government. It was to this peak that the sergeant was ordered to carry his instruments and to make an abiding-place for himself. And here, after two days' journey from the base, he arrived at night in a storm of snow and hail—the guides having cleared the way with axes—set up his instruments, and took observations above the clouds while trees and rocks were sheeted with ice, and there was no shelter for himself or his companions from the furious tempests. A hut was built after a few days, and here the observer remained with the lonely grave as companion, taking hourly observations during several months.

Another officer was sent to the top of Pike's Peak, where he lived in a rudely-constructed cabin until his health broke down: he was then replaced by another, who after a year was obliged to yield also. As soon as one soldier succumbs in these perilous outposts another goes forward. The rarity of the air at this great altitude (nearly thirteen thousand feet) produces nausea, fever and dizziness: added to this were the intense cold and exposure to terrific storms. Sergeant Seyboth records several nights when he with his companions were forced, in a driving tempest, to leave the shelter of their hut and work all night heaping rocks upon its roof to keep it from being blown away: beneath them, many thousand feet, was the rolling sea of clouds. Again and again these men were lost in the drifted snow of the cañons while passing from station to station, and barely escaped with their lives. So imminent, indeed, was their danger during the winter of 1873 that prayers for their safety were offered continually in the churches below.

Frederick Meyer, another of these signal-service soldiers, was sent on the North Polar expedition with Captain Hall. No such marvelous tale as that contained in his formal report was ever found in fiction. Sergeant Meyer made observations every three hours on the voyage north, and hourly when coming south, during a year and two months. At the end of that time, as is well known to our readers, he, with part of the crew of the Polaris, was deserted by the ship, and left on a floe of ice in 79° north latitude, the steamer going southward without attempting their relief. Even in that moment of extremity he made an effort to secure the case containing his observations, but it was washed away from him by heavy seas. For six months these nineteen human beings drifted on the mass of ice over the polar seas, through all the darkness and horrors of an Arctic winter, without fire except such as was made by burning one of their boats—a feeble blaze daily, enough to warm a quart of water in which to soak their pemmican—without shelter save such as the heaped ice and snow afforded, and on starvation diet. After four months the floe began to melt so rapidly that it was but twenty yards wide. "We dared not sleep," says Sergeant Meyer, "fearing the ice would break under us and we should find our grave in the Arctic Sea." Several times the ice did break beneath them, and they were washed into the flood, but scrambled up again on the fast-melting floe. During the whole of this time the signal-service soldier continued faithful to his work, taking such observations as were possible with the instruments left to him. The boat had been burned long before, and they warmed their water with an Esquimaux lamp. On April 22d their provisions consisted of but ten biscuits. Starvation was before them when a bear was shot, and they lived on its raw meat for two weeks. At the end of that time a steamer passed within sight. The poor wretches on the ice hoisted a flag and shouted, but the vessel passed out of sight. Another ship a few days later came within the horizon and disappeared. The next day was foggy: again a steamer was sighted, and for hours the shipwrecked crew strove to make themselves seen and heard through the fog, firing shots, hoisting their torn flag and shouting at the tops of their voices. They were seen at last, and taken aboard the Tigress, "more like ghastly spectres who had come up through hell," says one of the narrators, "than living men."

The pay of the signal-service soldiers is small, and it is hardly to be supposed that they are all enthusiasts in science, or so in love with meteorology that they cheerfully brave danger and hardships such as these for its sake. We must look for the secret of their loyalty to their steady, tedious work in that quiet devotion to duty which we find in the majority of honest men—the feeling that they must go through with what they have once undertaken. And, after all, the majority of men are honest, and loyalty to irksome work is so commonplace a matter that it is only when we see it carry a man steadily through great and sudden peril, or consider how in its great total the work of obscure individuals has lifted humanity to higher levels in the last three centuries, that we can understand how good a thing it is.

At some future time we shall ransack the lower floor of the little house on the beach and discover what is to be found there.

# Some Testimony in the Case

Atlantic Monthly, November 1885

The discussions of the negro problem in Northern and Southern reviews last winter, it is true, showed us the subject from widely different points of view. But if any Northerner, living quietly at home, surrounded only by white faces, supposes that these pictures of the great struggle of race in the South have discovered the whole of it to him, he is greatly mistaken.

An impartial traveler through the Southern States just now must feel that he is in the middle of a great game, which will decide the future of the negro, and in which every man or woman that he meets, white or black, is taking a part. The result of this struggle, if not a matter of life and death to either race, will certainly affect permanently their domestic relations, their commercial prosperity, and the place which the South will hereafter hold in the scale of civilized peoples. The Southern people everywhere are ready to talk freely of this matter, and every man has his own positive opinion about it. He looks at the problem from the standing-point of his own plantation, or family, or factory, and is quite sure that he of all men in the country sees it clearly and has found the answer to it.

It occurred to me, while in the Gulf States, last winter, that this conflicting testimony from actual witnesses in the case would surprise and interest other Southerners. It seems to be so difficult in that part of the world to understand why your neighbor differs with you in opinion!

Northern readers are apt to listen to all varying statements of troubles in the South as they might to the different slogans of clans who come into the world only to fight each other. It would be far more just if they would receive them as the candid utterances of men who, whether white or black, are, like ourselves, struggling honestly to live at peace and happily with each other, and to make life fuller and nobler for their children than it has been for themselves. The educated white Southerner seldom thinks or talks now of the war or of slavery. His hands are full of the immediate struggle for a living, and in this work the negro helps or thwarts him at every turn.

I have tried to set down fragments of conversation or letters, which will explain some of these complex relations, giving as closely as possible the literal words of the speakers.

First, then, let us hear a cotton planter near Montgomery, Alabama.

He was asked, "What is the difficulty in the way of the Alabamians? You ought to make a great commercial success, in five years. You have apparently limitless resources in iron and coal. You have good soil, and your planters understand their business scientifically. Capital is coming in steadily from the North. What else do you want?"

"White labor," he promptly replied, — "white labor. The abolition of slavery lifted a great weight from the shoulders of the ruling class in the South. I acknowledge that now. If the blacks could be lifted *en masse* and dropped into Africa, it would be still greater relief. If I, for instance, could work twenty intelligent Germans instead of two hundred negroes, I could double my cotton crop this year."

"You certainly have had time to train the negro as a laborer. Where does he fall short?"

He laughed. " 'Train!' Look at that fellow holding up the fence yonder. He is a fair specimen of the field hands on a large plantation. Laziness is inborn in him; it is part of his flesh and his blood. It is as incurable as leprosy. He will pretend to work for four days, and on the fifth go off for a fortnight without a word. It matters nothing to him that it is the most critical point of the year's work. He has neither reason, nor conscience, nor ambition, to which you can appeal. No, nor even greed. He would rather sneak off and sleep all day with a nickel in his pocket than work two days longer for ten dollars. He has the mind of an animal, and, I begin to think, can be governed, like an animal, only by the lash. However, the day is over for that," shrugging his shoulders.

"But his moral sense, — his gratitude?"

"He has neither. He takes a new wife every year, and he steals from me while I am looking at him. He reckons me an exceptionally kind 'boss,' too."

"But this is only one man, of millions."

"The great mass of field hands are alike. It is an ugly story, but it is plain fact."

An aged lady in Virginia, the head of a large family, who still lives on the old plantation: —

"These are not all my own old people that work the place now," she said, scanning the haymakers, as they came in, with a shrewd, kindly smile.

"Only one third were our own; the others gathered in from the old places in the neighborhood, when strangers bought them. They are not the lowest class of laborers, as you see. We pay them good wages, and they are not driven. I hear many complaints," she added, "about the idleness and incompetency of the negro. But he was just as idle and incompetent before the war. Only now the planter is poor; he hires the laborer instead of owning him, and he feels the necessity of getting the worth of his money from him."

"You do not think, then, that freedom has elevated these people?"

"I can speak only for my own plantation." She hesitated. "In one way, yes. Most of the young people now can read and write. The elder negroes are eager to get money, to push their children on, to make them, as they say, 'like the whites.' Further than that I fail to see any good results. Their education has not been put to any practical purpose. It cannot be used, as with us, in helping them up into trades or professions. It has made them ambitious and restless, and there is no outlet for them but manual labor. Their ambition usually ends in gaudy clothes, and their restlessness in a bitter antipathy and insolence to the whites. The old loyal affection of the negro to his master, though you may think the master did not deserve it, was an ennobling quality in the slave. He has lost it, and suspicion and self-conceit have taken its place. Merely teaching a child to read and write, or even to cipher, will not give it a higher character. These people here know less of the Bible and of God than when the old Methodist preacher and I taught them and they could not read. Now they read penny song books and the lowest flash newspapers. They are more tricky, vain, and vulgar than they were as slaves."

"Do you think the color line will ever be blotted out in the South?" asked one of her listeners. "The Civil Rights Bill was fought with inhuman prejudice here, it seemed to us."

"Inhuman?" Her fair old face reddened. "How was it in the North? How long was it after you had freed your slaves in Massachusetts and Pennsylvania before you admitted them to the cars and theatres? Do they sit at your tables now? Ah, no! 'We may make laws,' as Lady Mary said, 'but we all follow customs!' And how can the North, that has been so tardy in this matter, sneer at us or urge us to our duty? The negro will not receive social recognition in my day," with a sigh of relief.

Cloty (or Madame Clotilde, as the other freedmen called her) was a stout, neat, keen-eyed mulatto in a cotton-raising district on the Gulf.

"A very rich country," she told us, adding, with a certain pride, "Mos' of de planters yahbouts worked from three hundred to a thousand slaves. Dere idee of livin' was to dress 'n' drink 'n' go to de springs 'n' play kyards on de money dere people made foh dem. When we was took 'way from dem, it was like knockin' de bottom outen de tub. Dey 'jes fell, 'n' dey don' seem t' recober demselves. But it 's our time now! De good Lohd sees to dat! I reckon," she added, " 't was 's bad a any in de Souf. De rich planters, dey leab eberyt'ing 'n de han's ob oberseers, 'n' de hardest ob dem was Yankees. But de wust marsters was de pore folk who on'y owned one or two. Dey was such litty bit 'bove dere people dey keep de distance by countin' 'em as dogs."

Her husband was the owner of a carriage, in which he drove strangers about the town: a burly, Celtic-looking fellow, with sullen light eyes and straight brown hair, the passions of a colder-blooded race than that of the negro smouldering in his face. He, too, boasted proudly of the "old families," and the state they kept, until one of the strangers said carelessly,—

"I suppose all those stories of the cruelty of slavery were exaggerated."

He glanced sharply at the speaker, and did not speak for a minute or two; then he said in a low voice, "I'll be fah. 'T wa'n't so bad foh de house suhvants ob gemmen. Dey *was* gemmen. But dese low white marsters! Why, madam, s'pose yoh be a cook, 'n' you got two nice litty gals, 'n' some man he see one, 'n' want her, 'n' he go to ole mas', 'n' to sabe a fuss dey say to you, 'Send Susy to de stoh, foh matches, or soap, or somepin'.' An' she go, 'n' de man he waitin' at de stoh, 'n' you nebber see your chile ag'in in dis wurl'! Or, you be a man, 'n' you see you mas' or he's son knock you wife or you litty gal down, 'n' you dahsn't say, 'Please, sah, don't!' Cruel, did you say? Good Lohd! My ole mas' owned twenty people. He could n't read or write. He know'd no more dan a debbil fish, 'n' he keer no mo' what he kill. *I* knowed a boy—a boy of fohteen—bucked[1] head to feet, 'n' de lash laid on till he sick foh days." His eyes were set, and the blood settled in mottled spots on his jaws, as he talked. " 'N' as soon 's he could stan', a collar put on his neck 'n' a chain from dat to he's feet, 'n' him ploughin' all day wid he's head down, 'n' at night salt brine poured on his raw back. Great God in heaven! 'N' me only a boy of fohteen! I was ole mas's grandson, sah. He terr'ble temper! When he get in fury he tear he's hat off he's head 'n' tramp it like mad bull. 'N' one day when dey push me so hard I get fah wild, 'n' rush in from de field 'n' tell him to he's face to shoot me, foh God's sake! I could n't stan' libin' no longer. 'N' de folks tell me dat I tore de cloes off me, 'n' tramp em down; 'n' at dat, old mas' look at me scart 'n' say, quite quiet, 'Take him to de cabin.' "

He drove on in silence for some time and then said, "I t'ink sometimes dat pore boy hab hard times!" with an unsteady laugh. Pointing to a gibbet-like structure in the middle of the shady street, "Dah 's de ole whippin'-post," he said. " 'N' hyah," turning into a settlement of comfortable, tidy houses, "hyah 's whah we cullored folks lib now, 'n' dis is de college foh our chillen," stopping before a large brick house, which he told us had been built and endowed by a few wealthy ex-slaveholders. He was greatly pleased when he went in, and followed us, the teacher addressing him respectfully as "Mr. Paxton," shaking his hand, and telling him of his children's progress. After we had left the school, he asked if he might show us his house, which was a pretty, white, vine-covered cottage in a large garden. He called his three "litty gals" out, and was very proud and happy in them.

As we drove away, he said, "When we fus' start, my wife go out to cook, 'n' we banked every dollah, till we build dat house. Den I say, 'You stay home, Cloty, 'n' cook, 'n' patch, 'n' sew, 'n' de gals go to school, 'n' I scratch foh dem all outside.' 'N' next year I goin' build a sittin'-room to dat house foh de gals: 'n' I 'll paint it all up. 'N' mebbe," with a delighted chuckle, "when strangers from de Norf come ridin' by, same as you, dey 'll t'ink white folks lib in dat house! But sometimes I t'ink, sah, sposen my litty gals been born 'foh de wah, 'n' somebody want 'em, 'n' dey be sent down street to de stoh, 'n' come back no more!"

It is impossible to see the present of the negro in its true light without the background of the past.

Hear now the Northern owner of a plantation in one of the Gulf States:—

"I have owned this place for fifteen years, and I have tried honestly in that time to better the condition of the negroes I employ. Without being an active abolitionist, I was no believer in slavery. I did believe that these people, by patience and rational treatment, could be elevated. But I am totally discouraged. I had a good deal of feeling in the matter, and gave it my personal attention. We went to work practically. I built them decent cabins; my wife gave them some furniture and a few little comforts. I paid them liberally, and explained to them that the better their work, the better should be their wages. There was the foundation for useful citizenship. It was of no use. They will not understand the uses of work. Then they are gregarious in their filth and idleness. Build six cabins for six families, and in a month they will all be living (or kenneling) in two, and burning the others for firewood. My wife gave them hens, ducks, etc., promising to buy their eggs and poultry. But they immediately had a grand feast on the fowls, and ever since have robbed her hen-roosts. It is impossible to keep poultry, tools, or anything else which can be carried away. No, to be just, they are not all alike. Here and there, one, like Job, my coachman, is honest and truthful, and will work hard for my interest and his own. There are probably half a dozen such among our people. You will find such on every plantation. But the others borrow, beg, or steal from them. An industrious negro always has a load of lazy kinsfolk to carry, and he carries them without grumbling."

Job, however, on inquiry, was found to have "banked" enough to buy a house and patch of ground, in spite of his load.

A business man in New Orleans, a Southerner and former slaveholder: "It is hardly fair to judge of the place which the negro can hold in the future, among the workers of this country, by the present generation. They are still weighted by the ignorance of slavery and (what is perhaps as heavy a load) their intense self-conceit, which is largely due to the influence of the carpet-baggers who flooded the country after the war. They convinced the negro not only that he was entitled to freedom and suffrage, but that, without education, skill, or even a wish to work, he was as good a man as his master. Why, there are negroes holding office now in Louisiana, justices of the peace and post-masters, who can neither read nor write their own names. It would be hard, under these circumstances, to convince the rest of their race that success in life depends on knowledge, skill, honesty, or work. But in thirty years another generation, at least partially educated, will have supplanted the ex-slaves. They will have more intelligence and common sense than the present freedmen, and will have found out that a man's place, be he white or black, depends on the way in which he does his special work."

An outspoken Mississippian wrote, "As for the system of convict labor, it seems cruel to Northerners, no doubt. But we have a mass of ignorant paupers to carry. What better use can we make of them than to set them to open mines and build roads? They help civilization in that way as they can in no other."

A leading politician in another State said, still more frankly, "We were forced to give up slavery. But we have got hold of a better thing for us than slavery."

Many prominent Georgians denounced it as "an atrocious cruelty, a sin against humanity."

The editor of one of the most influential Southern journals: "We are accused by certain demagogues, both here and in the North, with injustice to our freed slaves; as for instance, in the system of convict labor, in social oppression, keeping them out of hotels, theatres, etc. I can only say in reply, The negro is a voter, and the South is giving him the education which will enable him to defend himself intelligently against legalized tyranny. She is taxing herself heavily for his schools; she is putting her own shoulder to the wheel to lift him out of the mire; she is, in short, helping him in the surest way to help himself. That is an argument which is, as yet, unanswered. As for social rank, that is a matter which, as you know, no legislation can reach. It was folly to attempt to do it."

A clergyman, born in the South, said, "These different attempts to describe the position of the negro and to define his future remind me of the fable of the travelers who met in an inn, and began to discuss the chameleon. 'It is green,' said one. 'It is blue,' said another. 'It is yellow,' said a third. 'I have one here and to convince you'—He opened the box, and the lizard came out—white. Mr. Cable,[2] Mr. Grady,[3] and other recent essayists see the same subject, but with different lights on it. The character and the claims of the colored man differ with each individual precisely as do those of the white. They have their political rights: they are receiving education. For the rest they must work it out. Admission to theatres, cars, etc., will come, probably, as they show their fitness to rank as the equals of refined and well-bred people. But it will be slowly, as in the North. One thing, however, I will say with full conviction, and that is that the freedman receives from nobody, not even his Northern teacher, as much real personal sympathy or intelligent comprehension of his character and wants as from the better class of his former owners."

A beautiful and educated woman, married to a man as white as any Englishman, in telling her story, said, "My father's family were wealthy Germans. I have my blood and my fair skin and gray eyes from them. There is nothing to show that my mother was an octoroon but these dark patches on the palms of my hands. But that is enough. My father, out of his love for me, sent me to a Northern school as a white girl. He would have done better to send me to the slave pens. I should never then have known what I had lost. Neither my husband's education nor mine opens the way for us to earn our living in any trade or profession occupied by educated people. The only way in which he can be admitted into the society of gentlemen is as a waiter behind their chairs."

"Why, then," she was asked, "if you are barred out from the white race, do you not ally yourself to your own,—make their cause yours, and try to elevate them?"

"Because they are not my own!" she cried passionately. "I am white!

Must I bring the curse which falls on every negro on my children, when there are not ten black drops in my veins? Are they to be held as lepers by the whites to whom they belong for these few drops? They *are* white children, sensitive, refined, lovers of books, music, and art. Are they to be classed and made to herd with field hands all their lives?"

A North Carolinian, hearing the story of this woman (which I have but hinted here), remarked that "the question between the two races in the South would be easily settled if one race were white and the other black. It is the mulatto that offers the impregnable difficulties. We Southerners are apt, when we talk of the future of the negro, to forget that the white and black man meet in the same individual. Given the temper, feeling, and ambition of a high-bred Carolinian, with the skin and lot in life of a freedman, and the problem is not easy to solve. When we talk of 'the implacable instinct which must forever separate the races,' we forget that the answer confronts us in the face of every mulatto that we meet. This mixed race is, in every case, the kinsman by birth of the white. We can predicate that the negro cannot become industrious, cannot comprehend mathematics, has a natural disability for skilled labor; but how can we assume these natural defects for our brothers and cousins?"

"Give us time," urged more than one Southerner of the more moderate, thoughtful class. "It is easy for Northerners to read us lessons of duty. They never seem to have realized how complete was the ruin that overtook us, or how frightful the social and financial overthrow. The old relations between the races still are fresh in the minds of the more ignorant whites. The freedmen are still slaves in their eyes. Give them all time. We are turning to new industries and new interests: these, and increased friction with the world, will wear away the prejudices and soreness in the minds of whites, while education will change the character of the negro. Wait until the fermentation is over, to pass judgment. The North must not and cannot force nor hurry it. She never had any right to interfere."

Two significant facts appear to me to offer suggestions worth consideration on this subject:—

The first is the universal increasing demand in every Southern State for skilled labor. Machinists are wanted, carpenters, joiners, shoemakers, weavers, plumbers, mill-hands,—every kind of craftsmen, in short, who can efficiently aid in the countless new industries which are struggling into existence in the South. So great and pressing is the need for them that most strenuous efforts are being made to induce European emigrants to come to this new-old field, instead of to the Northern ports; in fact to enter by New Orleans, and remain a few months before going West,—if West they will go.

The second fact was the negro exhibit at the New Orleans exhibition. It was significant and pathetic, because it showed what the free colored men wished to do, but never had been taught to do. Their schools and colleges made creditable displays of their intellectual progress. But the work of their hands was almost invariably the work of willing but untrained hands. There were attempts at every kind of handicraft, from shoes and rolling-pins to a steam engine cleverly made by a negro, who assuredly did not understand mechanics, as he could neither read nor write. Shoes, machines, tubs, even pictures, were, as a rule, proudly labeled as the work of a man or woman who never had been taught to make them. The whole exhibit was pitiable as a display of wasted cleverness. In suggestive contrast were the work from the Hampton Industrial School, and some really admirable specimens of saddlery and engraved glass made by colored men in Philadelphia who had "learned how."

General S. C. Armstrong, who has had seventeen years of experience in teaching the Industrial School for negroes at Hampton, writes, "There is now a large class of negro mechanics in the South, carpenters, blacksmiths, and bricklayers. The proof of the capacity of the negro for skilled labor is, I think, ample. I fully believe in it. The great difficulty is their lack of opportunity to learn. They have less chance to learn now than in the days of slavery, which, in a crude way, was a great industrial school. I have seen so much evidence here of the negro's desire to learn trades, and have had such satisfactory experience of the race as mechanics, that I consider its success a question of opportunity only."

There are several colleges and universities in the South for the freedmen which profess to rank with those for the whites, but I know of no other industrial school than that at Hampton.

No practical visitor to the South can help questioning whether the great mass of negroes and mulattoes do not, in this crisis of their history, need training in handicrafts rather than in Latin and metaphysics; and whether, too, granting that the negro and mulatto have the mechanical ability to receive this training, it will not be more to the interest of the Southern white man to keep the new industries, now opening with such splendid promise, under his own control, with his familiar freed workmen, than to surrender them to foreign capitalists and foreign laborers?

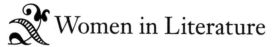

Women in Literature

Independent, May 7, 1891

There can surely be little doubt that women will occupy a much wider space in American literature during the next thirty years than they have done hitherto. Chatauquan circles, University Extension lectures, the innumerable literary, scientific, religious and charitable classes and clubs which young women are forming from Murray Hill to Montana ranches, are all doing a quickening work. They are, if one might say it, manuring the brain soil of the country. Some kind of crop must soon follow, and it will be a large one.

It is but reasonable to expect that all the avenues now open to women who can hold a pen will then be crowded by them. Increase of population will compel more of my sex to earn their own living, and literature (or journalism) will always be, as now, an easy, respectable way of doing it. It is a profession with many castes, but fewer Pariahs in it than any other. It is a path in which you can, if you choose, find the best of good company. Besides, there is always at the end of the path the possible crown to be won: a chance of gratification for that desire for personal notoriety with which the American soul, both male and female, seems of late to be so fatally tainted.

A few women, as men, will write for other reasons than these, simply because there is in them a message to be given, and they cannot die until they have spoken it. But these reasons are powerful and good enough to fill the ranks of literature during the next generation with a multitude of women who can not only write with ease but with sincerity and noble purpose, and who will help themselves and the world by so writing.

The question, What new fields in literature will be opened and tilled by this coming generation of women? is not easy to answer.

May I venture just here to hope that none of these coming women or men will ever try to give to us that much longed-for monstrosity — the Great American Novel. Imagine the huge canvas on which should be sketched all the phases of our national life, from the New Yorker in Wall Street to the Navajo Indian; the Virginian, rich only in forefathers and good breeding; the lepers in Acadia; the nihilist, the already dominant Jew, the Catholic, the German anarchist, each biding his time; the educated Negro still under the ban; the red man; the Mañan and Molly Maguire[1] brethren; and the Chicago millionaire! Who could paint the silent struggle between these people and a thousand other human types in one sketch? Who would wish it painted?

Genre pictures of individual characters in our national drama, each with his own scene and framing, we must have; and, indeed, we already have many of them, drawn with power and delicacy. It is a significant fact that so many of these distinctively American portraits and landscapes are the work of woman. A woman's quick perception of detail, her keen sympathy with the individual man or woman rather than with the masses, fit her, if she have any power of dramatic representation to catch the likeness of these isolated phases of our varied life.

Marion Harland[2] preserved for us the old Virginia plantation with its men and women. Miss Murfree[3] has made the mountaineer of Tennessee as immortal as his mountains. Mary Dean painted pictures of rural New York with a touch as fine and strong as Meissonier's own. Mrs. Catherwood[4] and Mary Halleck Foote[5] have sketched picturesque poses of the Western man. Miss Woolson[6] on her larger canvas inserts marvelous portraits of gentle, lazy, shrewd Southern women, and while Elizabeth Phelps[7] draws the educated Puritan woman from the life, Sara Jewett and Miss Wilkins give us pictures of the race in its decadence, the New England villager, hungry in soul and body, with fidelity equal to any other photographs of dying men.

Other women novelists have omitted local pecularities in their work, and there are still others, who in the last year or two have shown that they had the power to paint as masterly portraits as these, if they had not preferred instead to preach some pet dogma of belief, or unbelief.

Does not the fact, however, that so many American women have been successful in this kind of work hint that they will probably preserve it hereafter?

There is another field reaped with brilliant success by French writers, which is almost unknown in English or American literature. It is the Memoir, the Journal and the Autobiography. How the dead bones of French history put on flesh and blood in those scrappy, delicious if scandalous "Recollections" and "Histories of my Time!"

There are, as yet, very few such books to illustrate our own history. Even the Revolutionary and Civil Wars, with their infinite phases of individual tragedy and comedy, did not bring them out. Our people had not had time to keep journals, and our history is so short that we do not even yet understand how invaluable its details will be to our descendants. A few slight, powerful sketches by Mrs. Frémont[8] show what vitality such painting can give to an historic event.

With every year the class of educated, influential gentlewomen increases in this country; women who are *en rapport* with the literary, political, and social movements of their time; who have keen sight as well as sympathies, and whose sympathies, fancy and wit, seldom find their way into print.

I have a hope that this body of women who have the habit of broad and accurate thought will not always be content to expend their force in society, or even in charitable work. They will be stirred by the ambition to leave something more permanent behind them than reports of Sanitary or Archeological clubs, and will paint as they only can do, for the next generation, the inner life and history of their time with a power which shall make that time alive for future ages.

I do not mean to underrate the intellectual power of women when I prophesy that we will be more likely to succeed as painters of historic or domestic portraits than as theologians or scientific lecturers. I only can surmise what we shall do by the knowledge of what we have done.

The Newly Discovered Woman

Independent, November 30, 1893

I have intended for several weeks to call the attention of the readers of THE INDEPENDENT to an article by Helen Watterson Moody[1] in the September number of *The Forum*. It is on "Women's Excitement over Woman." And of all the countless arguments concerning my uneasy sex, which I have heard in the last twenty years, it seems to me the most rational and sane. It comes in the midst of the shrill feminine hurly-burly everywhere, like the sound of the bell in the church tower, calm and steady, striking the correct time, high over the babel of the marketplace.

Mrs. Moody quietly asks of us women, a few questions, which I am afraid we will find it difficult to answer.

While she understands the rejoicing of her sisters that they have pushed their way into the professions, trade, finance and men's attire (these being regarded by them as solid rungs on the ladder to fortune and self-development), she finds a false note in their rejoicing. There is too much sex-consciousness in it, and a great deal too much boasting.

She reminds them that women always have done one-half of the world's work, and that the women who did it in past ages were quite as able, as dignified and as usefully, if not as publicly, employed as those who so loudly trumpet their own achievements to-day.

She is perplexed, too, by the recent ecstatic announcement in Chicago, by the leaders of the new movement, that "a discovery has just been made more important than that of the New World by Columbus; the discovery, this summer—of Woman."

While she sees the difference in the kind of work done by past generations of her sex, and this present just discovered rival of man, she mildly asks, What is the difference between the workers? The only change in them that she can see is that "while women once were content to do their work unostentatiously, and without asking special recognition for it, they manifest to-day a disposition toward the title roles and the limelight and the center of the stage."

She asks, too, why women of to-day do not simply emphasize to the public the quality of their work, which is the only thing worth comment, but urge instead the fact that the worker wears skirts instead of trousers—a consideration which has no bearing whatever on the case. She cites, as an example, the Woman's Exhibit at Chicago.[2] If the work was creditable, as work, why was it not placed side by side with that of men?

Probably every rational woman of the myriads who entered the Woman's Building asked, with Mrs. Moody, "Why is our work set apart, like that of savages or feeble-minded children?" The mere setting of it apart was an acknowledgment of inferiority.

I may add, *en passant*, that the exhibit was a mistake if it was intended to show the advance made by women in the last four hundred years. With the exception of one or two creditable pictures and some decorated china, there was no important art nor handicraft represented by the women in their building in which their sisters who lived before Columbus did not excel them.

The advance made by our sex during that time has been the broadening of their fields of influence, the capture of new standing ground, the wider cultivation of the individual, and the methods and habit of combination. They cannot index these real gains by pictures or lacework.

The gains are so real and so great that the women who have struggled for them, in their intoxication of victory are not likely to listen with patience to any strictures, even when they are as gentle as those of Mrs. Moody.

The American Woman, who claims to have been discovered at Chicago this summer, is exultant and happy in her thousand new ways of work; in her congresses, her guilds, her Chautauquan circles and her colleges, in her political triumphs, in her charities, wise and unwise. She has so much reason to be proud and happy, that she will not hear the suggestion, that she has only advanced *with man* along these upward paths. She is fond of regarding the women who went before her as ignorant, weak thralls of a tyrant.

Mrs. Moody points out in detail that women of other ages were the equals in art and literature of those who are now so widely advertised.

She might have called attention also to the fact that the women who inherit political power have been gradually more and more cramped and stinted in its exercise during the last four centuries. Queen Bess would scorn Victoria's scepter, which that worthy bourgeoise old lady cannot touch except under the direction of half a dozen men.

Or what woman reigning in this century would make or lead her forces into the field with the skill in strategy of Margaret of Anjou or Joan of

Brittany, or any other of the warlike queens? It was a poor business; but we have lost their skill in it.

Or, to come down to the middle class, had not the wife of the English squire or Virginia planter, who superintended a great establishment—the weaving, the brewing, the clothing, the provisioning, the education and the morals of a host of children and servants, holding her place in social life also as a gentlewoman with grace and dignity—quite as much need of intellectual power and executive ability as if she had been a newspaper correspondent or had painted china saucers? Was not the influence of Mme. de Maintenon[3] as she sat knotting her lace, or de Staël[4] twisting her bit of ivy while she talked at dinner, at least as great over the age in which they lived as that of a woman lecturer in Chicago?

We are apt to look upon modern guilds and charitable works as discoveries of the newly discovered woman. Even Mrs. Moody suggests that the work of the Sanitary Commission first taught our sex its power in philanthropy. We forget that guilds of women exist, more powerful than any of modern origin, which for seven hundred years have carried on their sacred work. They were founded by women, and have always been conducted by women for the education of women, for their rescue from vice, and for the care of the sick and orphans and prisoners. They have succored, literally, millions who needed succor; and, whatever may be our religious faith, we must acknowledge that no modern association can surpass them in the purity of their purpose or the devotion, shrewdness or sagacity with which the purpose has been carried out.

The graduate of Vassar[5] or Smith[6] has a pitying contempt for her grandmother whose life was spent in her nursery and kitchen, and whose Bible and Cook-book constituted her library. But her grandfather's life also was bounded by his shop and field; his weekly *United States Gazette* gave him his sole glimpse of the world; he knew no more of science or foreign politics or the Unions and Organizations in which his grandson has bound himself than did his old wife of mathematics and Women's clubs. When Eve span, Adam delved. They march together always. If Eve is "enfranchised," as she declared at Chicago, it is because Adam first grew tired of old bonds and gained a wider, freer life. She has lost power as a sovereign and gained power as a citizen, just as man has done.

The difference between them now is that the man takes his development as a matter of course, and attributes it to the increased knowledge of science, to the public schools, to railways, the telegraph, newspaper— all things which bring the peoples of the world closer together. But the

Woman (as she writes herself) is *tête-montée*[7] with her success and attributes it wholly to her own efforts. The persistency with which she sounds her own trumpet, and calls attention to her virtues and perfections, makes the judicious grieve. As I write comes a report from the meeting of the foremost woman's club in the country in which the "blundering government of men" is arraigned and we are assured that "the future of the world is in the hands of Woman," who will bring it all right.

This Woman seized on the World's Fair as an opportunity to exploit herself. If she had had her own way it would have degenerated into a game of brag. She besought every woman in the country who had ever written a paper in a magazine or invented a mousetrap to send her paper and her trap, her portrait and her autograph for exhibition. In some of the States it was suggested that folding screens should be erected by each county, on which should be pasted the photograph and a sketch of the life of every woman who had "done anything," if it were only to keep a successful shoe-shop.

These are simply straws to show which way the current sets. It was fitting and right that women should take part in the management of the Fair, and that the papers, the shoes and the mousetraps should be shown. But, in the name of decency, why should the private lives and faces of their makers be given up to the staring millions?

The majority of women in this country, strange as it may seem to this pretentious, wordy Woman, prefer not to be "discovered." Their work may belong to the world; but their personality does not. This is the class whose individual influence will make them potential in the future of the country.

As for their active sisters, no one questions the value of their achievements nor their just cause for triumph. They are so strong and so wise that one wonders that they are not wise enough to see that their work and not their words should recommend them, and that loud boasting and swagger in public is a sign of bad taste and ill breeding as much in a club as in an individual woman.

It is the newly made peer who talks of his title; the prince of the blood drops it when he would be comfortable, and travels incognito. A man of sense is too busy with his work to ask what people say of him; it is the child who brags of what he has done and begs to be petted and applauded.

In the Gray Cabins of New England

Century Magazine, February 1895

An Englishman who recently visited this country wrote from Boston to a friend:

As I have so little time in America, I have decided to spend it all in New England. It is the American race that I wish to study, not their scenery nor towns. I have always heard that in New England was the brain of the country, and that the Puritan blood first gave the distinctive character to your people. My friends in Boston assure me that the influence of this section is still dominant throughout the States, and that the leaders of the nation in politics, in literature, and in religious inquiry come now, as they did at first, out of the little gray cabins on these bleak farms of New England. From the stories that they tell me of these Yankee cotters, their poverty, their thrift, and their hungry greed for knowledge, I can readily understand that they still supply much of the intellectual force for the complex mass which makes up the American people. I am going among them. I wish to study the power which moves the machine.

I do not know what was the result of his studies. The opinion of any foreigner about us really matters very little. But it matters a great deal if we are mistaken in our own opinion of ourselves or of the work which we are doing for our country.

When his friends in Boston talked to this stranger of the intellectual energy at work in the gray cabins of New England, they only repeated an old orthodox formula, which was true a hundred or even fifty years ago. They have repeated it so often that it never occurs to them to ask whether it is true now.

Is it?

Nobody who is not made imbecile by prejudice denies the influence of the intellectual life of Boston, and of two or three other cities in New England, upon the thought of the whole country. It is genuine life—that; the generation, birth, and growth of ideas. It is not merely the chafing of old, hackneyed opinions against one another, such as we sometimes find in the literary clubs of newer towns where the creeds and sayings of dead times and dead men, from Aristotle to Browning, are taken out and picked over and over and compared, as a housewife assorts the scraps from her rag-bag.

It is the fashion now to gibe at Boston and Boston culture. But if the meanest giber brings a bit of good work into the world, in book or score or picture, he knows that it is from Boston its first recognition will come, and that promptly and heartily. He will find no grudging jealousy there of his little success, no damning him with faint praise. The past master is not afraid to hold out his hand to the apprentice.

It is because I know so well the liberal, large justice of that class in New England who welcome intelligently the best work and best workers throughout the country that I venture to point out to them certain poor work and unable workers at home. They view the world at long range clearly enough: they take a keen interest in the conditions of life in the Ukraine, and the changes of belief in every Somaj in India; but they appear to be blind to conditions and beliefs in Vermont and Cape Cod. They think, apparently, that the old-time Yankee of Lowell and the Puritan of Hawthorne are still living in their farms and villages, producing brain force for the whole country. They neglect to look into the effect which a century of insufficient food, narrow interests, hard economy, and superfluous education has produced in them.

Perhaps a few scattered facts, if I try to set them down, will show what this effect is more clearly than any labored explanation.

About ten years ago I went for the first time to spend the summer in one of these lonely farming districts. I expected to find the same intellectual aspirations among these people that I had found in the class whom Doctor Holmes calls the Brahmins of New England. I looked at the unpainted little houses with gratitude and respect. Here, no doubt, the Emersons, the Websters, and the Hawthornes of the next generation were now being trained.

The village lay upon a solitary stretch of the Massachusetts coast. It had a picturesque and noble environment. Nature had made a fitting habitat for a high-minded and generous race. Silent, unbroken forests stretched down almost to the sea with countless limpid little pools shining in their recesses. Along the beach huge brown headlands, shaggy with seaweed, rose out of the surf; while the dog-seals crowded up on them to bark defiance at passing vessels—just as their grandfathers, perhaps, had barked at the *Mayflower* when she passed into harbor. For this was the very water up which the Pilgrim Fathers sailed; Plymouth Rock was in sight yonder.

In these old farm-houses some of their descendants still dwelt. Here, one felt, if anywhere, was to be found the soul of New England. Nature and blood and circumstance surely had combined to make the inhabitants of these neat, bare houses the flower of their race in its highest development.

But these inhabitants were, in fact, a few stooped, dull-eyed old men and lean old women. The young men and their wives had gone to Idaho or Kansas. The old people were employed in saving pennies. To that end they starved their cattle and themselves with patience and system. Most of them had been educated; but their only mental food now was the most sensational fiction in a circulating library in Plymouth. They knew, at least, that excitement was the nutriment lacking in their lives. They took no interest in any vital question, not even in the dogmatic theology dear to the hearts of their forefathers, though a few of them looked hazily into spiritualism. Some of them made a fetish of their homes: to pay for the little house, to scrub it, to keep it unaltered in its bare ugliness, took the place of worship in their lives.

One house, bigger, barer, and uglier than the others was the voluntary prison of an old woman who for five years had not allowed a human being to cross the threshold. Nobody thought her conduct odd or remarkable. I saw her once at the gate, and she poured out a flood of meaningless babble in delight at the possession of a listener. Her words were inarticulate, just as sour beer runs, choking itself, escaping from an uncorked cask.

"I've seen you passin' before. There's nobody ever passes but Len Moles goin' to his lobster-pots twicet a week. I locked my doors six year ago come July. The folks tramped on my kitchen floor, and I can't scrub it but once a day. The year afore that I spent at my married da'ater's on the Cape. She did n't charge nothin' for my keep. To be sure, I chored round an' knitted, reg'lar. But I took it kind in 'Liza, not chargin' nothin'. No board all winter!"

"Do children here usually charge their mothers for board?" I asked.

"No." with a scared look; "they send them to the house."

"You must be lonely."

"Me? No. I've got my cleanin' to do. An' Len Moles goes by reg'lar."

In the old days solitude, fasting, and praying for five years no doubt brought many a hermit very near to God or the devil; but a solitude of five years of scrubbing and watching for Len Moles?

Another village which I know well was once the thriving seat of a great industry. It was abandoned by the capitalists about fifteen years ago. The gray cabins are double, and inside you find now and then a gay carpet or a plush chair bought when the young people lived here and had high wages. They have gone to the West now, and the old men and women creep silently about with wistful, hungry faces.

Other villages which I could name offer to the eye of the casual visitor an air of cheerful prosperity. He is charmed with their chilly neatness. The grass plats are trimmed as with scissors; the glass in the windows glitters before the white curtains. Inside are the same subdued old men and ashy-faced women. Long ago the sons of the old men who should have married these women went South or West to some new community where food was cheap and the habit of thought broad and kindly. There their shrewdness, thrift, and respect for education usually helped them to success. But it is with the feeble remnant which they left behind that we have to do.

You find this remnant everywhere; in fishing villages from Maine to Rhode Island, in abandoned farms begging for buyers throughout Connecticut, Vermont, and New Hampshire. These people have not enough food for their bodies, or occupation for their minds. The niggardly economy forced upon their fore-fathers by the barren soil is not bewailed by them as a belittling necessity, but is honored as the chief of virtues. More food goes to the nutriment of a big, energetic Ohioan or Pennsylvanian in a day than would keep his listless, lean brother in these worn-out villages alive for weeks. If the first man is hearty and liberal the credit is partly due to his abounding beef and cider, and the lack of them helps to make the latter both avaricious and morbid. Neither has plain living lifted him into high thinking. He is stingy of love, of friendship, of emotion. Kindly words, enthusiasm, caresses, and laughter, are so much waste in his eyes. Divorces become more numerous with each year. He has given up the lofty Puritan faith, and has kept the objectionable Puritan temperament. He goes about his milking or planting as absorbed and reticent as a Hebrew prophet to whom God told the secrets of coming ages. But he has no secret: he has nothing else to think of but the milk-cans or potatoes. The most hopeless feature in his case is his absolute complacency. He believes his own to be the highest type of man. He is not even alive enough to see how paltry and torpid his life is. I do not deny that beneath this hard, bare exterior his soul is often true and generous and even tender; but it is certain that he has worn the iron armor of self-control bequeathed to him by his ancestors so long that his soul would feel indecently naked without it.

In the cities of New England, and in villages where there are prosperous industries, the condition of the people is in marked contrast to that which I have pictured here. So great is this contrast that the live New Englander does not see how fast the life is being sapped out of his unlucky brother. When he goes out to the lonely farms or coast places, his esthetic sense is pleased by the somber atmosphere, the gray cabins and gray rocks cropping out of the mat of grass and wild roses. The grim old men and delicate, sad-eyed women are fitting figures for the melancholy background. He does not see that the eventless drama of their lives is not a picture, but the symptom of the decadence of a race.

A significant fact that ought to startle him is that nine tenths of the children and working people whom he meets, even in these outlying districts, answer him with an Irish brogue or a Canadian patois.

Another is that the New England farmer, once the most vehement of sectarians, seldom cares enough for religion now to enter a church. The big meeting-houses are filled, if filled at all, by women. Spiritualism has many disciples; so has the faith-cure; so has Theosophy. Religion, in the descendant of the Puritan, seems to have died down into a feeble flicker of curiosity concerning the unknown world. Really the whipping of Quakers and the hanging of witches argued a better spiritual condition than this apathy. When Cotton Mather declared that "the smell of the roasting flesh of the savages was a sweet savor in the nostrils of the Almighty," he had at least a live faith in — something.

But the class which calls now most urgently for consideration and help is the large surplus of unattached women, widows, and spinsters, in all of these communities. They are educated, almost without exception; they have sensitive instincts, strong affections, and the capacity to do high work in the world. But from the sheer force of a single circumstance — the majority of their sex in certain States, — they have neither husbands nor children, and there is no occupation for them but household drudgery. Nervous prostration is an almost universal ailment among them, following, as it always does, long self-repression.

I know women of high culture and large wealth who spend the year flying from mountain to coast, from the Isle of Shoals to Florida, in the hope of gaining a night's solid sleep. They will look at you with wide, tragic eyes, and coolly inform you that "as they are descended from a long line of brain-workers — scholars — they can hope for nothing better than cerebral disease. The brain in their race has worn out the body." When it chances that these victims of atavism marry, they inevitably soon grow stout, energetic, and common-sensed; they joke, dote on their children, and skirmish with their servants like ordinary happy women. One hears no more of hereditary madness. A baby is a cure, as old-fashioned as the days of Eve, for a woman's morbid ambitions.

In the prosperous towns of New England this class of women find an outlet for their strength, if not in marriage, in active work, charitable or literary or social. With their culture, their broad outlook, the aplomb given by secure footing of birth and position, and perceptions usually delicate and *fines*, they are probably the highest type of the American gentlewoman. Friction with the world has kept them healthy in thought. I wish they would consider their sisters in the lonely country places, who for want of work and that friction are overtaken by neurosis, or driven to spiritualism, to Buddhism, or to opium.

One such woman was used to attack a new science or language every year, and, failing, from her lack of teacher or companion, would pile the text-books in heaps until walls of dusty volumes shut in every room of the house. She fell at last into a state of semi-idiocy, and wandered like a ghost around the village, jabbering scraps of foreign tongues which she did not understand.

It is a hereditary habit in certain families for the women who have a grief to shut themselves into a single room, and remain there for ten, twenty, thirty years. Nor are the morbid fancies of these women always gloomy and sad. They live sometimes in an enchanted land of their own.

One whom I know, a woman of sensuous temperament and motherly instincts, refused to marry a man whom she loved because he had gone to live in another town, and she would be forced to leave the old house and half acre which were the center of the world to her. The courtship went on for forty years, but she was true to the house!

Another drove her lover away on the day of the wedding because she could not bring herself to change the name of Wonson for any other. He was rich and she was poor; he remained faithful and ready as long as she lived. She died at seventy, a maiden Wonson still. Could pride of blood go further?

The intellectual training of these women only makes their cramped existence more intolerable. The New Englander is losing the shop and the church out of his life, but he keeps a hard grip on the school. In almost every village there are academies and libraries free to all comers. Education he believes to be the royal road to civilization. But to what does it lead in these villages—in fact, not in theory?

Ball, let us say, is a fisherman; his wife cooks, scrubs, washes, every day in the year. His daughter goes through an academic course, and learns more or less thoroughly the rudiments of astronomy, philosophy, art, mathematics, chemistry, etc. Nobody, meanwhile, teaches her good manners, or brings her into relations with the outside world. She is unfitted to be a cook or chambermaid, or the wife of any of the Irish or Canadian laborers who come in her way. There is no possible chance for her to be anything else. She remains, *plantée la*, idle, discontented, and useless. When will we learn in this country that the education which a human being can use for his own or his neighbor's benefit is a blessing; but the education which he cannot use is a burden and a curse!

But why do I try to show the emptiness and paralysis of the life of these people? Miss Jewett,[1] Miss Wilkins,[2] and Mrs. Slosson[3] were born among them, and have written the petty tragedy of their lives with a power which has held the whole country attentive, as a breathless spectator of a play. I am afraid that the very power with which the tragedy has been set forth has made the spectator forget to ask why these lives should be either petty or tragic. These genre artists show us the tender, heroic spirit in a famishing woman which makes her boil her last egg for a neighbor nearer starvation than herself. But if the heroic spirit be there, why should it not have a nobler outlet than the boiling of an egg? With the whole big, seething world around us full of God's highest work to do, one grows a little impatient of human souls who make a life-drama out of their hair pictures or muddied kitchen floors.

Heaven forbid that I should have a word of impatience for these thousands of morbid lonely women whom God sent into the world to be busy and happy. "But yet the pity of it. Iago! O Iago, the pity of it, Iago!"[4] Think of the process by which the possible mother in a young girl is starved into one of these dumb human machines! The slow torture of the water-drop is less lingering and sore.

What can be done for them?

One of these single women, after living alone in her little hut on Cape Cod until old age, a reticent, miserly creature, became at sixty suddenly and violently insane. Her physician, wiser than his kind, prescribed no medicine, but procured a huge doll and the clothes of a baby, and gave them to her. She was at once quieted. She treated the doll as if it were alive, fed it, slept with it in her arms, worried over its diseases, ran to the neighbors to tell of its sayings and pretty ways. It was her child; God had given it to her at last. While she lived it kept her occupied and happy.

But we cannot play this kindly trick upon all of these undedicate nuns.

What is to be done for them?

First, it seems to me, recognize the fact that they need help: that these villages offer not only *matériel* for the artist or author, but a problem of wasted human life and force. The cities of New England are full of noble men and women who use their influence and money for the freedman, the Indians, the lepers in India, and Nihilists in Siberian mines. Can they do nothing to free these starved, coffined lives at home?

It is not sympathy, but practical help that is needed by these women. First, they should have remunerative work. Establish industries among them. Give them a chance to earn money (and better still, to spend it) as bee-farmers, florists, saleswomen, shop-keepers, trained nurses, librarians, etc., or in any of the lighter handicrafts. Even in the larger towns all kinds of work are now almost monopolized by women from New Brunswick or Ireland. If work cannot be found for them at home, help them to emigrate to the Middle States, or to the West. Let them follow their brothers. They have enough of energy. They are like a steam-engine before the fire is kindled.

A few years ago the Amazons in Barnum's Great Consolidated Show, the riders of his fiery steeds, the Roman Queens who raced in his gilded chariots driving six horses abreast, were all the daughters of New England farmers. They came to him in a body, seeking employment—self-respecting, decent, virtuous girls; and they went back home as they came. These women can be trusted to play any part well if they have the chance.

There is a part ready for them to play. From every town and camp and ranch in the west comes the demand for house-servants, nurses, teachers, and—wives. I heard last spring of a clergyman who collected thirty respectable, modest New England girls, and sent them to a missionary in Montana, who at once found work for them. In six months every one of them was married—making, let us hope, a happy home and a happy life for some honest fellow. The good gospeller, I suspect, saved more souls by his little plan than by many sermons.

Why should not others try the plan?

Why should not the philanthropic women in New England, who form associations to help the Czar take care of his lepers, and the South to settle her negro problem, organize to find employment for these, their neighbors, out in the busy, living world?

And after that? Nothing need be done for them after that. Through wholesome work and intercourse with healthy-minded people they will soon find again what they have now entirely lost—their proper relations to their brother-man and to God.

# Two Points of View

Independent, September 9, 1887

Two papers have just been published which are of unusual significance to the friends of the Negro, as they express the different opinions held by the advanced men and women of that race as to its present condition, and its chances for the future. The first appeared in the *Atlantic* for August. It is by Mr. W. E. du Bois, an educated Negro, and is a summary of the prejudices of the whites and their injustice to the freedmen during the thirty years just passed. It is a bitter, vehement protest, as passionate as that despairing cry of Esau when his brother cheated him of his birthright, which has echoed through the world for ages.

Of the life of the free Negro and the weight dropped upon it at his birth, he gives us a glimpse in a pathetic little story of his childhood. He writes:

"I was a little thing away up in the hills of New England, where the dark Housatonic winds between Hoosac and Taghanic to the sea. In a wee wooden schoolhouse something put it into the boys' and girls' heads to buy gorgeous visiting-cards—ten cents a package—and exchange. The exchange was merry, till one girl, a tall newcomer, refused my card—refused it peremptorily, with a glance. Then it dawned upon me with a certain suddenness that I was different from the others; or like, mayhap, in heart and life and longing, but shut out from their world by a vast veil. I had thereafter no desire to tear down that veil, to creep through; I held all beyond it in common contempt, and lived above it in a region of blue sky and great wandering shadows. That sky was bluest when I could beat my mates at examination time, or beat them at a foot-race, or even beat their stringy heads. Alas, with the years all this fine contempt began to fade; for the world I longed for, and all its dazzling opportunities, were theirs, not mine. But they should not keep these prizes, I said; some, all, I would wrest from them. Just how I would do it I could never decide; by reading law, by healing the sick, by telling the wonderful tales that swam in my head—some way."

But he seems almost to have convinced himself that "there is no way," that the

> "shades of the prison-house have closed round about us all; walls straight and stubborn to the whitest, but relentlessly narrow, tall, and unscalable to sons of night who must plod darkly on in resignation, or beat unavailing palms against the stone, or steadily, half hopelessly, watch the streak of blue above."

He sums up the obstacles in the way of his race in their striving to "escape death and isolation and to husband and use their best powers: the ages of ignorance and poverty behind them: "the holocaust of war, the terrors of the Kuklux Klans [*sic*], the lies of carpet-baggers"; the effects on themselves of the accumulated sloth and awkwardness of centuries, all of which clogged their first steps into freedom and dragged them down. He paints, with a few powerful strokes, their desperate struggle to rise; how, finding that neither freedom nor the ballot put them on a level with the whites, they turned to books, as famished men would clutch at food.

"Here at last seemed to have been discovered the mountain path to Canaan; longer than the highway of emancipation and law, steep and rugged, but straight, leading to hights high enough to overlook life.

"Up the new path the advance-guard toiled, slowly, heavily, doggedly; only those who have watched and guided the faltering feet, the misty minds, the dull understandings of the dark pupils of these schools know how faithfully, how piteously, this people strove to learn."

And now, after thirty years—free, with the ballot in his hand, educated, earnest, self-respecting—the Negro, even in the North, finds his progress effectually barred by a shadow, an intangible, vague power which he can neither fight, nor placate nor pass. It is the unreasoning prejudice of the white against the color of his skin. "Before this nameless prejudice," says Mr. du Bois,

> "he stands helpless, dismayed, and well-nigh speechless; before the personal disrespect and mockery, the ridicule and systematic humiliation, the distortion of fact and wanton license of fancy, the cynical ignoring of the better and boisterous welcoming of the worse, the all-pervading desire to inculcate disdain for everything black, from Toussaint to the Devil—before this there rises a sickening despair that would disarm and discourage any nation, save that black host to whom discouragement is an unwritten word."

No candid white man can deny the justice of this passionate arraignment of the dominant race. The prejudice against the Negro in the Northern States has been as unjust and cruel in its effects as was slavery. We opened our schools and universities to him, and when he was ready and eager to earn his living we barred every way before him except those which led to the kitchen and the barber-shop. A man who had the ability and training which enabled him later fitly to represent the United States as Minister to a foreign country, was driven, by the groundless contempt of the whites in the Quaker city of Philadelphia, to earn his living as a cook. No merchant would dare to put behind his counters colored salesmen or women, however competent or curteous they might be.

The prejudice extends so far as practically to bar out a boy with black blood from the national schools which his race are taxed to maintain. It would require the courage of a Greek hero for him to pass through West Point or Annapolis and endure the tortures inflicted upon him hourly by the white cadets. These haughty lads apparently forget that they owe their education partly to money contributed by eight millions of Negroes.

This prejudice is as silly as it is cruel. Slavery at least had its advantages—for the slaveholder. But the angry whim which bars a large class of educated, able, moral, native American citizens out of the professions and the markets of the country because of the coloring matter in their skins, while it admits the lowest output of European slums, is blind and suicidal. So persistent and inexorable is it, however, that Bishop Tanner[1] so long a hopeful leader of his people, is just reported to have said publicly that he had now no hope of their ultimate progress in this country.

Mr. du Bois, too, when he declares that the Negro problem is "the stern test of the underlying principles of the great republic," does it with the accent of defeat; and when he tells us of the travail of the souls of a race whose burden is almost beyond their strength, there is already in the proud words a note of despair.

Now, what is the other side of this question?

For a paper issued by the Committee of the General Negro Conference at Hampton,[2] the other day, shows that there is another side; that a spirit which is neither that of despair nor defeat animates this struggling people. The paper is a message from their leaders, men and women of acknowledged high culture and ability to the whole Negro race.

I can call nothing in the history of this long struggle so prophetic of good as this paper. If the Negro bewails the past or despairs of the future, who can blame him? But there is no hint of wail or despair in this message. It is alive with energy and hope and common sense. It is throughout wholesome and practical. The Negroes are urged to become land-holders; to put their money into building associations; to establish business enterprises and industrial exchanges among themselves; to train their girls in domestic service; to put a stop at once to extravagance in dress, funeral ceremonies and church decoration; to bend their whole energies to the reform of the criminal propensities of their lowest class; to cultivate peace and harmony with their fellow-citizens, and a spirit of absolute reliance upon God.

The men and women who sent it out have stepped easily up on the platform where stand the leaders of mankind. They go straight to their work; they do not see nor encourage the whites in the matter. Nobody is present to them in this crisis but their race and God. In a word, the carter has ceased to pray to Hercules, and to upbraid him, and at last has got down and put his own shoulder to the wheel.

What are his chances? Will he ever get out of the mire? What are the facts in the case apart from all passion and prejudice?

The most hopeful fact is that, during the last two years, a certain tendency to cohesion, an *esprit de corps* has manifested itself among this people. It was strangely lacking at first. The mulatto graduate of Fisk[3] or Oberlin[4] was apt to cling to the race which disowned him and to curse the black drops in his veins—damned spots that would not out. He was slow to perceive (what policy, if no higher instinct, might have shown him) that success and distinction were possible to him as a leader of the hosts of Ham, while he would be but a servant in the tents of his brethren of Shem.

Such men as Booker Washington, W. E. du Bois and Bishop Tanner do not sound the gathering cry in vain. The dusky clans are fusing into one nation and learning to call each other brethren.

There are other facts which the Negro, when, like Mr. du Bois, he counts up his accusations of cruelty and injustice against the white man, would do well to consider. The accusations are true. Yet it is to the white man he owes his freedom, his right to vote, the chance of education— every chance that he has of a higher, climbing life. The prejudice of the white is strong, but it is weakening every day. In 1847 it was an offense punishable by law in the South to teach a Negro to read. In 1897 every district has its school or college for black pupils.

Last July, an educated mulatto in Philadelphia married a white woman, the daughter of a prominent journalist. The marriage was described in the morning papers as that of "two Philadelphians of high social position." I saw not a word of offensive comment. Thirty years ago they would have been in danger of a mob. Whatever our individual opinion of amalgamation may be, it is certain that this generation regards it with less horror than did their fathers.

The Negro should remember, however, that his progress depends, not on his affiliation, political, mercantile or social, with the whites, but on the development of his own people. The time that he spends in striving for recognition by the paler race, in denouncing them or upbraiding them, is only so much time wasted. He should remember, too, that he suffers from no more cruel prejudice than did the Goth in Italy, the Moor in Spain, our own Saxon forefathers in England, and the Jew in all Christendom.

Every man to-day has a weight to carry put upon him before he was born. It may be a dull brain, a diseased body, a hereditary tendency to drink or steal, a crooked spine, or a dark skin. He goes tottering up the hill under his bag of stones. The world about him, generations yet to come, and others not seen by him, will watch him climb and fall and climb again.

Victory always comes to him who climbs steadily; and he may be sure that at the end nobody will ask whether his weight was a broken back or a dark skin, but how far with it up the hill did he go?

Two Methods with the Negro

Independent, March 31, 1898

The recent Negro Conference at Tuskegee was especially useful, as it set before the public more clearly than ever before the black actor who is playing his part with the others on the national stage; and, what was more important, showed him the full meaning of his part and how he ought to play it. The public unfortunately was not very attentive to the Conference; with the noise of the "Maine"[1] explosion in its ears, it did not listen as it should have done to the plans of these earnest black leaders for the uplifting of their race, much less to the funny, pathetic speeches of the old Uncles and Mammys whose experience was so significant.

And yet a war with Spain is an affair of months, while the progress of this people will concern us for all time.

I know of no more important or dramatic action in contemporary history than the slow upgrowth of this nation within the American nation.

Mr. Booker Washington, its chief leader, has a common-sense which is as successful as genius, and never has used it more effectively than in his effort to combine his people, to give them coherence, the sense of race, the courage which comes to a man from the sound of other men marching in step with him.

Several Afro-Americans whom I have known have lost their chance in life by ignoring their birth, by not seeing that it was their business to be black, to identify themselves with their people. As spokesmen for their own race they would have won respect and fame; but among the whites they were lost in the mob of the rank and file.

The Tuskegee Annual Council and the many local conferences founded by Mr. Washington are among his devices to produce this kinship and unity. The most garrulous old woman, the most conceited young man had a hearing. There was a shrewd wisdom in this. Each one of them went home with the belief that he was at work for the whole; his hand, too, was on the rope for the tug of war. They carried back to their filthy cabins and weedy fields white with gopher hills, the report of other negroes as poor as themselves who had cleaned their cabins and plowed their fields; how much cotton they had picked and the money, to a cent, which they had cleared in the year. Nothing could be more homely than this council and nothing more useful. The Northern newspapers, which saw in it only matter for ridicule, failed to recognize a most able bit of generalship.

Note, too, the words by which this keen-sighted leader strove to inspire the ignorant, unable hosts before him. Not a hint of their wrongs, past or present; not a single mention of slavery; not a moan for their poor chance in life, but sharp, ringing orders, to be obeyed now and here.

"Go to work. Buy land. Build a cabin. Keep it clean. Don't buy bogus jewelry, sewing-machines you can't run, organs you can't play. Pay for a good teacher for your children. Be clean, be honest. Make yourselves decent Christian men and women. But, first of all, go to work."

One must travel through the South and see the interminable wastes of pine forests and swamps, with their wretched "clarins," swarming with half-starved idle negroes, and remember that these hordes are numbered not by thousands but by millions, to understand the task which this man has set himself. He shouts in their ears only such words as they can understand. He does not try to hide their shortcomings from themselves or the public. He knows that the surgeon must probe to the bottom of the ghastly sore before he can heal it.

Unfortunately, there are other leaders of this people who do not pursue so wise a policy. They are young, educated men, naturally made bitter and resentful by the cruel injustice of their treatment by the whites. They probably find themselves ostracized and insulted by people whom they believe, perhaps justly, to be their inferiors. They then make the mistake of considering their whole race as in the same condition as themselves, and try to instil into them their own antagonism to the whites.

I have before me now, for example, a pamphlet containing six lectures delivered to the pupils of Hampton and Tuskegee, by one of the most prominent men of their race in the country. They are avowedly intended for the teachers who "are beginning their life-work in the humble negro huts." They give to these teachers a brief *résumé* of the history of the black race in this country to be taught to their pupils. The horrors of slavery, bad enough in reality, as we all know, are intensified and exaggerated beyond measure. They are told that the masters, as a class, "spent their days in horse-racing, cock-fighting, gambling and grog-drinking." The slaves brought into the mansion-house "imitated the vices of their owners." The mansion-house influence "proved to be the very damnation of negro manhood and womanhood."

There is no mention of the fact that the Washingtons, the Madisons, the Marshalls, the patriots and lawgivers whose wisdom and integrity made this country honored among nations, the faithful gospelers, servants of Christ in every sect, and their kindly God-fearing flocks, generation after generation, were also slave-owners. There is no mention of the fact that whatever change had taken place in the negro, as he was at his emancipation, from the brutal savage who left the coasts of Africa, was due to the influence of these slave-owners, and their influence only. Nor of the fact that when they were freed the large class of respectable self-respecting negroes at the South were those who had been brought into contact with their masters, while the field hands bore and still bear too significant a resemblance to their imported ancestors.

I came from a slave State, and the evils that I saw in slavery made me an Abolitionist before these excitable young men probably were born. But facts are facts, and to ignore them fatally weakens any cause.

In these lectures we are also told that the "infernal mansion-house influence" still exerts its debasing and malignant power upon the waiters, chambermaids, etc., who are earning their living among us. The teachers are instructed, too, to tell the negro child that the failure of his race as laborers in the South, skilled and unskilled, is also due to the injustice of his white enemy, "The white Northern contractor, has stepped in. He has brought his own white workmen." The negro is thrust out of the field, etc., etc.

That negro child must be dull indeed who does not know that no contractor will import workmen at a high price if he can find equally good workmen on the ground, of any color.

If this discontented leader will go through the Gulf States to-day he will find farms, mills and phosphate works without number abandoned for want of laborers, while negroes by the thousand are standing idle. The explanation is everywhere the same. They would work for two or three days and then stop and live on the money earned, or they would throw up a job to move on in a body to another place.

These morbid cries of discontent from the educated Negro against the unjust white are natural, but useless. Let him face facts, and if he wishes to help his ignorant brother in the South, take Booker Washington's method to do it. Don't talk to him of slavery, which is dead and buried. Talk to him of his own laziness, which is a worse enemy to him than any slave-owner ever was or could be. Don't antagonize him to the people who gave their lives to free him and are now giving their money to educate and civilize him. If he ever succeeds in this country it must be with the white man as his neighbor and friend, not as his enemy.

There are tens of thousands of negroes educated and not educated in both the South and North who are leading useful, honorable lives. They are teachers, merchants, skilled craftsmen and helpers in the "mansion-house." They have their own self-respect and the respect of their white neighbors. No such men or women, I venture to say, are let or hindered in their quiet road to success by the whites. I know such men who own large farms and others who have built blocks of houses in the very heart of the old confederacy.

If the teacher who goes out from Hampton and Tuskegee wishes to convert the field-hands into such men, let him not waste his time in be-wailing the wrongs of his grandfathers or the malign influence of his white neighbors upon him; but let him say with Booker Washington:

"We have a splendid chance now to make of ourselves a great people. Let us go to work and do it."

The white Washington never spoke a wiser or more timely word.

# The Work Before Us

Independent, January 19, 1899

A suggestive item of news comes to us this week from England. The Sirdar,[1] it will be remembered, asked a month or two ago for £100,000 to found a Gordon[2] memorial college in Khartum. Having successfully avenged Gordon's death by the slaughter (planned for fourteen years) of tens of thousands of Dervishes and negroes, he now proposes at once to elevate the miserable conquered residue. A huge university is to be built in Africa. British teachers are to be sent out, and the sons of the head-men of the villages are to be the first pupils. It is distinctly stated that there is to be no religious instruction in this college, and no meddling with the opinions of the pupils upon questions of morality. Hence there can be no attempt to change their daily thoughts and actions on to a base of more decent and pure principle. The one thing which is promised is that the English language shall be taught. The undergraduate may worship his gods or serve Mohammed as he chooses, to the end of his days. But he must recite his creed in grammatical English. *Et voilà tout!* He is saved.

The last reports assure us that popular feeling in England is strongly in favor of this project. Half of the sum required has been subscribed, and the Queen and Prince of Wales have offered to become Patron and Vice-Patron of the college.

The reason why this incident is of peculiar interest to us Americans lies in the fact that it is a deliberate, well-considered effort by a civilized race to elevate a mass of human beings inferior and alien to themselves. How are they going to do it? Is the way they take the best way?

Now, the American believes that this work of elevating alien and inferior races is the one to which he, in the Providence of God, has been called. He has been busy with it ever since the first ship disgorged its load of emigrants on our coasts. He is experimenting on it now at Hampton and Tuskegee, in every reservation in the West, and in every public school in the East. He will soon probably extend his experiments among millions of Malays.

He of all men, therefore, is interested in the question: How shall an ignorant race, differing from ourselves in creed, habits and speech, be lifted to a higher place in the ranks of men?

The perfunctory answer which most of us would give is that of Lord Kitchener:[3] First, teach him to speak English, to wear our clothes, to copy our social customs, to force his life into our mold of life.

That is the only remedy urged by some of our reformers for all the Indian difficulty. Compel the Sioux or Cheyenne boy to believe that he is not red, but white. Put a hat and trousers and a football sweater on him, dub him "Sam Jones" instead of "The Eagle," blot out in him all memory of the woods and the ancient proud traditions of his tribe and the old blanket-squaw, his mother. If that does not make a man of him — what will?

But birth-marks are not easily rubbed out of body or mind. It is a singular fact that the individual man reaches his highest development on his own racial lines. Be he red or yellow or black, as soon as he forswears the blood which God gave to him he becomes a cheap, factitious copy of a man God may forgive, but Nature never does.

The boy who had he been true to the tendencies of his race might have been a leader among negroes or Hindoos or Indians, being false to them, goes skulking through life a mongrel unable white.

History is full of records of the defeat of such masquerading folk: of Russians who tried to be German, of Germans who tried to be French; of the hopeless struggle of England for four hundred years to persuade the Celt that he was English; of the triumph of the Jew who in spite of the persecution of nineteen centuries now holds alarming power among the nations that hate him, by simply persisting in being a Jew.

But in spite of these hints from history, the Sirdar apparently has no doubt of the success of his experiment. He evidently thinks that the Sudanese can be as easily turned into an Englishman as into a corpse. Backed by the Queen and applauding England and a hundred thousand pounds he grapples with the mass of Dervishes and negroes, orders their clothes and their language to be changed, gives them a smattering of modern science and policy, and presto! the work is done! They are Anglicized and civilized.

Now and then amid the applause which is given to his plan we hear a note of anxious doubt.

The *Spectator* says:

"We do not doubt the readiness of all the tribes, Shillooks included, if they can be persuaded to dress, to fill the classes to repletion, and become surveyors, engineers, doctors, traffic managers, and even men of learning. But we are afraid of one thing. Lord Kitchener is striking the note at which all future education in Ethiopia will be pitched, and we fear the note is wrong. He and his future colleagues evidently intend that the education they give shall be given in English—that is, shall lose almost all its vivifying power. They propose, it seems clear, to repeat the blunder which India owes to Macaulay, and which has spoiled the results of a splendid effort continued for half a century. That narrow man of genius insisted on English training instead of training in the vernaculars or in Persian—and we have as a product the "educated native," who, tho a much abler man than he is commonly taken to be, is the despair alike of the politician and the moralist. No race will ever be civilized through teaching in a tongue in which it does not think, and when the teacher is a Northern and the learner an Asiatic—that is, when the two men's thoughts turn on different pivots—the jar between their ideals produces nothing but mental bewilderment, and a breakdown of all the supports among which character is built up.

"The scholars of the Sudan will not be like the Baboos whom England has created and now regards with such scorn; but they will be people who are not wanted, saturated with surface-ideas which are not built up on their own ideas, but are only thinly veneered over them. We cannot, we well know, produce conviction, for the whole utilitarian world is bitterly against us. The English is convenient because you can get English teachers cheap, because it will smooth the path of all young officers, and because it will make the work of engineers, railroad managers, electricians, and all their kind—a most valuable kind in a way—somewhat easier to them; and for this convenience all else that is included in education will be sacrificed."

The calmness with which all moral and religious influence is ignored in this plan is amusing. The ordinary observer would probably regard the negro *per se* as of more importance than his dress or table-manners, or even his knowledge of chemistry or mathematics, and think that what he says is of more concern than the language in which he says it.

Sum up the requirements in the Sirdar's abstract of civilization—the English language, clothes, learning and habits—and the trickiest political boss among us can boast of them all, while it is certain that St. John himself could not pass muster on a single point!

The plain fact of the matter is that this extraordinary scheme of education has its root in the complacent self-conceit of the English race. We share it with our cousins across the sea. We are always right; hence all other races must be more or less wrong. Our language, our coats, our religion, our manners, even our whims are the best of their kind; so we use them as inch rules by which to measure the condition of inferior races. We hold that they are inferior, as a matter of course. When, therefore, we set out to raise and better them we naturally try to turn them into a poor copy of ourselves as quickly as possible. Hence the Sirdar's plan.

This monstrous content with ourselves is at the bottom of quiet English insolence and rudeness, and of American pretension and brag. Other races probably have it. But it is not their arrogance which lowers us. It is our own. It blinds us, too, to the possibilities in other races, and unfits us to deal with them intelligently. We have talked of "poor Lo," and of the negro as one of the servile races for two centuries, and never have seen that by nature one was a finer gentleman and the other a better soldier than ourselves.

This defect in Anglo-Saxon character becomes important just now, when two successful wars have thrown the control of millions of aliens into the hands of the English speaking peoples.

The Sirdar has shown us what England will do for her pupils. How will we deal with ours?

Reclothe them, change their speech, give them an inkling of arithmetic, geography and modern civilization? Nothing more? Is civilization after all a matter of railways or even the ballot box?

Beneath these outer casings of life, beneath even the differences of race is the Man whom we must make or mar in our handling.

The White Fathers are said to have been the most successful teachers of the heathen, because they wasted no time in changing his clothes, language or harmless customs, but struck straight at the soul of their pagan brother, and tried to make it faithful to God, true, clean and honest. It was a different plan from that of the Sirdars.

If we make ourselves the keepers of these teeming millions of aliens, there is something more to consider than rates of custom or military occupancy.

What condition is the American in just now to become the controller and guide of any alien brother?

Is his own domestic life clean and unselfish and noble with content and simplicity, or is it tawdry with vulgar display and mean ambitions? Are his public men working for their country, or for the next election? Is the press just and dignified and free from scurrility and filth?

Does he really at heart worship God—or money?

 # The Mean Face of War

Independent, July 20, 1899

Of all the gods on Olympus Mars is always the most popular figure. Especially is he heroic in the eyes of a nation which is just about to set the crown of Imperialism on its brows, to gird a sword on its thighs and drive another nation into civilization and Christianity—at the point of the bayonet.

By all means let us look this god of war closely in the face and see what he really is like. His features at a distance are noble and heroic, but seen at nearer range there are ugly smirches and meanings in them. Our campaign last summer, for instance, loomed before us in June a glorious outburst of high chivalric purpose and individual courage. But when we looked back at it in September war had come to mean polluted camps, incompetent officers appointed by corrupt politicians, decayed meat and thousands of victims of disease and neglect.

I lived through the Civil War on the border States, and two or three facts which I remember may help young Americans to see this great god Mars, whom we are about to make our tutelary deity, just as he is. They are not the kind of facts which the historians of a campaign usually set down.

A sleepy old Southern town of which I knew was made by the Government, at an early date, the headquarters of a military department. Martial law was proclaimed; the two good-humored, leisurely constables were remanded into private life: sentinels patrolled the streets all day long: the body guard of the general in command galloped madly up and down: bugles sounded and flags waved from every house.

But the flag did not always indicate the real feeling of the owners of the house. Almost every family was divided against itself, the elders usually siding with the Government, the young people with the South. The young men, one by one, made their way across the lines and entered the Confederate army.

Before the war the drowsy old town had boasted a hall, the upper floor of a tobacco warehouse, which was used as a theater or concert room. The whole building was now converted by the Provost-Marshal into a military prison. He also, with difficulty, raised a Loyal Guard, in whose care it was placed. As all the fighting men of the town were already in one army or the other, this Loyal Guard necessarily was made up of material which no doubt furnished a good deal of amusement to the corps of regulars stationed in the place. No man in it was under sixty; they were quiet, honest mechanics and tradesmen; church-going fathers and grandfathers who had trodden the same secluded path since their birth, never once probably tempted to break a law of the land. Their ideas of military discipline were vague. For two or three weeks they guarded the empty warehouse by sitting in a row of chairs tilted back against the front wall, smoking their pipes and telling over their old stories, occasionally joining in a hymn sung with much fervor.

But at last one day after a skirmish in the hills some prisoners were brought in and led through the streets to the warehouse. Some of them were wounded. The sight of these limping, bloody men produced a strange effect upon the townspeople, who hitherto had really regarded the war as a passing disaster, the work of politicians which might come to an end any day.

"To-morrow, perhaps," they would say, "we may waken and find the whole miserable business at an end, and comfort and peace come again."

But at the sight of these prisoners passing down the street a sudden passion of rage and malignancy seemed to poison the air.

Some of the men were wounded, one, it was said, mortally; he was carried on a litter, and his hand, torn and red with dried blood, hung down limp and swung to and fro. Other men, we were told, lay dead on the hill yonder, where we used to go to gather pink laurel and paw-paws in the spring.

This was—war.

Women cried out madly—gentle, delicate women—and ran from their houses shrieking into the street; men crowded together following the wounded with sharp, wordless yells of pity or of hate. That one sight of blood tore off the life-long mask of education or manners from each of us, and the natural brute showed itself.

When the prisoners were taken into the warehouse these kindly neighbors looked at each other with sudden suspicion and dislike. They hurried to their homes in silence. Who knew which man was his enemy? He might be next door—in the same house with him. The old friendships and affections of a life-time ended that morning and gave place to an unreasoning distrust. Brother quarreled with brother, husband with wife, father with son. Very often neither man nor woman understood the cause of the war. But the contagion of hate was in the air. Men caught it from each other, as they take the poison of a disease. The old men of the Guard became suddenly possessed with a fury of zeal. They looked upon the prisoners as their personal enemies. The orderly, devout grandfathers raged like wild beasts outside of the prison, and fired at the prisoners whenever they approached the windows. So bent were they upon their slaughter that it was found necessary at last to remove the old men from the post.

As time passed the bitterness deepened, the gentlest woman and most generous man in both factions often becoming the most unreasonable and malignant toward all who differed from them. Old lines of right and wrong were blurred in the sanest and most devout. There was no right and wrong to most people. Take a trifling example: Late in the summer one Sunday night, while the churches were still open, the bugles were suddenly sounded and cannon fired. The alarm spread that General Lee's army was advancing upon the town to burn it. There were no Federal troops in it at the time. So the staid citizens of the town mustered and shouldering their muskets boarded a train to go forth, as they thought, to meet the Confederate army. I can see their stooped shoulders and gray heads now as they marched past peering into the darkness through their spectacles. Oh, such sorry warriors! But it was as fine a blaze of courage as any that illumined the war.

The courage blazed in vain. When the train reached the hills it was found that there was not a Confederate soldier within fifty miles. What happened then was told to me by the officer commanding the expedition.

The men alighted, formed in column, and boldly advanced into the sleeping village near which the train had halted. When no one appeared they held a brief council, and then, to the dismay of their leader, made a rush upon the village firing their muskets. breaking into the houses and seizing upon whatever came first to hand—churns, rocking chairs, feather beds, sewing machines, etc. One man appeared with a huge copper kettle on his back. In vain their captain commanded them to give up their spoils, telling them that the people were harmless and poor, and most of them loyal to the Union.

They were crazed with excitement and rage, shouting: "Loot them! Loot them! Booty of war!"

He compelled some of them to leave their plunder behind them, but when the train arrived at home many of them marched away in triumph with their stolen goods, among them the conqueror of the copper kettle. Yet these men were class leaders, deacons, and pious members of the Christian church.

I remember a company of young men, the sons of Scotch and Scotch-

Irish families, honorable, devout, gentle folk, who enlisted in the Northern army to serve their country and as they thought (and it may be justly), their God. They went through the war gallantly. Whatever was best and highest in its discipline they took and assimilated; it became part of their character and life. Yet almost every one of those men brought home spoons, watches, and jewelry which he had taken out of a Southern home.

It was the breath of war which had made them and the old men for the time heroes, murderers, and thieves.

I remember another company recruited from the same class for the Confederate army. They fought bravely, remaining in the service during the full five years. Of those still alive at Lee's surrender every man sooner or later filled a drunkard's grave.

Since the close of that war I have read and listened to countless paeans in the South and in the North to the dauntless courage of the heroes who gave their lives for the cause which they held just.

All this is true. But I never yet have heard a word of the other side of the history of that great campaign, which is equally true, of the debilitating effect upon most men in mind and morals of years in camp, and the habits acquired of idleness, of drunkenness, and of immorality.

The American is not used to idleness, nor to military discipline. Put a gun in his hand, and give him nothing to do but wait for somebody to kill, and the monkey or beast in him will soon show itself.

After thirty years of peace, a sudden effort is now being made by interested politicians to induce the American people to make war its regular business.

The army is to be largely increased. Many young men of all classes expect to find an opening in it to earn their livelihood—to make a career for life. The talk of glory and heroism and the service of the country is very tempting these gallant immature boys.

What is really intended, of course, is the establishment of a uniformed guard to police the Philippine Islands in the interests of certain trusts.[1]

But our brave young fellow sees only the waving of the flag.

Before he goes to camp for the rest of his days, let him look more closely into the life of it, to see what in time it will do to him—to his mind, his manners and the soul inside of them.

Mars, as I said, is just now the most popular figure among the gods. But there are ugly, mean features in his noble face when we come close to him.

# Lord Kitchener's Methods

Independent, February 7, 1901

An English naturalist, who kept close company with the birds and reptiles for many years, used to say:

"There's no limit to the queerness of beasts! The longer you live with them the less you know about them!"

As we grow old, if we think at all, we have the same feeling about men and women. The countless millions of them that people the earth, renewed every thirty years, with all of their varieties, have not exhausted the "queerness" of the human stuff out of which they are made. You spend your life with a friend or a family or a race and think you know them to the marrow. And, presto! they turn on you faces alien and incomprehensible. As even Behemoth did to Job.

Your cousin Tom, for instance, with no blood in his body but that of a long line of dull, godly Presbyterian ministers—how did he get that unerring lightning flash of financial insight which has made him the head of a great trust and a hundred times a millionaire?

And Jose, the affectionate Italian boy, who used to sell us bananas, laughing at our jokes—where did he hide so long the black drops that drove him to murder a child in its sleep?

Nations, however, develop abnormal traits more rapidly than individuals.

What was there in the character of the French people to prepare the world for the Dreyfus case?

What American, ten years ago, could have conceived of his country as at war with the Filipinos, or as again a slave owner?

Who that knows and loves the German as he is at home, kindly, music loving, the good husband, the fond father, the loyal friend, was prepared for the devilish gusto with which the other day he butchered the helpless Chinese women and children? Not one or two in a sudden frenzy of rage, but masses of them, settling down to the work, as to his yearly pig killing, with keen relish.

It is our English cousin, however, who has startled us most of late, with his extraordinary development of new traits. Here is a fact or two taken from the English papers of last month. To the ordinary observer they are inexplicable.

Mr. R. H. Hudson stated in the *Saturday Review* that it long has been custom for English sportsmen when voyaging on the Pacific to fish with rod and line for the albatrosses that follow the ship. When one of these great birds—supposed to be the most innocent and gentle of flying creatures—was thus taken, it is dragged up on deck, its head cut off as a souvenir, its wing bones scraped for pipe stems and the white beautiful body pitched into the water to rot.

So universal was the disgust at this wanton cruelty that prohibitory laws for the protection of the bird have been passed in England and in all of her colonies. But it appears from Mr. Hudson's statement that some albatrosses were caught last October by the officers of the steamship "Star," of New Zealand, and were placed alive in the ice box in order that the captain might satisfy his curiosity as to how long the bird could sustain life under the freezing process.

> "One bird," he reports, "at the end of ten days, on being taken out with the lower half of its body frozen hard, emitted groaning sounds, and raised its head and gaped, staring around with wide open, living eyes. It was kept out in the warm air for two hours and then put back in the ice box."

The captain ended this account with declaring that he

> "would proceed with these scientific investigations on his return voyage with other birds."

But it is not likely that he will do so. The scientific captain has suddenly found himself the best abused man in England. His account was published by the leading newspapers and raised a storm of indignant horror throughout the kingdom.

Now this loud impulsive outburst of sympathy for a single tortured bird among our English kinsfolk must impress any rational observer as something wholesome and fine. The people whose instincts are so true must, we feel, rank very high in the scale of humanity. Christianity has softened and refined in them the original tiger blood which is in every man. It surely has evaporated quite out of them. They shiver with horror at the story of a freezing bird; ergo, they must be just and humane toward other human beings; beyond all, other men.

But in the very week which followed this incident the reports reached England of the methods resorted to by the English leaders in South Africa to put an end to the war.[1]

Let me premise just here that partisan feeling had nothing to do with this account. It was a bald official statement of facts.

England has spent over £100,000,000 in the war. The loss in men disabled, wounded and dead is estimated at 70,000. This is the price already paid in the effort to subdue thirty thousand Boers. They are still unconquered. During the last month Cape Town has been so closely threatened that for the first time since hostilities began the guns have been taken from the ships of war in the harbor to add to the defenses of the town.

These facts prove that for some reason, which we need not enter into now, British troops cannot cope with the burghers in actual fighting on the veldt.

There is, however, another kind of warfare to which they can resort, and which promises success: to starve out the Boer soldiers and force them to subjection by burning their farm houses and growing crops; by driving their women and children and aged folk out homeless to "live like baboons among the kopjes." This kind of warfare proved effectual in Ireland under Raleigh and Lord Gray;[2] in Burma during the war with the dacoits,[3] and it is being tried in China now, where the Russians and Germans are dealing with the heathen.

The English people, however, were not aware that it had been resorted to in South Africa until last month, when a full account of the new policy was given to them. The eleven reasons were published by which the English commanders officially justified the burning of farms, crops and houses:

"1. Because it would cow the enemy. — (Colonel Pilcher's devastation of thirty square miles of the Free State, January, 1899.)

"2. Because a railway was attacked. — (Lord Roberts's order, No. 602, to burn thirty-eight farms.)

"3. Because a whole district had to be devastated. — (See proceedings of General Campbell in Ficksburg, September 14th, General Rundle in Free State, General Paget in the Transvaal, Lord Methuen in Zeerust.)

"4. Because rifles were found on the premises. — (See among others the doings of Generals French, Rundle and Pole-Carew in Free State in April last.)

"5. Because Boer scouts were sheltered. — (Roberts's order, August 14th.)

"6. Because no man was on the premises. 'Absent on commando.' — (See letter of Boer officers at Green Point, November 1st.)

"7. Because the owner had broken his oath of neutrality.

"8. Because shots had been fired from the farm while the white flag was flying over the house.

"9. Because a fight had taken place in the neighborhood.

"10. Because the occupants were alleged to be in communication with the enemy. — (Miss Cronje's letter, October 15th.)

"11. Because they refused twice to go scouting against snipers. — (Roberts's order, October 24th.)"

The *Westminster Gazette* also made public the secret instructions issued by Lord Kitchener to the army:

"1. To seize all forage, horses, cattle, and other live stock belonging to any Boer who had broken his oath of neutrality, or whose son had gone on commando.

"2. To denude the country of forage and supplies so as to leave no means of subsistence for any commando.

"3. To seize all stock without payment or receipt of all disloyal farmers, or of those whose fathers or sons are in the field.

"4. To seize all stock on farms any member of whose household, after laying down arms, again goes on commando.

"5. To seize or destroy all crops on farms belonging to men on commando.

"6. To seize and remove all farming gear, leaving none whatever for farming and other purposes."

The announcement in England that these orders were now being carried out was received almost in silence. A feeble inquiry was raised as to the number of homes burned, which was answered by a letter in the *Times* from a "South African Volunteer" who avowedly "justified the burnings" because the houses destroyed belonged as a rule to the poorer class of farmers. He himself, he declared cheerfully, had helped to burn down fifty or more farm houses, but none of them belonged to rich Boers.

Private letters crept into print describing the wholesale destruction of food, the blazing homesteads, the women and children flying from the soldiery. One English lady, the wife of a Uitlander,[4] had enough womanly truth in her to write home of the outraged women, wives of respectable burghers, whom she had taken into her house to die after Tommy Atkins had wreaked his will upon them.

What was the effect of these reports upon the English people?

They had no effect. They have fallen upon the public, greedy for every word, like drops of a summer shower upon the deeps of a black, motionless sea. The very papers that had been moved to passionate eloquence by the sufferings of a bird calmly hinted that this method of warfare had proved successful in the Sudan. Lord Kitchener left no prisoners there to breed mischief. England must have no trouble hereafter in the Boer republic. The Boer that would cause least trouble doubtless was the dead Boer. Hence, crush the bird in the egg.

It is true that Labouchere,[5] Frederic Harrison,[6] and one or two other sane men showed the horror which any normal sane human being feels at the sight of a debauched soldiery starving children and outraged women.

But the English nation, the honorable kindly men, the mothers, the Christian teachers, have kept silence.

A few calm folk may remember that Great Britain hopes to make the citizens of these conquered republics loyal subjects to the King and may have a passing doubt whether the policy of fire and starvation is the one best calculated to accomplish the end. A nation is slow to forget warfare made on its women and children. The Fenian[7] in Munster to-day hates his Protestant neighbor because his grandfather helped to hang and burn the Kernes, his ancestors, by the thousands in the days of Elizabeth. The Hindoo loathes the Englishman because of the doings of Lord Clyde,[8] and even in our own country it is not political opinions which now hold the North and South apart, but the burned homes and the wanton destruction of household sacred things long ago. If any optimistic Northerner thinks we are again one loving band of brothers let him go to the South to live awhile and trace the effect of Sherman's march to the sea. It was doubtless a brilliant strategic movement, but it will hold the two sections apart for many generations.

However, we need not discuss the future effects of Lord Kitchener's warfare on homes and women and children. It is the silence of the English people as they watch the fight that concerns us now.

These are the people who beyond all others declare themselves lovers of fair play. The defenders of the weak. The followers of Jesus. Yet when Lord Kitchener is let loose on Boer mothers and children they are silent.

# The "Black North"

Independent, February 6, 1902

Mr. W. E. Burghardt du Bois[1] has lately finished his series of advisory lectures to the negroes. Just now our poor black brother is the most advised man in Christendom. First of all, he has as counselor Booker T. Washington,[2] whom God has sent to pull him out of the slough as surely as he sent Moses to bring his people to the promised land. The next generation may appreciate the common sense, the piercing sagacity, the moderation of this black leader, but his race do not appreciate it now. Each man among them who has achieved any kind of an education shouts out a differing order to the struggling dumb hosts below him.

"Aim at the highest," cries one. "Get a college education; get Greek, mathematics, logic, tho you have to earn your bread as a barber or a baker."

"Learn a trade," commands another.

"Go to the North."

"Stay in the South."

"Make friends of your old masters. To follow peace with all men is Christian and expedient."

"Fight for your rights! Organize! Drill! Form into companies. Be ready to strike when the hour comes!"

Is it any wonder that the negro, dazed and perplexed by this multitude of counsel, staggers this way and that on his upward road? The miracle is that he goes up it at all.

White men are equally noisy concerning him. "The negro" is the one theme on which every American feels competent to pronounce a final judgment. Down to the unwashed emigrant limping on shore in his rags each one of them is ready to decide the place and future of the negro. Is he not black? Are they not white? What other authority do you want? The ignorant white finds down among his squalid mean thoughts a dislike to a dark skin—just as he may dislike a harelip or a hunchback. But he parades it as "a racial instinct," God-given, irremovable, and because he has this puerile prejudice demands that a whole nation, noble in their high aim, their courage and their patience, shall be sentenced to perpetual defeat and ignominy. Could anything have been more ludicrous than the spasm which convulsed the country the other day when the President asked Mr. Washington to dinner? Your white American will sit calmly every day while a negro shaves him, rubs his face and hair, touches his eyes and lips with his black fingers; or he will eat bread kneaded by other black fingers, or meat which they have seasoned and cooked: he will put his child into the arms of a black nurse; he will come, in a word, into the closest personal contact with the ignorant and often unclean low class of negro, and yet, when Mr. Roosevelt asks one of the foremost leaders of thought and action among Americans, a gentleman by instinct and habit, to sit down near him and be helped to the same mutton and potatoes he shrieks with dismay the Republic is in peril! Unimaginable horrors will follow this recognition of the fact that a man with a dark skin is a leader in thought or a gentleman in instinct and habit.

The most absurd explanation of this action was given by certain Southern editors who gravely assured us that as soon as the negro was admitted to the table of the white, general miscegenation would follow! Nothing could stop the white woman of the South from marrying him. The white woman of the South certainly had no reason that day to thank her champion for his defense!

It is a significant fact that the negro journals were much more calm and temperate in their comments on this incident than were those of their white brethren. They were not unduly uplifted by the invitation to dinner from the President to one of their race. The fact is, the negro is less excited by the desire for social recognition than the whites imagine. This is partly due to a dignified self respect common to the upper class of colored people, and perhaps to a certain funny trait of self-esteem common to the lower class—a vanity which makes them ridiculous, perhaps, but which comforts them enormously in their desperate climb upward. It is like the conceit and self-confidence of a child which carries him over obstacles in youth, but which he outgrows, and at which he laughs when it is no longer necessary to him.

Mr. Du Bois in the papers lately finished takes his usual pessimistic view of the fortunes of his race, but his advice to them is good, except as it seems to me, when, after acknowledging that the negro can find work in the South, which he cannot find in the North, he insists that he must not for that reason remain there. "A certain sort of soul," he says, "a certain kind of spirit finds the narrow repression, the provincialism of the South almost unbearable."

This may be true of the young educated negro who has ambitions and longings in him for—he scarcely knows what—altho Booker T. Washington and my friend the venerable Dr. Crummles[3] and many other black men whom I am proud to call friends, who are doing steady, vigorous work for their race in the South, are apparently not tormented by any such vague discontent.

These sentimental objections to "the provincialism of the South" fade into nothingness in the face of the great fact that the negro to live must find work, and that his old masters will give him work, and his new friends in the North will not. The trades unions here shut him out. But there is not a town in the South to-day where a black mason or carpenter or black-smith cannot find work and wages. The real difficulty there in his way is that, as a rule, he will not work steadily. Every capitalist who has operated in the Southern States will tell the same story of the negroes who would work for a week and as soon as they were paid would "lay off to rest up" for a fortnight. It is this unconquerable habit of the negro workman that has closed factories and phosphate works from Carolina to the Gulf.

On the other hand, you will scarcely find a town or village in the South that has not its industrious, shrewd, successful negro—a mechanic, a trader; an employer of other men, self-respecting and respected by his white neighbors.

The sum of the whole matter is, that both the white and black leaders of the race have fallen too much into the habit of considering it as a unit, of urging it here and there, and of prophesying defeat or victory of it as a whole people.

The fact is that the defeat or success of the negro, as of the white, depends upon himself as an individual. He has, it is true, to contend against an absurd and cruel prejudice. But every man has to contend against some difficulty—a dull brain, or deafness, or a tendency bequeathed by his grandfathers to drink, or to lie, or to steal. Whoever he is, be sure that he has his fight to make.

The negro, almost without a fight, has gained freedom, suffrage and education—now he wants work and has difficulty in getting it, just as women had thirty years ago. *They have it now.*

In spite of this difficulty, I should like to show him that he can succeed, if he keeps his head, works steadily to his purpose, trusts in God, and deserves success.

I have in mind now a freed slave who came to Philadelphia in the sixties. He had only learned to read and write; he had not a dollar, nor a friend in the city. But he was honest, he had keen mother wit, unflagging capacity for work, and that fine natural courtesy in which his race so far surpasses ours. He began work as a waiter, then became a caterer; then employed other men and women and made his establishment a universal aid to housekeepers. He laid your carpets, he draped your curtains, he cooked and served your meals, he took charge of your moving and carried you from one house to the other as quietly as if you were on a magic carpet. In word and work he never was known to be slack. His business increased rapidly. He took enormous buildings into his care, his huge vans were seen in every street. When the town fell asleep in summer he went to a seaside resort and opened a great *café*. When he died he left a comfortable fortune to his children and an honorable name. Everybody felt that Philadelphia had lost one of her most useful and worthy citizens.

What one man has done others may do. It is a significant fact, however, that there was not an educated young negro in Philadelphia ready or willing to take the good will of this man's business or to carry it on when he died.

I have known other freed slaves in the same town who unaided made their way to comfort, even luxury, as purveyors, coal dealers, even brokers. Success waits for the black or white man who works for it. No man is the sport of any god. The negro leaders do irreparable damage to their people by their incessant melancholy wails of complaint and defeat.

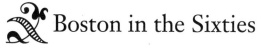 Boston in the Sixties

Bits of Gossip, 1904

In the garden of our old house there were some huge cherry-trees, with low growing branches, and in one of them our nurse, Barbara, having an architectural turn of mind, once built me a house. Really, even now, old as I am, and after I have seen St. James's and the Vatican, I can't imagine any house as satisfactory as Barbara's.

You went up as far as you could by a ladder to the dizzy height of twelve feet, and then you kicked the ladder down and climbed on, up and up, breathless with terror and triumph, and—there it was. All your own. Not a boy had ever heard of it. There was a plank nailed in for the floor and another for a seat, and there was a secret box with a lid. You could hide your baby in that box, if there were danger of an attack by the Indians, or you could store your provisions in it in case you had been on a long journey in the wilderness, and had gained this refuge from the wolves in the jungle of currant bushes below. All around you, above and below, were the thick wall of green leaves and the red cherries. They were useful, in case there was danger of starving when the siege by the redskins or wild beasts lasted long.

After I had grown old enough to be ashamed of my dolls, or of looking for wolves in the currant bushes, I used to carry my two or three books up to the tree-house. There were but two or three books then for children; no magazines, nor Kiplings, nor Stevensons, nor any of the army of cheery storytellers who beset the young people to-day; only Bunyan and Miss Edgeworth and Sir Walter.

Still, when Apollyon roared in the celery pits below,[1] and Mercy and Christiana sat under the locust-trees, and the tents and glittering legions of the crusaders stretched away to the hills, I don't know that any girl now, in a proper modern house, has better company than was mine up in Barbara's lodge.

One day I climbed up with a new book, the first cheap book, by the way, that I ever saw. It was in two volumes; the cover was of yellow paper and the name was "Moral Tales." The tales, for the most part, were thin and cheap as the paper; they commanded no enchanted company, bad or good, into the cherry-tree.

But among them were two or three unsigned stories which I read over so often that I almost know every line of them by heart now. One was a story told by a town-pump, and another the account of the rambles of a little girl like myself, and still another a description of a Sunday morning in a quiet town like our sleepy village. There was no talk of enchantment in them. But in these papers the commonplace folk and things which I saw every day took on a sudden mystery and charm, and, for the first time, I found that they, too, belonged to the magic world of knights and pilgrims and fiends.

The publisher of "Moral Tales," whoever he was, had probably stolen these anonymous papers from the annuals in which they had appeared. Nobody called him to account. Their author was then, as he tells us somewhere, the "obscurest man of letters in America."

Years afterward, when he was known as the greatest of living romancers, I opened his "Twice-Told Tales" and found there my old friends with a shock of delight as keen as if I had met one of my own kinsfolk in the streets of a foreign city. In the first heat of my discovery I wrote to Mr. Hawthorne and told him about Barbara's house and of what he had done for the child who used to hide there. The little story, coming from the backwoods, touched his fancy, I suppose, for I presently received a note from him saying that he was then at Washington, and was coming on to Harper's Ferry, where John Brown had died, and still farther to see the cherry-trees and—me.

Me:

Well, I suppose Esther felt a little in that way when the king's sceptre touched her.

I wish he had come to the old town. It would have seemed a different place forever after to many people. But we were in the midst of the Civil War, and the western end of the Baltimore and Ohio Railroad was seized just then by the Confederates, and he turned back.

A year later I saw him. It was during my first visit to New England, at the time when certain men and women were earning for Boston its claim to be called the modern Athens.

I wish I could summon these memorable ghosts before you as I saw them then and afterward. To the eyes of an observer, belonging to the commonplace world, they did not appear precisely as they do in the portraits drawn of them for posterity by their companions, the other Areopagites,[2] who walked and talked with them apart—always apart from humanity.

That was the first peculiarity which struck an outsider in Emerson, Hawthorne, and the other members of the "Atlantic" coterie; that while they thought they were guiding the real world, they stood quite outside of it, and never would see it as it was.

For instance, during the Civil War, they had much to say of it, and all used the same strained high note of exaltation. It was to them "only the shining track," as Lowell calls it, where

> . . . "heroes mustered in a gleaming row,
> Beautiful evermore, and with the rays
> Of morn on their white shields of expectation."

These heroes were their bravest and their best, gone to die for the slave or for their country. They were "the army" to them.

I remember listening during one long summer morning to Louisa Alcott's father as he chanted pæans to the war, the "armed angel which was wakening the nation to a lofty life unknown before."

We were in the little parlor of the Wayside, Mr. Hawthorne's house in Concord. Mr. Alcott[3] stood in front of the fireplace, his long gray hair streaming over his collar, his pale eyes turning quickly from one listener to another to hold them quiet, his hands waving to keep time with the orotund sentences which had a stale, familiar ring as if often repeated before. Mr. Emerson stood listening, his head sunk on his breast, with profound submissive attention, but Hawthorne sat astride of a chair, his arms folded on the back, his chin dropped on them, and his laughing, sagacious eyes watching us, full of mockery.

I had just come up from the border where I had seen the actual war; the filthy spewings of it; the political jobbery in Union and Confederate camps; the malignant personal hatreds wearing patriotic masks, and glutted by burning homes and outraged women; the chances in it, well improved on both sides, for brutish men to grow more brutish, and for honorable gentlemen to degenerate into thieves and sots. War may be an armed angel with a mission, but she has the personal habits of the slums. This would-be seer who was talking of it, and the real seer who listened, knew no more of war as it was, than I had done in my cherry-tree when I dreamed of bannered legions of crusaders debouching in the misty fields.

Mr. Hawthorne at last gathered himself up lazily to his feet, and said quietly: "We cannot see that thing at so long a range. Let us go to dinner," and Mr. Alcott suddenly checked the droning flow of his prophecy and quickly led the way to the dining-room.

Early that morning when his lank, gray figure had first appeared at the gate, Mr. Hawthorne said: "Here comes the Sage of Concord. He is anxious to know what kind of human beings come up from the back hills in Virginia. Now I will tell you," his eyes gleaming with fun, "what he will talk to you about. Pears. Yes. You may begin at Plato or the day's news, and he will come around to pears. He is now convinced that a vegetable diet affects both the body and soul, and that pears exercise a more direct and ennobling influence on us than any other vegetable or fruit. Wait. You 'll hear presently."

When we went in to dinner, therefore, I was surprised to see the sage eat heartily of the fine sirloin of beef set before us. But with the dessert he began to advocate a vegetable diet and at last announced the spiritual influence of pears, to the great delight of his host, who laughed like a boy and was humored like one by the gentle old man.

Whether Alcott, Emerson, and their disciples discussed pears or the war, their views gave you the same sense of unreality, of having been taken, as Hawthorne said, at too long a range. You heard much sound philosophy and many sublime guesses at the eternal verities; in fact, never were the eternal verities so disected and pawed over and turned inside out as they were about that time, in Boston, by Margaret Fuller and her successors. But the discussion left you with a vague, uneasy sense that something was lacking, some back-bone of fact. Their theories were like beautiful bubbles blown from a child's pipe, floating overhead, with queer reflections on them of sky and earth and human beings, all in a glow of fairy color and all a little distorted.

Mr. Alcott once showed me an arbor which he had built with great pains and skill for Mr. Emerson to "do his thinking in." It was made of unbarked saplings and boughs, a tiny round temple, two storied, with chambers in which were seats, a desk, etc., all very artistic and complete, except that he had forgotten to make any door. You could look at it and admire it, but nobody could go in or use it. It seemed to me a fitting symbol for this guild of prophets and their scheme of life.

Mr. Alcott at that time was their oracle, appointed and held in authority by Emerson alone. His faith in the old man was so sincere and simple that it was almost painful to see it.

He once told me, "I asked Alcott the other day what he would do when he came to the gate, and St. Peter demanded his ticket. 'What have you to show to justify your right to live?' I said. 'Where is your book, your picture? You have done nothing in the world.' 'No,' he said, 'but somewhere on a hill up there will be Plato and Paul and Socrates talking, and they will say: "Send Alcott over here, we want him with us." ' And," said Emerson, gravely shaking his head, "he was right! Alcott was right."

Mr. Alcott was a tall, awkward, kindly old man, absolutely ignorant of the world, but with an obstinate faith in himself which would have befitted a pagan god. Hearing that I was from Virginia, he told me that he owed his education wholly to Virginian planters. He had traveled in his youth as a peddler through the State, and finding how eager he was to learn they would keep him for days in their houses, turning him loose in their libraries.

His own library was full of folios of his manuscripts. He had covered miles of paper with his inspirations, but when I first knew him no publisher had ever put a line of them into print. His house was bleak and bitter cold with poverty, his wife had always worked hard to feed him and his children. In any other town he would have been more respected if he had tried to put his poor carpentering skill to use to support them. But the homelier virtues were not, apparently, in vogue in Concord.

During my first visit to Boston in 1862, I saw at an evening reception a tall, thin young woman standing alone in a corner. She was plainly dressed, and had that watchful, defiant air with which the woman whose youth is slipping away is apt to face the world which has offered no place to her. Presently she came up to me.

"These people may say pleasant things to you," she said abruptly; "but not one of them would have gone to Concord and back to see you, as I did to-day. I went for this gown. It 's the only decent one I have. I 'm very poor;" and in the next breath she contrived to tell me that she had once taken a place as "second girl." [4] "My name," she added, "is Louisa Alcott."

Now, although we had never met, Louisa Alcott had shown me great kindness in the winter just past, sacrificing a whole day to a tedious work which was to give me pleasure at a time when every hour counted largely to her in her desperate struggle to keep her family from want. The little act was so considerate and fine, that I am still grateful for it, now when I am an old woman, and Louisa Alcott has long been dead. It was as natural for her to do such things as for a pomegranate-tree to bear fruit.

Before I met her I had known many women and girls who were fighting with poverty and loneliness, wondering why God had sent them into a life where apparently there was no place for them, but never one so big and generous in soul as this one in her poor scant best gown, the "claret-colored merino," which she tells of with such triumph in her diary. Amid her grim surroundings, she had the gracious instincts of a queen. It was her delight to give, to feed living creatures, to make them happy in body and soul.

She would so welcome you in her home to a butterless baked potato and a glass of milk that you would never forget the delicious feast. Or, if she had no potato or milk to offer, she would take you through the woods to the river, and tell you old legends of colony times, and be so witty and kind in the doing of it that the day would stand out in your memory ever after, differing from all other days, brimful of pleasure and comfort.

With this summer, however, the darkest hour of her life passed. A few months after I saw her she went as a nurse into the war, and soon after wrote her "Hospital Sketches." Then she found her work and place in the world.

Years afterward she came to the city where I was living and I hurried to meet her. The lean, eager, defiant girl was gone, and instead, there came to greet me a large, portly, middle-aged woman, richly dressed. Everything about her, from her shrewd, calm eyes to the rustle of her satin gown told of assured success.

Yet I am sure fame and success counted for nothing with her except for the material aid which they enabled her to give to a few men and women whom she loved. She would have ground her bones to make their bread. Louisa Alcott wrote books which were true and fine, but she never imagined a life as noble as her own.

The altar for human sacrifices still stands and smokes in this Christian day of the world, and God apparently does not reject its offerings.

Of the group of famous people in Concord in 1862, Mr. Emerson was best known to the country at large. He was the typical Yankee in appearance. The tall, gaunt man, with the watchful, patient face and slightly dazed eyes, his hands clasped behind his back, that came slowly down the shady village street toward the Wayside that summer day, was Uncle Sam himself in ill-fitting brown clothes. I often have wondered that none of his biographers have noticed the likeness. Voice and look and manner were full of the most exquisite courtesy, yet I doubt whether he was conscious of his courtesy or meant to be deferential. Emerson, first of all, was a student of man, an explorer into the dim, obscure regions of human intelligence. He studied souls as a philologist does words, or an entomologist beetles. He approached each man with bent head and eager eyes. "What new thing shall I find here?" they said.

I went to Concord, a young woman from the backwoods, firm in the belief that Emerson was the first of living men. He was the modern Moses who had talked with God apart and could interpret Him to us.

When I heard him coming into the parlor at the Wayside my body literally grew stiff and my tongue dry with awe. And in ten minutes I was telling him all that I had seen of the war, the words tumbling over each other, so convinced was I of his eagerness to hear. He was eager. If Edison had been there he would have been just as eager to wrench out of him the secret of electricity, or if it had been a freed slave he would have compelled him to show the scars on his back and lay bare his rejoicing, ignorant, half-animal soul, and an hour later he would have forgotten that Edison or the negro or I were in the world—having taken from each what he wanted.

Naturally Mr. Emerson valued the abnormal freaks among human souls most highly, just as the unclassable word and the mongrel beetle are dearest to the grammarian or the naturalist. The only man to whose authority he bowed was Alcott, the vague, would-be prophet, whose ravings he did not pretend to fathom. He apparently shared in the popular belief that eccentricity was a sign of genius.

He said to me suddenly once, "I wish Thoreau had not died before you came. He was an interesting study."

"Why?" I asked.

"Why? Thoreau?" He hesitated, thinking, going apparently to the bottom of the matter, and said presently: "Henry often reminded me of an animal in human form. He had the eye of a bird, the scent of a dog, the most acute, delicate intelligence—but no soul. No," he repeated, shaking his head with decision, "Henry could not have had a human soul."

His own perception of character was an intuition. He felt a fine trait as he would a fine strain of music. Coming once to Philadelphia, he said, almost as soon as he entered the house, "So Philip Randolph has gone! That man had the sweetest moral nature I ever knew. There never was a man so lacking in self-consciousness. The other day I saw in the London 'Times' that 'the American, Randolph, one of the three greatest chess players in the world was dead.' I knew Philip intimately since he was a boy, and I never heard him mention the game. I did not even know that he played it. How fine that was!" he said, walking up and down the room. "How fine that was!"

Emerson himself was as little likely to parade his merits as Randolph, but not from any lack of self-appreciation. On the contrary, his interest in his Ego was so dominant that it probably never occurred to him to ask what others thought of him. He took from each man his drop of stored honey, and after that the man counted for no more to him than any other robbed bee. I do not think that even the worship which his disciples gave him interested him enough to either amuse or annoy him.

It was worship. No such homage has ever been paid to any American. His teaching influenced at once the trend of thought here and in England; the strongest men then living became promptly his disciples or his active antagonists.

But outside of this central circle of scholars and original thinkers, there were vast outlying provinces of intelligence where he reigned absolutely as does the unseen Grand Llama over his adoring votaries. New England then swarmed with weak-brained, imitative folk who had studied books with more or less zeal, and who knew nothing of actual life. They were suffering under the curse of an education which they could not use; they were the lean, underfed men and women of villages and farms, who were trained enough to be lawyers and teachers in their communities, but who actually were cobblers, millhands, or tailoresses. They had revolted from Puritanism, not to enter any other live church, but to fall into a dull disgust, a nausea with all religion. To them came this new prophet with his discovery of the God within themselves. They hailed it with acclamation. The new dialect of the Transcendentalist was easily learned. They talked it as correctly as the Chinaman does his pigeon English. Up to the old gray house among the pines in Concord they went—hordes of wild-eyed Harvard undergraduates and lean, underpaid working-women, each with a disease of soul to be cured by the new Healer.

It is quite impossible to give to the present generation an idea of the devout faith of these people. Keen-witted and scholarly as some of them were, it was as absolute as that of the poor Irishman tramping over the bogs in Munster to cure his ailments by a drink of the water of a holy well.[5]

Outside of these circles of disciples there was then throughout the country a certain vague pride in Emerson as an American prophet. We were in the first flush of our triumph in the beginnings of a national literature. We talked much of it. Irving, Prescott,[6] and Longfellow had been English, we said, but these new men—Holmes and Lowell and Hawthorne—were our own, the indigenous growth of the soil. In the West and South there was no definite idea as to what truth this Concord man had brought into the world. But in any case it was American truth and not English, Emerson's popularity, therefore, outside of New England was wide, but vague and impersonal.

It was very different with Dr. Holmes. Everybody who cared for books, whether in New York clubs, California ranches, or Pennsylvania farms, loved and laughed with "the little doctor," as he was fondly called. They discussed his queer ways and quoted his last jokes as if he had been the autocrat at their own breakfast-table that morning. His output of occa-

sional verses was enormous and constant. The present generation, probably, regard most of them as paste jewels, but they shone for us, the purest
of gems. He was literally the autocrat of the young men and women of his
time. He opened the depths of their own hearts to them as nobody else
had done, and they ran to him to pour out their secrets. Letters—hundreds in a day—rained down on him with confidences, tragic, pathetic,
and ridiculous, but all true. The little man was alive with magnetism; it
fired his feeblest verse, and drew many men and all women to him.

Physically, he was a very small man, holding himself stiffly erect—his
face insignificant as his figure, except for a long, obstinate upper lip ("left
to me," he said one day, "by some ill-conditioned great-grandmother"),
and eyes full of a wonderful fire and sympathy. No one on whom Dr.
Holmes had once looked with interest ever forgot the look—or him. He
attracted all kinds of people as a brilliant, excitable child would attract
them. But nobody, I suspect, ever succeeded in being familiar with him.

Americans at that time seldom talked of distinction of class or descent.
You were only truly patriotic if you had a laborer for a grandfather and
were glad of it. But the Autocrat was patrician enough to represent the
descent of a daimio,[7] with two thousand years of ancestry behind him. He
was the finest fruit of that Brahmin order of New England which he first
had classified and christened. He had too keen an appreciation of genius
not to recognize his own. He enjoyed his work as much as his most fervent admirers, and openly enjoyed, too, their applause. I remember one
evening that he quoted one of his poems, and I was forced stupidly to
acknowledge that I did not know it. He fairly jumped to the book-cases,
took out the volume and read the verses, standing in the middle of the
room, his voice trembling, his whole body thrilling with their meaning.

"There!" he cried at the end, his eyes flashing, "could anybody have
said that better? Ah-h!" with a long, indrawn breath of delight as he put
the book back.

He had the fervor, the irritability, the tenderness of a woman, and
her whimsical fancies, too. He was, unlike women, eager to help you out
with your unreasonable whims. One day I happened to confess to a liking
for old graveyards and the strange bits of human history to be found or
guessed at in them. The result was that he became my cicerone the next
day to Mount Auburn. It was an odd bit of luck to fall to a young woman
from the hills that she should have the Autocrat, to whom the whole country was paying homage, all to herself for a whole summer morning. He
took me to none of the costly monuments, nor graves of famous folk,
but wandered here and there among the trees, his hands clasped behind

him, stopping now and then at a green mound, while he told me curious fragments of the life which was ended below. He mentioned no names—they would have meant nothing to me if he had—but he wrested the secret meaning out of each life, pouncing on it, holding it up with a certain racy enjoyment in his own astuteness. It was a marvelous monologue, full of keen wit and delicate sympathy and acrid shrewdness. I must confess that I think he forgot the country and its homage and me that morning, and talked simply for his own pleasure in his own pathos and fun, just as a woman might take out her jewels when she was alone, to hold up the glittering strings and take delight in their shining. Once, I remember, he halted by a magnificent shaft and read the bead roll of the virtues of the man who lay beneath: "A devoted husband, a tender father, a noble citizen—dying triumphant in the Christian faith."

"Now this dead man," he said, in a high, rasping tone, "was a prize fighter, a drunkard, and a thief. He beat his wife. But she puts up this stone. He had money!"

Then he hurried me across the slopes to an obscure corner where a grave was hidden by high, wild grasses. He knelt and parted the long branches. Under them was a little headstone with the initials "M. H.," and underneath the verse:—

> She lived unknown and
> few could know
> When Mary ceased to be,
> But she is gone, and Oh!
> The difference to me!

"Do you see this?" he asked, in a whisper.

"Do you know who she was?" I asked.

"No, I would n't try to find out. I 'd like to know, but I could n't uncover that grave. No, no! I could n't do that."

He put back the leaves reverently so as to hide the stone again and rose, and as he turned away I saw that the tears stood in his eyes.

As we drove home he said: "I believe that I know every grave in the old villages within a radius of thirty miles from Boston. I search out the histories of these forgotten folk in records and traditions, and sometimes I find strange things—oh, very strange things! When I have found out all about them they seem like my own friends, lying there forgotten. But I know them! And every spring, as soon as the grass begins to come up, I go my rounds to visit them and see how my dead men do!"

But with all his whims Dr. Holmes was no unpractical dreamer like his friends in Concord. He was far in advance of his time in certain shrewd, practical plans for the bettering of the conditions of American life.

One of his hobbies was a belief in a hobby as an escape valve in the over-heated, over-driven career of a brain worker.

The doctrine was almost new then. The pace of life was as yet tranquil and moderate compared to the present headlong American race. But the doctor foresaw what was coming—both the danger and its remedy.

His camera and violin were two of his own doors of escape from work and worry. Under his library table, too, was a little box, furnished with a jig-saw, lathe, etc. It ran in and out on grooves, like a car on a railway. He showed it one day with triumph.

"I contrived that!" he said. "But only my friends know about it. People think I am shut in here, hard at work, writing poetry or lectures. And I am making jim-cracks. But if any of the dunces make their way in, I give it a shove—so! Away it goes under the table and I am discovered—Poet or Professor, in character—pen in hand!" and he chuckled like a naughty boy over his successful trick.

Holmes, Longfellow, Emerson, and George Ticknor, all chiefs of differing literary clans, formed a fraternity then in New England which never since has found its parallel in America.

There can be no doubt that their success as individuals or as a body in influencing American thought was largely due to their friend and neighbor, James T. Fields, the shrewdest of publishers and kindest of men. He was the wire that conducted the lightning so that it never struck amiss.

His little house in Charles Street, with the pretty garden sloping to the river, was then the shelter to which hied all wandering men of letters, from Thackeray and Dickens down to starving poets from the western prairies.

They were wisely counseled and sent upon the right path, but not until they had been warmed and fed in body and mind. Mr. Fields was a keen man of business, but he had a kindly, hospitable soul.

Hawthorne was in the Boston fraternity but not of it. He was an alien among these men, not of their kind. He belonged to no tribe. I am sure that wherever he went during his whole life, from the grassy streets of Salem to the docks of Liverpool, on Parisian boulevards or in the olive groves of Bellosguardo, he was always a foreigner, different from his neighbors. He probably never knew that he was different. He knew and cared little about Nathaniel Hawthorne, or indeed about the people around him. The man next door interested him no more than the man in Mozambique. He walked through life, talking and thinking to himself in a language which we do not understand.

It has happened to me to meet many of the men of my day whom the world agreed to call great. I have found that most of these royalties seem to sink into ordinary citizens at close approach.

You will find the poet who wrings the heart of the world, or the foremost captain of his time, driving a bargain or paring a potato, just as you would do. You are disappointed in every word and look from them. You expect to see the divine light shining through their talk to the office-boy or the train-man, and you never catch a glimmer of it; you are aggrieved because their coats and trousers have not something of the cut of kingly robes.

Hawthorne only, of them all, always stood aloof. Even in his own house he was like Banquo's ghost among the thanes at the banquet.

There is an old Cornish legend that a certain tribe of mountain spirits were once destroyed by the trolls, all except one, who still wanders through the earth looking for his own people and never finding them. I never looked at Hawthorne without remembering the old story.

Personally he was a rather short, powerfully built man, gentle and low voiced, with a sly, elusive humor gleaming sometimes in his watchful gray eyes. The portrait with which we all are familiar—a curled barbershop head—gives no idea of the singular melancholy charm of his face. There was a mysterious power in it which I never have seen elsewhere in picture, statue, or human being.

Wayside, the home of the Hawthornes in Concord, was a comfortable little house on a shady, grassy road. To please his wife he had built an addition to it, a tower into which he could climb, locking out the world below, and underneath, a little parlor, in whose dainty new furnishings Mrs. Hawthorne took a womanish delight. Yet, somehow, gay Brussels rugs and gilded fames were not the background for the morbid, silent recluse.

Mrs. Hawthorne, however, made few such mistakes. She was a soft, affectionate, feminine little woman, with intuitions subtle enough to follow her husband into his darkest moods, but with, too, a cheerful, practical Yankee "capacity" which fitted her to meet baker and butcher. Nobody could have been better fitted to stand between Hawthorne and the world. She did it effectively. When I was at Wayside, they had been living there for two years—ever since their return from Europe, and I was told that in that time he had never once been seen on the village street.

This habit of seclusion was a family trait. Hawthorne's mother had managed to live the life of a hermit in busy Salem, and her sister, meeting a disappointment in early life, had gone into her chamber, and for more than twenty years shut herself up from her kind, and dug into her own soul to find there what truth and life she could. During the years in which Nathaniel, then a young man lived with these two women, he, too, chose to be alone, going out of the house only at night, and finding his food on a plate left at his locked door. Sometimes weeks passed during which the three inmates of the little gray wooden house never saw each other.

Hawthorne was the product of generations of solitude and silence. No wonder that he had the second sight and was naturalized into the world of ghosts and could interpret for us their speech.

America may have great poets and novelists, but she never will have more than one necromancer.

The natural feeling among healthy, commonplace people toward the solitary man was a tender sympathy such as they would give to a sick child.

"Nathaniel," an old blacksmith in Salem once said to me, "was queer even as a boy. He certainly was queer. But you humored him. You *wanted* to humor him."

One person, however, had no mind to humor him. This was Miss Elizabeth Peabody, Mrs. Hawthorne's sister. She was the mother of the kindergarten in this country, and gave to its cause, which seemed to her first in importance, a long and patient life of noble self-sacrifice. She was a woman of wide research and a really fine intelligence, but she had the discretion of a six-year-old child. She loved to tell the details of Hawthorne's courtship of her sister, and of how she herself had unearthed him from the tomb of the little gray house in Salem, and "brought him into Sophia's presence." She still regarded him as a demi-god, but a demi-god who required to be fed, tutored, and kept in order. It was her mission, she felt, to bring him out from solitudes where he walked apart, to the broad ways of common sense.

I happened to be present at her grand and last *coup* to this end.

One evening I was with Mrs. Hawthorne in the little parlor when the children brought in their father. The windows were open, and we sat in the warm twilight quietly talking or silent as we chose. Suddenly Miss Peabody appeared in the doorway. She was a short, stout little woman, with her white stockinged feet thrust into slippers, her hoop skirt swaying from side to side, and her gray hair flying to the winds.

She lighted the lamp, went out and brought in more lamps, and then sat down and waited with an air of stern resolution.

Presently Mr. Emerson and his daughter appeared, then Louisa Alcott and her father, then two gray old clergymen who were formally presented to Mr. Hawthorne, who now looked about him with terrified dismay. We saw other figures approaching in the road outside.

"What does this mean, Elizabeth?" Mrs. Hawthorne asked aside.

"I did it. I went around and asked a few people in to meet our friend here. I ordered some cake and lemonade, too."

Her blue eyes glittered with triumph as Mrs. Hawthorne turned away. "They 've been here two years," she whispered, "and nobody has met Mr. Hawthorne. People talk. It 's ridiculous! There 's no reason why Sophia should not go into society. So I just made an excuse of your visit to bring them in."

Miss Elizabeth has been for many years among the sages and saints on the heavenly hills, but I have not yet quite forgiven her the misery of that moment.

The little room was quite full when there rustled in a woman who came straight to Mr. Hawthorne, as a vulture to its prey. I never heard her name, but I knew her at sight as the intellectual woman of the village, the Intelligent Questioner who cows you into idiocy by her fluent cleverness.

"So delighted to meet you *at last!*" she said, seating herself beside him. "I have always admired your books, Mr. Hawthorne. I was one of the very first to recognize your power. And now I want you to tell me about your methods of work. I want to hear all about it."

But at that moment his wife came up and said that he was wanted outside, and he escaped. A few moments later I heard his steps on the floor overhead, and knew that he was safe in the tower for the night.

He did not hold me guilty in the matter, for the next morning he joined his wife and me in a walk through the fields. We went to the Old Manse where they had lived when they were first married, and then wandered on to the wooded slopes of the Sleepy Hollow Valley in which the Concord people had begun to lay away their dead.

It was a cool morning, with soft mists rolling up the hills, and flashes between of sudden sunlight. The air was full of pungent woody smells, and the undergrowth blushed pink with blossoms. There was no look of a cemetery about the place. Here and there, in a shady nook, was a green hillock like a bed, as if some tired traveler had chosen a quiet place for himself and lain down to sleep.

Mr. Hawthorne sat down in the deep grass and then, clasping his hands about his knees, looked up laughing.

"Yes," he said, "we New Englanders begin to enjoy ourselves—when we are dead."

As we walked back the mists gathered and the day darkened overhead. Hawthorne, who had been joking like a boy, grew suddenly silent, and before we reached home the cloud had settled down again upon him, and his steps lagged heavily.

Even the faithful woman who kept always close to his side with her laughing words and anxious eyes did not know that day how fast the last shadows were closing in upon him.

In a few months he was lying under the deep grass, at rest, near the very spot where he sat and laughed, looking up at us.

I left Concord that evening and never saw him again. He said good-by, hesitated shyly, and then, holding out his hand, said: —

"I am sorry you are going away. It seems as if we had known you always."

The words were nothing. I suppose he forgot them and me as he turned into the house. And yet, because perhaps of the child in the cherry-tree, and the touch which the Magician laid upon her, I never have forgotten them. They seemed to take me, too, for one moment, into his enchanted country.

Of the many pleasant things which have come into my life, this was one of the pleasantest and best.

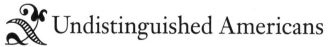# Undistinguished Americans

Independent, April 26, 1906

[Since we are very directly interested in "The Life Stories of Undistinguished Americans," we have given the book for review, not to one of our regular critics, but to Mrs. Davis, an author in whose independence of judgment our readers will have confidence. In our advertising pages we show our subscribers how they can obtain this book free. — EDITOR.] [1]

As far as I know, Mr. Hamilton Holt, in compiling this book, has struck an absolutely untrodden path in the field of literature. I have not seen anything so interesting or suggestive for years as it is. The thing that he has done is so satisfactory, so thoroughly well done, and withal so easy a thing to do that the reader wonders why he himself did not do it long ago. We all have felt the same uneasy grudge against Edison or Marconi or any other successful discoverer of every day wonders to which we ourselves have been stupidly blind.

The every day wonder which this little book discovers to us is the inevitable stratum of tragedy or comedy which is hidden in all of the ordinary lives around us; in the daily doings of the car driver, the cook, the farmer's boy and the myriads of other commonplace folk who jostle us on the streets.

Mr. Holt, as we are told in the preface, has tried to secure from themselves the history of the lives and condition of sixteen men and women. "His aim has been to include a representative of each of the races that go to make up our nationality and of as many different industries as possible."

We, the poor, anxious mongers of novels and stories, who, incessantly for years, have been dredging our brains and raking over the unclean swamps of bygone history to find characters and situations for our romances, naturally feel a grudge against Mr. Holt, who apparently stumbles against an original hero or heroine every time he leaves his office to cross the street. He has shown skill and fine insight in his choice from out of the crowd of the men and women who should take the *rôle* of the Ancient Mariner and tell us their stories. Each of these sixteen autobiographies is commonplace and normal enough to convince us that it is a confession from actual life, and a significant hint of the condition of the class to which the story teller belongs—be he Scotch farmer, negro peon or Italian bootblack. Nothing has happened to any of the heroes of these brief histories which is not likely to happen every day to tens of thousands of their fellows here in our streets. Neither are any of these narrators, in any sense, abnormal folk. The wandering Greek peddler does not turn out to be a blind Homer, the Polish sweatshop girl is not a masquerading Emma Goldman[2] with a dagger hidden up her sleeve; she is concealing nothing but her poor dimes in the savings bank, against the happy time when she shall marry Henry; neither is the itinerant preacher an unrevealed Saint John. They are simply what they purport to be, and the joys and miseries and chances in life which have come to them are likely to come today to countless other peddlers and shop girls and preachers. All these little gossips have an unmistakable flavor of truth in them. In that are their weight and value.

The collection of these confessions must have been no easy task. The uneducated man is not given to self-analysis nor to the study of the events of his life with a view to finding out their causes and effects. He very rarely sees his own history as a dramatic whole, as these have been set before us. Mr. Holt evidently has chosen men and women to tell their stories who have either some latent grudge against fate in its hard dealings with them, or some triumph in its unearned kindness—either of which convictions would give them that comprehensive view of their own lives which is the mental effort made most rarely by men of their class.

I remember that I once heard Horace Greeley[3] say that if any ignorant man—a man whose life had been entirely commonplace—would write an absolutely truthful account of it, with not a single concealment or apology, the story would have a power and value which no novelist that ever lived could give to it. In several of these histories we feel this rare peculiar force of the naked truth. It is the stronger because the editor has refrained from urging the meaning of the individual lives upon us by any comment whatever. He states the facts, and leaves the reader to find out for himself, with whatever wit or insight he may have, the meaning which each of these experiments in living spells out.

The purpose of the whole book, too, is not the gratification of the curiosity of even humanitarians as to the modes of life of their foreign born or needy neighbors. It means something higher.

It is but a little more than a century ago since Washington, Patrick Henry, Jefferson and a few other sincere men gathered in the little town of Philadelphia, resolved to try the experiment of giving to all the peoples of the earth a chance for life, liberty and the pursuit of happiness. Here was a vast, empty continent in which the teeming millions of the world for ages to come, might, if they chose, find plenty of food for their bodies, work for their brains and peace for their souls. They read this proclamation on the green square of the town; they rang the bell, whose motto was to "Proclaim liberty to all the earth and to the inhabitants thereof."

The gates were set open. The chance was ready for every man. Nobody can complain that the peoples of the world have slighted the invitation. They have come by myriads; there is not a tribe on the round globe which has not sent its deputation to find out what they could make of the opportunity. They are coming by myriads still.

Now, as far as I know, this little unpretentious volume is the first effort to show in detail how the experiment has succeeded; how the incomers have seized and used the chance.

Sixteen living men and women—the majority of them ignorant and poor, of differing races and religions and occupations, each tell us the story of their struggle for bread and for happiness in the United States.

The first is a young man in Chicago, who was the son of a peasant in Lithuania. He could not read nor write his own language; he was forced to go to Russian schools, to worship in the Russian Church, to serve five years in the Russian army, to pay taxes to the Russian Government that left him naked and starved. When his day's work was done he danced with his sweetheart, was content with her and his neighbors for company, mourned bitterly for days over his old mother lying dead. His life was bare and tragic. But there were in it wholesome, sweet human influences. Now, he is a prosperous cattle butcher in the Chicago Stock Yards. He bought the chance to work. In Chicago, he says, you have to buy all chances. He is married. He and his wife, he tells us, make a hard fight every hour for more money. They talk all day of money—of graft, graft. She dresses finely. They never go to church. "Church is too slow." Sometimes they are homesick for the green hills of Lithuania. They do not send their boy to church schools, "but to one where he is taught how to get on—get on." He sums up the moral of his American life. "To live well you must get money."

There is, too, the story of Rocco Corresca, an Italian bootblack, who worked for a fisherman, near Naples, for his food. The food was scarce enough, but the work was light, and there were dancing in the evenings, and lots of fun in the day. He learned from the priest to say his prayers, and that it "was bad to steal or tell lies." Now he has two or three bootblacking stands in Jersey City. He has saved $700 and wears smart clothes and a gold chain. He plays cards in the evenings and does not go to church or take lessons in conduct from priests any more.

There is also a significant story of a Greek pushcart peddler who landed in New York with a few francs in his pocket, and is now the owner of a fruit business valued at $50,000. He credits himself, apparently with justice, with push and honesty and shrewdness, but his success, evidently, was due to his alertness in adopting the Yankee practice of bribing the police, and thus securing good stands for his stalls on the best thorofares. He went back to fight for Greece in the last war. He is eager to make money in the American way, and to adopt American inventions and habits of life. But his religion, his zeal, his patriotism, all that is vital and human in the man, belong to his native land.

Among the most tragic and significant of these biographies is the story of a negro released from a Georgia peon camp. It is dyed so black with horror as to appear unreal. There is, too, the long drawn out complaint of a farmer's wife, who is a prosperous, wideawake American. Her grievance appears to be that the work set before her by the Giver of work, is that of a wife and mother, and not of a literary celebrity. This very fact, perhaps, makes her story a more typical utterance of her class of average women as they are at the present time.

There is a history of the life of a poor Scotch-Irish cook, who is a very fair example of the force, the honesty and the thrift of that most sane and virile race.

There are a Swedish farmer, a French dressmaker, an Itinerant Minister, a Syrian, a Japanese, a Chinaman, an Igorrote chief, and men and women of other races and occupations. All have been successful in this country in making money, and in securing more easy, comfortable lives.

But there are two significant traits common to all of these confessions. First, the importance of success in money making is given the first place in every one of them. Secondly, there is not in a single one of these histories of life, a word of acknowledgment or gratitude to the country which gave them the chance and the success.

Why is this?

Was there anything lacking in the gift?

 Notes

INTRODUCTION

Except where noted, page references to Davis's work are to this volume.

1. Rebecca Harding Davis, *Margret Howth: A Story of Today* (Boston: Ticknor and Fields, 1862), 6.

2. Glen Hendler, "The Limits of Sympathy: Louisa May Alcott and the Sentimental Novel," *American Literary History* 3 (1991): 689–90, argues that the sentimental novel only limits the seemingly unrestricted extension of sympathy by raising the threat of incest.

3. RHD to James Fields, January 26, 1861, Clifton Waller Barrett Collection, Alderman Library, University of Virginia. Further references to correspondence in this collection will be designated UVA.

4. Davis's title for her first version of *Margret Howth* was *The Deaf and the Dumb*.

5. RHD to James Fields, May 10, 1861, Huntington Library.

6. Jean Fagan Yellin, "Afterword" to *Margret Howth* (New York: Feminist Press, 1990), 271.

7. Judith Fetterley, "Introduction to *Life in the Iron Mills*," in *Provisions: A Reader from Nineteenth-Century American Women* (Bloomington: Indiana University Press, 1985), 313.

8. Jane Tompkins, *Sensational Designs: The Cultural Work of American Fiction 1790–1860* (New York: Oxford University Press, 1985), 124.

9. Davis's letters, filed with those of her son Richard Harding Davis at the University of Virginia, as well as her well-censored journal, are informative; yet, for the most part, they feel quite closed to me. I have not been able to find out who cut up her journal and what was destroyed. I have found no letters between RHD and her husband. Davis carried on a fascinating, intense, but brief correspondence during the sixties with Annie Fields, at the time the wife of James Fields, Davis's editor at the *Atlantic*, but sadly this correspondence waned because of conflicts of publishing loyalties. In her later years, there is a caring and maternal correspondence with Richard, some practical correspondence with her second son, Charles, and (of great curiosity to me) no correspondence and virtually no references to her daughter Nora. RHD's reminiscences, interestingly named *Bits of Gossip*, reveal the family history and

its legends, her early acquaintances with the Boston Brahmins, including her meetings with Ralph Waldo Emerson, Nathaniel Hawthorne, and Bronson Alcott, and significant recollections of the Civil War from the point of view of a woman who was raised on the border between the Union and Confederacy.

10. To date, the most complete and accurate bibliography of Davis's works is found in Jane Atterbridge Rose, "A Bibliography of Fiction and Non-Fiction by Rebecca Harding Davis," *American Realism*, Spring 1990, 67–86. However, no bibliography attempts to identify Davis's early pieces for the Wheeling *Intelligencer* or her later essays and editorials for the *New York Herald Tribune*.

11. The biographical details for this essay come from Rebecca Harding Davis, *Bits of Gossip* (New York: Houghton Mifflin, 1904); Gerald Langford, *The Richard Harding Davis Years: A Biography of Mother and Son* (New York: Holt, Rinehart and Winston, 1961); Charles Davis, ed., *Adventures and Letters of Richard Harding Davis* (New York: Charles Scribner's Sons, 1917); Sharon Harris, *Rebecca Harding Davis and American Realism* (Philadelphia: University of Pennsylvania Press, 1991); Arthur Lobow, *The Reporter Who Would Be King: Biography of Richard Hading Davis* (New York: Scribner, 1992); Helen Woodward Sheaffer, "Rebecca Harding Davis, Pioneer Realist" (Ph.D. diss., University of Pennsylvania, 1947); William F. Grayburn, "The Major Fiction of Rebecca Harding Davis" (Ph.D. diss., Pennsylvania State University, 1965); and correspondence in the Rebecca Harding Davis Collection, UVA.

12. Langford, *The Richard Harding Davis Years*, 6.

13. Ibid., 4.

14. Davis, *Bits of Gossip*, 68–69.

15. Ibid., 1.

16. Ibid., 4.

17. Ibid., 29.

18. Davis scholarship is indebted to the biographical work of Sharon Harris, who suggests that Davis wrote and edited for the *Intelligencer* before the publication of *Life in the Iron Mills*, which heretofore seemed to spring mysteriously from the pen of a young mountain woman.

19. Harris, *Rebecca Harding Davis and American Realism*, 24–26.

20. Ibid., 25. Later Davis dismissed these early journalistic pieces in discussing her development as a writer. To James Fields she wrote, "Whatever I wrote before the Iron Mill story I would not care to see again—chiefly verses and reviews written under circumstances that made them unhealthful. I would rather they were forgotten." RHD to James Fields, November 16, 1861, UVA. Although it is not really clear what the unhealthful circumstances were, to Archibald Campbell she wrote that an editorial had been written in "the intervals of that all important cooking" (ibid., 26).

21. Beginning in 1873, Mary Mapes Dodge edited *Saint Nicholas*, to which Davis was a frequent contributor. Sarah Josepha Hale served as editor of

Ladies' Magazine (1837–1877) and later of *Godey's Lady's Book* (1837–1877) (ibid., 25).

22. Hendler, "The Limits of Sympathy: Louisa May Alcott and the Sentimental Novel," 686.

23. Elizabeth Langland, "Nobody's Angel: Domestic Ideology and Middle-Class Women in the Victorian Novel," *PMLA* 107 (1992): 294.

24. Herman Melville's "The Paradise of Bachelors and the Tartarus of Maids" was published in *Harpers New Monthly Magazine* in April 1855. This story is generally credited with being the first portrait of industrial labor in American fiction.

25. Elaine Showalter, "Dinah Murlock Craik and the Tactics of Sentiment: A Case Study in Victorian Female Authorship," *Feminist Studies* 2 (1975).

26. Discussions of naturalism in "Life in the Iron-Mills" are found in Harris, *Rebecca Harding Davis and American Realism*; Sandra Gilbert and Susan Gubar, *The Norton Anthology of Literature by Women: The Tradition in English* (New York: Norton, 1985), 903; and Jean Pfaelzer, "Rebecca Harding Davis: Domesticity, Social Order, and the Industrial Novel," *International Journal of Women's Studies* 4 (May 1981): 234–44.

27. Davis does not escape the nativist stereotypes of her time in assigning debased animal behavior to the Welsh characters in this story. For the most part the Welsh were not totally impoverished immigrants. Because England's industrial revolution predated America's by about thirty years, Britain provided the skilled labor for new U.S. industries. Welsh miners and industrial workers crossed the Atlantic in both directions, responding to the laws of supply and demand in the period between the abolition of indentured labor and the recruitment of immigrant workers through foreign agents who offered stipends, bribes, and utopian descriptions of American life. The Welsh, tempted here mainly by letters from other Welsh immigrants, generally paid their own fares. See Philip Taylor, *The Distant Magnet: European Immigration to the U.S.A.* (New York: Harper and Row, 1971), 14ff.

28. William Dean Howells, "Review of *Miss Ravenal's Conversion from Secession to Loyalty* by J. W. De Forrest," *Atlantic Monthly* 20 (July 1867): 211.

29. Daniel Aaron, *The Unwritten War: American Writers and the Civil War* (New York: Knopf, 1973), xvii.

30. Ibid., xviii.

31. Hazel Carby similarly observes that "slavery is rarely the focus of the imaginative physical and geographical terrain" of American fiction ("Ideologies of Black Folk: The Historical Novel of Slavery," in *Slavery and the Literary Imagination*, ed. Deborah E. McDowell and Arnold Rampersad [Baltimore: Johns Hopkins University Press, 1989], 125).

32. Aaron, *The Unwritten War*, xviii.

33. Nathaniel Hawthorne, *Life of Franklin Pierce*, in *Complete Works* (Boston: Houghton Mifflin, 1888), 417.

34. Jane Tompkins, "The Other American Renaissance," in *The American Renaissance Reconsidered*, ed. Walter Benn Michaels and Donald E. Pease (Baltimore: Johns Hopkins University Press, 1985), 37.

35. Werner Sollors, "Of Mules and Mares in a Land of Difference; or, Quadrupeds All?" *American Quarterly* 42 (1990): 181.

36. For an influential discussion of the politics of the imagery of slave martyrdom, see Jane Tompkins, "Sentimental Power: *Uncle Tom's Cabin* and the Politics of Literary History," *Sensational Designs: The Cultural Work of American Fiction 1790–1860*, 122–46.

37. William Chafe, "Sex and Race: The Analogy of Social Control," in *Racism and Sexism: An Integrated Study*, ed. Paula S. Rothenberg (New York: St. Martin's Press, 1988), 334.

38. See Herbert Gutman, *The Black Family in Slavery and Freedom* (New York: Pantheon Books, 1976), 293–96, on how the relationship between ideas about class and gender reinforced racial stereotypes in the mid-nineteenth century.

39. See, for example, Mary Dearborn, *Pocahontas's Daughters: Gender and Ethnicity in American Culture* (New York: Oxford University Press, 1986), 132.

40. Quoted in Sterling A. Brown, "A Century of Negro Portraiture in American Literature," *Massachusetts Review* 7 (1966): 78.

41. Elizabeth Fox-Genovese, *Within the Plantation Household: Black and White Women of the Old South* (Chapel Hill: University of North Carolina Press, 1988), 291.

42. Marianna Torgovnick, *Gone Primitive: Savage Intellects, Modern Lives* (Chicago: University of Chicago Press, 1990), 9.

43. When he was sixteen, Tom Bethune was seen by Dr. Edward Seguin, who diagnosed him as an "idiotic genius." In this early report, written in 1866, Seguin suggests that in addition to biology and genetics (the common etiologies of the time), isolation and sensory deprivation would have produced sizable "intellectual defects" in Tom. According to Seguin's description, Tom had a vocabulary of less than a hundred words, but a musical repertoire of over 5,000 pieces. As a young child, noted Seguin, Tom was fascinated with sounds, and although he could scarcely walk and refused to speak, if someone seated Tom at the piano he would play beautiful tunes, a somewhat less sudden debut than that recorded by Davis. Apparently Tom was incapable of learning in any area other than music. By age six he could improvise as well as repeat music he had heard. By age seven, as Davis correctly notes, Bethune took him on a tour that is said to have earned $100,000 in the first year. By age eleven Tom played at the White House before President James Buchanan. After the Civil War, Tom continued to appear on stage, but his career ended when he was fifty-three with the death of his former master. He died in 1880, apparently lonely and alone, a tragic case of dependency and exploitation. I have been unable to discover what happened to the profits from

his many performances, but his solitary death suggests that the money did not go to him.

In addition to Davis's study, biographical information on Thomas Greene Bethune can be found in Edward Seguin, *Idiocy and Its Treatment By the Physical Method* (1866; rpt. New York: A. M. Kelley, 1971); Robert Goldenson, *Mysteries of the Mind: The Drama of Human Behavior* (Garden City, N.Y.: Doubleday, 1973); Benjamin Brawley, *The Negro Genius: A New Appraisal of the Achievement of the American Negro in Literature and the Fine Arts* (New York: Biblo and Tannen, 1966), 131–33.

44. See Jean Fagan Yellin, *Women and Sisters: The Antislavery Feminists in American Culture* (New Haven: Yale University Press, 1989) on the iconography of silence in abolitionists' representations of the slave—esp. pt. 1, "The Speechless Agony of the Fettered Slave."

45. It is likely that by 1862 Davis was aware of Charles Darwin's *Origin of the Species* (1859), published in the United States in 1860 and immediately widely reviewed.

46. Philip Fisher, *Hard Facts: Setting and Form in the American Novel* (New York: Oxford University Press, 1985), 94.

47. Ibid., 99.

48. Werner Sollars, *Beyond Ethnicity: Consent and Descent in American Culture* (New York: Oxford, 1986), 41.

49. Davis, *Bits of Gossip*, 116–17.

50. Davis, "David Gaunt," pt. 2, 404.

51. RHD to Annie Fields, January 10, 1863, UVA.

52. RHD to Annie Fields, dated Monday evening [probably late January 1863], UVA.

53. See Joanne Dobson, "The Hidden Hand: Subversion of Cultural Ideology in Three Mid-Nineteenth Century American Women's Novels," *American Quarterly* 38 (1986): 223–42, for narrative strategies in Susan Warner's *The Wide, Wide World* (1850), E.D.E.N. Southworth's *The Hidden Hand* (1859), and in A.D.T. Whitney's *Hitherto: A Story of Yesterdays* (1869), exposing those authors' clear understanding of the losses imposed by women's close adherence to the "societal text" of feminine identity. Dobson traces how anger and rebellion emerge through the clarification of personal oppression.

54. Ibid., 230.

55. See Carol Kolmerten's study of women's experiences in nineteenth-century intentional communities in *Women: The Ideology of Gender in the American Owenite Communities* (Bloomington: Indiana University Press, 1990), esp. 90–100.

56. With its religious overtones, celibacy in Rappite communities differed from celibacy in Shaker communities, which apparently stemmed from the founder Ann Lee's traumatic loss of her four children, her ensuing sexual traumas, and her eventual attacks against the carnal nature of men. Shaker

celibacy freed women from the risks of childbirth and the duties of child rearing, allowing women to assume significant leadership positions. Hence, celibacy deconstructed biology as a social determinant. See Don Blair, *The New Harmony Story* (n.d., n.p.); and Lawrence Foster, *Religion and Sexuality: The Shakers, the Mormons, and the Oneida Community* (Urbana: University of Illinois Press, 1984).

57. The Rappites were not atypical of nineteenth-century utopian communities in their treatment of women. In the American Owenite communities of the 1820s, conflict arose over women's political rights. In some Owenite communities, women were "wives of members" rather than members in their own right; unmarried women were simply not "members" at all. In others, women could vote only on domestic matters; elsewhere women could vote only in the "female department." See Kolmerten, *Women: The Ideology of Gender in the American Owenite Communities*.

58. Some passages from this discussion of "The Harmonists" appeared originally in "The Sentimental Promise and the Utopian Myth," *ATQ*, n.s. 3:1 (March 1989): 85–99, in which I argue that these early critiques of utopia expose the sentimental fallacy. Sentimentalism offered false security by promising female safety through the benevolence of male patronage despite its critique of male character. Even though it romanticizes the home, sentiment also exposed how female moral authority in the domestic sphere is meaningless without power in the public sphere; hence, sentiment in fact revealed the inconsistency in the ethical argument for gender segregation.

59. See Nancy Chodorow, "Gender, Relation and Difference in Psychoanalytic Perspective" in *The Future of Difference*, ed. Alice Jardine and Hester Eisenstein (Boston: G.K. Hall, 1980), 3–19.

60. Jessica Benjamin, "A Desire of One's Own: Psychoanalytic Feminism and Intersubjective Space," in *Feminist Studies/Critical Studies*, ed. Teresa de Lauretis (Bloomington: Indiana University Press, 1986), 80.

61. Ibid., 92.

62. Marianne Hirsch, *The Mother/Daughter Plot: Narrative, Psychoanalysis, Feminism* (Bloomington: Indiana University Press, 1989) argues that repression of the fictional mother "stands at the very basis of the marriage plot." Hirsch suggests that we need to include maternal absence, silence, and negativity in this analysis. She also considers the impact of eliminating the mother on the heroine's development and allegiances. See esp. 46–50.

63. Sandra Gilbert and Susan Gubar, *The Madwoman in the Attic: The Woman Writer and the Nineteenth-Century Literary Imagination* (New Haven: Yale University Press, 1979), 174.

64. Adrienne Rich, *On Lies, Secrets and Silence: Selected Prose, 1966–1978* (New York: Norton, 1979), 91.

65. Mary Kelley, *Private Woman, Public Stage: Literary Domesticity in Nineteenth-Century America* (New York: Oxford University Press, 1984) de-

velops the concept of the popular woman writer of this time as a "literary domestic."

66. Ann Wood, "The 'Scribbling Women' and Fanny Fern: Why Women Wrote," *American Quarterly* 23 (1971): 7.

67. Quoted in ibid., 8.

68. Ann Douglas [Wood], *The Feminization of American Culture* (New York: Knopf, 1977), 12.

69. Raymond Williams surveys the long history of these polarities in the English tradition.

70. Caroline Gebhard, "The Spinster in the House of American Criticism,"astutely surveys the critical attack on local color literature as trivial, senile, and sterile narratives written by unmarried women. Originating with the wave of masculinist nationalism around the turn of the century, this charge appears to have first been popularized by George Santayana in "The Genteel Tradition in American Philosophy" (1911), passing through reviews in the *Nation*, then on through Henry Adams, Van Wyck Brooks, V. L. Parrington, up through Ann Douglas's *The Feminization of American Culture* (New York: Knopf, 1977), 1–13. This quotation, cited by Gebhard, is from Warner Berthoff's summation of mainstream views of local color, quoted in Louis J. Renza, *"A White Heron" and the Question of Minor Literature* (Madison: University of Wisconsin Press, 1984), 44–45.

71. From the *Nation*, September 27, 1919, cited in Gebhard, "The Spinster in the House of American Criticism," 79.

72. George Santayana, "The Academic Environment," *Character and Opinion in the United States* (New York: Charles Scribner's Sons, 1920), 44.

73. Robert Spiller et al., *A Literary History of the United States*, 4th rev. ed. (New York: Macmillan, 1974).

74. Ann Douglas [Wood], "The Literature of Impoverishment: The Women Local Colorists in America 1865–1914," *Women's Studies* 1 (1972): 14.

75. Annette Kolodny, *The Land Before Her: Fantasy and Experience of the American Frontiers 1630–1860* (Chapel Hill: University of North Carolina Press, 1984), 6.

76. Ibid., 7.

77. L. J. Jordanova, "Natural Facts: A Historical Perspective on Science and Sexuality," in *Nature, Culture and Gender*, ed. Carol MacCormack and Marilyn Strathern (Cambridge: Cambridge University Press, 1980), 42.

78. See ibid., p 44–61; and Raymond Williams, *The City and the Country* (London: Chatto and Windus, 1973), 1–8.

79. See Annette Kolodny, *The Lay of the Land: Metaphor as Experience and History in American Life and Letters* (Chapel Hill: University of North Carolina Press, 1975), 4.

80. Kolodny defines the "maternal landscape" in ibid., 6, 22.

81. Ibid., 202.

82. See Josephine Donovan, *New England Local Color Literature: A Woman's Tradition* (Frederick Ungar: New York, 1983), for a discussion of American literary sources of local color, the relationship between local color and realism, and the connections between women local colorists that define them as a self-identified group.

83. Roger Stein, *The View and the Vision: Landscape Painting in Nineteenth Century America* (Seattle: University of Washington Press, 1968), 8–9.

84. Simone de Beauvoir, *The Second Sex* (New York: Knopf, 1953), 710–11. For an analysis of twentieth-century fiction along these lines, see Annis Pratt, "Women and Nature in Modern Fiction," *Contemporary Literature* 13 (1972): 477–90.

85. Nina Baym, "Melodramas of Beset Manhood: How Theories of American Fiction Exclude Women Writers," *American Quarterly* 33 (1981): 132.

NOTES TO THE FICTION

"Life in the Iron-Mills"

1. Alfred, Lord Tennyson, "In Memoriam A.H.H." (1833), sec. 12, l. 16; sec. 56, ll. 25, 27.

2. Pig-iron: iron first reduced from ore and then cast into small oblong masses called *pigs*. Larger masses were called *sows*.

3. Rain butt: tub used to catch rain water from the eaves of buildings.

4. Puddler: workman who stirred molten iron.

5. Arminian: initially followers of Dutch theologian James Arminius (1560–1609) who disagreed with the Calvinist doctrine of predestination and trusted the possibility of universal redemption for believers in Christ.

6. Rolling mill: immense iron works containing machinery to roll out or flatten metal.

7. Picker: machine that separated and cleaning cotton fibers; also the operator of the machine.

8. Begorra: nineteenth-century and early twenieth-century Anglo-Irish expression for "By God!"

9. Lashin's (lashings): generous portions of alcohol or food, more than enough.

10. Milesian: Irish term referring to descendants of King Milesius, a Spaniard whose sons are reputed to have conquered Ireland in 1300 B.C.

11. Flitch: slab of bacon or smoked meat.

12. Farinata Degli Uberti: thirteenth-century leader of Ghibelline faction in Florence who refused to raze the city after returning from exile; immortalized by Dante as the savior of his country.

13. Bitumen: generic name for inflammable mineral substances such as petroleum or asphalt.

14. Sinking funds: revenues, occasionally government revenues, set aside by companies in order to accumulate interest.

15. Immanuel Kant (1724-1804): German metaphysician and philosopher whose work in the theory of knowledge, ethics, and aesthetics influenced various schools of idealism.

16. Novalis: pseudonym of Friedrich Leopold Freiherr von Hardenberg (1722-1801), lyric poet and leader of early German romanticism.

17. Wilhelm von Humboldt (1767-1835): Prussian statesman, humanist, and linguist who argued for the inalienable value of the individual.

18. From the Latin: "They clamor [or call] from the depths."

19. Claude-Henri de Rouvroy de Saint-Simon, comte de (1760-1825), French philosopher and founder of French socialism and utopianism who advocated a "science" of society for abolishing inequities in the distribution of property, power, and happiness.

20. Aphrodite: Greek goddess of love and beauty.

"John Lamar"

1. Rebel Cheat counties: areas along the Cheat River in West Virginia that sided with the Confederacy. Cheat Mountain was the site of an early Union victory in September 1861.

2. 'Baccy-houses (tobacco houses): structures in which tobacco was stored during the curing process.

3. Snakehunters: members of an independent volunteer army from West Virginia that fought for the Union side.

4. Scrimmage: irregular encounter or skirmish between small bodies of armed enemies.

5. Maumer: slave mammy or mama, i.e., enslaved nanny.

6. Polypus: cuttlefish or octopus.

7. Eleven dollars a month: salary during the early years of the Civil War for privates in the Confederate artillery and infantry; comparable ranks in the Union Army received $13 per month.

8. William Tell: legendary Swiss patriot whose heroic deeds symbolized the struggle for political and individual freedom and galvanized the Swiss to rise up against Austrian rule in the thirteenth and fourteenth centuries.

9. Giuseppe Garibaldi (1807-1882): Italian republican, patriot and soldier of the Risorgimento who contributed to Italian unity by his conquest of Sicily and Naples.

"David Gaunt"

1. Christian and Appolyon: characters in John Bunyon's popular allegory *Pilgrim's Progress*, (1860) I, Fourth Stage.

2. Prospero's Ariel: attendant spirit in *The Tempest*.

3. Kalpas: duration of time that covers a complete cosmic cycle from the origination to the destruction of the world in Hinduism .

4. Bone and Joe perhaps share a common ancestor, and were perhaps half-brothers.

5. Puling: a contemptuous term for whining or querulous children.

6. Romney, West Virginia, was swapped back and forth between Union and Confederate troops three times during the first year of the Civil War.

7. Spatterdashes: long garters or leggings, often used while riding, that kept trousers and stockings from being spattered with mud.

8. Pythoness: female serpent from Delphi that protected the oracle of Gaia, often associated with mother earth.

9. Worm fence: zigzag rail fence common in Virginia.

10. William Jay (1789–1858): abolitionist who argued against the movement to rid the country of African Americans through colonization.

11. Johann Heinrich Jung-Stilling (1740–1817): German writer known for his autobiography that gave a vividly realistic picture of village life in an eighteenth-century pietistic family.

12. Baize: coarse woolen cloth with a long nap, generally used for lining or house-furnishing.

13. Bushwackers: term that originated during this period for those who lurked in woods or thickets to plunder or carry on guerrilla warfare.

14. Bacchante: priestess or female devotee of Bacchus, the god of wine.

15. Port Royal: island and town in South Carolina that was captured by the Union early in the war and used as a coaling and repair station.

16. Rods: common linear measure equal to 16.5 feet.

17. *Psalms* 13: "How Long, O Lord? Will you forget me forever? How long will You hide Your face from me?"

"Blind Tom"

1. Friedrich Melchior Grimm, baron von (1723–1807): friend of the Mozarts in Paris.

"The Wife's Story"

1. Psyche: in Greek mythology, a beautiful mortal loved by Eros.

2. Marie-Rosalie (Rosa) Bonheur (1822–1899): French painter and sculptor famed for the remarkable accuracy and detail of her portrayals of animals in particular. In 1865 she became the first woman to receive the Grand Cross of the Legion d'Honneur.

3. From the German: "license for happiness."

4. Marian: Mariam, the sister of Aaron and Moses, was known as a prophetess and a divinely inspired singer.

5. Posset: drink composed of hot spiced milk curdled with liquor, and seen as a remedy for colds.

"Out of the Sea"

1. Gaelic Oisin: Irish warrior-poet who became known throughout Europe in the late eighteenth century when the Scottish poet James Macpherson "discovered" his poems and published the epics of Fingal and Temora as translations from the 3rd. c. Gaelic originals. Actually, the works were inventions of Macpherson, and were more indebted to Homer, Milton and the Bible than to Oisin. Yet so-called Ossian poems were a central influence in early European romanticism.

2. From Barnegat Bay in Eastern New Jersey.

3. Marl: crumbling soil, heavy with clay.

4. Francois VI, duc de LaRochefoucauld (1613–1680): French author known for the "maxime" or epigram that briefly expresses a harsh or paradoxical truth.

5. Euroclydon: strong cold wind that blows from the northeast across the Mediterranean region, mainly in the winter months; referred to in Acts, 27:14.

"The Harmonists"

1. *Père Bonhours:* collection of tales published in 1691 by Pasquier Quesnel (1634–1719) about the defense of Port Royal against attacks by the Jesuits.

2. Rebel Thomas Jonathan (Stonewall) Jackson (1824–1863): Confederate General regarded as one of the outstanding tacticians in military history.

3. John Charles Fremont (1813–1890): Commander of the Dept. of the West who arbitrarily declared martial law and issued an order or proclamation on August 30, 1861, freeing the slaves in Missouri. As a result of this independent act, he was dismissed by President Lincoln.

4. Lemuel Shaw, (1781–1861) Chief Justice of the Supreme Judicial Court of Massachusetts from 1830–60, best known for two rulings, one which provided the first precedent for removing labor unions from the purview of the law of conspiracy, and another that upheld Boston's segregated schools in what would later become the "separate but equal" doctrine. The immediate effect of this ruling, however, was to stimulate the passage in Massachusetts of the most significant early desegregation law in the United States.

5. Conies: small hares or rabbits.

6. Auguste Compte (1798–1857): French philosopher, founder of positivism.

7. Saint-Simon; see "Life in the Iron-Mills," note 18.

8. *Vide* Trustees of Harmony Society *vs.* Nachtrieb, 19 Howard, U.S. Reports, p. 126, Campell J. [author's note].

9. Sohreiber *vs.* Rapp, 5 Watts, 836, Gibson, C. J. [author's note].

10. Beulah: the Promised Land (Isaiah 62.4). In Bunyan's *Pilgrim's Progress*, Beulah is the land where the pilgrims await their summons to the Celestial City.

11. From the German: "What do you need?"

12. From the German: "I am Joseph, the tavern-keeper."

13. From the German: "Oh! You darling! My pretty treasure."

14. From the German: "With another."

15. Benjamin West (1738–1820): American painter of historical, religious and mythological subjects.

16. Probably a reference to Tidoute, a town in northwestern Pennsylvania on the Allegheny River.

"The Story of Christine"

1. No translation available.

2. Levantine: a very soft and elegant twilled silk.

3. From the German: "dear treasure."

4. Redemptioners: indentured servants who agreed to serve their master for a fixed time in return for passage to the United States.

"In the Market"

1. Burin: an engraver's tool.

"Earthen Pitchers"

1. Bohemian was introduced as a term for an artistic person who leads an unconventional life by William Makepeace Thackeray in *Vanity Fair* (1848).

2. Dundreary whiskers: long side whiskers worn without a beard.

3. Jean-Leon Gérome (1824–1904): prominent academic painter, sculptor, and teacher whose historical and mythological compositions, such as "Pygmalion and Galatea," were anecdotal, melodramatic, and frequently erotic.

4. Bonheur: See "The Wife's Story," note 2.

5. Jean-Louis Ernest Meissonier, French painter and illustrator of military and historical subjects, especially of Napoleonic battles.

6. Fountain of Helicon: the privileged mountain abode of Apollo and his muses.

7. Pegasus: magical winged horse as swift as the wind, always in search of new springs.

8. Screw: slang for an excessively sharp, obsessive, and demanding person, often a teacher.

9. Cheviot clothes: garments made from fine wool of cheviot sheep.

10. Progs: to scavenge or forage for food.

11. Cape Henlopen: on the southern coast of Delaware, about three miles east of Lewes.

12. Gamaliel: one of the leading Pharisees and a famous legal scholar in Jerusalem.

13. Atalanta: legendary character, swiftest of all mortals, who announced that all her suitors would have to compete against her in a race; a defeated suitor would be beheaded.

14. Minauderies: affected expressions and coquettish airs.

15. A kind of white porcelain made at Meissen near Dresden, characterized by elaborate decoration and delicate coloring.

16. *Psalms* 19:2–3.

17. Settle: settee or sofa.

18. Boneset tea: medicinal tea made from eupatorium perfoliatum.

19. Dover's Powder: compound made of ipecac and opium used for relaxation, pain relief, and to induce sweating.

20. Pegotty's house in *David Copperfield* by Charles Dickens, was constructed out of a turned-up boat.

21. Mawthers (mothers): also large awkward girls.

22. Moiling: performing exhausting toil or labor.

23. Calenture: tropical disease suffered by sailors characterized by a delirium in which the victim supposedly believes that the sea is green fields and wants to jump into it.

24. *Nature morte*: still life.

25. Mignon: character from Ambrose Thomas's opera *Wilhelm Meister's Lehrjahre* (1866) based on Goethe's tale of the same name.

"*Dolly*"

1. Moravians: members of an evangelical sect, also known as the Renewed Church of the United Brethren, that came to the United States from Germany in the eighteenth century.

2. Gemein Houses: apparently the communal buildings or dwellings.

3. A hippodrome: course or circus for horse races and chariot races.

4. Boanerges: in the New Testament, a surname meaning the sons of thunder, given to James and John, the sons of Zebedee. *Mark* 3.17.

"*The Yares of Black Mountain*"

1. Punk: rotten wood, or a fungus growing on wood.

2. Ku Klux Klan: secret white supremacist organization founded in 1866

in Pulaski, Tennessee, used intimidation and terror to prevent newly enfranchised African Americans from voting, for example.

3. Salisbury: a Confederate prison in North Carolina. By 1864, 10,000 destitute prisoners occupied the inadequate prison, living in tents or burrowed into the earth in mud huts. Between October 1864 to February 1865, 3,419 prisoners died in Salisbury.

4. Albert Richardson (1833–1869): war correspondent employed by the *New York Tribune*, a paper to which Davis contributed. In 1860 he went to the South to investigate the secessionist movement. In May, 1863, while attempting to run a tugboat past the Confederate batteries at Vicksburg, Richardson was captured. After spending nineteen months in various Confederate prisons, he escaped from Salisbury prison, walked 400 miles to Union lines in Tennessee, and wrote several books on his experiences.

"Marcia"

1. Gérome: see "Earthen Pitchers," note 2.

2. George Henry Boughton (1834–1905): genre and landscape artist who lived in Albany, N.Y.

"A Day with Doctor Sarah"

1. Joint: probably refers to a cut of meat, such as a roast.

2. A 1881 survey performed by Dean Rachel Bodley of the Woman's Medical College of Pennsylvania, one of the few schools to train women physicians, found that among the 166 respondents who had graduated the school, 129 were married, 92 percent were still in active practice, over 50 percent were involved in gynecology and obstetrics, only five left the practice of medicine after they married. In 1905, the first year numbers are apparently available, 4 percent of graduates of American medical schools were women.

3. John "Benicia Boy" Heenan (1833–1873) and John Morrissey (n.d.) were professional boxers who competed for the title of American heavyweight champion in the late 1850s.

4. Probably a reference to Helen Watterson Moody (1859–1928), whose work on the condition of women would become significant later in the century.

5. Madame de Maintenon (1635–1719) married Louis XIV of France and provided the monarchy with a new dignity and stability necessary to survive. Margaret Fuller, transcendentalist and feminist, married Giovanni Ossoli, ten years her junior, in Italy in 1848.

"Anne"

1. Pier-glass: large tall mirror originally fitted to fill up the space over a chimney piece or between two windows.

2. Stroller: itinerant actor.

3. Thomas à Kempis (c.1380–1471): German theologian of the Low Counties, reputed author of the *Imitation of Christ*, one of the most widely circulated Christian devotional books.

4. Happed: covered up, as with extra bedclothes; tucked in bed.

5. Morris Whites: kind of peach.

NOTES TO THE ESSAYS

"Men's Rights"

1. From chap. 2 of John Bunyan, *The Pilgrim's Progress*, "The Slough of Despond."

2. Frederick William Faber (1814–1863): widely known British convert to Catholicism, compelling preacher and hymnodist. "The Children of the Abby" (1816) by Regina Maria Roche (1810–1887), was an extremely popular novel that was frequently republished throughout the nineteenth century, although there is no evidence that Faber reviewed it.

3. Joseph Ernest Renan (1823–1892): French philosopher, historian, and religious scholar.

4. Theseus: king of Athens, whose father, Aegeus, hid his own sword and sandals underneath a large boulder, vowing that when his son was strong enough to raise the boulder, he would inherit the crown.

5. Rose Bradwardine: character in Sir Walter Scott's *Waverley* (1814).

6. Amelia: clever, ambitious and unscrupulous character in William Makepeace Thackeray's *Vanity Fair* (1847–8).

7. Caroline Wells Healey Dall (1822–1912): reformer and writer in the Women's Rights Movement during the 1860s and 1870s.

8. Lucretia Mott (1793–1880): reformer and preacher in the Society of Friends, promoter of the Women's Rights Convention held in Seneca Falls, New York, in 1848, and a friend of RHD.

9. Virginia Penny (1826–?): writer on women, work, and wages.

10. Miss Penny's book would be more useful if the scale of prices in it for work, were those of the present time. It would be worth her while to correct this in another edition. The book woutld then be a more efficient aid to woman than a dozen treatises on her rights [author's note].

11. Rosa Bonheur: see "The Wife's Story," note 2.

12. Jean Ingelow (1820–1897): nature poet, influenced by Wordsworth and Tennyson, whose poetry is characterized by pathos and religious introspection.

13. Frances Anne (Fanny) Kemble (1809–1893): popular actress and author of plays, poems, reminiscences of theatrical and social history.

"A Faded Leaf of History"

1. François Jean Chastellux (Marquis de) (1734–1788): French general and author of *Travels in North America in the Years 1780, 1781, and 1782,* his observations of the northeastern United States from the Blue Ridge Mountains through Pennsylvania into New England.

2. Ashley River: joins the Charles River at Charleston, South Carolina, to form Charleston Harbor.

3. Paduasoy: strong corded or grosgrain silk.

4. Santa Lucia: probably a reference to a town on the northwest coast of Cuba.

5. Perre-augoe: *perrogue,* or large canoe or dugout.

"The Middle-Aged Woman"

1. "Let husbands . . . sour." *Othello* 4.3.94ff.

2. One of the seven stars in the constellation Pleiades is invisible to the naked eye. Some accounts say it is Merope, who married a mortal and hides in shame; others say it is Electra, who hides in grief over the destruction of Troy.

3. Yclept: archaism meaning named, or called.

4. Greatheart: in Bunyan, *The Pilgrim's Progress,* the character appointed to guide Christian's wife and children on their pilgrimage.

"The House on the Beach"

1. Thomas Carlyle (1795–1881): British essayist and historian.

2. Ulfila the Moesogoth: fourth-century missionary who evangelized the Goths, created the Gothic alphabet, and produced the first German translation of the Bible.

3. Theophrastus (ca. 370–ca. 288 B.C.): collaborator and successor of Aristotle as head of the Lyceum.

4. Cambyses: most likely Cambyses II, king of Persia from sixth century B.C., who conquered Egypt. He was accused by Herodotus of madness and violence, traits discounted by Egyptian sources.

5. Sir John Frederick Herschel (1792–1871): British astronomer who produced a catalogue of 5,079 nebulae and clusters.

6. Henry Wilhelm Dove (1803–1879): German-born physicist and meteorologist who mapped the mean distribution of heat at the earth's surface, demonstrating the influence of winds, seas, and land masses on climate. His "law of motion" was a significant system for predicting weather changes.

7. Henry J. Rogers (1811–1879): inventor of telegraphic communication who patented the marine signaling system in 1844 that was adopted by the U.S. Navy.

"Some Testimony in the Case"

1. Bucked: bucking was a punishment administered by tying the wrists together, passing the arms over bent knees, and inserting a stick over the arms and beneath the knees; to tie a person across a log, before flogging.

2. George Washington Cable (1844–1925): author of stories and novels about Creole life, as well as a social crusader and religious leader.

3. Henry Woodfin Grady (1850–1889): journalist and orator known as the "national pacificator." He believed that the South must cease "waving the bloody shirt," acknowledge its defeat in the Civil War, and bend its energies to constructive endeavor.

"Women in Literature"

1. Molly Maguires: secret organization of anthracite coal miners formed in 1862 in Pennsylvania. It advocated militant and terrorist tactics against mine owners and landlords. The "order" was disbanded in 1876 after being infiltrated by Pinkerton detectives. Ten members were hanged for murder.

2. Marion Harland (Mary Terhune, 1830–1922): author of advice books and twenty-five novels and short stories set in the antebellum South; her works have highly sentimental resolutions, although she suggests that women should also be educated and able to support themselves.

3. Mary Noailles Murfree (1850–1922): author of detailed stories of Tennessee and Cumberland mountains under the pseudonyms Charles Egbert Craddock or R. Emmet Dembury. Her greatest achievement was *In the Tennessee Mountains* (1884).

4. Mary Hartwell Catherwood (1847–1902): originally known as the first novelist to write popular romantic historical novels, now recognized for her critical realism and pioneering regional material, using the settlement of the West and Canada as background.

5. Mary Halleck Foote (1847–1938): illustrator for texts by Longfellow, Whittier, and Hawthorne and author and illustrator of her own material set in mining camps and areas in the West.

6. Constance Fenimore Woolson (1840–1894): regionalist novelist and poet whose works focused on Georgia and Florida. Wrote for the *Atlantic Monthly*, *Harper's*, *Appleton's*, and *Lippincott's*.

7. Elizabeth Stuart Phelps (1815–1852): one of the earliest regional authors of the domestic scenes in rural New England.

8. Jessie Ann Benton Fremont (1824–1902): author of Civil War memoirs,

travel sketches, western stories; also wrote in defense of controversial husband (General) John Charles Fremont. Close friend of RHD.

"The Newly Discovered Woman"

1. Helen Watterson Moody. See "A Day with Doctor Sarah," note 4.
2. The Woman's Exhibit occurred during the World's Columbian Exposition in Chicago in 1893. Following the efforts of Susan B. Anthony, women played an active role in the Exposition, and maintained a Women's Building that exhibited women's accomplishments in education, arts, science and industry. Linked to the fair was the World's Congress of Representative Women, addressed by Frances Willard, Elizabeth Cady Stanton and Susan B. Anthony.
3. Mme. de Maintenon. See "A Day with Doctor Sarah" note 5.
4. Mme. Germaine de Stael: French author, established a famous intellectual and political salon; expelled from France several times for criticizing Napoleon.
5. Vassar College: founded in 1865; first American women's college of merit.
6. Smith College: founded in 1875; a liberal arts college for women.
7. Tete-montée: (literally, raised head) overexcited, agitated or worked up.

"In the Gray Cabins of New England"

1. Sarah Orne Jewett (1849–1909): important regional writer of Maine and New England.
2. Mary Wilkins Freeman (1852–1930): author of regional tales and novels set in New England focusing on women's lives.
3. Annie Trumbull Slosson (1838–1926): author of dialect stories. Her novel *The China Hunter's Club* (1878), along with Jewett's *Deephaven* (1877), was considered an early example of the local color genre.
4. *Othello*, IV.i.207.

"Two Points of View"

1. Benjamin Tucker Tanner (1835–1923): bishop of African Methodist Episcopal church, editor and founder, in 1884, of the "African Methodists' Episcopal Church Review," a leading black journal that argued for racial solidarity as a means of combating racist violence.
2. Hampton Normal and Agricultural Institute, founded in 1868 as a training center for ex-slaves.
3. Fisk University: founded in 1866 as a college primarily for African-

American students, although it has always accepted students regardless of race.

4. Oberlin College: founded in 1833, one of the first colleges to accept African-American students.

"Two Methods with the Negro"

1. On February 15, 1898, the USS *Maine* exploded off the coast of Havana, Cuba. Despite differing explanations by the Spanish and the Americans for the explosion, the hysteria generated by the popular press led to a declaration of war against Spain on April 25, 1898.

"The Work Before Us"

1. Sirdar: British commander-in-chief of the Egyptian army; also a term for military leader in India and other colonized areas.

2. Charles George Gordon (1833-1885): British general who became a national hero for reckless exploits in China during the 1860s. Praised as a martyred warrior for the ill-fated defense of Khartoum against Sudanese rebels.

3. Horatio Herbert Kitchener, first Earl (1850-1916): English military leader and colonial administrator, British commander-in-chief (1900-1902) in the Boer War.

"The Mean Face of War"

1. At the outbreak of hostilities between Spain and the United States in 1898, the U.S. consul promised President Aguinaldo independence to the Philippines if U.S. troops could occupy trenches there in the Spanish-American War. After victory, the United States purchased the Philippines from Spain for $20 million, and President William McKinley announced a policy to "civilize and Christianize" the Filipinos before recognizing their independence. An insurrection against the United States began in February 1899. Although Aguinaldo swore allegiance to the United States in April 1901, resistance continued until 1906, and the Phillipines did not become independent until July 4, 1946.

"Lord Kitchener's Methods"

1. The Boer War, also called the South Africa War, (1899-1902) between Great Britain and the Transvaal (South African Republic) and the Orange Free State following the British claim to South African lands, mining opera-

tions and commerce. The Boers, white residents of Dutch, German and Huguenot descent, carried out extensive guerrilla warfare that the British ultimately crushed with great brutality. The Union of South Africa was formed in 1910.

2. Sir Walter Raleigh (1552?-1618): enforced the orders of Queen Elizabeth's appointee Lord Deputy Arthur Grey (1535-1593) to kill the Spanish and Italian adventurers who landed at Smerwick in Ireland, an event that was seen as cold-blooded butchery.

3. Dacoits: armed robbers and plunderers in Burma and India.

4. Uitlander: Afrikaans for *outlander*, any British or non-Afrikaaner immigrant in the Transvaal in the 1880s and 1890s, lured to Southern Africa by the prospect of gold. Led by an aristocracy of wealthy mine owners, they became a majority. Afraid of being overwhelmed, the Boers passed laws to restrict Uitlander influence.

5. Henry Du Pre Labouchere (1831-1912): British politician and foreign correspondent. As member of Parliament (1865, 1867-1868, 1880-1906), he urged abolition of the House of Lords and opposed the expansionism that led to the South African War of 1899-1902.

6. Frederic Harrison (1831-1923): British author who publicized the positivism of Auguste Compte.

7. Fenian: militant Irish nationalist, member of the secret Fenian Brotherhood.

8. Baron Colin Campbell Clyde (1792-1863): British commander-in-chief during the Indian mutiny of 1857 who was criticized for being overly cautious during the mutiny, but his successes were cheaply won and his campaigns were thorough.

"The Black North"

1. William E. B. du Bois (1868-1963): Influential African-American teacher, editor, and author of *The Souls of Black Folk* (1903).

2. Booker T. Washington (1856-1915): Influential African-American author and educator who served as principal of Tuskegee Institute in Alabama from 1881-1915.

3. Dr. Crummles: probably a reference to Alexander Crummell (1819-1898), freeborn missionary, abolitionist, and author. He was the tenth African-American clergyman ordained in the Episcopal church (1844) after private instruction because the General Theological Seminary refused to enroll him. Author of "Defense of the Negro Race."

"Boston in the Sixties"

1. Cf. Bunyan, *The Pilgrim's Progress*, chap. 6, "The Valley of Humiliation."

2. Areopagites: those who favor censorship, a term derived from John Milton's speech "Areopagitica" (1644).

3. Amos Bronson Alcott (1799–1888): educator, author, mystic, transcendentalist, and father of Louisa May Alcott.

4. Second girl: household domestic in a subordinate position.

5. Refers to the character Dermott O'Duivna, in the Irish folktale "The Gruff Gillie," who drinks from a silver horn hung from a branch by a holy well, then fights the Champion of the Well.

6. William Hickling Prescott (1796–1859): wrote histories of Ferdinand and Isabella and of the conquest of Mexico and Peru.

7. Daimio: territorial noble in Japan, vassal of the mikado.

"Undistinguished Americans"

1. Original note.

2. Emma Goldman (1869–1940): Russian-American Jewish anarchist.

3. Horace Greeley (1811–1872): reformist lecturer and journalist who championed labor reform, abolition of slavery, women's rights, and anticolonialism; was editor of the *New York Tribune*, to which RHD was a contributor.